▼

Declare

Other Books by Tim Powers

▼

Declare

Tim Powers

WILLIAM MORROW
75 YEARS OF PUBLISHING
An Imprint of HarperCollins*Publishers*

DECLARE. Copyright © 2001 by Tim Powers. All rights reserved. Printed in the United States of America. No part of this book may be used or reproduced in any manner whatsoever without written permission except in the case of brief quotations embodied in critical articles and reviews. For information address HarperCollins Publishers Inc., 10 East 53rd Street, New York, NY 10022.

HarperCollins books may be purchased for educational, business, or sales promotional use. For information please write: Special Markets Department, HarperCollins Publishers Inc., 10 East 53rd Street, New York, NY 10022.

FIRST EDITION

Designed by Nancy Singer Olaguera

Printed on acid-free paper

Library of Congress Cataloging-in-Publication Data has been applied for.

ISBN 0-380-97652-8

01 02 03 04 QW 10 9 8 7 6 5 4 3 2 1

To Fr. Gerald Leonard SVD

And with thanks to Chris Arena, John Berlyne, John Bierer, Jennifer Brehl, Charles N. Brown, Beth Dieckhoff, J. R. Dunn, Ken Estes, Ben Fenwick, Russell Galen, Patricia Geary, Tom Gilchrist, Lisa Goldstein, Anne Guerand, Varnum Honey, Fiona Kelleghan, Barry Levin, Marion Mazauric, Ross Pavlac, David Perry, Serena Powers, Ramiz Rafeedie, Jacques Sadoul, Claire Spencer, and Eric Woolery—

—and especially to Jennifer Brehl and Peter Schneider and Serena Powers, for that long discussion about Kim Philby, over dinner at the White House in Anaheim.

▼

Birthdays? yes, in a general way;
For the most if not for the best of men:
You were born (I suppose) on a certain day:
So was I: or perhaps in the night: what then?

Only this: or at least, if more,
You must know, not think it, and learn, not speak:
There is truth to be found on the unknown shore,
And many will find what few would seek.
>   —J. K. Stephen, inaccurately quoted in a letter from
>   St. John Philby to his son, Kim Philby, March 15, 1932

Where wast thou when I laid the foundations of the earth?
Declare, if thou hast understanding.
>   —Job 38:4

▼

Declare

Prologue

▼

Mount Ararat, 1948

. . . from behind that craggy steep till then
The horizon's bound, a huge peak, black and huge,
As if with voluntary power instinct,
Upreared its head. I struck and struck again,
And growing still in stature the grim shape
Towered up between me and the stars, and still,
For so it seemed, with purpose of its own
And measured motion like a living thing,
Strode after me.
   —William Wordsworth, *The Prelude*, 381–389

The young captain's hands were sticky with blood on the steering wheel as he cautiously backed the jeep in a tight turn off the rutted mud track onto a patch of level snow that shone in the intermittent moonlight on the edge of the gorge, and then his left hand seemed to freeze onto the gear-shift knob after he reached down to clank the lever up into first gear. He had been inching down the mountain path in reverse for an hour, peering over his shoulder at the dark trail, but the looming peak of Mount Ararat had not receded at all, still eclipsed half of the night sky above him, and more than anything else he needed to get away from it.

He flexed his cold-numbed fingers off the gear-shift knob and switched on the headlamps—only one came on, but the sudden blaze was dazzling, and he squinted through the shattered windscreen at the rock wall of the gorge and the tire tracks in the mud as he pulled the wheel around to drive straight down the narrow shepherds' path. He was still panting, his breath bursting out of his open mouth in plumes of steam. He was able to drive a little faster now, moving forward—the jeep was rocking on its abused springs and the four-cylinder engine roared in first gear, no longer in danger of lugging to a stall.

He was fairly sure that nine men had fled down the path an hour ago. Desperately he hoped that as many as four of them might be survivors of the SAS group he had led up the gorge, and that they might somehow still be sane.

But his face was stiff with dried tears, and he wasn't sure if he were still sane himself—and unlike his men, he had been somewhat prepared for what had awaited them; to his aching shame now, he had at least known how to evade it.

In the glow reflected back from the rock wall at his right, he could see bright, bare steel around the bullet holes in the jeep's bonnet; and he knew the doors and fenders were riddled with similar holes. The wobbling fuel gauge needle showed half a tank of petrol, so at least the tank had not been punctured.

Within a minute he saw three upright figures a hundred feet ahead of him on the path, and they didn't turn around into the glow of the single headlamp. At this distance he couldn't tell if they were British or Russian. He had lost his Sten gun somewhere on the high slopes, but he pulled the chunky .45 revolver out of his shoulder holster—even if these survivors were British, he might need it.

But he glanced fearfully back over his shoulder, at the looming mountain—the unsubdued power in the night was back there, up among the craggy high fastnesses of Mount Ararat.

He turned back to the frail beam of light that stretched down the slope ahead of him to light the three stumbling figures, and he increased the pressure of his foot on the accelerator, and he wished he dared to pray.

He didn't look again at the mountain. Though in years to come he would try to dismiss it from his mind, in that moment he was bleakly sure that he would one day see it again, would again climb this cold track.

▼

Book One

Learn, Not Speak

▼

1

London, 1963

Of my Base Metal may be filed a Key,
That shall unlock the Door he howls without.
　　—Omar Khayyám, *The Rubáiyát,* Edward J. FitzGerald translation

From the telephone a man's accentless voice said, "Here's a list: Chaucer . . . Malory . . ."

Hale's face was suddenly chilly.

The voice went on. "Wyatt . . . Spenser . . ."

Hale had automatically started counting, and Spenser made four. "I imagine so," he said, hastily and at random. "Uh, 'which being dead many years, shall after revive,' is the bit you're thinking of. It's *Shakespeare,* actually, Mr.—" He nearly said *Mr. Goudie,* which was the name of the Common Room porter who had summoned him to the telephone and who was still rocking on his heels by the door of the registrar clerk's unlocked office, and then he nearly said *Mr. Philby;* "—Fonebone," he finished lamely, trying to mumble the made-up name. He clenched his fist around the receiver to hold it steady, and with his free hand he shakily pushed a stray lock of sandy-blond hair back out of his eyes.

"Shakespeare," said the man's careful voice, and Hale realized that he should have phrased his response for more apparent continuity. "Oh well. Five pounds, was it? I can pay you at lunch."

For a moment neither of them spoke.

"Lunch," Hale said with no inflection. What is it supposed to be now, he thought, a contrary and then a parallel or example. "Better than fasting, a—uh—sandwich would be." Good Lord.

"It might be a picnic lunch, the fools," the bland voice went on, "and here we are barely in January—so do bring a raincoat, right?"

Repeat it back, Hale remembered. "Raincoat, I follow you." He kept himself from asking, uselessly, *Picnic, certainly—raincoat, right—but will anyone even be there, this time? Are we going to be doing this charade every tenth winter for the rest of my life? I'll be fifty next time.*

The caller hung up then, and after a few seconds Hale realized that he'd been holding his breath and started breathing again. Goudie was still standing in the doorway, probably listening, so Hale added, "If I mentioned it in the lectures, you must assume it's liable to be in the exam." He exhaled unhappily at the end of the sentence. Play-acting into a dead telephone now, he thought; you're scoring idiot-goals all round. To cover the blunder, he said, "Hello? Hello?" as if he hadn't realized the other man had rung off, and then he replaced the receiver. Not *too* bad a job, he told himself, all these years later. He stepped back from the desk and forced himself not to pull out his handkerchief to wipe his face.

Raincoat. Well, they had said that ten years ago too, and nothing had happened at all, then or since.

"Thank you, Goudie," he said to the porter, and then walked past him, back across the dark old Common Room carpet to the cup of tea that was still steaming in the lamplight beside the humming typewriter. Irrationally, it seemed odd to him that the tea should still be hot, after this. He didn't resume his seat, but picked up his sheaf of handwritten test questions and stared at the ink lines.

Ten years ago. Eventually he would cast his mind further back, and think of the war-surplus corrugated-steel bomb shelter on the marshy plain below Ararat on the Turkish–Soviet border, and then of a night in Berlin before that; but right now, defensively, he was thinking of that somewhat more recent, and local, summons—just to pace the snowy lanes of Green Park in London for an hour, as it had happened, alone and with at least diminishing anxiety, and of the subsequent forty hours of useless walks and cab rides from one old fallback location to another, down the slushy streets and across the bridges of London, cursing the confusing new buildings and intersections. There had been no telephone numbers or addresses that he would have dared to try, and in any case they would almost certainly all have been obsolete by that time. He had eventually given it up and taken the train back to Oxford, having incidentally missed a job interview; a fair calamity, in those days.

At least there was no real work to do today, and none tomorrow either. He had only come over to the college so early this morning to use fresh carbon paper and one of the electric typewriters.

Between the tall curtains to his left he could see clouds like hammered tin over the library's mansard roof, and bare young oak branches waving in the wind that rattled the casement latches. He would probably be *wanting* a raincoat, a *literal* one. God knew where he'd wind up having lunch. Not at a picnic, certainly.

He folded the papers and tucked them into his coat pocket, then ratcheted the half-typed sheets out of the typewriter, and switched the machine off.

He hoped it would still be working right, and not have got gummed up by some undergraduate teaching assistant, when he got back—which would be, he was confident, in at most a couple of days. The confidence was real, and he knew that it should have buoyed him up.

He sighed and patted the pockets of his trousers for his car keys.

The wooded hills above the River Wey were overhung in wet fog, and he drove most of the way home from the college in second gear, with the side-lamps on. When at last he steered his old Vauxhall into Morlan Lane, he tossed his cigarette out the window and shifted down to first gear, and he lifted his foot from the accelerator as the front corner of his white bungalow came dimly into view.

When he had first got the job as assistant lecturer back in 1953, he had rented a room right in Weybridge, and he remembered now bicycling back to the old landlady's house after classes in those long-ago late afternoons, from old habit favoring alleys too narrow for motor vehicles and watching for unfamiliar vans parked or driving past on the birch-shaded lanes—tensing at any absence of birdcalls in the trees, coasting close by the old red-iron V.R. post-box and darting a glance at it to look for any hasty scratches around the keyhole—and alert too for any agitation among the dogs in the yards he passed, especially if their barking should ever be simultaneous with a gust of wind or several humans shouting at once.

The old, old saying had been: *Look to dogs, camels don't react*—though of course there had been no camels in Weybridge anyway.

There had still then been periods when he couldn't sleep well or keep food down, and during those weeks when he was both too jumpy and too quickly tired to pedal the bicycle, he would generally walk home, kicking a stone along ahead of himself and using the opportunity to scan the macadam for skid-marks, or—somehow not implausible-seeming on those particular afternoons—for a stray bowed metal clip carelessly dropped after having had cartridges stripped off it into the box magazine of a rifle, or for the peel-off filter-cover from a gas mask, or for any bits of military-looking cellulose packaging or wire insulation . . . or even, though he had never actually let this image form in his mind and it would have been hard to see anyway on the black tarmac, for circles scorched into the pavement, circles ranging in size from as tiny as a pinhead to yards across. Sometimes on clear evenings he would simply hurry right past the house and on to the public house by the Bersham road, and come back hours later when the sky was safely overcast or he was temporarily too drunk to worry.

In '56, with the aid of one last shaky Education Authority grant, he had finally got his long-delayed B. Litt. from Magdalen College, Oxford and been promoted to full lecturer status here, and soon after that he had begun paying on this house in the hills on the north side of the University College of Weybridge. By that time he had finally stopped bothering about—"had outgrown," he would have said—all those cautious vigilances that he remembered the wartime American OSS officers referring to as "dry-cleaning."

And he had felt, if anything, bleakly virtuous in abandoning the old souvenir reflexes; fully eight years earlier C himself, which had been white-haired Stuart Menzies then, had summoned Hale to the "arcana," the fabled fourth-floor office at Broadway Buildings by St. James's Park, and though the old man had clearly not known much about what Hale's postwar work in the Middle East had been, nor the real story about the recent secret disaster in eastern Turkey, his pallid old face had been kindly when he'd told the twenty-six-year-old Hale to make a new life for himself in the private sector. *You were reading English at an Oxford college before we recruited you,* C had said. *Go back to that, pick up your life from that point, and forget the backstage world, the way you would forget any other illogical nightmare. You'll receive another year's pay through Drummond's in Admiralty Arch, and with attested wartime work in the Foreign Office you should have no difficulties getting an education grant. In the end, for all of us,* "Dulce et decorum est pro patria vanescere."

Sweet and fitting it is to vanish for the fatherland. Well, better than *die,* certainly, as the original Horace verse had it. Hale had known enough by then to be sure that he had effectively vanished from the ken of even the highest levels at Broadway, and all but one of the ministers in Whitehall, long before that final interview with C.

So what dormant, obsolete short-circuit was this, that was still occasionally using the old codes as if to summon him? No one had made any kind of contact with him in Green Park on that day in the winter of '52, and he was sure that no one would be there today, on this second day of 1963. The whole fugitive Special Operations Executive had finally been closed down for good in '48, and he assumed that all the surviving personnel had been cashed out and swept under the rug, as he had been.

Here's a list, he thought bitterly as he stepped on the clutch and touched the brake pedal: Walsingham's Elizabethan secret service, Richelieu's Cabinet Noir, the Russian Oprichnina, the SOE—that's four, speak up! They're all just footnotes in history. Probably there's an unconsidered routine at the present-day SIS headquarters to call agents of all the defunct wartime services and recite to them an uncomprehended old code, once every ten years. He recalled hearing of a temporary wartime petrol-storage tank in Kent that had been wired to ring a certain Army telephone number whenever its fuel level was too low; somehow the old circuitry had come on again during the 1950s, long after the tank itself had been dismantled, and had begun once a month calling the old number, which had by that time been assigned to some London physician. Doubtless this was the same sort of mix-up. Probably SIS had telephoned the old lady's boardinghouse in Weybridge before trying the college exchange.

Still, *do bring a raincoat.*

He had stopped the car in the narrow street now, half a dozen yards short of his gravel driveway and partly concealed from the house by the boughs of a dense pine tree on the next-door property. Of course the only cars parked at the curbs were a Hillman and a Morris that belonged to his neighbors. From here he couldn't see the bowed drawing room windows, but the recessed front door certainly didn't give any obvious sign of having been forced since he'd locked it early this morning, and the driveway gravel didn't look any different; even the cleaning woman wasn't due until Friday.

The television antenna on the shingled roof swayed faintly in the wind against the gray sky . . . and now, for the first time, it reminded him of the ranked herringbone short-wave antennae on the high roof of the old Broadway Buildings headquarters of the SIS, and on the roof of the Soviet Embassy in Kensington Gardens, and then even of the makeshift antenna he had at one time and another furtively strung out the gabled windows of a succession of top-floor rooms in occupied Paris . . .

Et bloody cetera, he thought savagely, trying not to think of the last night of 1941.

In the old SOE code, *raincoat* had meant "violated-cover procedures," and until the false-alarm summons ten years ago he had never heard it used in a domestic context.

There was a gun in the house, though he'd have to dig through a trunk nowadays to find it: a .45 revolver that he'd modified according to Captain Fairbairn's advice, with the hammer-spur and the trigger guard and all but two inches of the barrel sawn off, and deep grooves cut into the wooden grips so that his fingers would always hold the gun the same way. It wasn't a gun for competition accuracy, but Captain Fairbairn had pointed out that most "shooting affrays" occurred at distances of less than four yards.

But it wouldn't be of much use across the expansive lawns of Green Park. And according to violated-cover procedures, he must consider himself blown here; his address was even printed in the telephone directory. Play by the old rules, he told himself with a shaky sigh, if only in respectful memory of the old Great Game.

He could get along without an actual raincoat, and he had at least ten pounds in his notecase.

He relaxed the pressure of his foot on the brake pedal and let the Vauxhall roll back down the street until he was able to turn it around in a neighbor's driveway, and then he shifted rapidly up through the gears as he drove off toward the road that would take him to the A316 and, in an hour or so, to some tube station not too far from the old Green Park in London.

Only three days earlier he had been out in his lifeless garden hanging blocks of suet on strings from the bare oak limbs. The stuff stayed hard in the winter air, and the wild thrushes that would have worms to eat come spring were able to sustain themselves on this butcher shop provender until those sunnier days arrived. He was absently whistling "There'll Be

Bluebirds Over the White Cliffs of Dover" now as he drove, and he tried to estimate how long those suet blocks would last, before new ones would have to be hung; not all the way until spring, he thought fretfully. But surely whatever happened he would be back long before then.

His restless gaze was jumping from the windscreen to the driving mirrors and back, and with a chill he realized that he was once again, after a hiatus of about seven years, reflexively watching the vehicles around him, and noting sections of the shoulder where he could leave the road if he should have to.

It took Hale nearly half an hour to amble around the margin of Green Park this time, through the mist under the dripping oak and sycamore branches, and when at length he slanted for the second time past the gazebo by Queen's Walk, the old man in the overcoat and homburg hat was still there, still leaning against the rail. Without ever looking directly at the man, Hale passed within fifty yards of him and then strode away across the wet grass toward the benches that lined the north-south path.

His heart was pounding, even as he told himself that the old man was probably just some Whitehall sub-secretary taking a morning break; and when he groped in his pocket for cigarettes and matches, he crumpled the pages of test questions he had thrust there a little less than two hours ago. That was his real world now, the Milton classes and the survey of the Romantic poets, not . . . the dusty alleys around the embassy in Al-Kuwait, not the black Bedu tents in the dunes of the Hassa desert, not jeeps in the Ahora Gorge below Mount Ararat . . . he killed the thought. As he shook a cigarette out of the pack and struck a match to it, he blinked in the chilly damp breeze and squinted around at the lawns. The grass in the park was mowed these days, and he doubted that sheep were ever pastured here anymore, as he recalled that they had been right after the war. He puffed the cigarette alight and nodded calmly as he exhaled a plume of smoke.

He had driven no farther into the city this morning than West Kensington and had parked the car in the visitors' lot of Western Hospital across the rail line from the Brompton Cemetery, then conscientiously trudged up a sidewalk against oncoming one-way traffic to the West Brompton tube station.

When he had been uselessly summoned in '52, he had got off the Piccadilly Line at Hyde Park Corner, and before walking away up Knightsbridge he had nervously traced a back-tracking counterclockwise saunter among the splashing galoshes and headlamp beams and drifting snow flurries by the Wellington Arch, frequently peering down at the skirt hems and trouser cuffs of the otherwise interchangeable figures in over-coats and scarves that passed him, and trying to remember the one-man-pace evasion rhythms he had learned in Paris more than a decade earlier.

This morning he had ridden the underground train right past the park and got off at Piccadilly Circus, and climbed the tube station stairs to a gray sky that threatened only rain.

And he had known he should start straightaway down Piccadilly toward the park, being careful once or twice to glance into shop windows he passed and then double back to them after a few paces, as if reconsid-ering some bit of merchandise, and note peripherally any figure that hesi-tated behind him, and after a few blocks to enter a shop and stuff his coat into a bag and re-comb his unruly blond hair and then leave with some group of men dressed in white shirts and ties, as he was, and if possible get right onto a bus or into a cab; but he had not been on foot in Piccadilly Circus since the war, and for several minutes after stepping away from the station stairs he had just stood on the pavement in front of Swan & Edgar and stared past the old Eros fountain at the Gordon's gin advertisements and the big Guinness clock on the London Pavilion, which was appar-ently a cinema now; he remembered when it had been occupied by the Ministry of Food, and housewives had gone in there to learn the uses of the new national flour. And for the first time in years he remembered buy-ing an orange from a Soviet recruiter on the steps of the Eros fountain in the autumn of '41. At last he had stirred himself, though his walk down the wide boulevard, past the columned portico of the old Piccadilly Hotel and then the caviar displays in the windows of Fortnum's, had been slowed more by nostalgia than by watchful "dry-cleaning."

I'll give it an hour, he thought now as he puffed on the cigarette and stared at the top stories of new buildings above the bare tree branches; then an early lunch at Kempinski's if it's still there off Regent Street, and after that the long trip home. To hell with the fallbacks. Forget the back-stage world, as you were ordered to. *Dulce et decorum est.*

But he looked behind him, and for a moment all memory of the busy concerns of these last fourteen years fell away from him like a block of snow falling away from the iron gutters of a hard old house.

Though still far off, the man from the gazebo was walking in his direction at a leisurely pace across the grass, glancing north and south with no appearance of urgency. And the pale face under the hat brim was much older now, wrinkled and hollowed with probably seventy years, but Hale had encountered him at enough points during his life to remember him continuously all the way back—to the summer of 1929, when Hale had been seven years old.

Andrew Hale had grown up in the Cotswold village of Chipping Campden, seventy-five miles northwest of London, in a steep-roofed stone house that he and his mother had shared with her elderly father. Andrew had slept in an ornate old shuttered box bed because at night his mother and grandfather had had to carry their lamps through his room to get to theirs, and on many evenings he would slide the oak shutters closed from outside the bed and then sneak to the head of the stairs to listen to the stilted, formal quarreling of the two adults in the parlor below.

Andrew and his mother had been Roman Catholics, but his grandfather had been a censorious low-church Anglican, and the boy had heard a lot of heated discussions about popes and indulgences and the Virgin Mary, punctuated by thumps when his grandfather would pound his fist on the enormous old family Bible and exclaim, "Show it to me in the Word of God!"—and well before he was seven years old he had gathered that his mother had once been a missionary Catholic nun who had got pregnant in the Middle East and left her order, and had returned to England when her illegitimate son was two years old. The villagers always said that it was penitential Papist fasting that made Andrew's mother so thin and asthmatic and cross, and young Andrew had not ever had any close friends in Chipping Campden. He had known that in the opinion of his neighbors his father had been a corrupt priest of one species or another, but his mother had made it clear to the boy when he was very young that she would not say anything at all about the man.

Andrew's grandfather had restrained himself from debating religion with the boy, but the old man had taken an active hand in Andrew's upbringing. The old man always said that Andrew was too thin—"looks like bloody Percy Perishing Shelley"—and was forever forcing on him health-concoctions like Plasmon concentrated milk protein, which all by itself was supposed to contain every element required to keep body and soul together, and Parrish's Chemical Food, a nasty red syrup that had to be drunk through a straw to avoid blackening the teeth.

Andrew had frequently escaped to hike the couple of miles to the windy Edge-of-the-Wold, the crest of the steep escarpment that marked the western boundary of the Cotswolds, below which on clear days he could see the roofs of Evesham on the plain and the remote glitter of the River Isbourne. In his daydreams his father was a missionary priest, and Andrew tried to imagine where the man might be, and how they might one day meet.

Before retracing his steps across the hills and stubbled fields to the straw-colored stone houses of Chipping Campden he would sometimes follow the old cowpaths south to look, always from a respectful distance, at the Broadway Tower. Actually it was two mottled limestone towers, with a tall narrow castle-keep wedged corner-on between, and the vertical window slits and the high, crenellated turrets gave it a medieval look that had not been dispelled when he'd learned that it had been built as recently as 1800. Years later, when he had gone to do wartime work for the Secret Intelligence Service in London, the SIS headquarters had been in Broadway Buildings off St. James's Park, and known simply as Broadway; and not until his assignment to Berlin in 1945 had the London offices entirely lost for him the storybook associations with this isolated castle on the Edge-of-the-Wold.

The houses and shops along High Street in Chipping Campden were all narrow and crowded up against one another, the rows of pointed rooftops denting the sky like the teeth of a saw. Though when Sunday morning skies were clear Andrew and his mother would take her father's little 10-horsepower Austin to the Catholic church in Stow-on-the-Wold, in threatening weather his mother would give in to her father's demand that they attend the Anglican church in town, and Andrew would hurry along the High Street sidewalk to keep up with the longer strides of his mother and grandfather; the houses weren't set back at all from the sidewalk pavement, so that if Andrew turned his head away from the street, he'd be peering through leaded glass straight into someone's front parlor, and he had always worried that the old man's flailing walking stick would break a window. Andrew had wished he could walk down the middle of the street, or walk entirely away, straight out across the unbounded fields.

On Easter, Andrew and his mother would attend midnight Easter Vigil Mass in Stow-on-the-Wold, and then after they had driven back home, before the little car's motor had cooled off, all three of them would climb into the vehicle and drive to the dawn service at the Anglican church in Fairford. Little Andrew would sit yawning and uneasy through the non-Catholic and therefore heretical service, sometimes peering fearfully at the medieval stained-glass western window, where a huge Satan was depicted devouring unhappy-looking little naked sinners; Satan's body was covered with silver scales, and his round torso was a grimacing, pop-eyed face, but it was the figure's profiled head that howled in the boy's dreams—it was the round-eyed head of a voracious fish, almost imbecilic in its inhuman ferocity.

Many years later he would wonder if he really had, as he seemed to remember, heard in a childhood nightmare a voice call out to this figure, *O Fish, are you constant to the old covenant?*—and then a chorus of the voices of the damned: *Return, and we return; keep faith, and so will we . . .* And he would suppose that he might have, if the dream had been on the very last night of some year.

Andrew had formally renounced Satan by proxy and been baptized in the actual Jordan River, according to his mother—"on the Palestine shore, at Allenby Bridge near Jericho," she would occasionally add, very quietly—and when he was seven years old he had taken his first Holy Communion at the church in Stow-on-the-Wold. After the Mass, instead of driving back up to Chipping Campden, his mother had for once driven away from the church heading farther south. Explaining to the boy only that he needed to meet his godfather, she had piloted the little car straight on through Oxford and on, eventually, to the A103 into London. Andrew had sat quietly beside her in his new coat and tie, trying to comprehend the fact that he had just consumed the body and blood of Christ, and wondering why he had never heard of this godfather until this day.

In 1929 the Secret Intelligence Service headquarters was on the top floor and rooftop of a residential building across the street from the War Office, in Whitehall Court. When Andrew and his mother stepped off the lift on the seventh floor, they were in the building's eastern turret; through a narrow window the boy could see some formal gardens in sunlight below, and Hungerford Bridge spanning the broad steely face of the Thames beyond. The lift had smelled of latakia tobacco and hair oil, and the warm air in the turret room was spicy with the vanilla scent of very old paper.

Andrew didn't know what place this was, and from the frown on his mother's thin face as she glanced around at the paneled chamber he guessed that she had never been here and had expected something grander.

The man who stepped forward and took her arm had been in his late thirties then, his raven-black hair combed straight back from his high forehead, his jawline still firm above the stiff white collar and the knot of his Old Etonian tie. "Miss Hale," he said, smiling; and then he glanced down at Andrew and added, "And this must be . . . the son."

"Who has no knowledge that would put him at peril," Andrew's mother said.

"Easier to do than undo," the man said cheerfully, apparently agreeing with her. "My dears, C wants you shown right in to him," he went on, turning toward the narrowest, steepest stairway Andrew had ever seen, "so if you'll let me lead you through the maze . . ."

But first Andrew's mother crouched beside him, the hem of her linen dress sweeping the scuffed wood floor, and she licked her fingers and pushed back the boy's unruly blond hair. "These are the people who got us home from Cairo," she said quietly, "when . . . Herod . . . was looking for you. And they're the King's men. They deserve our obedience."

"Herod!" laughed their escort as Andrew's mother straightened and led the boy by the hand toward the stairs. "Well, Herod is no longer in the service of the Raj—and he's doing any harrying of *Nazrani* children in Jidda nowadays, for an Arab king."

Hale's mother snapped, *"Uskut!"*—an exclamation she sometimes used around the house to convey *shut up.* "God blacken his face!"

"Inshallah bukra," the man answered, in what might have been Arabic. He and Andrew's mother nearly had to shuffle sideways to climb the tight-curving counterclockwise stairs, ducking their heads around a caged and buzzing electric light, though Andrew was able to tap up the stairs comfortably.

Andrew was excited by the air of secret knowledge implicit in this place and this man, and he was impressed that his mother had had dealings with whoever these mysterious King's men were; still, he didn't like the cruel sort of humor that seemed to be expressed in the lines under the black-haired man's eyes, and he wondered why these stairs had evidently been built to keep very big men from ascending.

Their escort stopped at a door on the first landing and pulled a ring of keys from his trouser pocket, and when he had unlocked it and pushed it open Andrew was startled at the sudden sunlight and fresh river-scented air. An iron pedestrian bridge stretched away for twenty feet over the rooftop to a rambling structure that looked to Andrew like a half-collapsed crazy old ship, patched together out of a dozen mismatched vessels and grounded on this roof by some calamitously high tide. Partly the structure was green-painted wood, partly bare corrugated metal; Marconi radio masts and wind-socks and the spinning cups of anemometers bristled on its topsides, and interrupted patterns of round windows, and several balconies like railed decks, implied stairs and irregularly arranged floors within. From various brick and iron and concrete chimneys, yellow and black smokes curled away into the blue sky.

The three of them strode clattering across the bridge, and Andrew watched his mother's graying brown hair toss in the wind. *Got us home from Cairo,* he thought; *when Herod was looking for you.* And the man she called Herod is with an Arab king now, in a place called something like *jitter.*

Andrew's mother had instructed him in geography, as well as mathematics and Latin and Greek and history and literature and the tenets of the Catholic faith, but except for the Holy Land she had always dealt cursorily with the Middle East.

At the open doorway on the far side of the bridge two men stood back to let the trio pass, and Andrew saw what he guessed was the steel-and-polished-wood butt of a revolver under the coat of one of them. His mind was whirling with potent words: *Cairo* and *revolver* and *the Raj* and *the body and blood of Christ,* and he wondered anxiously if it was a sin to vomit after taking Communion. He did almost feel seasick.

The black-haired man now led Andrew and his mother through a succession of doors and narrow climbing and descending hallways, and if Andrew had known where north was when he had come in, he would not have known it any longer; the floor was sometimes carpeted, sometimes bare wood or tile. Then they turned left into a dim side-hall, and immediately right under a low arch, and scuffed their way up another electrically illuminated staircase, this one turning clockwise. Net zero, Andrew thought dizzily.

At the top was a door upholstered quilt-fashion in polished red leather, with a green light glowing above it. Their guide pressed a button beside the door frame, and by this time Andrew wouldn't have been very surprised if a trapdoor had opened under them, sending them to their destination down a slide; but the door simply swung open.

The black-haired man swept a hand into the little room beyond. "Our Chief," he said. Andrew was the first to step inside, his nose wrinkling involuntarily at the mingled smells of curry, oiled metal, and a cluster of purple foxglove flowers that stood in a vase on the big Victorian desk.

A stocky man in the uniform of a British colonel was standing beside the room's one small window, and he appeared to be trying to disassemble a spiderweb with a brass letter opener. Without stepping away from the window he turned toward his visitors; he was bald, with bristly gray hair above his ears, and his weathered jaw and nose were prominent like granite outcroppings on a cliff face. After a moment his chilly gray eyes narrowed in a smile, and he held out his free right hand. "Andrew, I think," he said.

"Yes, sir," said the boy, crossing the old Oriental carpet to shake the man's callused hand.

"Splendid." The old man returned his attention to the spiderweb then, and Andrew watched him expectantly, soon noticing that the loose left thigh of the old man's uniform trousers, though clean and pressed, was riddled with little half-inch cuts; but after half a minute had passed Andrew let his eyes dart around the dim room. Six black Bakelite hook-and-candlestick telephones hung on extendable scissors-supports against the wall, and several glass flagons half-filled with colored liquids stood on a table beside them; one wall was all shelves, and models of submarines and airplanes served as haphazard bookends and dividers for the vast collection of leather-bound volumes and sheaves of paper that were crowded together and stacked every-which-way on the shelves. On the walls were hung rubber gas masks, tacked-up maps, diagrams of radio vacuum valves, and a photograph of a group of European villagers lined up against a wall facing a Prussian firing squad.

"There's a fly here," said the Chief, without looking up from his work.

Not sure who was being addressed, Andrew glanced back at his mother, who just widened her eyes in helpless puzzlement. Even the man who had led them here was simply blank-faced.

"Andrew, lad," the Chief went on impatiently, "look here. Do you see this fly, in the web? Waving his legs like a madman."

Andrew stepped up beside the burly old man and pushed back a lock of his long blond hair to peer at the windowsill. A bluebottle fly was struggling in the spiderweb. "Yes, sir."

"Can you kill it?"

Bewildered, assuming this was some token sort of test of ruthlessness, the boy swallowed against his nausea and then nodded and held out his hand for the letter opener.

"No," said the Chief impatiently, "with your will alone. Can you kill the fly just by looking at it?"

Andrew really didn't know whether he wanted to laugh or start crying. He heard his mother shift and mutter behind him. "No, sir," he said hoarsely.

The old Chief sighed, and turned to stare for several seconds straight into the boy's eyes. "No," he said at last, gently. Then he hugely startled Andrew by stabbing the letter opener into his own left thigh, which gave out a knock that let the boy know it was a wooden leg. Through ringing ears Andrew heard the Chief go on, "No, I see you could not—and good for you. Are you interested in radio, lad?" He rocked the letter opener out of his leg and tested the point with his thumb.

Chipping Campden had only got electricity the year before. "We don't own one," Andrew answered. He had fainted in church once, and the remembered rainbow glitter of unconsciousness was crowding in now from the edges of his vision—so he abruptly sat down cross-legged on the carpet and took several deep breaths. "Excuse me," he said. "I'll be all right—"

Andrew's mother was crouching beside him, her hand on his forehead. "The boy hasn't eaten since midnight," she said in an accusing or pleading voice.

"Good Lord," came the Chief's voice from over Andrew's head. "Where did they drive from, Scotland? I thought you said they live in Oxfordshire."

"That's right, sir," the black-haired man said, "in the Cotswolds. This is some Catholic fast, I believe."

"Of course. Polarized, you see? Like Merlin in the old stories, christened. Nevertheless—Andrew."

Andrew looked up into the old man's stern face, and he felt clearheaded enough now to get back up onto his feet. "Yes, sir," he said when he was standing again. His mother had stood up too, and he could feel that she was right behind him.

"Remember your dreams." The Chief scowled. "Dreams, right? Things you see when you're asleep, things you hear? Don't *write them down,* but remember them. One day Theodora will ask you about them."

"Yes, sir. I will, sir." Andrew was simply postponing the effort of trying to imagine some no doubt frightening-looking woman named Theodora interrogating him about his dreams at some future date.

"Good lad. When is your birthday?"

"January the sixth, sir."

"And why the hell shouldn't it be, eh? Sorry. Good. Your mother has done very well in these seven years. Do as she tells you." He waved his hand, suddenly looking very tired. "Go and get something to eat now, and then go home to your Cotswolds. And don't—*worry,* about anything, understand? You're on our rolls."

"Yes, sir. Uh—thank you, sir."

Andrew and his mother had been abruptly led out then, and the black-haired man had taken them down to a narrow dark lunchroom or employees' bar on the seventh floor, and simply left them there, after telling them that their meal would be paid for by the Crown. Andrew managed to get down a ham sandwich and a glass of ginger beer, and he had guessed that he shouldn't talk about the affairs of this place while he was still in it. Even on the drive home, though, his mother had parried his questions with evasions, and assurances that he'd be told everything one day, and that she didn't know very much about it all herself; and when he had finally asked which of those men had been his godfather, she had hesitated.

"The man who led us in," she'd said finally, "was the one who . . . well, the wooden-legged chap—you saw that it was an artificial limb, didn't you, that he stabbed himself in?—he took the . . ." Then she had sighed, not taking her eyes off the already shadow-streaked road that led toward Oxford and eventually, beyond that, home. "Well, it's the whole service, really, I suppose."

On our rolls.

Shortly after the visit to London his mother had begun receiving checks from an obscure City bank called Drummond's. They had not been accompanied by any invoices or memoranda, and she had let her father believe that the money was belated payment from Andrew's delinquent father, but Andrew had known that it was from "the Crown"— and sometimes when he'd been alone on the windy hill below the Broadway Tower he had tried to imagine what sort of services it might prove to be payment for.

Remember your dreams.

In his dreams, especially right at the end of the year and during the first nights of 1930, he sometimes found himself standing alone in a desert by moonlight; and always the whole landscape had been spinning, silently, while he tried to measure the angle of the horizon with some kind of swiveling telescope on a tripod. Once in the dream he had looked up, and been awakened in a jolt of vertigo by the sight of the stars spinning too. For a few minutes after he woke from these dreams he couldn't think in words, only in moods and images of desert vistas he had never seen; and though he knew—as if it were something exotic!— that he was a human being living in this house, sometimes he wasn't sure whether he was the old grandfather, or the ex-nun mother, or the little boy who slept in the wooden box.

He always felt that he should go to Confession after having one of these dreams, though he never did; he was sure that if he could somehow manage to convey to the priest the true nature of these dreams, which he didn't even know himself, the priest would excommunicate him and call for an exorcist.

And he had begun to get unsolicited subscriptions to magazines about amateur radio and wireless telegraphy. He tried to read them but wasn't able to make much sense of all the talk of enameled wire, loose couplers, regenerative receivers, and Brandes phones; he would have canceled the subscriptions if he had not remembered the one-legged old man's question—*Are you interested in radio, lad?*—and anyway the subscriptions had not followed him to his new address when he went away to school two years later.

In her new affluence Andrew's mother had enrolled him in St. John's, a Catholic boys' boarding school in old Windsor, across the Thames and four miles downriver from Eton. The school was a massive old three-story brick building at the end of a birch-lined driveway, and he slept in one of a row of thirty curtained cubicles that crowded both sides of a long hallway on the third floor—no hardship to someone used to sleeping in an eighteenth-century box bed—and ate in the refectory hall downstairs with an army of boys ranging from his own age, nine, up to fourteen. To his own surprise, he had not suffered at all from homesickness. The teachers were all Jesuit priests, and every day started with a brief Mass in the chapel and ended with evening prayers; and in the busy hours between he found that he was good at French and geometry, subjects his mother had not been able to teach him, and that he could make friends.

Obedient to his mother, he had told his new companions about his youth in the Cotswolds but had not ever mentioned the circumstances of his birth, and never told them about his peculiar corporate "godfather."

His mother had motored down to visit on three or four weekends in each term, and had written infrequent letters; her invariable topics of discussion had been the petty doings of her neighbors and an anxious insistence that Andrew pay attention to his religious instruction, and politics—she had been a Tory at least since Andrew had been born, and though glad of the failure of MacDonald's Labour Party in '31, she'd been alarmed by the subsequent general mood in favor of the League of Nations and worldwide disarmament: "Not all the beasts that were kept out of the Ark had the decency to perish," she had said once. Andrew had known better than to try to introduce topics like his father, or the mysterious King's men in the rooftop building in London. In the summers Andrew had taken the train home to Chipping Campden, but he had spent most of his time during those months hiking or reading, guiltily looking forward to the beginning of the fall term.

In the spring of 1935 one of the Jesuit priests had come to Andrew's cubicle before Mass to tell him that his mother had died the day before, of a sudden stroke.

Andrew Hale let the dapper old man in the homburg hat walk on past him at a distance of a dozen yards, while Hale squinted through his cigarette smoke and scanned the misty lawns back in the direction of the gazebo and Queen's Walk. The only people visible in that direction were a woman walking a dog in the middle distance and two bearded young men beyond her striding briskly from north to south; neither party was in a position to signal the other, and they were all looking elsewhere in this moment of the old man's closest approach to Hale; clearly the old man wasn't being followed. And neither was Hale, or the old man would have seen it and simply disappeared, to try to meet later at a fallback.

Now the old man had halted and pulled a map from an inside pocket. Hale's eye was caught by the flash of white paper when the man partly unfolded the map and began frowning at it and glancing at the distant roofs of buildings. In fact the building on top of which Hale had first met him was only a ten minutes' walk to the east, past St. James's Park and Whitehall, but Hale knew that this flashing of the map was a signal; and so Hale was looking directly at him when the old man caught his gaze and then raised his white eyebrows under the hat brim.

Hale took one last deep draw off the cigarette, and tossed it away onto the grass, before walking over to where the man stood. His heart was still thumping rapidly.

"Lost, Jimmie?" he said through exhaled smoke, with muted sarcasm.

"Without a clue, my dear." Jimmie Theodora folded up the map and tucked it back inside his overcoat. "Actually," he went on as he began strolling away in the direction of Whitehall, with Hale following, "I do hardly know where I am in London these days. The Green Park *I* remember has a barrage balloon moored back there by the Arch, and piles of help-yourself coal lining the walks. You remember."

"No beatniks, in those days."

"*Aren't* they frightful? Makes you wonder why we still bother."

"You—we?—are still bothering, I gather."

"Yes," Jimmie Theodora said flatly. "And yes, you had bloody well better say 'we.' "

It's "we" when *you* say it is, Hale thought as he followed the old man across the wet grass, not sure whether his thought was wry or bitter.

The day of his mother's funeral in Stow-on-the-Wold had dawned sunny, but like many such Cotswold days it had turned rainy by noon, and the sparse knot of mourners on the grass by the grave had been clustered under gleaming black umbrellas. They were shopkeepers and neighbors from Chipping Campden, mostly friends of Andrew's grandfather—but the solemn, frightened boy had glimpsed a face at the back of the group that he was sure he recognized from his First Communion day trip to London, six years previous. Andrew had tugged his hand free of his grandfather's to go reeling away from the grave toward the black-haired man, who at that moment seemed like closer kin than the grand-father; but Andrew had caught a surprised and admonishing scowl on that well-remembered face, and then the black-haired man had simply been gone, not present at all. Later Andrew had concluded that the man must have stepped back out of sight and quickly assumed a disguise—false moustache? cheek inserts, contrary posture, a sexton's dirty work-shirt under the quickly discarded morning coat and dickey?—but on that morning Andrew had gone blundering through the mourners, tear-fully and idiotically calling, "Sir? Sir?" since he hadn't even known the man's name. Jimmie Theodora had no doubt been embarrassed for him and made an unobtrusive exit as soon as possible.

The priests at St. John's had known the name and address of a solic-itor Andrew's mother had been in touch with, which proved to be a pear-shaped little man by the name of Corliss, and after the funeral ser-vice the solicitor had driven Andrew and his grandfather to an office in Cirencester. There Corliss had explained that the uncle—he had paused before the word and then pronounced it so clearly and deliberately that even Andrew's grandfather had not bothered to object that no such per-son existed—who had been paying for Andrew's support and schooling would continue to do so, but that this benefactor would now no longer be persuaded that an expensive and Roman Catholic school like St. John's was appropriate. Andrew's grandfather had shifted to a more comfortable position in his chair at that, clearly pleased. Andrew was to be sent to the City of London School for Boys instead, and would inci-dentally be required to add the study of German to his curriculum.

During the long drive back south to Windsor, where Andrew could at least finish out the present school term at St. John's, his grandfather had gruffly advised the thirteen-year-old boy to get into the Officers' Training Corps as soon as he could; war with Germany was inevitable, the old man had said, now that Hitler was Chancellor, and even the blindly optimistic Prime Minister Baldwin had admitted that the German Air Force was better than the British. But Andrew's grandfather had been an old soldier, having fought with Kitchener in the Sudan and in South Africa during the Boer War, and Andrew had not taken seriously the old man's apocalyptic predictions of bombs falling on London. Andrew's only goal at this period, which he had known better than to confide to the eld-erly Anglican hunched over the steering wheel to his right, had been a vague intention to become a Jesuit priest himself one day.

▼▼▼

Within a year that frail ambition had been forgotten.

In those days the City of London School had been housed in a four-storied red-brick building with a grandly pilastered front, on the Victoria Embankment right next to Blackfriars Bridge and the new Unilever House with all its marble statues standing between the pillars along the fifth-floor colonnade; and it was only a short walk to the Law Courts at the Temple, where barristers in wigs and gowns could be seen hurrying through the arched gray stone halls, and to the new Daily Express Building in Fleet Street, already known as the Black Lubyanka because of its black-glass-and-chrome Art Deco architecture. Like the other boys at the school, Andrew wore a black coat and striped trousers and affected an air of sophistication, and his aim now was to become a barrister or a foreign correspondent for some prestigious newspaper.

The older boys, enviably allowed to use the school's Embankment entrance and to have lunch out in the City, had all seemed to be very worldly and political. Some, captivated by newsreels of the splendid Olympic Games in Berlin as much as for any other reason, subscribed to *Germany Today* and favored the pro-German position of the Prince of Wales, who had become King Edward VIII in early 1936. Others were passionate about Marxism and the valiant Trotskyite Republicans fighting a losing war against the fascist rebels in Spain. It had all seemed very remote to Andrew, and he had tended to be tepidly convinced by whatever argument had most recently been brought to bear. Any decision about his grandfather's advice had been taken out of his hands when *all* the boys at the City of London School had been drafted into the Officers' Training Corps, and so Andrew had twice a week put on his little khaki uniform and got into a bus to go to a rifle range and obediently shoot at targets with an old .303 rifle loaded with .22 rounds; the idea of an actual war, though, was still as exotically implausible as marriage—or death.

But Edward VIII abdicated in order to marry an American divorcée, and the Russians and the Germans made a pact not to attack each other, and Parliament passed a law declaring that men of twenty years of age were to be conscripted into the armed forces. And in September of 1939 the newspapers announced that Germany had invaded Poland and that

England had declared war on Germany, and all the boys were evacuated to Haslemere College in Surrey, forty miles southwest of London.

For an uneventful eight months Andrew lived with two other boys in a cottage that got so cold in the winter that the chamber-pot and its contents froze, and went to makeshift classes in the now-very-crowded Haslemere College buildings; then in May of 1940 the German Army finally moved again, sweeping through Holland and Belgium, and Prime Minister Chamberlain's government collapsed, to be replaced by Churchill's National Government; and in September the bombs began to fall on London.

▼

2

London, World War II

The game is so large that one sees but a little at a time.
    —Rudyard Kipling, *Kim*

A schoolmate of his had been given permission to live at home in the West End of London during that summer, and, when the autumn term in Haslemere had subsequently started up, the boy had shakily described to Andrew the new silver pin-heads of barrage balloons stippling the blue horizon to the east on the balmy early evening of September 7, and the uneven roar of Heinkel bomber engines in the distance, and then the rolling, cracking thunder of bombs exploding on the Woolwich Arsenal and the Limehouse Docks ten or twelve miles away; and that night, closer, perhaps only half a dozen miles to the east, the bright orange glow of the flames on both sides of the river that had lit the whole sky when a fresh lot of German bombers had flown over after eight o'clock and somehow kept up the nightmare engine-roar and thumping of bombs until four-thirty the next morning, simply incinerating whole districts of British streets and shops and homes. The boy had been sent back to Haslemere on a crowded morning train, and for the first twenty miles of the trip he had been able to see the storm cloud of black smoke behind him; the inconceivable bombing had been repeated every single night since then, and Andrew's friend relied on daily telegrams now to know that his parents were still alive. By the time he had told all this to Andrew, the eight-page wartime newspapers were describing the rows of old trucks that were being set out on any English fields big enough for an enemy airplane to land in, and ditches freshly dug in Kent to stop invading tanks. Already butter and sugar were being rationed.

Perhaps because he had grown up knowing that he had been born abroad in a perennially insecure region, this abrupt prospect of the invasion and defeat of his homeland galvanized Andrew Hale. He was eighteen now, and he was suddenly determined to enlist in the Royal Air Force at once, without waiting to finish school and the Officers' Training Corps program. He wrote to Corliss in Cirencester, demanding his birth certificate, but when the lawyer finally wrote back it was to say that that document was in the hands of the uncle, who was some sort of secretary in Whitehall. Corliss was willing to give Andrew what little information he himself had: a Post Office box number, a telephone number, and a name—James Theodora.

Andrew remembered the one-legged old colonel telling him to remember his dreams—*One day Theodora will ask you about them*—and though the prospect of recounting some of his dreams made him uncomfortable, he knew he was on the right track.

The telephone number had been a challenge; Andrew had had to get permission to use the instrument in the Haslemere College warden's office during a study hour, with the cost laboriously calculated and added onto his tuition balance. And the trunk line to London had been slow to connect numbers even before the bombing began, and now, though the service still worked, calls were frequently cut off, or interrupted with abrupt bursts of static, or even shifted somehow among startled parties, implicit testimony to the reported hundreds of high-explosive bombs that were hammering the City every night. After interrupting several calls, and even breaking in on what sounded like a military radio transmission, Andrew heard a woman answer, "Hullo?"

"I need to speak with James Theodora," Andrew had said, sweating under the warden's by now impatient stare. "He's my—my uncle—I met him at his office, and his Chief, who had a wooden—"

"—Indian out in front of his tobacconist shop in Boston, I dare say," the woman interrupted breezily. "Nobody cares about any of that. If we've got a James Theodora at the firm here, I'll have him call you. What's the number there?"

Andrew nervously asked the warden, and then gave her the office telephone number. "It's about my—"

"No use telling me, my good man. And what's your first name? Don't give me your last name." Andrew told her. "Right, very well, Andrew. If we've got this fellow here, I'll see he gets the message." Abruptly Andrew was holding a dead telephone.

He hung it up, humbly thanked the warden, and left the office; but an hour later the warden had him summoned back from class. The telephone earpiece sat waiting for him like an upside-down black teacup on the desktop, with the warden staring as if these City boys must all be W.1 district plutocrats. Andrew picked it up and said hello.

"Andrew," came a man's impatient voice. "What's the trouble?"

"Uh, is this—who I called—"

"*Yes,* this is who you called. *The odor o'* sanctity should be detectable even over the line."

"Oh, heh, yes. Well—no trouble, sir, it's just that I want to—" Peripherally he saw the warden still staring at him. "It occurred to me that I don't have all my personal records in my possession here at the school; you know, medical records, birth certificate . . ."

"You want to *enlist,* you bloody little fool, don't you? No, put it out of your mind. The Crown will call for you in good season, and it's not for you to . . . volunteer your own suggestions, your invaluable suggestions. Your mother once said that you owe obedience, do you recall that? 'On our rolls' cuts both ways. We also serve who only stand and wait, boy."

Again Andrew was holding a dead telephone receiver. "Thank you, sir," he told the warden as he set it back down on the table.

That had been on a Friday in early October of 1940. After his last class he had skipped dinner, packed a bag, and hiked to the railway station in town, determined to catch a train to London or to whatever station—Battersea? *Wimbledon?*—might be as close to the city as the railway line extended these days. He would tell the RAF recruiters that he was a London resident, which had been true until only a year ago, and that his birth certificate had been burned up in the bombing. They would surely take him—he had read that they were in desperate need of air crews.

But as he pushed open the heavy glass-paneled doors of the Haslemere railway station lobby, a moustached man in a tweed cap and heavy coat had stood up from a bench, smiling at him, and walked across the tiled floor to hook his strong left arm around Andrew's shoulders.

"Andrew Hale," the man had said fondly as he forced him to walk toward a row of empty benches at the far end of the lobby, "what *have* I got here?" His right hand was inside his coat, and Andrew saw the silvery point of a knife blade appear from behind the lapel and then withdraw. "Rhetorical question, lad. You're on the strength, you know, on the rolls; and you were given an *order*, is what that was, today. Do you know what the penalty is for disobeying orders during wartime?"

Andrew was sure he had not yet irretrievably disobeyed the order; he was still in Haslemere. But he couldn't help glancing into the man's eyes, and the utter, almost vacant remoteness of the returned gaze was so at odds with the man's affected cheer that Andrew felt diminished and sick. In the months to come, on crisp sunny days in the rural Surrey winter, he would sometimes doubt it; but on this gold-lit late autumn evening he had been convinced that the terrible finality of his own death was as casually possible, and could be achieved as indifferently, as the lighting of a cigarette or the clearing of a throat.

"I—hadn't realized," he said hoarsely, not looking at the man and trying to lob the words out into the lobby, as if they weren't addressed specifically to him. "I won't do it again."

"You'll do what you're told?" The voice was jovial.

"*Yes*," Andrew whispered.

"Then happily no exertions are called for. I've got a car in the yard— I'll drive you back to your school. Come along."

"No. Please." Andrew's forehead was sweaty, and his mouth was full of salty saliva. "Let me walk back." How could the man imagine that Andrew would willingly sit in a car with him, or prolong this intolerable proximity for one moment more than he had to?

The man—the agent? the domestic assassin?—shrugged and strode away, and Andrew left the station and trudged back to the college. Generally he only suffered what he thought of as his "Arabian Nightmares" in the week after Christmas, but that night in a dream he was suspended over a moonlit ocean, watching, or perhaps even propelling, horizontal beams of light that moved across the dark face of the waters like spokes of a vast turning wheel; and when he convulsed awake before dawn, clammy with sweat, he was muttering feverishly in a language he did not understand. He had not been able to get back to sleep, and he'd kept remembering the voice, eleven years earlier, of the man who had turned out to be Theodora: *Herod is no longer in the service of the Raj— and he's doing any harrying of* Nazrani *children in Jidda nowadays, for an Arab king.*

Hale was glad he would not be telling his dreams to the Theodora person any time soon, and he did not try again to enlist.

We also serve who only stand and wait.

In November he successfully sat for an exhibition scholarship to Magdalen College, Oxford, and in the spring of 1941 he went up to that college to read English literature.

His allowance from Drummond's Bank in Admiralty Arch was not big enough for him to do any of the high living for which Oxford was legendary, but wartime rationing appeared to have cut down on that kind of thing in any case—even cigarettes and beer were too costly for most of the students in Hale's college, and it was fortunate that the one-way lanes of Oxford were too narrow for comfortable driving and parking, since bicycles were the only vehicles most students could afford to maintain. His time was spent mostly in the Bodleian Library researching Spenser and Malory, and defending his resultant essays in weekly sessions with his merciless tutor.

A couple of his friends from the City of London School had also come to Oxford colleges, and the three of them would sometimes go pub-hopping up and down Broad Street in the shadow of the old Sheldonian Theatre dome; and Hale eventually even followed their example and joined a student wing of the Communist Party, more in the hope of meeting girls at meetings and getting free refreshments than from any real ideological sympathy.

Before the war, attendance at chapel had apparently been compulsory in Magdalen, except to such students as cared to arise early and report to the Dean to have their names entered in the roll-call; now it was optional, and it seemed that everybody chose to sleep in and skip chapel. Andrew had stopped going to church during the period of evacuation to Haslemere, or perhaps a little before that, and lately on school forms he had begun writing AGN, for agnostic, when his religious denomination was asked for, rather than RC for Roman Catholic. At least from a distance, communism had seemed to offer a realistic, contemporary and even *geographical* alternative, in dealing with the vague yet nagging sense of spiritual duty, to the remembered devotions and gospel texts and rosaries; and in any case international "solidarity" seemed to be the only pragmatic hope for defeating Nazi Germany.

Remembering the cold man in the Haslemere train station, he had first taken the precaution of writing to the London post office box and asking Theodora if there was any objection to his joining the Party; but he'd had no reply, and decided *qui tacit consentit.*

In fact the Party meetings were dull, uninspiring affairs, full of earnest speeches about Marx and Stalin and five-year-plans, with occasional films of laboring iron foundries and farm machinery; Hale was entranced with the Dublin accent of one Iris Murdoch, but she was an elegant twenty-two-year-old Somerville student, and he couldn't imagine suggesting to her that she come out for tea with him sometime. By the end of the first term he had pretty much stopped attending meetings, and so he was surprised to get an invitation through the post from a girl at St. Hilda's College, asking him to join her at a big meeting in the London Party headquarters in King Street on a Friday night in September.

He didn't even consider refusing; and on the appointed evening he was able to get a train to the underground station in St. John's Wood, and he alighted at Covent Garden at dusk and walked to King Street. Though German armies had now swept through the Balkans and Greece and were presently threatening Africa, the London bombings had finally stopped in May. Even shops with their front walls and windows blown out had BUSINESS AS USUAL banners strung across the ragged gaps, and cheerful brassy Glenn Miller songs echoed from radio speakers out into the streets; but after dark, taxis still drove with their headlamps out and were hailed by pedestrians blinking electric torches at them. Hale managed to share a taxi with an elderly gentleman going to the Garrick Club, and when Hale asked to be let off at Number 16 King Street the driver embarrassed him by saying, as the cab slowed in front of the dark office block, "Communist Party Headquarters, sir."

"Thank you," Hale mumbled, wincing under the clubman's peripherally glimpsed glare as he counted out shillings in the spotlight of the driver's cigarette lighter. He did recall that the St. Hilda's girl had been pretty.

Six or eight people were standing on the pavement in front of the tall entry arch, and as Hale stepped away from the departing cab and blinked around, trying to get back his night vision, a figure approached him out of the darkness and a man's Cockney voice said, "And are you a Party member as well, sir?"

"That's right," Andrew told him. "Student branch in Oxford. I'm here for the meeting. I'm to meet a young lady."

"Ah—well, I'm afraid our jail cells are segregated by gender, sir. Perhaps you'll be able to write her a letter, if the censors have no objections."

Belatedly Hale noticed the shape of a City police helmet, and his ribs tingled and his face went cold several seconds before he realized that he was frightened—if only he had answered, *Certainly not, isn't this Garrick's?* a mere twenty seconds ago!

"It's not . . . against the law to belong to the Party," he said, trying to speak in a reasonable tone. Three months earlier Germany had finally invaded Russia, violating their non-aggression pact and making the Soviet Union at least nominally a British ally.

"Espionage and subversion still are, sir, very much so. There's a document on our air strategy that's been lifted from the Air Ministry's files. Our men are inside, trying to stop you lot from incinerating papers." Hale now saw that a dark van was parked farther up the street, with a dimly visible blur of smoke fluttering at the exhaust. "I'll have to ask you to come with me," the policeman said, taking Hale's elbow.

At last Hale realized what it was that he was afraid of: not the police, not jail, nor even possible expulsion from Magdalen College, but the man in the Haslemere railway station, or another of his sort, one Hale wouldn't even recognize. Being here tonight suddenly looked a lot like *disobeying orders during wartime.*

With a despairing moan, Hale yanked his arm free of the policeman's grip and began running back the way his taxi had come, panting more from panic than from exertion as the hard soles of his shoes skidded noisily on the unseen pavement. Suddenly there were torch beams and tall-helmeted silhouettes everywhere in the darkness—what were *City* police doing out here in Covent Garden?—and after sprinting and dodging for two hundred yards, Hale was cornered on the moonlit steps of the little St. Paul's church in the Piazza. He held up his hands palms-outward against the dazzling yellow lights until the pursuing figures had cautiously shuffled close enough to seize his arms and twist him around and yank down the shoulders of his jacket; he heard a seam rip, and the autumn evening breeze was chilly through his sweat-soaked dress shirt.

The policeman who had grabbed him down the street came puffing up as others were snapping manacles onto Hale's wrists and rifling his pockets. "If your name," the man wheezed angrily, "isn't—bloody *Hale,* I'm going to thrash you—right here on the church steps."

"The name's—in my notecase," panted Hale. He could hear the van accelerating in reverse, audibly weaving in the lane as it came fast the wrong way up King Street in the dark. Had there been nobody else to arrest? "Andrew Hale."

Makes you wonder why we still bother.

Hale had started to slant his stride to the right, away from the direction Theodora was taking across the wet grass of Green Park, and after a moment he realized that this was the old training kicking in; the plot here said that he had given an elderly stranger advice to do with the map, and that the two of them didn't know each other, weren't together. Hale squinted to the right, as if considering walking west toward Hyde Park Corner tube station, but dutifully kept the figure of the old man clearly in his peripheral vision.

Now Theodora reached up with his gnarled left hand had took off the black homburg. Even out of the corner of his eye Hale could see the spotty bald scalp and the neatly styled white hair, so different from the black locks he remembered seeing as a boy; and he nearly didn't notice the signal—the old man had whirled the hat on one finger before flipping it back onto his head. *Get in the car,* that move meant.

"Not so fast," Hale whispered through clenched teeth. These were real enemy-territory contact procedures, and for the first time in many years he was experiencing the old anxiety that was somehow more immediate than fear of capture—*don't slip up, don't let down the side.*

Beyond the beech trunks ahead, he could see vehicles driving east down the lanes of Constitution Hill, all their colors drab on this gray day. Keep your pace steady, he told himself. Don't try to help. They'll have got this timed.

This? he wondered helplessly. What, did Khrushchev only *pretend* to back down from Kennedy's ultimatum about the Cuban missiles two months ago, have all the legal Soviet and Sov Bloc residencies disappeared from their embassies at once, gone covert and illegal, is war the next card to be dealt? But why are *we* miming? Or has there been some sort of in-house coup at SIS, so that old peripheral agents are being reactivated and concealed from the present victors? Am I in a *faction* here?

When he passed the bordering trees and stepped off the grass onto the pavement, the old man was an anonymous figure twenty yards away to his left, and Hale just hoped no more signals were being given. When Hale paused at the curb—even as he shrilly wondered, *What car?*—a blue Peugeot sedan came grinding up to rock to a halt right in front of him. The passenger-side door was levered open from inside, and he bent over and climbed in; and the car had pulled away from the curb even before he had yanked the door closed.

The driver was a thin woman with iron-gray hair, and he thought he recognized her chin-up profile from the fourth-floor offices at Broadway during the war. He knew better than to ask.

"There's a jacket on the floor," she said. "When I dogleg through Pall Mall, ditch yours and put it on. Not now."

She made a fast but controlled left into the narrower corridor of Basingstoke Road and sped between the briefly glimpsed gray stone porticoes of St. James's Palace and Lancaster House, and then turned left again into the westernmost block of Pall Mall. Hale was gripping the strap on the inside of the passenger door.

"Now," she said, her gaze darting from the cars ahead to her mirrors and back as she juggled the Peugeot rapidly across the lanes. "Glasses and a moustache in the jacket pocket." Hale smiled nervously at the notion of a false moustache, but his face went blank when, after a beat, she added, "Iron anchor in the inside pocket."

He heard his own voice say, "Shit." With his feet braced against the floorboards he shrugged out of his coat without conspicuous contortion, wondering remotely if he would ever get the coat back and if his test questions would still be in the pocket if he did, but his attention was on the gray wool jacket he now snatched up from the floor; he squeezed the lapel, and even through the cloth his fingers found the heavy iron shape of the looped Egyptian cross, properly called an *ankh*. And he was bleakly sure now that the route his driver was tracing would be widdershins, a counterclockwise circle, and that it would loop right around Buckingham Palace to end in Whitehall.

"And lose the tie," she said. "You'll be getting on the back of a motorcycle pretty prompt here."

They were speeding up St. James's Street now, past gentlemen's hat and shoe shops, but as he obediently pulled loose the knot of his tie, Hale didn't look out through the windscreen nor at his driver; he was staring blindly at the fascia panel, remembering the ankhs that had failed to work as anchors for the men he had led up the Ahora Gorge below Mount Ararat in '48, on the night that the starry sky had spun like a ponderous unbalanced wheel over their doomed heads. He was certain now that this new year's business would have nothing to do with any recognized Soviet residents in London, nor with factions that could possibly still be on the active force at SIS.

He pulled his necktie out of his collar and undid the top button of his shirt. "I wish I *could* 'lose the tie,' " he said, his voice sounding child-ish and frightened in his own ears.

This was going straight back to what had been the most-secret core of espionage in the first half of the century, the hidden power he had become dimly, fearfully aware of only in the last three and a half years of his service, after Berlin in '45; the operational theatre that it had been mortally perilous even to know about, more restricted by far than the German Ultra traffic had been during the war, or the Soviet Venona decrypts after; this had been the concealed war that, ironically, facili-tated its own concealment simply by being beyond the capacity of most people to believe.

Like someone tonguing a carious tooth to see if it still ached, he asked himself if *he* still believed it.

He sighed finally and focused on the traffic, and then glanced around to be sure they were in fact passing the Tory Carlton Club, and Brooks's. "They let buses drive in St. James's Street now?" he asked.

"Just in the last year or two," said the woman at the wheel.

He remembered Theodora saying, *I hardly know where I am in London these days.* Me too, Jimmy, he thought. And how do you suppose things are in Erzurum, Al-Kuwait, Berlin? Even Paris?

He was to learn later that the old police station in Temple Lane had been exploded across the flower beds of the Inner Temple Garden by a November bomb; but even at nineteen and in the dark he had known at once that the dimly seen hut he'd been driven to in the police van was a

wartime makeshift. Its roof was a semicircular arched sheet of corrugated metal, and as he was marched up to the door, he saw that the
building sat like a sled on bolted steel beams in the middle of a patch of
cleared pavement, a hundred yards from the pillared entry arch and rak-
ing cornices of St. Paul's Cathedral—the big St. Paul's, at this end of the
ride, Christopher Wren's masterpiece, its dark dome seeming to eclipse
a full quarter of the cloudy nighttime sky.

And even in his despairing panic he shivered at the sight, for he had
motored past St. Paul's Cathedral when he had been a student at the
City of London School—and only the top of its dome had been visible
then above the close-crowding newer buildings. Now it stood alone in
the center of a bomb-cratered plain of low uneven walls, itself miraculously undamaged, like a durable mirage from a previous century.

The night sky was quiet, and no searchlights swept across the
patchy clouds; but the BUSINESS AS USUAL signs he had seen earlier in the
evening, and the brave radio program music he had heard echoing out
of gutted shops, seemed intolerably gallant and sad when recalled to
mind on this viciously broken landscape, and the breath caught in his
throat to imagine this supremely British old church, this heart of London, surrounded by walls of roaring flame as it lately must have been.

"In you go, Ivan," said one of the policemen, gripping his upper arm.

After being ducked through a pair of velvet blackout curtains Hale
had found himself in a little office lit by unshaded electric bulbs dangling from the curved ceiling, and in front of a tall desk or lectern he
was unshackled so that each of his fingers in turn could be rolled on a
stamp pad and then pressed onto squares printed on a card—an
unusual procedure in a standard arrest, he believed. A teakettle hissed
on a tiny electric stove in the corner.

A white-haired officer was standing behind another desk, leaning
forward with his hands flat on the blotter. "You're being detained, Mr.
Hale," he said, speaking straight down at the desk, "for subversion and
espionage. Treason too, I expect." He looked up and stared across the
little office at him, and even the shivering, distracted Hale could see the
glitter of suspicion in the man's narrowed eyes. "I'm told that you're to
be handed over to the Special Branch section of Scotland Yard within a
few hours, but that we're to formally charge and question you first. A
redundancy. And there was a directive an hour ago that the Metropoli-
tan police were not to be involved in your apprehension, though Covent

Garden is properly in their jurisdiction, not in ours. Yours is a damned peculiar case, young man."

"Yes, sir," said Hale in a humble tone, in fact cautiously grateful that the man had not mentioned resisting arrest.

For a few minutes then Hale perched on a chair in front of the officer's desk and answered questions, but they were all to do with the schools he had attended and his membership in the Communist Party. Twice Hale had ventured to say that he had only gone to tonight's meeting in King Street to meet a girl from one of the Oxford women's colleges and that he hadn't known anything about the missing Air Ministry document, but his interrogators had each time just nodded and repeated a question about the Party meetings at Oxford, or his stint in Haslemere College in Surrey, or about the technical magazines he had subscribed to.

Eventually the questioning was done, and he was told that since he was apparently to be handed over to officers of the Special Branch soon, he would simply be shackled to a chair here in the station in the meantime and not driven over to the holding cells in Ludgate Hill. The officers even offered him a cup of tea, but he refused, fearing that his hands would shake too badly to hold a cup.

And so for several hours Hale dozed in a stout chair against the curved ceiling-wall, jolting awake whenever the wind outside knocked the wooden shutters against the window frame over his head or when involuntary twitches rattled the chains that connected his ankles to the chair legs; much later two men were brought in and booked for looting, having grabbed some bottles of brandy and a couple of bicycles from a boarded-up shop in Eastcheap, and Hale watched with morbid interest as they were curtly interrogated and then sent away under stern guard to the Ludgate Hill cells.

Hale almost envied them. He was fairly sure that his imminent transfer of custody must have been arranged by the James Theodora person he had spoken to on the telephone last year, but he had no idea at all what the man's response to this detainment would be. Why the apparently deliberate confusions in the details of his arrest? Chained to a chair in a police station, charged with subversion during wartime—so far from his bed in Magdalen College, so very many cold dark miles and years from the old box bed in Chipping Campden!—Hale wasn't able to quite dismiss the possibility that Theodora would simply have him taken away somewhere, under the fog of contradictory paper-work, and killed.

If there was any solace to be derived from the Communist philosophy in the face of death, Hale had not studied Marx deeply enough to find it; but at the same time the feverish *Our Fathers* and *Hail Marys* that droned in his head and even twitched his lips from time to time seemed to lack some crucial carrier wave, so that they propagated no farther than the inside of his skull.

He awoke from a deeper sleep when his chair was shoved aside by two men who unlatched the shutters and folded them back with a businesslike clatter; and he was squinting against the bright daylight as they unshackled his ankles and brusquely hoisted him to his feet.

"Time to go, Ivan," one of the men told him. "The Special Branch lads are here for you."

Oddly both disoriented and calmed by the glare of the summer morning visible beyond the pulled-back blackout curtains, Hale absently thanked his captors and shuffled across the unworn wooden floor and out into the sunlight. At first he didn't see anyone waiting for him.

St. Paul's Cathedral stood in solitary grandeur out there on the bombed plain, silhouetted by the rising sun like a god's baroque ship arrived too late in a ruined land; the impression was strengthened by the sea smell from the high-tide river that lay somewhere close beyond the broken skyline of Upper Thames Street to the south. Seen in daylight, the humped and pocked ground was a field of purple-blooming wildflowers, and Hale walked a few steps along a path of mismatched masonry fragments trodden flush with the black dirt, blinking downward through stinging, watering eyes at his dress shoes and the cuffs of his recently pressed trousers—wondering for the first time if his Oxford evening clothes would have been quite right for a City meeting of the International Workers' Party.

At one of the Oxford Branch Party meetings, over tea and cucumber sandwiches, he had heard an earnest, white-flannel-clad undergraduate observe that it was a melancholy necessity that all the old English universities be razed when the Proletariat Dictatorship was achieved; and this morning Andrew Hale shivered with a big emotion that could only be grasped—right now, inadequately—as a fierce determination to stop any more English buildings from being knocked down.

"Makes you feel like Macaulay's New Zealander," came a plummy voice from behind him in the open air, "doesn't it?"

Hale sighed and turned around.

The hair was more gray than black now, but Hale recognized the man who had escorted his mother and him into the office of the one-legged colonel twelve years earlier. He must have been fifty years old now. The man was hatless, but his black dinner jacket and white shirt indicated that he too had been out all night.

"A tourist in the future," Hale said, in spite of everything not wanting to seem to have missed the reference, "visiting the ruins of London." He looked past the figure that must have been James Theodora, and he was only vaguely depressed to see three men in coveralls—no, four—standing well back on the far side of the police hut, clearly watching. "I—did write to you," Hale said unsteadily, "about joining the Communist Party. Whatever this is about a missing Air Ministry document—"

"Impromptu is what it is," said Theodora, shaking his head. "Let's walk." He started away eastward against the morning breeze in a long-legged stride, his black coat-tails flapping up below the hands clasped at the small of his back. Hale shrugged, though only the surveillance men could have seen the gesture, and hurried to catch up.

"The old ARCOS raid was the only example they could think of," Theodora said. He squinted sideways at Hale. "Right? ARCOS? 'All Russia Co-Operative Society,' in Moorgate? Huh! Some Communist you are. Well, that's what it was, Special Branch went in hoping to find evidence and found only a lot of burned papers; this was fifteen years ago. Excuse enough to break off diplomatic relations with Moscow, at least. So when we needed a story last night, they just re-enacted the ARCOS raid, but on the King Street headquarters this time. Still, it did get you a police record, didn't it?—verifiable detention, for proper espionage, right in front of the Communist headquarters! You're at liberty right now, but nevertheless formally in the custody of Scotland Yard while you 'assist in the inquiry.' You'll be sent down from Magdalen, of course." He snickered. "Scandal, disgrace."

Hale was dizzy, and when he looked at his formally dressed companion in this field of wildflowers he actually thought of the white rabbit in *Alice in Wonderland*. "Not killed," he said.

"Good heavens no, my dear! We'd have had to *order* you to join the Party, if you hadn't done it on your own. No, you're doing splendidly. We'll even reinstate you at Magdalen one day, if you like—there *were* some irregularities about your detention last night. The service taketh away, and sometimes giveth back. What else would you like? An Order of the British Empire is entirely feasible. You're too young for a CBE. *Tell me about your dreams.*"

"My dreams?" Hale had to keep remembering his mother's words: . . . *they're the King's men; they deserve our obedience,* because on this surreal morning he could easily have persuaded himself that Theodora was insane; for that matter, he wasn't necessarily confident about his own sanity either. What would happen here if he were to demand a knighthood? Would he be told it was his?—would he *believe* it was? "I suppose I'd like to be an Oxford don one day—"

"No, my boy, *dreams,* visions you see when you're asleep."

"Oh." Coming right after thoughts about insanity, this topic was an uncomfortable one; perhaps the older man could be deflected to some other. "Well, I didn't have any dreams last night, certainly," he said with a forced laugh, "being chained in a chair. Did you know they chained—"

"Not in *September,* of course not," snapped Theodora, abruptly impatient. "You're nineteen now—has puberty occluded you? Even so, you must remember, nineteen winters, you must know what I'm talking about. What dreams have you had at the shift of the year, say on the last night of the year, any year?"

Hale took two long steps away from Theodora, his face suddenly stinging, and he had to force himself to keep breathing normally. He waved the older man back, not looking at him. What *else* did this man know about him, what could he *not* know, if he was already aware of so intimate and disturbing a secret? "Why," Hale said carefully, if a little too loudly, "did you ap-apparently *want* me to be-be-be arrested by the police?" He frowned, for usually he was only afflicted with a stutter right after Christmas, around the . . . around the time of *the new year.* "Sent down from college—disgrace, you said! And now you've been t-talking about an *OBE!*—for God's sake!—What's all this about, what are your— *plans* for m-me?"

The older man was laughing, his eyes wide open. "Oh my! He is touchy about his *dreams,* after all, isn't he! *Allahumma!* But we can put that off for a while, for a few hundred yards here." He had resumed picking his way over the canted pavement fragments, walking toward the sun that shone way out there over the bombed docks, and Hale exhaled and then plodded along beside him.

"Plans," Theodora went on, "for you. It's not so much *our* plans that are at issue." He was staring at the ground as he walked, and he held up a hand to forestall interruption. "I don't think I'll say much more than this: you speak and read German, you've subscribed to technical wireless magazines, and you've been arrested at a Communist Party meeting. I believe I can promise you that you'll soon be approached by—well, by a recruiter. We want you to be persuaded by this person. Don't *act*, that is don't pretend to hate England or anything of that sort; just be what you seem genuinely to be, a politically ignorant young man who's drifted into communism because it's the fashion, resentful now at being detained by the police and expelled from college for what strikes you as a trivial offense." He was looking away from Hale, squinting toward the rising sun. "Probably you'll be leaving the country illegally. There will in that case be a warrant issued for your arrest, charges of treason and whatnot. We'll see that it's all dismissed, afterward."

"I'm to be . . . a *spy*?" Having grasped the concept and come up with the word, Hale was too exhausted to go on and make a judgment about it.

"Would it upset you to be?"

"Ask me after I've had about twelve hours of sleep," said Hale absently, "and a big plate of eggs and bacon and grilled tomatoes, and a couple-or-three pints." Then he blinked around at the craters and the outlines of foundations, the rectangular pits of forlorn cellars, and his yawn was more from sudden nervousness than from exhaustion. This broken city was London, this besieged country was his own England, the England of Malory and More and Kipling and Chesterton—of lamp-lit nights with the rain thrashing down beyond the leaded-glass windows over miles of dark Cotswold hills, of sunny canoeing on the placid Windrush, the England his poor Tory mother had loved—and he couldn't pretend that he didn't ache to defend it against any further injury.

"No, actually," he said then. "No, I don't think it would upset me, working for the Crown."

Theodora had crouched beside a bush dotted with pale-yellow flowers. "All these flowers are supposed to be extinct," he said, "grown from seeds that were preserved under the old floors, freed at last and thrown onto plowed ground, rich now with ash." His gaze was oddly intent when he squinted up at Hale. "Do you know what this flower is? *Sisymbrium irio,* known as the London Rocket. It bloomed all over the City right after the Great Fire of 1666." He picked two of the little flowers and handed one to Hale after he straightened up.

"London recovered from that," observed Hale, dutifully sniffing the thing. "They rebuilt her."

"Perhaps it was the flowers that sustained her life. Some can do that, I think." Theodora glanced back, so Hale did too—the four surveillance men were following them at a distance. "Of course," said Theodora, "you won't say anything to this recruiter about *me,* nor about having been to that building where we met. You're a very clean player—your mother was admirably thorough, for an amateur, about leaving no tracks; even 'Hale' isn't the name under which she joined her religious order. Oh I say, you did know about that, didn't you?" When Hale smiled wanly and nodded, the older man went on, "Well, we've advanced a pawn here, and it's Red's turn to move. You won't see me again for a while, after this morning; they can't possibly be aware of you yet, which is why I'm able to talk to you face-to-face. Whenever you come back, we'll meet again and I'll have a lot of questions for you."

" 'Come back,' " echoed Hale. "From where?"

Theodora gave him an irritable look. "From wherever they *send* you, where did you think? You'll know when it's time to make your way back to England, and if you're clever you'll even find a way. I will almost certainly be aware of it when you return, and meet you; but if I can't meet you, wait for me—that is, don't tell *anyone* about me, nor about your secret purposes. Not even Churchill."

Perhaps from memory, Hale heard in his head a young woman's voice say, in French, *You were born to this*—and he shivered, not entirely in alarm. "What *are* my . . . 'secret purposes'?"

"Tell me about your dreams."

Hale sighed, then deliberately tucked the stem of his little London Rocket into the buttonhole of his lapel. "All right." This seemed to be a morning outside of time, in which anything at all could be said, no matter how crazy-sounding, without immediacy nor fear of skepticism or judgment. "Do you remember the 'wheels within wheels' in Ezekiel . . . ?"

Two mornings later Hale's trunk was packed and stowed in the porter's lodge at Magdalen; the lorry that was to take him and his things back to Chipping Campden wasn't due for half an hour, and as he paced the sunny Broad Street pavement he was careful not to meet the eyes of any of the apparently carefree students who strolled past. The formal letter of dismissal from his tutor was tucked in his coat pocket—what use now had been all his study of the Caxton *Morte d'Arthur,* the pageantry in *The Faerie Queene?*

When he did inadvertently glance at one of the passing faces, it was because he had noticed that a slim woman in a plaid skirt with a leather purse was for the second time walking past where he stood—and he found himself meeting a pair of brown eyes over high slanted cheekbones in a face framed with short dark hair. Her gaze was coldly quizzical, and he looked away instantly, certain that she must somehow know of his disgrace.

He exhaled and impulsively strode across the street, hoping he appeared to have some purpose besides hiding from the disapproving public view. On the far side of the street he walked under the Roman arch into the Botanical Gardens, bright green ranks of shrubs and midget trees spread across four acres under the empty blue sky, and he crouched by one of the flowering herbs beside the footpath as though to read the description on the little sign in front of it, though in fact he couldn't focus on the letters.

Andrew Hale, barrister, he thought in bitter bewilderment; foreign correspondent Hale of the *Times;* the great Oxford dons Lewis, Tolkien, Bowra, Hale. Sweet fuck-all seems more like it.

He straightened abruptly and took several deep breaths, not wanting anyone to see tears in his eyes here.

Eyes; those were *Slavic* eyes, he thought, in the instant before someone behind him touched his elbow; and when he turned around without surprise it was the woman in the plaid skirt standing there, still with the look of a dubious purchaser. She appeared to be in her thirties.

"I've seen you in the Party meetings," she said.

He was fairly sure she had never been to a meeting he had attended, but he nodded. "Not unlikely," he said. His heart was thumping under the expulsion papers in his coat pocket. "I'd advise you not to go to any in London."

"I heard of your misfortune," she said with a nod, gripping his elbow and leading him along the crushed-stone path. "We are all allies against the monster Germany. How strange that cooperation should be called espionage, and a crime! We're all working for world peace." She spoke with no accent, but he thought he detected the spiky cadence of eastern Europe.

"I—wasn't even doing espionage," Hale stammered.

"To belong to the International Workers' Party is implicitly to commit what they call espionage," she told him sternly. "We're citizens of a bigger thing than any nineteenth-century empires, aren't we?"

We want you to be persuaded by this person. But *Don't act.* "I've hoped to be," he said. "Things look unpromising right now."

"Knowing the danger now, are you still with us?" She had stopped walking and was staring intently into his eyes. "Now?"

"Yes," he told her, and he was surprised at the assurance with which he said it; she did represent his only hope of eventual reinstatement at Magdalen, but he had spoken from a sudden conviction that he had been waiting for this *en garde* ever since visiting the SIS headquarters at the age of seven; a conviction that all along he had been more a member of the world that included Theodora and this woman than of the world of St. John's and the City of London School and Oxford.

She nodded, and they resumed walking between the rows of flowers. "Do you know what they do in Blenheim Palace?" she asked.

Hale glanced at her, but she was looking ahead. Blenheim Palace was six miles north of Oxford. "The, uh, Duke of Marlborough lives there."

"He has turned it for wartime spy purposes over to MI5, a branch of the British secret service. We have comrades working there, covertly." She opened her purse and tilted it toward him; he could see a folded buff envelope tucked in there. "In this envelope is a list, copied from the MI5 Registry files, of Comintern agents known by the British to be working in London. I am not a person who ordinarily meets comrades face-to-face, as I am doing now with you; this is important. We need to convey this list right away to a still-unsuspected agent in London, so that Moscow Centre will know who must be reassigned, where fresh agents must be put in place. Also here in photographic miniature are full specifications of the new Rolls-Royce Merlin motor that is powering the Boulton-Paul Defiant aircraft; the British government has classified these specifications as 'most-secret,' not to be shared with allies. It is Soviet Russia that now is doing the greatest work of fighting Germany, at Riga and Minsk and Kiev; if—*espionage*—helps the Soviets to do this, is it right to impede it?"

"No," said Hale, trying to look resolute and not to think of the undergraduate who had advocated the destruction of all the Oxford colleges.

"I cannot leave here today," the woman said. "We want *you* to take a train to London, now. I will give you a hundred pounds for the travel and inconvenience. Tonight at eight o'clock you are to be standing under the—Eros?—statue in Piccadilly Square, you know what that is? Good. Hold a belt, you know?—for trousers?—in your right hand. A man carrying some fruit, an orange perhaps, will approach you and ask you where you bought the belt; you will tell him that you bought it in an ironmonger's shop in Paris, and then you will ask him where you can buy an orange like his; he will offer to sell it to you for a penny. Hand this envelope to him then. He will have further work for you."

"Just . . . go, right now?" said Hale, wondering what would become of his trunk. "This seems awfully precipitate—"

She interrupted him with, "Where did you buy the belt?"

"In—an ironmonger's shop," he said. "In Paris."

"You were born in Palestine, I think," said the woman.

He blinked at her in surprise, wondering if Theodora would be unhappy to know that she was aware of this. "Yes," he said. "How did you know that?"

Without a smile she said, "A little bird told me. Here." She handed him the buff envelope, and he folded it more sharply and tucked it into his coat pocket next to the letter from his tutor. "And here's a hundred pounds," she went on, handing him a letter-sized envelope. "I'll need you to sign a receipt for it."

In spite of Theodora's vapory assurances, Hale was numbingly aware that this constituted real, deliberate espionage, documentable treason; and he could feel the sudden heat in his face. "My—real name?"

She had obviously noted his involuntary blush, and for the first time she smiled at him. "Yes, comrade," she said softly, "your real name. Don't worry, I won't let it fall into the wrong hands."

And what, he wondered a moment later as he signed *Andrew Hale* in the notebook she had unwedged from her purse, would constitute the wrong hands, here?

I'm on *somebody's* rolls now.

God help me, he thought.

3

▼

London, 1963

But cannot the government protect?
We of the game are beyond protection. If we die, we die. Our names are
blotted from the book. That is all.
Thou art safe in the te-rain, at least.
Live a year at the great game and tell me that again!
   —Rudyard Kipling, *Kim*

The driver of the Peugeot swung in to a jolting halt in front of Overton's oyster bar in Terminus Place, and the now bespectacled and moustached Hale followed her curt directions and sprinted through the restaurant and out the back, then down a breezeway to Victoria Street, where the specified black BMW motorcycle hummed at the curb. The rider was anonymous under a visored black helmet, and Hale swung a leg over the seat and sat down. Luckily the rider waited until Hale had got his feet onto the pegs and got a grip on his leather jacket before he let the clutch spring out and gunned the machine away up Victoria Street, weaving between the slower cars like a barracuda.

In spite of the glasses, the headwind battered tears out of the corners of Hale's eyes as the motorcycle left behind the mediocre modern buildings of 1963 London and leaned alarmingly fast to the right around the north side of Westminster Abbey and then left up St. Margaret and Parliament streets to Whitehall; Hale pressed his face against his own shoulder to keep the moustache from being peeled off. When they passed the Cenotaph monument in the middle of the street, the rider began rapidly downshifting, and he pulled in to the curb by the new Cabinet Office in the old Treasury building, not far from Downing Street. As Hale shakily got off the back of the machine, his sweaty trousers clinging to his thighs, the rider nodded toward the entry stairs.

A familiar white-haired figure in an overcoat and a homburg hat was just then strolling up the pavement, and in spite of himself Hale had to suppress a smile at the neatness of it all as he followed Theodora through a door marked PRIVY COUNCIL OFFICE below the main steps.

"Anchors aweigh," whispered Theodora after the door had closed and audibly locked behind them. He pulled a black iron ankh from his overcoat pocket and waved it at the pair of guards who stood behind a desk at the side of the fluorescent-lit passage; when they had nodded he tucked the thing into a vest pocket and then shrugged out of his overcoat and hat and laid them them across the papers on the desk with thoughtless Etonian arrogance.

Hale obediently fumbled the ankh out of his new jacket and held it up as he passed the two men, who stared at it as carefully as if it were a top-security pass.

The Foreign Office was at the far end of this building, and Hale wondered if they had come here with such elaborate precautions merely to help get permission for some proposed SIS-connected operation. Hale recalled that, in his day, FO permission for routine projects like infiltrating an agent into a hostile country could be taken for granted; planting a microphone in a consulate required that C consult the FO liaison, who would likely call on the Permanent Secretary to authorize it. Only if bad political consequences looked possible would C have to clear an operation with the Foreign Secretary in person. Who *was* Chief of SIS these days? Not still Menzies, surely.

"Who's C now?" he whispered to Theodora as he dropped the ankh into his pocket and wiped his hand on his lapel. A moment later he took off the glasses and tucked them in after it.

"You don't need to—oh hell, it's Dick White. He was in MI5 when you were a player."

Hale raised his eyebrows; MI5 was the domestic Security Service, generally looked down on by the cowboys in SIS.

"Bothering the Foreign Secretary for this, are we?" Hale said.

Theodora gave him a blank stare. "We're going through the green door for this."

"Oh," said Hale humbly. They weren't going to the Foreign Office at all; even the Cabinet Secretary, who was the one responsible for all the secret services, the one who accounted for Parliament's Secret Vote funding of them and who oversaw the Joint Intelligence Secretariat, was not the ultimate authority. And though the Cabinet Office was separated from Number 10 Downing Street only by a connecting green baize door, the door was always locked, and even the Cabinet Secretary had to telephone the Prime Minister's Principal Private Secretary to get clearance to step through.

The approval of the Prime Minister himself was required for the most secret, most robust operations—big sabotage, substantial loss of life, serious risk of war. "We're to see *Macmillan?*" whispered Hale, wishing he had been allowed to keep his own coat.

"This is nothing." Theodora's withered old face creased in a strained smile. "Know, O Papist, that White was in the *Vatican* two weeks ago, having a secret audience with *Pius XII.*"

In fact, they did not literally go "through the green door"—the glossy plaster walls of the downward-slanting corridor soon gave way to old Tudor brick, and by the time they arrived at a set of ascending stone stairs, Hale thought they must have traversed the fabled eighteenth-century Cockpit Passage, and even skirted whatever might remain of Henry VIII's tennis court, a wall of which had been revealed by a 1940 bomb. The stairs led up to a tiny ivy-hung garden under a plane tree; a red-roofed building blocked the view in front of them, and Hale realized that the door Theodora now knocked at must be a side entrance to Number 10. His right hand instinctively sprang up to make the sign of the cross, but after a momentary hesitation he covered the twitch by pulling off the false moustache.

It was the Prime Minister himself, Harold Macmillan, who opened the door. The lean old patrician face was expressionless, but Hale thought there was banked fury behind the hooded eyes. Macmillan apparently recognized Theodora, and wordlessly stood aside to let them enter.

Theodora led the way down a hall to a small windowless room that was paneled up to waist height, with white plaster and framed portraits above; a couple of middle-aged men already sat in two of the tall green leather chairs around the narrow table, and as he followed Theodora's example and joined them, Hale supposed that one of them must be Dick White. Sconces on the walls threw yellow electric light across the bare, gleaming tabletop.

Macmillan didn't sit down, but stood behind one of the chairs with his arms crossed over the top of it. The air in the room was warm and smelled faintly of furniture polish.

"We haven't all been introduced to one another," said Theodora, "and I think we can leave it that way. We're here to deal with the culmination, one way or another, of Operation Declare."

The ankh was suddenly heavier in Hale's pocket. "*Declare* is still live?" he burst out, almost irritably; he had been confident that it had been closed as a failure nearly fifteen years ago. Then, abashed at having spoken up, he sat back and mumbled, "That's a . . . long-running operation."

Theodora smiled lazily at him. "It was an old operation before any of us were born, my dear. *Lawrence of Arabia,*" he said, in a patronizing drawl that probably indicated distaste for the popular David Lean movie of the year before, "was a second- or third-generation agent in it."

Hale had never seen Theodora this relaxed before, and it occurred to him that the old man was in some trouble here; and that therefore he himself probably was too. Theodora reached into his coat pocket and pulled out an ivory stick, which proved to be a folding Chinese fan when he flicked it open and began waving it under his sagging chin. The fan rattled faintly at each stroke.

One of the men who had already been at the table leaned forward now, his lean face creased in a frown. "You are still bound by the Official Secrets Act, at the very least," he said quietly to Hale. He pursed his lips and then went on, "In fact our Registry books now indicate that you never left the force, that you've been taking your full pay all along, in the capacity of deep-cover recruiter and safe-house proprietor, working out of your Weybridge college. Salary in cash, of course, no endorsed checks needed to be forged. So you've got more than twenty years of uninterrupted service, on paper. Are you still a willing player?"

"Yes, of course," said Hale stiffly. This was evidently the current C, Dick White, who according to Theodora had come out of plodding MI5.

"You didn't need to wave the pension at him before you asked," said Theodora to the man who had spoken. "Andrew has always been the Crown's good servant."

Across from Theodora sat a lean red-headed man whose well-cut gray wool suit was somehow made to look flashy by his tan and the deep lines in his cheeks. His quick and obviously characteristic grin flicked back to a squinting frown, and Hale wondered if he was frightened, and who he was in all this.

White blinked, then nodded. "I—do apologize!" He ran his fingers through his graying hair. "Mr. Theodora will give you the details of your final assignment, after the rest of us leave here. Suffice to say right now that Moscow is the entity behind Nasser's recent, ostensibly Egyptian, imperialism in the Middle East—three months ago his Yemeni rebels seized our main gulf fueling station at Aden, and in Cairo Nasser's men are obediently painting Turkish insignia over the Soviet markings on Tupelov TU-16 aircraft, and Russian pilots are flying them to Ankara. We've even traced the distinctive radar echo of the eight-blade propellers on the big Tupelov TU-95 Bear bombers over Kurdistan, but that's stopped in the last month—probably just because they've developed non-metallic composite propellers. The Arab countries are mostly using the Swiss Hagelin cipher machines, and even a lot of the old wartime German Enigma machines; we can break their traffic, but everything they imagine they know is soapy Soviet front-story—the Soviets themselves are using the new Albatross-class cipher machine, and just in the last ten days the Soviet residencies have all switched to new call signs and cipher keys."

Hale nodded. This looked like prelude to a big Communist takeover in the Arab states; bad enough, certainly, but where precisely did Declare come in? Why had White consulted *the Pope?*

"This government won't be able to weather it," growled Macmillan, leaning on the chair across from Hale. "The wage-freezes in '61 hurt us politically, and it looks too likely that de Gaulle will veto Britain's entry into the European Economic Community within the month, because we've agreed to take American nuclear missiles on our submarines; but since the Suez Canal fiasco the Americans won't support us very far. And if our Conservative government falls, and the Liberals do step into power in Whitehall, the Soviets will have no substantial difficulty in taking what they've wanted to get ever since the Versailles Treaty—the Bosporus and the Dardanelles and thus free passage of shipping from the Black Sea to the Mediterranean—and all the most oil-rich countries in the world!—in fact, the Ottoman Empire, all of Moslem Asia as it existed before the First World War." He stared at Dick White, and then, alarmingly, straight at Hale. "I wasn't in the government in 1948, when this unsanctioned Declare operation was somehow . . . exercised, in eastern Turkey; I've simply *inherited* it. You commanded it, I think."

And saw the five men in my charge driven mad or killed, thought Hale; along with some number of Russians. "That 1948 operation, yes." Not for the first time, he wondered what had become of the two members of his party whom he had briefly seen on the road down out of the Ahora Gorge, on that night. Beds in British military mental asylums? Begging bowls, or unmarked graves, in the Kurdish villages around Lake Van?

"Britain needs you to end the damned misbegotten thing now," said Macmillan, with a sweeping gesture that took in all three of his listeners. "Silently and invisibly, and taking your Soviet opposite numbers and their filthy agenda with you."

"We do have a sort of agent-in-place," said Theodora, "closely involved in this Soviet enterprise. A somewhat *shaky* agent, but . . ." He looked around at Macmillan and the other two. "Quis?"

Macmillan just scowled.

"Ego," said the red-haired man. He leaned back in his chair and smiled at Hale. "I was Head of Station in Turkey in '51—summers in the old consulate building in Constantinople, but winters up in Ankara. Kim Philby had been gone for three years, but his old jeep was still in the Ankara embassy motor pool, and there was still a yard-long length of rope tied to a hook on the dashboard; everybody said Philby put it there so his drunk Foreign Office chum Burgess could hang on, when the two of them went *surveying* in the mountains out beyond Erzurum. Being mere *SIS*, of course, we didn't know about *Declare*."

He had paused, so Hale shifted in his chair. "I remember the rope," he said cautiously. He was disoriented by the incongruous public school *Quis?* and *Ego* exchange, which roughly meant *Who wants this?* and *I'll take it*. A cigarette would have been a godsend, but there were no ashtrays in sight.

Theodora raised a lean finger. "And several of us don't want to hear about it," he said.

The red-haired man nodded, conceding the point. "I'm told," he went on, still speaking to Hale, "that after the bash in '48 you reported Philby as a double agent, one secretly working for Moscow."

"His suspicions were, of course, not reported to my predecessor," said White to the room at large, staring at the high plaster ceiling.

As if he were being cross-examined in a courtroom, Hale waited for an objection. When no one spoke, he said, "I filed a report to . . . my superior officer, stating my reasons for suspecting that. But," he went on, forcing himself not to glance at the glowering Macmillan, "Philby has been exonerated since."

Just from having read the newspapers Hale knew that Kim Philby had been working in Washington under some diplomatic cover until 1951, and that after his friend Guy Burgess and another Foreign Office diplomat named Maclean had fled to Moscow, Philby had been suspected of having been a spy himself, and of having warned Maclean that MI5 was about to arrest him for espionage. Philby had apparently been relieved of his SIS duties after that, though not formally charged with anything, and in 1955 an MP in the House of Commons had challenged Macmillan, Foreign Secretary at the time, to answer the accusation that Philby had been the "third man" in the alleged Soviet spy ring. Macmillan had subsequently read a prepared statement saying that the British government had no reason to suspect Philby of any collusion or wrongdoing.

At the moment Macmillan's hands were clenched on the green leather chair back; Hale didn't dare look up into the man's face. "As far as SIS knew to advise," said White stiffly, "that exoneration seven years ago was valid. No one in Broadway knew that the old wartime Special Operations Executive had covertly survived its official dissolution and was still doing intelligence work."

White's face was stiff with obvious suppressed anger, but the red-headed onetime Head of Station in Turkey flashed his brief grin again.

Hale blinked and didn't change his expression—he had certainly known that a core group in SOE had ignored its shutdown order at the end of the war; he himself had gone on working for the divergent branch of the service for another three years—but he was chilled to hear his suspicion about Kim Philby apparently confirmed, after all this time. It had been one thing to be convinced, but it was quite another to virtually hear it from the Prime Minister.

"Declare wasn't finished yet," said Theodora mildly, "and it needed an independent, secure agency to run it. A number of the overseas wartime agencies didn't actually close down when the war ended, but stayed on the rolls under ambiguous categories." He paused, languidly waving his rattling ivory fan, and Hale knew White must be wondering what other splinter secret services might still be hidden in his trackless payroll.

"We took the warning about Philby seriously," Theodora went on. "We investigated and concluded that in fact he was, and had for some time been, a KGB agent."

Hale felt sick all over again, remembering the ambush into which he had led the men in his command. *What were you all doing up there?* Philby had blandly asked him, afterward. *A thousand rounds of ammunition fired off in the Ahora Gorge!*

"And," Theodora went on, "late in '52 we braced him—confronted him with facts and threats—and turned him double." He smiled at Hale. "We even called you up then with the old signal—now didn't we?—but it all happened too fast: he was in Turkey, on the Soviet border, and it turned out that Burgess was waiting for him right there on the red side of the Aras River, and they were on the verge of . . . trying *it* again. We managed to abort it and at the same time save Philby's face with the Russians, but I'm afraid we did leave you rather at loose ends in Green Park, that day."

Hale gave a tense flip of his fingers; the job interview he had missed ten years ago—even his current position at the University College of Weybridge—seemed like inconsequential pastimes now that he was again an active player in the deadly Great Game.

"We," said White, "don't know the Soviet timetable on this; but I'm afraid we've got a deadline of our own. A year ago a KGB officer named Golitsyn defected to the CIA in Helsinki and was extensively debriefed in Maryland; and this last August a woman in Israel, one Flora Solomon, contacted an old MI5 agent and told him a secret she'd been keeping since the '30s. The upshot of their stories is that, as Mr. Theodora has known for ten years, Philby has been Moscow's man all along, probably since 1934. And we at SIS—not having been told that he had already been confronted and turned!—well, I'm afraid steps are being taken, beyond my control now, to arrest him and offer him immunity in exchange for coming back to England and making a full confession. MI5 is aware of this too, and insists on getting him to their tough interrogation center at Ham Common in Richmond."

Hale remembered Ham Common—he had in fact been interrogated there himself, and by Kim Philby, some twenty years ago.

"I don't like that," said Macmillan. "All these spies we've been arresting, exposing, admitting to! The Kroger couple and Lonsdale two years ago, the homosexual Vassal in September, this Fell woman giving MI5's secrets to the Yugoslav Embassy just last month! Damn it, when my gamekeeper shoots a fox, he doesn't nail it up in the Master of the Foxhounds' drawing room; he buries it, out of sight. I suppose we can't simply shoot spies, as we did in the war—but they should be discovered and then played back in the old double-cross way, with or without their knowledge—never *arrested*."

"Philby is too likely to jump at the proposed SIS offer of immunity, you see," said Theodora. He shrugged and pursed his lips. *"We, the old SOE, didn't offer him immunity in '52—we just told him that we'd kill him if he didn't fully report to us any further contact the Soviets might have with him; and, if the day came, participate in any operation they might want him for, but do it working for us now.* So he must be . . . induced to refuse the SIS offer when it's made to him, and to follow through on his old agreement, go through with this big Soviet operation as our agent. He won't want to, he's boxed and . . . *outfoxed.* He'll want to come home and leave the Russians to play out their present game without him."

Hale managed a tight smile. "How am I to induce him to refuse the immunity offer?"

Leather creaked faintly as the other men relaxed without changing their positions.

"By pointing out to him," said Theodora, "that *our* offer, SOE's, takes precedence and still applies; that is, he can either work for the Russians in this thing as a double, reporting to us and doing what we tell him, or he can be killed. No other choice exists, regardless of what he may soon be hearing from an SIS representative."

"To what extent will that be a bluff?" asked Hale carefully. Would the Great-and-the-Good of the Foreign Office endorse the SOE's old lethal ultimatum?

Macmillan sighed, and White said, "It will not be a bluff at all." He looked up. "You'll do it, then."

"Yes, of course," said Hale.

White stood up. "Then we'll leave you to get the details from Jimmie."

Macmillan gave Hale a respectful nod as he left the room, though the red-haired man, who probably knew more than the Prime Minister, didn't look at him.

After the interior door clicked shut, Theodora stared at Hale and said, wonderingly, "Clearance from the top! We're legitimate, finally!"

"This room is clean," guessed Hale.

"Right you are, nobody wants any hint of what I'm going to tell you now." He stared at the door. "Arrests, spy scandals! He doesn't know the half of it yet, poor man. This Conservative government is doomed already. His War Secretary, Jack Profumo, has been having an affair with the mistress of a Soviet naval attaché—and it's not unrelated to our current problem that two weeks ago this bit of gossip was passed on to a *Labour* Party MP. It will be in the papers before the month is out." He sighed. "I wonder who the new PM will be, and what his attitude will be toward the poor old services." He clicked his ivory fan closed and laid it on the table.

"And of course he's wrong to imagine that the Russians want any part of Turkey east of Erzurum," Hale noted bleakly. *Britain needs you to end the damned misbegotten thing now,* Macmillan had said. Carefully keeping any irony out of his voice, Hale now said, "I hope this isn't going to involve"—a return to Ararat, he thought—"Turkey, at all?"

Theodora frowned at Hale, all his earlier relaxation gone now. "This is going to be brutal, Andrew. 'Crown's good servant' notwithstanding, are you still surrendered to the service?"

Hale sighed. "Yes, Jimmie."

"Would you break the laws of England, if we ordered it?"

"Are you confirming me again? I went through this before graduating from the Fort." In the summer of 1945 Hale had belatedly gone through a six-week SOE training course in the paramilitary arts at Fort Monkton near Gosport, studying unarmed combat and "opposed border crossings" and the use of explosives; and the course had ended with a catechism that had begun this way. Theodora was frowning more deeply, so Hale hastily said, "Yes, I would."

"And go to prison, in disgrace, if it was the will of the Crown?"

"I would."

"You already know—I hope you remember!—that this operation has sometimes involved—" Theodora paused and pursed his lips, as fastidious as a Victorian schoolmaster forced to refer to venereal disease.

"Would you go into a situation in which you were likely to have to . . . fight magic with magic, if we ordered you to?"

Of course this had not been in the paramilitary arts litany, and Hale forced himself not to touch the bulge of the ankh in his pocket. "For the Crown," he said flatly, "I would." But his mouth had gone dry, and he could feel the old forlorn wail starting up in his head.

"Would you kill an apparently innocent person, on our orders?"

A relative relief: "Yes."

"Would you kill your brother, in those circumstances?"

"I haven't got a brother."

"If you did, child."

"Yes, Jimmie." He yawned tensely, squeezing tears out of his eyes. "Am I to resolve Philby's status?" he asked, using the old SOE euphemism. Hale had never done an assassination, but now that he was assured that Philby had indeed been a Soviet saboteur during that debacle in Turkey in 1948, he thought he could. "Establish the truth about him?" he added, using a related euphemism.

"Why do you ask that?"

"Why wouldn't I? It doesn't seem like a remote possibility that you might want him verified, resolved, at the end of this." And I should be the man to do it, he thought.

"Oh. No, quite the contrary. Though as a matter of fact you will at some point be called on to *seem* to try to kill him—you're to shoot him with a load of .410 birdshot."

Hale nodded tiredly and reminded himself that plain revenge was seldom the shrewdest move in espionage. "I'm sure that will make sense, when we come to it."

"You won't like the math, but it will make sense." The old man glanced around at the high corners of the room, then leaned sideways in his chair to reach into his coat pocket. "All this business with Nasser and Yemen and the Arabs is of course incidental to the main Soviet purpose." From his pocket he lifted out a white handkerchief wrapped around something no bigger than a couple of pens; he laid the little bundle carefully, without a sound, on the tabletop. "The Soviets have their own . . . *fugitive SOE,* as you recall, quite a bit older than ours."

Rabkrin, thought Hale with a suppressed shiver. "I do recall." He cocked an eyebrow curiously at the bundle.

Theodora picked up his fan again and flicked it open. "Well, for five hours last month we had the . . . the tsar of *kotiryssas* in our lap." Hale knew the term—literally it meant "house Russian," derived from *kotikissa*, "house cat," and it referred to a Soviet spy who has defected to the West.

"We actually managed," Theodora went on, "to get a director of that oldest Russian agency to jump ship and come over to us, right here in London—a sickly, hypochondriacal old fellow called Zhlobin. His cover among his own people was as a KGB colonel, and the general-consumption cover for *that* was First Secretary in the Soviet Embassy. We were suspicious of him because he was posted here, right after Khrushchev knuckled under to Kennedy, apparently as a replacement for another old fellow whose main job had turned out to be flying kites on the embassy roof on moonless nights, hmm? Apostle to the Heaviside Layer. And clearly this Zhlobin was another joker in the residency deck—he had no apparent embassy duties, but he didn't seem to be meeting any agents either; and he obviously wasn't a cipher clerk, since he did go out into the city unescorted. Our watchers were right on him every time he stepped outside the embassy gate in Kensington Park Gardens, and even a brush-contact in a crowd would have been difficult to hide from them. He did nothing. But finally last month he went along on an official cultural outing—all aboveboard, with proper F.O. permission to go beyond the ordinary eighty-kilometer limit-on-travel for Eastern Bloc diplomats—a field trip to view the Roman ruins in Dorchester, out in Dorset. Our watchers went along, and Zhlobin got off the train by himself at Poole and took a taxi to a churchyard near Bovington, where, thinking he was unobserved, he commenced rooting around at one particular grave. Later in the day he caught the return train at Poole and went back to the embassy with his comrades, who no doubt assumed he had met some KGB-run agent."

"And whose grave was that?" asked Hale dutifully.

"Thomas Edward Lawrence," pronounced Theodora. "Lawrence of Arabia himself, dead since 1935." He cocked his head at Hale. "You'd never have met him, I suppose, but do you know you *look* like poor old Lawrence—same thin, worried face, same flyaway sandy hair."

"Thanks, Jimmie. Was your man Zhlobin trying to dig him up?"

"Well, he was looking for *fulgurites,* actually—brittle tubes of glass and sand, imbedded in the dirt, generally caused by lightning strikes.

He didn't find any, so never mind." The old man fanned himself more rapidly.

Hale just nodded; but he remembered coming across lightning tubes, in a desolate region where huge basalt stones moved like smoke and sand dunes roared like low-flying bomber aircraft engines, south of the well at Umm al-Hadid in the Arabian Rub' al-Khali desert, in early 1948. The wail in his head was louder, and he thought he might be sick.

"But we knew what he was now, you see," said Theodora. "So we worked to achieve definition of his motivations for defection, as recruiters say—that is, exacerbate his problems. An agent of ours in the embassy was able to tell us that Zhlobin was forever taking pills and measuring his own blood pressure and running to the embassy doctor."

"So you—you crash-turned the doctor."

Theodora smiled. "Did we not. We showed that poor man KGB documents we'd got from our own sources and told him how we'd claim to have got them from him, and showed him composed photographs of himself in bed with an MI5 woman—he quickly agreed to give Zhlobin a convincing diagnosis of pancreatic cancer." Theodora shrugged. "We figured that might soften him up for a pass, you know; we could even promise a cure as a prerequisite to any questioning, miracles of modern British medicine, since he didn't have the cancer anyway; but before we could approach him, Zhlobin went out solo, and he *dived*—he used every elusion trick in the book, pogo-sticking like a twenty-year-old all over Bloomsbury and Holborn, and even a quick four-car team of our watchers could scarcely keep him in sight! Well, he wasn't hiding from *us,* he was hiding from his own security people. And where do you think he went?"

To a pub, thought Hale; to a whorehouse. "To St. Paul's."

Theodora looked nettled. "Why did you say that? You're almost right—he went to a Catholic church near the Old Bailey and went to Confession! The Papist sacrament of that name! Some of our fellows were all for quick-miking the confessional, but I said to back off. I braced him on his way out of the church, and he immediately broke down weeping, in that Slavic way, and agreed to everything I said. I promised him citizenship and a new identity and stacks of money and total medical care—I didn't want to get too specific there—and we got him to one of our safe houses right off the Holborn Viaduct. For five hours he answered every question I put to him." Theodora sighed.

"Then he said he wanted a bath, and he pulled a radio into the tub with him, and that was the end of Zhlobin."

Hale blinked. "Deliberately?"

"He had to plug the radio into a closer outlet, for the cord to reach."

"Huh! That rather negates his confession—the one to the priest, I mean."

"Perhaps that was the penance the priest assigned. I felt that, if anything, it enhanced his confession to us."

For a moment neither of them spoke, and Theodora's fan swished and rattled faintly in the warm air; then the old man stirred and said, "You're right, the Russians have no intention of annexing eastern Turkey—but they are preparing to send a team in again to Mount Ararat, as they did in '48 and tried to do again in '52; if all goes as planned, you and Philby will be members of the team."

The ankh in Hale's pocket was twitching with his rapid heartbeat, and he had to take a deep breath to speak. "Back to Ararat," he said, "to finally kill the—"

Theodora waited with raised eyebrows for him to finish, then laughed softly when Hale lapsed into silence. "If I had thought there was any chance of you completing that sentence, I would have shushed you. But your instincts are still good; what do *I* know about the microphone situation here, really, right?"

"Sure." Hale stretched his arms out and yawned again. "Is *lunch* a prospect of any imminence? What on earth can you *mean*, Philby and I will be 'members of the team' when the—Russians go up Ararat again?"

With his free hand Theodora reached over to the silk bundle he had laid on the table and flipped the edges of the handkerchief aside. Lying on the fabric was a tiny hand-drill like a screwdriver, a dental pick, and a plastic cylinder no bigger than a cigarette filter with a fine antenna wire projecting two inches from one end.

Hale nearly forgot his hanging question as he stared at the kit in disbelief. The plastic cylinder was clearly a miniature microphone, an electronic bug, and the tools were for installing it.

"Well," Theodora said smoothly, "the expedition probably can't succeed without Philby; the—the Russian equivalent of our SOE, at least, is convinced that it can't, and I think they're right. Philby is in a privileged position, relative to the thing on Ararat, that the Russians know they can't duplicate with anyone else—you'll be told about that shortly, when you get to Kuwait. They may serve some sort of tiffin on the plane."

The archaic word reminded Hale that Theodora had long ago served in the Indian Civil Service, the Raj—where high-handed schemes had been the standard *modus operandi*. "When I—get to Kuwait," Hale said in a monotone. He gave the old man a wide-eyed questioning stare and waved his spread fingers stiffly at the kit.

Theodora frowned impatiently and snapped his fan closed to use it and both hands in a pantomime of drilling and inserting.

He wants me, thought Hale incredulously, to plant a bug in this secured conference room! In Number 10 Downing Street! *I wonder what the new PM's attitude will be toward the poor old services*—the old man doesn't intend to wait for hints.

Theodora held up his free hand. "But!—when we grabbed Philby at the Turkish–Soviet border in the winter of '52 and forced him to switch sides, there wasn't time to set up a sabotage of the Russian attempt on the mountain; we had to force them simply to abort it, so that they'd have to try it again at some later date, when we'd have something prepared."

Would you break the laws of England, if we ordered it? thought Hale as he tried to pay attention to what Theodora was saying; *Yes, I would.* God help me. He sighed and glanced around the room as Theodora had done. There was no telephone, nor any window frame at all, much less a nice metal one to damp the microphone's electromagnetic field, and Hale finally shrugged and pointed down at the table.

The old man nodded judiciously, and then went on, "We had to ask Philby himself!—who had then been a double agent of ours for only about ten minutes—what development would cause the Russians to call it off; and in his imperturbable way he advised fomenting an uprising among the native Kurds, with the Turkish government goaded to respond in force."

Hale leaned forward to lift his chair by the arms, hike it back a yard, and then slowly and silently lower it to the wooden floor; then he slid the handkerchief and its burden closer to him and knelt carefully between the chair and the table.

"So we hastily burned some Kurd villages in the area," Theodora said, waving his ivory fan to make it rattle, "shot a couple of the Oscars with Kurdish rifles, and got an excitable Turk captain to radio a grossly exaggerated report of it to Ankara, and then we bribed a Security Inspectorate bureaucrat there to send in the Turkish Air Force."

Hale recalled that *Oscar* had been the enduring American mispronunciation of the Turk word *asker,* which meant soldier; and fleetingly, remembering the hospitality of a Khan in the Zagros Mountains, he hoped the Kurds had come through the contrived skirmish without too many casualties. He nodded, then picked up the tiny hand-drill and ducked his head under the tabletop and peered up at the underside; a hole for a counter-sunk screw in the corner-block nearest him looked like the best spot, and he pressed the bit of the drill at an angle into the hole and began twisting the handle, cupping his free hand under it to catch the curls of sawdust. The knees of the old man's neatly pressed striped trousers were only a couple of feet in front of his face.

Theodora wasn't speaking any louder than before, and Hale had to cock his head to hear him as he kept twisting the drill: "It was a proper circus around Ararat for a week or so, with the ignorant KGB and the Red Army panicking on the Russian side of the Aras River, and therefore the Shah sending Iranian aircraft out to patrol *their* border—and the Russian expedition was indeed canceled, with no evidence that the circumstances had had anything to do with Philby, who obviously had no choice then but to return to England. So far so good, you'll say."

Hale straightened up from under the table to replace the drill and lift the pick and the little microphone. "Consider it said," he told the old man in a conversational tone, and then ducked under the table again. The drill bit had been well chosen—the plastic cylinder slid tightly into the new, oblique hole without needing any help from the pick, and its fine antenna was invisible in the shadows. He knew Theodora wouldn't be sending an activating signal to the microphone, making it vulnerable to electronic security sweeps, until such time as Macmillan's government fell and a Labour Party Prime Minister took office.

"But the secret Russian directors were suspicious of Philby anyway," he could hear Theodora saying over the rapid, covering rattle of the ivory fan, "clearly wondering if he had been turned there in Turkey, or in London the year before when MI5 interrogated him about Burgess and Maclean, or even right after the failure in '48. They've always been so leery of Ararat, since Lenin got killed fooling with it, that they'd jump at any honorable excuse to leave it alone; we've had to nudge them at every turn to encourage them to try it again, so that we'll be able to step in at the last moment and finally close down the whole show. And so we had to leave Philby out trailing his coat, for another six years, before they worked up the nerve to get back in contact with him."

Hale pocketed the sawdust and wiped his hand on the pocket lining, then stood up and laid the pick on the handkerchief. "Six years of it," he said respectfully as he slowly sat down in his chair, "and he wasn't working for SIS anymore." He reached for his own handkerchief, but it was in the coat he had left in the Peugeot; so he mopped the sweat from his forehead and cheeks with the new coat's rough sleeve.

"No," agreed Theodora, nodding with evident satisfaction as he reached forward to fold the handkerchief and sweep it back into his own pocket, "he was as attractive as we could make him—virtually bankrupt and doing odd ghost-writing jobs, drinking too much, his wife going crazy, avoided by all his old friends. And then after the Prime Minister exonerated him in Parliament, SIS gave him some charity chicken-feed jobs in Beirut, where he's been doing journalistic piece-work. And Angleton's CIA men in Lebanon have been harassing him and getting him arrested on trivial suspicions, which certainly hasn't made it look as though he had any *usefulness* to anybody. We painted them a proper picture, with him. And still it was mere KGB that finally approached him, very tentatively, in '58. But he continued to look genuinely abandoned—brilliant man, he even tried to get Indian citizenship in 1960!—and now he's fully back on the old Russian force, as trusted by them as anybody ever is." He finally clicked his fan closed and tucked it back into his pocket.

Hale pushed away the fresh memories of having installed the microphone, trying to do it so thoroughly that he would even be able to deny the action convincingly in a polygraph interrogation. He focused all his attention on the old man's story. "And—me?" he asked now. Hale recalled Theodora telling him, in 1941, *It's not so much our plans for you that are at issue.*

"Yes. Well, this has to move fast. Last night in Beirut"—he glanced at his wristwatch—"sixteen hours ago, someone shot Kim Philby as he stood too near the bathroom window of his Beirut apartment; it was a .30-caliber rifle round, fired from the roof of a building across the street. He's alive—the bullet nearly missed, cracked his skull instead of exploding it. He's had it put about that the injury was caused by a drunken fall, but he very nearly bled to death, and the wound took twenty-four stitches at a local hospital, and he isn't expected to be receiving company for a few days. Peter Lunn has been head of the SIS Lebanon station in Beirut since October, and of course the hospital staff will have let *him* know that it's a gunshot wound, and he knows that Philby has been doing allotment work for the service since his semi-vindication in '55; Lunn doesn't know yet about SIS's new evidence against Philby, and the impending immunity offer, but he will certainly be calling Philby up soon, wanting to ask about this assassination attempt."

Hale's heartbeat had nearly slowed to normal. "Who would the shooter represent?" he asked. "Not *us*, I gather, nor the broader SIS, and not any of the powers out of Moscow."

Theodora shrugged expansively. "The Turkish Security Inspectorate? The *Service de Documentation Extérieure et d'Contre-Espionage?* Mossad? Any of them would like to spike this covert Russian expedition, if they knew about it and didn't trust us to effectively infiltrate a"— he waved at Hale—"a Trojan horse; or if they feared England might try to harness the Ararat power for herself, instead of simply killing it. We're aware now of a woman with a forged Canadian passport who flew from Istanbul to Beirut yesterday morning, and a Beirut taxi driver remembers driving her to the Rue Kantari, where Philby lives, at sunset. She was carrying a case for a musical instrument the size of an alto saxophone. We made the Istanbul Head of Station get whatever he could out of the room she had vacated; but the room had been cleaned, and all they found was two slips of paper that had been in the waste bin—on one was written '*Bueno Ano,*' and on the other '*Medio Ano.*' "

Only old practice kept Hale from twitching, and he narrowed his eyes to prevent Theodora from noticing his surely dilated pupils. "Spanish!" Hale said easily. "Good Year and Medium Year, those mean."

"Yes. I suspect there was a third slip that said '*Malo Ano,*' Bad Year; most likely a brush-pass signal, with three possible messages, and she only knew yesterday morning which one to pass. I suppose the one she took away with her, *Malo Ano,* meant *I'm going off now to kill Philby.*"

Hale's ears were ringing, and he felt dizzy. *I should have spoken up when he first mentioned the two slips,* he thought; *they've got nothing to do with any brush-pass signal. And if I don't speak up now, I'm concealing vital information from him, concealing it from the service.* "The Crown's good servant" indeed! But—is she still working for the French Secret Service, the SDECE, as an assassin now? Or could she possibly be involved in this as an independent actor? Those slips of paper were no indication that she's working with anyone, as Theodora thinks. Could her attempt to kill Philby have been *personal?*

To his surprise he felt an extra surge of anger toward Philby, and recognized it as jealousy.

She must actually have looked, this time—and got *Malo Ano.*

I need to get there, he thought. Soon.

He remembered crawling out of bed in his rented room in Weybridge on many nights in 1953 and '54, when nerves and resisted memories had made sleep impossible, and tuning the landlady's short-wave set to random points near the 40-meter bandwidth, and then just sitting there in the dark parlor listening to the indecipherable dots and dashes of code groups being transmitted from God knew where in England or Western Europe—and wondering if one of those lonely signals was originating from *her* finger on a sending key, far out there in the night in some boulevard garret or harbor boat.

"If I'm to be a part of the Russian team," he said evenly, "I expect I'm to do some coat-trailing myself, and fast. What is *my* story to be, this time, what can they hope I'll give them? What *will* I give them, good enough to convince them that I'm a real traitor? Why am I going to Kuwait, if Philby is in Beirut?" With all of Arabia between, he thought.

Again Theodora glanced at his wristwatch, and Hale thought the old man looked uncomfortable. "Yes. Well, we've painted them a proper picture of you too." He looked up with a frosty stare. " 'Surrendered to the service,' right? 'Go to prison, in disgrace.' "

"Good God, Jimmie!" said Hale in unfeigned alarm. "What have you scripted?"

"A good way to make something look plausible is to make it appear to be just one more of an established ongoing series, right? We've been, that is, MI5 has been, exposing a lot of corruption in the secret service files lately, turning up old shamefuls like the ones the Prime Minister mentioned a few minutes ago; and the Russians are certainly aware of Profumo's imminent fall, and they probably know about the new evidence against Philby. The liberal press always headlines each new instance of it, it's been like a running serial, and Macmillan is known to hate it, and it's terrible for the country. One more would not look at all deliberate."

"I follow you. I'm not a longtime *Soviet* plant, obviously, since they'd know that wasn't so. Mossad? Have I secretly been a Zionist all along?"

"I'm afraid you're just a crook, Andrew. Our new, unimpeachable evidence indicates that when you were in Kuwait from '46 to early '48, you were involved in betraying British Petroleum interests in the Persian Gulf by selling strategic secrets to the Americans at Standard Oil, and a couple of murdered Bedouin guides now appear to be on your conscience; and you used your cover post as Passport Control Officer to sell forged British passports to fugitive Nazi war criminals stranded in Oman. Oh yes, and you took money from a now deceased Russian illegal to break a couple of Soviet agents out of a Turk prison and smuggle them safely back across the Soviet border; the illegal kept no records, it can't be disproved. There's a good deal more, you'll be briefed in Kuwait."

Hale was frowning as he listened to this, his lips pressed tightly together. "Right," he said finally. So much for all the good work I did do there, he thought. This will be the version preserved in the Registry Archive files. "The murdered *Bedu*," he said, correcting Theodora's pronunciation, "probably aren't a helpful element, but very well. None of that old stuff will get me into the papers, though."

"No, something immediate is doing that. You remember Claude Cassagnac, the MI5 consultant."

"Yes," said Hale in a tight voice. "Fondly." It occurred to him that this would be the version *she* would get. Even if he managed to find her in Beirut, he could hardly tell her the true story and thus compromise this operation—Macmillan had personally cleared it, and it was Hale's unlooked-for chance to finally right the big defeat of his espionage career, and in some sense justify the deaths of the men he had commanded on Ararat.

Across the table, Theodora's withered old face was expressionless, his eyes blank as slate. "Cassagnac called you on the telephone at your college this morning, it appears, and gave you an old SOE code proposing a meeting; that covers any clumsiness you might have exhibited during the call, you see. The two of you met at your house in Weybridge about two hours ago, and he told you that all of these old crimes of yours had been discovered; he wanted you to accompany him back to Century House—that's the SIS headquarters now, we're not in Broadway anymore—and give yourself up, so that you could at least avoid a publicized arrest. Among the elect there will be hints that he wanted you to participate in this Philby affair as an advisor, that you might have been able to ask for immunity in exchange for telling us everything about Philby and Ararat in '48. You resisted Cassagnac."

"What—have—you—done?" whispered Hale. "Is he dead?"

"He's been shot," snapped Theodora, "with a gun of yours, in your house, I can tell you that. And—"

"That's a *.45!* Dum-dum bullets! And he must be as old as you are!"

"And!" Theodora repeated. Again he looked at his watch, raising his frail fist to do it, "And right about *now,* a minute and a half ago, technically, you are shooting a policeman not two miles from here, with the same gun, just to help cover it in case you were recognized on the train or in the park. I don't know if he's dead either."

Hale's mouth was open.

The old man slumped in his chair and flapped a pale hand at Hale. "Ah, lad, run you now to your old haunts in Kuwait, as you would if you were on the run from SIS—which you are, absolutely; by nightfall you'll be on the Middle Eastern watch list for forcible detainment, and Dick White is able to prove he wasn't even in London today. Run to the ambiguous leave-behind networks and spare identities you must certainly have established during your posting there, like every other agent-runner. The Russians will find you, you'll be approached by a recruiter; and we—want you to be persuaded by them."

This is the version *she* will get, Hale thought again. He remembered Claude Cassagnac telling the two of them, in a vaulted cellar near the Seine in 1941, *It is the indispensable agents who are always the first to be purged* . . . Claude, Claude! thought Hale now. Did you finally get trapped into becoming indispensable?

Hale took a deep breath and let it out. "If I'm to sell myself to them as a—a *koti-ahngleeyski,* a turncoat, they'll expect me to give them my whole story—our Ararat plans, everything. What script do you want me to give them?"

Theodora stared at him dubiously. "I won't tell you now." After a full second he gave a decisive nod. "It would be redundant—you'll be told that in Kuwait, *that* much certainly, even if the briefing falls through and our agent has to write it on his forehead and walk past you on the street. I warn you that you won't like it; you'll probably doubt its validity and want confirmation, which won't be possible. So this right now, what I'm saying, is your confirmation-in-advance. *If you hate it, it's the genuine instructions,* have you got that?"

Hale felt sick. Good God, he thought. Who or what on earth does he want me to betray?

"Have you got that?" Theodora repeated.

No confirmation possible, Hale thought; if it's abominable, it's genuine. And whatever it is, it's so abominable that he's evidently afraid I'll bolt if I learn it right now. "Yes," he said hoarsely.

"Very good. A lorry out front will take you to a stolen car in Hammersmith. There's a great deal of money in the glove box, and an airline ticket out of Heathrow, and a passport, in the name of Andrew Hale; that's unhandy, I know, but it's a nice indication of haste. Inside the passport is a Kuwait address, and a name; go there untraceably to hear all the details of this and to pick up your equipment. And when you get back—probably by the end of the month!—we'll set you up with a complete new identity anywhere you like, and you can even have the OBE I promised you once. Hell, you're old enough for a Commander of the British Empire now."

Hale got shakily to his feet, not sure he was being dismissed. He wanted to find out one more thing here, first. It had to do with the wild birds that subsisted on the suet hung from his oak tree, as much as anything.

"Put the moustache and glasses on again," said Theodora. "You can toss them when you're in the lorry—your picture won't be released to the press until after your flight has taken off."

"Chipping Campden," said Hale, mumbling as he pressed the wilted moustache back onto his upper lip.

"I beg your pardon?"

"Chipping Campden, in the Cotswolds, is where I'd like to retire. I haven't been there since I was thirteen—I'm forty now. Nobody'd recognize me, and I presume I'll have been reported dead somewhere."

Theodora stared at him, and Hale wondered if he had asked for too much to be able to detect anything valuable in the old man's response.

"No, Andrew," Theodora said. "You're going to be in the *papers,* remember? Reporters will be all over that place. *Remote* England, if it's to be England at all, right?"

"I suppose." He had indeed overplayed it; but if Theodora had agreed to so insecure a proposal, Hale would have been *sure* the old man intended to have him killed at the end of this operation. Now he could only speculate.

The old euphemisms echoed in his head: *resolve his status, establish the truth about him, give him the truth.* He recalled a dinner in Berlin in '45 at which Philby himself had said, of an erratic agent who seemed bound for resolution, "There is truth to be found on the unknown shore, and many will find what few would seek."

She had been at that dinner too, as an agent of the French Direction Générale des Services Spéciaux, the headquarters of which had still been in Algiers then, so recently had the war ended; and of course she had loved Claude Cassagnac too.

In Broadway he had heard rumors that the 1935 motorcycle crash that had killed T. E. Lawrence had not been an accident—a black van had been seen passing him just before his crash, and witnesses were told not to refer to it in the inquest. Lawrence had supposedly found some ancient Biblical scrolls in a cave south of Jericho in 1918, by the Dead Sea, and been an unreliable agent ever since deciphering the primitive Hebrew texts; *Knew too much,* had been the laconic verdict. *Makes a man unpredictable.*

Do you know you look like poor old Lawrence.

It occurred to him that he would be protesting more, here—denouncing the shooting of poor old Cassagnac, demanding to be told his script right now, even frankly raising the mathematical possibility of his own assassination like a chess problem that needed to be solved—if he had not stepped out of honesty with Theodora, if instead he had instantly told the old man what he knew about the woman who had apparently shot at Philby.

"I should tell you—" he said impulsively; he wanted to get out of this unfocused, less-than-honest posture right away, restore the perfect loyalty to the Crown which had always been his defining moral anchor, and which he had not violated in any of the hard conflicts in Paris and Berlin and the Arabian desert and the Ahora Gorge below Ararat; but if he explained who the woman was, Theodora would very likely have her killed, have *her* status resolved. Whatever her motivations, if she had tried to kill Philby she was imperiling Declare.

Theodora was staring at him like an ancient, weary lizard.

"—that I'm outraged by your use of Claude Cassagnac." How pedestrian it sounded! And he had not stepped back into the old perfect accord. Where *am* I, now? he wondered. How am I to navigate, now?

Theodora said, " 'Would you kill an apparently innocent person, on our orders?' He was a player, boy, like us all. Go now. We've set you up, it's Red's turn to move."

▼

4

Paris, 1941

Across the margent of the world I fled,
And troubled the gold gateways of the stars,
Smiting for shelter on their clangèd bars;
      Fretted to dulcet jars
And silvern chatter the pale ports o' the moon.
I said to Dawn: Be sudden—to Eve: Be soon . . .
      —Francis Thompson, "The Hound of Heaven"

He had first met her in German-occupied France in October of 1941, after doing two weeks of hasty training and occasional desultory courier work for what he had still assumed was the Comintern, in rural Norfolk eighty miles northeast of London. The Comintern was Communist International, a worldwide association of national Communist parties united in a "popular front" again fascism.

Hale had pulled his own belt out of his pants before crossing Regent Street to step up to the Eros fountain in Piccadilly, and a smiling little fat man with an orange in his hand had indeed approached him and asked him about the belt; after the formal dialogue—"Well, I got it in an *iron-monger's* shop, actually, believe it or not, in *Paris*"—Hale had taken the orange along when the little man escorted him up Regent Street. The man had not touched nor even looked at the envelope Hale had brought down on the train, but had advised him to leave it on the fountain coping, presumably either because it would be picked up by someone watching or because it had not contained any secrets in the first place.

But over goulash and dark beer at Kempinski's the little man's nervous cheer had abruptly evaporated, and in fact he had been visibly frightened, when he learned that Hale did not, in fact, know anything about radios or wireless telegraphy.

"But," the man sputtered, "are you *sure?* Our people have the idea that you're an expert!"

"I did subscribe to several magazines for a while," Hale said, "about it. But I never really read them." His companion just stared at him in dismay, so Hale shrugged, wide-eyed. "My mother wanted me to learn a trade! But I wanted to be a teacher, not a wireless operator. I'm sorry— was this crucial?—you can have back what's left of the hundred pounds, uh, less what it'll cost me to get back to Oxford." Would this be the end of the whole thing? Hale didn't know whether he was relieved or alarmed—or angry. "The woman who approached me there should have asked me about this radio business, I gather it would have saved me this trip." And what's become of my trunk by now? he wondered. I shouldn't even have mentioned the hundred pounds to this fellow.

"Woman? Don't tell me about any woman." The man was nodding rapidly, his bald head shiny with sweat now. "And you can't go back to Oxford, our people in Europe approved your profile and specifically asked for you. A teacher! Damn it! WT was the main description for you, that's wireless telegraphy. I'll have to interrupt the transfer, send on an explanation and a—a recommendation, God help me! Either way is bad, but I think I'd be *most* remiss if I didn't ask for a two-week post-ponement on delivery of you, so as to run you through the accelerated course at our hedge school in Norfolk. There'd be no facilities across the Channel." He stared at the bewildered Hale as if at an armed lunatic. "I'll have to drive you up to Norfolk tonight, on the unsupported assump-tion." A drop of sweat had rolled down the man's jowls, and it occurred to Hale, for the first time, that being a spy might be to live constantly in the shadow of people like the coldly jovial man he had met in the Hasle-mere railway station.

Of course he never saw the little fat man again after being dropped off that afternoon at a pub off the A12 up in Norfolk, where two men bought Hale a pint and then walked him to an old farmhouse up an unpaved track somewhere near Great Yarmouth; and for the next four-teen days Hale sat with a dozen other uncommunicative men in a swel-tering barn and studied wireless as he had never studied anything before.

He learned about the Heaviside Layer, an atmospheric blanket of ionized air molecules that would reflect radio waves and let them "skip" across great distances; the layer was only about sixty miles above the earth during the day, with the sun pressure forcing it down, but at night it sprang up to a height of two hundred miles and split into two layers, and though transmission was clearer and stronger at night, signals could sometimes get caught between the layers and bounce along for thousands of miles before finally escaping to earth. The skipping effect was necessary for long-distance transmission, but Hale's instructors spoke of the Heaviside Layer with a sort of irritated respect, for its capricious billows and varying height often scattered signals and caused fading in the reception. Illicit spy broadcasts were referred to as *les parasites,* flickering covertly between the bandwidths of official transmissions, but sometimes his instructors seemed to use the French term for the knots of turbulent activity in the nighttime Heaviside Layer.

He learned to file and tin a soldering iron, and where to use a metallic flux and where to use a non-conducting rosin flux in connecting wire splices; and he learned how to re-wire the heater circuit of a direct current radio set so that it would work off alternating current, and what socket and vacuum valve needed to be changed, and how to avoid getting squealing and dead spots from the more sensitive cathode valve. At various points on the roofs of the barn and the barracks-like farmhouse he practiced setting up a Herz off-center-fed aerial, stringing the enameled wire at maximum angles to existing power lines or house wiring to avoid picking up accidental induction currents, and using ceramic coffee creamers and Coca-Cola bottles as makeshift insulators.

But mainly he learned the dit-and-dah characters of the International Morse code, concentrating on the numbers rather than the letters.

And he learned to use one-time pads. These were tiny books whose flimsy pages were nothing but columns of random four-digit numbers; given a practice sentence to encipher, he would assign a number to each letter of it—usually just 1 for A, 2 for B, and so on—and then after having written the message out in this pedestrian substitution-cipher he would add to each of the numbers one of the numbers from the one-time pad, taking them in order off the pad page from left to right. None of the one-time pad's numbers was so high that the addition of any two-digit number would make it a five-digit number. When he tapped out the resulting code groups, his partner on the other side of the table would copy the numbers and then use a duplicate one-time pad to subtract the pad's numbers and derive the original substitution-cipher message, and then quickly convert that all the way back into letters. Immediately after sending and copying, both copies of the used one-time pad page would be formally burned or eaten.

Accuracy was more important than speed here, and the students were constantly warned against the danger of losing their place on the flimsy pages, or turning two pages at once, as this would put the signal out of correspondence with the receiver's deciphering, and the message would be lost in gibberish. Oddly, the instructors sometimes called such nonsense results *les parasites* too.

His photograph was taken at the end of the first week, and when he left the Norfolk farm he was given a Swiss passport in the name of LeClos, with his picture in it. He was driven in a closed van down to Gravesend, where it turned out that LeClos was listed as a passenger aboard a Portuguese merchantman bound for still-neutral Lisbon.

At the dock he nearly bolted—he had not been abroad since the uncomprehending age of two, and now he was apparently expected to enter some Nazi-occupied country, *pretending* to be a *Comintern spy*. A British prison seemed infinitely preferable . . . until he remembered his haggard mother taking him to the ship-like rooftop building in Whitehall Court. *These are the people who got us home from Cairo . . . And they're the King's men. They deserve our obedience.* And he remembered his resolve at seeing the ruins around St. Paul's . . .

In the end, with the aid of some whisky provided by one of his sympathetic escorts, he had got aboard the ship.

Immediately on his arrival in Lisbon, after having spent the four-day voyage mostly secluded in his cabin with a stack of ragged old Belgian newspapers, he was met on the dock by a Soviet agent carrying an orange and taken to a crowded hotel across town near the Sintra Airdrome; Hale surrendered the LeClos passport and was given a Vichy-government French passport in the name of one Philippe St.-Simon, who was a cork buyer for a Paris-based company called Simex and who had airline tickets to Paris on the next weekly flights of both Air France and Luft-Hansa. As St.-Simon, bewildered and disoriented and wearing a secondhand European business suit, Hale had wound up taking the Air France flight at midnight on the thirtieth of September—and she had met him in the chilly dawn of the first day of October in the terminal at Orly Airport.

With no luggage besides a briefcase full of assorted cork washers and gaskets, and a thoroughly stamped passport that indicated a business traveler who had been checked and cleared many times before, Hale had been passed through Paris Customs without a second glance. His mouth had been dry and his ears ringing with the knowledge that he was all alone in an enemy-occupied foreign country now, and the loudspeaker announcements in flat, German-accented French had seemed to batter at him physically, but he had managed to keep a steady, distracted frown on his face and to answer the routine questions in relaxed French—though the interior of his head had been echoing with unvoiced, astonished British curses.

When the thin girl caught his eye and nodded to him outside the Customs shed, he assumed that the Comintern was using schoolgirls as inconspicuous couriers, for she appeared to be no more than eighteen years old, if even that, and the loose gray skirt and blouse and black sweater could have been a convent school uniform. Until she spoke to him he thought she might be of Irish descent, with her auburn hair and blue eyes, but her French was animated with the full vowels and razory consonants of Spain, and when she pronounced St.-Simon it was with the back-of-the-teeth lisp of Castile.

"*Rien a declarer, Monsieur St.-Simon?*" she said with a tight smile as she took his elbow and led him through the crowded terminal.

"Uh, *non,*" agreed Hale in a voice that was only now beginning to shake. He certainly had nothing to declare, and the infinitive verb had no significance to him beyond the concerns of Customs.

She led him to a tiny right-hand-drive Citroen in the car park, and as soon as Hale climbed in on the left side and she pressed the starter, she said in her lively French, "If the police stop us, you are my brother, understand? We are both fair, it is believable. My name during this drive is Delphine St.-Simon. Say something quickly now, in French."

Nervously but smoothly, and with a sincerity that surprised him, Hale recited the first several lines of Ghelderode's *Death of Doctor Faust,* in which the frightened old mage complains that everything in the modern world is so false that one can blunder into one's own self in the darkness; Hale even managed to mimic her Castilian accent. "Is that good enough for our purposes, sister Delphine?" he added in Spanish, feeling all at once absurdly pleased with himself. His shirt was damp with sweat, and he had to restrain himself from giggling.

She laughed delightedly as she clanked the car into gear and steered toward the exit. "Good! Your accent is peculiar, but not British at all. We grew up in Madrid, you and I, with our aunt Dolores . . ."

In a few quick sentences she gave him the outline of their immediate family history. "You work for the company Simex, where I have friends working, as a buyer of Portuguese cork, which is used for engine gaskets. Simex provides most of the construction materials to the Todt Organization, which is the branch of the German occupation force involved in building barracks and fortifications."

The little car was roaring north in one of the right-hand lanes of a highway that passed between green forests of beech and oak, and the sun was just clearing the fringe of treetops off to his right. Hale cranked down his window to take deep breaths of the fresh air and let the chilly breeze sluice through his hair.

"Four months ago," she went on, "you would have been sent to a special school in Moscow, to learn about things like microphotography and secret inks, and—oh, arson, and bomb construction and placement, and guns. But there is no time for any of that now. *None* of us *ever* believed that the non-aggression pact between Germany and Russia was anything more than cunning *realpolitik,* buying us time to prepare; and now the fascist beasts have invaded Russia, as expected, and preparation has given way to enactment."

Hale nodded, but he detected guilty relief in her voice, and he guessed that in fact the Molotov–Ribbentrop pact had for a while shaken her faith in the Communist cause. Hitler's invasion of Russia in June, violating and ending the pact, must have been a welcome return to virtue for devout Communists everywhere; and Hale wondered how this earnest girl's faith would survive if Stalin should again find it efficacious to align himself with fascism.

"A Soviet network has been in place for some time," she went on, "in Paris—perhaps several have been, unknown to one another—but apparently there is a shortage of radio sets. Certainly the Soviet military attaché in Vichy fled to Moscow in June without providing a single one. The established networks are not allowed to ask the local Communist parties for help in this, as they are considered insecure; but new, parallel networks may get this help from the local parties without compromising any others. You and I are members of one such independent network. We needed a wireless telegrapher who had no local acquaintance at all, and you are what Moscow Centre has finally delivered to us. When we get to my apartment we will pack up all records of St.-Simon, and you will become someone fresh."

"Am I still to be a cork buyer?" asked Hale in French. "At . . . Simex?"

"You are only that if the police stop us in the next half hour. Once we're at my apartment, you and I will forget everything about St.-Simon and his job, and Simex too, until such time as you may need to leave the country. In your new name you will be a Swiss student lying low in Paris—an *embusqué,* a shirker of your national duty." She glanced away from the traffic to give him a quizzical look. "Centre may ask you to pose as a homosexual. You do look like a Romantic poet, with your blond hair and cheekbones, and it would bolster your *embusqué* status."

"The Romantic poets weren't homosexuals, and neither am I," said Hale in alarm, barely remembering to keep speaking French. He scowled at her. "Cheekbones or no cheekbones."

She was looking ahead through the windscreen and she didn't quite smile, but Hale saw a dimple appear in her cheek. "Oh, you like girls?"

"D'un tumulte," said Hale with dignity.

"D'un tumulte!" She laughed and added, in English, "Oh my!"

Traffic slowed and the air was fumy with automobile exhaust as they entered the city of Paris in a tangle of cars and horse-drawn carriages and bicycle traffic at the Porte de Gentilly. Hale saw a cluster of guards in tan uniforms with swastika armbands standing alertly in the back of a muddy flatbed truck by the side of the highway, and he must have flinched, because in her exotic French the girl told him, "The ones to fear, the Gestapo, aren't so obvious." She licked her lips and nodded at the shiny black truck that was idling ahead of them. "You see the license plate? WL is Wehrmacht Luftwaffe. They, and the Gestapo and the Abwehr, are the ones who come after us, tracking our wireless transmissions with direction finders."

"Bloody hell," said Hale in English. After that neither of them said anything until they were on the Boulevard St.-Michel, driving past the Luxembourg Gardens; and even then she only spoke to tell him, in a subdued voice, more about their imaginary childhoods in Madrid, though according to her he was just about to abandon that identity.

Most of the traffic on the boulevards appeared to be green military trucks with the black German cross on the hoods.

But Hale peered up curiously at the tall nineteenth-century building fronts, and when the girl steered the car into a right turn onto the Boulevard St.-Germain and passed the open-air market at the Place Maubert, already crowded in the bright morning sunlight, he was as forcibly cheered by the plain fact of being in Paris as he would have been by a fast pint of champagne. And he couldn't repress a delighted yelp when she swung the car left and drove across a bridge over the Seine onto what was obviously a little island city in the middle of the river. She smiled and rocked her head in a gesture that acknowledged the charm of the place.

She drove to a narrow street off the six-block Rue St.-Louis-en-Île that was the center line of the island, and after she switched off the engine Hale got out and obediently helped her lift the front end of the car and swing it toward the curb; they stepped around to the back bumper and did the same there, then returned to the front to do it again, and within a minute they had walked the tiny car crabwise until its right-side wheels were up on the curb in a gap between two old panel trucks. Not good for a fast escape, Hale thought; but perhaps a car wouldn't be much good for fleeing in anyway, in the narrow streets on this little island.

The street was the Rue le Regrattier, and the girl's apartment was a couple of high-ceilinged rooms on the third floor of a subdivided seventeenth-century town house. The first thing she did when they were inside was to take from him every bit of paper that had to do with St.-Simon, including the passport, and give him instead a set of documents that identified him as Marcel Gruey, a Swiss student. Then, over a kitchen table breakfast of bread, garlic sausage, scallions, and a rough red wine, his hostess told him that he would have an apartment in this same building, but that he would be spending most nights in a locked custodian's closet on the roof, transmitting and receiving signals from midnight until sometimes dawn or later. "Of course a high-voltage battery is used to get oscillation of the set," she went on quickly, "but the set is equipped with a cathode-type vacuum valve heated by an alternating current for better distance reception, so you'll be using household current in the heater circuit."

But Hale's attention had snagged on her previous statement. "Midnight until dawn?" he said uneasily. That couldn't be right. "Are you sure? That's . . . quite a bit more air-time than I was told there would be, at the school in Norfolk." In fact, his instructors there had told the students that uninterrupted sending for more than an hour at a time was asking for detection and arrest; the operator's job as they had described it involved a couple of scheduled evening times a week for two-way traffic, with several designated hours on other days when Moscow would be listening for possible urgent reports, and other hours when the operator would be expected to monitor the Moscow band for instructions addressed to his call-sign.

"Since June we are at war," she reminded him, "we Communists. In war one takes outlandish risks, isn't that right? We have agents in many factories and businesses, even in the German military, and what they bring us must be transmitted fully and immediately; Moscow will be listening at your bandwidth twenty-four hours a day now."

"Oh." He was numb—this seemed like suicide.

"But don't worry *too* much. We have watchers, and they will warn us if the Abwehr vehicles come within a few blocks of us—their trucks always have a meter-wide circular aerial swiveling on the roof, for direction-finding to locate black transmitters, as they call our sets. And even if the Abwehr should manage to get very close, their standard procedure when the radio source is in a block of houses is to cut off the current to each house in turn and note which house loses its lights in the same moment that the radio stops sending; and your radio is wired to the current of the house next door." She smiled. "If you should lose power in your heater circuit and fall off the air, and we see police breaking into that house, we'll know it is time to relocate."

"I hope they're in the habit of leaving some lights on all night, next door," said Hale, "just so that the Abwehr will clearly see which place to hit." His eyes were stinging with lack of sleep, and the wine was a weight on the top of his slightly bobbing head. His brain wanted a rest from translating and composing French sentences.

"We keep a light on in the foyer of this house. Now I must go to Paris to meet a cut-out, who will relay messages between me and one of the parallel networks," she said, "and—"

"Aren't we *in* Paris?"

"We're on the Île St.-Louis. Louisiens say they are going to Paris when they cross one of the bridges. You are a Louisien now. But I must go meet an ignorant message carrier, who doesn't know what I look like and who will ideally assume that I'm only a cut-out myself. It may take time to make contact, with possible fallbacks. You can sleep on the sofa here for a few hours."

"That does sound splendid," sighed Hale, glancing at the sofa and looking forward to forgetting all these distressing concerns for a while.

She reached across the table and shook his shoulder. "Don't sleep yet. Listen with your full attention, comrade. I am your contact with Moscow Centre, and my code name is the Latin phrase 'Et Cetera'—remember it. ETC is our group's radio call-sign, though if we are fortunate you will meet none of the others. You or I or both of us may have to relocate from time to time, at a moment's notice—I've only been here for a week, and might be somewhere else tomorrow—and if you lose contact with me for more than three days and have no access to a wireless set, you must go to some unoccupied country, Switzerland probably, and get in contact with the Soviet military attaché there. Are you following this?"

"If I lose track of you, I go to the military attaché in Switzerland," Hale recited. He could not imagine how he would get to Switzerland, if the need should arise.

"You must see the attaché personally, alone, and if anyone else tries to deflect you, you must threaten them with reprisals from the NKVD; that's the Soviet secret police, the threat should scare them if you deliver it in a mild voice. Don't show your passport to anyone, not even the attaché—give all of them only your code name, which is 'Lot'—and get the attaché to send a message to Moscow saying that Lot has lost contact with ETC and needs to get in touch with the director. The attaché will let you wait there until a reply comes, with instructions for you. What's your code name?"

"Lot."

"And my code name?"

"Et Salinae." He shook his head. "Et Cetera."

"That was Latin—and *salina* is 'salt mine' in Spanish, probably the same. You were thinking of Lot's wife, who was changed to a pillar of salt, in the Book of Genesis."

Hale was embarrassed, for the name Lot had put him in mind of the Biblical Lot, and so he probably had been thinking of this girl in terms of Lot's wife. But what business did a young Communist have knowing Bible stories?

She had stood up, and now she crossed to the hat stand by the door and pulled her black sweater back on. "Just you work at being worth your salary"—the French word was *salaire*—"to the Party. You will be paid a hundred and fifty United States dollars a month, plus justifiable expenses. The Red Army never pays in any other currency—"

Hale had stood up too and started for the sofa, but now he paused. "The Red Army? I thought we were working for the Comintern."

She bit her lip. "No, we are working for the secret service of the Red Army—Razvedupr, or GRU, both terms are short for Glavnoe Razvedy-vatelnoe Upravlenie—the Chief Intelligence Administration."

"Oh." I should have known, he thought, that Theodora wouldn't have gone to all this trouble just to set me spying on the Communist International.

From her pocket she dug out a brass key and tossed it to him. "That is a duplicate key to this apartment. You are to use it only in an emergency having to do with our Party work, understand?"

"Yes," he said humbly.

"If we should ever meet accidentally on the street, don't acknowledge me—if I'm working I might be under surveillance, by either side." She had her hand on the doorknob, but paused and looked back at him. "And—if we should find ourselves in a situation where the motivations and identities aren't clear—there is a code phrase which means, *Things are not what they seem—trust me.* It is 'Bless me.' Have you got that?"

"Bless me," Hale echoed.

She nodded, and her stern manner relaxed for a moment as she grinned and made a cross in the air with her forefinger. Then she was gone, and the tall door closed behind her, and he heard her steps tapping away down the stairs. Many years later he was to learn that they had not even really been working for the Red Army, or not entirely.

If a perfectly oscillating radio circuit is connected to an aerial, it becomes a transmitter, sending a uniform whistle out over the airwaves on its particular frequency; and if a telegraph key is wired into the leads from the high-voltage battery that maintains the oscillation, the key can break the steady carrier wave into the dots and dashes of International Morse. A receiving set tuned to a point just short of oscillation on the same frequency will pick up the stuttering whistle at great distances—as long as the Heaviside Layer isn't curling and flexing in the vagaries of *les parasites.*

But it often was. On many nights, hunched under a bare lightbulb in the ammonia reek among the brooms and buckets in the custodian's closet on the roof, with sweaty earphones clamped to his head, Hale would be hearing the signal from Moscow on the 39-meter band—ETC ETC ETC—but be unable to get them to acknowledge his answering signal—KLK KLK KLK DE ETC—on the prescribed 49-meter band or any bandwidth near it. Sometimes he would get weird ghost-echo responses, old signals of his own from the day or week before, as if they had been stuck quivering in the sky until his present agitation of the airwaves had shaken them loose, distorted in their rhythms now and riding a signal as faint as an electromagnetic sigh.

Very late on one such night in mid-October, when in fact the close-pressing blackness beyond the closet window had just begun to coalesce into jagged rooftop and chimney shapes against a receding sky, he blearily imagined that the rhythm of the *parasite* ghost-signal was a syncopated counterpoint to his own heartbeat, and so he impulsively began tapping out his call-sign in that same skipping, halting beat; and after only a few newly rhythmic passes he was rewarded with the clear answering signal ETC ETC OK DE KLK QRK RST 599 KN. In the international Q-code this indicated that Moscow had received his signal with perfect strength and clarity and asked him to go ahead. Hale immediately tuned his condenser to the designated working bandwidth and began tapping out the messages he had laboriously encoded with a one-time pad that afternoon:

FROM PIERRE B-T TOTAL STRENGTH OF THE GERMAN ARMY COLON 412 DIVISIONS COMMA 21 IN FRANCE NOW PERIOD 3 DIVISIONS PREVIOUSLY SOUTH OF BORDEAUX NOW BEING SHIFTED EAST . . .

He realized that he was able to send faster than normal when he matched his keystrokes to the quicker-tempo rhythm dancing in his head, even though it involved sometimes slapping the key on a hard double beat, and he realized that he no longer needed the metronome of his own heartbeat in order to follow it—

. . . FROM EMIL B-T NEW GERMAN GASES COLON NITROSYLFLUORIDE COMMA CACODYLISOCYANIDE . . .

—he was almost able to hum the single line of barbaric melody that the fractured intervals seemed to hint at—

. . . GERMAN HIGH COMMAND MOVING HEAVY COASTAL AND NAVAL GUNS TOWARD THE MOSCOW FRONT FROM KONIGSBERG AND BRESLAU IN PREPARATION FOR A PROLONGED SIEGE . . .

—but he had to grip the edge of the table with his free hand, for the whole building seemed to be rotating with ponderous and increasing velocity, and at the back of his brain and in his spine he was sure that centrifugal force was about to tug him out of his chair. He was blinking sweat out of his eyes to keep reading the numbers he was tapping out, and then tears; the harsh castanet sound of the key seemed to be accompanied by a monstrously slow, far-subsonic pounding that he could feel in his blood, like a slow-motion giant's running footfalls across the dome of the sky.

But he kept doggedly tapping out the code groups in the new ether-born syncopation, glad that the window was not directly in front of him and hoping that the stars were already invisible in the rising glow of dawn. At the end of his transmission he received the curt OSL NK on the Moscow bandwidth, signaling that his message had been received in its entirety and that contact was ended.

He shuddered convulsively, and then let his face follow the shaken-loose drops of sweat down onto the desktop, and for several seconds he just panted with his lips against the wood.

His mind scrabbled fearfully for an explanation of what had happened, and eventually came up with the reassuringly abstract phrase *self-hypnosis*. Fatigue and anxiety, and the irregularly repetitious action of tapping the telegraph key, had apparently—had obviously—pushed him to concoct a natural rhythm that allowed effective, spontaneous sending. The dizziness and the fear must simply have been childish reactions to the inadvertent self-hypnosis. Freud would have made short work of it.

Finally he unplugged the set and wearily tucked it and the key and the earphones away behind a sliding panel in the wall; but instead of going downstairs to his bed he pulled open the slanted roof door and climbed out onto the scooped iron gutter between two gables. Pigeons had clattered away into the brightening sky at the squeak of the door, and the fresh river breeze was cold in Hale's lank sweat-damp hair as he leaned half-sitting against the slanted roof shingles, with his heels braced in the gutter, and stared northwest toward the still-shadowed spires of Notre-Dame Cathedral on the bigger island, the Île de la Cité.

Below him in the chilly darkness he could see the channel that separated the islands, though he couldn't quite see the Pont St.-Louis that linked them like a tow rope.

One afternoon a week ago he had walked all the way out to the northwest end of the Île de la Cité. Trudging along like an idle *embusqué* but at the same time watching for Nazi police as he made his way up Baron Haussmann's broad, beech-lined avenues, he had avoided a couple of *motards,* motorcycle policemen, by ducking through a pair of open iron gates into what had proved to be the courtyard of the Palais de Justice; then, realizing with poker-faced horror that he was standing directly between the police headquarters and the courts, he had turned his steps sharply left through a driveway tunnel into a crowded parking lot surrounded on all four sides by government offices—and found himself looking upward from the roofs of the cars to the gray gothic columns and high arches of Sainte-Chapelle against the blue sky.

He had recognized it immediately from a picture in a history book he'd studied at St. John's, and then he wondered if he might subconsciously have come this way on purpose. The towering thirteenth-century chapel had been built by St. Louis, the only canonized French king, to house the relics he had brought back from Venice during a crusade: Christ's crown of thorns, a nail from the cross, and several drops of Christ's blood. Hale was skeptical about the genuineness of the relics, and he supposed that the Catholic Church must have spirited them away to the Vatican as soon as the German Panzers had crossed the Meuse River in May of last year, and he still considered himself an agnostic, if not an outright atheist—but he had shivered at the thought that these evidences of God's redeeming death had perhaps actually reposed behind the tall stained-glass windows not twenty steps in front of him.

He had quickly fled out through another arch to the river-fronting pavement of the the Quai des Orfèvres, and hurried on northwest across the broad lanes of the island-transecting Pont-Neuf to the cobblestone lanes and chestnut-shaded groves of the narrow Square du Vert-Galant, where fishermen sat in the grass on both sides of the lane, trailing lines in the water. Standing above the sloped cement piling at the very tip of the island on that recent afternoon, it had been easy for Hale to imagine that he was at the bow of a vast stone ship pointed downriver toward the distant sea, and that the Île St.-Louis on which he lived was a barge towed behind.

Leaning now on the roof of the house in the Rue le Regrattier with the sun coming up behind the steep shingles at his back, it occurred to him that the Seine was flowing in the direction he was looking—it was the barge that was cutting the water, and the grand ship with Notre-Dame and Sainte-Chapelle on it was just wallowing along in its wake. The thought disturbed him—and he could still see a couple of bright stars in the gray sky—and so he hurried back inside to shuffle down-stairs to his bed.

He generally met for an early twilight dinner with the girl whose code name was Et Cetera. Their favored spot was a restaurant called Quasi-modo on the Quai d'Orléans around the corner from their apartment building, and she sometimes brought the concierge's big black Persian cat, who would sit in the third cane chair at their window table; the golden-eyed beast would wait, silently, through their soup and omelettes and the eventual lighting of the table candle, and its patience would be rewarded with bits of cheese at the end of the meal. The girl's cover name was Elena, and Hale thought it might be her real Christian name too, since she responded to it naturally and it fit with her Spanish accent. She never spoke of her past, and he was left helplessly thinking of her as having grown up in Madrid with her aunt Dolores, which was the cover story she had told him during the drive from Orly Airport on that first morning, when her cover name had been Delphine.

She did say that she was eighteen years old, which seemed plausi-ble. The only lines on her face were a crease underlining each lower eye-lid, implying habitual humor or skepticism, and the summer sun had brought out a scatter of freckles across her smooth cheeks, and Hale never saw her broad mouth touched with lipstick; but her walk had the careless balance of a woman's hips and shoulders, and after his third glass of vin bouche he would find himself uncomfortably aware of her breasts under the invariably loose blouse.

In spite of her lack of any make-up, she always had a small tortoise-shell-backed mirror in her pocket, and with uncanny perception she would pull it out whenever his gaze drifted below her face, and turn it toward him and say, merrily, "Want to see a monkey?" With repetition it had become daunting, if not actually annoying.

The faintly flirting tone he thought he had detected in their first conversation was certainly absent these days. She was generally cheerful, but there was no extra interest in her blue eyes when she listened to him, and their talk was either oblique references to the material she got from the couriers and cut-outs she met during the day, or speculative gossip about their neighbors, or heated arguments about modern poetry and painting. She admired the work of Picasso and Matisse, while Hale considered that painting had reached its zenith with Monet and had been rapidly deteriorating since; and Hale had thought he was progressive in liking Eliot and Auden, but her favorite poets were obscure Spanish and South American modernists like Pedro Salinas and Cesar Vallejo. Sometimes she brought him books and magazine articles about Switzerland, and at dinner he would often recite for her details of his ever-more-rounded cover identity. He and Elena both kept track of police activity in their neighborhood and cautioned each other about suspected Gestapo agents, but though the messages she relayed to him from her agents generally had to do with the German offensive against the Soviet Union, somehow she and Hale nearly never discussed the war itself.

After dinner the sky would be some dark shade of purple behind the chimneys, with Hale's radio set waiting for him on the roof of their old town house. Elena would gather the cat to her bosom for the stroll back, and Hale, beginning to be nervous about the perilous hours of concentration now stretching ahead of him, would puff on a cigarette and make aimless small talk and try not to think about the cat's position. At least he was beginning to get used to the vertigo effects of sending with the newer, faster beat.

Because his work frequently involved encoding and transmitting bulletins about German bombing flights, Hale quickly noticed that the periods when Moscow Centre abruptly went off the air corresponded to scheduled air raids over that city; and when Centre's transmission ceased in the middle of a message during the night of October 19 and had still not resumed after a week, he guessed that the Razvedupr communications headquarters was being relocated to some site away from Moscow.

Elena nervously agreed with his guess, and by relaying inquiries through her furtive contacts she established that all the networks had lost the radio link with Centre. All any of them could do was remain in place and monitor the airwaves, she said.

Hale continued to listen dutifully to the busy ether, but none of the inscrutable messages skipping across the underside of the night sky gave any indication of being from Centre; and for half-hour periods he would monotonously and perilously tap out his call signal, with no reply to justify the risk of detection.

During his first week at the rooftop post, he had spent the occasional idle hour listening to broadcasts not addressed to the ETC network, and he had maintained his copying proficiency by making sure he could transcribe the indecipherable numbers as fast as they were sent; now, with nothing at all being broadcast around the 40-meter band, he unfolded those old lists of numbers and studied them. During the stretches when the tense work had filled whole nights he had not always remembered to burn or eat the used pages from his one-time pads, and so he was able to dig a few of these out of the waste bin now and test his deciphering speed by idly subtracting the pad numbers from the unknown code groups, of course getting random nonsense results.

But late one night at the end of October he was chilled to find one three-week-old message whose numbers visibly corresponded to the numbers on a couple of his discarded one-time pad pages, and after a moment's work he found that the pad pages could actually decipher the message. This was a violation of protocol on Moscow's part, for the whole point of one-time pads was that they were to be used one time only—if Centre was using the same pad more than once, for more than one network, it gave the Abwehr a sporting chance to deduce what the pad's numbers were, and thus at least in theory enabled them to render out the basic substitution-code, which in turn could be broken easily.

The message was evidently addressed to another network somewhere in France, and it proved to be a complaint about *him*. Its text ordered the recipient to find out why the ETC network apparently wasn't broadcasting—this must have been sent before he had figured out the efficient sending rhythm—and it gave the full address of the house in the Rue le Regrattier.

Hale reread the text, his face suddenly cold. How many other messages had been sent using this particular one-time pad? And had he now stumbled by chance across the one message that had given the address of this house, or was this message just one of several, addressed to all of the other networks, as seemed more likely?

This was a clear breach of security. The carelessness of some over-worked cipher clerk in Moscow had irretreivably compromised the location of the ETC network—three weeks ago!—and Hale knew that the rules now required him to pack up the radio set and instantly escape across the rooftops and make his way alone to the military attaché in Switzerland; Centre would eventually send someone to escort Elena to safety, if the Abwehr had not broken the code and arrested her in the meantime. And Gestapo soldiers with socks over their boots to muffle their footsteps might be stealing up the stairs at this very moment.

Without pausing for thought he tucked the earphones and tele-graph key into the set's carrying case, unplugged the power cable and stuffed it in beside the earphones, and closed and latched the case; he swept all his papers into the waste bin and shook them all into the chute that led down to the building's furnace, but carefully tucked his rubber-banded deck of still-unused one-time pads into his pants pocket. Then he paused, looking out through the little window at the moon hanging low in the dark western sky. Daylight and all its dangers couldn't be more than a couple of hours away. He glanced for one yearning moment at the slanted roof door, then shook his head and unlocked the bigger door that led to the interior stairs.

He hurried down the unlit carpeted stairs to Elena's apartment on the third floor and unlocked her door with the brass key she had given him, and which he had carried with him ever since, more for sentiment than for security concerns.

The lights were out in her apartment, and at least there were no uni-formed figures ransacking her bookcases yet; in the moments until his eyes adjusted to the darkness he just stood still and sniffed the warm air, but smelled only her soap and the stale reek of her Gauloises cigarette butts. Hale lowered the radio onto the drawing room rug and tiptoed to her bedroom door.

She didn't awaken when he turned the knob and pushed the door open on silent hinges—he could dimly see her long body in the bed, lying on her side facing him, and he could hear her regular breathing. The window was open to the autumn night breeze, and the blanket was down around her waist; moonlight faintly highlighted her bare shoul-ders, and he knew that he would be able to see her breasts if the electric light were on.

"Elena," he said softly—and then froze, for when she sat up he heard the snap-and-click of an automatic pistol being chambered.

"Bless me," he said clearly, recalling that she had said the phrase was code for *Things are not what they seem—trust me*. "It's Lot," he went on, keeping his voice level. "Or Marcel Gruey," he added, giving his cover name.

In the thick silence he heard the snick of the safety catch being pushed up, and then the gun clunked faintly on the bedside table. She glanced around quickly, as if to make sure this was her own room, and he realized that she was still half-asleep. "What have I—" she muttered in Spanish. "Lot? Yes, it is you. What have I said to you here? I did say—" She was clearly confused, and he opened his mouth to explain that he had only this moment stepped into the room, and that she had not said anything to him, when she spoke again, in a hoarser voice: "Oh, but do take off your clothes."

Hale's breath caught in his throat. *Yes,* he thought; the compromising message is three weeks old!—and if the Abwehr had broken it we would have been arrested by now. "I—love you, Elena," he stammered, stepping toward the bed. He would tell her about the message afterward, in the morning.

And what would she think of him then, when she learned that he had kept her ignorant in mortal danger for several extra hours? Or even for half an hour?

Still in Spanish, she whispered, "And I know I have said I love you." She shifted in the bed, clearly to make room for him.

He could pretend to find the message later today . . .

. . . Thus not only keeping her in unknowing danger but lying to her as well. What would he think of himself, if he did that?

"Ah God," he wailed softly. "Remember that I love you. I've deciphered a message that was sent to one of the *other* Razvedupr networks—you understand?—it was enciphered with a one-time pad that Centre used more than once. The message"—Will we ever be in this position again? he thought despairingly—"refers to our network and gives the address of this house."

She was out of bed in an instant, and he glimpsed her naked body in the moonlight only for as long as it took her to scramble into her skirt and blouse.

"You should have run, with the radio set," she said in clipped French as she buttoned the skirt and stepped into her shoes.

"And left you to the Gestapo," he said in a shaky voice. "Yes, of course."

"I'll have to report your dereliction of duty, once we're clear," she panted, stuffing the gun into her purse. "We are loyal to each other only in service to the Party."

"I'll add a postscript to your report, when I send it," he said giddily. " 'I did it because I love her.' "

"Oh, you fool." She kissed his cheek as she stepped past him into the drawing room. "I won't make a report. Let them imagine that I was with you when you deciphered it, and we will both forget foolish things said while half-asleep in the middle of the night. That's the radio set? Good. Come on, we leave now. Peculiar evasion measures are called for, and it's high time you got practice at them—though you will never speak of them again after the sun comes up this morning, not even to me."

They descended the stairs to the ground floor, and then paused in the dark entry hall just inside the street door while she explained how they were to walk. Two people, she explained, even a young couple, risked drawing suspicious attention; so they would emulate the *clochards,* the homeless gypsies who slept under the bridges and bathed in the Seine. "The *boche* do not like to trouble the *clochards,*" she said nervously, "even during the day, when they can see them. I learned this from a Hungarian agent named Maly, who had been a Catholic priest before the Great War, and they say that a man ordained as a Catholic priest can never divest himself of that status. He was later sent to run agents in England, and then recalled to Moscow."

Her voice was sad. Hale knew that she hated Catholic priests, and he had gathered that a recall to Moscow by Centre was often a summons to execution; but he couldn't tell which of these facts it was, if indeed it was either of them, that grieved her.

"You are from Palestine," she went on, "and you had the sending difficulties people from there often have, and then all unaided you found out the sending rhythms that placate—that *overcome* those difficulties and ultimately make for the best DX sending of all. They can't be taught—one needs to discover them unaided, from one's own heartbeat."

DX meant long-distance, and Hale nodded uncertainly.

"Poor Maly made a study of those rhythms," Elena went on as she stared out through the glass at the empty street, "with the idea of achieving some sort of immortality: that is, a way to evade God's judgment. He did not, I think, achieve that—in the end I think he chose not to avail himself of it."

"I—I was born and baptized in Palestine," said Hale, "but I left there well before I was two years old. I really don't think this—"

She waved him to silence. "We will be doing an *imitation* as we walk," she said. "We will walk one behind the other down the gutter in the center of the street, our footsteps combining into one of these rhythms, like two hands on the keys of a piano; later I will show you how a single person walking can do this nearly as well. You will pick it up quickly, I think. The sound of our footsteps will be likely to . . . *confuse* anyone who hears it and tries to locate us; they will look the wrong way, or imagine that it is a noise from the sky like an airplane, or even forget that they had looked for something."

Hypnosis again, he thought defensively; or plain superstition.

"We will be doing an imitation of *'nothing right here,'* you see?" she went on. "If the street were a painting, we would be a semblance of a blank shadowed spot. I can walk to the Quai d'Orleans stairs and the riverbank without looking up from my feet, and you too must keep your eyes downcast, watching nothing but my feet ahead of you. Do you understand? Above all you must not look up into the sky."

Hale was uncomfortably reminded of his childhood end-of-the year dreams—nightmares—and he realized that his breathing had become rapid and shallow. "Whatever you say," he told her gruffly.

"We go," she said, pulling open the door. Cold air sharp with the sea smell of the river fluffed Hale's hair and chilled his damp chest between the buttons of his shirt. "Watch my feet," she said as she stepped out onto the sidewalk, "and complement my pace."

They hurried out across the dark cobblestones to the sunken cement-lined gutter that ran down the middle of the Rue le Regrattier, and as she started south, toward the quai, Hale was following at her heels, the heavy radio case swinging beside his right knee. He was acutely aware of how vulnerable he was to arrest, carrying an illicit short-wave set and a bundle of one-time pads.

The heels and toes of her shoes were tapping out a hesitant, skipping beat that echoed between the close housefronts and batted away into the open sky above, as if dancing around some absent or inaudible bass line, and with the practice he had got from playing the telegraph key he quickly found himself stepping along in a choppy rhythm that made arabesques around her pace but still avoided placing a toe-tap squarely on the implicit metronomic thudding that he almost imagined he could hear.

"Good," she said softly over her shoulder. "You were born to this."

"Oh, thanks—very much," he said, breathing and speaking only sketchily, from the very tops of his lungs. The dark sky behind his lowered head seemed ponderous with momentum.

Born to this, he thought; *had childhood dreams about this, nightmares.* He was too tense and exhausted to sustain long thoughts, and these phrases echoed loudly inside his head. *Born to these nightmares. Born in Palestine, found out the rhythms that placate.* And then simply the phrase *Born to this* was pounding over and over again in his thoughts, weaving itself into his compulsively rhythmic pace.

Elena had mentioned two hands on a piano keyboard. Hale's mind now separated into two attentions, as if a pianist's hands had diverged to pursue separate scores, or as if the pianist himself had devoted one mind to following the notes perfectly and a second mind to catching every syllable of a backstage conversation.

—sign the Official Secrets Act, for six hundred pounds a year, new banknotes in a blank envelope, no taxes—hurrah—and no pension either!—but I'm free to make pension arrangements with the service's own Drummond's in Admiralty Arch, am I? No, thank you, when I retire it will be to the place where nobody needs money.

It was a voice in Hale's head, but not his customary one. Even mentally, this one had a much more pronounced Oxbridge drawl, and it was deeper, older, than Hale's. The challenge of following Elena's tricky footsteps down the Rue le Regrattier fully occupied Hale's own attention.

—Iberian sub-section of Section V, exposing German agents by buying the passenger lists from Aero Portuguesa and Trafico Aero Español, and then matching the Enigma-traffic code names and itineraries to the passengers who consistently took the same flights that were specified in the traffic, Madrid to Barcelona, Madrid to Seville, and alerting Lisbon Station to them. Have to

work from out here in the British countryside in St. Albans it's true, War Sta-tion XB, nineteen miles north of London . . . The alien thoughts were accompanied by the warm, roofing-tar taste of Scotch whisky, and Hale felt drunk from the hallucinated fumes.

He took several deep breaths of the chilly river air, mostly to estab-lish to himself that he was still in Paris. The world was spinning and he clung desperately to the grip of the radio case, and he was afraid he would somehow lose Elena before they got to the river and were able to look into each other's eyes again. "Elena!" he called unsteadily, without looking up from her heels. "Marry me."

—Marry me? mused the other voice in his head. *Well, she's taken my name by deed-poll, advertised it in the* London Gazette. *Still, with a child now, and more to come, I ought to do it properly, for them. I can think of nothing more rewarding than the sight of a row of descending heads at the breakfast table.*

Hale was uncomfortable with the other attention's image. Chil-dren . . . ? A very personal duty, voluntarily undertaken . . .

—volunteer for night duty in Broadway, drive down to London once or twice a month and get to read freshly deciphered telegrams from Heads of Sta-tion all over the world—stop in at 58 St. James's Street to say hullo to the MI5 lads, give Dick White a peek at the latest Enigma-Ultra decrypts, in exchange for some gossip—but—

The emotion that now smoked in Hale's head was frustrated rage, and his sudden panting through clenched teeth threatened to interfere with his complicated pace.

—am I even now in the Secret Service, the real *one? The SIS Registry is right here in St. Albans, but the German incendiary bomb a year ago suppos-edly burned up all the old SIS files, all the way back to when the service was called MI-1C. Really? All of them? Even the microfilm copy? Or has a deeper or higher secret service used the bomb as a plausible pretext to spirit those files away to some more secret registry somewhere? How far in have I got to get, to know what Lawrence knew?*

The voice faded, and immediately Hale found its thoughts as hard to remember as the details of a dream, once one has awakened. Lawrence? Something about Drummond's? He was relieved to see that the Seine embankment was only a few steps ahead of Elena, for he was sure that the *clochard* effect of their footsteps had ceased and that he could safely look up into the sky now if he cared to—and in fact Elena's pace had subsided to a normal walk.

How long have we been walking? he wondered as he finally allowed himself to breathe deeply. I asked her to marry me, at some point! Has she answered yet? Did I even speak the words out loud?

He opened his mouth to say it again, but in that instant she stepped onto the grass between the riverside chestnut trees and turned around. The moon was behind her, just over her shoulder, and so her face was in darkness.

"I am glad you ask," she said, "because you need to understand that I am married to the Communist Party. The Soviet State is my husband, and I am a devoted, obedient wife. In Madrid I made my vows, after my deluded father and mother were killed by the fascists and my aunt Dolores took me in, and showed me the engine of human history, the real salvation, the real adventurous surrender to a supreme power. It is not just for the duration of this war—my life will always revolve around Moscow, and I will always take what Moscow gives me."

Hale nodded, and didn't speak. Since abandoning the religious faith of his youth he had had no such sun to fix the orbits of his whirling philosophies, but loyalty to England was secure in the central orbit. "I— follow you," he said miserably.

He saw the profile of her head turn to look up and down the embankment, and then again, more quickly; and she sighed deeply. "You follow me," she said in a new voice, flat and controlled. "I wonder what we both followed. We are in the Square du Vert-Galant, at the far end of the Île de la Cité. Look! This is where the old men fish, that is the Louvre across the river, we"—her voice was shaking— "must have walked right past the Palais de Justice, with you carrying an illegal radio! Past the police station!" Perhaps seeing his blank look, she said almost angrily, "We are on the other island now."

"We—" Hale glanced around, trying to identify landmarks by the moonlight.

She was right. This was the spot where he had stood on a recent afternoon and imagined that this island was a boat pointed downriver, and that the island on which they lived was a barge being towed behind. Somehow the two of them must tonight have walked north instead of south from their house, and across the short metal bridge that connected the islands, and past Notre-Dame.

The wind from off the river suddenly felt chillier, and he found that he had sat down in the damp grass. What had happened to him, when his mind had seemed to split into two? There had been another voice in his head, he remembered that much—

"You are a trouble to me, Marcel," Elena said remotely. "You make me unfaithful to my husband . . . for I believe I will not put this event into my report either."

▼

5

Paris, 1941

"How am I to fear the absolutely nonexistent?" said Hurree Babu, talking English to reassure himself. It is an awful thing still to dread the magic that you contemptuously investigate—to collect folklore for the Royal Society with a lively belief in all the Powers of Darkness.
—Rudyard Kipling, *Kim*

They were alone in the windy moon-streaked darkness at the tip of the island—the furtive *clochards* must all have been clustered on the smaller island, or been frightened away by the approach of this particular semblance of *"nothing right here"*—and for a while during the hour or so before dawn Hale and Elena debated in whispers what to do with the radio.

Hale, still angry that Centre had broadcast their address to agents using duplicated one-time pads, was for throwing the machine into the river; Elena objected that it might be one of only a few sets in Paris available to the Party, perhaps in fact the only set, though she did think that carrying it through the city streets was unconscionably risky; it looked like a typewriter case as much as it looked like a valise, and even a typewriter was a suspicious thing to be carrying around in occupied Paris. In the end they groped among the leafy chestnut trees overhanging the river until they found a branch with a three-pronged crotch above eye level, and with Elena standing on tip-toe to help they wedged the case there, hoping that daylight wouldn't make it conspicuous. Hale was glad to get rid of it for now, and his step was a good deal springier as they walked away from the incriminating set.

When dawn had fully claimed the sky and the sparrows were a chattering noise in the leafy branches, Hale and Elena took one last anxious glance at the tree in which the radio was hidden—they could see nothing suspicious from up on the path, and Elena said they shouldn't approach that tree now that they could be seen from the south bank—and then they dutifully assumed the cover of a pair of early-rising lovers and strolled arm-in-arm across the Pont-Neuf to the south side of the river.

"We need a fish," she said when they had reached the broad pavement of the Quai de Conti on the southern shore. Seeing his blank look, she went on, "Anything obvious that one would call a fish—a real one, a toy, a *painting* of a fish."

"A recognition signal," hazarded Hale, and she nodded impatiently.

It took an hour. No shops were open yet, but after walking a hundred yards down the embankment, and approaching several of the old fishermen who looked as if they had been trailing their lines in the river all night, they at last found one old fellow who had actually caught something, and they bought a thoroughly dead trout from him. Elena slung it in a handkerchief and carried it with the fish's silvery head and tail hanging out at either side.

Then at an aimless-seeming pace that led them several times back across their own trail, they walked through the drafty narrow streets of the St.-Germain district, and after an expensive but suspicion-deflecting *petit déjeuner* at Aux Deux Magots—rolls and ersatz tea served by waiters in black waistcoats and long white aprons—Elena led him south to the gray stone fountain in the square in front of the Church of St.-Sulpice, which she described as her place of conspiracy.

"Ideally," she told him quietly as they leaned on the side of the coping that was not wet from wind-flung spray, "the place of conspiracy would be in a neighboring country—probably Belgium, if the Germans had not occupied it, or Switzerland, if the Germans had given Centre time to plan thoroughly." She sighed and brushed the disordered auburn hair back from her forehead, and Hale's heart ached at how young she looked. "But this is probably secure enough. Someone is assigned to watch this fountain until noon every day, and when they see us, with the fish, they'll refer the fact of us up the chain of command; we'll get a room somewhere tonight, and then come back here again tomorrow. And then, or the day after, or the day after that, a return message will have been sent back down the chain, and someone will approach us with instructions."

"Tomorrow's the first of November. Can you still meet the courier who'll have our pay?"

"Oh, certainly, that's in the afternoon. And I have to, don't I? Anyway, I don't see any reason to think the courier would be compromised."

Hale nodded and squinted curiously around at the Parisians who were beginning to populate the slantingly sunlit square. On the Îsle St.-Louis he had generally slept until noon, and made lunch of whatever bread and cheese and wine Elena had bought on the black market the day before; she would return from her clandestine meetings late in the afternoon, and after a shared glass or two of wine Hale would begin encoding the material she had brought home. Aside from their dinners at Quasimodo and occasional furtive walks to glance at the gargoyles and flying buttresses and ranked saints of Notre-Dame, he had not seen much of Paris at all.

And he was surprised now by all the bicycles. He had seen bicycles in the traffic jam at the Porte de Gentilly and on the island boulevards, but in this square and the adjoining streets of St.-Germain he saw people riding in the perambulator baskets of bicycle rickshaws, and groups of businessmen in suits and ties pedaling soberly across the cobblestones, and elegant ladies whose wide skirts were clearly designed to project out away from spokes and sprockets.

One man's bicycle had a green kite or paper flag rattling on an upright pole behind the seat—and Hale realized that it was a paper fish, ribbed with wooden dowels. The man was just riding in a big circle around the fountain.

"There's a fish," Hale said softly to Elena.

"I see it," she said—but she was looking back toward the pillars at the church entrance. Hale followed her gaze and saw on the steps a woman whose broad skirt had a big red-flannel sunfish stitched onto it.

They both saw the next one, a portly little man only a dozen steps away, carrying a dead trout like Elena's slung in a newspaper.

"Is it a coincidence?" whispered Hale.

The little man halted to stare at the fish Elena was carrying, and then he looked up at her and Hale with an expression of alarm.

Elena slid her hand behind her and dropped the trout and handkerchief into the fountain water. She stood up away from the coping and said softly to Hale, "Bless me!"

Things are not what they seem—trust me.

He nodded and followed her as she stepped away from the fountain.

They walked away north up the Rue des Canettes, in the first block passing several more people carrying fish emblems, and Elena didn't say anything until she paused below the Romanesque tower of a church on the north side of the Boulevard St.-Germain.

She turned an anxious glare on him then, but he knew she was thinking of all the fish in the square by St.-Sulpice. "Does Centre *want* their networks rolled up? They obviously gave the same place of conspiracy—even the same recognition sign!—to—it might be *dozens* of agents! Of what use is that? Is the watcher supposed to go down into the square with a notebook at noon, have them all line up and give their code names? It's even worse than reusing the one-time pads, and that was blatantly bad security. How alert would a Gestapo officer need to be to wonder about the . . . this *fish* festival at St.-Sulpice?"

Hale pushed away the memory of a voice from his childhood nightmare: *O Fish, are you constant to the old covenant?* "Can it be normal," he said, "for that many people to be at their place of conspiracy at the same time?"

In his head echoed the ritual answer to the dream's challenge: *Return, and we return; keep faith, and so will we . . .*

She blinked. "Good point. No. All those agents on the run at once! There must have been a big reverse, perhaps some centrally informed agent has joined sides with the Gestapo. There is not supposed to *be* any such agent, but after these last hours nothing would surprise me." She shook her head and resumed walking north, toward the river. "We don't dare try to get my automobile, but we've got to get our radio set back. This isn't Centre's fault, entirely."

Hale trotted up beside her and matched her pace; and when she glanced at him he raised his eyebrows enquiringly.

"Hitler didn't care about Spain," Elena said. "The Spanish Civil War was just a practice ground for him. Among other things, he learned there how to do the *Blitzkrieg,* and thus he was able to sweep through France much faster than anyone had allowed for. The networks used to send information as microphotographs carried by couriers from Berlin here to Paris, where the Soviet attaché could send the information on to Moscow by the consulate wireless. But with the overnight fall of France that became impossible, and all the weight of intelligence-relaying fell onto the illegal networks. Arrangements had to be made in haste."

"And agents are expendable."

She nodded, apparently choosing to ignore his irony. "Individually; even networks, individually. But not—*everything!*"

A Great Dane in a gated courtyard barked at them as they hurried along the sidewalk, and for a moment Hale was surprised that the dog was barking in the same dialect as English dogs.

"Perhaps," Elena went on, nodding at her own thought, "Moscow has established a perfect hermetic network in Europe, with some *sanctum sanctorum* intelligence access, and can afford to let the Gestapo roll up all the others."

"Can afford to deliberately betray all the others," suggested Hale cautiously.

"It is *realpolitik*, Marcel," she said in an almost pleading tone. "You are one of us, you know that the outcome is what matters. One day the peace of worldwide communism will be here, will be real. Until that day—"

"We are expendable," he said again.

"Yes," she said emptily.

They crossed the river by the Pont des Arts just downstream of the islands, and in the embankment street below the Louvre they bought roasted chestnuts wrapped in newspaper. Elena told Hale not to start eating them until they had crossed back to the Île de la Cité and were back in the Square du Vert-Galant. "It is cover," she said. "Spies don't generally bring treats along when they're doing risky work."

The sun was above the crenellations of the Louvre castle, and Hale no longer wished for a sweater. Scents of fresh-baked bread warmed the morning breeze, and he hoped they would get a more substantial breakfast, and some wine, before long.

"Where would you watch from, to catch anyone retrieving the radio?" asked Hale quietly as they approached the spot where they had waited for dawn. "If you were the Gestapo."

"I would have a boat out in the river," she said; and then she peered between the trees at the water. A rowboat floated out there, apparently at anchor, and the man in the boat wore a big straw hat, which would be very noticeable if he were to wave it. Thoughtfully she cracked a chestnut and chewed the hot nut. "And I'd," she mumbled around it, "have men in ordinary clothes sitting close by."

Two burly men were sitting on a low wall playing chess only a few yards ahead of them, and Hale glanced at the board as he and Elena strolled past. Both red bishops were on black squares. Three other men were squatting on the grass farther away, passing a bottle of white wine back and forth. All of them looked younger and healthier than the fishermen and *clochards* Hale had seen so far.

He turned to Elena and said, in a loud and irritated voice, "Very *well!* I *love* you! God!"

Elena stared at him in surprised embarrassment, then shook her head. "Oh, you are a beast!" She began snuffling and turned back toward the broad lanes of the Pont-Neuf.

Hale turned too and strode after her, not glancing back at the men. "Did I *misunderstand* you, somehow? God knows I'm trying to be cooperative here! I—"

She took his arm and shook it as they hurried below the statue of Henri IV. "That's enough," she said quietly. "And that was clever, very naturally *in media res*—we couldn't simply have turned in our tracks and walked away without a word after we saw them, and the rudeness of it was a completely convincing touch." She smiled at him, again looking very young. "You are angry that I love the Soviet State, and not you."

"You love the Soviet State *more* than you love me," said Hale, "was how I understood it." He shrugged. "Actually."

"We must try to get another wireless set," she said. "It's likely that the local Communist Party has at least a couple that they are afraid to use, or even admit to. I wish I still had the automobile." She was snapping her fingers as she thought. "I must assume that my own agents are sound. I will get black market passports for us, the clumsy things known as *gueules casses,* worthless to show the Gestapo but good enough to fool the concierge at a pension somewhere, so that we can get rooms; we don't dare try to get good new passports, for I believe all the networks have used the *pass-apparat* services of Raichman"—she glanced at Hale—"another man from Palestine, and our best cobbler of forged passports and supporting cover documents—and he might be the agent who has gone over to the Germans."

Hale nodded and helped himself to some of the nuts in the newspaper sheaf she carried. "And we must find some lunch," he said.

She shook her head. "Breakfast was too expensive, now, and I have to buy two *gueules casses,* and we can't be certain of my meeting the courier with our pay tomorrow. We'll eat after sundown—cheaply."

▼▼▼

Elena found rooms for them in the attic of a house in the Latin Quarter, on a street that, at least for the moment, had continuous electrical current. She made Hale wait in the empty, slant-ceilinged chambers while she went out to meet the courier and then try to establish contact with the Communist Party—she knew the names of two Party members and where they lived, and she was confident that she could get a radio through them if they knew of one to be had.

Hale sat on the gable windowsill overlooking the medieval street, scanning the roof and gutters and chimney pots for good places to string an aerial and an earth wire, and late in the afternoon he saw her appear in the apricot sunlight for a moment from around the corner by the Panthéon, then come striding forward into the shadow of the ranked housefronts as she forced a perambulator over the cobblestones rapidly enough to scramble the brains of any baby in it; but he was bleakly sure that it concealed a new radio, and he hoped she was breaking the filaments and leads by shaking it up. He hurried down to the street door to help her carry the baby carriage up the four flights of stairs.

There was indeed a new radio in the carriage—along with, somehow, a Dutch book on architecture—but there was also bread and cheese and a bottle of Italian grappa, and Elena sat down on the room's bare floorboards and pulled the cork out of the bottle and took several deep swallows before she spoke.

"I got our money, right at the first meeting place," she gasped, holding the bottle out toward him, "but it was a different courier—and he spoke to me."

Hale took several gulps of the brandy himself. "So?" he said, exhaling. "Don't they usually speak?"

"Not more than the password phrases. He gave me that book and said it contains some messages that need to be sent off to Moscow immediately. The money courier isn't supposed to have any access to intelligence. And when he gave the book to me it was wrapped in bright red paper!"

"Ah!" The book wasn't wrapped now, and of course the colored paper would have been a vivid aid for any Gestapo agent assigned to follow her. "You must have taken a very roundabout route to your friends' houses," he said, "after you ditched the wrapping paper."

She nodded, reaching out and flipping her fingers for the bottle. "I bought another book," she said after she had drunk some more brandy, "and in a lavatory I wrapped the red paper around it, and then gave it to a girl who looked somewhat like me; I gave her twenty francs to deliver it to the Sorbonne library. Meanwhile I shoved this book under the waistband of my skirt and spent an hour going up and down apartment stairs, and out the kitchen doors of restaurants, and hiding among a crowd of Moslem women who were leaving La Mosquée de Paris. They were short, I had to crouch."

Hale frowned at this intrusion of Islam into her story, though at the same time it seemed to him that it had been a particularly good evasion move, or . . . *related* to a good evasion move. He tried to trace the thought, but could only think of the vagaries of the nighttime Heaviside Layer.

Elena got wearily to her feet and lifted the book from the perambulator. "Comrade Charlotte is going to have to *carry* her baby around town for a while," she remarked idly as she riffled through the pages. "She probably would have given me the baby too, if I'd insisted—she was so relieved to get the set out of her house. There have been a lot of arrests, apparently." Then she lifted out four sheets of paper that had been laid between the pages, and scanned them. "German troop movements, battle plans." She waved the sheets at him. "These might be real, you know. The red paper might have been innocent."

Hale took the sheets from her and glanced at them—ROMMEL, 15TH PANZER DIVISION, HALFAYA PASS—they could be real, or not. "Assuming the radio works and I can get Centre on the air," he said thoughtfully, "I'll rephrase these, and send them with a lot of dummy code groups mixed in." He nodded toward the window and the city outside. "That's in case it's a Gestapo trap and they've got their monitors listening for messages of these particular lengths to be sent. If I sent the verbatim texts, they could easily recognize them and then derive my enciphering numbers."

Elena nodded. "Which might not be as unique as they're supposed to be."

"Right. Any other agent using the same pad might as well be sending *en clair.*" He looked at the window, calculating how he would attach the earth wire to the drain pipe he had noted earlier. He would string the aerial so as to get a low angle of radiation, good for long skip distances, and hope for clear receptions and a brief time on the air.

Beyond the frame of the window the eastern sky had darkened to deep indigo. Elena switched on the electric wall lamps, and Hale tore the blank endpapers out of the architecture book and spent twenty minutes enciphering an explanation of their current circumstances and of the dubious messages Elena had got from the courier; and then he paraphrased the message texts, adding a lot of *x*s and *y*s which Centre would recognize as null groups.

"Let's look at Comrade Charlatan's apparatus," he said, getting to his feet.

"I really should report you for spontaneity," she sighed. "Do you want some of this cheese and bread?"

"We can eat as I work. Don't get crumbs in the mechanism."

Hale lifted the radio case out of the perambulator, laid it on the floor, unlatched the lid and flipped it open. The radio inside was equipped with a cord for alternating current, and earphones and a telegraph key and a coiled aerial wire were tucked neatly into a gap at the side. There was even a packet of sharpened pencils. "It does appear to be a radio," he allowed. He used a centime coin from his pocket to unscrew the facing plate and look at the works.

The set had a regenerative hookup powered by a high-voltage battery to maintain oscillation and amplify weak signals, with a Hartley oscillator instead of a crystal for transmitting on a broad range of bandwidths, and a Bradleystat resistor to prevent key-click sparks, which might otherwise interfere with radio reception for a mile around.

"Not bad," he said. He turned the condenser and rheostat knobs, noting a gritty tightness in their action. The set had apparently never been used.

"So how soon can you be on the air? We need instructions."

"As soon as I string the aerial and the earth, and—" He glanced around the plaster walls of the bare room for an electrical outlet, and saw none. "And figure a way to hook the plug into one of the light sockets."

At last Hale sat on the floor with the headphones on and several of the book's endpapers laid out in front of him, and he turned up the set's rheostat until the valve glowed yellow; then he turned the condenser knob, and the set began oscillating—he could hear the rushing sound in the phones, and when he touched the wire between the grid condenser and the secondary coil he heard a satisfactory *thud*. For a few seconds he could hear a faint high-speed clicking that would be caused by the sparks in the distributor of some nearby automobile, a problem he had seldom had on the Île St.-Louis, but it soon faded.

"So far so good," he said. "Let's see if Moscow is back on the air yet."

He tuned the condenser knob to the 49-meter bandwidth and tapped out KLK KLK KLK DE ETC on the key, then reset the dial to the 39-meter bandwidth for receiving. Even transmitting for only a few seconds had misted his forehead with sweat—the current he was using was not wired in from a neighboring house anymore, and the Abwehr and SS direction-finders were supposedly always noting illicit broadcasts and laying out direction lines on street maps; already if they were quick they might have triangulated this block.

Abruptly he was getting a strong Morse signal over the phones, and he lunged for the pencil to begin copying.

ETC ETC ETCETCCCTTTEEE. The dits and dahs were coming so quickly that they were nearly a rattle. He could only lift the pencil from the paper and wait for the signal to slow down.

"It's crazy," he said in a tight voice. "It's clear, but he's sending like a lunatic."

"That tube is glowing purple," said Elena softly, pointing.

Hale glanced at the alternating current valve through sweat-stung eyes—there was a purple glow in the glass, which generally meant ion-ized air in the vacuum; that would weaken the signal, though, and in fact the signal was coming through with razor clarity—

—but so rapidly now that it was just a rough buzz, and so painfully loud that he clawed off the headphones and tossed them onto the floor. Even so he could hear the noise clearly.

It wasn't musical, but it seemed to be pulsating in a deliberate rhythm—and both Hale and Elena inhaled audibly as they recognized the drop-and-double-beat measure they had patterned their footsteps on last night. Hale's pulse was twitching the collar of his shirt, and so he could *see* that the rhythm was in perfect counterpoint with his heart-beat, and he guessed that Elena's heart was pounding in exact synchro-nization with his, and with the barbaric drumbeat or inorganic chanting that was shaking out of the headphones. His ears popped as if with increased air pressure, and he was irrationally sure that something out of a nightmare had come down from the stars to hang over the house, filling the sky.

Hale flinched and dropped the pencil, and from the corner of his eye he saw Elena start back too, at the clear impression of attention being paid to them. *It knows me,* he thought, *and now it knows where I am.*

Horizontal beams of light moving across the dark face of the sea like spokes of a vast turning wheel . . .

How far in have I got to get, to know what Lawrence knew?

Elena was gasping, "Turn it off, turn it off," even as Hale became aware of an uneven gusting of wind at the window and a rattling of the roof shingles outside, and the smell of wood burning.

Almost reluctantly, almost despairingly, Hale grabbed the alternating current wire and yanked on it, and the set went dead as the wall lamp and pieces of plaster clattered to the floor.

Both of them were crouched tensely on the floor, staring at the window, but only the evening breeze sighed in over the sill, with no sounds but distant motors and sirens. In the glow from the lamp on the opposite wall, Hale could see wisps of smoke spin away to invisibility in the fresh air.

At last he let himself relax, slumping backward to rest on his elbows and rock his head back. The night air was chilly in his damp shirt. "Damn me!" he panted. "Where's that brandy?"

Elena's face was sheened with sweat as she got up on her knees to hand it to him. "Maybe," she said shakily, "that's why Centre is letting all the networks be rounded up. Cut off a gangrenous limb." She took the bottle from him after he had gulped several swallows and tipped it up herself. When she lowered it and licked her lips, she said, "We need to consult Claude Cassagnac as soon as it can be arranged—he's the only other member of our network that I know, and he's been in the game since even before the last time Moscow rolled up the networks."

Hale wanted to ask her what she had seen—and heard and smelled, and *thought*—here; but he found that he couldn't frame the words, and he felt himself blushing to realize that it was self-consciousness, or shame, that was choking his question. And he didn't want to ask himself why he should feel *ashamed* of what had happened. This had been some electrical phenomenon—static charge in the atmosphere causing inter-

ference and unsynchronized duplication of the signal, turbulent air preceding a thunderstorm. Exhaustion had made him impose the familiar
rhythms on the random noise, just as it could conjure voices or the ringing of a telephone out of the sound of a filling tub; and only exhaustion
could be the reason he was reminded of his boyhood reluctance to tell
his year's-end dreams to the priest in the confessional.

But he was shivering, and he couldn't make himself ask Elena about
what they had just experienced.

"Really?" he said instead, in a brittle voice. " 'The last time'? Easy
work for the Abwehr and Gestapo, just wait for Moscow to hand over
her spies again."

Elena too seemed to be distracted. "Moscow works in ways that
needn't be explained to us."

"Her wonders to perform," agreed Hale in English.

"Marcel," she said in what struck him as an inordinately angry tone,
"I have no choice but to report your—flippancy! Can't you—"

"What's that?" he interrupted.

Looking past the radio set, he had noticed a shadowy delta of spots
on the floor, fanning out toward the window; and when he walked over
on his knees to look at it more closely, he saw that it was hundreds of
hair-thin rings scorched into the polished boards. Some of the faint
rings could be traced to be a yard across, but most were no bigger than
a penny, and some were such tiny black pinpricks that he assumed a
magnifying glass would be needed to see that they were actually rings.
He swiped at a patch of them with the damp palm of his hand, and they
had been so lightly burned in that the blackness rubbed away almost
completely.

Elena had stood up and crossed to the window. "It's on the sill too,"
she said humbly. "Some kind of electrical discharge . . . ?"

"Ball lightning, probably," he agreed almost shrilly, crawling back to
where they had left the bottle. It could have been ball lightning, he told
himself as he pulled out the cork. It could have been.

"I think we sleep in our clothes tonight," she said, stepping away
from the window and tugging the frames shut over the aerial wire and
latching them. Clearly she was wishing there were curtains to pull
across the view of the darkening sky. Still facing the glass, she said, "I
think we should sleep together, with the light on." She exhaled sharply.
"Once I would have prayed."

Hale glanced at the faint black soot marks on the palm of his hand—and he thought he understood why Adam and Eve had hidden from Yahweh, in the Garden, for he wouldn't be praying tonight either. *I heard Thy voice in the Garden, and I was afraid, because I was naked; and I hid myself.* "Once I would have too," he said. It occurred to him that she probably assumed that because he was British he had been brought up as an Anglican. "I was a Roman Catholic," he said, barely loud enough for her to hear.

"Oh, you are a bad influence!" She turned and looked at him. "You do understand *in our clothes,* don't you?"

I was naked, and I hid myself. "Yes, Elena." In this half-light, with her hair pulled back and her rumpled skirt and blouse looking too big for her, and the eyes in her narrow face wide with uncertainty, she looked twelve years old; and Hale himself was wishing that he was back in Chipping Campden and could climb into the old upstairs box bed.

"Dawn, be sudden," she said in English as she lay down next to where he sat.

Hale thought it was a quote from a poem he had read, but suddenly he was too exhausted to ask her about it.

Next day they bought fresh clothing at a black market stall by the river and moved into a different apartment, and that night Hale gingerly strung his antenna and aerial again, and plugged in the radio set—but though they braced themselves for another bout of wind and scorched floors and idiotically accelerated signal, or contrarily for the disappointment of finding that the set had been wrecked, in fact it was a session just like the ones he had experienced during the last ten days in the Rue le Regrattier house—the radio worked perfectly, but his call-sign drew no response from Centre.

Elena composed a note to the agent Cassagnac, proposing a meeting, and she went off by herself to put it in what she called a *dubok,* which she told Hale could be any agreed-upon space that was not likely to be disturbed—a gap behind a loose brick in a quiet alley, a knothole in a remote tree, a flap of loose carpet in a cinema. *Duboks* were generally used only once, and the recipient often hired some random passerby to walk ahead and make the pickup. The best *duboks,* she told him, were often to be found in the ornate, dusty vestibules of churches, which led

Hale to believe that wherever the security-minded girl was going to put the note, it would not be in a church.

At the end of the week they moved again, and on the following Monday morning they went to meet with the agent Cassagnac. When Hale asked how she had learned where and when to meet the man, he was told that of nine broken windows in an abandoned convent in Montparnasse, three had been repaired with cardboard.

To meet Cassagnac they bought an electric torch and then passed through a low door in the Rue de la Harpe, which Elena said was the oldest street in Paris; and when by the torch's beam they had picked their way down a zigzag succession of worn stone stairs, their hair fluttering in the cold clay-scented breeze from below, they found themselves in a cavernous chamber lit only in sections by paraffin lanterns hung on pillars that flanked gaping arches. The yellow glow of the lanterns disappeared far overhead in stray gleams on a concave stone ceiling, and wooden tables were arranged on the broad flags of the floor.

A man's voice spoke—"Et Cetera!"—and in spite of the echoes Hale was able to locate a figure sitting at one of the farther tables. The man went on, in French, "And Monsieur Lot." He pronounced it *Low,* which nettled Hale. "Join me, please."

Hale and Elena shuffled forward across the uneven floor, and from the cold drafts Hale got the impression that a number of tunnels extended out of this chamber, perhaps even under the river—and he was sure that this floor was Roman architecture, if not older. Catching a nimble fugitive down here would be impossible.

A bottle sat on the man's table, and after they had sat down on a bench opposite him, he poured two glasses full of what proved to be a vaporously aromatic cognac. He appeared to be about forty, with graying brown hair curled back over his ears and falling onto his forehead, and his lean face was lined with Gallic humor and melancholy. He wore a gray sweater under a battered dark jacket.

"You are adrift," he said, "and the relocation apparat isn't working."

"Centre seems to be abandoning us," Elena said, and she told him about their address having been broadcast insecurely, and described the disorder at the place of conspiracy in front of St.-Sulpice. Hale noted that she did not mention the weirdly accelerated signals and the burned floor of a week ago.

"Call it a testing," Cassagnac said, "or a distillation. Survival of a few, which will include an increased percentage of the most genuinely committed. Before he himself was executed, Yezhov of the NKVD used to say, 'Better that ten innocent people should die than that one traitor should go undetected.' "

"I met Theo Maly," Elena said in a cautious voice, "the Hungarian illegal agent, the ex-Catholic priest. He knew he was going to his death, when he obeyed the NKVD summons back to Moscow."

"You were a child, and Maly had great charm." Cassagnac sipped his brandy. "Charm, wit—intelligence, even—these are I think preliminary catalysts, like picture books for children: useful ladder rungs for awakening people, but not things for the people to cling to, once they've been awakened. I believe Russia has a . . . a primitive guardian angel, which must be denied at every turn; and those who persist in loving the angel, and merit her special assistance, must be killed—ideally after they have given their full measure of acceptable benefits to the Party, and not one benefit more."

"Is that the way?" asked Elena forlornly.

"The angel will always be there, my dear," Cassagnac said kindly, refilling her glass. "Five years ago Centre purged all the great illegals, the non-Russian Communists who could work outside the diplomatic channels and who in times of trouble could be disowned with no risk. They were educated Europeans, men and women who came to communism through literature and philosophy and the wounds of atheism, and they served their intercessory purpose, and then Yezhov killed them all lest their intercession proceed to become invocation; each morning the NKVD executioners were given their rifles and their vodka, and after they had shot their dozens and bulldozed them into pits dug by convict labor, they went back to the guardrooms and drank themselves insensible. The present generation in both the Razvedupr and the NKVD are correspondingly less attractive, to people like you and me, and even less tolerant of the guardian angel. But they will be summoned to the Lubyanka basement in their turn, and the ones who will follow them will perhaps be a little more to our liking; or else the ones who follow *them* will be."

"For three weeks we haven't been able to raise Centre on the radio," put in Hale, who wanted only concrete advice from this man. Somehow Hale couldn't help liking Cassagnac—the man's sad eyes and humorous mouth, and his rich voice, seemed vibrant with humane wisdom, but

Hale thought his statements were damnable, and it hurt him to see Elena bravely trying to assimilate them.

Cassagnac turned his warm eyes on Hale. "They will respond, my friend, as soon as they are set up in the new provisional capital at Kuibyshev. Keep listening until they do. And in the meantime—" He laughed gently. "You two are not malleable playback material. Elena, you must suspend contact with all agents and couriers and cut-outs; if you do establish wireless contact with Centre, change your address as frequently as you can, using cheap *gueules casses*. A month ago Centre sent a message to the head agent in Belgium, giving the addresses of three of the Brussels agents; that message will be deciphered by the Abwehr, and that network will inevitably be rolled up, and then played back against Moscow. It is almost certainly Centre's intention that this occur now, deliberately rather than accidentally. If you are not in a position to be used in this way, Centre will not ask it of you."

"Moscow," said Elena, and Hale remembered her saying, *I will always take what Moscow gives me.* "Moscow Centre wants this to happen, this 'playback'?"

"Does a fencer *want* to be disarmed or break his blade when he does the *passata sotto,* the low pass? It is the common event. Playback is the natural last stage of any spy network. At first a couple of agents are arrested, and their motive for cooperating with the Gestapo at this stage is simply fear of torture and death, and the hope that cooperation will buy them mercy; so they use the security passwords and signals to lure other agents into capture. And these newly captured agents follow the example of their duplicitous companions, with uncanny ease, and soon the whole network, though unchanged in its routines and codes, has switched polarity—the network goes on with its radio work uninterrupted, but now it is conducted by the Gestapo, intending to deceive Moscow and discover her secret urgencies. In the agents a mood of mocking cynicism quickly replaces, or evolves from, their previous principles and ideals. And for the agents who have switched sides, for the best of them, at least, the governing passion now is no longer ideology but a disattached, professional pride in the art itself. If they survive, such agents can be reclaimed at a later date, can still be useful, in limited ways."

"What are we . . . *hoping* for?" asked Hale. Dutifully he tried to assess what information he had learned in these five weeks abroad, for clearly the time had come for him to get out of France and find a way to return to England—but Elena would never accompany him on that trip, and so he was hoping that Cassagnac would provide him with some justifiable reason to stay on in France, to stay with her.

"You are a radio operator who was born in Palestine." Cassagnac's pouchy eyes were merry. "Deny it as they will, Moscow does value the assistance of a few people like yourself, albeit on the old illegal basis— with the left hand, at arm's length, unacknowledged and deniable. If you stay out of the action in this current wave of purges, Centre will certainly go on using you . . . for at least another couple of years. And if by then you are alert enough to see the next purge coming, you may hide through that one as well. *I* am one of the old illegals, reduced now to working in my own country; but I hope to live to see real communism achieved in the world, and to that end I disappear from time to time, and I see to it that my skills are never indispensable—it is the indispensable agents who are always the first to be purged, because their very existence proves an inadequacy in the Party as a homogenous whole."

Hale blinked at the man. "You're saying don't trust the Party," he said levelly, hoping Elena was paying attention and that her faith in her corporate "husband" might be shaken.

"Not at all, comrade, don't misquote me. I'm saying the Party can be trusted absolutely to do what's best for humanity—and if you can find no way within the rules to avoid a death-sentence, you should trust the Party to be doing the best thing, and cooperate. Maly agreed with this, and obediently assented to his own death."

"That's right," said Elena slowly, nodding. "If I'm to die for the Party, I would prefer that it be at the Party's hand. So Lot and I will be obedient but not evident for a while."

Hale realized that he couldn't run back to England now, and abandon poor idealistic Elena in this insane chess game. "I'm glad to understand you correctly," he said. "That's what we'll do." But he drained his brandy and poured himself another full glass, understanding for the first time in his life something of what drunkards sought in alcohol.

Cassagnac rapped the table with his knuckle, and he said abruptly to Elena, "Thistles, flowers—plants; did Maly ever talk about such things with you, my dear?"

She stared at him. "I don't think so. He cooked a dinner for us once, he might have talked about herbs."

Cassagnac crinkled his eyes and nodded, then turned his penetrating gaze on Hale. "You were recruited in a garden. Why were you there?"

"I was in Piccadilly Circus—oh! the woman, before that. The botanical garden at Oxford." *I was naked, and I hid myself,* he thought. "I don't know. It was across the road from my college." He wondered helplessly if a new secret chemical weapon were based on a plant extract, the way some medicines were; he had read that aspirin was derived from willow bark.

Cassagnac stared from one of them to the other for a few seconds, then exhaled a laugh and tossed back his head. "Forgive me, I was instructed weeks ago to ask you both this at the earliest opportunity. And now I have." He pulled an envelope from inside his jacket and slid it across the table to Elena. "I have received no other instructions regarding you," he said, "so I certainly have no reason not to give you this lot of American dollars and French marks and deutschmarks; it should sustain you for several weeks. When I may next be in contact with Centre, I will relay your ignorance of botanical matters, and your request for instructions, and no doubt I will at that time be given orders having to do with you."

"I think it would be best if we—did not meet with you again," said Hale.

Cassagnac shrugged and smiled. "The arch directly to your right will lead you up a set of stairs to the basement of an ironmonger's shop in the Rue de Savoie. No one will be surprised to see you appear. Buy a belt there, before you go out onto the street. You won't forget?"

Through steamy windows at the back of the shop, Hale could see that it was raining outside, and water plunked into pails on the wooden floor. Hammers and shovels and tool kits crowded most of the racks under the dim electric bulbs, but when Hale asked about belts he was directed to a bin up by the street windows, next to a stack of rusty lightning rods. Elena lifted a belt from the bin and handed it to him.

Aside from pictures of the Egyptian looped cross in history books, this black iron belt buckle was the first ankh that Hale had ever seen. It looked too crude and bohemian even for his neglected *embusqué* cover, but it was the only sort of belt the shop sold, so he obediently bought it;

and he wasn't pleased to look at it out in the lowering gray daylight and see that a stylized pattern of circles had been burned decoratively into the leather strap. Thunder rumbled away on the north side of the river.

"You should be the one to wear it," he told Elena as they paused on the sidewalk under the shop's awning; rain was drumming loudly on the canvas over their heads and tapping rings in the puddled gutter. "I'll bet it's a woman's belt."

"No," she said, "look at it, it buckles right over left—it's a man's belt."

Hale nodded and shrugged irritably, and only when he glanced at her a moment later, and saw her deadpan expression, did he realize that of course the belt could be worn either way.

"I don't think either of us should wear it," he said, his breath steaming away in the cold fresh air. "It's conspicuous—and since he insisted on it, it must be some kind of recognition signal, and he said himself that we don't want to be recognized for a while."

Elena stepped quickly out into the rain, and Hale followed, stuffing the belt into his coat pocket. She started to say something, then paused; finally she squinted back at him and said, "The guardian angel he mentioned—did you get the impression that it was real, or a figure of speech?"

"A figure of speech," he said tightly. Implicit in his tone were the words, *of course.*

"Oh." His answer seemed to have disconcerted her. She stopped in the rainy street and turned around to take hold of his shoulders and stare straight into his eyes; and, in English, she said, " 'Where wast thou when I laid the foundations of the earth? Declare, if thou hast understanding.' "

"I'm missing this," he said helplessly, in French. He blinked away cold water that was dripping from his eyebrows. "That's from the Book of Job—and not the Catholic Douay Version. It doesn't say 'Declare' in the Catholic version." He pushed a lock of sodden blond hair back from his forehead with his free hand, while she just kept frowning up at him. "We should have bought an umbrella back there," he said at last, awkwardly. "Though probably all they had were *iron* umbrellas."

She let go of his shoulders and resumed trudging across the wet pavement toward the Boulevard St.-Germain and their current home. Amber lights glowed behind the leaded glass of shop windows, but there were no other pedestrians out on the street. "It was an Englishman," she said over her shoulder, "no doubt a Protestant, who quoted it to a group of us in Albacete. He'd been pretending to be a Comintern recruit in the International Brigades, but actually he was a spy, a member of the British secret service. The Party had caught and exposed him, and Andre Marty shot him through the forehead a moment after he quoted that Bible verse; Marty used to be the leader of the Party here in France, before he went to Spain to command the Brigades. Nine-millimeter Luger. Blood flew forward as well as back, and some got on my dress. I was twelve . . . or thirteen or so, and I was a wireless telegrapher for the Brigades."

"Good God." Hale shivered, and not just because of the cold rain-water that was battering his face, as he lengthened his stride to catch up to her. "I'm—that must have been horrible. But why quote that verse to me now?"

"I *can* work a radio," she said. "I can copy and send International Morse, and I've been the assigned WT agent in several Soviet networks before this: here, and in Belgium, and back then, in Albacete. But in this current configuration I'm the one who travels around and meets couriers, and Centre wants each network to have one agent whose sole job is to manage the ciphers and the radio, and they don't want anyone else besides that person to do any sending; their operators in Moscow quickly learned the characteristics of your 'fist,' as they call it, your particular style on the telegraph key, and they'd get suspicious if I or anyone but you was to do any of the sending for our network now. But I *could.* And I think—I'm certain—that, if I'd been working the radio a week ago, we wouldn't have got the accelerated signal and the burned floor."

Hale nodded nervously, not wanting to discuss that night. "And that's why you quoted Job to me."

"Marty killed hundreds of Comintern agents in Spain, on the pretext that they had Trotskyite sympathies. But I think he was trying to weed out agents who had gradually become members of a transcendent order, a category so subtle and secret that the agents themselves didn't even know they were in it—that is, didn't know that they were in it *too.* I think there are more than one of these higher orders, I think there are partisan divisions. That English agent that Marty killed had been driving around the airfield at Guadalajara in a jeep, taking photographs—but it seemed he was taking pictures *away* from the airfield! Guadalajara was a

Moorish city once, Moslem—its old name was Wadi al-Hijarah, Arabic for River of Stones, and the *campesinos* say black basalt stones walk in those hills at night. The Englishman may not even have known he was involved in something bigger than the British secret service . . . though he did seem to mean something when he quoted the verse from Job."

A roar in the sky that Hale had thought at first was thunder grew louder and droning, and then he flinched and glanced up as a tri-motor Junkers 52 sailed heavily across the gray sky several hundred feet over-head, its broad silver wings rocking as it banked in for imminent touch-down at Orly.

"The verse from Job," he said too loudly, embarrassed at having been startled by the plane. "Well, it means nothing to me, besides Yah-weh telling Job, rudely, that if the world is run according to any rules at all, those rules are beyond Job's comprehension. Let's move along faster here, we're getting soaked."

"If the belt is a recognition signal," she went on doggedly, almost pleadingly, "I don't think we need to worry about its being one that would be recognized by any mere Razvedupr or Gestapo agents."

"Except Cassagnac," Hale objected, "and whoever told him about it; and the man in London who told me to say I'd bought a belt in an iron-monger's shop in Paris, as a password phrase." He smiled and reached out and squeezed her shoulder under the sodden sweater. "Your angel will be able to recognize it even in my pocket."

"Eyeless in Gaza!" she burst out in English, suddenly very angry. Hale stepped back from her in bewilderment; this was another quote from an English poem—Milton? *Samson Agonistes?*—and Gaza was a town in Palestine. Elena turned away from him and strode on ahead, and Hale thought her voice was choked with tears when she called back to him, "You be sure to quote the *Catholic* version, when they shoot *you.*"

Hale splashed hurriedly through the puddles at her heels, not at all sure of what she had meant; did she suspect that he too was a member of the British secret service? Surely not—he had almost forgotten it him-self, until Cassagnac's talk today had made him consider fleeing back to England, and he was certain that she would instantly turn him in if she ever suspected that he was a spy. No, she had simply seen him as one of these hypothetical agents who unwittingly begin to . . . what, operate in a higher category, like her friend Maly, and perhaps like herself.

The thought made him consider again the idea of running, of finding his way back to England. *If it had been one of the big Focke Achgelis helicopters, instead of a plane, with big rotor blades turning slowly enough to be seen* . . . Resentfully, he thought of his year's-end childhood nightmares, which Theodora had been so interested in; and then he remembered his and Elena's predawn *clochard* walk ten days ago, which had somehow transported them from one island in the Seine to the far end of the other—*You were born for this,* she had said that night—and he recalled the terrible near-music in the earphones the next night, and the weirdly scorched floor . . .

The implications of all this were simply too morbid and medieval to be true, or at least to be *consistently* true—he had been vaguely hoping that all these things would recede without consequence or sequel, and he had convinced himself that the emotion he had felt, when the radio had gone mad and the wind had been rattling the shingles outside the apartment window on that night, had not been fearful eagerness.

To wear the belt would be to voluntarily participate in this filthy old business . . . which, really, he had started to do when he had begun tapping out his wireless signals in the insistent, pulse-hopping rhythm.

Recognition, he thought bleakly as he pulled the belt out of his pocket and slung it around his waist; and perhaps some awful sort of *protection,* by God knew what means, from God knew what threat.

He sprinted through the rain to catch up with her, and after tapping her on the shoulder he pointed to the ankh buckle cinched at his waist. She gave him a broad, relieved smile, and they walked back to the apartment arm-in-arm.

The radio behaved normally that night, and once again Moscow did not respond.

▼

6

Paris, 1941

There was a Door to which I found no Key:
There was a Veil past which I could not see:
Some little Talk a while of ME and THEE
There seemed, and then no more of THEE and ME.
   —Omar Khayyám, *The Rubáiyát*, Edward J. FitzGerald translation

On the last day of 1941 Centre sent orders that both Hale and Elena were to report in person to Moscow immediately, and that the ETC network was to be retired.

Radio contact with Moscow Centre had been reestablished for a month by that time, and right away Elena had been ordered to take over half of the radio duties, while at the same time resuming her job of meeting the furtive couriers and sources. And at the end it was Elena who deciphered the summons order—probably only moments before the Gestapo broke down the front door of the latest of the Rive Gauche *pensions* in which she and Hale had been renting rooms.

Moscow Centre had not come back on the air until November 29. During the two weeks preceeding that, Elena had got work as a typist at the Simex offices in the Lido building on the the Champs-Élysées, while Hale had developed a rudimentary network among the unemployed and alcoholic *clochards*.

Neither of them had accomplished much in that interlude.

Though she was given only innocuous clerical work to do, Elena had learned that Simex was the main procurement firm working for the German occupation authorities—Simex executives were allowed free access to Wermacht installations, and the Abwehr actually consulted

Simex engineers on secret German construction projects, and of course the company had a sophisticated radio system—and she guessed that Simex, and its sister corporation Simexco, in Brussels, were the perfect hermetic Soviet network she had speculated about to Hale, the intelligence source that was so secure and omniscient that Centre could afford to, and therefore arguably would be shrewd to, give the Gestapo the delusive satisfaction of rolling up all the other networks. Elena had begun carrying her little automatic pistol with her in her purse after she had deduced that, and Hale had known it was for killing herself if she should be captured, lest her conclusions should be wrung out of her by Gestapo interrogators.

And Hale had become a drinking companion of the ragged old riverside *clochards*. Their language was a mix of French and something that might have been Gypsy Romany, but he picked it up quickly, and his custom of always bringing a bottle of grappa or burgundy to their makeshift bridge shelters endeared him to them. Among them he felt as though he had drifted into a *lower* order of secret service—they were largely indifferent to last year's shift in government, and the only secrets they had were their modest thefts of food and clothing and liquor, and the locations of the best pools along the riverbanks for catching trout. But they flew kites with pinwheels on them on moonless nights, and somehow always knew to reel the kites down when a formation of German planes was within half an hour of passing overhead; and one morning in the middle of November one of them told Hale, as he passed him a bottle in the shade under the Pont St.-Michel, "They were stopped at Vyasma, the *boche* were, that's a hundred and sixty kilometers west of Moscow—the weather's better right now, no rain to turn the roads into mud, and today their trucks and tanks are moving east again—tanks move better than trucks through mud, being on tracks instead of wheels, though all their provisions are in the trucks—but the rain and snow will be back on them within a day or two, and they know it; they're all reading Caulaincourt's *Memoires,* about Napoléon's failed siege in 1812." The old man could have had no way of knowing any of this—unless, as the *clochards* claimed, their kites sometimes gave them true dreams—but Hale would have been tempted to encipher it and send it as unconfirmed rumor anyway, if Moscow had been on the air then.

Hale missed the vinous company of the eerie old men when he had to resume his all-night radio duties at the end of November; he had been listening as usual on the 49-meter bandwidth on the night of the twenty-ninth, and after all this time of dead air he had been hugely startled when Centre's signal had abruptly started chattering in his earphones, in fact completing a sentence that had been interrupted six weeks earlier. And in spite of her Party stoicism he could tell that Elena was unhappy to be ordered to take half of the radio work in addition to her old duties, and quit the Simex job. The six weeks of radio silence from Moscow had been a vacation, and this new pace was more strenuous than early October's had been, with even more hours spent at the telegraph key and the perilously live, oscillating transmitter.

By Christmas both Hale and Elena had been short-tempered and absentminded from lack of sleep, frequently hungover and hungry, and clumsy in darkness and dazzled by daylight. Hale had begun meeting some of Elena's contacts in her stead—wearily trudging to the meeting places, speaking the password phrases she gave him and pocketing the illegal reports to take back to whatever garret they were occupying on that day, and begin enciphering the texts—and any sluggish thought he gave to the Abwehr direction-finders was by this time in fatalistic terms of *when* rather than *if*. Hale's only remaining goal was a cold determination to somehow get Elena away when the inevitable arrest occurred.

At noon on the last day of the year, Hale was hurrying back to the *pension* at which they'd been staying for the last two nights; he had been to a *boulangerie* by the ruins of the Roman Arena off the Rue Monge, and he was carrying baguettes and a terrine of goose liver pâté wrapped in newspapers. Elena was sending on that morning, and she would be hungry when she could finally take off the earphones and switch off the set's power. There had been no snow yet in Paris that year, but cold winds and rain had set the two miserable young spies to stuffing papers and scraps of cloth into the gaps between the window frames, and huddling together in coats and scarves during the few hours when they both had time to sleep, and now the cold wind at his back made Hale trot along more quickly.

As always, he glanced quickly around at the pedestrians in front of the boardinghouse—and his frail attention was caught by the odd sight of a man whose briefcase was connected to his ear by a thin wire.

Direction-finding was done with trucks, Hale believed; it needed heavy machinery and big rotating aerial rings. Not yet suspicious, he nevertheless glanced at the nearest vehicle, a grocer's lorry that was even now driving up onto the curb and squeaking to a halt, and though the men levering open the doors and climbing out were dressed in grimy coveralls, the licence plate bore only two letters: WL. Hale's face and hands stung with sudden heat even in the instant before he remembered what Elena had told him they stood for.

Wehrmacht Luftwaffe.

Hale didn't change his half-running pace, nor glance again at the men or the lorry; he ran on, past the alley on the far side of the board-inghouse, and tapped up the brick steps of the next house on the street, pushed open the front door and stepped inside. To the woman in the warm hallway who started to object he said, "Food, eat," as he thrust his package at her; then he was pounding away up the carpeted stairs.

The stairs appeared to end at the fourth floor, with no roof access that Hale could instantly see, so he kicked open a door on the side of the hall facing his *pension* and hurried past a couple of scared-looking chil-dren to the tall window in the far wall. He unlatched it and pushed it open, popping old rust deposits and shaking black dust down from the top edges, and the cold air billowed the curtains around him as he leaned out. Down on the street to his left he could see the back end of the Wehrmacht Luftwaffe truck, still rocking on its springs.

The slanted shingled roof of the *pension* was a couple of yards below him and straight ahead, but separated from this building by the alley he had passed; and the alley appeared to be about ten feet wide.

For a moment he could vividly imagine leaping across that gap, col-liding hard and uselessly with the *pension*'s gritty brick wall about six feet below the roof edge, and then spinning through thirty feet of cold, rushing air to abruptly snap his bones and rupture his guts against the unyielding paving stones so far below; broken teeth, wet white bone torn through his trouser fabric, split flesh torn wider open as the rough hands of Gestapo men hauled him to his feet . . .

But Elena was crouched not far below the shingles of the gable roof that he could see so clearly; he could even see the aerial and earth wires strung out across the sloping main roof to the gutter over the street. Hale could almost see her, her pale forehead no doubt creased in a frown of concentration as she tapped at the key, her auburn hair falling around her narrow face, her brave little automatic pistol probably within easy reach . . .

Breathing in whimpers through clenched teeth, Hale ran back to the room's door and braced himself against that wall; then he pushed away from it hard enough to crack the plaster, took two running steps across the floor and launched himself at the airy gap that was the open window. One foot shoved back against the windowsill with all the power in his torso, and then he was flying through the cold air, one hand clawed out in front of him.

His other hand clutched the iron buckle of his belt—and the air was driven out of his lungs as he folded over the narrow belt, which seemed to be following the trajectory of his jump, independent of gravity; and the rooftops and chimneys of the Latin Quarter spun around him in the instant before he crashed full-length onto the shingles of the other building.

Impossibly, his face was in the roof edge gutter and his legs stretched up toward the roof peak. Hot blood smeared his mouth and chin and ran up his face into his hair, and there was no breath in his stunned, aching throat, but he slid himself around so that his feet were braced against the roof gutter, his skinned hands splayed out on the shingles as he furiously willed his blood to be sticky, and then he crawled rapidly to the peak of the little gable that projected out over the main roof. A stovepipe chimney jutted from the upper slope of it, and he hooked one knee around the iron cylinder as he leaned out over the street-side slope of the *pension's* roof and rapped his fist against the gable window glass.

He heard it break inward. He had no breath to shout her name, so he waved the scraped palm of his hand where she would see it.

He heard her voice through the broken pane: "Marcel?" and then he heard the window creak open. Unable to see below the end of the gable roof peak against his cheek, he clenched his fist and then opened it wide again.

Then her hand gripped his wrist strongly, and he gripped hers, and he wrenched every muscle and cracked rib in his body as he clamped his knee around the chimney cylinder and *pulled* her right out of the room, through the window; through her forearm he could feel flexing and twisting as she scrambled over the windowsill to keep her balance.

A moment later she had climbed up beside him on the roof. He was able to croak the word *"Run."*

But she got her arm under his shoulders and dragged him with her across the roof to the side away from the street, steering wide around a dusty skylight and the insulators at the mooring of a high-voltage cable. Hale pushed himself along with his feet and hands, but his vision was dissolving in rainbow glitters, and he wished she would just drop him and run away on her own.

Another brick house abutted this one, the gutter of its roof hanging a yard over the surface of the one they were on; and when they had limped and scuffled over to it, Elena pulled Hale upright and shoved him onto the slope of the adjoining roof, then hopped up onto it herself and dragged him up the shingled incline. Hale was able to climb along beside her now, and once they had hoisted themselves over the roof peak of this house and down the other side, they were on a hidden slope, facing the canyon of a street that was not connected at all to the house they'd started from.

She let him lie then, while she slithered down to this gutter and peered over it; after a few seconds she climbed back up to where he lay spread-eagled on his back.

"Gestapo?" she panted.

Close enough, and he was able to nod. His heaving chest was beginning to draw breath into his lungs, and each exhalation blew bloody spray; a few drops spotted her taut face, but she didn't blink.

"There's a drainpipe," she said; "follow me. We've got to climb down it, or slide. Just *keep your hands on it*, right?"

"Right," he croaked.

Her face was pale as she crawled backward down the roof on her stomach, and when her legs were below the edge, she slowly let her weight go over, while her white hands clutched the gutter. She disappeared by cautious inches, but she gave him a strained smile before her head receded out of his sight.

His pulse was roaring in his ears so that he could not tell if there was any commotion yet on the street side of their own building, or on the rooftops behind him, and as he rolled over to face the shingles and begin to slide down, scrabbling with his feet to know when he had reached the roof gutter, he became aware that he was panting in the pulse-counterpoint rhythm he had learned to use in working the telegraph key.

Ten minutes later they were sitting at a table in a café in the Mouffetard Market, sipping a second couple of brandies after having gulped the first two.

After they had shinnied and slid down the drainpipe to the street and hurried across it and through the next building to the sidewalk of a broader boulevard, Elena had looked at Hale in the gray daylight and then pulled him into a recessed shop doorway, where she lifted her sweater to wipe his face with her blouse and used her fingers to push his blond hair back into some order. His nose had stopped bleeding, and at her suggestion he reluctantly took off his own blood-spotted sweater and folded it under his arm, shivering in the chilly wind. "Now you merely look as if you got into a fight," she had told him as they resumed their deliberately leisurely walk, "and not as if you'd been dragged behind a car."

Elena now clanked her glass down on the wooden tabletop with more force than she probably had intended. "Thank you," she said quietly.

His nod was jerky. "You're—welcome." He touched his glass. His hands had stopped shaking in the warm, tobacco-scented air of the café, and he hoped he would get a third drink. "Can we even pay for these? I mean, can you? All I've got—if it didn't fall out of my pocket—"

"We're fine," she told him. She glanced around the room; the tile walls and floor echoed with clatter from the kitchen, but no one was sitting near the two of them. "The radio began roaring like a lion trying to sing, and then a second later you hit the roof—that was you, wasn't it? You sounded like a sack of coal dropped from an airplane—and I thought all the devils and Gestapos in the world were about to break into the room." She patted her skirt pocket and sat back and gulped more brandy. "I grabbed my gun, and the one-time pads and the papers, and the money, and that's when you broke the window. The *machine* is gone, but we're still mobile and nothing is compromised."

He exhaled more air than he had thought was in his lungs. *The radio began roaring like a lion,* she had said. And something, some inertial force, had undeniably held him up and spun him around in his jump to the *pension* roof. He opened his mouth to tell her about it, but found that he could not; in this moment he was sure that she would believe it, but he was stopped by embarrassment, or shame, as if the gaudy, outré event was proof of some moral failing on his part. "So what do we do now?" he said instead, dully. "Find another machine?"

She was looking away, toward the street door.

"No," she said, after a pause. "The last message I deciphered was an order, for both of us." Very quietly, still without looking at him, she went on, "We are ordered to report in person to Moscow, using our old Vichy-issue St.-Simon passports—going by way of neutral Lisbon, via an Air France flight to Istanbul and then by railway to Samsun on the Black Sea coast; none of these trips is out of character for employees of Simex, but in Samsun there will be a cigarette smuggler's boat waiting to take us to Batumi in the Georgian Soviet Socialist Republic. Russian Intourist railway tickets will be waiting for us in Tbilisi, two hundred miles east of Batumi." Her voice was tense, even frightened, and she blinked rapidly. "They don't like agents to travel by Intourist; the *in* is short for *inostranets*, which is Russian for foreign—it brands the holder of the passport as a foreigner in good favor with the Soviet state. Passports with Intourist visas in them can't be used again. Delphine and Philippe St.-Simon will have to be retired."

Hale's heartbeat quickened. This was the opportunity for escape, for both of them, from the frightening mysteries, natural and unnatural, of wartime Paris.

He reached out and took hold of her cold hand on the tabletop. "We won't go," he said. She was frowning, clearly about to interrupt, so he went on in a fast whisper, "You know what a summons to Moscow means; you know what it meant for your friend Maly, in spite of his filthy *clochard* rhythms. 'Retired' is right. Listen, in the entire rest of your natural life you'll surely be able to do *something* for the Communist cause, something you *wouldn't* be able to do if you let them kill you now. Cassagnac said that this generation of the Soviet secret services will be killed in their own turn before long, and that the next lot is likely to be more reasonable. Wait for them, with me. I love you. Come to England with me." His voice was shaking, and for the first time in three months he thought of her again as Lot's wife. "Don't look back."

Now tears spilled down her cheeks; she cuffed them away. " 'Come to England'! You might find it difficult getting to England yourself, as Marcel Gruey the *embusqué* Swiss student. Answer me honestly, once and for all: will you come with me?"

"I won't go to Moscow." He tried to sound confident when he added, "I really think you won't either."

Tears still streaked her face, but her expression was blank. "I would sooner try to . . . live on the river bottom, and breathe water like the fishes, than disobey my masters. If it is their will that I be shot in the Lubyanka cellars in Moscow, then that is my will too. You and I will not see each other again, I think."

"Elena," he burst out, "the jump from the house to the *pension* roof was too far—I would have fallen into the alley, but"—he took a deep breath and looked away from her—"Cassagnac's damned belt—*didn't fall.* It kept moving in a straight line, like a gyroscope resisting a sideways pull. Your radio was going mad, right?" He was sweating. "Something was *paying attention* to us ten minutes ago, something like what burned the floor of the garret in the house by the Panthéon. If you go to Moscow, you'll be getting more deeply involved in this, this *God-damned* stuff!"

She was pale, and her head swung back and forth wearily. "Moscow found it efficacious to ally herself with Germany," she said, "for a while. If *realpolitik* requires that she ally herself with other abominable forces now, it is not my place to be . . . scrupulous, fastidious."

Put it off, Hale thought. "Very well." He sighed shakily. "But we can travel a little way together. To hell with Marcel Gruey—I can travel with you, as far as Lisbon, as Philippe St.-Simon the cork wholesaler. He's an established business traveler, a collaborator, traveling with his sister—he'll have no problems."

Her momentary control broke, and now she was sobbing softly. "Oh, Marcel!—Lot—but you should have *lied* to me, pretended to be willing to obey the order, and then just run away from me in Lisbon. Now I cannot possibly give you the St.-Simon passport."

He stared at her, his mouth open. Her determination was as obviously genuine as her distress. It didn't even occur to him to be angry—he had known from the first that she was as deeply committed to communism as he was to England, as he had once been to Roman Catholicism.

"What chance," he asked slowly, watching his pulse jog his relaxed hand on the brandy glass, "do you think Marcel Gruey has of getting a flight to Lisbon?"

The padded shoulders of her sweater jerked up and down in a shrug. "He's a citizen of a neutral country, wanting to visit another. Buy a round-trip ticket, it will look better, if you are able to afford it. You've studied your Swiss cover well enough to get through any interrogation they're likely to bother with. At worst, you'll have to stay in France— live with your *clochards* until Russia defeats the fascists." She brushed splinters of roof shingle from her hair onto the tabletop, and her blue eyes stared at him miserably. "You're a bad man, I think—no, a good man but a bad agent, a bad Communist—but nevertheless I hope you don't hate me."

He drained his glass, hoping that the alcohol would maintain a perspective that he feared he wouldn't have when he was sober. "I love you, Elena," he said hoarsely when he had clanked the glass back down. "And I'm—*glad* that I didn't lie to you." About that one thing, at least, he thought.

She nodded, and stirred herself to pull the old mirror out of her pocket. She turned it toward him and asked softly, "Do you want to see a monkey?" The glass had been cracked at some point since the last time, probably during her climb down the drainpipe, and Hale saw two reflections of himself. "We have not got to know each other, you and I," she said. Then she sighed and blinked around at the corners of the high ceiling. "Centre did not allow for today's intrusion by the Gestapo; the Lisbon tickets being held at the Orly Air France desk are for tomorrow. This is the very last day of the year—if we can find a room to rent somewhere, we can spend this very last night together." She smiled sadly as she tucked the broken mirror away. "For once, we will not have to find an *arrondissement* that's scheduled for round-the-clock electricity."

Hale wondered if the Biblical Lot had paused to touch his crystalline wife before continuing on his way alone. "I won't sleep," he said unsteadily. "I'll just . . . look at your face, for the hours we have left together." He knew he was talking adolescent nonsense, but he was frightened by this sudden ending of the furtive life they'd had together in Paris and by the prospect of piloting the frail Gruey identity to Lisbon; and he simply wanted to cling to her for any period of time that could be had.

"Not if there's no electricity," she said, "for the light. And I think you will sleep."

That night they found a room on the Île de la Cité, at the northeastern corner above Notre-Dame Cathedral, in one of the narrow old lanes of sixteenth-and-seventeenth-century houses that had escaped Baron Haussmann's demolitions and street-widenings a hundred years earlier. Since the German officers had apparently not discovered the place, they had dinner at La Colombe by the old pavement that was the remains of a Roman wall; abundant vases of fresh-cut wildflowers and cages of fluttering doves made the restaurant look like one of the lamplit nighttime street markets, and they sat under the low beamed ceiling at a window table overlooking the embankment and the dark river, eating rabbit in mushroom sauce and even sharing a bottle of the fabulous Château d'Yquem with the sentimental owner.

Back in their room, Elena lit the lamp and then began writing on a sheet of blank paper from her skirt pocket. Hale frowned, wishing espionage wouldn't intrude now, but when he peered over her shoulder he saw that she had simply written *Bueno Ano, Malo Ano,* and *Medio Ano,* and now she tore the sheet into three strips, with one of the phrases on each.

She looked up at him with a defensive smile in the flickering amber light. "It's the only one of my mother's superstitions I've kept." She folded the paper strips, took off her sweater and then stood up and crossed to the bed. "Tonight is New Year's Eve. I put these under the pillow, and then sleep on them; and in the morning I draw one out, and it is an omen for the coming year." After having tucked the papers under the pillow nearest the window, she pulled back the bedspread and began unbuttoning her blouse, though the room was nearly cold enough for Hale to see her breath.

"Is it—ac-accurate?" he stammered. His hands lifted toward the buttons of his shirt, then fell away. He managed to kick off his shoes without too much trouble, and he slid the belt out of his trousers and tossed it to the farthest corner of the room.

"Would you call my mother a fool?" She dropped her blouse and, shivering, quickly began to unfasten her skirt.

Hale glanced at her pale breasts and then away; but he did dare to twist free his cuff and collar buttons. "You've f-found it reliable, then," he said, dizzily wondering which augury she would find in the morning.

"To tell you the truth—" she began as she stepped out of her skirt and slid naked between the sheets. "Oh, it *is* cold! Take off your clothes and come here!" She pulled the blanket to her chin, visibly shivering. "To tell you the truth," she went on when the bed at last shifted with Hale's weight, "I have never dared to unfold the paper and look."

Hale did eventually sleep, and it was the last night of the year.

In his dream the stars might have been spinning, but thick clouds masked the sky, and rain thrashed so heavily down onto the Île de la Cité that as it hit the pavement clouds of spray were thrown up to surge along the streets like waves.

His viewpoint floated away upward and hovered over the island, and the spires of Sainte-Chapelle stood above the waves like the fore-castle of a ship; the river was flowing strongly backward tonight in his dream, and dark water crashed up on the embankment at the Square du Vert-Galant like a bow wave.

In the roaring downpour he could no longer see the city on either side of the island ship—a turbulent sea appeared to extend out past the limits of perception—but he could see a dark square shape wallowing astern, a bargelike vessel apparently being towed by the ship. He didn't want to look at it, and so he looked ahead.

Dimly through the rain he could see the silhouette of a mountain rising above the sea, with vast columns or towers on the peak—and then he was reminded of the German plane that had flown low over his and Elena's heads in the Rue de Savoie in the rain forty days ago, for he felt the wind of some massive shape rushing past under the clouds, toward the mountain, and he saw that some sort of aerial dogfight was going on over the dark mountain castle.

And after a moment his stomach went cold, for a gust in the veils of rain made him revise his perspective, and he realized that the murky mountain was miles farther away than he had at first thought, and the swooping and diving shapes were much bigger than any airplanes.

The combatants seemed not so much to fly through the air as to appear sequentially at a smoothly continuous number of points across the sky—like the moving intersection of closing scissors blades, or the tip of a crack rushing through a pane of glass. In the dream he under-stood that the battle was fought every year, but that in a bigger sense it was the identically same event each time, since the position of the stars overhead was the same; in a sense the battle only seemed to occur again and again because the night sky kept rotating around to the same position every year.

Hale's viewpoint was closer to the mountain now, and he could see a white dome amid the turrets at the top; the dome had not been there a few moments ago, and he understood that the dome was . . . the phrases came into his mind . . . "the Destroyer of Delights and the Sunderer of Companies," which meant Death.

The sky and the mountain faded then, but the dome was now fully visible as an oval, and there were dozens or hundreds of similar vast eggs around it, light and dark and black, crowded and piled as if on an undulating plain. There must have been thousands of them, perhaps millions. Hale was trying to estimate the scale of them, and the height from which he must be looking down on the plain, when a foamy wave rushed forward from behind him and hid them under bubbles and foam.

The size of the bubbles jolted his perspective, and he lifted his head and saw that he was on his hands and knees in warm surf on a sunlit beach; the egg shapes had been grains of sand in the relative darkness of his shadow.

A middle-aged man in a modern, rumpled sport coat and a cravat was striding toward him down the dazzling sand slope; the man's face was pouchy and tired, but it creased in a jovial smile as the mouth opened—from the man's arrogantly casual Marks & Spencer–style clothes Hale almost anticipated a plummy Oxbridge drawl—

But it was a shrill piping like the cries of birds that came skirling out of the open mouth, and Hale flinched at the savage rhythm of the harsh whistling—the mouth opened wider, cleaving the face vertically, and the division quickly extended down through the neck—and then the man had split down the middle, and it was two dressed men standing on the sand facing Hale. One was the middle-aged original; the other appeared younger, but Hale had a sudden conviction that if he were to look into the face of that one, he would die.

He spun away and threw himself toward the surf, but it had receded, and he fell toward the grains of sand; but as they rushed up in his vision, he saw that they were as immense and widely separated as planets or even stars, and then he was simply falling through a black abyss while incomprehensible constellations spun with titanic momentum around him.

When he awoke, Elena was gone, leaving the faint cut-grass smell of her hair on the pillow and half of their money on the table for him. And just as he had begun to worry seriously about Marcel Gruey's chances of getting a flight to Lisbon, he saw the note she had left:

The stone dog at the north corner-edge of the first house we lived in is a dubok *—the head is loose and can be lifted off. The Philippe St.-Simon passport and travel papers are in a hollow inside; the Air France flight is at 1800. I compromise my proper husband to tell you this. Destroy this note, as you value my life. We will not meet again. I love you.—ETC.*

Hale carefully burned the note in an ashtray and stirred the ashes. When he got to the Air France desk at Orly Airport, Philippe St.-Simon learned that his sister Delphine had arrived at the airport at dawn and had taken an empty seat on the 8 AM flight.

When the sturdy Air France Dewoitine 338 had finally begun its roaring descent over the Tejo River valley and banked around to land at the Sintra Airdrome on the outskirts of Lisbon, the sun had long since gone down over the Estremadura mountains, and electric lights illuminated the airfield runways and the terminal buildings; the glaring lights, and the sight of British, German and Italian insignia on the airplanes parked nearly side by side at the edges of the tarmac, were a forcible reminder to Hale that Lisbon was indeed a neutral city.

The first thing he did after climbing down the wheeled metal stairs to the pavement was to sprint in to the Air France desk and ask when the flight to Istanbul was; he learned that one had left two hours earlier, and that the next was to leave at noon tomorrow.

By showing the clerk his passport, Hale was able to coax the man into checking the passenger list, and it turned out that Delphine St.-Simon had once again taken an empty seat on the earlier flight. And as he stumbled away from the desk, Hale wondered if that had been the real plan all along, if Moscow Centre had arranged for unoccupied seats to be available on the earlier flights, so that he and Elena would be able to exit countries hours sooner than they were officially scheduled to, as a measure to impede capture.

Aware that Razvedupr agents might already be looking for the delinquent Philippe St.-Simon or Marcel Gruey, he used the one-man *"nothing right here"* walk that Elena had taught him as he strode out of the terminal; and it might have been effective, for no one approached him as he made his way out to the cabstand.

The St.-Simon ticket had been paid for by Moscow Centre through Simex, and so Hale had easily enough money to take a taxi from the airdrome into Lisbon—but for several minutes he just stood on the curb between the brightly lit sidewalk and the dark street pavement, actually considering waiting at the airfield until tomorrow and catching the noon flight to Istanbul. He probably wouldn't be able to get on the same train to Samsun, and he would have no hope at all of finding the smuggler's boat to Batumi—but finally it was only the bleak certainty that she would be unhappy to see him, and that he would be unable to talk her into retreating west with him, that made him spit out a harsh curse and wave for one of the idling cabs.

"Take me to the best hotel in town," he told the driver in Spanish.

But in the crowded lobby of the Hotel Aviz on the Avenida de Libertade he learned that there was no apartment or hotel room to be had in the whole city; refugees from all of occupied Europe had found their way to Lisbon, hoping for transport onward to England, or North Africa, or America; many were Jewish, or Americans who had had to flee occupied countries when the United States had entered the war three weeks earlier, and it seemed to Hale that all the conversations he overheard, in French and German and Spanish and English, were about rumored Basque fishermen who could take passengers to Tangier, or Spanish freighters bound for Brazil, or a Greek passenger ship soon to sail for New York. No more refugees were being permitted by the Portuguese government to enter the country, and Hale realized that he would never have been issued a Lisbon ticket in the Marcel Gruey identity, even a supposedly round-trip one.

The hotel newsstand carried papers from all over the world—the *New York Times,* the *Deutsche Allegmeine Zeitung,* the *Lavora Fascista*—and Hale bought a copy of the London *Daily Mail* and found a corner to sit in and wait for the British Embassy to open.

When his stinging eyes finally grew too blurry to read the print at all, he found that he had for some minutes been trying to project his thoughts to Elena, perhaps somewhere over Majorca or Sardinia by now—*Turn back, turn back.*

▼ ▼ ▼

The passport control officer at the British Embassy in Lisbon was a tired, cheerful man named Philip Johns. His collar was open and his tie was already loosened at eleven in the morning.

"My dear boy," he said to Hale, who was sitting in a straight-backed wooden chair on the other side of the desk, "Special Branch can operate in Malaya and the Far East colonies—Singapore, Hong Kong—but not in Portugal. And," he added, touching Hale's St.-Simon passport on the desk, "they certainly don't operate with phony passports in German-occupied countries. What sort of 'investigation' were you 'assisting' them with?" He sat back and grinned at Hale in irritable puzzlement. "Are you sure it was Special Branch?"

Hale had finally been relayed to Johns by the Repatriation Office on the second floor, and he was afraid that the Embassy staff's next step would be to turn him back out into the street. He wished Theodora had given him a place of conspiracy and a recognition signal, as the Razvedupr had. His only plan was to somehow get word of his situation to the solicitor Corliss in Cirencester, who would in turn surely contact Theodora.

"I'll tell you the truth." His basic cover story was bound to come out soon anyway, so Hale took a deep breath and said, "I was arrested for espionage in London, in September, at a Communist Party meeting in King Street. I was released into the custody of Special Branch, and I eluded them and fled the country. Illegally." He had hardly spoken a dozen words in English since the end of September, and he found that he had to think about his phrasing. "Since then I have been living in Paris. Now I want to go home and . . . face the music."

"I hope you'll forgive me for assuming that you've been working these past three months as a Soviet spy. This passport says you're an employee of Simex. It seems to me I've heard of Simex." He leaned forward and said, clearly, "I am the passport control officer. At the British Embassy. Are you sure you don't have anything to"—he paused, almost seeming embarrassed—"declare?"

Hale realized that Johns must be the British Secret Intelligence Service representative in Lisbon, and that the man was inviting him to admit to working for SIS himself. But in Paris he had learned about hermetic, parallel networks, and he didn't think Theodora would want him sharing any information here.

"Just that Special Branch will want me shipped home." He smiled wanly. "In shackles, I expect."

Johns nodded a number of times, then stood up from his desk and crossed the carpet to the tall window. For several moments he just stared down at the street. "Hitler could take Portugal, you know," he said at last, "just by picking up the telephone. But I suppose the place has its value for Germany too, as a common ground between the occupied countries and the rest of the world. God knows every country in the world has spy networks here, all concentrated and distinct like . . . bacteria cultures on a petri dish, and the Germans probably do a fair job of infiltrating them, monitoring them."

He slouched back to his desk and sat down. "When I was a boy," he said, not looking at Hale, "we had one of those Russian dolls that twist apart in the middle to reveal a smaller one inside, which also twists apart, and so on *ad infinitum;* it was years before we discovered that what we had thought was the last, smallest one could be opened too, and that there was one more tiny one inside it. Astonishment, uproar among all of us children . . . though probably there was still another to be discovered, several more, microscope required finally." He sighed and stared at the ceiling. "There's value in . . . duplication, in having another, having a more secret one inside the already secret one. You didn't deny being a Soviet spy."

"I'm sorry, I thought denial went without saying. Surely no one *admits* to that here."

"Surely not. Who is Delphine St.-Simon?"

Hale exhaled so abruptly that it was a grunt. "Have you—*detained* her?" he asked with sudden hope. Perhaps the Air France clerk had been wrong in saying that she had caught the earlier flight.

Johns's right eyebrow was arched. "No, she was off to Istanbul before we even registered that she had arrived, and we didn't attach any importance to her anyway until you showed up downstairs this morning. So who is she?"

Hale slumped in his chair. "I don't know. I suppose St.-Simon is a common name."

Johns was nodding again, though suddenly he seemed very tired. "Your case is, marginally, interesting enough for me to check your bona fides—or mala fide—with the Security Service, of which Special Branch is the executive arm, in London. Not my outfit, but I'll see who I can reach over the WT. In the meantime I can hardly place you under detention—I don't even have any documentation to indicate that you're a British subject."

"I'd be happy to sign something," said Hale eagerly, "attesting that I am."

"You *want* to be detained? Is it the Gestapo you're afraid of, or the NKVD?"

"I'd—certainly hate to come to the attention of either agency."

"But you want to go back to England in shackles." He shrugged. "To be preferred, under the circumstances, I do see. Look, sit in the lobby downstairs for a few hours, right? Anybody who queries you can be told that you're waiting for me. If I haven't found grounds to arrest you by nightfall, I'll have security chase you out."

"Fair enough," said Hale, struggling to his feet and wishing he'd had a spare shirt and socks to bring along.

Hale did wear shackles when he flew back to England, accompanied by two British soldiers and the King's Messenger and the diplomatic bag, aboard an RAF Catalina flying boat that took off from the consulate dock at Cabo Ruivo. The seaplane landed six hours later, chopping the tops off the low gray Channel waves just northeast of the Dungeness lighthouse and then chugging up on the plane's pontoons to the RAF dock at New Romney.

Hale was immediately bundled across a chilly, snow-drifted yard into the back of a military lorry, along with two Army corporals who wore automatic pistols on their belts and who had apparently got the idea that he was a German spy; a tarpaulin had been laced over iron poles to make a windowless boxy tent of the truck bed, illuminated by an electric bulb that swung over the benches as the truck's engine ground through the gears along some sequence of icy rural roads, and one of his guards solemnly passed across to Hale an unskilled and obscene pencil caricature of Hitler, and then one of Goebbels, and then one of Goering. Hale simply nodded politely after scrutinizing each one and handing it back with both manacled hands, and when the little ceremony was done his guards sat back with a satisfied air. Hale was nearly choking on the fumes of diesel exhaust, though it was cold enough for him to see his breath.

When the lorry finally halted and the engine was switched off, the tarpaulin was pulled away from the rear of the vehicle and Hale was helped down to stand on the deeply rutted gravel driveway of a sprawling Victorian mansion; a gated iron fence was stitched in black poles and barbed wire across the snow behind him, and a forest of pine trees hid the surrounding countryside. He could hear the stationary roaring motor of a generator, but there were no sounds of city or even suburban traffic. When he was forcibly turned toward the house and kicked into a march, he noticed the bright metal filaments of new aerials sprouting from the snowy roof, and iron bars on several, but not all, of the windows. His manacled hands were clasped in front of him as if in prayer.

He was interrogated in what might have been a dining room—a green baize cloth was draped over a trestle table in front of a tall stone fireplace, and pale sections of the wood floor indicated where vast carpets had once lain; and the empty room echoed when one of the officers at the table asked him for his name and date of birth.

"Andrew Hale," said Hale, swaying with exhaustion and wondering if it would be rude to ask for a chair. "January 6, 1922."

"When did you join the Communist Party?"

"Last semester sometime—spring of last year. At Oxford. My solicitor can clear all this up." Corliss would surely contact Theodora, as he had done before. "His name is Corliss, and he's in Cirencester—"

"Sir!"

Hale blinked at the man, who was apparently a colonel. "Yes?"

"Damn you, *you* will address *me* as sir!"

"Yes, sir, sorry. Henry Corliss, sir, can provide—"

"Describe the Communist spy network that smuggled you out of England."

"Sir, I must insist that you contact Henry Corliss—"

"*Insist?*" The colonel thumped his fist on the table, spilling a glass of water. "*I* insist that you answer my question!"

One of the other officers, a younger man, leaned forward. "This is wartime," he said in a helpful tone. "You don't get to have your solicitor present."

"I don't want him *as* a solicitor," Hale said loudly. The involuntary raising of his voice, and a sudden chill in the pit of his stomach, startled him; and for the first time it occurred to him that he might be in some enduring trouble here. And he was horrified to realize that hunger and anxiety and lack of sleep had brought him very near to tears. Where the hell was Theodora? "I don't even need to talk to him," he went on more quietly. "Sir. But he'll be able to . . . point you toward an explanation of all this."

"Where and how did you get the Philippe St.-Simon passport?"

"I don't think I can answer these questions," said Hale. The dripping of the spilled water onto the wood floor was distracting him. "Please get in touch with Corliss." He wanted to wail, *Ask James Theodora, of the Secret Intelligence Service!*—but he kept remembering Theodora's order: *Don't tell anyone about me, nor about your secret purposes. Not even Churchill.*

A sickening punch to the kidney knocked Hale right down onto his knees and forehead and the fingertips of his manacled hands—one of the soldiers who had been in the truck with him had apparently walked up unheard from behind and got a signal from someone at the table—and now Hale was sobbing helplessly and drooling onto the cold floor. His nose had started bleeding, and blood and saliva streaked his chin when the soldier hauled him back up onto his feet.

"Who is your Party contact in England?"

The younger officer again spoke, in his helpful tone: "Spies can be executed in wartime, without the necessity of a trial."

A man in a plain business suit who sat at the end of the table and had not spoken yet now crushed out a cigarette and said quietly, "Let him rest for now. We can talk to him again later."

Hale was marched off to an emptied room that had been converted to a makeshift doctor's office, with a wheeled metal cabinet and an upright set of green-enameled scales in the corner and eye charts on the wall, and finally the manacles were unlocked and his hands were freed. The soldier stayed in the room while a man in white coveralls asked Hale if he had any family history of tuberculosis or insanity, and listened to Hale's chest with a stethoscope, and then asked Hale to read letters off the eye chart; finally Hale was escorted to a room with a barred window and a narrow, military-looking bed, and locked in.

He hadn't eaten anything since a quick sandwich in the Lisbon embassy lobby the day before, and with frail bravado he thought he would have endured another punch for a cigarette, or many more punches for a tall glass of brandy; but as soon as he lay down on the bed, his cumulative exhaustion seemed to fall onto him like the rubble of a bombed house.

His last, fragmented thought was of Elena, bravely bound for Moscow, and it might have become a prayer if his consciousness had not been almost instantly snuffed out.

When a guard shook him awake, it was dark outside the window.

Hale was not manacled again, but neither was he given anything at all to eat, before being led back to the green-baize-draped table in the stripped dining room; but a padded office chair had been wheeled in to face the table. Hale gratefully sat down in it and squinted at the faces of his interrogators in the electric lamplight.

The civilian in the business suit was the first to speak. "We did send a man to talk with your solicitor, Henry Corliss," he said. "And Mr. Corliss expressed only bewilderment at your activities. He was not able to suggest any contacts nor to 'point us toward an explanation,' as you claimed he would, and he is not willing to represent you in this action."

Hale didn't let his expression change or his shoulders sag, but he was hugely relieved; obviously the only reason Corliss would have failed to mention Theodora was that Theodora himself had ordered him not to. So Theodora was, as he had promised, aware that Hale had returned to England. *If I can't meet you, wait for me.*

Hale had decided at some point that he could tell all of his story except for his conversations with Theodora and the "secret purposes," which he was certain were the pieces that were connected with his New Year's dreams: the dreams themselves, and the "Palestine" rhythms that had transformed his wireless sending and led him and Elena on their weird predawn *clochard* walk to the end of the Île de la Cité, and the night of the accelerated Moscow signal and the scorched floor. He was even looking forward now to questions about his Communist contacts.

But the direction of their questions had changed. "What," asked the old colonel, "did you discuss with James Theodora, on the morning after your arrest in Covent Garden?"

Live your cover, Hale thought. "With whom? Sir?"

"The man who accompanied the Special Branch operatives—he talked to you alone, walked with you through the bombed area by St. Paul's Cathedral."

"Oh, that gentleman. He told me that my scholastic career was over, but that I might avoid the full consequences of my . . . error, if I would abandon the Communist Party and cooperate fully with the Special Branch."

"And you convinced him that you would; convinced him so thoroughly that he took full custody of you in the name of—his legal authority, and allowed you to return to your college alone."

"Yes, sir."

"But you were lying to him, weren't you? Instead of cooperating, you made contact with the Party and fled the country with their help. Is there any way to conclude that Theodora was not a naïve fool?"

"I wouldn't know, sir. He seemed intelligent enough. Perhaps he knew I would run, and had me followed."

"Theodora 'seemed intelligent enough,' " said the civilian dryly. "When had you met him before?"

"I never did, sir, before that morning."

"I should tell you," the civilian went on as he lit a cigarette with a gold lighter, "that James Theodora has been relieved of his duties and may even face criminal charges." He exhaled a plume of smoke that glowed in the lamplight. "Why have you for twelve years now been getting monthly payments from Drummond's Bank?"

"Those are payments from my father," Hale said promptly. "At least that's what my mother told me. They weren't married."

"Who is your father?"

"My mother never said, sir. She would never speak of him."

"He was a Catholic priest, wasn't he?"

"That was the opinion of our neighbors, sir. My mother never said."

From the hall behind Hale came a man's cultured drawl: "It was Jimmie Theodora who told you to joe-join the Com-Communist Party, wasn't it, Mr. H-Hale?"

Hale knew before he turned around to look that he had heard the voice before, but under some peculiar, disturbing circumstance—in the radio-amplified buzzing of *les parasites?* in a dream, in a nightmare?—and so he was not completely startled to recognize the smiling, dark-haired man who now slouched into the electric light, his suitcoat rumpled as if from recent constriction under an overcoat and his dark brown hair flattened at the top and dusted with snow over his collar. He appeared to be in his early thirties, though his features were already heavy with evident dissipation.

It was the man Hale had dreamed about two nights ago, who in the dream had walked down a sunlit beach toward Hale, speaking in bird cries, and had subsequently split apart into two men.

Braced by the familiarity of the voice, Hale was able to meet the man's intense stare without any change in his worried, earnest expression—though before the man strode around to the front of the room Hale did furtively button his coat to hide the ankh belt buckle. But his heart was thudding in his chest, for he now realized how very profoundly he had been hoping that all of this morbid and alarming dream stuff would prove to have been left behind in Paris.

Hale glanced levelly past the newcomer at the men behind the table; the civilian nodded and said, "Answer Mr. Philby's question."

"I didn't meet Mr. Theodora until after I had been arrested, sir," said Hale in a voice no shakier than it had been before. "It was a friend from CLS, who was attending one of the other Oxford colleges, who suggested I join. He was a member already."

Philby nodded genially. "You're all C-Communists these days, aren't you? Jimmie p-probably didn't even have to suggest it. Why was it the *sss*—the *City* Police, rather than the Metrop-po-politan force, that detained you in Covent Garden?"

Hale lifted his hands and let them fall. "I have no idea, sir." There was a sheen of sweat now on the Philby man's forehead, and Hale wondered if he always stammered.

"I don't believe your father is a C-Cath-cth—a priest," said Philby. "Was he, is he, in the s-secret service? Drummond's is the preferred secret service bank. Theodora could h-h-hardly be your father— who is?"

"I don't know," said Hale clearly.

Philby's pouchy face was still cheerful, but his voice was strident and almost angry as he said, "You were born in P-Phh—fucking— *Palestine,* allegedly on the Feast of the Epiphany—and you're a, a *Catho-lic,* Roman variety, Papist!— 'Our Father which art in Amman, Hajji be thy name!'—so you m-must know that Ep-p-piphany is when the Three Why-Wise Men arrived at last in Bbbeth!-lehem! just south of Jerusalem, 'following yonder star.' " He took a deep breath and let it out, and then gave Hale a bright, boyish smile. "True?"

Hale remembered telling Elena his own interpretation of the passage she had quoted from the Book of Job: *If the world is run according to any rules at all, those rules are beyond Job's comprehension.* And beyond mine too, he thought now fearfully; even here at home, in England.

"Uh," Hale said, "Yes, sir." His hesitation in answering had probably not looked unnatural—even the men behind the table were now staring at Philby uncertainly.

Philby sighed, and then went on in a more quiet voice, "Theodora *stage-managed* your skewed C-Covent Garden arrest, in order to set you up as one of his p-private spies to undermine the Soviet n-networks in France—and he did it in d-d-isobedience to his masters at . . . in Whitehall."

Hale supposed this was the exact truth; but "not even Churchill," Theodora had said; and ever since his mother had taken Hale to meet his "godfather" in '29, Theodora had for good or ill been his image of the King's Man, the representative of the Crown.

"But I wasn't doing *anything* the Theodora person had told me to do," said Hale, "and I certainly wasn't undermining the Sov—"

Philby interrupted him: "Theodora's politics calcified in about 1920. You are aware, Mr. Hale, that the S-Soviet you-Union is at present an—*ally*—of England?"

"Well, exactly, sir," ventured Hale, "though I *believe* I'm being detained now for working *for* them, at considerable personal risk, against Germany." It was a fairly cheeky thing to say here, but Hale believed it was in character for his cover.

"You—*unspeakable* little shit," said Philby. "Do you expect anyone to b-believe that the service's most rabid anti-Communist took c-c-custody of a young Party member and *accidentally* let him escape to Europe, to work for a Soviet spy network in P-Paris?—with no nn-intentions to impede that n-network's efforts against Hitler, nor to d-damage the frag-ile alliance between the Soviet Union and Ig-Ig-England?" He took a deep breath and let half of it out, like a marksman preparing to fire. "Is it then your claim that Theodora was so smitten with your willowy figure and blond locks that he freed you in exchange for indulgence in activi-ties with which I suppose upon reflection you cannot be unfamiliar?"

Managed to say that straight out, thought Hale sourly. He opened his mouth to begin to answer, but the old colonel spoke up first.

"Catholic priest or no," the colonel growled, "I doubt Mr. Hale's father was ever engaged in activities prejudicial to the safety of the Realm."

Philby turned on the officer with an expression Hale wasn't able to see; but the man went on imperturbably, staring straight back at Philby from under lowered white eyebrows, "And we'd certainly have heard if Mr. Hale had ever been editor of, oh, any periodical like *Germany Today.*"

Bewilderedly, Hale wondered if these things were true of Philby's father and of Philby. Certainly the remarks had been offensively meant.

Philby gave a harsh laugh. "I c-*came* here to off—to offer Broadway's ass—assiss-assiss—Broadway's *help,*" he said. "Unofficially, as a volatile—damn it—as a voluntary *li-ai-son* between the s-services." He waved behind him toward Hale. "This man came out of your—out of Europe through Lisbon, and even as head of the Iberian sub-section in Broadway I c-could have simply taken Hay-Hay-Hale's case right out of your hands. And allow me to inform you, in case you haven't b-been to *town* lately, that I am presently acting head of the entire counter-espionage section."

The civilian at the table had steepled his fingers and was nodding thoughtfully. "You could have," he agreed, frowning. "I think we would contest it now; in which case the Cabinet Secretary would likely just move to defer the question until the real head of section returns. I doubt your C would argue with that."

"Hale has ob-obviously been doing work for an officer of . . . for one of *our* old Robber Barons in Broadway."

"Possibly. Even probably. Not obviously."

The phrase *Iberian sub-section,* in that Oxbridge voice, was still echoing in Hale's head, and it had almost reminded him of something; but an officer who had not previously spoken now asked, plaintively, "So is bloody Hale a British spy or a Communist spy?"

The civilian at the table pushed back his chair and stood up. He wasn't looking at anyone, but Hale got the impression that his words were addressed to Philby: "We'll keep him—safe, here— until we can find out. He's had a medical examination and proves out fit; it would be very puzzling indeed if he were to—die, say, before all this is sorted out to everyone's satisfaction. Guard, escort Mr. Hale back to his room. Mr. Philby, it is good of you to have given us your time."

The place where Hale was being confined, he learned, was known as Camp 020, and it was only half a dozen miles southwest of London, at

Ham Common in Richmond. The makeshift compound was an interrogation center and a prison for spies, and as a combination of those functions it was also a sort of espionage retooling center, in which captured German spies were induced to use their call-signs and their smuggled radios to conduct a deceptive traffic with Berlin, the receptions being monitored and the transmissions scripted by the counter-intelligence division of the British Security Service, known as MI5. Hale was reminded of Cassagnac's fatalistic dictum: *Playback is the natural last stage of any spy network.*

The civilian member of the board that had interviewed Hale proved to be an MI5 agent called Speas, and Speas would frequently escort Hale on walks around the camp's snowy perimeter and have him talk about the Communist networks he had had dealings with in England. "MI5 is concerned with espionage in England and the colonies," Speas told him more than once. "I'm not interested in whatever you did in France." And Hale was glad to tell the MI5 man about the woman who had approached him at Oxford and about the secret wireless school in Norfolk. True to his word, Speas never asked about the Paris network, and his references to Hale's arrest at the King Street Communist headquarters were incidental and only mildly ironic.

The playback operation was a joint effort among the three military services and SIS and MI5, but it was the B Division of MI5, the counter-espionage division, that ran the camp and maintained the various shacks and Quonset huts and the Victorian edifice of Latchmere House. Hale soon gathered that the opinion of his MI5 captors was that Philby had been correct, that Hale was just a very covert agent of Theodora's, though they were determined not to turn over custody of Hale to SIS before the head of Philby's section returned to England.

After a week Hale noticed that his door wasn't being locked at night, and, when he asked a guard if he was expected to grow a beard here, an unarmed orderly began leaving a basin and shaving kit on the windowsill. But the little mirror in the kit reminded him too clearly of Elena—*Want to see a monkey?*—and so he began carrying his razor and brush downstairs to the common staff lavatory. During one of their outdoor walks, he asked Speas if there was any way to trace a Soviet agent who had been summoned from Europe to Moscow, and Speas told him that that would be an SIS matter, difficult even for them, and that anyway any such agent would probably have been shot soon after arrival in

Moscow; Hale then asked about the availability of liquor, and that night Speas brought him a nearly full bottle of Ballantine whisky, which was no longer nearly full by morning.

Hale was soon given cooking duties in the Latchmere House kitchen—the German prisoners were reportedly amazed to find meat and butter in England, after having been assured by their own intelligence service that the country was expiring in famine—and it was on the second day of February 1942, while he was bent over a pot of pea soup on the stove and singing along to "Somewhere Over the Rainbow" as it was being sung by Judy Garland on the battered old kitchen radio, that Theodora found him.

"I *shouldn't* be angry," Theodora interrupted from the kitchen doorway. Halted in his singing, Hale glanced up and recognized the man, and dropped the ladle into the soup. "I *should,*" Theodora went on, "recall that you must have had some hair-raising experiences in Europe, no doubt a good deal worse than what I've been having in London. Nevertheless, to find that I risked my career and possibly my liberty in order to make a good kitchen scullion out of you is . . . maddening."

For a moment neither of them spoke. Hale slowly reached up to the shelf to switch off the radio, noticing Theodora's rumpled suit and tie and aware of his own stained apron.

"Are you here in authority," Hale asked finally in the sudden quiet, "or as another prisoner?"

"Oh, I'm reinstated in SIS, my dear." He smiled, but Hale thought he had lost weight, and the dark circles under his eyes implied that he had not been getting much sleep lately. "And I've come to take you to Broadway, where you will make a detailed report of your undercover experiences. It might take a couple of days."

"Can you find out the status of a Soviet network agent who's been summoned from Paris to Moscow?"

Theodora was probably about fifty then, but for a moment he looked older. "That would be Delphine St.-Simon," he said, and sighed. "Sometimes we can. We haven't heard anything about her."

Hale turned off the fire under the soup pot and began untying his apron. "My felonies—" he began.

"Are dismissed, erased, forgotten. Cowgill is back from North America, all is forgiven—it's quite safe now for you to leave this camp. Cowgill is the head of Section Five, the counter-espionage section of

SIS; he was opening a branch of the British secret service in New York, flogging some most-secret decrypts of ours to the Americans, even as the Japs bombed Hawaii. Gave some extra force to his arguments, I gather."

Hale scouted up one of the other cooks and told him that he was leaving; and as he followed Theodora down the hall toward the duty officer's desk, the older man said quietly over his shoulder, "It would probably be possible now to get you back into your Oxford college."

Theodora's drawl had been more pronounced as he said it, and Hale asked cautiously, "What would be the alternative?"

"A post in Broadway. Continue working for SIS, but on the official payroll now. It could be argued that your country needs you there."

And, as he was to find again twenty-one years later, his academic career seemed like an inconsequential pastime now that he had become a player in what Kipling had called the Great Game.

"When do I start?"

"Well, today, lad. Did you think you'd get a period of leave? We're at war, you must have read about it."

▼

7

Kuwait, 1963

You want to know the Secret—so did I,
Low in the dust I sought it, and on high
Sought it in awful flight from star to star,
The Sultan's watchman of the starry sky.
    —Omar Khayyám, *The Rubáiyát*, Edward J. FitzGerald translation

And behind the temporary overt war had been an enduring secret war, one that had started long before Hale was born and was apparently still churning—above or below the radar of newspaper headlines, in the remote border regions and the fastnesses of unnamed government corridors where the Great Game was played.

From his window seat on the starboard side of the big BOAC DC-8, Hale stared out at storm clouds over the Persian Gulf, and the unchanging background whine of the four jet engines seemed to emphasize the astronomical silence of the miles-distant storm front.

The Great Game. Kipling had used the term in his book *Kim,* a novel about an orphaned British boy, raised as a native beggar in India, who had become a roving agent of the *fin de siècle* British secret service; and Hale wondered now if the one-legged Chief he had met thirty-three years ago had been a youthful agent in the service in those days. During the long night in the Anderson bomb shelter below the angry peak of Ararat in '48, Kim Philby had told Hale that he himself had been born in India in the last days of the colonial Raj, and had spoken Hindi before he spoke English, and that his father had given him his nickname after the Kipling character. And now Hale was winging his way back to "somewhere east o' Suez," under the indelible cover of disgrace and treason, to threaten Philby with death and then to accompany him . . . to Ararat, again.

The sun was setting over the Arabian desert on the other side of the plane, lighting the seats and overheads in window-fragmented orange. In other years, on other flights, Hale had looked out through a Perspex window at the shadow of his airplane cast by a dawning sun onto the surfaces of close white clouds, and the silhouette of the plane, growing and shrinking abruptly as the cloud contours moved past, had always in those moments been at the center of a complete rainbow, a perfect prismatic circle unbroken by any horizon; but this evening the clouds at the eastern nadir seemed to be half a world away, towering gods carved out of the old ivory sky by a supernatural Rodin. Where the DC-8's shadow would be, and it would be far too tiny to see at this infinite distance, a golden cumulus column filled an eighth of the sky, and world-spanning beams and fans of shadow radiated as dark as nicotine from the heart of it.

Soon the Saudi coastline was nearly invisible in the darkness below, and the lights of El Qatif or Qasr es Sabh were hardly more than clusters and strings of yellow light-points. Under the purple sky-vault the eastern horizon was ringed with the tall clouds, lit from within by flashes as continuous as a barrage—Hale saw no arcs of lightning, just the glaring bright flares inside the clouds, sometimes nearly simultaneously rushing from south to north like a relay sequence of timed charges.

Hale shivered and wondered how the storm sounded to any luckless sailors who might be out on the gulf tonight—and how the light might be seen to move over the water.

He couldn't pry his gaze away from those towering, incandescing sentinels on the edge of the world; and though he resisted it, and even waved his emptied glass at the stewardess for yet another refill of Scotch, the thought muscled its way into his consciousness: *They can see me, they know I've come back.*

He didn't sleep through the remaining hour of the flight, and when the DC-8 touched down at the new Al-Kuwait international airport, he was among the first to exit the plane and climb down the aluminum stair to the tarmac.

It was not raining tonight in Kuwait. The well-remembered Shamal wind was blowing cold from the Iraqi marshes below the Tigris and Euphrates Valley to the northwest, and Hale knew he would have to buy an overcoat at the first opportunity; but he knew too that by morning the wind would have shifted to come more bearably from the west. And just being back in Kuwait again, even after nearly fifteen years, gave him again the Bedu's instinctive gratitude for winter winds; the hot Suhaili winds would not start up until April, and along with the drying up of the desert grasses they signaled the onset of the murderous summer, when the Bedu would be deprived of grazing and would have to camp miserably on their wells until the appearance of Canopus in the southern night sky in September. On the very next day after Canopus was finally sighted, as he recalled, the summer heat was palpably broken, and water-skins left out that night would be cold by morning.

Tonight, as he hurried into the spotlit terminal building and patted the angularity in his coat pocket that was his Andrew Hale passport, he thought that any such water-skins would be jangling with frost by morning.

After a routine procession past the Customs desks—as Theodora had promised, Hale's name and passport number clearly had not been flagged yet—a quick cab ride took him to the new Kuwait-Sheraton, which as best he could estimate stood where the crumbling old mud wall had once defined the southwestern corner of the city. Now, from the balcony of his sixth-floor room, he could see bright-lit highways and shopping arcades stretching away in every direction, and all the buildings seemed to be modern concrete and glass.

He struck a match to a cigarette, wishing for a drink.

During the last hour of his flight, he had wondered whether or not to register at a hotel. It was a move calculated to make it easier for the very secret Soviet service to track him, of course, but eventually he decided that it was in character as well. According to his cover story, he wouldn't have had time to acquire a contemporary forged passport in England, and so the airline and Customs records would clearly indicate that Andrew Hale had fled to Kuwait in any case; and checking into a hotel showed a confident knowledge of the workings of SIS—his imminent status as a "person to be detained" might have got him arrested at Customs, but would not quickly provoke a canvassing of local hotels by the Kuwait Head of Station.

And it made sense that he would not try to look up his old contacts in the changed city immediately upon his arrival, like a desperate fugitive. Obligations of hospitality and protection were taken with religious seriousness among the Arabs, but Hale's relationship with his contacts had been as an agent-runner, and he had not been dealing exclusively with the most honorable citizens in those old days . . . and he remembered the Arab proverb: *When the camel kneels down in exhaustion, out come the knives.*

Before stepping back inside, he glanced to the west, now as dark as the rest of the sky. Far away in that direction, out beyond the Syrian desert and past Damascus, on the eastern shore of the Mediterranean, Philby awaited him unaware in Beirut. What would the man's response be, on being approached and threatened by a retired agent of the disbanded SOE?

Hale remembered the lines from *Cymbeline* that Philby had quoted in the bomb shelter below Ararat: *When from a stately cedar shall be lopped branches, which being dead many years, shall after revive, be jointed to the old stock, and freshly grow . . .*

And Elena was in Beirut too—she had apparently been there last night, at least, and had not then succeeded in killing Philby. How soon would it be until she heard Hale's cover story, got the scripted news that he had treacherously shot old Cassagnac? If Hale were to meet her, he could not tell her the absolving truth about that; wherever her loyalties lay now, clearly her plans were at radical odds with Operation Declare. And Hale did desperately need to complete the long-delayed assault on Ararat, needed to justify the deaths and broken minds of the five men he had led up that terrible road in 1948. And so Elena must be allowed to believe that Hale had shot and perhaps killed their loyal old friend, who had saved their lives in Berlin.

According to Theodora, *Malo Ano* was the slip of paper she had picked yesterday morning in Istanbul.

In these past fourteen years Hale had often dreamed about his brief times of intimacy with Elena in Paris and Berlin; and even during his wakeful hours, as he had graded test papers or trudged across the green lawns of the University College, Weybridge, he had imagined somehow meeting her one more time, imagined himself impossibly convincing her to marry him at last, in spite of their histories, in spite of their last words on the Ahora Gorge road in 1948. He had never married, and he had liked to imagine that in the unguessed course of her life she had not either.

The captain of a ship can perform marriages, Cassagnac had said with exhausted merriment on that Berlin night in 1945—the three of them had been crouched below the gunwales of a makeshift Ark on the bed of an American truck just east of the Brandenburg Gate, and though each of them had held a loaded pistol it had seemed likely that all three would be killed within minutes—*and so I hereby pronounce you two man and wife. Kiss the bride quick, Andrew, before you die.*

Hale had kissed her, tasting blood from her cut lip, and then she had kissed Cassagnac too.

Hale now flicked the cigarette out past the hotel balcony rail, over the broad new streets of the Kuwait that was no longer the city he remembered, and he watched the coal arc away through the night like a tiny shooting star.

Now his bleak prayer was that he and Elena would not suffer the useless hurt and bitterness of meeting again, ever.

Until the end of World War II, the standard cover for an SIS agent abroad had been passport control officer, attached to the local British Embassy; but when Hale had been an SIS agent in Kuwait in the late '40s, the cover organization had been the Combined Research Planning Office, CRPO, known as "Creepo." It had been run independently of the embassy and consulate, and largely even of Whitehall control, since a coincidence in the initials meant that a good deal of the secret correspondence from London was sent by mistake to the Combined Regimental Pay Office in Jerusalem, where it was generally lost.

Hale had not been the first agent-runner in the Middle East to note the unique qualities of the Bedu—the nomadic herdsmen were as unregarded as gypsies, one tribe hardly distinguishable from another except among themselves, and they were free to cross the Iraq, Saudi Arabia, and Trans-Jordan borders with no notice or record—but probably few British agent-runners aside from Lawrence and the elder Philby had lived among them as closely as Hale had. Hale had recruited agents from among sheiks of the Muntafik and Mutair and Awazim tribes of the Kuwait-area Bedu, and even from tribes as far off as the Jerba Shammar in the Tigris and Euphrates Valley and the Bani Sakhr in Trans-Jordan, and like all agent-runners he had kept his networks a secret from his fellow SIS officers.

In this winter season the tribes he had known would no doubt be scattered across the deserts of Iraq and Saudi Arabia, chasing the rainfall for the grazing of their camel herds, but he had also established solid leave-behind networks among the *Hadhira,* the town Arabs, and he had hopes of finding some of these still in place.

The next morning he set out under an overcast winter sky to reacquaint himself with the city. He took his passport and cash with him, not just because it was second nature for an agent but also because he hoped to avoid staying at the Kuwait-Sheraton for another night.

The Kuwait oil boom had been going on for about ten years when he had last been here, but evidence of the country's wealth was lavishly obvious now. On the sidewalk of the boulevard called Fahad al-Salim he walked past nothing but modern architecture—gleaming stores and office buildings were separated by broad parking lots, and the design of the buildings was not Arab at all; Hale thought that some of the gigantic edifices he passed must in fact have been modeled on toasters, or unfolding lawn furniture, or the grillwork of modern American cars. The clusters of women he passed still wore the traditional black *aba,* but many of the Arab men had forsaken the *dishdasha* robes and wore Western business suits under the *kaffiyehs* that still covered their heads.

At the eastern end of the city, yellow bulldozers spouted plumes of black diesel smoke and ground their gears on fenced-off lots of raw cleared dirt, but Hale was cheered to see that the metal hard hats the laborers wore were incised with arabesque floral motifs as intricate as any fretwork he'd seen in Cairo mosques. And toward the gulf shore, down among the neon Pepsi-Cola signs and the petrol stations, he found an old neighborhood of mud-and-coral-walled houses that still hadn't been reached by the bulldozers.

In a broad, packed-sand alley behind a row of whitewashed houses, a dozen old men were sitting cross-legged on three plaid-print couches that appeared to be dry, and therefore must have been carried outside since the last rain. The men were dressed in what Hale thought of as Saudi fashion, with calf-length white shirts and cloaks, and white headcloths held in place with black woolen head-ropes; a new Olympic television set stood on a table in front of them, connected to an orange extension cable. They had arranged their sandals on the ground below their crossed knees and were sipping tiny cups of coffee as they watched the American President Kennedy in ruddy color while subtitles in Arabic scrolled across the bottom of the screen. A stainless-steel electric coffeepot sat on top of the television.

Hale stood a dozen feet behind one of the couches, facing the other. "*Salam 'alaikum*," he said. *Peace be with you.*

" *'Alaikum as salam*," replied one of the bearded men. *On you be peace.* He lowered his brown feet into his sandals, stood up, and crossed to the coffeepot to refill his china cup. He turned to Hale and smiled as he offered it to him.

As soon as it became clear that Hale spoke Arabic, he was included in the conversation and invited to sit down. They asked him his name and he told them he was Tommo Burks, from Canada—it was one of the names he had used in dealing with his agents, unknown to the SIS, and it would be plausible that he would to try to revive it—and then his companions resumed an apparently ongoing discussion of real estate transactions. In their speech Hale recognized the classical accent of the Murra tribes of Qatar—pronouncing the capital of Najd as *Riyal* rather than *Riyadh*—and the softened *j* of the Manasir who ranged south of Abu Dhabi; and with a touch of nostalgic sadness he realized that these were Bedu, who had given up the nomadic life for a secure city existence. In Hale's day their discussion would have been of good grazing areas for the camels, and of when the dhows would be coming into port with the season's dates, and of which tribes were having feuds with which; and Hale wondered how long it would be before their descendants spoke the flat, Egyptianized Arabic that already prevailed in the Hadhramaut and Yemen.

Among other cover endeavors in the late 1940s, Tommo Burks had opened a news agency for the distribution of British news to Arab radio stations, and now Hale mentioned the names of some of the Kuwait Radio executives he had dealt with; his companions were able to tell him the current status of several of them, and Hale noted for possible contact the ones with whom he had done undercover business. And he reminisced about favorite restaurants, and learned that two were still owned by Arabs who had sometimes sold him information.

And finally, since these men sitting in the alley were Bedu, he asked them, "Is there news of Salim bin Jalawi, of the Mutair tribe?" Bin Jalawi had been Hale's main lieutenant in the operational days, and had accompanied him on a memorable trek into the Rub' al-Khali desert to the Wabar ruins in early '48. The Bedu passion for news and gossip could not have subsided, and these men might know what wells bin Jalawi's tribe had been seen at recently.

A couple of the old men, probably Mutair tribesmen themselves to judge by their accents, now looked away from the television to stare curiously at him. "Bin Jalawi lives in Al-Ahmadi," spoke up one. "He works as a guard at the Ministry of Education." He stepped into his sandals and stood up. "You can use my *hatif,*" he said modestly.

Hale smiled and thanked him, but he was experiencing the old unreasoned chill at an operation that seemed to be shifting out of his control, and as always it almost made him want to crouch like a fencer or a boxer to keep his balance. It had started on the airplane last night, when he had thought that something had sensed his return to the East; and now, in spite of the example of these men in the alley, he was disoriented to think of bin Jalawi as a town Arab, for in Hale's mind the man's identity was inextricably that of a Bedu kneeling far back on the flat saddle of a camel, his old brass-bound .303 Martini rifle slung over his shoulder and gripped by the muzzle in the universal Bedu fashion, squinting as he scanned the horizon or stared down to decipher wind-blurred camel tracks in the sand with such thoroughness that he could tell which tribe had passed, how many of them, and even whether or not any of the camels were in calf. If bin Jalawi had a garden now, or an automobile, or a bank account, could he in any sense still be the man Hale had so relied on fifteen years ago?

And, in an instance of the kind of portent that Hale had learned not to ignore, this man today had used the word *hatif.* Admittedly it was as common a word for telephone as the derivative *tilifon,* but in old Arab folklore a *hatif* was a mysterious voice from out of the night that foretold the death of some prominent figure. Hale wondered who this bad-luck portent was for.

"*Mutsakkira,*" Hale said again. *Thank you.* Thank you for putting me on my guard, at least. "But I'll call him later."

Before leaving England Hale had eaten the slip of paper with the address and name on it which had been tucked into his passport, but of course he had memorized it, along with all the fictitious Customs stamps in the passport pages. *Go there untraceably,* Theodora had said not twenty-four hours ago, *to hear all the details of this and to pick up your equipment.*

The address was ostensibly that of a marine welding shop by the Mina al-Ahmadi quays, and Hale took a series of public buses down the modern desert-transecting highway back south to the airport, watching the Arabs and Westerners who got on and off the buses as he arbitrarily transferred, and sitting always by the back door so that he could get out fast if he had to and could watch the cars behind from the bus seat's high elevation. He could see no indication that he was being followed, and his coat and tie were not conspicuous dress.

At the airport he went to the Pan Am desk and stared at the posted schedule of international flights while he thought about any surveillance that might be focused on him. Would it be Arabs? He knew from experience that Arabs tended to find all fair-haired white men in European clothing indistinguishable from one another. Unobtrusively, as if checking a flight plan or tickets, he took his passport and cigarettes out of his coat, fumbled with them, and finally stuffed them into his front pants pocket.

He looked at his watch and then strolled away to a recessed shoe-shine booth under a sign in English and Arabic letters, consciously knocking the hard-leather soles of his shoes against the green linoleum floor in one of Elena's old attention-deflecting rhythms; and after getting his shoes shined, and palming a bottle of liquid white polish while making Arabic small-talk with the proprietor, he stepped away from the booth, again carefully tapping his soles on the floor. He noted where the nearest men's room was, and then walked across to a news kiosk and bought a pair of sunglasses and a copy of the *London Times*; he tucked the sunglasses into his pocket and flipped open the paper as he walked thoughtfully back the way he had come. Pretending to read, he was not conspicuous leaning on a pillar near the men's room.

Arabs in snow-white robes swept past him, and pilots and European businessmen strode by, but always singly or in pairs. Hale kept staring at the newspaper, though his attention was focused in the periphery of his vision above the paper edges.

At last he saw what he wanted—a group of Western businessmen hurrying this way, Texans by their accents, all wearing fedora hats. They clearly had no time to spare, and they would be trotting right past the men's room door, so Hale did a restrained tap-dance in the old rhythms across the linoleum, pushed open the lavatory door and stepped inside.

At the sink he quickly broke open the shoe-shine bottle and combed a couple of splashes of the white liquid liberally through his blond hair and eyebrows; then he whipped off his coat and tie—torso-cover being the inevitable primary flag in any surveillance—and dropped them on the floor. Finally he kicked off his shoes and shoved them inside his shirt, unfolded the sunglasses and slid them onto his nose, picked up the white metal waste bin and strode in his stocking feet to the door to listen.

When the Texas accents were loudest, he crouched and pushed the door open, shoving it against elbows and ribs.

"Hey!" came an annoyed yelp. "Steady, dipshit!"

" *'Eh-sif!*" Hale mumbled apologetically. "*Is mahlee!*" He waved his arm up in a placating gesture and succeeded in knocking one man's hat off.

And then Hale was walking rapidly away, his feet making no noise at all on the linoleum floor now, carrying the waste bin over his shoulder with a determined air of practiced ease.

The man whose hat he had knocked off was going on about it as the voices receded behind him, and Hale hoped any watchers would note the complaint and give extra scrutiny to any figure among the Texans who might look as if he had just put on the hat in question and joined the group.

Hale, meanwhile, was to at least a hasty glance a hunched, white-haired, pot-bellied figure in noiseless black footwear carrying a waste bin toward the nearest unmarked door; service personnel tended to be invisible, and when he had pushed open the door and stepped into a hallway lined with glass-windowed offices, none of the people at the desks gave him a second glance.

At the end of the hallway he set down the waste bin, pocketed the sunglasses and put his shoes back on, then hurried on through a series of corridors that eventually led to an outside door.

He was still tucking his shirt back into his trousers when he saw a cabstand, and he managed to wave as he hurried up to the first cab in line.

"Mina al-Ahmadi," he panted when he had climbed in.

Before looking for the marine welding shop he walked around the diesel-reeking waterfront yards, frequently pausing to stare past the docks, and past the close harbor boats and the expanses of open gray water, at the vast Kuwait Oil Company tankers moored way out at the T-end of the mile-long quay. The nine pipes that extended the whole mile looked like the fallen pillars of a temple that could have held up the marble sky if they had been standing, and Hale thought the angular black hulls out on the ashy Persian Gulf horizon, overhung with long streaks of smoke as if from sacrificial fires, looked like the remote tents of gods.

The wind was shifting around to come from the west, as he had expected, and it was replacing the diesel-and-seaweed smell with the remembered scent of the yellow Arfaj-grass flowers that would be blooming in this season across the infinite miles of dunes and gravel plains at his back.

And in spite of the landscaped lawns around the newer pastel office buildings, and the tall fiberglass GULF OIL signs and the modern asphalt of the streets, at the south end of the docks Hale saw ragged Arabs crouched over the old checkers-like *dama* boards by the side of oiled-sand roads, and beyond them the teak hulls and reefed lateen sails of fishing dhows dragged up onto the shore slope.

Judging by the street numbers, he was now within a few doors of the welding shop's address; and he was glancing around at the carpet-sellers' shops and car-repair garages as he strode purposefully down an awning-overhung sidewalk, when a car horn in the street tapped out the old SOE code group that meant *emergency attention.*

It was a crazy old yellow Volkswagen weaving down the oiled road, and its Arab-dressed driver was convincingly trying to get the attention of someone over by the beached boats on the shore. The man tapped out another series of honks as he drove on past, looking squarely away from Hale, and the nasal electric beeps were the fugitive-SOE code for *go to* and *W-I-N-D-O-W* and *here.*

Hale had permitted himself only the most casual glance at the Volkswagen, and now he returned his attention to the shops he was passing. Obediently he looked at the windows, and behind the dusty glass display flanking the recessed doorway of a pearls-and-antiques shop he could dimly see a bearded figure in a black robe.

Hale walked on past, then stepped in under the awning and glanced up and down the street, shivering in the eddying wind and wishing he had not lost his jacket at the airport. When he glanced at the old man behind the window six feet away, he saw that the man had breathed a patch of steam onto the inside of the entryway glass, and with a finger-nail had written in tiny English letters: STAND + DECLARE. The letters were painstakingly drawn, and Hale guessed that the old man probably didn't even know the meaning of the symbols he was tracing in reverse on the glass.

Hale closed his eyes in a slightly protracted blink to show that he had understood; and then he looked the other way. This was fairly extreme caution—not even to go to the indicated address, and now to be redirected by this evanescent writing. And it occurred to him that only someone standing as close to the shop as he was would even see the old man in the darkness inside, much less the faint letters in the dampness on the glass.

Hale glanced back and saw that the old man had wiped out the two words and written, less legibly but still readably in the moisture: WATCHED—BRIEF IN BEIRUT.

Hale was apparently not being redirected, here.

His stomach churned, and his face was hot in the cold breeze as he turned away from the window. The planned briefing here in Kuwait had apparently been called off, with no fallbacks until he somehow got to Beirut. But he needed his script, he needed to know what story he was supposed to give the expected Rabkrin recruiter. Damn it, he thought worriedly, what am I supposed to *say*?

The unwelcome answer was written in a fresh patch of steam when he glanced back after another blind look in the other direction: GIVE '48 ARARAT MATH: ALL WRONG.

This time he looked away to hide his face, even just from this stranger behind the glass.

Hale was numb and dizzy, and for a moment his mind simply recoiled from comprehending the words he had read. The math—the strategy and the calculations and the orders given to the men he had led up the road below Ararat—had been of his own devising. "All wrong"? Was it actually possible?

With a desperate leap of logic he decided that it was not. Cold sweat of relief dewed his forehead as he told himself forcefully that his secret purpose here had been found out by the Rabkrin, that this was a gambit to trick him into revealing to their recruiter the valid deductions and strategy that he had assembled in '48. His mission here was blown, Cassagnac had been shot uselessly, but at least Hale was not guilty of having killed his own men through a *mistake* fourteen years ago. It was obvious, so obvious that he didn't need to prove it by trying to get confirmation of this "order," even if he could make contact with Theodora . . .

But the thought of Theodora brought back the old man's words yesterday morning—*You'll probably doubt its validity . . . this right now, what I'm telling you, is your confirmation-in-advance. If you hate it, it's the genuine instructions.*

Too obviously this was exactly what Theodora had been referring to.

Hale closed his eyes and let his thoughts collapse into an unvoiced shrill wail of abysmal dismay; and he didn't realize that he was clenching his jaws until the pain in his teeth made him involuntarily open his eyes, and then he had to blink away tears to see the street clearly.

He remembered wondering who or what Theodora expected him to betray in his script. But apparently it was not to be a script after all, and the betrayal had happened fourteen years ago.

All wrong. The words seemed in this moment to describe Hale's whole life.

He blotted his eyes on his shirt cuff and took a deep breath and forced his gaze to be blank as he looked back again at the window.

The old man was gone, and the word GO was barely visible in the fading steam. A moment after he had seen it, a wet squeegee drew an obliterating streak of runny cleanness across the inside of the glass.

All you can do now is justify the losses, avenge them, Hale thought emptily. If Declare knows the '48 math was bad, Declare must have some better sort to work with now—there's nothing for it but to push on and further that effort. Lines from a Bartholomew Dowling poem dirged in his head: *'Tis all we have left to prize. One cup to the dead already—hurrah for the next that dies!*

He looked at his watch and then began trudging away on down the sand-gritty sidewalk. Forcing himself into the familiar cold professionalism, he considered whether it was likely himself or the welding shop that was being watched. Probably it was the shop—he was fairly sure he had evaded any watchers on the buses, or at the airport. He wondered what the rest of the missed briefing would have consisted of, and what "equipment" he would have been given.

But speculation was useless. He had no choice here but to follow such scanty instructions as he had been given, and look up Salim bin Jalawi and any other covert operatives he could find from among his old networks. He made a mental note to wash the shoe-polish out of his hair in the first men's room he found—it would be counter-productive to seem anxious about anything at all.

And as for equipment, he could *make* an ankh, if he had to—tinfoil rolled and bent into the right shape would do, since it was the Klein bottle topological shape of the thing that compelled the attention of djinn, not any property of what it was made of.

He filled his lungs with the sea air, then exhaled it all in a deep sigh. Since it *might* be himself who was being watched, he conscientiously stepped into a carpet shop to ask about some of the waterfront merchants he had known fifteen years ago. After half an hour of this, he could catch a bus back north to Al-Kuwait and call Salim bin Jalawi. Whatever agency might be watching, this would be behavior consistent with his fugitive cover, and the troublesome tail-evading route he had taken down here from Al-Kuwait could only make it look more genuine.

Old, reawakened practice permitted him to nearly forget the intolerable words drawn in the steam—ALL WRONG.

Salim bin Jalawi's house was air-conditioned, and in the aggressive chill Hale sipped a glass of tea and politely ate some cashew nuts from a bowl on the Danish Modern table. A refrigerator hummed out in the white-tiled kitchen next to an electric range, and fluorescent lights held back the dark of the late afternoon. Through the sliding glass door at his right Hale could see, as bright dots on the iron-colored southwest horizon, the beacons of natural gas flares out on the Burgan oil fields.

Bin Jalawi's beard was ivory white now, but his face was still as dark as coffee and as lean and angular as a Notre-Dame gargoyle, and he bared white teeth as he grinned at Hale.

"You must be a director," he said, "or a vice president, by now, of the Creepo."

There was knowingness in the man's voice, but Hale couldn't tell if it meant that bin Jalawi was somehow already aware of his fugitive status or, more likely, if it was just the equivalent of a wink at the long-compromised pretense of the old Combined Research Planning Office.

Hale had called the man from a nearby telephone, and though they had only exchanged the old recognition signals over the wire, bin Jalawi had greeted him at his door with Bedu enthusiasm, holding both of Hale's hands and joyfully shouting, *Shlun kum? Kaif hal ak, kaif int, kaif int, kaif int?*—and much more, all of which had essentially meant: *How have you been?*

Hale now put down his tea glass with a soft knock, absurdly wishing it were a cup of the coffee they had made at camp in the old days, harsh with the foul water of the desert wells.

"I've retired," he said in Arabic. "I felt like a change of water and air. Tommo Burks will, I think, begin a new life in the Arab states. And I thought you might be able to help me."

Bin Jalawi nodded, still grinning. "Allah is all-beneficent!" he said. It was one of the standard lines Arabs gave to importunate beggars, meaning *Look to God, not to me*—the equivalent of the British *Tell your troubles to Jesus, mate*—and Hale couldn't tell if the man meant it coldly or jokingly. "Many Arabs trusted Creepo," bin Jalawi went on in a jovial tone, "until they learned that the Israelis invaded Nasser's Suez with Creepo help, based on betrayed Arab confidences."

Nasser's Suez, thought Hale bitterly. As if the Arabs could have built the canal, or could even keep it dredged!

"I'm a landless man now," said Hale; "but you know that the British declared Kuwait to be a sovereign nation, more than a year ago." The remark was in character—to be too anti-British here would be to overplay his hand.

"Kuwait was never a long-term commitment, to England," said bin Jalawi. "Your policy here, and in all the Arab states, has been to get out as much oil as you could, before the indigenous peoples looked around and noticed that they were living in the twentieth century."

Hale supposed that was true. But he let his face stiffen as he said, "My policy?"

Bin Jalawi plucked several times lightly at the neck of his robe, then lowered his hands, palm down—an Arab gesture conveying something like, *You and I have nothing to do with these villains.* "I apologize, bin Sikkah," he said quietly, using Hale's Bedu nickname. "You were always a generous friend to the Bedu. 'Honor him who has been great and is fallen, and him who has been rich and now is poor.'"

The radio cabinet had been producing muted conversation for these twenty minutes, but now music started, some Islamic-style single-line melody, and the Arab got up from his couch, crossed to the radio and turned up the volume. The stylized, quavering singing of an Arab woman rang out of the speakers.

"Do you know her?" he asked.

Hale blinked. "Who, the singer? No. I suppose I might have heard her before."

"She is Um Kalthum," said bin Jalawi in a tone of reproof. "Every Thursday evening she is on Radio Cairo. In Cairo you don't even need a radio to hear her, because every set in the city is tuned to her, and her voice seems to emanate from the stones and the sky."

"Do you visit Cairo often?" Hale asked.

"Dogs can hear things that people cannot," said bin Jalawi, staring down at the radio console, "and so they know when to be vigilant, and which way to look, which way to run to safety. So can the Bedu perhaps hear things that Westerners cannot, singing out of the sky." He turned to give Hale a blank look. "You are maybe Bedu enough to hear also, if you clean out your ears. 'When thine enemy extends his hand to thee, cut it off if thou canst, else kiss it.' You in the old days cut off some *metaphorical* hands; now, my friend, is time to kiss the hand."

Hale smiled cautiously. He had often had to use the word *metaphorical* in dealing with bin Jalawi and the tribes, and the Arab had here pronounced the word in English, in imitation of him.

"I visit Cairo often," bin Jalawi went on. "You will be able to as well, I think, if you have invested the money you were paid by the American Standard Oil. Of what tribe were the Bedu guides you killed?"

Hale raised his eyebrows at the other man. "Saar," he answered. The Saar roved far to the south, above the Hadhramaut, and were feared by most of the other tribes. "It was self-defense."

This was of course his cover story, which hadn't been activated by Whitehall until late yesterday, according to Theodora. Perhaps to his credit, Salim bin Jalawi was not bothering with pretense, but Hale wondered sourly if the man had been taking Soviet pay in the '40s too; perhaps Hale would have been told, in the aborted briefing. Certainly the Soviet forces at Ararat had been able to prevent Hale from using the meteorite that he and bin Jalawi had found at the Wabar ruins in the Rub' al-Khali desert . . .

But . . . Hale's math had been bad. Apparently the meteorite had *not* been the Seal.

Still, if bin Jalawi had tipped the Soviets to Hale's activities then, he had no doubt helped the Russians kill Hale's men; those men who had been shot, at any rate, if not those who had been pulled screaming up into the sky . . .

Before speaking again, Hale carefully smothered the sick, remorseful anger this thought raised in him. You can't be sure bin Jalawi was doubling then, he told himself; and even if you could be, what would you do differently here?

"At Wabar," Hale said lightly, "you and I met a man who had long ago killed half of himself, to hide from the wrath of God. Is that a good way to live?"

"*Half* of you, you think it would be?" said bin Jalawi cheerfully. "Cut your hair, cut your toenails, and you'll have dispensed with more."

Hale knew that his companion—his oldest friend in the Middle East!—was referring to Hale's patriotism, his sense of duty to the Crown. In fact Hale suspected that it was more than half of himself, but his cover story required him to pretend far otherwise. Again he reminded himself not to get angry at bin Jalawi—the man simply believed the Whitehall-scripted cover story, which presented Hale as having been a crook for years, and which Hale had not denied here.

"More than that," Hale said. "A hand."

"A finger. A left-hand finger."

Hale fumbled a pack of Player's cigarettes out of his coat pocket. "Ramadan's fast ended two days ago," he said hoarsely. He could safely let his agitation show, as it would be interpreted as anxiety at the prospect of doubling, changing sides. "Do you have any old Ikhwan prejudices against your guests smoking?"

"Allah knows that djinn and ghosts without number clustered around our fires when you and I perfumed the desert with tobacco smoke," bin Jalawi protested. "Smoke like a refinery, if you like. The Russian we are to go to meet now, he smokes."

Hale was aware of his own knocking heartbeat. "You called him right after I called you?"

"That trouble was not required. His people placed a *bug* in my *hatif* last night. It is working as a microphone even now."

The Russian's house was in an old neighborhood in Al-Jahrah, twenty miles west of Al-Kuwait. It was a one-story coral-rock house with a tall square wind tower standing over the roof. The enormous front doors, visible in the headlights of bin Jalawi's Chevrolet, were of carved teak, studded with big iron nails in serpentine patterns, and a conventional-sized door had been cut and hinged into the right portal. When they had climbed out of the car and walked up to the small door, Salim bin Jalawi turned a wooden key in the wooden lock, and when the door had squeaked open, he stepped back and waved Hale toward the lamplit courtyard dimly visible within.

A drop of cold sweat rolled down Hale's ribs under his shirt, and he remembered the cheery greeting of the American OSS men in London during the war: *Is anything okay?*

As he trudged toward the flagstone threshold, he was rapidly, uselessly, trying to calculate the *cui bono* of his position. Who would benefit from having him killed here? Theodora would hardly have bothered to send him to Kuwait just for that; and the Soviet Ratkrin service was supposed to want his seemingly freelance expertise for the new Ararat operation, and even if they had found out that Philby had been doubled back, it was unlikely that they could know that Hale too was a Trojan horse.

I think *this* is okay, he told himself with frail confidence as he stepped through the low doorway.

A voice from a chair under the branches of a pomegranate tree said, in unaccented English, "You can have a drink, if you like, Mr. Hale. Scotch or vodka?"

I won't be obsequious, Hale thought. "Scotch, please." He squinted in the flickering amber lamplight, and saw that it was a lean man in a white Arab robe and head-cloth that sat in the chair. The garden walls appeared to be sheets of tarpaulin, their hanging folds gleaming dully in the muted light.

"Call me Ishmael," the man said without a smile. "John Christie is the SIS Head of Station in Kuwait, and the only cable he has got regarding you is an order that you be detained. Christie's office is of course now aware that you have arrived in Kuwait."

Hale just nodded, confident that his tradecraft had been logical and trusting the Russian to see that.

"Salim," said Ishmael, "you can go. Bring the car back at dawn."

Bin Jalawi had been standing in the doorway; now he nodded and retreated out of sight, closing the door.

"Sit," said the Russian, waving toward a palm tree a dozen feet from where he sat; a green or black rattan chair stood there, and Hale crossed the flagstones to it and sat down.

Hale looked more closely at the Ishmael person; he was much older than he had seemed at first glance, perhaps in his late seventies, and he didn't look well. His eyes glittered in dark sockets, and his leanness seemed a symptom of fever.

"You knew Kuwait in the old days, I'm told," the old man said. "Do you remember the flood of '34? No? Well, you'd have been a child, wouldn't you. On the first day of the Ramadan fast, four inches of rain fell in three hours—no drainage, the streets were five feet deep in water, and all the mud houses collapsed. Homeless, destitute. This was in May, when ordinarily there is never any rain. But the desert bloomed, grass for grazing was everywhere, and so butter and mutton and wool were suddenly as cheap as water. They *were* water, first destructive and then nourishing. You must remember when water was boated in from Iraq."

"Yes." Hale could vividly recall the teak *booms* that had sailed south daily from the Shatt-al-Arab, anchoring off Ras al-Ajuz to let the silt settle out in the topside tanks; then the itinerant Arab *candaris* would sell the water from goatskin bags, while established merchants sold it out of carts and trucks.

Beyond the door Hale heard bin Jalawi's car engine start up and then shift into gear.

"And when the sandstorms were fierce from Syria and Iraq," Ishmael said, "the boats couldn't sail, and Kuwait went without water for days." He coughed, and drank from a tumbler of what might have been vodka; when he put the glass down again on the table beside him, Hale noticed an automatic pistol lying beside it. The growl of bin Jalawi's Chevrolet diminished away down the road outside. "Nowadays," the old man went on weakly, "the Westinghouse distillation plant at al-Shuwaikh produces millions of gallons of water a day, so pure that brackish water has to be added to give it taste. Do you think the engineers could have accomplished that, if they had not first learned the secrets of rainstorms?"

"I suppose not."

"And still it rains." What Hale thought was more coughing appeared instead to be laughter. "Other, bigger, powers that can destroy or enrich remain—and if they cannot be tamed as thoroughly as rain and water can be, at least we owe it to ourselves to press for whatever accommodations we can get."

The old man gave Hale a quizzical look, and then picked up a cigar from the table and lit it with a gold lighter. In the glare his face was furrowed and lined. "If," he went on between puffs as the lighter flame rose and fell, "for no other reason—than to prevent inimical nations—from getting such accommodations—for themselves." He clicked the lighter shut and seemed to disappear in the sudden darkness. "You *are,* clearly, acquainted with the power I speak of," came his voice from behind the dim red coal of the cigar, "and you are at the moment a knight without a lord. Will you listen to persuasions?"

"Yes. Listen."

A barefoot Arab boy in a dark turban appeared at an inner doorway and stared with obvious expectancy at Ishmael; and the old man set down the cigar and waved a frail hand in a circle and then made a pulling-down gesture.

The boy nodded, and went to the nearest section of garden wall and yanked the tarpaulin down, exposing a bright metal mesh with dark movement behind it, and then went to the next tarpaulin. Hale guessed that the boy was a deaf-mute and had been summoned by the aroma of the cigar, in which Ishmael now appeared to have lost interest.

Brief staccato flutterings and mumbling and a smell like bad cheese on the chilly evening breeze let Hale know that the wire mesh structures the boy was exposing were tall birdcages; and when the boy had yanked the tarpaulin cover from the sixth and last cage, he scampered to a fuse box on the wall and stood on tip-toe to pull a switch, and floodlights lit the garden in a dazzling glare, illuminating dozens or perhaps even hundreds of finches and pigeons and doves and huge green-and-red parrots on perches inside the cages. Squinting, Hale even saw hens and roosters standing up and stretching their stubby wings.

Ishmael said nothing, simply stared at the nearest cage, until the birds had begun a fairly continuous din of cawing and chirping, punctuated by shouts from the parrots and crowing from the roosters.

"Why did you flee England yesterday morning?" Ishmael asked. Hale had to lean close to hear him, and he realized that the birds had been awakened in order to prevent any microphone from catching this conversation. And Hale was bleakly sure that the man wanted to prevent the KGB from eavesdropping as much as the SIS.

"I was about to be arrested, for old crimes," Hale answered.

"You are said to have killed two men yesterday, an MI5 consultant and a policeman. This would mean you can't go back to England ever again, if it's true, and that the SIS would work hard to find you, even here, and extradite you." He smiled, wrinkling his face. "These must have been extraordinarily bad old crimes."

"Bad enough." The news that Cassagnac and the policeman were dead hit Hale like profound weariness. He took a deep breath and made himself go on: "But in fact the MI5 consultant offered me at least partial immunity from prosecution, if I would do some work for them on an old operation." Living his cover, it didn't occur to him to urge the Russian to check out the facts of the story for himself. "They've probably been sitting on the criminal charges for some time, and dusted them off now just in order to compel me to work on the operation."

The Russian sat back, and for a moment seemed at a loss as to how to continue. At last he said, "Do you know which of the Soviet secret services I represent?"

"Rabkrin."

Ishmael raised an eyebrow. "I hope that name is not common knowledge in the SIS. Do you know our history?"

"No. I know you were aligned with both the KGB—or NKVD, as it was called then—and the GRU, before the war, and independent after."

"Like your SOE," Ishmael agreed. "A secret service that is secret even from the secret service, isn't it? In 1880 Tsar Alexander II founded the Department of State Police to protect him from assassins, and the special department in charge of stopping political crimes was called the Okhrana. As it happened, the Tsar was blown up with a grenade in the following year, but the Okhrana, at least, was already a power unto itself. In 1883 an earthquake in eastern Turkey knocked down cliffs in the Ahora Gorge on Mount Ararat, and, after Kremlin scientists investigated the situation on the mountain, it became necessary for the Okhrana to establish a foreign agency, the Zagranichnaya Agentura. Its headquarters were in Paris—and still were when you did work for their ETC network there."

The news forced a harsh laugh out of Hale. "We thought we were working for the Razvedupr, the GRU. That was . . . Rabkrin?"

"Under one of its names, yes. Where is Elena Teresa Ceniza-Bendiga these days?"

"I don't know. I last saw her in Berlin in the summer of '45. She was working for the French DGSS then, out of Algiers." Hale wondered uneasily what he might have been told to reveal or hide, if the briefing today had not been aborted.

"You are lying. Good, you were almost seeming too perfect, too cooperative; but this lie is nicely vain, ill-considered. In fact you saw her in the Ahora Gorge in 1948, when you had tried to stifle the thing on Ararat for the SIS. She called you a rude name."

Cannibale. Hale could feel shame heating his face as he realized that one of the Russian gunmen must have survived that carnage, and heard her. It had to have been one of the Russians, surely . . . not something in the sky . . .

Hale breathed slowly. "You're right," he said. "I forgot."

"Is she so forgettable? I met her, in 1942, in the Lubyanka." He stared at Hale for a few seconds, then went on: "In 1913 the Zagranichnaya Agentura was ostensibly shut down to mollify certain French Catholics who had got wind of its real work and were threatening to involve Pope Pius X; but it went on under another name, in greater secrecy."

Hale was leaned far forward to hear, and now he said, "You mentioned a— drink."

The Russian nodded, as if Hale had made a conversational point; and his hand rattled among the items on the table beside him, at one point striking a flame from the cigarette lighter, and then he tossed out onto the flagstones a tiny cardboard cylinder that commenced whirling furiously and whistling and shooting out colored flame like a road flare. The Arab boy hurried up to him, and Ishmael gestured.

A parrot behind the mesh at Hale's right elbow said, *"Allaho A'alam,"* and Hale glanced at the bird curiously, for what it had said was a deprecatory phrase, usually preceding some dubious story; but the parrot appeared to have nothing else to say.

The boy had scampered away, and now skipped back to where Hale sat and expressionlessly handed him a tall glass of neat Scotch, without ice. Hale tasted it—it was lukewarm, and he recognized the smoky, almost tarry taste of Laphroaig.

Ishmael nodded, and then went on: "When the Labor Party split into the Bolsheviks and the Mensheviks in 1903, the Okhrana had penetrated both groups; and when six Bolshevik deputies were elected into the Duma parliament in 1912, two of them were the Okhrana's. The Bolshevik Lenin, motivated by both opportunism and idealism, came to a secret agreement with the Okhrana—they arrested the most troublesome of the Mensheviks for him, as well as any Bolsheviks still agitating for reunification of the Labor Party, and in return Lenin saved the core of the Okhrana, the onetime Zagranichnaya Agentura, and transplanted it into the new Soviet secret police, the Cheka."

"*Hayhat!*" said the parrot; the word was Arabic, meaning roughly *alas,* or *far be it from you and me.*

Ishmael frowned at the bird. "Revolutionary mobs," he continued, "broke into the Okhrana headquarters in 1917 and burned all the records there, but the soul of the Okhrana had moved on, and the head of the Cheka was Feliks Dzerzhinsky—a man who, in his youth, had aspired to be a Catholic priest; a certain spiritual perspective had by this time proved to be necessary in the highest levels of state security and espionage. It was Dzerzhinsky who convinced Lenin to switch from the Julian to the Gregorian calendar in 1918, adding thirteen days, so that the previous year's October Revolution was retroactively made to have happened in November; Dzerzhinsky knew the value of concealing true birthdays, though Lenin later became overconfident of it." Ishmael stared at Hale. "Mr. Hale, when is your birthday?"

"January sixth. I'll turn forty-one in three days."

The old man nodded thoughtfully, apparently weighing Hale's answer—though he must have known it. And Hale remembered that Philby had appeared to question his birthday, at the Ham Common camp in '42.

Ishmael went on, "Lenin himself instituted the autonomous Rabkrin directorate, with provisions to keep it independent of, and even secret from, the other services; he did not trust Stalin, who in fact later purged the services unmercifully in an unsuccessful effort to eliminate the Rabkrin element. Stalin had a horror of spiritual warfare, the possible wrath of God. Since then we have at different times been known as the OMS, which was the International Liaison Department of the Comintern, and as Smersh and Smernesh even under Stalin's very nose during the war, and at other times as flickering sub-directorates in the KGB; but since 1917 it has always been Rabkrin, under the shifting titles. Why didn't you accept Whitehall's offer of 'at least partial immunity from prosecution'?"

"I don't know that it was Whitehall's offer," Hale said over the noisy bickering of the birds. "In any case, I'm convinced that it was an offer of immunity from prosecution on account of death. Other agents who have got too informed about this operation have had a way of dying prematurely."

The old man nodded tiredly. "T. E. Lawrence was bludgeoned off of his motor-bicycle; the code-breaker Alan Turing was fed a poisoned apple. You were probably right. This MI5 advisor you killed yesterday, this Cassagnac—he was one of ours, once, and I am grateful that you succeeded in killing him at last—what did he tell you about our current operation? What does Whitehall know?"

This was moving very fast—everything since his arrival in Kuwait had been fast—and Hale felt badly uninformed, and he wasn't happy that this man had told him so much about the Rabkrin. "Am I working for your people now?" he asked nervously. "Does the Rabkrin offer me immunity from prosecution?"

"You think we'll resolve your status, as your service jargon has it? Establish the truth about you? No, I can demonstrate, to your most exacting satisfaction, that it would be against our interests to kill you afterward. As you proposed to Salim bin Jalawi, Tommo Burks can begin a new life in the Arab states—a very comfortable one at that, more privileged than you can now imagine. What did Jimmie Theodora talk to you about?"

"When?"

"When you last spoke with him. When was that, to the best of your vain, ill-considered memory?" He shifted in his chair. "Any further lies will seriously impair the note of mutual respect you and I have established here."

Hale had to assume that the Rabkrin was unaware of his summons to London yesterday. "It was just before Ararat in '48," he said evenly. "We discussed . . . that operation, damn it. And I didn't ever see him again, after that."

"It was Cassagnac alone, then, who came to your house yesterday morning, with the news of your imminent detainment and possible immunity?"

"He was alone, yes."

"Incautious of him—but then you and he had been friends, I believe." Ishmael smiled. "In the *old days*."

Hale took a quick gulp of Scotch and then stood up and paced to the farthest birdcage and stared at a couple of angry-looking roosters. "I guess it's a lucky thing for you that SIS braced me when they did," he said tightly.

"Not coincidence," came Ishmael's voice from behind him, barely audible above the birds' squabbling. "Your masters are clearly aware that we are preparing for another attempt on the mountain—and you were the man in charge, working against us, when we tried it fourteen years ago. They would naturally want to compel your counsel and assistance in trying again to counter it. And when instead you fled England, ringing all the alarms, I was activated in case you decided to hole up among your leave-behind *Hadhira* or Bedouin networks. Other Rabkrin agents were activated in other places, or sent, to watch for you. Paris, Rome, even Chipping Campden, pitiably."

Rome? thought Hale. Because I used to be a Catholic? Theodora said Dick White had consulted the Pope . . . And Paris? That would have to be in case I had gone looking for Elena, through the French SDECE; apparently the Rabkrin really doesn't know her present whereabouts.

He walked back to his chair and sat down. "Right," Hale said, "now *you* want my . . . counsel and assistance. What if I'm not worth it, as things work out? I might not be much help, even with the best will in the world, you know. I'll tell you right now, if I . . . go with you, it'll cost you a lot." This shaky, defiant tone was good. "And—and I might not go with you in any case, you understand. I've never been disloyal, not to the service, at least."

"Only to your country, as in the matter of steering oil concessions to the Americans out from under the British Petroleum Company, and as in aiding Nazi war criminals to escape proper retribution. I do see. But how do you reconcile—I'm simply curious, my dear fellow—how do you reconcile having killed Cassagnac with 'not being disloyal to the service'? I would have thought that was a memorable event."

It was a good thrust, and Hale had stared at Ishmael and shrugged before he had thought of an answer; but without a measurable pause he said, "Cassagnac? But he wasn't SIS, was he? He was GRU, or Rabkrin, or French DGSS. At best he was part-time MI5."

Ishmael laughed, and again it was nearly coughing. "I like 'at best'! Interdepartmental rivalry! You don't have to tell me about it. Well, but you must admit you've shaved your patriotism down to a very narrow reed. It will not support you." He leaned forward, and the birds all clamored in their cages. "Break it now. Say, 'I break it now.' "

"Before I would—"

"You bought that coat you're wearing today after losing your previous one at the airport, and you have some kind of ankh or drogue stone in your pocket. I know you do, because if you did not have it, I would not have had to raise smells and flares here to summon the servant; and the birds are inhabited tonight. Do you understand? Assassins from Russia or England are not what you should primarily be afraid of."

Hale remembered the storm clouds he had seen over the Persian Gulf last night; but he forced himself to laugh and say, "I'll admit that—on Ararat itself—"

The old man got to his feet and was nearly shouting to be heard over the controversies among the birds. "What sort of *personage* did your Lawrence of Arabia learn of, in the *brontologion* scroll he found at the Qumran Wadi in 1917? Why did the American President Wilson suffer a stroke immediately upon returning to America from the Paris Peace Conference in 1919, where he had reluctantly agreed to take the League of Nations mandate to occupy eastern Turkey, in spite of the advice of the experts—experts on ancient Persian languages and the Crusades!—in his secret Inquiry group? Why did Lenin suffer the strokes that killed him in '22 and '23, after the Red Army had recaptured and then lost the Kars and Van districts in eastern Turkey? Idiot! Will you walk out of here still a knight without a protecting lord, without a covenant? Where will you walk—how far? I offer you a staff—say to me, about your old betrayed reed, 'I break it now.' Your statement will be witnessed."

Ice would have been rattling in Hale's glass, for his hand was trembling—but with sheer excitement, for this was the very highest-stakes table of the Great Game, and he didn't suppress a tight smile as he said, "I break it now."

Ishmael was breathing hard, as if he had just run up a flight of stairs. "Surrender your weapon."

Hale reached into the inner pocket of his new coat and dragged out the tinfoil ankh, and as the parrots and roosters shouted around him he tore it apart into impotent glittering shreds and let them fall like twisted airplane wreckage onto the spotlit flagstones.

"I break it now," he repeated.

Ishmael said, "Would you die for our cause, your new cause?"

Hale barked out two syllables of a surprised laugh. "No!"

"I would. Would you kill for us?"

"Well, it's your cause, isn't it? Makes a world of difference. I haven't got one of those any longer, aside from enlightened self-preservation. Kill for you?" Hale shrugged. "In some circumstances."

Ishmael pursed his wrinkled lips, clearly recognizing that this indifference, distasteful though he might find it, was a small point in Hale's favor—an infiltrated double might well have been told to feign more commitment. "What did Cassagnac say?" the old man snapped. "What does Whitehall know?"

Hale took a deep breath and opened his mouth—and then discovered that he had an almost physical difficulty in telling Ishmael the answers. As recently as yesterday, Hale would have undergone torture rather than tell a Rabkrin operative these things.

He exhaled without speaking, aware of a chill of sudden dampness on his forehead. But it's *all wrong,* he told himself, you can tell this man the old math because it's—apparently—invalid; *but!*—but it is nevertheless the math I put together, *discovered!*—to deceive and checkmate Ishmael's people—and it's so internally consistent, so convincing—

Ishmael was staring at him with eager attention, and Hale realized that his own hesitancy here was obviously genuine . . . and he knew that Theodora had arranged all this so that it would be.

And so at last Hale began talking, haltingly telling his questioner everything the Declare operatives had known in 1948, and describing, as if it were the still-current plan, his own earnest, painstaking strategy for countering that Soviet attempt to awaken what slept uneasily on the top of Mount Ararat.

The birds appeared to want to listen, and Ishmael had to summon the boy and make him beat the cages with a stick to get them all shouting and cawing again.

▼

8

Ain al' Abd, 1963

*. . . it was noticeable that whenever the Church of England dealt with a
human problem she was likely to call in the Church of Rome.*
—Rudyard Kipling, *Kim*

When the stars had begun to fade in the east, Hale and his host
shared a breakfast of hot saffron rice with eggs beaten into it, accompanied by a choice of beer or camel's milk, of which Hale chose beer; and
then Ishmael gave him a clearly secondhand set of Bedu clothes to change
into: a patched cotton *dishdasha* smock with an *aba* robe to drape over
it, and a once-white *kaffiyeh* head-cloth and an *agal* cord to tie it on
with. Ishmael looked like a prosperous town Arab in his long white shirt
and robe and white *kaffiyeh,* while Hale's smock had been patched with
so many different fabrics that he sourly thought he looked like a
dervish; and his bare feet were obscenely white, and soon achingly
numb with cold from standing on the dewy flagstones.

In the frosty overcast dawn Salim bin Jalawi returned with the
jaunty blue Chevrolet, and Hale and Ishmael climbed into the back as
Ishmael gave bin Jalawi directions to a place off the highway south of
Magwa.

Bin Jalawi was moody, and several times frowned at Hale in the rear-
view mirror. Hale had gathered that they were to travel to some desert
location to consult some very old person.

Hale thought about how to phrase a question. "Is it a place I know?"
he asked finally, leaning forward over the seat back. They were driving
down a big new divided highway under a clearing sky, and for nearly
half a minute now had been gunning around the perimeter of a traffic

circle almost wide enough to contain another airport; but the interior of the circle was just tractor-leveled sand, as were the expanses on either side of the highway, and the only other vehicles between the flat north and south horizons were a couple of miles-distant water tankers.

Bin Jalawi spat against the inside of the windscreen. "It is a place you have heard of. It is to the south, in 'Awazim country, and I am Mutair. We will meet guides at Magwa."

"Are the 'Awazim at war with the Mutair?" asked Hale. "Do we need a *rafiq?*" When trekking through hostile country, it was the Bedu custom to talk a member of the local tribe into coming along as a guarantor or peacemaker, known as a *rafiq* in these northern countries around the gulf.

"We wouldn't want a *rafiq* from the tribe of the one we go to see," said bin Jalawi in a tight voice.

"And the only tribe at war with us here is the KGB," said Ishmael, his watery old eyes blinking ahead. "Khrushchev is not hostile to my agency, but the Presidium is growing tired of Khrushchev, and Semichastny of the KGB is pursuing Stalin's old line toward us."

"Horror at the wrath of God," recalled Hale.

They had been speaking in English, but now bin Jalawi burst out, "*Yahrak kiddisak man rabba-k!*" It meant *Burn the saint who brought thee up,* and Hale, startled, met his eyes in the rear-view mirror. Bin Jalawi glowered back at him. Still in Arabic, he said to Hale, "Speak you of horror at the wrath of God?"

And Hale almost smiled, for he realized at last that bin Jalawi was, illogically, angry at Hale for giving in to his cut-off-the-hand-or-kiss-it argument and turning double for this Russian. I have disappointed you, Hale thought, haven't I, Salim? Were you dutifully waiting for me to condemn your duplicity?

"Allah is all-beneficent," Hale told him mildly. Look to him for reproof, not to me.

A few miles south of the palms and apartment blocks and petrol stations of Magwa, bin Jalawi slowed the car and then steered it off the pavement onto a rutted dry-mud track, and through the jolting windscreen Hale could see, a hundred yards ahead, the glint of sunlight reflecting from the bumpers of several jeeps parked on the sand. Around the vehicles stood the old familiar silhouettes of robed Bedu and baggage-laden camels.

"These are Mutair and 'Awazim," said Ishmael rapidly in Arabic, "there is no enmity among them. Our destination is on the Saudi border, at the southern edge of the Neutral Zone—motor vehicles or helicopters in that region would draw the attentions of all the nations involved in this, so we will travel with these Bedu, as Bedu. They understand that you are a Frank"— Hale smiled, recalling that Bedu somehow always confused all Westerners with the French—"but do try to behave as one of them. They have each a *khusa* dagger and a rifle, naturally; you have no weapon; try to make up for that with an air of authority. You have the advantage of having more experience, than they, with the sort of thing we go to consult."

Hale could feel his scalp prickling. He remembered the man he and bin Jalawi had encountered at Wabar in 1948, the lower half of whose body had so long ago been transformed to stone that the immobile knees had been weathered to grotesque flattened flipper shapes by sandstorms; and for the second time in three days his right hand twitched in a reflexive impulse to make the sign of the cross. He made a fist instead, and took several deep breaths, and because bin Jalawi might be looking at him in the rocking rear-view mirror, he kept an impassive expression on his face.

The car began to slew like a boat in the loose sand when they were still some distance from the jeeps, and bin Jalawi sighed theatrically and trod on the brake; and when he switched off the engine, Hale heard and remembered the windy silence of the Arabian desert.

They levered open the doors, and bin Jalawi plodded around to unlock the trunk, from which he lifted two rifles which Hale recognized as old U.S. Army .30-caliber BARs, with blocky magazines protruding down in front of the trigger guards. Bin Jalawi handed one to Ishmael and held on to the other himself, and he ostentatiously did not look at Hale as the three of them began striding barefoot over the cold sand toward the jeeps.

It was clearly meant as a snub, so that Hale would lose face in front of these Arabs—but the tops of the low sand hummocks were furred green with the desert grasses that the rains always conjured up in the winter, and when Hale saw the yellow blossoms of the *Alqa* waving in the wind, he forgot his naked feet and his lack of a rifle and was cheered simply by this promise of good grazing ahead; and this very Bedu thought gave him the confidence to smile easily at the Arabs around the jeeps.

Two of the camels were white, clearly from the herds of the Dhafir, and the other five were the characteristic red-brown beasts of the Mutair and 'Awazim; all were laden with saddlebags and glistening water-skins and northern saddles with tall pommels fore and aft.

The camels were being tugged away into a walk toward the open desert to the west—apparently the party was to set off immediately—and one old graybeard by the jeeps was jangling a set of car keys impatiently; in Arabic he said to Hale, "An ill welcome to a face that will never prosper!"

Now the smells of old sweat and camels and automobile exhaust on the clean desert breeze had at least for the moment completely shaken away all memory of the years at Weybridge, and when one of the Bedu held out the reins of a Mutair camel to Hale, he took them and automatically tugged to bring the walking camel's head swinging heavily down.

And as Hale took a long step forward to set his bare right foot on the camel's neck and then was lifted up past the swaying saddlebags to the height of the saddle, he looked over his shoulder and called back to the man, "*Ya ibn al-kalb! Kaif halak?*"

It meant *O dog-son, how have you been?*—for Hale had recognized the man's voice as that of a Muntafik shepherd who had long ago been given the nickname Al Auf, which meant The Bad, because of his deceptively gruff manner.

Hale settled onto the flat saddle platform, kneeling far back as the Bedu did, and he heard Al Auf wonderingly call after him, "Bin Sikkah?"

Hale waved without looking back. He had been given the nickname bin Sikkah by the Mutair tribe when he had traveled with them in the winters of 1946 and '47. It meant Son of the Iron Road, which was the railway—the Arabs had always identified Europeans with the trains and rails that transected the coastal regions, and the steel rails were said to confound the attention of djinn.

Several of the Bedu had mounted their camels, and now as they rocked along up on the saddles they were peering curiously across at Hale, and he heard them mutter to one another, "It is bin Sikkah, back from the land of the Franks!" "It is bin Sikkah the *Nazrani!*"

Nazrani was almost a synonym with Frank, but it meant specifically Christian, and at least in Hale's day Christians had been held in very low esteem among the Bedu; so Hale decided to force a defining greeting before the despised term could be fully considered.

He glanced at the Bedu nearest him, a young Mutair to judge by the red mare he was riding, and nodded and said, "*Al kuwa,*" a common Bedu greeting which was a short way of saying *God give you strength.* If the man responded in kind, he would be nearly as bound to Hale as if he had invited Hale to drink a cup of coffee in his tent.

The man looked away from Hale toward his companions, but they were all absorbed in scanning the bumpy western horizon far out beyond the long blue shadows that stretched ahead of them across the reddish sand. At last the young Bedu nodded at Hale and gave the reply, "*Allah-i-gauik,*" which meant *May God strengthen you.*

After that the other three whom Hale had not met swung their camels into closer parallel around him as they rode west, and as soon as the customary pious greetings had been exchanged, Hale was included in the conversation as they reviewed the news of the last ten years or so. He learned about deaths and births and winter rainfalls and botched circumcisions, but altogether it appeared that most of the Bedu he had known were now living in new cement houses out near the airfield, and apparently all owned American trucks. His new companions in turn asked about the health of the Frank queen, and Hale assured them that she was well. From behind him, Hale heard the car and jeep engines start up and recede, sounding very far away because of the desert wind in his face.

The tufted, placid head of Ishmael's camel bobbed into view on Hale's left, and Hale saw that the old man was riding astride the saddle, rather than kneeling on it; from experience Hale knew that in this posture the saddle edges would eventually bite uncomfortably into the thighs, and he wondered if the old man would get down and walk beside his camel after a while. Ishmael carried his rifle slung over his shoulder, military fashion.

"We ride west," said Ishmael crossly in Arabic, "to the Ash Shaq valley, which we will follow south along the Saudi border, to avoid the Burgan oil fields. Nothing should obstruct us before we camp for the night, which should be at the mouth of the valley but nowhere near the Dughaiyim water hole; do, therefore, nothing of a *signaling* nature, am I understood?"

Hale nodded impassively; but he wondered what sort of signal the old man imagined he could give, from here, and to what sort of entities. As to camping away from the water hole, that was simply common sense—a known water hole was likely to be the destination of any travelers out on the desert, and the custom was to refill the water-skins and let the camels drink as quickly as possible and then to move off before any other, unknown parties might approach the place.

The Bedu had presumably had their coffee and made their morning prayers before Hale's party had arrived at the meeting place, and now they all, bin Jalawi included, began the monotonous falsetto singing that they could keep up for hours—a high trilling chatter of *La ilaha illa 'llah,"* which meant *There is no God but God,* repeated until it became as meaningless to Hale as the songs of birds.

As his legs and back rediscovered the postures of riding, Hale gradually became aware of wrongnesses in his clothing—he missed the constriction of the woven leather belt Bedu wore over the kidneys and abdomen; and without a dagger at his waist his robe didn't fold into the natural pocket in which he used to carry the comforting weights of compass and notebook and camera; and most of all he missed the strap over his right shoulder, the wooden stock by his elbow, and the rifle muzzle bobbing always ready in his peripheral vision.

The Ash Shaq was a gravel plain between eroded cliffs, and in the patches where low dunes transected it Hale could see little wake trails in the sand on the south sides of the solitary *abal* shrubs, indicating the prevalence here of the Shamal wind. Late in the afternoon Hale's party came upon the al-Sur water hole—bin Jalawi rode his camel up the western cliff slope to scout ahead along the higher ground and be sure that no other desert folk were pausing there for water—and then when he waved broadly from a farther promontory Hale and the others goaded their camels past the water hole in a fast walk. The gravel was polished and packed in paths radiating from the ring of stones, but there were no very fresh camel droppings visible.

Twice a fox scampered across their path, and Hale's companions told him how the desert foxes would sometimes stand in front of a man on his knees praying and imitate the man's gestures, distracting him from his devotions; and how Al Auf had once set up a head-cloth and robe on a stick, and when the fox imitated the scarecrow's immobility, Al Auf had succeeded in catching the creature. Hale nodded without envy, remembering but not sharing with these Bedu a time when, at his approach, solitary foxes had run with evident deliberateness across the unstable slip-faces of dunes and provoked the roaring of the sands, like courtiers summoning kings.

At dusk rain began to fall from the low sky, and by the time the darkness forced them to make camp, the rain was thrashing down with a numbing constant hiss onto the gravel. They had not found any wood or brush for starting a fire, and when they had all dismounted and unloaded the camels, Ishmael distributed cheese sandwiches, commercially sealed in cellophane.

Hale unrolled the sleeping bag that had been strapped to his camel, and he covered it with the rug and sheepskin from under the saddle, but as he lay on the humped mattress of gravel, the icy water found its way in and gathered in unwarming pools at his elbow, hip, and knee. Even though he had not slept at all the night before, he slept now only fitfully, often shivering awake to glance around at the dim shapes of the camels sitting facing away from the wind.

In the gray light of dawn Hale was awakened by the Arabs calling to one another as they roused the hobbled camels; frost crackled on the sheepskin as he pushed it off, and the camels' breath was white plumes in the dawn air. Hale sat shivering and rubbing his bare feet while all his companions except Ishmael knelt in the wet gravel facing west toward Mecca to pray, and then he struggled stiffly to his feet when bin Jalawi started a fire of old heliotrope roots which he forced into flame with gasoline and scrapings from a bar of magnesium. The brassy ringing of a pestle pounding coffee beans in a mortar promised hot coffee, and another Bedu was soon mixing flour with water and kneading it into lumps to flatten and drop onto the embers of the fire. The camels had wandered off to a patch of green *arfaj* and were chewing noisily.

One of the Arabs had walked away to dig a hole in a sand dune, and he came back with the news that the rain had penetrated the sand as deep as his forearm. All the Bedu were cheered, and glanced around to fix the area in their memories, for a good soaking rain would produce grazing that would be green for years to come.

But though the sun was a red disk in the cleared eastern sky, throwing a watery rose light over their labors as they lifted the wet bales and saddlebags back onto the camels and strapped them securely down, the

Bedu were soon moody and grumbling, for the course now lay due east, toward salt flats and the sulfur spring at Ain al' Abd.

Hale now recalled hearing of the place—the Bedu he had traveled with had never visited it, for the water was foul and the place was said to be a haunt of djinn. He assumed Ishmael was paying a stiff price for these guides.

By midmorning they had reached the border of the desert where the red sand gave way to the gray-white salt flats, and before they could proceed across they had to dismount and tie knotted cords under the hooves of the camels to keep them from slipping.

It had not rained here last night, and at first the salt sheets grated crisply under the camel's hooves, and Hale's companions looked unearthly with their chins and eyebrows underlit by the glare of reflected sunlight; the camels walked carefully, for fossil sea shells and the stumps of dead 'ausaj bushes projected sharply from the gray surface; then their hooves began to break through the salt to the greasy black mud, and their progress became a slow, sliding dialogue between balance and gravity, punctuated by the curses of the riders and the camels' panicky braying. When at last the beasts climbed long-legged up the shallow slope of the first of a succession of white dune chains, they had spent two hours traversing less than two miles.

The glaring gray expanses of salt still stretched away around them into the flickering horizon, and the Bedu muttered and kept their hands on their rifles, for in the universal dazzlement of the reflecting flats and the rising sun, every distant bush or rock seemed to be a cluster of tents or mounted men. And Hale thought too that he saw whirlwind shapes rising from the distant expanses of desert, among the dark spots in his vision that were just sun glare on his retinas; and he wondered what topologically effective shapes he might be able to make with the reins and his camel stick, if he should have to in a hurry. Once in Berlin he had made an ankh out of a dagger and a length of rope.

At dawn the Bedu had been sniffing the breeze for any whiff of alien campfires, but now they swore and spat, for the breeze from the ten-miles-distant ocean was fouled with the rotten-egg reek of sulfur. And the camels were moving slowly even across the sand, for their long necks were down low so that they could sweep their big heads back and forth and graze on the green 'ausaj bushes as they walked; among the desert Arabs the 'ausaj was considered to be haunted by djinn, and they would never use it as campfire fuel.

At noon the Bedu insisted on stopping for a smoke. When they had dismounted, bin Jalawi ceremoniously shook some dry tobacco from a leather pouch into an old .30 caliber cartridge shell, then struck a match to it and took several deep puffs from the hole where the primer had once been; then he passed it to the man next to him. When the makeshift pipe came around to Hale, he inhaled the harsh smoke deeply, wishing that Moslems could bring themselves to indulge in liquor as well.

Before getting back up onto the camels, the Bedu had to chat for a few minutes in the warming sun, and as they swapped old stories that they must all have heard many times before, they checked their rifles— the men carrying automatic weapons popped the magazine out and worked the action to eject the chambered round, while the ones with bolt-action rifles stripped the bolt out and wiped it off before sliding it back into the breech. Hale knew that the desert Arabs were forever idly stripping and reassembling their rifles, but today it seemed to him that they performed the habitual actions more deliberately than was usual, and he noticed that when the men finally got to their feet, each rifle now had a round ready in the chamber.

They had ridden for another hour across the low white dunes when the young man who had first returned Hale's greeting pointed ahead. "Ain al' Abd," he said uneasily.

The rotten-egg smell had grown stronger, and Hale had followed the example of his companions and pulled his *kaffiyeh* across his face, tucking the ends into the black *agal* head-ropes; now from the narrow gap between the lengths of cloth he squinted ahead and saw a dark shadow line that proved to be the edges of a depression in the marshy sand.

A meteor strike? wondered Hale. He remembered seeing a meteor crater some thirty miles southwest of here, near Abraq al-Khalijah, which meant high stony ground in an empty region—the crater had encompassed forty acres, and its cliff sides were twenty or thirty feet high; the meteorite had fallen in the 1860s, and the 'Ajman and 'Awazim tribes had avoided the place because of the Bedu superstitions about the Shihab, the shooting stars that knock down evil spirits who fly too near to heaven. The Coptic Christians in Egypt had a similar notion about the

Perseid meteor showers in August, calling them "the fiery tears of St. Lawrence," whose feast day was August 10.

St. Lawrence, thought Hale with a nervous grin. The patron saint of Declare, perhaps. A martyr to it, certainly.

In early 1948 in the ruins of Wabar, at the southern end of the ancient dry Dawasir-Jawb riverbed that stretched for more than two hundred miles from the Al-Jafurah valley by the Gulf of Bahrain, Hale and bin Jalawi had found what Hale had believed was a Solomonic seal, an iron meteorite as big as a tire, among the scattered black pearls that were lumps of fused sand, and Hale had radioed an RAF base in Abu Dhabi to fly out a DC-3 Dakota to take the thing away . . . and too at Wabar they had found and conversed with the half-man king who had made a covenant to evade the . . . the *wrath of God* . . . which had destroyed his city and stopped the river and buried his pastures and farmland under the dead sands of the desert . . .

But as his camel rocked steadily closer to the shadowy streak in the white sand, Hale soon saw that this was not a meteor crater; and it was almost with disappointment that he finally looked down at the sunken black pool, forty feet across at the widest, that lay at the bottom of this six-foot depression in the desert. In the center of the pool the water rolled and swirled over a natural spring, and Hale could see that on the eastern side a channel curled away toward the Maqta marshes and the eventual sea.

Only Ishmael had ridden up to the edge of the slope with him. The five Bedu sat on their grazing camels several hundred feet back.

Hale squinted around at the remote horizon: *'ausaj* bushes and sand and salt and far-traveling wind, nothing else. Ishmael, perched awkwardly in the saddle on top of his camel, was staring down at the desolate sulfur-fouled spring.

"When is he going to be here?" Hale called, shifting to sit cross-legged on his own saddle. "The person we're supposed to talk to?"

Only Ishmael's eyes showed over the tied-across flap of his head-cloth, but Hale thought the old man looked sick. After a few seconds Ishmael sighed visibly, then nodded toward the water and said quietly, "He is here."

Hale followed the man's gaze—the rainbow-smeared surface of the water was more bumpy and irregular now, as if the wrecked chassis of a locomotive were rising up from the depths, humping the sliding water above it and about to break the surface—and then Hale's face went cold, two full seconds before his ribs tingled like a mouthful of bubbling champagne.

Nothing was pushing up from below the surface. The surface of the pool had *clenched,* in defiance of gravity, into gleaming folds and hollows, like the consistent standing shapes in a boat's wake; and the glassy ridges and depressions were moving, slowly and laboriously, sometimes shattering into explosive spray but more often holding their shapes. Curling streaks of tan silt rushed like pale flames across the gleaming black surfaces.

Two parallel ridges of water, ten feet long and tapered at the ends, flexed into symmetrical contours, and Hale thought they now resembled vast lips; beyond the ends and behind them, two upswelling domes suddenly seemed to be yard-wide bulbous eyes. Webs of silt flowed over the domes like eyelid membranes; the whole surface of the pool had swollen into a gleaming mound and now looked something like a blind amphibian head.

It was hard to grasp the scale of the pool—surface tension couldn't hold this volume of any liquid in this shape, and Hale's optic nerves apparently supposed that some magnification was going on—his vision kept blurring and he had to keep refocusing on the thing.

After a moment the eye hemispheres cleared of silt and were glistening black orbs, while turbulent whirls of sand still clouded the rest of the monstrously bulging pool. The eyes had nothing like irises, but there was focused attention, if not intelligence, in the gaze that was directed straight across thirty feet of heated air at Hale and Ishmael.

The faltering breeze from the pool was not only hot, but damp. The pool's convoluted surface was steaming now, at least in the twenty-foot quadrant between the huge lips and the sand slope below Hale's camel, and among the foggy wisps Hale could see that in the instant of its first appearance each puff of steam was a perfect ring, too brief to glimpse unless he happened to be staring at the right spot at the moment when one of them sizzled. Most of the flashbulb-quick rings were as small as coins, but some were as big as steering wheels, and a few were just segments of circles that would have been wider than radar dishes. The water was hissing and popping, and now a counterclockwise breeze had started up around the pool, raising a haze of sand.

Hale stared back at the blank face sculpted on the steaming and uncollapsing water out there. He didn't flinch, for he had been up close to this sort of creature before, but he was suddenly so dizzy that he wanted to jump down from the saddle and fall to his knees for sheer steadiness: the mere *fact* of this phenomenon was so incongruous and *wrong* that the landscape around it seemed to fade to a colorless two-dimensional sheet, with no reliable horizontal.

Ishmael muttered, "*Ikh! Khrr, khrr,*" to his camel and tapped her neck with his stick, and the mare obediently folded down onto her knees, lowered her hindquarters to the sand, and then shuffled her knees forward until she was sitting as comfortably as a big cat. Clearly nothing so far had struck the beast as alarming. *Look to dogs, camels don't react.*

Hale's mount too was calm, and sat down with a leisurely shifting of weight when he had tapped her neck and huskily given her the "*Khrr, khrr*" command.

Ishmael stepped down from the saddle to the sand. His hand brushed the rifle stock that swung by his hip, but he left the weapon slung over his shoulder.

Hale noted the instinctive gesture and bared his teeth behind the flap of his *kaffiyeh*. The rifle could be of no use against something made of water and wind. The makeshift tinfoil ankh would have been a comfort—but he told himself that this djinn was apparently confined to this water, and probably diminished in power.

Ishmael had plodded several steps down the sand slope from the crest, and his robe was suddenly flapping as he stepped into the localized whirlwind. He scowled back over his shoulder at Hale. "Come over here!" he snapped in Arabic.

Hale took a deep breath. "Aye aye," he said hoarsely in English, boosting himself down from his saddle. The crusty sand was jagged under the soles of his bare feet, and he walked carefully down the slope to halt beside the old man. He was squinting now against the flying sand.

With a crash that almost made him jump back, the crudely formed eyes and lips broke apart into spray like wave-tops sheared by a gale, and for several seconds the space for ten feet above the pool was blackly opaque with whirling water; it looked like glittering smoke and hissed and crackled like a heavy rainstorm.

The separating and reforming sheets of black water were whipping past only a few yards in front of Hale's face, and the reek of sulfur filled his head. His knees were shaking—it was a moment-by-moment strug-gle for him not to break and run away.

Beside him, Ishmael called out in Arabic, "O Fish, are you constant to the old covenant?" Though loud, his voice was thin against the wind.

Abruptly the spray fell back, and the black water was a rushing whirlpool now, with a column of steam spinning above a tapering hole in the center. And from the wobbling hole echoed a deep oily voice like shale plates sliding in a cave: *"Return, and we return,"* it said in Arabic. The funnel of water shook as the steam was sucked down into it, and then the voice said, *"Keep faith, and so will we."*

Hale's heart was thudding in his chest, and he knew that it was fear that had narrowed his vision and made his fingertips tingle, but with an electric exhilaration he knew too that there was no place on earth where he would rather be right now. He was sure that after this was over he would forget, as he had forgotten before—but in these rare moments of confronting the supernatural he always surprised in himself a craving to *get farther in,* to participate knowledgeably in this perilous, vertiginous, *most-secret* world.

Irregular ridges like spokes whirled around the gleaming hole now, giving the pool the appearance of a rapidly turning black glass wheel. Again the big voice rang in the air: *"Is this . . . the son?"*

Ishmael croaked, "You tell me, O Djinn."

With another crash the water exploded as if something big had plummeted into it, and when it had fallen back like glittering coal it smoothed out into the crude amphibian-like head again, veiled with hissing bursts of steam. In the silt-streaked swell the two gleaming black domes stared straight into Hale's eyes, with nothing but fixed attention. While the thing was focusing on him in this way, Hale's thoughts were a fluttering scatter of speculation and alarm and excitement, like a radio receiver picking up too many bands at once.

The two lip-like ridges separated with a splash, and from the yard-wide gap between them the *basso profundo* voice sang to Hale, *"O man, I believe you are the son."* White clouds of steam blasted away into the blue sky with each syllable.

Hale couldn't think of anything to say—but he was able to recall the old rule, *Never startle them, never reason with them*—and so he simply echoed Ishmael. "You tell me, O Djinn."

Ishmael was speaking again, desperately: "We think he is. He will tonight be flying west over the sands, to the western sea. Your brothers and sisters are awake, but they will not approach him—"

The black globes collapsed and then bulged up from the convex surface again, and when they had cleared of silt they were palpably focused on the old man, and Hale was once more able to think. Whose son did they believe he was? Did they mean it literally? Could the Rabkrin, and this elemental creature, know something of Hale's actual father?—but a moment later he was distracted by the flat crack of a rifle shot behind him; and as he turned to look back he heard two more shots.

The five mounted Bedu were looking away from the spring, toward the southeast, and Hale saw that bin Jalawi had the BAR rifle in his hands. Looking beyond them, Hale was able to see on that horizon a cluster of moving dots that were mounted men, not mirage.

If the strangers were friendly, they would soon be waving their head-cloths in the air and then dismounting to toss up handfuls of sand.

So far they were not doing it.

" 'Al-Murra?" asked Hale nervously, unable to keep himself from glancing back at the pool. The bulbous approximations of eyes and lips had broken up into churning random shapes below the curls of vapor. "Manasir?"

"As much as our party is Mutair, probably," Ishmael said in a flat voice. "But they're KGB—or conceivably Mossad, or the French SDECE. We have no time." He tugged back the fluttering flap of his *kaffiyeh,* and his exposed face was gray. "Bin Jalawi!" the old man shouted.

Hale's friend looked away from the unknown riders, toward the pool, and goaded his camel into a fast walk this way when Ishmael beckoned.

Ishmael's raised arm swept down with surprising weight onto Hale's shoulder, turning him back around to face the djinn in the pool.

"Say 'I break it now,' " the old man hissed in Hale's ear.

Hale crouched, clawing the sand and digging in with his toes—for an instant he thought he was about to fall into the pool—and then he realized that the nearest ten-foot quadrant of it had tilted up more than forty-five degrees, like a slanted glass bunker wall. Steaming black spray was fringing away along the rounded top and sides of the raised section of water, and as he watched, the smoothly convex surface began churning in a dozen concave vortices.

Hale straightened up dizzily, but Ishmael's hand was bearing down on his shoulder.

"Kneel," said Ishmael's voice urgently.

The vortices deepened into holes like clarinet bells, and as steam puffed out of the deep chambers, a dozen deep voices in unison said, *"My name is Legion. Worship us."* Two, then three of the holes combined into a bigger one.

Break it now, Hale thought as his heart thudded like a hammer in his chest. You've been coat-trailing for the opposition, and it's worked, they've been fooled so far, they've picked you up. They've at least provisionally bought into your role as a renegade ex-Declare agent. Live your role, "Know, not think it." And . . .

And it would be membership, initiation, a way to get leagues *farther in!* What on earth—or above it or under it!—might you not learn, and become able to do, if you obey this creature or cluster of creatures and kneel to it, prostrate yourself before it? What kingdoms in the clouds . . .

To his own surprise Hale realized that he had not even shifted the weight on his bare feet; and a moment later he knew coldly that he was not going to obey.

Ishmael had stepped back, to Hale's right, and at a glimpsed glint of silver in the old man's hand Hale turned toward him. Ishmael was holding an American .45 Army Colt automatic pistol pointed straight at his face.

"Kneel, damn you," Ishmael snarled.

Don't worry about anything, C had told him in 1929, when Andrew Hale had been seven years old. *You're on our rolls.* And that had been the very day of Hale's first Holy Communion, when he had consumed the body and blood of God.

Steam like sulfurous breath touched his left cheek, but from the corner of his eye he could see that the black wall was holding its position for now, ten feet away down the slope.

It had been a .45 for Cassagnac, at the end, out of a revolver. Hale had seen men hit by the .45 slug. It had knocked them right down, breathless and pale and dying.

I am the Lord thy God; thou shalt not have strange gods before Me.

But you don't *believe* in God anymore! he told himself tensely. You kneel to check the air pressure in a tire, or to open a low dresser drawer—why can't you kneel here? Finish Operation Declare, redeem the deaths on Ararat, save your own life—

He could hear the hooves of bin Jalawi's camel, and he heard the stamp-and-slither as bin Jalawi must have seen the uptilted section of the black pool and frantically reined in the camel.

Speak you of the wrath of God? bin Jalawi had asked angrily on the drive down to Magwa.

Hale glanced to his left, squinting down the slope against the sandy whirlwind. All the holes had merged into one yard-wide mouth, and a ring of jagged rocks whirled around its circumference like a wheel of wet tan teeth.

A deep, inorganic voice groaned out of the black-water mouth: "*Adore—us,*" it tolled, "*bin Hajji.*"

Hale was still able to think. Bin Hajji meant *son of a pilgrim,* son of a devout Moslem who has made the pilgrimage to Mecca. Perhaps it was a taunt, a challenge. At the Ham Common camp in '42, Philby had said, *Our Hajji which art in Amman . . .*

Finally, it was simply impossible to prostrate himself before this unnatural thing in the sight of his old Bedu friend, Soviet tool though the old friend might be.

"I—won't do it," Hale said, exhaling. The old man was just a few paces too far away for Hale to have any hope of springing at him and grabbing the gun before it would be fired; and to dive to Ishmael's right, forcing the old man to swing the barrel out to the side, would be to jump down the slope and right into the spinning mouth. Better to stand still and only *perhaps* die. He looked past Ishmael and the monster, at the infinite extent of the Arabian desert, and he was oddly contented with the possibility that he had come back here at the age of forty to be killed. Elena was long lost to him. "Who is my father?" he asked curiously.

"*This is the son,*" groaned the spinning hole in the wall of black water. The whole surface was quivering, and the fringe of steamy spray was flying away, beading up in the sky or kicking up splashes and sand below it, as if flung by centrifugal force. "*This is the Nazrani son.*"

Abruptly Ishmael surprised Hale by throwing the gun to him, and then the old man reached inside his robe and pulled out a walkie-talkie-sized radio and yanked up the telescoping antenna.

Hale had caught the gun carefully by the grip, and he half-tossed it to grasp it firmly, his finger outside the trigger guard. He realized that he had been holding his breath, and he began panting. It was all he could do not to point the muzzle, uselessly, at the turbulent wall of water.

"Kill Salim bin Jalawi," Ishmael snapped. "That's an order, a condition of employment, a proof of your sincerity." He twisted a dial on the radio and then cupped his hand around the microphone and began to speak into it quickly in Russian, his eyes on the no-longer-distant riders.

Bin Jalawi knelt atop his camel fifteen paces across the sand toward the south; his voice now was loud and steady, and it must have required courage for the Bedu to speak at all in the terrible presence of the djinn: "Will you shoot me, bin Sikkah?"

Ishmael gave Hale a fierce nod. For the first time, he seemed more frightened than irritable. Peripherally Hale could see that the ring of stones was spinning more rapidly in the steaming mouth.

Hale laughed dizzily, still doubtful that any of them would live to leave this place. "No, my friend," he called over the whistling wind to bin Jalawi. And I do wonder if *you* would not shoot *me,* if our positions were reversed, old friend.

Ishmael stared at Hale, then after a moment of open-mouthed hesitation pronounced some flat, clear Russian syllables into the radio, after which he dropped it onto the sand. "There is a ship off the Ras Khabji headland"—he spat out the words in English—"and a helicopter from it is now heading this way, fast, tracing the Al-Maqta stream. It is Rabkrin, get aboard it." He stepped sideways to face Hale squarely. "Kill *me,* then," he said. "I have told them on the radio that you are genuine—the devil confirms your identity, and certainly no SOE infiltrator would have perversely refused my orders—my part of the task is finished. The things of the water demand a life in exchange for their testimony, and we cannot possibly offend any ambassadors of theirs right now—kill me."

Hale heard the rapid multiple crunch of camel hooves, and saw that Ishmael's group of Mutair and 'Awazim had goaded their camels into a rolling gallop toward the east; in the southwest the unknown riders were close enough for him to see that their camels also were running—stretching their long legs and holding their heads low. Bin Jalawi was still sitting imperturbably on his camel close at hand, but all of them needed to get moving right now.

Nevertheless Ishmael had clearly meant what he had said, and it was probably true. If they cheated this, this *oracle,* the entire Rabkrin Soviet operation *might* misfire, which meant that Declare would misfire too.

Hale flexed his hand on the checked wooden grip of the .45—but it had been nearly eighteen years since he had shot a man, and he had never simply *executed* anyone, and somehow the sight of the old man's gray face and bare feet made shooting him impossible. "Kill yourself, then," said Hale thickly. "But do it quickly—I need your rifle if we're to get away from this hole."

The old man unslung the BAR from over his shoulder and simply tossed it through the air upright to Hale, who caught it by the stock with his left hand. The polished wood was warm, and the steel barrel was hot, and Hale noticed belatedly that the sky had cleared and the sun was a caloric weight on the landscape.

Then Ishmael simply turned toward the pool and started walking down the crusty sand slope—and the fringes of black water were as distinct as tentacles now, though water and steam still flew from their ends; as Hale watched, they began to bend forward, like the spines of a huge black Venus's-flytrap. The spinning rocks clattered like weighty castanets, and Hale could see the whirlpool mouth constricting and dilating until Ishmael knelt in front of the opening, blocking Hale's view; then the old man raised his hands and bowed forward.

Hale quickly slung the rifle and bent to pick up the radio, and then he stepped across to his couched camel and scrambled up onto the saddle. He tapped her neck to get her to stand, and as she rocked up onto her feet, he tucked the .45 and the radio into a saddlebag by his ankle, and neither he nor bin Jalawi looked back as they goaded their mounts into a gallop after their fleeing companions, away from the pursuing riders and the living sulfur pool and the splashing, sucking, cracking sounds behind them.

Hale thought of Elena's friend Maly, who had voluntarily gone to Moscow to be killed, and he wondered fleetingly if Ishmael had also been a religious man, once.

Hale was straddling the saddle and clinging to the rifle as his camel began lumbering after her fellows against the hot breeze, her hooves pounding the sand and the saddlebags flopping as she picked up speed. Hale braced himself with one hand on the forward saddle pommel, and he craned his neck to look back.

The strangers were gaining; he could clearly see the fluttering white robes and head-cloths, and the brandished rifles. And not all of the weapons were simply being waved in the air—his ribs went icy cold as he heard the chatter of a short burst of full-automatic gunfire, and then another.

He had just glanced down at the trigger assembly of the rifle that was jolting in his lap and flicked the change lever from single-fire to auto when he was startled by a loud and wildly prolonged burst from only a few yards to his right. Bin Jalawi had turned around on his own saddle and raked the whole quarter of the compass behind them.

More jackhammer racket replied, and Hale saw simultaneous spurts of sand kicked up along the ridge of a low dune ahead of them.

"Bloody hell," he wailed through clenched teeth. He clamped his legs on the saddle and then twisted his body around to point the heavy rifle's muzzle at the riders. When the front sight was bouncing closely across his view of the figures he pulled the trigger and released it, sending three or four 7.62-millimeter slugs toward them. The barrel jumped out of line, and he swung it back and fired briefly again.

When he glanced ahead he saw an underslung, streamlined olive-green shape scudding low over the dunes—it was the helicopter, flying toward them half in profile, and now he could hear the thudding of its rotors.

He lunged forward over the hot barrel of the rifle and snatched the radio out of the saddlebag by his ankle; he found the set's power switch, and he yelled into it in English, "Rabkrin! I'm the two riders! Shoot the ones behind me!"

He didn't know whether they understood English or had even heard him, but a moment later he saw a bright spot of fluttering muzzle fire in the dark rectangle of the helicopter's open cargo door; for several seconds the nearly continuous flashes didn't cease, and he could hear the choppy whisper of bullets ripping through the air over his head; then the muzzle flashes went dark and his ears were belatedly battered by the stuttering roar of the machine gun.

Clouds of sand scooped up into the air a hundred yards ahead. The helicopter was apparently settling down for a landing, its tail elevated as if the pilot was afraid of hitting one of the low sand dunes with the tail rotor.

The camels began hitching and lifting their heads as they pounded closer to the hovering aircraft, and when they were still fifty yards short of it they wobbled to a halt and balked at going any farther.

"—not bothered by a bloody *genie*," Hale snarled as he gripped the rifle and the .45 and simply jumped from the saddle. He knocked his chin with one knee when his bare feet hit the hot sand, but a moment later he had got up into a crouch and was limping to bin Jalawi's mount.

And Salim bin Jalawi rolled off of his saddle, slid facedown across the glistening water-skins and thumped heavily to the sand on his hip and shoulder. He was facing Hale, and the front of his robe was bright red with blood.

The sunlight seemed to dim, and there was a shrill keening in Hale's head. Ignoring several crackling, megaphone-amplified shouts from the helicopter, Hale crouched helplessly beside the dying Arab.

"Salim!" Hale's breath wavered in his throat. "Salim!"

The Arab opened his eyes. The flap of his *kaffiyeh* had been pulled away from his white-bearded face, and Hale saw blood on the man's teeth when he grimaced. "Get out of this, bin Sikkah," he whispered. "These men—traffic with devils—"

"Salim," said Hale urgently in Arabic, "I am still working for Creepo, under deep cover. This is a pretense, a trick, to confound this lot's plans. Are you hearing me? I—I pretend to kiss the enemy's hand, the better to be sure of cutting it cleanly off."

Bin Jalawi's mouth opened in what might have been a pained smile, as if he were trying to laugh. " 'You're a better man than I am, Gunga Din,' " he said in English, quoting the Kipling poem that Hale sometimes used to recite when drunk; and then he shuddered and died.

Hale looked back the way they'd come—the riders who had been pursuing them appeared to have stopped and dismounted several hundred yards back, and Hale thought there were fewer of them now. They weren't shooting.

The Mutair and 'Awazim with whom Hale had ridden here were somewhere to the east, on the far side of the small sandstorm around the hovering helicopter—they or these southern tribes would no doubt take possession of the camels and, being Bedu, give bin Jalawi a Moslem burial.

Hale got to his feet and jogged painfully across the sand toward the drifting helicopter. Squinting against the stinging sand kicked up by its whirling rotors, he could see in the cargo doorway a short-haired man with sunglasses and earphones, waving at him; the man had apparently put down the megaphone, and the steady booming of the rotors was too loud for Hale to hear anything the man might have been shouting. Hale forced his aching legs to run faster over the uneven sand, and when at last he exhaustedly set one bare foot on the metal skid and grabbed the edge of the door frame, the man took Hale's free hand and dragged him in to sprawl onto the corrugated steel cargo deck between two .60-caliber machine guns mounted on pylons.

Hale's rescuer, who was wearing dungarees and a sweatshirt and appeared to be European, waved toward the pilot's station, and then Hale felt heavier as the big rotors thudded more loudly with their pitch angle increased for a fast ascent. There was no shaking or vibration from the engine, and Hale realized that it was some kind of turbine, not one of the piston engines that had powered the old Sikorskis and Bristols he had flown in after the war. He got cautiously up on his hands and knees and only then realized that he had at some point dropped both the BAR and the .45.

After several seconds the helicopter banked to the north, tilting the open cargo door up toward the sky, and Hale impulsively crawled forward and gripped the bottom edge of the steel-and-ceramic laminate of the craft's exterior armor, and he peered over the door sill, down through a hundred feet of swirling sand clouds, at the rippled desert of the Kuwait–Saudi border; he could make out bin Jalawi's camel, though he couldn't see his friend in the beast's shadow, and farther west he saw the shadows of other camels and the scattered white dots of robes sprawled on the reddish tan ground. Not far away to the north was the sulfur pool, though it was a featureless black disk from this height and distance. Farther off he could see the white of the salt flats, and dimly beyond them the long shadow of the Ash Shaq valley, while the tan horizon was the broad interior deserts of the Summan and Nafud.

The man who had pulled him into the aircraft now grabbed him by the ankles and dragged him back from the door.

"They still have rifles," the man told Hale, shouting to be heard over the rotor noise through the open door. "Come up by the pilot's station." Even shouting, he had a German accent. He pulled the heavy door closed along its track, and in the relative silence after it had slammed shut he said, "You look like hell. Are you shot already?"

"No," said Hale, bracing himself against a gun pylon as he got wearily to his feet.

The two high-backed seats up in front were nylon mesh strung across aluminum frames, and in the right-side one the pilot was hunched over the cyclic control stick—Hale saw that as he moved it, the stick in front of the empty left-side seat moved too, and for one childish instant, before he realized that the control sticks were linked, he nearly flinched.

"Ishmael killed himself?" asked the man standing beside Hale, still speaking loudly.

"Yes," said Hale, wondering if these men would believe a description of the action at the pool. They appeared to be in their late twenties or early thirties—and Hale, stiff and sore after sleeping on the ground in the rain and riding a camel for two days, felt incalculably old and decrepit and unreliable. "I didn't see it, but—I heard it."

The pilot nodded. "Years now, that old man's been looking for an excuse."

The German gave Hale a quizzical look. "The genie ate him?"

Hale found that he was laughing, though not hard enough to justify the tears that were blurring his view of the switches and circuit-breakers on the console in front of him. "That's what it sounded like, yes." *You're a better man than I am, Gunga Din.* "Do you gentlemen have any *drink* aboard?"

The pilot groped by his left knee and then, without looking away from the Perspex windscreen, lifted over his head a half-full pint bottle of Smirnoff vodka that swayed in his hand with the motion of the aircraft. "Bung ho, eh, what?" he said in an affected British drawl.

"*Skol, Prosit,*" agreed Hale absently, catching the swinging bottle. He unscrewed the cap and took several deep swallows of the warm, stinging liquor. In his mind he saw bin Jalawi as he had been in 1948, dark-bearded and whipcord-thin; and then as he had looked two days ago, his beard white now, listening to the radio in his Al-Ahmadi house with the electric range and refrigerator in the modern kitchen. Hale thought, *It was not a good day for you, old friend, when I came back into your life.* "Where are we—going?"

"Kuwait International Airport," the German told him. "Ishmael said you have been confirmed, so now you are to get on an airplane, a private jet, there."

"To go . . . where?" Hale asked. "Do you know?"

The German gave him a blank stare. "Somewhere intermediate, I suppose. Probably several intermediate places. You are at home in them, I think."

Hale nodded and tipped the bottle up for another couple of swallows. "Oh sure," he said hoarsely. "Me and intermediate go way back."

"Soon we will be at the airport," said the pilot. "There are airport staff clothes and shoes in a locker in the cargo bay—get into them now." He glanced back at Hale with a cold smile. "You can take the bottle."

Hale found the locker, and after sloughing off his bloody, muddy old Bedu costume he put on the tan uniform, complete with name badge, of a Kuwait International Airport baggage handler. He bundled up the Bedu clothes and shoved them into the locker, and then he sat down cross-legged below a couple of bright steel bolts where a passenger seat could have been installed. He sipped at the warm vodka and tried to take satisfaction in the thought that he was now successfully injected into the opposition's machine, and that Theodora would be pleased; but in his mind was droning the old refrain, *You can't relax yet.*

The next twelve hours were a series of destinations and layovers, seen through a haze of intermittently renewed alcohol and persistent exhaustion.

At the Kuwait airport he simply walked from the helicopter across fifty yards of tarmac to a sleek British Aerospace commuter jet that the German had pointed out to him, and climbed aboard. The only crew members Hale saw were two young Arab men in snow-white Saudi-style robes and head-cloths, and they didn't speak to him beyond ordering him in terse Arabic to take a seat in the cabin and, in English, "Belt up." When the plane had taken off and reached cruising altitude, somewhere down the gulf coast over Oman, he was given a Savile Row suit to change into, and a shaving kit, a French passport, and an Alitalia Airlines ticket. Four hours later the jet landed at Benina International Airport near Benghazi, and he followed the directions he'd been given and got right aboard the next Alitalia flight bound for the Ciampino Airport in Rome, having spent less than forty minutes in Libya.

Slumped in a window seat in the turboprop Alitalia Vanguard, he drank Canadian whisky and watched twilight darken to full night over the purple expanse of the Mediterranean; and he kept reminding himself of what Ishmael had said to the djinn in the sulfur pool—*He will be flying tonight west over the sands, to the western sea—your brothers and sisters are awake, but they will not approach him . . .*

At the Alitalia gate in Ciampino he was met by a cheerful young couple who greeted him by the name on his new passport and drove him to a modern apartment in the Parioli district of Rome, and behind drawn curtains he managed to eat most of a quick, hindered dinner of lukewarm gnocchi and red wine even as the woman was cutting his hair in a bristly brush cut and then dyeing it and his eyebrows dark brown. When his hair was dry they took his photograph, and a couple of hours later he was given a British passport in the name of Charles Garner, with his new picture in it. The sky was pale above the electric trolley lines when he was bundled out of the apartment building and boosted into the back of a newspaper delivery van, and he fell asleep among bales of the daily *Corriere della Sera* as the van sped north up one of the new autostrade express highways. Finally at noon a dark-haired Charles Garner walked haggardly into the Malpensa Airport outside Milan and boarded a TWA flight for Beirut.

The Beirut airport was at Khalde, on the coast seven miles south of the city. The terminal was a long white two-story building with louvered ground-floor windows and a modernistic but vaguely Arab-looking lattice over the broader windows on the upper floor. After presenting the entry visa he'd been given, and getting his passport stamped on one of the artfully few remaining blank pages, Hale shambled aimlessly out into the linoleum-floored lobby, blinking up at the painted airplane models hanging on wires from the high ceiling. He could smell his own stale sweat, and even though his shoes were too big for him to lift his feet comfortably, he walked outside to the car park; but the pine-scented afternoon breeze was chilly, and he soon pushed his way back in through the glass doors.

This was Lebanon, and the loudspeakers broadcast arrivals and departures in English and Arabic and French; and a pair of Maronite Catholic nuns who stepped past him nodded and said *Bon jour* instead of *Sabah al khair.* Hale echoed their greeting—guiltily, for he was a lapsed Catholic and had spent time the previous day talking with a creature whose name was Legion.

A big dark-bearded man by the auto-rentals desk was baring white teeth at him in a grin—he wore a blue-striped gown under a French-cut jacket, and a white *kaffiyeh,* and Hale thought he was probably an Arab, altogether—and now the man strode over and said, in English, "You flinched, Mr. Garner! Confess, you were taught by nuns."

"Jesuits, actually," said Hale. "Same general effect."

The man laughed jovially and led Hale back out through the doors to the sidewalk. "That accidental encounter was a nice confirmation," he said, his voice just loud enough for Hale to hear in the cold open air. "It is odd how many of the people destined for our wielding were tempered in the Church—Dzerzhinsky, Theo Maly, even our late friend Ishmael—and the SIS would never have the wit to cook us a *Papist* double out of their Anglican fish-pot."

You don't know Jimmie Theodora, thought Hale. "No," he said tiredly, "they're not running me. They'd *like* to run me."

"And they would kill you afterward. This Volvo is ours," he said, waving at a little gray station wagon among the ranks of Mercedes-Benzes and Oldsmobiles and Peugeots in the car park. "I tried to kill you, in 1948—I was with the Russians on the mountain, and if I had not been knocked unconscious by a British bullet, I think I would have been killed or driven mad. I am an Armenian—it is our mountain, not the Russians' and not yours."

The steering wheel was on the left side, American-style, and Hale pulled open the passenger door. "Nothing's mine anymore," he said over the roof to his companion before getting in and closing the door.

"True," said the Armenian as he got in on his side, closed his door and started the engine. Hale noticed that the man's breath reeked of garlic and licorice. "I am Hakob Mammalian, and I am your handler in this undertaking. I am not interested in killing you anymore." He held out his big right hand toward Hale.

Hale smiled and shook the warm, dry hand. "You people killed three of my men that night, I think."

Mammalian released Hale's hand to shift the engine into reverse. "Consider what it was that *you* were trying to kill. The heart of the mountain! Do you still seek . . . *vrej?*"

The word, Hale knew, was Armenian for *revenge*. "Nothing's mine anymore," he said again. "I'm not after *vrej*."

"Remember that Charles Garner has no grudges. Much will be his, soon."

The road north to Beirut was a flat dirt track wide enough for two cars to pass comfortably. The lowering sun reflected off the Mediterranean to light the undersides of the clouds in gold, and the occasional roadside clusters of leafy cypresses threw blue shadows across the apricot-colored road.

"Charles Garner is a journalist," Mammalian told Hale, "a sometime foreign correspondent for the London newspapers *The Observer* and *The Economist*. A brief biography of him and a book of tear-sheets of his articles are in your room at the Normandy Hotel for you to study, so that you can make small talk. He is not a real person, but an occasional pseudonym used by another member of our team, who is a genuine journalist; you are welcome to the Garner identity and career."

Soon Hale could see the rocky beaches and the white office buildings of the Beirut promontory ahead of them, and within minutes they were driving along a new highway, with cliffs and the sea to their left and modern hotels and restaurants on their right. Hale stared at a place called Le Réverbère, which according to a sign was THE STEREO WITH A TOUCH OF PARIS.

"Beirut is become an American city, indistinguishable," Mammalian said, nodding. "Bowling alleys, and stereo clubs for the rock-and-roll and dancing. But it is, being in neutral Lebanon, the most wide-open city in the Middle East. No faction is truly in charge, not the Maronite Christians nor the Sunni Moslems, and nobody cares what you do if you keep your mouth shut about it; everyone is plotting something, and Nasser would not annex Lebanon if they begged him." He glanced sideways at Hale. "Ishmael sent us a radio message before the two of you left his house on Friday morning—a brief radio message. Did you explain to him what offer Cassagnac made to you on Wednesday morning? Did you inform him of what are Whitehall's plans, what Whitehall knows about the mountain and its longevitous citizens?"

"Yes," said Hale. "Fully."

"Tonight you will tell it all again, to me, even more fully, with a wire recorder operating. We will drink a good deal of arak, I think."

Hale suppressed a smile, for he knew now where the licorice smell came from. Arak was one of the anise-flavored liquors, like Pernod and absinthe. He had never cared for the taste, though, and he didn't like the way the stuff turned milky white when water was added.

"I might stick to Scotch," he said.

"Charles Garner drinks arak," Mammalian said. "You must get used to it."

They had taken a right turn inland, and Beirut suddenly didn't look American at all. Latticed balconies fronted the windows above the narrow shops, the signs of which, except for the big Pepsi-Cola trademarks, were all in French and Arabic. Women in bright-colored European skirts and high heels stepped from the curb to the street to make way for flocks of sheep being herded along the sidewalks by Arab women in long black *abas,* and soldiers in black berets stood on the corners holding automatic rifles whose stocks were decorated with glued-on colored glass beads. At one intersection traffic was halted for a Christian funeral procession, noisy with wailing, and Hale stared at the bearded priests and the tall swaying crosses garlanded with flower blossoms, and on the air from the vent by his feet he caught a whiff of incense.

At last they reached the north shore. The curved front of the five-story Normandy Hotel stood in white splendor just across the street from the beach, between a stand of palm trees and a men's hairdressing, manicure, and pedicure salon.

A valet hurried up when Hale and Mammalian climbed out of the Volvo, and as the car was driven away the Armenian led Hale up the steps and through the glass doors into the carpeted hotel lobby.

"You will want to shave and . . . freshen up," observed Mammalian, "but we could certainly have a drink, first."

Hale followed the man's pointing finger and saw the hotel bar, off to the side of the lobby behind a beaded curtain.

"Arak, I suppose," he growled, nevertheless starting toward the bar archway. Anything at all, actually, he thought—any ethanol at all, at all. Hale reached the arch before Mammalian and pulled back the rattling curtain—and then he stopped, the breath stilled in his throat.

A man and a woman sat with their heads close together in intimate conversation at a table by the street-side window. The man appeared to be in his late forties, and under a white bandage his face was deeply lined and pouchy; he looked fit enough, though, and his rumpled jacket was clearly a product of British tailoring. But it was the woman that Hale stared at—slim and still youthful-looking in spite of her salt-white hair, she was smoothing her linen skirt with one hand and tapping the ash from a cigarette with the other.

She was Elena—Elena Teresa Ceniza-Bendiga, ETC, Hale's beloved partner during the fugitive months in occupied Paris, the woman whom Claude Cassagnac had whimsically pronounced Hale's bride on a perilous night in Berlin in 1945. *Kiss the bride quick, Andrew, before you die.* Hale could taste the remembered kiss now, rusty with blood and earnest with love and the imminent prospect of merciless violent death. He ached to run between these little tables to her now, as he had done when he had first seen her on that night in Berlin, and tell her who he was, and take her hands in his and just babble out his whole truthful story to her.

But the man with her was Kim Philby. At least from across the dim room he looked no older now than he had when he had been the SIS Head of Station in Turkey in 1948—secretly in the pay of Moscow even then, it had turned out, and responsible for the betrayal of Declare. But Hale's instant memory was of his first encounter with Philby, in early 1942, when Hale had been a prisoner at the MI5 compound at Ham Common in Richmond and Philby had been trying to get custody of him, very likely in order to kill him.

Three nights ago Ishmael had asked Hale where Elena was—and she was here, with Philby, who evidently didn't know she was the one who had shot him in the head. Did Philby know the Rabkrin was looking for her? Was Mammalian aware of her, and who did *he* think she was? Again Hale wondered what he would have been told at the canceled briefing in Kuwait.

Now Philby raised his bandaged head and glanced around the bar—his gaze didn't pause on this hollow-cheeked, dark-haired figure silhouetted in the doorway—and he leaned over the table to kiss Elena on the lips. She might or might not have responded—in any case she did not push him away.

Hale let the beaded curtain swing across his view of the bar as he took a step back into the hotel lobby, bumping into Mammalian.

"I'm . . . too filthy," he said hoarsely, "for . . ."

"Well," said Mammalian in a judicious tone, "it's true, you are. You smell like an Iraqi Bedouin, my friend. I will take you to your room."

Hale let himself be led away past the couches and the registration desk toward the stairs; he didn't look back, but he felt as though this were a ghost that the Armenian was leading away, and that the real, physical Andrew Hale was still standing back there, transfixed with dismay, staring in through the bar archway.

▼

9

Berlin, 1945

It was said once to me that it is inexpedient to write the names of strangers concerned in any matter, because by the naming of names many good plans are brought to confusion.
—Rudyard Kipling, *Kim*

Hale's second encounter with Kim Philby had been in February of 1942, a month after their brief and hostile first meeting in the Latchmere House dining room at Ham Common.

Hale had been working at the SIS headquarters in Broadway Buildings in London for only three days, and he was startled to see striding toward him down the linoleum hallway the same stuttering man who had berated him on that well-remembered occasion. Philby was wearing the brown wool tunic of an Army uniform now, but without any badges of rank on the epaulettes, and he was deep in conversation with an older man in shirtsleeves.

But the intelligent eyes in the blunt face lit up on seeing Hale. "Why it's J-Jimmie's *boy!*" Philby drawled; and then in an affected, whining voice he quoted what Hale had told the interrogation panel a month earlier: " 'But I wasn't doing *anything* the Theodora person had told me to do!' " In his normal Oxbridge accent he went on, "And yet I d-discover that you are somehow working in S-Section One, on loan from Juh-Jimmie's det-te-*test*-able SOE!" He turned toward the older man beside him, whom Hale belatedly recognized as his own boss, David Footman, the head of SIS Section One. "What work is our dishonest boy here d-d-doing for you, David?"

Footman peered uncertainly at Hale. "It's 1-K, isn't it?" he said.

"Yes, sir," said Hale. 1-K was the code designation of the misplaced person whose job Hale had taken over.

"What *are* you working on, 1-K?" asked Footman.

Hale swallowed, but said levelly, "At the moment, statistics on infant death and insanity, sir, in the Kirov and Arbat districts of Moscow . . . uh, in the period from 1884 through 1890."

"Oh no, d-don't *t-tell* me, 1-K!" Philby was laughing so hard that he could barely speak. "You never n-know, I might be a sp-spy! Loose lips—sink ships, b-boy! Insane Russian in-fin-fants in the 1880s! I trust the Church"—he had to draw a hitching breath to finish the sentence—"the Churchill g-government is being advised daily of your p-progress!"

Hale's face was hot, but he nodded civilly and stepped past the two men to push open the door to the electrically lit white-tiled stairway. And as he tapped down the steps toward the third floor, he heard Philby's echoing voice say to Footman, "Do you know why the st-stairs in this place look like a p-public lavatory? Because only sh-shits ever come in here!"

Philby's laughter rang on the tile until the door clanked shut.

In fact, it was not to be until the war had been over for six weeks, and he was sent to Berlin, that Hale himself took his SIS job seriously.

Broadway Buildings was a nine-story office building at 54 Broadway, two streets south of St. James's Park and just across the street from the St. James's Park tube station. A brass plaque by the front entrance read Minimax Fire Extinguisher Company, though the only such precautions Hale noticed in the dark corridors of the place were red-painted fire buckets filled with sand and hung on hooks beside each of the frosted-glass office doors.

On Hale's first morning at Broadway, Theodora had taken him in to Footman's fourth-floor office.

"David!" Theodora had said jovially. "What vacancies have you got on the Section One staff?"

Footman had looked at Theodora and Hale with caution. "Well, 1-K never responded to the Reserve call-up."

"Then here he is at last. This is Andrew Hale, and he's on loan from the Special Operations Executive. We'll see to his pay—all you need do is tell the War Office that 1-K is onboard and has been seconded to SOE for special duties."

And so Hale had been given the identity of the missing 1-K, complete with an in-house lapel badge that gave his birth-date as having been in 1870, which would make him seventy-two years old now. The twenty-year-old Hale supposed that the real 1-K had probably died of old age.

Immediately after his release from the Ham Common compound, Hale had given Theodora a long and nearly complete account of his three months in occupied Paris—though he had found himself unable to tell the older man about things like the scorched garret floor, the quasi-voices from the radio head-phones, and the way his ankh belt had appeared to carry him across the gap between the rooftops—and he was still far too Catholic and young to tell Theodora that he had gone to bed with a Red Army agent—and now he wondered if his reticences at that interview had been noticed and had somehow led to this dead-end position.

He often had to remind himself, *We also serve who only stand and wait.*

Out in the world, the German Panzers fought their way east toward Stalingrad and the British Eighth Army defeated Rommel at El Alamein, but through some apparently random bureaucratic fiat Hale's time was spent in becoming an expert on obscure facets of late-nineteenth-century Moscow. The SIS mathematicians at Bletchley Park were rumored to have cracked a high-level German code, and the SOE cowboys were reportedly blowing up bridges in North Africa and parachuting agents into the Balkans, but the files routed to Hale's desk were all . . . treatises like "Evidences of Secret Construction in the Basement of the Anchor Insurance Company in Moscow in 1884" and "Coriolis Force Singularities: Incidence of Anomalous Rotational Meteorological Phenomena in Moscow, 1910–1930" and "Metallic Debris in Moscow Rainstorms (Spec.: Wedding Rings and Tooth-Fillings)."

Many of these files were addenda to older investigations, and in order to sign them off in good conscience Hale frequently had to locate and read as much as he could of the primary work. The SIS registry was a chaotic mess, with operational and personal files just stacked in boxes along the corridors, so he often took a car from the motor-pool garage and drove north to St. Albans, where the tidy MI5 Registry archives were kept in a Victorian mansion in King Harry Lane. To his initial surprise, his SOE/SIS credentials got him access to even the most-secret files, many of which were kept in cellophane envelopes and handled with tweezers because of having been charred in a 1940 bombing.

And for getting Russian documents translated he found himself having to consult the weird old women in the MI5 Soviet Transcription Center. This was located in another St. Albans house, in a tiny room which these fugitive White Russians had converted into a little anachronistic corner of Tsarist St. Petersburg, with carved wooden saint-icons standing among the dictaphone cylinders and acetate gramophone disks on the shelves, and a perpetual perfume of tea from the steaming samovar in the corner. To these wizened *babushkas* the NKVD was still the Cheka or even the pre-revolution Okhrana, and they took a particularly intense interest in Hale's researches, often pausing to cross themselves as they translated some musty old report of a Russian expedition to Turkey in 1883 or a description of burned grass around little coin-sized eruption holes in the grave plots of Moscow cemeteries. All of these old grandmothers were of the Russian Orthodox faith, but Hale noticed—uneasily—that their use of the term *guardian angel* was hesitant and fearful, and always accompanied by them splashing their lumpy old fingers in the holy water font by the locked door.

When carbon-copy transcripts of current SOE interrogations began to be delivered to his desk, relayed to him because of their being cross-referenced under the "Ararat" or "Lubyanka" or "Tsar Alexander III" categories, he felt that he had no honest choice but to visit the SOE establishments where the prisoners and refugees were being kept, and through translators ask the rootless foreigners about his antique concerns. The SOE had rented so many old country estates, in Buckinghamshire and Hertfordshire and Surrey, that the acronym was said to stand for "Stately 'Omes of England," and Hale became accustomed to the sight of sandbags and iron tripods on old Tudor stairways, and trestle tables and wire baskets in paneled bedrooms, and cheap colored photographs of the King on walls where pale patches indicated grander pictures recently taken away.

Most of the foreigners he questioned knew nothing relevant to his disjointed researches, and the SOE personnel were sometimes impatient with his interruptions of operational interrogations, but his credentials led them all to believe that at the very least he was compiling some sort of official history, and they were often respectful and generally civil.

Ultimately Hale did begin to suspect that there was a single story behind many of the old reports and rumors he was investigating: from Armenian fugitives he learned that an earthquake had shaken Mount Ararat in eastern Turkey in 1883 and knocked down a lot of ancient standing stones around the 17,000-foot level; Russian and Turkish scientists had visited the site, and subsequently a Russian team went to the mountain with wagons, and then went away by train to Moscow; and until the Turkish Army evacuated all the Armenians from the area in 1915, Armenian blacksmiths had hammered on their anvils every day, even on Sundays and holidays, hoping by their staccato ringing noise to keep something from descending the mountain. And from White Russians and exiled Trotskyites he heard stories about ancient carved stones set up in the deepest cellars of the Yakor or Anchor Insurance Company at Bolshaya Lubyanka 11, which in 1918 became the headquarters of the Cheka and was known and dreaded forever after as the Lubyanka.

And there were clues that seemed related, but which he couldn't connect. He was told that an effigy had been made of the tunic and death mask and plaster-cast hands of Feliks Dzerzhinsky, the first head of the Cheka, and set up in a glass coffin at the NKVD Officers' Club near Red Square; and that novice NKVD officers were required to lay flowers and wreaths before the thing in certain seasons and pray to it, and that the thing sometimes shifted its plaster hands or even spoke through the parted plaster lips in response, though not in Russian. And he learned that the ancient name of Ankara might have been a Greek word for *anchor,* and that ancient Turkish coins bore the bas-relief of an Egyptian anchor, which was a rectangle with a loop at the top; the Egyptian anchors had been carved out of stone, and one of his informants drew a picture of one for him, and even drew a cross on the rectangle, so that the resemblance to the Egyptian looped cross, the *ankh,* was obvious. And many of the Muscovite fugitives mentioned the peculiar rancid, metallic smell of Moscow air, which was attributed to cheap Soviet diesel oil.

Hale pondered the words *anchor, Ankara, Yakor, Lubyanka*—and *ankh.*

In his capacity as a special agent on loan to the SOE from Section One, he was able to ask for many categories of current files, and he pressed hard to get any information on a female GRU agent who had run a black radio network in Paris in late '41 and who might be known as Delphine St.-Simon. He learned that the French and Belgian Soviet networks, among which he and Elena had worked, had been collectively known to the Gestapo as the Rote Kapelle, which meant the Red Orchestra or the Red Chapel, and that most of the agents in it had been arrested before Christmas of '42; quite a number of them were executed very quickly, because of a German tradition that no executions occur between December 24 and January 6. The rest of the captured Rote Kapelle agents were turned to playback uses, and Hale wondered where Claude Cassagnac had wound up. Information from Moscow was harder to get, and though he read secondhand accounts of many executions in the Lubyanka cellars, none of the victims seemed to have been Elena.

In the summer of Hale's twenty-third year the London air-raid sirens seemed to wail all day and all night, punctuated by the hammering of anti-aircraft guns and the clatter of shrapnel falling in the streets and the regular window-rattling thunder of the new German buzz-bomb explosions. He slept on a cot in his office, and on many nights when sleep was impossible he would get drunk and join the midnight revelers in Green Park, and in the diffuse white searchlight glow around the army encampment known as the Bomber's Moon he would try to lead the wild spontaneous dancing into a park-spanning *clochard*-style nothing-right-here step that would shelter the whole city of London from the roaring sky. He succeeded only in exhausting himself enough to make sleep possible, and in the hungover mornings the sirens still wailed.

But across the Channel the Allies had landed on the Normandy beaches in June and liberated Paris by September, and Rome fell to the American Fifth Army, and the Russians pushed the Germans all the way back into Lithuania and Poland, and American B-29 Superfortresses were bombing Berlin. From his office window Hale could see the vapor trails of the flying bombs in the blue sky, but the lilacs and plane trees and apple trees in St. James's Park were all in vivid bloom as if it were spring instead of late summer, and all the old hands in Broadway Buildings were confident that the war would be over within six months.

Of course Hale never set foot in the senior officers' bar in the Broadway basement, where the Robber Barons drank and traded old stories and current news, but he did pick up interdepartmental gossip. In that summer he heard rumors that Colonel Felix Cowgill, the head of the counter-espionage Section Five, whose return from New York in February of 1942 had saved Hale from falling under Kim Philby's authority, might be cracking under the strain of his work. According to the office talk, Cowgill had lately summoned all his sub-section heads and told them that he had to go on another consulting mission to the the Americas—he hadn't clearly said why, only that private researches of his own made the trip imperative, and he hinted at some huge, hostile service that threatened his counter-espionage department; and he had finished with the puzzling declaration, "My own view is that it has something to do with the Arabs. Wherever I look in this case, I see Arabs!" Cowgill's mysterious overseas mission dragged on for a month and turned out to include visits to unspecified points in the Middle East—but when Cowgill finally returned in late September, he found that in his absence Kim Philby had effectively taken his job away from him: a new section, Section Nine, had been created specifically to penetrate Soviet espionage networks in the imminent postwar world, and the old Section Five was being incorporated into it, and Philby had been made Head of Section Nine. Whatever information Cowgill had found during his trip was now Philby's to deal with or dismiss.

Cowgill resigned on New Year's Day of 1945, bitterly describing the action as "a birthday present for bloody Philby." Philby had previously been working at the Ryder Street headquarters of Section Five, in the elegant neighborhood of the Boodles and Brooks's clubs just east of Green Park, but now as a section head he had a fourth-floor office in Broadway Buildings and was a constant figure in the cluttered hallways.

Hale tried to keep out of his way. Section One, where Hale toiled away in his tiny alcove, was a corridor of cramped offices on the third floor; here Footman's staff assembled summaries of current political intelligence from all the foreign stations, amplified and connected by the researches of people like Hale. Their main "customers" were "CSS & FO"—the SIS Chief and the Foreign Office—but in February Philby got the Foreign Secretary to agree to an expanded charter for Section Nine, and after that Philby too was on Section One's direct circulation list, and everyone knew that Philby's recommendations for postwar budget cuts would be respected.

C was Stuart Menzies, who was now fifty-five years old, the mandatory retirement age; but Churchill had persuaded him to stay on, and Menzies relied on the ambitious, thirty-two-year-old Philby for day-to-day in-house decisions.

Though Philby was either jovially derisive or coldly rude to Hale when they passed in the corridors, Hale discovered that the man was generally admired; he reportedly had great personal charm, and women found his stutter endearing, and he was perceived as a welcome infusion of new blood into a service that had for too long been dominated by retired policemen from the Indian Civil Service.

Hale hadn't seen Theodora nor even received any note from him in more than a year, and it seemed clear that Hale could hope for no career in an agency in which Philby was a rising power; Hale's thoughts were of postwar Oxford, and during slow afternoons he mentally phrased a letter of resignation that he planned to write when the war and the wartime draft should finally be ended.

In the gossipy corridors of Broadway, Hale was eventually able to monitor the close of the war with an intimacy that the *Times* couldn't come close to providing. He learned that the American General Eisenhower, supreme commander of the Allied Forces, was reluctant to accept anything less than an unconditional surrender from Germany, and that this delay permitted the Russians to cross the Oder River; and then Eisenhower refused to allow British forces in Hanover to move east past the Elbe, and instead let the Red Army be the power that took Berlin.

Germany finally surrendered on May 8, but Hale had known four days earlier that Hitler had committed suicide in a Berlin bunker.

The war in Europe was over, and in Broadway Buildings a festive, end-of-term mood quickened the steps and brightened the voices of the young clerks and secretaries whose lives had been interrupted by the war, and many of them were glancing through out-of-town newspapers at their desks and talking about the Autumn term at Durham or Hull or Oxford.

As it happened, though, Kim Philby had been out of the country for two months when Germany surrendered; as the new Head of Section Nine, he had been off visiting Paris and Athens and other capitals of the newly liberated countries, reestablishing the prewar alliances and the old *cordon sanitaire* against the Soviet Union. Hale postponed writing his letter of resignation, and for now simply kept reading and signing off the fifty-year-old files that were still piled on his desk every Monday.

And on the morning of June 20 he received crash-priority SOE orders to report immediately to a German city called Helmstedt, at the western end of the Helmstedt–Berlin Autobahn.

He was flown in an RAF De Havilland Mosquito to a landing strip in newly conquered Gottingen, and then spent a long afternoon riding in a train compartment with half a dozen morose and hungover American soldiers who were returning to Braunschweig from leave time spent in Paris; in the crowded Braunschweig railway station, all the windows of which had been broken out by Allied bombs, he changed to a local line that ran east, and he watched the sun go down over ruined buildings as the train crossed the Oker River on a temporary iron bridge, a stone's throw from the broken piers and twisted deck of a previous bridge.

Outside of the city limits he glimpsed German civilians in the rubbled lanes carrying big bundles of twigs in perambulators or on the backs of bicycles, and he realized that coal must be scarce—and he probed his conscience for guilt. But crowding out these immediate scenes were memories of panic in the faces of women and old men in London streets, and of feeling the same expression tightening his own eye sockets, when the throbbing motorcycle-roar of a V-2 rocket suddenly stopped—and of the subsequent ten seconds of scrambling for cover, before the air shook with shotgunning glass fragments as the almighty crack of the detonation seemed to reach right down into whatever corner he crouched in and pry the clawed hands away from his ducked head. He could still recall the chemical stink of high explosives, and the horrifying reek of living blood instantly rendered into a spray as fine as perfume out of an atomizer. And finally he took a bleak solace from the fact that he was able to discover in himself no particular satisfaction, at least, at the plight of these defeated Germans.

Like apparently all German railroad stations, the Helmstedt station platform was crowded with rootless-looking people sitting on luggage and napping or staring or listlessly eating bread; but at the back of the platform he saw the tall, thin figure of Theodora, and when the now-gray-haired man turned away and walked toward a row of cars on the pavement outside the station, Hale followed at a distance. He lost sight of the spare silhouette between a couple of buses in a row far away from the electric arc lights, and was standing uncertainly on the pavement when a Renault roadster slowed beside him and the passenger door squeaked open.

Theodora was at the wheel, and Hale climbed in and pulled the door closed.

"Ready for action at last, Andrew?" asked Theodora with fatigued cheer as he shifted up through the gears. In the headlamp beams Hale could see only rushing pavement between lightless brick buildings. "Oh good God, I say, you can drive an automobile, can't you?"

"Yes," Hale told him, hanging onto the door panel strap. "But the war's over. You must have read about it."

"The *real* war didn't start in '39, my dear, and it surely didn't end six weeks ago. Listen, the Soviets have taken a third of Germany and apparently mean to keep it. But away out in the middle of that Red sea is Berlin, moored to the rest of the free world by one long autobahn, and though the Russians have the eastern half of the city, we Brits and the Americans and the French have each got a third of the western half. Hah! God knows how long this equilibrium can be maintained—the Russians might close the highway tomorrow, except for outgoing traffic. Who'd do anything more than protest? Truman? Churchill? *Attlee?* We've got a safe house you can sleep at tonight, but tomorrow you go down the hole alone."

"Down the hole," echoed Hale, though he had already guessed what the phrase meant. For the first time since stepping into the sanctuary of the British Embassy in Lisbon three years ago, he had the sensation of having left his heart and lungs and guts somewhere behind, replaced by a durable emptiness, and his hearing and vision seemed more acute.

"Down the Helmstedt–Berlin Autobahn, a hundred and four miles to Berlin. You're a London-based scout for an American chemical fertilizers manufacturer, you see, I've got a couple of Yank government pamphlets on the subject you can swot up on. In a nutshell, the Berliners are using plain shit to fertilize their fields—all the nitrogen factories were converted to wartime use for explosives manufacture and then properly bombed. The Yanks are making some nitrate fertilizers, but they need to import ammonia from the French Zone, and coal from ours, which we haven't got any of to spare anyway. The thing is, you've got a contract with an American company in an industry the Russians need. They'll let you pass, into the American sector; we don't want to trouble our own people with this."

"This," said Hale.

"Surveying work, actually. The Soviets are going to be installing a bench mark somewhere in the city tomorrow night at midnight—June twenty-second and twenty-third, the summer solstice, when the plane of the ecliptic will be at its northernmost point for the year, and the eventual noon sun will be directly over the Jabrin oasis in Saudi Arabia. The Soviets are going to put down a sort of reference point in Berlin, a cornerstone for a wall they might build one day. It's a heavy stone, and we've tracked the lorry carrying it all the way from Moscow, and it was in Warsaw yesterday, trundling steadily west." Theodora was nodding as he stared out through the windscreen. "The Crown needs you to note with precision exactly where they plant the stone."

Hale's breath was shallow. "Is it—by any chance—a big, rough, rectangular stone, with a loop carved at one end?"

"Ah, good lad, you've done your prep this time, unlike the job with the radio magazines back in our youths. Yes, and you won't by any means be the only man in town observing this . . . undertaking. Some will be acting as security for it, some trying to impede it. You just note, and be careful not to be seen noting. When it appears to be starting up, you instantly go into total evasion procedures, am I understood?"

"Total evasion procedures when it starts up," said Hale obediently. "Understood."

The safe house was one of a row of apartments across a gravel yard from the road. The building had not been bombed, but a hole had been cut into the stucco wall to fit a stovepipe through, and when they had got inside and locked the door, Hale saw that a wood-burning stove had been moved in to replace the prewar central heating. An unshaded electric lamp threw stark shadows on the grimy white walls.

Theodora pointed at one of two cots by the boarded-over window. "That's yours. I'm turning in right now, but I'll give you your reading material and show you where the Scotch is. The alarm is set for six."

At seven the next morning, Hale sat in the driver's seat of the Renault, fluttering the throttle pedal to keep the cold engine from stalling. Two cups of hot coffee and a couple of biscuits sat heavily in his stomach, and he was acutely aware of the German automatic pistol that was fitted up among the springs of the passenger-side seat.

Theodora was leaning against the driver's-side window frame and breathing a sour smell of coffee at him. "Your passport and travel order are solid," the older man said. "You've got nothing to worry about at the checkpoints. Now on the autobahn?—remember, don't stop, and don't take any less than two hours covering the hundred miles—the guards at the first checkpoint will radio ahead, and if you go too fast you'll be in trouble. If you break down, stay by the car, and you're not allowed to go more than fifteen feet off the pavement in any case. If you haven't arrived in Berlin in four hours, I'll hear from my SHAEF chum, and I'll—send someone looking for you, if possible." The gravel crunched as Theodora stepped back. *"Gute Fahrt,"* he said dryly.

It was German for *Have a good trip.* "Oh, the same to you," said Hale, letting out the clutch and then steering the car toward the road that led to the border. The sky was blue behind the smokeless factory chimneys, with only a few clouds mounting in the east.

As Theodora had predicted, Hale had no difficulties with the border checkpoint guards. They waved him to a halt with submachine guns, but when he had got out of the car and gone into their shack, they simply wrote down his name and stamped his American travel orders. "Okay," one of them said in English, pulling the lever that lifted the bar outside.

The autobahn beyond was a wide, two-lane highway, and the cherry and pine and birch trees on either side were soon a blur of varying shades of green as Hale shifted up to the prescribed eighty kilometers per hour. Long stretches of the median between the eastbound and westbound lanes had been cemented over, but it wasn't until Hale noticed heavy black skid-marks on one stretch of it that he realized that these paved expanses had been the makeshift, last-resort airstrips of the Third Reich.

German-language signs stood on posts on the roadside shoulder and hung from the overpasses, but they all appeared to be pro-Soviet propaganda—ONE BERLIN, and AMERICANS GO HOME, and one in English: ORDER THE INVASTIGATORS OF WAR TO PUT A STOP TO!

Hear hear, thought Hale.

At the Gleinecker Bridge over the Havel, in the southwest suburbs of Berlin, he slowed for the second Soviet checkpoint and braked to a stop while two guards pointed submachine guns at the grille of his car; but the soldier in the guard shack had clearly been expecting Hale, and only glanced at his papers before waving the bar up. Nevertheless Hale felt by now like a visitor to a high-security prison, nervous about doing anything that might make it hard to get out again.

Directly ahead was a stark black-on-white sign announcing the border of the United States Sector, and it was with relief that Hale put the car into first gear and drove toward it. The American soldiers wore khaki uniforms with white helmets and belts and holsters, and one of them waved Hale to a shed like a toll booth.

"Where you headed, Mr. Conway?" he asked after looking at Hale's travel order and handing it back through the rolled-down window.

"I'm supposed to—" Hale's voice was hoarse, and he cleared his throat before trying again. "I'm supposed to meet a Hubert Flannery, of the SHAEF, at the U.S. Sector Headquarters." SHAEF was the Supreme Headquarters Allied Expeditionary Force.

"That's on the Zehlendorf, straight ahead and turn left on Onkel Tom Strasse, no joke. Don't turn right at all, and if you go more than six miles, stop, you've missed it. Don't drive around the city without looking at a map—most of the streets lead into the Soviet Sector. They're not all barricaded and patrolled, and if you drift across with any incriminating items on you, like a newspaper or money, you'll have a very bad time getting back out. Enjoy your stay."

"Jesus. You too."

Many of the brick buildings he drove slowly past were hollowed and roofless and missing walls, with stairs leading nowhere anymore and windows that opened on the sky from any angle. The center lanes of the streets were clear pavement, but where gutters and sidewalks must once have been were shoulder-high piles of broken masonry, from which old women were picking up bricks two at a time and loading them into horse-drawn wagons. Hale was careful to watch his odometer and to avoid any right turns, and he wondered if Elena, who had disappeared into the world that crowded so close here, was still alive.

Flannery was a big, red-faced man who smelled of juniper berries; and when he closed the door to his office after Hale had stepped inside, he intensified the juniper smell by pouring Gordon's gin into two fragile china teacups, one of which had not been dry.

"Drink up," he said cheerfully. "Mithridates principle, right? Accustom yourself to the poison in advance, and after that nobody can harm you with it."

Hale nodded and drank half of the cup in one gulp.

"Oh, you're bound for immortality," Flannery said. "So Jimmie says your cover is fertilizers—chemistry and agriculture. I'll make an appointment for you with Sandy Bennett, that's Sanford Bennett on our agricultural staff. He's safely out of town until after the weekend, and tomorrow I'll erase it from his calendar, but for these twenty-four hours you can mention the appointment and his secretary will back you up. Your boss was already onto her today to get some fly-spray. And say you intend to talk to Fred Cavanaugh—he's in charge of repatriation and refugees. You can claim to want to hire Displaced Persons from the *Fluchtlingstelle* refugee center at Marienfelde, it's in this sector."

"Good Lord, I don't want forced labor!"

"For the fertilizer factory you're not even going to start up, right— live your cover. It'd be seen as a mercy, though, if you wanted Soviets who've been German prisoners of war. We've been repatriating them, by force—we had a crowd of Russian soldiers who were captured by the Germans in '42, and we had to tear-gas 'em to get them into the east-bound train cars to go back home. Eleven of them actually managed to kill themselves, rather than return. I gather Moscow doesn't look kindly on Communists who've been too long in the West, even if the time was spent in prison camps."

Again Hale thought of Elena. The gin was suddenly as sour as varnish in his mouth, and he put the teacup down on the desk.

"You're going to be walking around?" asked Flannery.

Hale nodded. "I—expect so."

"Here." Flannery crossed to a closet, and after unlocking a padlock on a hasp he opened the closet door and handed Hale two cartons of Chesterfield cigarettes. "Easiest thing is don't carry money at all. A pack of cigarettes is worth, very roughly, five dollars, clean currency any-where in the city. As a favor to Jimmie Theodora, the United States will part with some smokes—but if you need actual cash, I can't requisition that. I assume you didn't bring much down the hole—but you'll get any you need from the British Sector HQ on the Kurfursten Damm, right? You've even got your boss here to authorize it."

This was the second time Flannery had referred to Hale's "boss."

Hale tried to think of a way to get Flannery to say who he was talking about, then just asked, "Who do you mean by my boss?"

"Philby, Kim Philby. Visiting SIS dignitary. He was through here today talking to our OSS brass about what's to become of Berlin."

Hale nodded, and he didn't change his expression or pause in tucking the cigarette cartons into the inside pockets of his coat. "Oh sure, the Section Nine man," he said, making sure to speak carelessly. "I'm SOE— only vaguely connected. But yes, I can touch the HQ for cash."

After thanking Flannery, and then discussing the bleak local restaurant situation for a few minutes to take the closing emphasis away from the name *Philby*, Hale walked down the stairs to the street.

Hale realized that Berlin must be the current stop on Philby's goodwill tour of liberated European capitals. But why in God's name did the man have to be in Berlin on this particular day?

Hale left the pistol under the car seat in the U.S. Sector HQ parking lot when he set out into the city's streets to reconnoiter.

For pedestrians the sector divisions of the city appeared to have little meaning—Hale saw men in Soviet uniforms mingling with American soldiers at the sidewalk tables along the Kurfursten Damm, where the only drinks available seemed to be imitation orange juice and ersatz coffee; and electric streetcars with their broken windows covered by wooden panels clattered down tracks in the center of the street, their step rails jammed with passengers whose bags and suitcases clearly marked them as fugitives from the east. Hale soon gathered that the local civilian population was sharply divided between native Berliners and "rucksack" Berliners, and the local traffic policemen—oddly medieval-looking figures in coal-scuttle hats and short-sleeved dark tunics over long-sleeved baggy white shirts—kept trying to rout the shabby immigrants away from the once-elegant café tables.

When Hale ventured to walk east—past the sawed-off tree stumps and the ruined pavilions of the Tiergarten, to the unmarked Soviet border that was understood to run down the broad lanes of the Koniggratzer Strasse—he found that the Soviet police were a good deal harsher.

He had paused on the western Koniggratzer Strasse sidewalk, drawn by the smell of grilled meat to a wood-and-canvas stand selling

Fleisch Bratwurst, and by the fact that he could pause there without being conspicuous. He gladly wasted a pack of Chesterfields on one sizzling sausage served on a cracker, and as he chewed small bites of the thing in the shadow of the waving uncooked sausages that fringed the stand's roof he squinted out at the broad street. On the far side, the south face of a modern nine-story office building curved around out of his sight as the Leipziger Strasse swung away to the north over there, and though half of the high office windows that he could see were boarded up, the shops under the awnings on the sidewalk level were bustling with shoppers.

Russian soldiers with red cap-badges and purple shoulder-boards stood out in the center of the cracked boulevard pavement, mostly clustered around an eccentrically placed tobacco kiosk that Hale thought must be a disguised guard shack, but from time to time one of them would stride out to stop some figure crossing the street. The guard would look at the hapless pedestrian's papers, while dozens of others crossed in both directions unmolested, and would then invariably nod and step back to the kiosk.

Hale was reflecting that it would be hard in this city of bomb craters to find evidence of a hole being dug for a big stone to be put into, and that he didn't have many more hours until the installation would commence—and he was considering buying another *Bratwurst*—when the *pop* of a gunshot snapped his attention back to the soldiers in the street.

A ragged man was running north, away from a dropped bag and from a soldier who was carefully aiming a handgun at him for a second shot; Hale realized that the soldier had stepped toward the west side of the street so as to be sure of firing only back into the Soviet Sector.

Another Soviet soldier was sprinting away from Hale north along the western Koniggratzer Strasse gutter, matching the fugitive's pace but apparently not trying to stop him. And then Hale noticed two other soldiers doing the same on the eastern side of the boulevard. Were they *herding* the man?

Hale followed, jogging up the western sidewalk and just keeping the fugitive and his pursuers in sight. The cigarette cartons bounced awkwardly under his coat.

With Hale trailing watchfully behind, the desperate procession moved quickly up the street, and now that the fugitive and his calmly jogging pursuers had moved north from the spot where the shot had been fired, many of the pedestrians clearly didn't even notice the several men running tensely past them through the sparse crowd. The buildings on either side of the boulevard were bizarrely scaffolded with their own ruin—exposed floors, sagging roof sections, and beams dangling on snagged cables—and Hale thought that this terrible pursuit seemed to be taking place in some stray hour after the end of the world.

The fleeing man had crossed two streets without being able to run into the western sector, and now he crossed another street and was running out across the wide square in front of the towering mottled-gray pillars of the Brandenburg Gate. Soldiers up by the Reichstag ruins on the far side appeared to be simply waiting for him, though Hale saw a jeep swerve onto the square from between two of the wide-spaced pillars to cut him off from running east. Roadblocks around a tall lorry-mounted crane blocked the man from slanting west.

Hale stamped to a halt beside a broken wall on the south side of the square and then just panted and watched the pursuit through the fringe of his disordered hair.

The fugitive out there on the broad pavement was slowed by rubble and shell-holes, and he was shouting something at his pursuers, probably surrender—but while he was still yelling, the chilly summer afternoon air shook with the bang of a rifle shot, and the man out in the middle of the square fell to one knee, silent now.

Hale felt cold air on his bared teeth, and realized that he was gritting them. He had never seen a man die, but he was suddenly sure that he was about to see it happen now. The very air seemed achingly tense, like a flexed pane of glass.

The man was half-crawling, half-hopping, back east toward the temple-like gate—until another rifle shot rang out, and a plume of dust sprang from the pavement in front of him; he began struggling away north, and then for several long seconds his tiny figure, dwarfed by the hulk of the Reichstag and the battered gray Brandenburg Gate columns, was the only moving thing in the gray stone world.

The distant toiling figure stopped at the broken edge of a wide shell-crater, perhaps considering hiding in it; but another shot hammered the air and he collapsed at the edge.

One of the soldiers now strode out across the square to the still-feebly-moving form, and with a handgun, carefully, fired one last shot. The figure on the ground was still.

Hale was acutely aware that there was one person less in the square now, and he thought of the Donne line, *Every man's death diminishes me*—but the thought finished with the unwilled phrase, *except when it enhances me;* and for just a moment Hale was seeing a double exposure as he stared at the pillars of the Brandenburg Gate: he was seeing the gate from where he stood, nearly end-on and not able to see between the pillars, and at the same time he was seeing it from a perspective that allowed him to look through the pillars and down the Unter den Linden boulevard on the eastern side.

Hale's forehead was suddenly damp. The intrusive thought and the apparent dislocation reminded him of the night when Elena and he had inadvertently walked to the end of the Île de la Cité, in Paris. He leaned against the broken stone wall now and rubbed his eyes until rainbows churned across his retinas, and when he blinked out at the pillars again, he was seeing them properly overlapped and receding in perspective. The storm clouds in the east had moved in to cover half the sky. A breeze sighed across the square, and Hale exhaled sharply at the oily metallic smell on it.

A couple of old men in homburg hats had shuffled up to the wall beside which Hale stood, and one of them now said sympathetically to him, in German, "Soviet diesel oil, that smell is." Hale saw that he was wearing a necktie and a high, threadbare collar under his overcoat, and he knew that these must be native Berliners.

The other old man was staring out at the square. "Easy enough to bury that Slav—push him into that hole he's on the edge of." He snickered. "You could bury the Russian bear in that hole."

His companion pointed at the crane on the western side of the square. "And there's a crane to hoist the bear in with."

"Easier to just shoot a dozen or so more immigrants," said the first man, "and pile them in. Pave right over them." He smiled at Hale. "Right?"

But Hale had had enough of Germans and Russians. He simply shook his head and blundered away, back toward the Western sectors.

By the end of the day Hale had seen actual excavations going on in only two places.

One was in the Soviet Sector. Before crossing the momentous lanes of the Koniggratzer Strasse he had nervously checked his pockets several times to make sure that he carried no money at all, but in fact the Soviet soldiers had not stopped him as he walked across; and at the end of a ruined block in that sector he had found Russian workmen digging a hole in front the shell-pocked neoclassical façade of what must have been a government building. Hale blinked curiously up at the four floors of glassless windows, and then noticed a tall, scarred brass plaque on the inset wall at the top of the steps—on it, below an eagle-and-swastika bas-relief, were the raised letters PRASIDIALKANZLE DES FÜHRERS UND REICHSKANZLERS. This gutted ruin was Hitler's Chancellery.

No Soviet soldiers were in evidence, and dozens of people were wandering in and out of the doorless Chancellery portal and leaning out of the gaping upstairs windows to shout to companions, or crossing the sidewalk to climb up on the black cement roof of what Hale gathered was the very bunker where Hitler had reportedly killed himself less than two months earlier. Among the spectators, "rucksack" and native Berliners mingled with foreign soldiers and civilians who might have been foreign press correspondents.

The workmen had broken away the pavement and were spading up gravelly dirt at a spot halfway between the Chancellery steps and the bunker, and one of the native Berliners placidly told Hale that it was on that spot that the bodies of Hitler and Eva Braun had been burned.

A slim, dark-eyed Arab-looking woman in a black sari appeared at first to be listening intently to the dignified old German, but when she caught Hale's glance she made a clicking sound with her tongue and rocked her head toward the dark Chancellery doorway—and the breath stopped in Hale's throat, for in that instant the motion had seemed to be an explicit sexual invitation. But the echoing halls of the building were full of sightseers, and Hale assured himself that he must have misread her gesture.

He had glanced away from her, awkwardly—and when after a few moments of listening to the old man's droning he furtively looked at her again, she was still staring hungrily at him, and fingering her necklace. Hale stared at the necklace instead of into her eyes, and he registered the fact that the it was a string of dozens or even hundreds of gold rings.

He stumbled away from the crowd without speaking or looking at her again, back down the rubbled streets toward the American Sector, feeling tiny under the vast gray sky. And when he had got to the Konig-gratzer Strasse and had strode halfway across the four broad lanes, two of the Soviet soldiers blocked his way and stopped him. They squinted hard at his passport and searched his pockets and even smelled his breath, as though suspecting that he might be drunk—but after they had grudgingly let him proceed to the western side he still felt trapped, and he kept remembering having glanced back at the dark woman, after having walked a good fifty paces up the street away from the bunker and the Chancellery and the morbid crowd: she had been staring after him, and she must even have followed him at least a little way, for she had appeared to be bigger, taller, than the other people back there.

The other digging site was in the French Sector, under the Column of Victory, which had been erected to commemorate the German invasion of France in 1871 and now served as an ornate flagpole for the tricolor French flag. French soldiers with pickaxes and shovels were ostensibly trying to get at the water mains. Several Red Army soldiers were observing the work, but they certainly weren't advising.

There might well have been other excavations going on, but Hale saw no signs of any. The rubble-choked streets to the south were as empty of life as some Roman ruin, the only signs of recent human habitation being graffiti: KAPITULIEREN? NEIN! in red paint on a bullet-pocked wall, and chalked names and destinations and messages left on the entries of bombed apartment buildings; below some of the chalked family names he saw the underlined scrawl LEBEN ALLE, meaning that all had survived, but he saw many repetitions of the single word TOT, dead.

Hale suspected that the excavation by Hitler's bunker was where the Russians were planning to install the stone, and he was dreading the thought of crossing back into the Soviet Sector late at night; but he trudged back to the fenced-in U.S. Sector HQ parking lot and showed the guard his travel order. When the guard had waved him in, Hale walked slowly down the rows of cars to Theodora's Renault and unlocked it—and after tucking one of the cigarette cartons under the driver's seat, he unclipped the holstered German pistol from under the passenger seat and with shaking hands shoved it into his coat pocket. He clamped his elbow against his ribs to keep that side of his jacket from swinging too heavily when he walked back out of the parking lot past the American guard.

The gray sky was darkening over the rim of the Olympic Stadium to the west, and he decided to find a restaurant so that he could put some decent food down on top of the *Bratwurst* that still burned in his stomach, and blunt the ringing edge of his nerves with a bit of strong drink.

Flannery had recommended several places to eat at in the Kurfursten Damm, but had added that they were generally frequented by American and British officers; but he had also mentioned what he called "a humble *imbiss*" on the banks of the Spree River at the eastern point of the British Sector, by the skeletal dome of the burned-out Reichstag; he had said it was a smoky little hole, and drafty in spite of the boards over the windows, but that one could get real liquor and generally some decent sort of *Happenpappen* there.

It proved to be in an old three-story stone building with rows of square windows that reminded Hale of the Bodleian Library at Oxford; but the windows at the end closest to the Reichstag hulk were black holes, and, at the nearer end, the light from the restaurant was visible from the street only as yellow streaks glowing between mis-matched boards. Hale hesitated on the chipped stone steps—the memory of the man being shot below the Brandenburg Gate this afternoon was still recent and vivid enough to twist his stomach—and just the smell of cooking onions on the cold breeze might not have decided him; but then he heard a pattering in the dark street, and felt the chill of a raindrop on his hand, and he tapped up the last two steps and pushed the door open.

Warm air redolent of sauerkraut and roasted pork stung his chilled cheeks and twitched at his hair, and a radio was playing a nostalgic melody from the *Polivtsian Dances*, and with a self-conscious smirk of surrender he stepped forward into the smoky hall.

By the light of candles in glass jars, he dimly saw a dozen diners seated at long tables below walls and arches of rough stone, and when a man's face was lit in laughter at one of the far tables Hale shivered with something like vertigo, for he was certain that he had seen this man before, in this very place—then a moment later he recognized him, and realized that it had been in a candlelit basement in Paris that he had met him, nearly four years ago. This was . . . Claude Cassagnac, his hair perhaps more silvery than brown now, his youthfully animated old face unchanged.

Cassagnac had been one of the Rote Kapelle agents then, in '41— and he might be in Berlin tonight to participate in the installing of the stone. The street door had closed behind Hale, and he had turned to open it again and leave, when he heard a woman's voice, speaking French words loudly enough to be heard over Cassagnac's laughter.

Hale didn't catch the words, but the voice vibrated in his chest like an electric shock. It was Elena's.

With no memory of having crossed the stone floor, he was standing over their table. In the amber candlelight the creases under Elena's eyes were more visible, and Hale could see faint lines down her cheeks, but her angular face had not aged.

Her hair, though, was now as white as salt.

Moscow doesn't look kindly on Communists who have been too long in the West . . .

But here she was, vividly not killed after all, and not more than a hundred yards west of the Soviet Sector line. Was she still working as a Communist agent?

Cassagnac was holding a smoldering cigarette in his left hand and looking up at Hale with polite inquiry, but he had pushed his chair back and his right hand hung loose by his side. Elena had darted her hand into her purse and then given Hale a blank look—which an instant later tensed into narrowed eyes and flexed jaw muscles.

"Elena," Hale gasped, "I—"

"You have mistaken the lady for someone else, my friend," said Cassagnac coldly in French. He took a drag on the cigarette and then said through exhaled smoke, "This woman is my wife, not your—Elena? Go away now." Without looking at her, Cassagnac clearly conveyed that it was her turn to say the same.

But she said, "Marcel!" in a wondering tone, and Cassagnac shrugged and rolled his eyes as he waved toward the bench on the other side of the table.

"I meant to say," he sighed, "do sit down, my friend."

Hale yanked back the bench and collapsed onto it, never taking his eyes off of Elena. "I," he said helplessly in French, "have thought about you—I've tried to find you—"

"Bon Dieu," said Cassagnac softly, "it is the English boy, Lot." At least he pronounced the *t* this time. "Listen to me, boy—she and I are in Berlin with the French forces. We assume—"

"Ahh!" exclaimed Hale. "Good, good." He hoped Cassagnac was telling the truth and that Elena had freed herself from Moscow.

Cassagnac lifted an eyebrow. "We're pleased that you approve. *And* we assume that you are here with the British. We do not need to have this assumption confirmed, and I'm confident that none of us would be so *gauche* as to discuss our histories or present tasks with one another. The past is past. You will have one drink with us, and then you will go away we know not where. You have seen that the lady is well; surely that has been your main concern, and now you can be relieved on that score." Cassagnac waved toward the brighter-lit arch from which the aromatic smoke was billowing. "What will you have to drink?" When Hale didn't answer, Cassagnac said to the aproned old waiter who shambled up to the table, "*Eine Berliner Weisse mit Schuss, bitte.*"

Hale realized that he could not ask Elena any of the questions that were clamoring in his head, nor explain anything to her, and so he just smiled at her and took hold of her free hand in both of his. Her hand was cold.

"No, Marcel," she said firmly, pulling her hand free. "Now is now."

Hale closed his hands in loose fists. "You are married to him?"

"*Oui,*" she said, and to Hale the unconsonanted syllable had the finality of an echoing gunshot.

Hale's drink was clanked down on the table then, and he glanced at the glass mug, then looked at it for several seconds. It appeared to contain pink beer. He sighed, and then turned to Cassagnac and made the effort to lift his eyebrows.

"Weak beer with raspberry syrup," Cassagnac explained.

Hale nodded, comprehending that he had been given a child's drink. For a moment he was tempted to speak the old code phrase, "Bless me!"—*Things are not what they seem—trust me*—just to let Elena know that he was in Berlin on covert SIS business; but a moment later he felt himself blushing, for he recognized this impulse as just a vindication of the spirit in which he'd been given the drink.

On the table in front of Elena stood a smaller glass of some brown liquor, and he humbly reached across and picked it up. "I want to drink to your—happiness," he said, "and not with weak beer. May you—be always contented and often joyful—*bueno ano, multos buenos anos*—and may you never forget one who has loved you."

He took a sip of what proved to be brandy and set the glass back down softly. Then he picked up his mug and swallowed a mouthful of the pink beer—and it was not bad.

"Thank you," said Elena in a level voice, but Hale saw her blink several times. From the tinny radio speakers on the other side of the room skirled a serpentine violin melody from Rimsky-Korsakov's *Scheherazade*.

And Hale remembered the night in Paris when their radio had roared with inorganic chanting, and the garret floor had been scorched by the focus of some terrible attention; afterward Elena had said, *Once I would have prayed,* and then had quoted a line of verse in English; and now the verse came back to him, and he recalled that it was from Francis Thompson's "The Hound of Heaven."

"*Across the margent of the world I fled,*" he recited now, almost idly, since nothing he said could matter anymore here,

> *And troubled the gold gateways of the stars,*
> *Fretted to dulcet jars*
> *And silvern chatter the pale ports o' the moon . . .*

Elena frowned deeply, but nodded, and in a whisper recited the next line—"*I said to Dawn: be sudden—to Eve: be soon . . .*"

"Finish your drink, young man," said Cassagnac, briskly tapping ash from his cigarette, "the hour grows late, and—"

A rich, plummy voice interrupted from behind Hale, in English: "Those sh-*shoes* I left out this afternoon weren't c-c-cleaned," said Kim Philby's well-remembered voice, "and yet I find you here d-*drinking,* Andrew?"

Hale was jolted by the bench being pulled out, and then Kim Philby had sat down heavily beside him, smelling of tobacco and whisky and some British after-shave lotion, and crinkling his eyes and showing his teeth in a smile.

Philby's gaze fell on the mug of pink beer. "And what *are* you d-drinking, Andrew?" He picked it up in one brown hand and sniffed it. "Is this s-some *boche* digestive aid? Have you got an upset st-*stomach,* my boy?"

Cassagnac leaned forward and tossed his cigarette butt under Philby's nose into the pink beer. "It was someone else's," he said in a bored tone. The waiter had walked up at Philby's arrival, and now Cassagnac said to him in German, "Where is the brandy our friend ordered?" as he pointed at Hale. Turning to Philby, he added, "And for you, sir?"

"A brandy as well. N-no, *two* glasses of b-brandy for me." He squinted speculatively at Hale. "You can't have flown here," he said. "It was hard enough for *me* to get a f-flight into the Gatow airport, with our Soviet allies l-laying claim to all altitudes and all directions and all ow-hours for their own scanty flights. Did you d-drive down the hole? Is this more of J-Jimmie's n-n-nonsense?" Less jovially, he asked, "What is the name and number of your passport here?"

"The *name* on it?" asked Hale, certain that Theodora would not want Philby to know about the Conway identity. "My *own* name." He tried to return Philby's gaze as if he were expecting, instead of fearing, some further question.

"We have thought it best," said Cassagnac, "not to discuss our jobs."

Philby frowned at Hale for another moment, then turned to Cassagnac with a smile. "Oh, that's all right, Andrew here is just a j-junior f-fetch-and-c-c—*errand-boy,* in my firm. A c-custodian, actually." Then Philby glanced back at Hale with mock concern and smacked his forehead. "Oh, I say, *I'm* sorry—you've probably been h-hinting to your friends about b-big secret g-government work! I should have considered your—your fragile young man's pride."

Hale took a deep breath, then just leaned back and smiled tiredly at Philby. "I'll thank you to leave my fragile young man out of this."

Cassagnac laughed. "Doubtless he has no pride," he said.

Philby's gaze fixed on the old Frenchman. "I'm Kim," he said, reaching across the table to shake hands. "And you are . . . ?"

"Louis Pasteur," said Cassagnac, smiling.

Philby nodded ponderously and swung his face toward Elena, opening his mouth as if to say something more in the same bantering tone; but then he just exhaled, frowning with what seemed to be surprised and tentative recognition. After two full seconds of staring at her, he closed his mouth, then looked away from her and said to Cassagnac, "And th-this lovely g-girl—is she your w-wife, Mr. Pasteur?"

"Bless me, no!" said Elena suddenly. "Actually I am *not* married. My name is . . . Marie Curie."

The waiter walked up then with a tray and set one glass in front of Hale and two in front of Philby—who emptied one of the glasses in a single gulp.

Hale's breathing had suddenly gone shallow and a smile was tugging at his lips, and in his head her words were still echoing: *Bless me, no! Actually I am not married.*

But Philby was still frowning at Elena, and now he said to her, abruptly, "Nineteen-forty . . . *one!* New Year's Eve. I d-do remember you—viv-viva-*vividly.*" He smiled, then went on quickly, "Who were you with, on that night?"

Hale's face tingled in sudden alarm, and he concentrated on taking hold of his brandy glass, and lifting it to his lips, and *not* glancing at Elena. New Year's Eve of '41 had been their last night together in Paris, the night he had thought of ever since as their wedding night. What intelligence sources did horrible old Philby have access to? Had *he* somehow been in Paris then?

Hale heard Elena's breezy reply: "On New Year's Eve?—I am sure I was with some handsome young man."

Peripherally Hale could see Philby nod and turn toward him; but the choppy murmur of conversation in the long room was muted then by the sudden roar of rain falling outside the building, and Hale saw dark lines of water begin to streak the boards across the glassless windows.

Philby shifted on the bench to look toward the leaking windows, and Hale heard him mutter, "Constant to the old covenant." Philby glanced back and smiled faintly as he met Hale's startled gaze. "St. Paul's epistle to the Crustaceans," he said lightly. From his pocket Philby took a corked bottle of some clear fluid, and then he popped it open and poured the liquid into the brandy glass he'd emptied. Hale caught a whiff of something like turpentine and ether. "Flit," Philby said. "A sample of bug killer, fr-from our American c-cousins."

Other diners in the room had turned to look at the rain-streaked boards over the windows, and now an unshaven man in a baggy old business suit came shuffling diffidently up to the table. In German he said, "Rain washes away blood."

Philby frowned at him, and answered in English. "You wish it were so, *mein H-Herr Schimpf.* I've t-told you before to s-sell your f-f-filthy old secrets to the Om-Om-Americans." He pointed sharply to the street door, and the man shambled away in evident confusion.

Hale knew that *schimpf* meant disgrace or insult, and he was intrigued to see a dew of sweat on Philby's forehead.

"The city's f-full of ex-Abwehr who've t-turned into freelance intelligence agents," said Philby to the table in general, "and the American Counter-Intelligence Corps and OSS are p-paying them; the British s-simply arrest them. Creatures like that f-fellow will sell you a Soviet code book on Monday, and then c-come back on Wednesday to sell you the news that the relevant coded traffic will be all d-deception now, since on Tuesday he sold word of the original tr-transaction to the Russians; and then on Thursday he'll go b-back to the Russians again." He scowled in the direction the diffident man had taken. "It's a g-g-good way to achieve abrupt, total retirement at the hands of some double-crossed g-government agency. 'There is truth to be found on the unknown shore, and many will find what few would seek.' " With that he snatched up a glass and drained it—and then grimaced and spat, for it had been the glass of insecticide.

"Hah!" he coughed. "*That* wasn't brandy!" He blinked through watering eyes at Hale. "Better than the l-local g-g-gin, at least, hey?"

"I—haven't tried the local gin," said Hale blankly, wondering if Philby had seriously poisoned himself just now. He looked at Elena and Cassagnac, and they were both staring at Philby in moderate alarm. "I guess I won't," Hale added, just to be saying something. But Philby's action had reminded him of something from his Section One archival researches, and he wanted to get away from the man's physical presence for a moment, away from the intrusive insecticide smell, and pin down the memory. Hale sneaked a glance at his wristwatch below the table edge; it was nearly ten o'clock. "How does one get food here?" he asked.

"There is a table by the kitchen wall," spoke up Elena in French, "and they will serve you a plate of potato pancakes or lung hash or Sturdy Max."

"Sturdy Max sounds good," said Hale, who didn't know what it might be. He stood up and walked through the tobacco and cooking smoke toward the indicated far table, where two big moustached men were stirring pots and clanking ladles on plates; and he wondered if he were drunk, for he felt an almost centrifugal resistance to progress away from the table, as if he were walking uphill.

Intrusive. That was it—six months ago Hale had been reading a file of brittle 1916 Secret Service telegrams from the Arab Bureau in Cairo, whose telegraphic addresss had been INTRUSIVE CAIRO; the group had included Gertrude Bell and the young T. E. Lawrence, and Hale had read about a controversial initiation ritual which had consisted of drinking a half-and-half shot of gin and insecticide, a concoction they had reportedly referred to as "Gin, Repellent."

Hale stumbled up to the serving table and blinked at the pots and platters laid out on it. Sturdy Max appeared to be ham and eggs on black bread, and he was about to ask for some—

—But at that moment the music on the radio was drowned out in a sudden barrage of static, and for a moment Hale thought lightning must have struck somewhere nearby; then the roar of the static began to flail itself into a wild drop-and-double-beat momentum, an articulated cacophony that was tantalizingly *almost* a coherent rhythm. As in that Paris garret nearly four years ago, the effect of drumming and chanting seemed totally free of any organic or rational source, but it was nevertheless urgent, and quickened with an "emotion" at once so alien and so strong that it could only be comprehended, inadequately, as rage.

Rain washes away blood.

True enough, Hale thought dizzily. This downpour will soon disperse the blood of that man who was shot by the Brandenburg Gate.

The Russian soldiers seemed to *herd* the fugitive to that spot, before killing him. And there was a crane nearby, useful for lifting a large stone. This is early, two hours ahead of schedule—but so were the flights Elena caught in Paris and Lisbon, three and a half years ago.

It's at the Brandenburg Gate, he thought with sudden total certainty, and it's right now.

When it appears to be starting up, you instantly go into total evasion procedures, am I understood?

Hale glanced back at the table, trying to catch Elena's gaze. But I can't just disappear *now*, he thought desperately. If I leave right now, when will I ever see her again?

But even if I go back to the table, when will I ever see her again?

. . . the king's men. They deserve our obedience.

. . . working for the Crown.

And too he felt again the vertiginous temptation he had felt in that Paris garret, the fascination that he imagined had led Adam and Eve to eat the fruit of the Tree of Knowledge of Good and Evil.

. . . and I hid myself.

He walked around behind the serving table, and then sidestepped through the arch into the kitchen.

He hurried past the busy cooks and the flaring stoves to a door in the back, and when he had pushed it open and stepped out into the darkness, he was in the cold rain, on a porch railed with broken iron posts. He skipped down the steps to the lightless street pavement, and then sprinted away south, toward the lacy Reichstag dome that showed in lines of darker black against the black sky, and toward the Brandenburg Gate beyond.

It was a night for irrational speculation, and fleetingly he wondered if Elena had caught his image in her old broken pocket mirror, so that as he now ran away from her toward a bloody hole in the Berlin pavement, a semblance of himself might still be sitting at the table, laughing and looking into her eyes.

▼

10

Berlin, 1945

A specter is haunting Europe—the specter of communism.
    —Karl Marx, *The Communist Manifesto*

The Reichstag had been the German Parliament building until it burned in 1933—in Broadway Hale had been assured that Goebbels had organized the arson in order to blame it on Communists—and until recently its ruined profile must have been a grotesque flaw in the stately Berlin skyline. Now the rest of the city had caught up to it. And Hale, having walked away from Elena, running now across dark squares in the rain with a gun bouncing in his pocket, had the uneasy feeling that he was on his way to catching up to it as well.

Big trucks were moving in the rain on the east side of the towering Brandenburg Gate, their glaring headlamps throwing brief sequential flashes between the pillars to the western side, and in the darkness at the southwest corner of the square Hale could hear the thudding of a big piston engine. The expanse of pavement on this side of the pillars glittered with rain splashes in the sweeps of headlamp glow, and Hale could clearly see the patch of darkness out in the middle of it that was the crater where the man had been killed this afternoon.

He could also see, spaced around this western perimeter of the square, the hooded silhouettes of soldiers carrying rifles—he counted four such figures, then saw four more, and concluded nervously that there were simply *very many* of them.

With his collar up and his head down, Hale hurried diagonally away from the broad square. He strode south across the lanes of the Charlottenburger Chaussee to the curb a good hundred yards within the British

Sector, and then he walked still further south, down the Sieges Alee, the old Avenue of Victory, below the stone statues of long-dead German kings. Several times he doubled back briefly in his course, but he saw no figures behind him at all. His plan was to walk back up the western sidewalk of the Koniggratzer Strasse to the broken wall from which he had watched the man killed—from that point he should be able to get bearings on landmarks so as to fix the hole's precise location later.

The *Bratwurst* stand was closed now, the fringe of uncooked sausages taken down from the dripping wooden roof, but Hale saw the falling rain glitter in yellow electric light around a high scaffold on the western side of the Potsdamer Platz square, and when he walked out to the curb and looked back he saw that the British had erected a huge sign across which thousands of light bulbs spelled out current news headlines for the benefit of the Berliners in the darkness of the Soviet Sector; before striding north up the splashing sidewalk, away from the lights, Hale read that Australian troops had captured Brunei Bay in Borneo from the Japanese.

The thighs of his trousers and the front of his shirt were soaked, and his shoes were sloshing with cold water, when he came crouching up to the broken wall. He was well south of the trucks and any evident soldiers, but his view of the expansive square was fine—in the shadows ahead of him to his left he could dimly see men climbing on the idling crane lorry, and he could even see the smoke from the lorry's throbbing exhaust—and since he was now seeing the Brandenburg Gate almost end-on, he could clearly make out the lorries on the eastern side through the waving veils of rain.

One was a big American flatbed truck, and Hale was bewildered to see that it had a boat braced up on the bed of it, an Arabic-looking vessel with an extended tapering stempost that projected over the truck cab, and a long, downward-curved yard moored to the mast.

The sheer *inappropriateness* of the thing, here, frightened him. Hale's breathing was quick and shallow, and he was glad of the low clouds that hid the stars; his chest went abruptly cold when he caught a gleam far up in the air over the stone horses on the high pediment of the gate, and he only relaxed a little when he realized that it was a low-hanging weather balloon, perhaps tethered to the boat.

His thoughts were of the stones, the *anchor* stones, that had been taken from Mount Ararat to Moscow in 1883 and set up in the Lubyanka basement—big rectangular stones with rings carved at the top—and he remembered the Trotskyite fugitive in Surrey who had drawn a picture of one for him and had drawn a cross on the rectangle to emphasize the fact that the thing was a form of the Egyptian *ankh*.

Hale gasped and his hand darted into his pocket to touch the gun when he glimpsed movement not far away to his right, to the east—but it was two figures over on the far side of the Koniggratzer Strasse, in the Soviet Sector, hunching north, away from him, through an unlit bombed lot. As he exhaled his indrawn breath and slowly let his fingers unclamp from the gun's grip, he watched them appear and disappear against the more distant lights, darting from one low section of broken masonry to another, and he wondered who on earth they could be, and what their purpose was in being here.

Hale heard the rain getting suddenly louder to the east, and so he was braced against the wall when the gust struck—and then he turned his face to the bricks, away from the stinging drops that were flying at him almost horizontally.

The wall moved against his hands, and his first thought was that a truck had coasted silently up from the other side and struck it; then his feet slid out from under him on the wet pavement and he was kneeling, and the pavement was rocking.

This was an earthquake, though he had never heard of an earthquake in Berlin. And only belatedly did he realize that the rain was warm, and that the wind that flung it was sour with a metallic, oily smell. In a moment the ground had steadied, and he was able to get back up on his feet in the darkness.

When he raised his head and squinted at the trucks on the east side of the pillars, something tall and blurry was moving now in the air over the boat, where the balloon had been—it was a whirlwind, a glittering black funnel of rain-haze that swayed and flexed like a reared cobra. And with a sinking heart he remembered one of the reports he had read in Broadway, "Coriolis Force Singularities: Incidence of Anomalous Rotational Meteorological Phenomena in Moscow, 1910–1930."

It's over there— The thought was a panicky wail in his head. *I've got to go over there.*

Before he could think about it, before he might remember the terror of his New Year's dreams, he pushed away from the wall and ran heavily against the battering warm wind that flipped his coat-tails up behind him, across the four broad, empty lanes to the Soviet side of the boulevard.

In a shadowy doorway he leaned against a wall and tugged the pistol out of his pocket. Theodora had said it was a captured German gun, a Walther P-38, with eight 9-millimeter rounds in the magazine and one in the chamber. Hale had read the circulars on it, and knew that the first shot would be a long double-action pull on the trigger, lifting and dropping the hammer, but the remaining eight shots would be single-action, with each brief trigger-pull simply dropping the recoil-cocked hammer.

He shoved it back into his soggy pocket, numbly wondering if he would be able to fire a quarter-ounce leaden slug, moving at the speed of 1150 feet per second, into a living man's body. Perhaps soon he would know—to his cost, surely, either way.

The two figures he had glimpsed on this side of the road a minute ago had seemed to move with furtive assurance, so when he stepped out of the doorway he strode to the lot they had crossed.

In moving north after them he imitated their approach and darted from one patch of masonry shadow to the next, pausing before each new shift of position to glance behind him and to the sides—as well as straight ahead, where a couple of hundred feet away the tall whirlwind still spun and glittered in the refracting headlamp beams. As he watched, the boat's long yardarm broke free of the mast and cartwheeled away into the darkness.

Perhaps the Russians had big radio speakers up there on the Unter den Linden pavement—for even above the whistle-chorus of the wind he could hear the pounding chant of *les parasites*. He did at least feel anonymous out here in the rubbled, gravelly dark—there was no sensation of big *attention* being paid to him.

He hurried to a fallen pillar, and peered over it—and then didn't move, for the two figures he had been following were crouched behind a broken wall just twenty feet in front of him. Keeping his white face down in the shadows, he looked left and right, and to his left he saw the tall crane swaying against the dark sky as its platform rolled slowly northeast, toward the gate from the western side. The warm rain tasted oily and salty in Hale's open, panting mouth.

Hale was having trouble focusing his eyes on the twisting rain funnel over the boat. The space it occupied in the perceived landscape didn't change, but at one moment it seemed to be rushing directly away from him and increasing in size, and at the next seemed to be shrinking rapidly and flying straight into his eyes.

And the inorganic articulated roaring was clearly coming from *it*. Its sinuous form curled in the rainy air, and he found himself momentarily seeing vast shoulders, or an outcropping hip, or long flowing hair, in its contours. The noise it made was like the throbbing of a bomber's engines now, but Hale was unhappily sure that it was forming the syllables of some language—and though it was made of nothing but wind and water and smoke, he was sure it was female.

You were born to this, Elena had told him in Paris.

The truck carrying the boat shuddered visibly as it was shifted into gear, and then it was rolling slowly west toward the Brandenburg Gate as if to meet the crane there, and the ever-more-solid-looking whirlwind moved with it like a living tower; another flatbed lorry accelerated up from the south to pace it, and on the bed of this one Hale could see a gray rectangle with a bump on the top that might have been a loop.

The *parasites* roar was recognizably musical now, though conforming to no human scale, and Hale's first thought was a paraphrase from the King James Book of Job: *When the midnight comets sang together.*

The clouds overhead flickered with interference fringes, illusionary flashes of red and gold in the moiré patterns where the whirlwind's veils and tresses overlapped and seemed even to brush the contours of the underlit clouds—Hale's thoughts fragmented into conflicting moods and half-phrases and one alien but complete sentence: *Zat al-Dawahi, Mistress of Misfortunes, look favorably upon our sacrifice!*—and then one of the figures twenty feet in front of Hale stood up from a crouch and aimed some sort of handgun up at the churning column of storm. Hale fell back into the shadow of his own concealment, horrified that this person was about to draw attention to this area.

Bang. Hale saw a reflected flashbulb wink of muzzle flash, and then the ringing night seemed to erupt in shouts and thudding boots. He crouched lower behind the broken pillar, not even breathing at all, his hand gripping the pistol in his pocket.

He heard scuffling, and then he heard a woman's voice cry out in angry pain—and he stood up, for the voice was Elena's.

Figures were struggling against the broken wall, but closer to him two Russian soldiers had wrestled someone to the pavement, and Hale saw that they were trying to pry a gun from a woman's clenched hand; and it seemed to Hale that the woman was trying desperately hard to turn the gun on herself rather than toward the soldiers.

Kill herself, flashed a horrified thought through Hale's mind, sooner than go back to Moscow.

"Elena!" he screamed as he yanked the Walther out of his pocket and pointed the muzzle at the broad back of the closest soldier, *"wait!"*

The other soldier hitched around toward Hale, reaching for a holster, and Hale swung the muzzle toward him and pulled the resistant trigger.

The hard *pop!* of the gunshot battered his ears and the muzzle flash dazzled him, but Hale simply crouched to make sure of not hitting Elena and then blindly fired another shot, upward toward the man wrestling over her.

He could see past the flash-glare in his retinas now, and he raised the barrel of his pistol as Elena rolled to her feet and fired her own gun once at the man Hale had just shot at, and then a second time toward the figures rolling along the irregular wall.

Another gunshot flared and cracked close at hand, and then through the ringing in his ears Hale heard Cassagnac's voice: "Is it Lot? We must run north, look."

Cassagnac nodded behind, toward the hollowed buildings to the south, and when Hale looked back that way he saw silhouettes with rifles jogging this way.

Elena grabbed Hale's arm and yanked him forward, after Cassagnac, and then the three of them were simply running north across the shadowed, rubbled lot, hopping over chunks of stone and skidding in puddles. Hale glimpsed her face under the flying white hair—dark blood slicked her mouth, but her teeth were bared in what might have been at least partly a desperate grin.

The lorry with the gray rectangular stone in the bed of it had sped up, and now rocked to a halt right next to the Brandenburg Gate columns on the eastern side; and on the western side the crane had been driven up to within a hundred feet of it. Through the hot rain Hale could see men carrying the end of a cable east between the columns.

Hale saw a man briefly tumble through the air as the roaring whirlwind moved out across the pavement away from the boat, toward the gate; its droning inhuman syllables shook the air and seemed to rattle Hale's teeth even at this fifty yards' distance, and bits of stone were falling from the gate's high pediment.

Though Hale and his companions were being pursued from the south, none of the Soviet soldiers around the lorries appeared to have noticed the intrusion yet—their attention was doubtless focused on the stone and the crane and the living tornado, and certainly radios wouldn't work correctly on this night.

But a jeep at the west end of the square had started forward, and though it halted at the edge of the lot, the driver was backing and filling to keep the headlamp beams on the three fugitives who were running toward the Unter den Linden pavement and the Arab boat, and Hale could hear the jeep's horn honking out the old Rote Kapelle radio code for *danger, danger.*

And now to the east he saw headlamps moving north along the boulevard that passed Hitler's Chancellery; and from somewhere out there a searchlight beam swept the lot in a moving fan of long black shadows on white-lit pavement, and after passing Hale and his companions once, it swung back and fixed on them.

Cassagnac hopped and skidded to a halt, crouching, and Hale and Elena stopped beside him and stood bent forward with their hands on their knees. They were within sprinting distance of the north edge of the lot now, with the gleaming lanes of Unter den Linden beyond.

Cassagnac's wet face seemed to have been carved out of granite in the harsh white light. "They," he panted, "won't shoot—into the Western sectors. But the soldiers—will be here—in moments. You," he said to Hale, "can surrender. Elena and I—must not be captured."

Hale permitted himself a glance at Elena. Under the sopping white hair her youthful face was drawn and pale, with blood at her lips; and too he considered the fact that he had just shot two of the soldiers who were trying to capture them. "I'll die with you," he panted dizzily.

"Good," Elena gasped, reaching out to squeeze his hand briefly. "We must get—in the boat. The soldiers must be afraid—of the monster, and perhaps won't—chase us there."

"Let us all die on the boat," agreed Cassagnac with a jerky nod.

The thing Elena had described as *the monster* was a whirling, flexing tower of concentrated wind and rain against the Brandenburg Gate pillars, and now with a grinding of gears the crane arm hitched strongly upward, and the rectangular gray stone was swinging in wide arcs on the western side of the gate columns. The whirlwind crashed in eddying spray against the pediment at the top, seeming to rock the whole battered structure.

Hale felt physically squeezed between the soldiers coming up from behind him and the huge supernatural creature ahead; and it took an effort for him to keep his throat open, so that he could breathe without a keening whimper.

"Go," said Cassagnac, and then he and Hale and Elena were running full-tilt straight toward the old Arab boat on the bed of the truck; Hale didn't look left or right, and he gritted his teeth and ignored the bangs of rifle fire he heard from the west and from behind.

Two splintered holes were punched into the boat's wooden hull strakes as Hale jolted across the final yards of street pavement toward it, but over the thudding of his heart and the roaring of his breath he heard a megaphone-amplified voice shouting urgently, and no further shots were fired.

Feeling naked in the glare of many pairs of headlamps, Hale clambered up onto the corrugated steel truck bed and helped Elena up beside him. The boat's hull was a high wooden curve at his shoulder, but Cassagnac had already jumped and caught the bundle of rope that was the vessel's rail, and after he had swung himself over it, he reached back down; Hale grabbed Elena by the waist, bunching her raincoat to get a good hold of her ribs, and boosted her up; she caught Cassagnac's hands, and after a few seconds of scrambling and grunting, the three of them were lying in shadow on loose tangles of rope on the boat's deck.

"They will shoot through the hull," said Elena, getting up on her knees. The hot rain was dripping rapidly off the spiky fringe of her white hair.

Hale had rolled over onto a leather boot, and when he picked it up to toss it aside, it felt heavy. He looked into it and saw glistening meat and stumps of wet bone.

With a smothered yell he let go of it, then kicked it away across the deck—and he noticed lengths of smeared white bone scattered among the ropes, and a gristly piebald sphere that, when he couldn't help but focus on it, he recognized as a stripped human head.

He had tucked his gun back into his pocket to climb aboard, but now without thinking he snatched it out again, and he exhaled so harshly that the breath came out in a grating moan.

Cassagnac had lifted his head to peer over the gunwale, but Elena looked back at Hale.

"I think they won't shoot the boat," said Hale carefully. "I think it's the monster's boat."

Elena looked past him at the disordered deck, and shock made the skin of her face seem to contract, widening her eyes and pulling her lips back from her teeth. Perhaps involuntarily, her right hand darted to her forehead and she made the sign of the cross. *"Bozhe moy!"* she whispered.

Cassagnac had heard Hale and glanced back, and now he too had taken in the spectacle of the boat's deck. "Ah, God," he said bleakly. "I think Lot is right. They will have to . . . storm the boat, board us."

As if to illustrate his statement, a thump and clatter started up at the stern, and Hale saw a blinking head in a rain hood appear beside the tiller. Cassagnac pointed his pistol at it and fired, and the head abruptly dropped out of sight.

"How many bullets have we?" Cassagnac asked.

"—Seven," said Hale.

"Seven," said Elena.

"And seven here as well," said Cassagnac. "Is that good luck? Count carefully as you shoot, and save the last round for yourself." He laughed. "We should be finished here in less than a minute."

Elena was peering forward, over the bow. "The monster is on the far side of the Brandenburg Gate."

"You—*shot* at it?" Hale asked Cassagnac. "From the lot back there?"

"With a flare-gun," the Frenchman agreed. "A specially manufactured round, an iron cylinder cored from a Shihab meteorite. The DGSS wizards in Algiers believed it contained the death of one of these creatures, and that firing the death into this one would kill this one. It appears they miscalculated—and I wish they were here now."

Hale knew that DGSS was de Gaulle's Direction Generale des Services Spéciaux, which had operated out of Algiers during the last two years of the war; and for a moment he wondered what crazy trail had led Elena to employment with them.

The paired posts of several ladders now clunked against the gunwales on both sides, and Hale sprang to the nearest port-side ladder and wrenched it sideways, feeling the resistance-to-leverage of a man's weight on the bottom end of it; Elena and Cassagnac both shot at figures crowding up on the other side, and then Hale and Cassagnac were able to scramble around the gruesomely littered deck and push all the ladders away toward the tapering bow. A couple of shots from the street whipped the rainy air over their hands, but neither of them was hit.

Hale spat out the hot, foul rain. "Elena," he called, "I love you."

"Marcel," she cried with exhausted merriment in return, "I love you too."

"My name is Andrew."

"Andrew, I love you! *D'un tumulte!*"

Cassagnac was laughing again. "This is the spirit for dying. The captain of a ship can perform marriages—and so I hereby pronounce you two man and wife. Kiss the bride quick, Andrew, before you die."

Hale crawled through the downpour over to where Elena knelt, and dropped his pistol to take her face in her hands and kiss her passionately on the mouth. And her hand was in his hair, pulling him to her, and he tasted the hot blood from her cut lip on his tongue.

Their lips parted, but for several seconds their gazes stayed still linked, to the seeming exclusion of time and the world; but then Elena had turned away to crawl toward Cassagnac, and Hale blinked several times and picked up his pistol with shaking fingers.

Elena was kissing Cassagnac now, and Hale heard them murmuring to each other. Then Elena had abruptly convulsed away from him and scrambled backward until she collided with the mast.

"*She's* coming back," she called, in a voice that she barely kept from sliding up the scale to a scream.

And *she* was—the tall wild crown of the whirlwind was stirring the clouds as *she* surged strongly back toward the east, filling the night sky, glittering in the rain-refracted electric light of headlamps and the searchlight. The inhuman singing battered Hale's eardrums with an emotion to which he could only hold up the inadequate word *triumphal*. And though his mind and very self were diminished and downcast by the intolerably close imminence of her, and terror was an implosive pressure against his skull, Hale found himself thinking, *She walks in Beauty, like the night/Of cloudless climes and starry skies . . .*

—But it was not his thought. Hale was suddenly sure that it was the thought of someone else, someone watching this scene from a vantage point, a safe vantage point!—on the western side of the gate.

He turned away from the terrible looming sight of her, and he forced himself to hold on to one thought as he crawled across the deck to shake Cassagnac's shoulder. "A knife!" he shouted in the man's ear.

Cassagnac just shuddered and did not look away from the advancing whirlwind, but his hand reached into his coat and pulled out a double-edged commando dagger. Hale took it from him and cut free a foot-and-a-half length of the tangled rope; then, working rapidly with trembling fingers, he stripped long fibers from the remaining rope-end and used them to tie the short length to the crosspiece and pommel of the dagger, in a loop.

The result was an *ankh,* though the loop was bisected by the dagger's grip. Hale could hear Elena loudly reciting the *Ave Maria* in Spanish behind him, and he took a deep breath and tried to whisper some syllables of the Latin *Pater Noster*—and then he gripped the dagger by the base of the blade and stood up, lifting the makeshift ankh over his head—and he had to *push* the thing up through the air, as if through magnetic resistance.

For an instant all thought and identity were blown out of Hale's head, and his knees sagged and he would have fallen if the ankh had not suddenly been pulling upward in his fist; then the intensity of the thing's surprise was abruptly gone, and Hale was again self-aware, a tiny sentient presumption in the face of something like a god.

He staggered and swung his upraised arm to the left to steady himself—the ankh could only be dragged slowly through the nearly unyielding air, like tugging at a big gyroscope—

—And with a shrill whistling that lashed spray up from the street, the whirlwind leaned over that way, seeming to overbalance the sky. Numbly, Hale flexed all the muscles in his arm and shoulder to force the ankh across the other way, to starboard—and the whirlwind stood up straight against the clouds and then swayed out over the bombed lots to the north.

"What," shouted Cassagnac shrilly to be heard over the wind and the drumming percussion—the man was frowning, and Hale knew what a struggle it was to hold on to a thought here for more than a couple of seconds—"are—you doing?"

"I have an ankh," yelled Hale. "An anchor."

"Give it to me."

Cassagnac struggled to his feet against the wind, and Hale leaned his weight toward him to reach across and press the hilt of the dagger into the man's palm.

"The Russians," said Cassagnac loudly in his ear, "have certainly fallen back, for dread of this. Start the truck, and take Elena away." And he climbed one-handed over the rope-topped gunwale and pulled the resistant ankh down with him to the truck bed. Hale stumbled to the gunwale, but he could already see Cassagnac jogging strongly away across the boulevard pavement toward the Western sectors, holding the ankh over his head like a heavy torch.

"He's buying our lives," Hale shouted to Elena. "Get in the truck cab."

Elena cast one long, wide-eyed look after the running figure of Cassagnac—and once again, but with obvious deliberateness this time, she made the sign of the cross—then she bit her bleeding lip and nodded, turning away to grip the starboard bow gunwale and swing one leg over it.

Hale climbed down to the cab, and he was gripping his pistol when he pulled open the left-side driver's door, but any driver there might have been earlier had long since fled. The truck was vibrating, already idling in neutral, and after Elena had hoisted herself in beside him and pulled her door closed, Hale pressed the clutch to the floor and clanked the gear-shift lever into first gear.

He let the clutch up, and they were rolling, and he steered toward the curb and the flattened masonry beyond the north side of the Brandenburg Gate. No one was shooting at them yet, and he stamped on the accelerator pedal.

Hale glanced out the window to the south, and through the whipping veils of hot rain he saw Cassagnac plodding heavily, desperately, toward the western side—but sheets of water were being blown away from the pavement in all directions around the laboring figure, and the whirlwind was slowly bending down over him. Cassagnac lost his footing for a moment, touched the pavement with his knee and free hand as the wind slid him sideways around the compass of the ankh in his fist, and then he was up again, crouching low and thrusting himself forward with each contested step.

Impulsively Hale shouted out the window, *"O Fish, are you constant to the old covenant?"*—and in the same moment he shifted up into second gear and again tromped the accelerator pedal flat against the floorboards.

As he had shouted the words at the roaring wind-thing that leaned down out of the sky, he was giving pictures to the ideas behind the words—the Devil fish in the old stained-glass window in Fairford, and a row of soldiers standing resolute, and the boxy litter shape of the Ark of the Covenant as it had appeared in his school textbooks—but a moment later he wasn't sure he had shouted in English.

In any case he had drawn the attention of the storm away from Cassagnac and onto himself and Elena. He clung to the truck's steering wheel as his weight increased and the Brandenburg Gate pillars swung from left to right beyond the streaming windscreen, and the engine was roaring as the rear wheels spun free of traction in the air.

But their momentum was still westward, and when the truck crashed back down onto its wheels it was on the rubbled raised pavement at the north end of the gate, uprooting bushes and exploding bricks and broken stones in all directions; the back end was sliding around to the right as the truck rocked down off the west side of the raised pavement in a hail of leaves and mortar fragments, and the windscreen was abruptly crazed with a white spiderweb pattern of cracks as the boat's bow crunched a dent into the steel roof over Hale's head, and in the driver's mirror he glimpsed the boat's toppling mast and upturning keel as the vessel rolled heavily off of the truck bed.

He whipped the steering wheel to the right and shifted back down to first gear, and when he hit the accelerator, the truck shuddered and coughed, then ground forward across the western Charlottenburg Chaussee lanes, thumping and shaking on at least two flat tires. The crane stood off to their left, apparently abandoned in place over the hole where the man had been shot that afternoon. Hale and Elena were now west of the place where the anchor stone had been installed.

And so was Cassagnac, now. As Hale spun the wheel to steer south, staring out the open side window back toward the Unter den Linden lanes beyond the Brandenburg Gate, he saw a closer figure, running west—and when Hale trod on the brake pedal and tapped out the Rote Kapelle *here* code on the horn, Cassagnac slanted his course toward the truck.

Cassagnac was waving both empty hands, and on the whipping wind Hale heard snatches of the man's shouting voice: *"Alibi—go back there—all evening, dinner—I'll—tomorrow—"*

Hale waved acknowledgment, and he switched off the headlamps as he steered the laboring truck back to the right, leaning his head out of the window into the rain to see where he was going. Figures scattered away in the darkness, but he couldn't tell if they were Soviet soldiers or civilians.

When he had driven the wrecked truck more than halfway across the distance to the skeletal dome of the Reichstag, he stamped on the brake. None of the anonymous pedestrians had followed them.

"Now we go back to where we had dinner," he said breathlessly as he levered open the driver's-side door. "We want to establish that we never left."

"Incredible," said Elena as she climbed out on her side.

Hale led Elena back through the kitchen entrance into the smoky restaurant, so that they wouldn't be seen to have entered through the street door; and the table at which they had sat earlier was still unoccupied. Both of them were soaked, dripping on the stone floor, but many of the dozen other diners were nearly as wet. Hale was at least profoundly glad to look around the long room and see that Philby was no longer present.

Hale paid for a plate of Sturdy Max with a cellophane-sealed pack of Chesterfields, and when he had carried the plate across to their table and sat down, he discovered that he was in fact very hungry.

Elena apparently was not. When the same old aproned waiter came to the table, she just ordered another brandy, frowning and speaking almost too quietly to be heard, without looking at him or at Hale; and Hale curtly told the man to make it four brandies.

Elena had taken off her long woolen coat and laid it with unnecessary care on the bench beside her; the long-sleeved blue sweater she'd had on underneath it was not obviously wet, and she had pulled her white hair back over her shoulders. Hale's sport coat glistened with moisture, but he didn't take it off because his clinging shirt would look worse.

He wasn't eager to speak, either. He could still vividly recall the heavy inertia of the dagger-ankh in his right hand, and in his mind he saw again the whirlwind bowing to one side and then the other as he had swung the ankh back and forth. And the thing had *heard* him, had *responded,* when he had called to it the old challenge from his dreams. He knew that soon he might discount these recollections, but he could not do that yet, and the realization that he had seen the supernatural tonight kept him chilly and shaking even in the warm, sauerkraut-scented air of the candlelit restaurant.

The old waiter brought over a tray with four glasses on it, and Hale and Elena each took a glass and gulped it at the same instant, without looking at each other. Then for a minute or so Hale just stared down at his plate and chewed his ham and eggs and black bread, and carefully sipped his second glass of brandy.

Figures in dripping macintoshes entered by ones and twos through the street door, and soon Hale could hear the phrases *"Brandenburger Tor"*—as well as *"boat"* and *"teufel,"* boat and devil—in the louder conversations from the other tables.

But no one was sitting close to them, and he needed to at least refer to the events of the evening, so he leaned forward—Elena looked up at him warily, and after a moment's hesitation he said in French, "We wound up wrecking the monster's boat."

She didn't stop frowning, but a nervous smile kinked her swelling mouth, and in spite of her white hair she looked very young. "That's right," she said in a low voice. "It wasn't still on the truck, at the end."

Hale took a deep breath. "The thing in the sky—" he began.

"Don't speak of it!" She shook her head and then took a noisy sip of brandy, wincing at the alcohol on her cut lip. "We will speak of worldly things only. Claude—Cassagnac—he would not have told you about the Shihab meteor-bullet, if he had thought we might survive."

Hale sighed. "Well, the meteor-bullet didn't work, in any case."

"No," she said bleakly, "it did—not—work." She looked straight into his eyes then, and suddenly he felt the warmth of the brandy. Her voice when she spoke again, though, was brisk. "And on the same assumption he told you that we are working for the French DGSS. I would venture to declare," she went on, using the French infinitive *déclarer,* "that you are working for the British secret service now . . . ?"

Hale opened his mouth, hesitated, and then said, "Yes." The abrupt question, coming from her, had caught him off-guard. *We will speak of worldly things only.* He knew that Theodora would have expected him to live his cover—deny any SIS connection and talk about his work in fertilizer manufacture—but this was *Elena!* And France *was* an ally. Nevertheless he could feel himself blushing at having so instantly broken his cover, and he bolted the rest of his second glass of brandy and glanced around for the waiter.

"Duplication," she said, "parallel sections, secrets within secrets. That arrogant man, Kim—we know he is an SIS section head, but he didn't know you had been sent here. It is informative to know that the SIS was aware of the action tonight, and had two men independently observing. They have not held it against you, the work you did for the GRU in Paris?"

Again Hale opened his mouth without speaking, and he felt his face getting hotter. "—No," he said. The waiter had walked up to the table, and Hale hastily ordered four more brandies. The old man nodded and walked away without picking up the four emptied glasses.

Elena's frown had deepened. "Ah, you were working for the British secret service even then. You were—a double."

Hale was stung by the tone of accusation. "You work for the French now," he protested. "Against the . . . the Party." Which you once described to me as your husband, he thought sourly. He wanted to ask her what had happened when she obeyed the summons to Moscow in January of 1942, but while he was trying to phrase the question, she spoke again.

"I work for them honestly," she said, "as I worked then for the Party—honestly."

Hale remembered her leaving the Philippe St.-Simon passport in a *dubok* for him, but that had been too gallant an act, and too beneficial to himself, for him to raise it now as an objection. "You would not now do undercover work for the DGSS?" he asked instead.

"I would. My loyalties have changed."

"Mine have not."

She leaned forward and gripped his hand in her cold fist. "But it was—*you and me,* do you understand? I was sincere."

The four fresh brandies arrived then, and with his free hand Hale dug out two packs of cigarettes to pay for them. When the waiter had again retreated, Hale said, "I was sincere too, where it was you and me. Hell, I was sincere in the *work*, that must have been obvious. Russia and England were allies against Germany."

"But you went home and reported it all." She was still holding his hand, loosely, but she was staring down at the table.

"I'm being honest here," Hale told her, "and I promise you I did not report . . . *you and me.*"

"Thank you." She shrugged, still looking down. "But there was a core of deceit. I would not have—gone to bed with you, if I had known who you were really working for."

"I—well, no, I suppose not," conceded Hale.

She sighed, and met his eyes. "I really was an atheist, you know; then, in Paris."

"I know." He had noted her exclamation *Bozhe moy!* tonight on the boat, and he knew that the phrase was Russian for *My God!*—and he had heard her reciting the *Hail Mary* in Spanish, and twice she had made the sign of the cross. Avoiding any mention of the events of the evening, he simply said, "And I know you are not anymore."

She squeezed his hand, and he returned the pressure. "Actually," she said, "I think I was *never* an atheist. But I realized it in the Lubyanka basements. They had not called me back from Paris to kill me, as it turned out, but to initiate me into the transcendent order of Soviet espionage. It involved imprisoning me in the Lubyanka, and at one point there they—seemed to kill me. Outside of the prison I had by then learned the truth about my—cherished *communism;* and when I seemed to die, there in the Lubyanka, I prayed to the Virgin Mary. I made a vow to her—I swore that, if she would intercede to free me, I would come back to Moscow on my fortieth birthday, and light a candle in St. Basil's Cathedral right there in Red Square, at high noon; and I promised her that I would . . ."

After a few seconds Hale said, "That you would—?"

Her answering smile seemed sad. "I won't tell you."

"When were you born?"

"Never mind." Then she shrugged. "Oh, but you could find it out, I'm sure—April 22, Andrew, in 1924!" She went on hastily: "But do *you*—imagine that you are an atheist—*still?*"

It wasn't God that we saw tonight, he thought. And the thing we saw—it bowed, when I waved the ankh, and it came to me when I called it.

He had been terrified, and had tried, without success, to recite the *Pater Noster*—but there had been immense fascination, too, and immense approachable power. And he had shot at two men, had perhaps killed them, and now he was disturbed but relieved to find that, for the moment at least, that action was in some concussed part of his memory, numb.

He knew that if he were to go to a Catholic priest in a confessional, all of this would look very ugly indeed.

Which perspective is true? he thought. Which do I want to be true?

He looked at her and shook his head. "I don't know."

She laughed fondly. "You are frank, but not honest. And I think you are a fool. But you have again blithely put yourself in mortal peril to save my life, and tomorrow morning Claude and I must fly back to Algiers to report our failure, and God knows when or if you and I may see each other again. I do love you, *Andrew—d'un tumulte!*—and—if you have no scruples!—I would very much like us to find a room together, on—on this fearful night." She was blushing, and Hale realized almost incredulously that she was hardly more than twenty years old. "Perhaps it will not be a sin," she said, pushing her bench back and reaching for her coat. "Cassagnac did marry us, tonight."

"Yes," Hale said unsteadily. "God, yes." His heart was thumping under his wet shirt. "Cassagnac formalized it," he added as he stood up, "but in my heart we have been married ever since our last night in Paris."

He touched one of the remaining full glasses of brandy, but then just deliberately knocked it over on the table, and with trembling hands helped Elena put on her wet coat instead.

The lower two or three floors of most Berlin residential buildings had been looted by the Red Army soldiers, but Hale and Elena found a fourth-floor suite in a rooming house near the Tempelhof Airport in the American Sector. The high ceiling was adorned with frescoes of angels and bearded saints, the tables and chairs were all black claw-footed shapes out of Gustave Doré, and the bed was an enormous old four-poster with a tapestry canopy.

Rain thrashed against the leaded-glass windows and a draft fluttered the candle flame until it eventually guttered out, and Hale and Elena weren't aware of any of it. But an hour before dawn the rain stopped, and a wind from the north rattled the window frames and opened the clouds so that moonlight silvered the old cobbled street and the gable roofs, and Hale and Elena wrapped themselves in blankets to get up and stand in the moonlight by the window, and for a little while they watched the red and green wingtip lights sweep overhead and on past them as Western airplanes descended for landings at Tempelhof.

Elena whispered in French, "I'll say it now, while it's still not immediate: Good-bye, Andrew, my love."

"I will not say it ever," he told her, leading her back away from the window.

At dawn Elena got dressed and went away to meet Cassagnac, and Hale put on his damp clothes and walked through the slanting sunlight north, back to the square by the Brandenburg Gate.

He hung well back past the western curbing of the square, by the sawed-off tree stumps on the south side of the Charlottenburg Chaussee, but he was able to see red-striped wooden barricades around the patch of wet cement that now covered the shell-crater in the pavement; and he surreptitiously made sketches from several vantage points, indicating the locations of landmarks, so that Theodora would know precisely where the anchor stone had been installed.

Of course the truck, with its flat tires and crushed roof, had been towed away during the night, and from this southern position Hale could see no evidence of lumber—or bones—up at the north end of the broad square, where he remembered the boat overturning. His head throbbed with a mild hangover as he panted in the cool morning air, and he was already beginning to wonder how much of what he seemed to recall could really, literally, have happened.

In a rubble-strewn alley he dropped the Walther pistol down the well of a broken drainage pipe—and then there was no reason to linger. During the walk southwest to the SHAEF U.S. Sector Headquarters, past gutted houses and curbside cooking fires and old women loading broken masonry into wagons, he tried to decide what report he would make to Theodora.

He reclaimed the Renault from the American lot and finally used some of his German marks to refill the petrol tank, and then he drove carefully back down the southwest segment of highway, past a brief view of green woods and the broad sunlit lakes of the Havel River, to the U.S. Sector gates and the Russian checkpoint at the outskirts of Berlin. In the Russian guard shack a taciturn Soviet soldier checked the Conway name and passport number against a posted list, then sighed and stamped the travel order. Hale got back into the idling car and drove on, out of Berlin.

Soviet military lorries passed him in both directions during the two-hour drive west, but he resisted the surprisingly strong impulse to race out of the Russian territory; and before slowing for the final checkpoint at the Helmstedt border crossing, he wiped the sweat from his face and managed to breathe deeply and slowly. A number of German diesel lorries were halted on the shoulder so that the loads could be checked, but when the checkpoint guard looked at Hale's stamped travel order, he simply waved, and the barrier was lifted.

Hale drove through, into the British Zone of conquered Germany. Abandoned brick warehouses fronted the street, and on the nearest curb stood a figure in an overcoat and a homburg hat—Hale recognized Theodora even as the figure began waving. Hale pulled over, and Theodora opened the door and climbed in, setting his hat on his lap.

"Don't talk," the gray-haired man told him shortly, "the Americans probably miked the car. Just drive straight ahead here."

Hale nodded and let out the clutch; and when the road had led them past the last outlying farmhouses of Helmstedt to shaggy green fields, Theodora said, "This will do. Pull over to the shoulder here. I'm not flying back with you, and I might not see you again in London. You'll give me your report now."

Hale nodded and steered the car onto the muddy shoulder, and when it had squeaked to a halt he rocked the shift lever into neutral and set the hand brake, and then clanked open the driver's-side door.

Theodora leaned forward, frowning. "I hope the report will be *lengthy* enough," he said, "to make it worthwhile turning off the damned *engine.*"

"Oh, yes, sir, of course," said Hale, reaching back to switch off the ignition. In the sudden silence he swung his legs out of the car and straightened up; blinking over the car's roof before Theodora unfolded himself from the passenger seat, Hale looked out across what he now recognized as wheat fields. No farmer was visible, and Hale wondered if there were still working tractors here.

When Theodora had stood up straight and replaced his hat, he strode west along the shoulder, his hands clasped behind the tails of his coat and his head down to be sure of keeping his shoes out of puddles. Hale trudged along after him.

When they had walked a hundred feet away from the Renault, Theodora turned around and fixed Hale with a chilly stare. "Well?"

"The stone is buried under fresh cement, sir," said Hale, "about two hundred feet from the Brandenburg Gate on the western side, pretty much centered. I've done drawings," he added, reaching into his pocket for the diagrams he had made that morning, "indicating the exact position—I can amplify them to make them more precise, now."

Theodora took the papers and glanced at them. "Good, I think this is clear." Again he turned his cold eyes on Hale. "Go on. Tell me every detail."

Hale began easily by telling him about his visit with the American Flannery and hearing that Kim Philby was in Berlin; then he recounted the pursuit of the fugitive from the Soviet Sector, and told Theodora how the man had seemed to be herded to the spot where the stone would soon be buried, and how the fugitive had been killed there. Hale became aware of a reluctance when he came to describing meeting Elena and Cassagnac at the restaurant by the Reichstag, and Philby's intrusion and odd behavior with the insecticide. And when his narrative got to the point when he had stood up from the table to go get food, he abandoned the story he had concocted on the drive west to Helmstedt and just stopped talking.

"Food," said Theodora impatiently, "right. Did you get some bloody food, or what?"

"No, sir, not then." Hale felt dizzy, and he didn't even know whether he hoped he was ending his SIS career here, or not. At last, slowly and deliberately, he went on: "There was a radio playing in the restaurant, and the music it had been playing was interrupted by—by an interference which I had learned in Paris meant—supernatural—attention—being paid." He was sweating again, and he discovered that it was no easier going on with this than it had been starting. "Magic, that is, sir," he said, feeling as if the words were coins he had tried to smuggle out, surrendered now as he pushed them out past his lips. "I think I should amplify the report I made to you concerning my three months in occupied Paris in '41," he added, "by the way."

Theodora exhaled, and Hale wondered how long the man had been holding his breath. "Good lad. Good lad. So many promising agents manage to convince even *themselves* that they didn't see what they saw—but go on. And *don't* tell me, in tones of apology, that *'It gets more weird'*—I do know that."

"Right. Well . . ." Hale ground out the story of the rest of the night, omitting only the gallows-marriage on the boat and going to bed with Elena—in this version of the story, he and Elena had parted outside the restaurant.

The sun was high when at last, with relief, he described ditching the gun and driving back up the hole to the Helmstedt checkpoint.

Theodora strode away across the mud, careless now of his shoes. He was nodding, and after a few paces he turned around again to face Hale. "Good. I did want to know where the stone was put, and I'm glad to learn of Philby's participation—oh, he was there about the stone too, lad, don't doubt it—and I think I'm alarmed at how aware the French DGSS is—but this was a test, too, to find out if you're worth all the years and money we've expended on you. Happily, you are. And I trust you are discreet with your little Spanish judy, no secrets revealed over the pillow. Eunuchs for agents would be best, I sometimes think. Impossible to get it past the Foreign Secretary, of course. Your work will be—of a different nature, now that you're an initiate. You've learned all you can from the old files, I expect, and it's time to put you in the field. When you get back to Broadway, you'll be sent to Fort Monkton for a six-week training course in the paramilitary arts, and then you'll be posted to the Middle East, Kuwait probably, under the cover of the Combined Research Planning Office, known jocularly as Creepo."

"The Middle East," said Hale thoughtfully. He had been hungry all morning, but now he felt distinctly nauseated; and he knew that it was fear that had quickened his heartbeat—but this was the next step *farther in,* on the way to learning the very deepest secrets of the world, of the most powerful and most hidden world. He flexed his right hand, remembering how the whirlwind had bowed in the rain when he had waved the ankh . . .

Theodora nodded. "Not totally a surprise, I daresay. Before you go, I will acquaint you with the big picture, the biggest picture—and then, finally, indoctrinate you for clearance to what we have called Operation Declare."

▼

Book Two

Know, Not Think It

▼

11

Beirut, 1963

And the two of them, laying him east and west, that the mysterious earth currents which thrill the clay of our bodies might help and not hinder, took him to pieces all one long afternoon—bone by bone, muscle by muscle, ligament by ligament, and lastly, nerve by nerve.
—Rudyard Kipling, *Kim*

Kim Philby sat back in his chair by the window-side table in the Normandy Hotel bar, and he licked his lips, tasting her lipstick. The woman on the other side of the table simply stared at him for a moment, then took a long inhalation on her cigarette. Out beyond the window glass the late afternoon sky was gold over the purple sea.

Philby smiled at her, but he was nettled. He found her prematurely bone-white hair very erotic, but her lips had been as inert as the back of her hand would have been; and he wished his head were not ludicrously wrapped in white bandages. "I do b-beg your p-pardon, Miss C-B. My Sov-oviet *handler* was in the l-lobby, with some cadaverous specimen, j-just now. They d-didden *did not* come in, but if you do in-snit—*insist* on meeting me in my—office this way, we had b-better pretend to be h-having an extramerry-extramartial-extramarital—"

"I understand," said Elena Teresa Ceniza-Bendiga in careful English. She sighed out a puff of smoke, then picked up her glass of Dubonnet. "In our work we have to emulate Judas sometimes." She finished the red drink in two gulps, raising her disconcertingly dark eyebrows at him over the rim. "Your office, this hotel bar is?" she asked when she had put the glass down.

"I g-get my mail here, and the c-concierge keeps a tah-tah-typewriter here, for my use. I'm a j-*journalist,* you know, these days." He picked up his own glass, swirling the gin among the diminished ice cubes. "But Judas, you say? The outfit I pro-propose to b-b-b—betray!—is hardly the aqua-equi-equivalent of the Son of man, even in my atheistic c-consideration." He smiled more broadly. "Or maybe you mean I turn out to have betrayed *you?*"

Elena stubbed out her cigarette. "I haven't seen you since Turkey in 1948," she said, getting to her feet and smoothing her skirt. "If you and I had a—had anything at all—then, I'm sure I can't recall it." She glanced around at the tables and the beaded curtain that led into the lobby. "Is there another way out of here? I'd never have been so careless as to approach you here, if I'd known you still had a—damned *handler* about. Bad craft, I apologize—we asumed you were in retirement here in Beirut." She spoke calmly, but he could see a quicker pulse in the side of her neck.

Philby tipped up his glass for the last mouthful of gin. "Beirut is a neutral city," he told her. "And my employers are not ee-eager right now to be doing any such—con-conspicuously *robust* operations—as k-kidnapping agents of a f-f-foreign power. But you're right, we proba-bly shhh—should not be seen together." He waved toward the bar. "Anwar will let us leave by the delivery dock in back." He set down his glass, reached under the table to be sure the snub-nose .38 was still secure in the elastic ankle holster and that his trouser cuff was tugged over it, and then he stood up.

As they walked across the tile floor toward the mahogany-and-brass bar, he said, " 'If we had anything at all, then—you're sure y-you can't recall it.' I have a fucking b-bullet-hole in my head; do take note of the f-fact that you have n-n-not got one in yours."

He was pleased to see her face redden, at that.

"I—I know," she said as she stepped behind the bar and nodded dis-tractedly at the simpering moustached Anwar. "I do remember."

They walked out the back door and down the alley behind the Nor-mandy Hotel, past the fire escapes and the hot-air fan vents, and when they emerged into the early twilight on the main street sidewalk Philby waved at a passing Service taxi and called *"Serveece!"* The taxi pulled in to the curb, and for once there were no other passengers already inside. Philby opened the back door for Elena, then went around to the street side and climbed in himself. He gave the driver 125 piastres, and said, in quick French, "I'm paying for all five spaces, right? No other passengers, right? Take us to Chouran Street, by the Pigeon Rock." He beamed at Elena and draped his right arm over the seat back behind her. In German, he said, "I'm fascinated that the"—the French SDECE, he thought, Pompidou's secret service; but the driver *might* speak German—"that they chose to send *you.*"

She answered in the same language. "The thinking was that since I have known you in the past, I would be best able to gauge whether your offer is genuine or not. And I'm an off-paper operative—if your offer is a trap, if I am arrested, then I am disownable, not traceably in their employ. But if I judge that it is genuine"—the German word she used was *richtig*—"my employers will exfiltrate you from here immediately, and give you a new identity and much money in my country. If you renege in any way, we will . . . *give you the truth,* as your people say."

Philby folded his arm back and clasped his hands in his lap. They *could* kill him, if they worked at it. In English he said, softly, "Oh, it's *richtig,* all r-right."

I have got to jump *somewhere,* he thought—and damned soon. The British SIS is being very slow in responding to old Flora Solomon's kind and timely betrayal of my past to MI5—don't they *want* the confession of their most damaging spy?—and Angleton's CIA wouldn't trust me to give them a recipe for *Borscht,* and Indian citizenship isn't possible. And Theodora's old SOE deal was for me to go on working for Moscow! But somebody's got to take me out of Burgess's control, out of *Moscow's* control—I will kill myself before I'll go up onto Ararat, alone as I am now. Our Hajji which art in Hell, now.

The driver steered the taxi up the Rue Kantari on the way to Hamra Street, and Philby leaned forward to hide his bandaged head well under the taxi's roof, in case his wife might be looking out from their fifth-floor balcony. I'll tell you about it if it works out, Eleanor my love, he thought. I won't trouble you with advance notice—and you'd enjoy living in France.

At last they had doglegged south on Chouran Street and were driving along the cliff road, past Lord's Hotel and the Yildizlar Restaurant, with the dark-indigo Mediterranean on their right. Philby could see the two enormous rocks out in St. George's Bay—traditionally the site where England's patron saint had killed the dragon. The weary St. Kim, he thought, will settle for just hiding from the dragon.

A crowd of Arab and European tourists was waiting at a taxi rank by
the Pigeon Grotto pavilion on the cliff, and after Philby and Elena had
got out of the taxi he took her bare elbow and led her south along the
railed cliff-top sidewalk. To their left, under the modern white façade of
the Carlton Hotel, Rolls-Royces and Volkswagens slowed as an Arab on
a donkey plodded away across the lanes. Only a few of the cars had
turned on their headlamps, and the clean smell of surf spray in the air
was still faintly perfumed with the afternoon aroma of suntan oil.

Seagulls spun in the darkening blue sky overhead, but their shrill
cries were muffled by the gauze taped over Philby's ears.

He turned toward the sea, where a quarter of a mile out across the
water a motorboat had just shot through the tunnel at the base of the
bigger rock, with a water skier just visible bouncing along in the spreading white fan of the wake. The four-hundred-foot-tall rock was flat on
top, a remote backlit meadow furred with wild grasses, and he wondered forlornly if anyone had ever climbed up there.

"I'll m-miss Beirut," he said in English. "I've b-been here six years."

"You'll like France," Elena told him. The red sun was low over the
horizon beyond the rocks, and she fished a pair of sunglasses out of her
purse and slipped them on. "Why do you want to leave the Soviet service? I gather you're still an active player, not just selling your memoirs."

"My f-father is d-d-dead." Our Hajji which art in Hell, now, he
thought again. "He died here t-two years ago, and he was my . . .
recruiter, in a, in an unspecific but v-very real sense, into the G-Great
Game. He wasn't a t-*traitor*—in spite of being j-jailed during the war for
making pro-Hitler talk, 'activities prejudicial to the safety of the
Realm'!—and he never p-pushed me toward the S-S-Soviet services *per
se*, but in the twenties and thirties he was studying under one of the
S-Soviet illegals who were all eventually p-purged by Stalin in '37 and
'38—a p-para-do-*dox*ical old Soviet Moslem called Hassim Hakimoff
Khan, in J-Jidda, which is the port city for Mecca."

"I—I met one of the great old illegals," said Elena quietly. "In
France, when I was quite young. What was your father studying?"

Philby barked out one syllable of a mirthless laugh. "Oh—what was
he not. Did you know that a g-god called al-Lah was worshipped in the
Ka'bah in Mecca a thousand years before Mohammed? According to the
Koran, the Thamud tribes refused to w-worship him, and were annihi-

lated by something remembered as both a thu-thunderbolt and an earthquake. My father f-found and deciphered more than ten thousand Thamudic inscriptions, and he didn't t-turn over all of them to the scholars. And he studied the Gilgamesh v-version of the Biblical flood story in the Chaldean cuneiform tablets at the B-British Museum, supplemented by others that he had f-found for h-himself in Baghdad." More slowly, he went on, "In 1921 he was appointed Chief B-British Representative in Jordan, ruh-ruh-replacing T. E. Lawrence, who w-was being p-posted to Iraq; my father—s-s-s-*stole* Lawrence's old files, and from reading them c-carefully one c-could deduce quite a lot about the files that were m-missing, the ones Lawrence had apparently ddd*destroyed:* the tr-translations of some ancient d-documents he had found in one of the Qumran Wadi caves by the Dead Sea in 1918."

Elena yawned, clearly from tension rather than tiredness. "You're talking about the Dead Sea Scrolls, right?—that were found—found again—in 1947! Do you know what the documents were?"

"Yes, I—I read the L-Lawrence files myself in 1934." After breaking into my father's safe, he thought, and photographing his papers. "According to h-his inventory files, there were a n-number of Semitic j-jars in the cave, but he took away an anomalous one that h-had an ankh-type c-cross for a h-h-*handle.* In it were s-several brittle old Hebrew scr-scrolls— apparently one was what is c-called a *brontologion,* which means 'what the thunder said'; these were usually di-di-divination and astrological t-texts, derived from l-listening to thu-thunder; but Lawrence's references to it s-seemed to indicate a—more specific and deliberate m-message from the thunder. Another of the s-s-s-scrolls seems to have been a variant v-version of either the Book of Genesis or the apocryphal Book of Enoch—the story of Noah and the great f-flood, in any case. My f-father never obtained the ack-ack-actual transcriptions Lawrence made of these, so I n-never saw them either. Lawrence became unreliable, after he t-translated them." Philby yawned too, creaking his jaw, and he clenched his hands into fists to stop them trembling. "I photographed what there was, and gave the foe-foe-photographs to Guy Burgess, who was always my m-main Soviet handler in those d-days."

"And Lawrence died in a motorcycle crash the following year. How does all this relate to your decision to—quit the 'Great Game,' leave the Soviet service, and seek the protection of the SDECE?"

"My f-f-*father*—initiated, t-tried to initiate me—into—" He let the sentence trail away.

Elena clicked her tongue impatiently. "If you're going to be evasive about the supernatural element of your story, the SDECE is not buying."

"Evasive." Philby laughed shortly, aware of the weight of chunky steel on his ankle and wondering if he might ever be faced with the necessity—and have the courage—to turn the gun on himself. "It is v-vaguely *shameful*, though, isn't it? Didn't you feel that, in B-Berlin?"

"And if you're not willing to face *shame*, we're not going to get anywhere."

" 'O valiant wheel! O most courageous heaven!' You g-give me back the s-same reproach I gave you, in T-Turkey. Yes, very well." For several seconds he just blinked out at the shadowed, eroded faces of the two giant monoliths standing in the bay, and at a flock of seagulls flying in a ring just to this side of the rocks. A new identity in France, he told himself. You cannot go up onto Mount Ararat.

Still, his voice shook when he finally spoke: "My father was b-baptized, but renounced Kruh-Christianity and converted to Islam in 1930, and took the name Hajji Abdullah, 'One Who Has Made the Pilgimage, Slave of God'—and I never was b-b-baptized at all, he saw to that. He had been born on Good F-Friday in 1885, in Ceylon, and a c-comet was clearly v-visible in the sky on that day—once when he was a baby he was accidentally left behind at a government rest stop during a journey, and the s-servants rushed back and found him being n-nursed by a *djjj*—by a 'gypsy' woman." Philby glanced at Elena, but her blue eyes were hidden behind the sunglasses, and he looked back out at the rocks. "In fact she was n-nursing two identical infants, b-both dressed in my father's B-British baby clothes. Later one of the infants was apparently l-lost—in any case, when they got home again, there was only one."

"They were both him," said Elena, "right? Don't hint, say."

Philby bared his teeth in a difficult smile. "My motto has always been 'know, not think it, and learn, not speak.' The short course for spies. But yes," he agreed wearily, "they were b-both him. At around the age of s-seven he lost that ability to be in two p-p-places at one time. I was born in Ambala, in the Punjab in India, and I s-spoke Hindi before I s-spoke English. I used to d-dream—"

With an emotion no stronger than perplexity, he discovered that he was unable to tell her about the year's-end dreams that had blighted his boyhood in India and England: dreams of a bearded bronze man as tall as the rotating night sky, holding an upraised scythe that glittered like a constellation; or of the whole world turning ponderously on the celestial potter's wheel; or of an *Arabian Nights* magician whirling a flaming fishing net right into his scorching eyes—from his own studies in the Old Testament's First Book of Kings he knew that the Hebrew words for *burn, excommunicate, magician, potter,* and *blasphemy,* as well as *sword,* all began with the Hebrew letters *cheth* and *resh*—and the dreams always ended with his head being forcibly split in two, so that before he awoke he imagined that he had been broken into two personalities. In adulthood he had come to suspect that the dreams expressed dim memories of some anti-baptism to which he had been subjected as an infant.

"Well," he said, covering his hesitation by jumping back to the last topic, "I didn't just *dream* it—I *was* able to be in t-two p-places at once myself, as a b-boy. One of me could be in studying, while the other was out h-hiking in the woods. My p-parents had always been aware of it, and simply t-told me to be d-d-discreet, circumspect. I wasn't b-baptized, and so I didn't lose that ability until . . . until precisely on my t-t-tenth birthday."

"When is your birthday?"

Never, he thought. It is never, and I will never tell you. "New Year's Day," he said lightly. "My f-father had been g-grooming me, he wanted his s-son to become—what his b-baptism had barred h-h-*him* from becoming. Until he was f-forced to resign in 1924, he was a m-major in the Raj, with the Political and Secret Department of the Indian government—the MI-lC, actually, f-forerunner of the present-day SIS. He became great p-pals with Ibn Saud, then king of the Najd r-region in central Arabia, eventually to become eponymous king of all S-S-Saudi Arabia, and when Ibn Saud's son Feisal p-paid a state visit to England in 1919, the Foreign Office appointed my f-father as the boy's escort. I was aye-aye-eight years old at the time, going to a Westminster-prep school in Eastbourne, and they v-visited me there. Feisal presented me with a t-twenty-carat d-diamond. The Russians have always wanted to g-get it away from me—not to be v-v-*vulgar,* but I had to *swallow* it, during the episode in Turkey in '48—and I'll wager Feisal h-himself would like to have it b-back now, now that air travel is so c-common."

"What has the jewel got to do with air travel?"

"I'm not going to g-give it to you people either. B-but what it d-does is—it constitutes a *rafiq,* it makes the bearer an emissary, with d-diplomatic immunity to any r-r-*wrath* from the powers that prevail . . . up high, from roughly a thousand feet above sea-level on up . . . to the m-moon, I suppose."

"Why did your ability cease on your tenth birthday?"

"I—don't know. My f-father was alarmed, dismayed; he was in Amman, in Jordan, but my m-m-mother must have written to him about my sudden *singularity.* He ordered me to m-meet him in Amman in the s-summer of my eleventh year, and though it was ostensibly a holiday, for a couple of months he . . . tt*tested* me, and the jewel. We traveled to Damascus, and Baalbek, and Nazareth, always hiking among the oldest t-tombs and watching the w-weather. We fl-flew over Lake Tiberias in a De Havilland biplane and saw a waterspout that he said was Sakhr al-Jinni, a djinn that had been c-confined to the lake by King S-S-Solomon, but it didn't approach us . . . and we went to the J-J-*Jordan River* near Jericho, and he collected samples of the river w-water." Philby shivered, recalling even now his father's frustrated rage as he had corked the dripping bottles. "He wanted to send the samples to the B-British Museum, to see if the water really d-d-did have any measurable special p-properties. I think he was worried about s-s-someone, some infant, who had been b-baptized there—not long before."

"He was *testing* you?"

"Yes, and I f-failed. When I lost the ability to be two b-boys, I apparently also lost the ability to . . . conjure, or c-control, the old entities. I became ill—shakes and fever—with what he elected to d-d-diagnose as malaria, though I've never had the usual r-relapses. And I was sent home to Ig-England. A year later I went off to Westminster school, and my f-f-father made it clear that I was to go on to T-Trinity College, Cambridge, as he had done, and which I d-did. But I had a—a n-nervous b-b-*breakdown,* at Westminster! Do y-you know why?"

Elena looked away from the circling gulls to face him, and she laughed in surprise. "No," she said. "Why?"

"Because of the *unrelenting* Christian instruction. Really! They did j-just k-keep *on* at us about Original Sin, and our individual s-sins, and how each of us m-must either submit to k-k-Christ, surrender our wills to His, or s-suffer the eternal wrath of God. I dee-dee-*denied* all of it. I was an atheist even then—though, thanks to my f-father, I was an atheist who was m-mortally afraid of graveyards, and of the Roman Catholic s-sacraments, and of tall storm clouds and th-thunder at twilight."

He looked out at the sea. The red sun had sunk below the horizon, leaving glowing golden terraces of cloud hung across the whole western half of the sky, but no cumulus clouds were rearing their shoulders and shaggy heads out there. The ring of seagulls was closer, though—a quarter of a mile away, halfway between the rocks and the cliff highway now.

"We should g-go inside somewhere," he said nervously. "Get something to d-drink."

"They're only birds. And no microphone can detect our talk out here. When were you actually inducted into the Soviet service? You say your father was your recruiter in an unspecific sense—who recruited you specifically?"

"Recruited. Into a t-t-*treasonous cause,* right? You resent that, the fact that s-secretly I was an agent of communism all along. H-how old were you in 1931?"

"Older than most my age."

"Well, exactly, your p-parents were k-killed by fascist monarchists, the right-wing C-C-Catholic lot, isn't that so?—in Madrid, when King Alfonso fled Spain; and a few y-y-years after that you were an orphan precociously working as a wireless t-telegrapher among the Loyalists. You see *I* r-r-remember everything about us. But in England in 1931 the b-betrayed Labour Party was v-voted out, and a coco—a Conservative National Government!—was voted in. You sh-should sympathize—the common p-people had been viciously fooled by sin-sin-*cynical* propaganda, and anyone could see that mere d-democracy could never lead to real p-peace."

He realized that he was frowning when the bandage over his forehead tightened, and he wondered, Do I still even believe that? Really?

"And *so,*" he went on, thrusting the thought away, "when another Cambridge student, this Guy B-B-*Burgess* fellow, approached me about d-doing s-secret work for Mother Russia, I was—*amenable.* Burgess had me tr-travel to Austria in the autumn of '33, when I was twenty-one years old; and with my B-British p-passport—and Cambridge accent!— I was able to be a useful network courier, c-carrying p-packages from Vienna to Prague and Budapest. In '34 I was s-sent back to work in England by one of the great old European illegals—he was a dedicated Communist and a Cheka officer, but he had been a C-C-Catholic p-priest before the horrors of the first war made him lose his f-faith, and when he was d-drunk he used to weep about the Cheka work he'd done, imposing collectivization on the Russian f-farms—"

" 'I could not bear the women wailing, when we lined the villagers up to be shot,' " said Elena in a quiet voice, clearly quoting. " 'I simply could not bear it.' "

And Philby was suddenly nauseated. He leaned on the cliff railing and stared at the circling birds in the gathering twilight. "You—*knew* Theo Maly?" he croaked.

"I met him in Paris, in 1937." Philby could barely hear her voice through the gauze over his ears. Her shoes shifted audibly on the pavement, and when she went on it was in a stronger voice, and she again seemed to be quoting someone: "Thistles, weeds—plants. Did Maly ever talk about such things with you, my dear?"

"Jesus!" burst out Philby, so loudly that a European tourist couple stared at him as they wheeled a perambulator along the sidewalk. "Yes, *my dear,*" he went on more quietly. "Yes, he did m-mention the *amomon* root to me—right at the end, when he had received his s-summons to Moscow and he knew he was g-going there to be g-given the, the *schluss*. And in fact he did tell me he was going by way of Paris."

"The *Stirnshluss,*" said Elena. "The bullet in the forehead."

Philby shifted to look around at her, and she was touching her own forehead, under the white bangs.

"Yes," Philby said, "th-that was the word he used. We were drinking in a London p-pub in early '37, and he t-told me, 'They will kill me if I go to Moscow—Stalin won't any longer continue to employ an ex-priest. But if I don't go, they will simply send someone to kill me here; and I don't want to give them the vindication of any disobedience on my part.' And then he—he said that, as a p-parting gift, he could offer me . . . *eternal life.* When I asked him what he m-meant, he explained that a C-C-Catholic p-priest can n-never abdicate his sacramental powers, and he offered to b-baptize me right there at the table, and then—he was drunk—to hear my c-c-*confession,* absolve me of my s-*sins,* if I would repent and have a f-firm purpose of amending them, and finally to order some bread and wine so that he could consecrate them and give me the"—he paused, and spoke carefully—"the Communion, the Eucharist."

"Ah, God," said Elena softly, taking off her sunglasses.

"Pitiful to see him b-break *down* so, at the end," agreed Philby. "I told him, 'No, th-thank you'—civilly enough, for he was an old f-friend, and drunk—and then he sighed, and said he could in that case offer me a more p-p-*profane* sort of eternal life."

The seagulls had been joined by pigeons from the cliffs, and the two sorts of birds were flying together in a wheel against the sky, which had lost its gold now and showed only the colors of blood and steel. Philby touched his chest, where Feisal's diamond hung on a chain under his shirt.

"There is apparently a k-kind of plant," he said slowly, "like a thistle, that g-grows at remote spots in the Holy Land. And you and I, my dear, have each seen enough of the sh-shameful supernatural to be at l-l-least ho-ho-*open-minded* to the idea that some specimens of this plant are *inhabited,* by the old entities. Maly said that when the r-rebel angels f-fell at the beginning of the w-world, some weren't quite bad enough to rate *Hell,* perhaps weren't developed or c-complete enough to have fully assented to the rebellion. In any case, they were truncated, compressed, c-condemned to live forever unconsciously as a k-kind of thistle— immortal still, in the a-a-*aggregate* at least, but on a sub-sentient level. They can be awakened, b-briefly, by a certain p-primordial, antediluvian rhythm, something s-similar to what the old illegals and the Rote Kapelle called *les parasites."*

The wheeling seagulls had disappeared in the darkness below the cliff at his feet. Low tide, he thought vaguely. They'll be feeding.

"And if a p-person awakens one of these vegetation-bound angels," he went on, "and then eats it with the p-proper *sacramentals,* sugar and garlic and l-liquor and such, that p-person will share in the angel's immortality, will n-never grow old or suffer f-fatal injury or illness. My father had known something of this—in the Gilgamesh story, a g-god tells the man Upanishtim to build a boat and take into it 'the seed of all living creatures,' and Upanishtim and his family do it, and s-survive the flood—and long afterward, Upanishtim gives Gilgamesh a th-thorny plant that will restore youth. But b-before Gilgamesh can take it home to his people, an old s-s-*snake!*—comes out of a well!—and eats the plant, and immediately c-casts off its old skin and returns, y-young again, to the well. So the plant w-w-worked as promised, but Gilgamesh d-didn't get it."

"Maly *did* talk to me about this!" exclaimed Elena. She went on, almost to herself, "Oh, I think he did; I will have to tell old Cassagnac that my answer in 1941 was not accurate." She looked up at Philby, her eyes gleaming in the light from the hotels across the street. "I was only twelve, but Maly said that the Serpent in the Garden of Eden tempted Eve with the fruit of the Tree of Knowledge of Good and Evil in order to keep her and Adam away from the *other* tree, the Tree of Life, which—"

"*Who's that?*" Philby shouted.

He had grabbed her arm with his left hand, and with his right he was pointing at the taller of the two rocks out in the bay—for he had just noticed a silhouetted figure standing in the meadow on the inaccessible top. It was far too remote for him to be able to tell if it was a man or a woman . . . but one of its arms was waving. It was beckoning.

"Don't move," he added in a whisper, for with a sound like sudden rain the birds now swept up from the abyss below the cliff and were circling low over Elena and himself—the pigeons and gulls made no cries, but the flutter of their wings was like rushing banners, and Philby was now aware of an invisible third person here. Had the third person drawn the attention of the birds, or of the thing that animated the birds?

Philby's chest was suddenly cold. Is that thing aware that I'm trying to beg off, here? he thought. Trying to forsake the old covenant?

The tourists along the cliff rail had been startled when he shouted, and now they hurried away as the low-flying pigeons and seagulls did not disperse—and Philby became aware of the ringing of a telephone.

Hatif, he thought breathlessly—the call from the dead at night, foretelling another death—but where is it? He glanced at the figure out on the rock, fearful that *it* might be flying toward them through the twilight; but it was still there where he had first seen it, still beckoning.

Rocking into cautious motion, Elena took two stiff steps toward a purse and a couple of abandoned toys that a woman had left behind on the sidewalk after snatching up her baby and hurrying away from the intrusive birds. Philby squinted at the toys and saw that one of them was a yellow plastic telephone; and then he realized that the ringing was coming from this toy.

"Don't—*answer* it," he croaked.

But Elena had bent down awkwardly, her white hair blown into her face by the battering breeze of the close wings, and she lifted the receiver, which was connected by a string to a plastic box with a smiling dial-face printed on it.

She held the little receiver to her ear; the mouthpiece was pressed against her cheek.

His face hot with humiliation, Philby babbled, "It will only be my w-wife, my l-last wife—she d-d-died five years ago, and she's always c-calling me—d-don't listen to her f-f-filth—"

"It's—a man," Elena said tonelessly. "I—I think I know him." She lifted the plastic receiver, with the telephone swinging below it on the string, not connected to anything else and with no antenna, and held the impossibly speaking thing toward him, as if for an explanation.

Philby reached out—slowly, for he feared that any sudden move might provoke some kind of calamitous definition of the birds—and as he kept his eyes on the beckoning figure on the distant rock he pressed the toy receiver to his ear.

"Their thoughts are kinetic macroscopic events," said a British man's voice from the unperforated earpiece, clearly enough for Philby to hear through the bandages, *"wind and fire and sandstorms, gross and literal. What the djinn imagine is done: for them to imagine it is to have done it, and for them to be reminded of it is for them to do it again. Their thoughts are* things, *things in* motion, *and their memories are literal things too, preserved for potential reference—wedding rings and gold teeth looted from graves, and bones in the sand, and scorch-marks on floors, all ready to spring into renewed activity again at a reminder. To impose—"*

The woman whose child the telephone belonged to had for several seconds now been yelling something from several yards away. "Shut her up!" yelled Philby now to Elena.

The voice in the toy had paused, as if it had heard him; then it went on, *"To impose a memory-shape onto their physical makeup is to forcibly impose an experience—which, in the case of a Shihab meteorite's imprint, is death."*

The speaker had not raised his voice, but at the word *death* the volume had increased, and Philby dropped the toy telephone when the abruptly loud word impacted his eardrum.

And the birds scattered away into the darkening sky, as if all released at once from invisible tethers. Philby turned awkwardly from the waist to watch as many of them as he could—he had no peripheral vision—and when he saw a Chevrolet sedan swerving in toward this cliff-side curb he whispered, "Fuck."

But perhaps they were simply stopping because of the birds and the panicky tourists.

He was shaking from the enigmatic encounter with the animated birds and the figure on the rock and the *hatif* call, and from the ordeal of having begun at long last to confess his real career before that; he had been living on nerves and gin ever since passing his proposal to the SDECE five days ago—and he was fifty years old now and felt every conflicted day of it.

He took Elena's elbow and led her away, toward the nearest crosswalk. "Don't look b-back," he said; "That's r-rogue CIA in the Chevrolet behind us, n-not working through CIA Beirut, but sent independently by the head of their Office of Special Operations in Washington."

Could they be here for *me?* he wondered tensely; could they be planning finally to *grab* me, kidnap me out of Beirut? Why?—why *now*, after three years of simply harassing me, and putting surveillance on me, and bribing the Lebanese *sûreté* to detain me from time to time for fruitless interrogation? Have they now learned about Mammalian, and the imminent Ararat expedition? Is this a pre-emptive detainment, meant to frustrate the operation I've for-Christ's-sake *already decided* I cannot perform? If the Americans *arrest* me, with the intention of flying me back to Washington and publicly *trying* me for espionage against their government back in '49 and '50, the French will surely withdraw their offer. The SDECE might even have told Elena to kill me, if I look like getting out of the French net. She might be able to do it too. And even if she did not, I'd spend all the rest of my birthdays in an American prison. The CIA, and Hoover at the FBI, will never agree to any immunity deal. And if my Soviet handlers thought I was about to be arrested by any Western government, they would surely kill me. I am being torn to pieces by East and West. I am being torn to pieces between East and West.

Sweat rolled down his forehead from the bandage, and he blinked it away. They'll have heard I was shot, I'm conspicuous in this bloody bandage.

When they had crossed the street to the landward sidewalk, he took Elena's shoulders and faced her, so that she was blocking their view of him; and quickly he hiked his ankle up and snagged the revolver out of the elastic holster and dropped it into his coat pocket.

Elena had raised one eyebrow at the momentary glimpse of the gun, but now she fell into step beside him as he began walking south along the sidewalk below the amber-lit lobby of the Carlton Hotel.

"I suppose *they* suspect your *KGB* complicity," she said. Her emphasis confirmed that she was well aware of his work for the deeper, older, vastly more secret agency.

"Suspect, yes—they've s-s-*suspected* me ever since Burgess d-defected to Moscow eleven years ago. Listen," he said, speaking quickly, "I won't let them arrest me. The deal I'm offering your people is jjj-genuine, damn it, it's *richtig,* understand? This isn't a Soviet t-trick, I swear by—by the heart that is still beating beneath your b-breast. My father was my protector, my *shield,* in this business, and he's gone now, and I can't do what the Rab—what the Soviets—well, what the *Rabkrin* wants me to do now. I cannot go up the mountain." In spite of his frantic unhappiness, he found that there was something distinctly *sexy* about exposing his momentous secrets to her; and even though his cold fingers were clamped on the grip of the revolver, he found himself thinking about their unsatisfactory kiss in the bar. "Have you g-got SDECE w-watching us now? Exfiltrate m-me right now, this nin-nin-instant."

She shook her head. "We can exfiltrate you from Beirut as soon as I am convinced that you'll tell us everything. I need to know—" She didn't go on, and he glanced at her. For a moment her face was blank, neither young nor old but as cold as a statue's. "—I need to know what happened on Mount Ararat in May of 1948."

"I can t-t-tell you all of th-that. If we get so-so-separated tonight, I'm meeting the S-Soviet team tomorrow m-morning at eleven—I've toe-told them to meet me on the t-terrace at the St. Georges Hotel. After that I sh-should be mom-mom-*unobserved*—follow me from there."

"I'll get in touch with you again, no fear. I'll decide when and where."

"You think I have no capacity for loyalty," he said hoarsely, "but I will be honest with your people. I was l-loyal to the rrr*Russians* for decades, for far longer than anyone would be who was not genuinely in l-love with the Communist ideal. I was a p-protégé of Maly's, and they feared he had told me the s-secret of the *amomon* rhythms, so in the great purr-purr—*purge* season they tried to kill me too—on my b-birthday in 1937—"

Instantly he glanced to the left, past her shoulder, and said, "Let's get off the street. A drink in the Carlton, what do you say?"—but he was horrified to realize that in his besotted confessional passion he had nearly betrayed his real birthday. I'm falling apart, he thought remotely. Breaking in two, at least; who *was* that, talking about djinn on the *hatif* telephone?

As he led Elena through the glass doors and across the carpeted lobby toward the bar—a good deal dressier than the Normandy's, with wood paneling and upholstered booths—he was remembering that frosty *last day of 1937,* when he had been out driving from Saragossa toward Tereuel, in Spain, under cover as a war correspondent for the *London Times;* an artillery shell had landed squarely on the car he and three other correspondents had been driving in, and his three companions had been blown to pieces, while Philby himself had suffered only a couple of cuts. The shell had been a Russian 12.40-centimeter round, certainly deliberately aimed, even deliberately scheduled—but, because it *was* his true birthday, Philby had taken the precaution of wearing the bright green, fox-fur lined Arab coat his father had given him, and so he had survived the explosion with only scratches. He had received a telegram the next day from his father in Alexandria—the old man had abruptly fainted the day before, bleeding from the nose and ears, at the very hour when Philby's car had been hit, and the elder Philby had been anxious now to know if his son had been hurt.

Philby had been wearing the fox fur this last Tuesday too—but with his father now dead *and* gone, the bullet that had been fired at his head had come much closer to killing him.

"Your birthday in '37?" prompted Elena when Philby had walked her to a booth against the doorway wall. She was looking at him as she sat down.

"Maly g-gave me a simple code with which to write hopefully innocent-looking l-letters to a cover address in Paris, a safe house where s-some NKVD courier would p-pick up the mail," Philby said, sitting down across from her and waving to the waiter. "You know the kind of code: 'Six *couches* arrived yesterday, but *the midwife* says they're not the *edible* kind—the *dog* needs more *toothbrushes.*' Not that bad, I suppose, but definitely d-disjointed; one hoped that the censors saw a lot of mail from genuine chatty l-l-lunatics." He was beginning to relax—this story was verifiably true, and Maly *had* given him the code sometime very early in '37, and it might even *have been* on his ostensible New Year's Day birthday. "I only found out in 1945, when I was Head of Section Nine and v-visiting the liberated c-capitals of Europe, that the address I had been writing to on the rue de Grenelle eight years earlier *had been the Soviet Embassy!* There was n-no safe house at all, n-no s-security measures—any censor who might have gone to the t-trouble of checking the address I was writing to would have r-reported me as a Soviet agent in an instant!"

Elena had fished matches and a pack of Gauloises from her purse, and she looked at him through narrowed eyes as she lit a cigarette. "Careless and negligent, surely—contemptuous, even—but I'd hardly call that an attempt to *purge* you, *kill* you."

She was not deflected. "Well," he said with affected mildness, "to *me* it seemed as if they had g-given me a ticking time bomb to hold. Two G-Gordon's gins, please, neat," he said then to the waiter who had finally come to the table. "Those are for me," he added, giving Elena his most charming grin. "What will you have? I believe you were drinking b-brandy, in Berlin."

"Can the bartender make a *Berliner Weisse mit Schuss?*" Elena asked the waiter. "That's beer with raspberry syrup," she added.

The waiter concealed any repugnance and simply said, *"Mais oui, madame,"* and bowed and stepped away.

Philby remembered the mug of odd pink beer that had been on the table in Berlin. "That was *your* drink, that night?"

"Do you disapprove? As I recall, *you* were drinking *insecticide.*"

Philby nodded glumly. "Djinn repellent, the old Cairo hands used to call it. If my f-father had thought to give me a glass of insecticide before we flew over Lake Tiberias, I would not have c-contracted 'malaria.' They . . . bud off, like cactus, in periods of activity, and the l-little . . . djinnlings! . . . can be attracted to and c-*cling* to someone who has—someone who bears the m-mark of previous djinn-recognition. They get in through your m-mouth, and they interfere with your thoughts, and exorcising them later is a tiresome bother. My father t-told me that some of the old lads in the Arab Bureau in Cairo would even rinse their m-mouths with a shot of petrol, if they were going out to some place where the m-monsters were likely to be. Volatile smells repel them, the y-young ones, at least, and a couple of shots of warm jjj-*gin* here ought to drive off any who came up over the cliff just now with the b-birds."

Elena was blushing, and Philby remembered asking her if she had not found this business vaguely shameful. "That was a, a female one, in Berlin," she said.

Philby could feel the hairs standing up on his arms, even at this late and cynical date, as he said softly, "That was Russia's very g-guardian angel, my dear—Machikha Nash, Our Stepmother—inspecting the n-new boundaries of her k-kingdom in person, in stormy person. I was there to monitor the installation of her boundary stone, and I watched it all from a parked car in the Charlotteburg Chaussee on the western side. She was . . . *splendid,* wasn't she? I remember thinking of Byron's line, *'She walks in Beauty, like the night/Of cloudless climes and starry skies.'* What w-were you doing there?"

Philby didn't look away from her, but he was aware of the two men who walked into the bar, and he simply shrugged and gave her a frail smile when they stopped in front of his table.

One of the men seemed to say, "Allah, beastly ass," but a moment later Philby realized that he had said, in an American accent, *I'll obviously ask;* and the man went on, "Who's your girlfriend, Kim?"

Philby looked up at his CIA inquisitors. Both were sandy-haired Americans in gray suits with wide lapels, and they both seemed offensively fit and young.

"Miss Weiss is a French m-magazine editor," Philby said. "I'm t-trying to sell her s-some nonfiction work."

"*We'd* love to read some of your non-fiction work, Kim," said the taller of the two. "Scoot over, Miss Weiss." When Elena shifted away across the booth seat, the man sat down beside her.

His companion folded himself into the booth beside Philby, so that Philby and Elena were both blocked in. "I'm Dr. Tarr," said the man beside Philby, "and my colleague there is Professor Feather. Our boss across the water is very curious about this *gathering of the old hands* that's going on here in Beirut."

"I'm not aware of it," said Philby carefully. He wanted to pant with relief, for clearly this was not to be a kidnap. With some confidence he went on, "Are you g-going to have the *sûreté* h-h-haul me in to their p-p-*police* station one more time, just so I can s-say the same th-thing there for a few hours?"

"More like watch-and-wait," said the man identified as Professor Feather. "You still do odd jobs for your old firm, don't you, Kim? Peter Lunn gives you off-paper travel assignments?"

Lunn was the SIS Head of Station in Beirut now, and in fact he had not had any professional conversation with Philby at all. But until three months ago the Head of Station had been Nicholas Elliott, an old friend of Philby's and one of his loyal defenders in the Burgess defection scandal that had cost Philby his SIS job in 1951. And in these last two years Elliott had indeed given Philby all kinds of off-paper assignments—to Riyadh, and Cairo, and Baghdad, and a dozen other Middle East cities—to mingle with the Arabs who had known Philby's father, and gauge the extent and purpose of the huge increase in the number of Soviet military advisors throughout the Arab nations.

Philby had been in a quandary: it had been starkly clear that Burgess at the Rabkrin headquarters in Moscow, as well as Petrukhov, Philby's more pedestrian KGB handler in Beirut, both required him to pass on immediately any information he might learn about the SIS response to the Soviet escalation—but Philby had been aware too that the SIS chiefs in London who believed him guilty of espionage would see to it that he was given "barium meal" information, custom-scripted false data that might later be detected in monitored Moscow traffic. If that were to happen, Philby would logically be isolated as the only possible source of the information, and the SIS could then arrest him for treason; and until this last September, when Philby's pet fox had been intolerably killed and further work with the Rabkrin had become unthinkable, Philby had not wanted the SIS to arrest him. Even now, he wanted to surrender only on specific terms, what he thought of as his three non-negotiable "itties": immunity, a new identity, and a comfortable annuity. Definitely *not* the deal Theodora's old fugitive SOE had offered him in '52.

"Or isn't it for Lunn?" went on Professor Feather. "Are you still running errands for—" He looked across the table at Dr. Tarr. "What was his name?"

"Petrukhov," said Dr. Tarr. "Of the Soviet trade mission in Lebanon. He's the local handler, runner."

"Any t-traveling I do," Philby said mildly, "has b-been for the stories I write."

"That's odd, you know," said Dr. Tarr. "You always charge your airline tickets on your IATA card, don't you? Well, we've clocked your stories in *The Observer* and *The Economist,* and compared them to the records from the International Air Transport Association in Montreal, and we find that your travel grossly outweighs your journalistic output. Could I have a bourbon-and-water, please," he said to the waiter, who had just then walked up with the two gins and the pink beer on a tray.

"Same here," said Dr. Tarr.

The waiter set the drinks on the table, nodded and strode back toward the bar.

Ignoring her ludicrous drink, Elena picked up her purse from beside her and said, "The dealings of the American Internal Revenue Service do not interest me. Mr. Philby, I'll be in touch—"

Professor Feather didn't budge. "Stay, Miss Weiss," he said coldly. "You play a musical instrument, don't you? Something about the size of a saxophone?"

"The U.S. government will pick up the drinks tab," added Dr. Tarr cheerfully, "though not precisely in its IRS capacity."

Philby thought the saxophone remark had seemed to jar her; but now she just sighed and said, "No, I don't play any instrument. But—I suppose I can't resist the opportunity to deplete the American treasury." She put her purse back down.

"And we even took your pseudonyms into account," said Professor Feather to Philby. "Charles Garner and all. It still doesn't add up."

Philby had already begun shaking his head dismissively, and he didn't stop now—but he was chilled by this new factor. The CIA knew that Charles Garner was one of his pseudonyms!—and Mammalian's new agent was to be using that identity as cover! Philby wondered if he should warn Mammalian, or let the CIA discover the Garner impostor; if Elena's SDECE people could "exfiltrate" him very soon, it wouldn't matter.

"You obviously know n-nothing about j-journalistic work," said Philby, picking up one of his glasses of gin. "Some of the seeds fall upon st-stony places, and w-wither in the sun because they have no root. For every story I file, a d-dozen prove to be false alarms." He lifted the glass to his lips and swirled the warm liquor over his tongue.

"That's from the thirteenth chapter of Matthew," said Dr. Tarr, "your seed analogy is. It properly refers to people, of course—and do remember the next verse: *'And some fell among thorns; and the thorns sprang up, and choked them.'* "

And to Philby's embarrassment, a trickle of the gin slipped down his windpipe, and he coughed gin out through his nostrils; the stinging liquor burned in his nose and brought tears to his eyes, and the CIA men laughed as he continued coughing.

"Oh, a palpable hit!" said Dr. Tarr. "You like to act as if you're out of play these days, Kim—the retired cold warrior—but lately Moscow is scrambling to make the Red Sea a Red Army sea, and make the Persian Gulf a . . ."

"Potemkin bluff?" suggested Elena. She was staring at Philby with distaste.

"Too reached-for," said Professor Feather, shaking his head.

"Anyway," Dr. Tarr went on, "they were ready to make the Caribbean a Soviet pond too, until Kennedy made them back down two months ago. Now the last time the Soviets tried a big grab like this was in '48, when they blockaded Berlin and incidentally annexed Czecho-slovakia and got a Communist Party member in as president of Hun-gary. *Less overtly,* there was also some action at that time around the Aras River, between Turkey and Soviet Armenia—specifically in the Ahora Gorge on Mount Ararat. And there are a lot of people in Beirut right now who were there then; including Miss Elena Teresa Ceniza-Bendiga herself."

Elena lifted her glass of pink beer in a tired salute and took a gulp of it.

"A couple of the old cast are *not* here, though," said Professor Feather, "or not obviously or not yet. Your old house-mate Burgess is unlikely to show up, I suppose, Kim; our Brit colleagues would arrest him if he strayed out of the Soviet Union. But Andrew Hale fled England on Wednesday, the second, and the SIS managed to track him to Kuwait, but lost him the next day. It seems timely. Have you heard any-thing about him?"

"N-no," said Philby, "I s-scarcely remember the boy." But his mind was whirling, trying to figure out how this new piece on the chessboard might change the lines of consequence. Hale was Theodora's star pro-tégé, Philby thought, and he *appeared* to be fired after his failure on Ararat; was that a feint? God help me if Theodora is still *in* this in any

way. Surely that old ultimatum with the SOE no longer applies! He
remembered Theodora's words at the Turkish–Soviet border in 1952:
*Report to us any contact from the Soviets; and participate in any action they
order you into; and report it all to us; or die.*

Elena took another sip of her polluted beer. " 'Fled England,' " she
said; " 'lost him the next day.' Is he a fugitive?" And with a chill Philby
remembered that Hale had been bitterly in love with her, in '48, and he
remembered the high-low seven-card stud game he had played with
Hale in the Anderson bomb shelter on that last terrible night: *Low hand
wins Maly's amomon instructions.*

"The news is five days old, even at newspaper-level," said Professor
Feather; "I'm surprised the SDECE hasn't relayed it to you. Hale was to
be arrested for old embezzlements committed during his residency in
Kuwait right after the war—on Wednesday MI5 sent an agent to negoti-
ate a possible immunity deal with him, contingent on doing some work
for the SIS, and Hale killed the agent and fled. He killed a cop too."

"Claude Cassagnac," said Dr. Tarr.

"What about Claude Cassagnac?" asked Elena quickly.

Philby recalled that she had mentioned the name Cassagnac earlier
this evening: *Maly did talk to me about this! I will have to tell old Cassagnac
that my answer in 1941 was not accurate.*

"That was the MI5 agent Hale killed," said Dr. Tarr. "I gather he was
more a consultant than an agent, actually."

"What proof is this?" demanded Elena, quaintly using in English
what Philby recognized as an old bit of Spanish Civil War slang.

"This is two hundred proof, ma'am, solid spirit right over the top of
the still," said Professor Feather, staring curiously at her. "Like I said, it's
even newspaper-level." He stood up out of the booth, unblocking her
way. "If you're through with your drink, you can leave."

"I'm not through with my drink," she said.

"Kim's not really for sale right now, Miss Ceniza-Bendiga." Professor
Feather looked across the table to where Philby sat hemmed in by Dr.
Tarr. *"We intend to read your non-fiction, Kim. And not as . . . excerpts,
in a French translation."*

Right, you haven't got a "special relationship" with the SDECE,
thought Philby, the way you have with the SIS. But neither you fellows
nor, apparently, my disappointing old SIS colleagues, are offering me
any itties. *Tout au contraire,* in fact.

The prolonged nervous strain of this evening, along with the cumulative effects of drink and his throbbing, wounded head, was goading Philby toward something like hysteria. I've got to end this, he thought.

"Oh well," he said with desperately affected breeziness, "Miss Weiss is only interested in—d-d-domestic reminiscences, human-interest m-material. Travels with my f-father, the traumas of a raw-raw-*religious* education, the d-death of my pet ffff*fox*—upon my honor, nothing that would attain to your 'n-newspaper level.'" He finished his first gin and picked up the second. "And now if you'll both excuse us . . ."

Dr. Tarr stood up from beside Philby and leaned down over Philby's bandaged head. "Applewhite doesn't think you were ever a spy for the Soviets," he said; Applewhite was the CIA station chief in Beirut. "The Philbys and the Applewhites go out together for picnics in the mountains by Ajaltoun. Applewhite thinks we're scoundrels for hassling you and rousting you all the time."

Cautiously, Philby allowed himself an indulgent laugh, and it came out convincingly enough; but when he tried to speak he found that he was babbling nervously: "Oh, th-that successive—that's excessive, surely—you s-seem like a couple of clean-cut Woodminster—I mean, Midwestern—"

"But *we're* not *under* Applewhite," Dr. Tarr went on almost in a snarl. "We work directly for the Office of Special Operations in Washington. And *our* boss"—he pressed his lips together—"*our* boss is very aware of your father, your pet fox."

Philby felt as though the man had punched him in the stomach. The *CIA* knows that my father's ghost was *inhabiting* that fox? But they *can't* know much *more* than that, they can't even *know that,* not with any certainty.

He had raised his eyebrows, and now he tensely opened his mouth to to try to express . . . weary puzzlement, impatience, mounting irritability . . .

But Professor Feather stepped well back from Elena and delivered another punch: "While you're dickering with the SDECE, ask Miss Ceniza-Bendiga to show you where she lay prone on the roof of a Rue Kantari office building Tuesday night, across the street from your place. She brought the rifle in a saxophone case, and I guess she must have joggled the telescopic sight a little during the taxi ride."

"You two have a pleasant evening now, hear?" said Dr. Tarr cheerfully, and the two CIA men strode out of the bar.

Philby had snatched the revolver out of his coat pocket and was now pointing it under the table directly at Elena's abdomen. "Dumdums," he said evenly, though he was breathing hard. "Paralysis, peritonitis—those would be *good* news."

He was remembering last Tuesday night—the stunning blow to the head while he stood in front of the toilet in his bathroom, and then his own drunken, confused effort to bash his head *again*, against the radiator, to conceal from his wife the fact that he had been shot—his wife dragging him half-conscious to the bedroom, with blood jetting from his scalp and spattering the wall and ruining the pillows—and then the Lebanese doctor that poor Eleanor had somehow got to come over to the apartment, and Philby's inarticulate reluctance to be taken away to a hospital while an assassin might be waiting outside for a second shot—

Elena smiled at him coldly and slowly lifted the palms of both hands from the table. "I don't have the rifle now. And that was just . . . personal regards, Tuesday night, disobedience—not my orders. France *is* willing to buy you—even if France's temperamental emissary would rather have seen you dead, that night—and you do still need a nation that will give you protection and immunity. You don't dare go up the mountain with the Russian expedition, do you, now that your protector and shield is *all the way* gone? You told me that your father's *body* died two years ago—when did the *fox* die?"

"September," whispered Philby, lowering the barrel of the gun. "Somebody p-pushed him over the railing of our apartment. Pushed *her,* if you like—the f-fox was a female. Fifth floor."

"I'll deny having shot at you," she said. She took a deep breath, and then, her eyes bright with tears as she stared straight at him, she added with clear deliberateness, "And what would have been the point of trying to kill you last Tuesday, in any case?—since"—she visibly braced herself—"since during our talk tonight I've gathered that January first isn't your true birthday after all? Your real birthday, the real day on which you're mortally vulnerable, is the date when something happened to nearly kill you in '37, right?"

The barrel was up again, leveled at her, but he made himself lift his finger out of the trigger guard. No, he thought, she's only giving you the truth: you will not be permitted to keep any part of you opaque; in the end you will be left with no secrets at all. "You—nearly got it, just then," he said, his whisper very shaky now. "Did you—*know* you were attempting suicide, by saying that to me?"

"I—I know you're solicitous of suicidal women." She exhaled on a downward whistling note, and her shoulders sagged. "And so you leave me with a *different* person to try to kill."

Philby nodded slowly, comprehending. "Andrew Hale," he said.

▼

12

Beirut, 1963/Wabar, 1948

The child turned on the cushion of the huge corded arms and looked at Kim through heavy eyelids. "And was it all worthless?" Kim asked, with easy interest.
    "All worthless—all worthless," said the child, lips cracking with fever.
—Rudyard Kipling, *Kim*

Earlier in the evening, when the sky had still been gold beyond the blowing gauze curtains, Hale had reluctantly pulled up a chair at one side of his hotel room desk.

He stared without enthusiasm at the glasses of arak that Mammalian had poured before sitting down in the chair opposite him; and as Hale watched, Mammalian topped up each glass from the water pitcher on the desk, and the clear liquor was abruptly streaked with milky cloudiness. Hale had never been seasick or airsick, but he was sweating and nauseated right now with a profounder sort of deficiency in traction. The Mezon wire recorder at Mammalian's elbow hissed faintly as its spools turned.

"You are ill at ease," said Mammalian quietly, stroking his black beard as he looked out the window at the purple Mediterranean sea. "You are like a man nerving himself to climb a steep mountain, anticipating all sorts of chasms, hard challenges, muscles flexed to cramping. But it is not a mountain—it is a flat beach, and you are only going to walk into the surf." He shrugged and rocked his head. "It will be cold, and the breath will perhaps seem to stop in your throat at times, but you will get through it by *relaxing*. All your adult life you have kept up a tense guard, a tight, clinging posture—your task tonight is simply to lower the guard, let your fists unclench." He turned away from the window to look at Hale, and he laughed softly. "Drink, my friend."

Hale nodded and lifted one of the glasses with a shaky hand. The liquor was sharp with the taste of anise, but when he had swallowed it he was glad of the expanding heat in his chest.

"What," said Mammalian thoughtfully, "has the British secret service learned about our plans involving Mount Ararat?"

"We—got the first hints of it when—Volkov—tried to defect from the Soviet NKGB, in Istanbul in '45," said Hale. He clanked the glass down, and a few drops flew out and beaded like pearls on the polished dark wood. In spite of what Mammalian had said, he was so tense that it was a conscious effort to breathe. Somehow it didn't help that he had gone over this same ground four days earlier with Ishmael. Ishmael's subsequent death had been a reprieve, a negation of it.

"But the NKGB *killed* Konstantin Volkov," said Mammalian, "before he could defect."

"True," said Hale. He forced his shoulders to relax, and he spread his hands on the desktop.

"Just wade slowly into the surf. It is cold, but still very shallow."

Hale nodded. "Volkov was a walk-in," he said. "He apparently just went to the British Consulate General building one day in August of '45, and said he wanted to sell information; he had a lot of—names of Soviet agents, even of doubles working in the British service, but the—the big item—was details about a most-secret impending Soviet operation in eastern Turkey."

"Go on. Take your time."

Hale filled his lungs, and then just let the words tumble out in a rush: "Volkov was the NKGB deputy resident, under cover as the local Soviet consul general, and in exchange for his full deposition he wanted a lot of money and a *laissez-passer* to Cyprus for himself and his wife. Unfortunately our ambassador was on vacation, and his *chargé d'affaires* didn't approve of espionage, so he didn't relay the offer to Cyril Machray, the SIS station commander. Both Machray and the ambassador had been indoctrinated into the outlines of our fugitive-SOE operation and would have relayed him to our man in Turkey. As it happened, though, Volkov's offer was simply sent by diplomatic bag to the SIS Section Nine in Broadway, in London, where Kim Philby was in charge. Philby took control of Volkov's case and somehow didn't manage to drag himself down to Istanbul until a month had passed since Volkov's visit; and by that time Volkov and his wife had been loaded into a Moscow-bound airplane—on stretchers, wrapped in bandages."

He had been unable to keep the bitterness out of his voice, and Mammalian smiled sympathetically. "Ah, well, Philby was one of ours, you know. He couldn't let Volkov talk to you people. In fact he told his London handler about it immediately, and Moscow Centre took care of the rest."

Hale wiped his damp forehead with his shirtsleeve and took another sip of the arak. "*But!*—our consulate office had taken routine photographs of the contents of Volkov's samples-package, the documents he had brought in to show his authority, before sending the originals to Philby in London; I was stationed in Kuwait then, and prints were eventually circulated to me for study."

"Why to you?"

"Because during the war I'd become one of the listed referees in the topics the documents dealt with—Volkov's samples included aerial photographs of Mount Ararat, with maps of the mountain's Ahora Gorge indicating the locations of what he called 'drogue stones,' which are—"

"Anchors," said Mammalian.

Hale nodded uncommittally; then he went on, more easily than before, "Or the five points of a pentagram, say, if there's a ring of these drogue stones, as there appeared to be on Ararat. A containment, an imposed ground state." The sea breeze from the window was chilly on his sweaty face, but now he felt as though a fever had broken; and he recalled that he had felt this way with Ishmael too, after a few minutes of talking. "It was autumn of '47 when the neglected Volkov prints were finally relayed to my office in the British Embassy at Al-Kuwait, and by that time I had got to know the local Bedu tribes—I had even traveled with the Mutair during the previous winter, and I had—"

Hale paused and took another sip of the candy-flavored drink. He was always vaguely but specifically humiliated to refer to experiences with the supernatural.

"I had by then met several of the oldest inhabitants of the desert," he said flatly, not looking at Mammalian. "Do you know the creatures to whom I refer."

He shivered as he remembered at times cowering before tall sandstorms that boomed out the old rhythmic syllables across the dunes, and remembered at other times actually conversing in cautious, archaic Arabic with depleted or confined members of the unnatural species: by means of radios carried down into wells too deep to receive human broadcasts, or with codes plucked by box canyon winds on Aeolian harps, or in flocks of caged birds that generally died in the stress of conveying vigorous answers to questions. *Never surprise them,* he had learned; *never reason with them.*

Mammalian reached across the hotel room desk to squeeze Hale's shoulder with one big brown hand, and his bearded face was creased in a wincing smile. "They are *angels,* Charles Garner!" he said earnestly. "Fallen, yes, but they are nevertheless pure spirits, who must take up the physical matter at hand in order to appear to us at all. They are a bigger category of *thing* than we are, and their proximity must needs diminish and humble us, by comparison."

Hale sat back in his chair, freeing his shoulder from the other man's hand; *sympathy* in this, even companionship, seemed perverse. "I had seen one of them in the summer of '45," he said in a resolutely matter-of-fact tone, "in *Berlin.* And from my wartime studies I knew that the drogue stone that had drawn it there had ultimately come from Mount Ararat in 1883. So Volkov's long-delayed information did two things for me: it bolstered my suspicions that a colony of djinn existed on Mount Ararat, and—"

"A kingdom," said Mammalian.

"Very well, a *kingdom* of djinn. And it let me know that the most-secret agency of the Soviets was planning to go again to the Ahora Gorge on Ararat—perhaps to fetch out another of the creatures, perhaps to establish some diplomatic alliance with the whole tribe." He smiled. "Perhaps both."

"It is both," said Mammalian. He looked away from Hale, out the window at the darkening sky. "And ultimately it will be an alliance with *mankind,* rather than with this nation or that. You, and even Kim Philby, and even myself, are in fortunate positions in this transcendent work. We will live forever, and we will be like gods." He blinked several times, and then looked back at Hale. "Your Operation Declare—it was a frustrated attempt to kill the angels on the mountain. How was it intended to work?"

And here we are at last, thought Hale. "It was," he began, and then he paused, waiting to see if God would provide an interruption; but the wind kept fluttering the curtains, the wire spools rotated steadily, and Mammalian simply stared at him. "Oh well." He sighed deeply. "I was trying to forcibly impose upon the djinn the experience of death."

"Yes, of course. But how?"

"It was a refinement of a technique the wartime French DGSS had used to try to kill the one in Berlin. Their scientists in Algiers had cut a cylinder from what was allegedly a Shihab meteorite, one of the spent 'shooting stars' that has knocked down and killed a djinn. Our SOE was able to get the specs on the operation, and the meteoric iron the French had used did have a peculiar internal structure: fine straight fissures— something like the Neumann lines that are found in ordinary meteorite cross-sections, and which result from interstellar collisions—but these were all at precise right angles, and the French had concluded that this configuration was a unique result of fatal collision with a djinn. The scientists believed"—how had poor old Cassagnac put it?—"that the iron 'contained the death of one of these creatures,' and that firing the death into the Berlin djinn would kill it."

"We had not known all this," said Mammalian softly. "We knew only that someone had fired some sort of gun at the angel."

"And of course the DGSS bullet didn't affect your *angel* at all. So I went back and studied the djinn. I read the oldest fragments of the *Hezar Efsan*, which was the core of the *Thousand Nights and One Night*; and in the Midian mountains of the Hejaz I found communities of Magians, fire-worshippers, and traded gold and medical-supply whole blood and thermite bombs for the privilege of witnessing their distressing mountain-top liturgies. And I found that in all the very oldest records, djinn are described as being killed by . . . trivial-seeming things: someone carelessly throwing a date-stone at one of them, or accidentally hitting one with a misaimed fowling arrow, or even by taking a sparrow out of a hidden nest. Eventually I decided that the way to kill a djinn was to change the shape of its animated substance in a particular way."

"I am glad we stopped you on Ararat fourteen years ago," said Mammalian, lifting his own glass and draining it in one gulp.

"I decided that a Shihab meteorite *would* comprise the death of a djinn—not in the stone's internal structure, but in its melted and rehardened *shape*. The meteorites are always pitted with round holes, like bubbles, uniform in their dimensions but of all sizes, even down to microscopic; I concluded that the concavities in the surface of the meteorite are the imprint of a djinn's death, repeated at every possible scale, and that if I could summon the djinn down from the mountain peak to the stone in the gorge, and then explode it in the midst of them, the pieces would be propelled into the substances of the creatures, forcing their *stuff* to assume the complementary convex shape."

Hale paused. For the last several seconds he had been hearing a telephone ringing in some nearby room; but Mammalian hadn't paid any attention to it, and now Hale realized that it had stopped.

"The djinn are supposed to have existed before mankind," Hale went on, "and in many ways they are a more primitive sort of life, more crude. Their thoughts are kinetic macroscopic events, wind and fire and sandstorms, gross and literal. What the djinn imagine is done: for them to imagine it is to have done it, and for them to be reminded of it is for them to do it again. Their thoughts are *things,* things in *motion,* and their memories are literal things too, preserved for potential reference—wedding rings and gold teeth looted from graves, and bones in the sand, and scorch-marks on floors, all ready to spring into renewed activity again at a reminder. To impose—"

He jumped in his chair then, for he had clearly heard a British man's voice shout, *"Shut her up!"*

It must have come from the beach outside, and Mammalian was simply waiting for him to go on.

Hale wiped his forehead on his shirtsleeve again. "To impose a memory-shape onto their physical makeup is to forcibly impose an experience—which, in the case of a Shihab meteorite's imprint, is death."

Mammalian's eyes were wide, and he was shaking his head mournfully. "In 1948 your people brought a big chunk of meteoric iron to the mountain and set it high in the Ahora Gorge, with explosives under it. The meteorite is still on the slope there now, rusting—though as soon as we finish talking here I will radio instructions that it be retrieved and ground to dust. Where did you get it, and how do you know it has killed a djinn?"

Ground to dust, thought Hale dully. This is all part of your *plan,* Jimmie?—that we lose the meteorite that poor Salim bin Jalawi and I worked so hard to find, worked so hard to retrieve—

"We got it," he said, "at the site of an ancient city that had been wiped out by a meteor strike—it's mentioned in the Koran—south of the well at Um al-Hadid in the Rub' al-Khali desert—the A'adite city of Wabar."

As he began to tell Mammalian the story, and the reels of wire hissed slowly between the recorder's spools, Hale did finally relax; the meteorite was gone, Elena was gone, and perhaps if he told his own story with objective, emptying thoroughness, drinking as much as possible as he told it, he might at least for a while lose the unwelcome burden of his own identity.

The Volkov documents had been the initial clue.

It had been late in 1947 when Hale concluded from them that the Soviets had in 1945 intended to mobilize a covert expedition to Mount Ararat; and when he had made some inquiries with the Ankara SIS station and Broadway in London, and then traveled out to the Hejaz to talk with the reclusive old fire-worshippers in the mountains, he concluded uneasily that the Soviets had not yet *done* it, but intended to start very soon. Overflight photographs indicated that big new hangars and pools and railway yards were being constructed at the secret research stations in Soviet Armenia, just on the other side of the Aras River from Ararat; and Hale was told by the Bedu who roamed the Hassa desert west of Kuwait that all over the Arabian peninsula sandstorms were lately calling urgently to each other across the wastes, and that *hatif* voices from the darkness were keeping Bedu up praying loudly all night, and that the roaring of the djinn who were confined to desolate pools could be heard for miles over the sands.

The most-secret agency of the Soviets was planning to go again to the Ahora Gorge on Ararat, for the first time since 1883—perhaps to fetch out another of the creatures, perhaps to establish some diplomatic alliance with the whole tribe. Perhaps both.

Hale had come up with the plan to cart a genuine Shihab meteorite way up into the Ahora Gorge on Mount Ararat, and use ankhs to summon the djinn down to the stone, and then explode it in their midst. It would be an SOE operation rather than an SIS one—and since the SOE no longer officially existed, the only person whose clearance he needed was Theodora's. The decipher-yourself code message okaying the plan arrived at Hale's CRPO office in the Al-Kuwait British Embassy less than an hour after he had telegraphed the proposal.

And so the twenty-five-year-old Captain Hale of the Combined Research Planning Office had set about finding a Shihab meteorite.

He learned that there was a covert traffic in the objects in the black-magic Al-Sahr shops down by the Ahmadi docks south of town, but the stones offered for sale in those furtive establishments had no real provenances and were often simply smoked sandstone or granite. He had turned to historical records then, hoping to find mention of a meteor strike that might be said to have killed a djinn.

It proved to be easy to find, in a book called *The Empty Quarter*, published by Holt as recently as 1933; and the very name of the author was intriguing—the book had been written by H. St. John Philby, the father of Kim Philby. In the book the senior Philby recounted his expedition into the Rub' al-Khali desert to find the lost city of Wabar.

Many passages in the Koran described Allah's angry destruction of the city of the idolatrous A'adites, and Arab folklore recalled the city as having been called Wabar or Ubar, and placed it in the great southern Arabian desert. St. John Philby had trekked by camel caravan to the reputed site, but instead of ruined foundations he had found the black volcanic walls of two meteor craters; in his book St. John Philby described black pellets of fused glass which his Bedu guides had thought were the pearls of perished A'adite ladies, and he mentioned a Bedu legend that a big piece of iron lay somewhere in the area, though Philby had not succeeded in finding it.

The elder Philby had assumed that the vaguely constructed-looking black crater walls must have been the only basis for the Bedu identification of the site as the legendary Wabar; apparently it had not occurred to him that the fabled city might actually have stood there, and literally have been destroyed by fire from the heavens.

Several times during Hale's research the old, half-welcome excited nausea had kept him fearfully reading all night, drinking contraband Scotch and wishing he could bring himself to follow Elena's example and return to the Catholic faith.

In the chapter on Wabar, St. John Philby had described the dreams he had had as his caravan had approached the craters—nightmares of the desert spinning around him in radiating rays of gravel, while he tried uselessly to take bearings with a surveyor's instrument.

And in the fragmentary *Hezar Efsan*, Hale was troubled to read the story enigmatically preserved as "The Fisherman and the Genie" in the

Thousand Nights and One Night. In the ancient story, a genie tricked a fisherman into catching fish from a miraculously preserved lake in the desert; when the fish were put into a frying pan, a solid wall opened and a black giant described as "a mountain, or one of the survivors of the tribe of A' ad" appeared and asked the fish, "O Fish, are you constant to the old covenant?"—to which the fish replied, "Return, and we return; keep faith, and so will we."

Clearly, in his childhood end-of-the-year nightmares, Hale had been *in touch* with some hidden world—a disturbingly contra-rational world, perhaps older than rationality, but still secretly alive and active.

Hale was nervously certain that the A'adites had been fallen angels, and that Wabar had been a kingdom of djinn, destroyed by some kind of meteor strike—and he resolved to find the meteoric stone that St. John Philby had failed to find there.

And so Captain Andrew Hale had quietly taken a vacation from the CRPO—while, as the Canadian Tommo Burks, he had flown to Al-Hufuf and begun outfitting an expedition to the Rub' al-Khali region of Saudi Arabia, under forged authorization documents from the National Geographic Society in Washington, D.C.

In the Jafurah desert settlements outside Al-Hufuf he hired ten Bedu tribesmen for the expedition, including several from the 'Al-Murra tribes to act as guides and *rafiq* escorts, and he set his agent Salim bin Jalawi to assembling thirty desert-bred 'Umaniya camels and purchasing enough rice, dates, coffee, first-aid supplies, and ammunition for a month-long trip.

He had planned to leave at the end of January in 1948, and had applied to King Saud for permission to travel in the Saudi interior—but on January 6, his birthday, Hale had received word that the king had forbidden the trip. The 'Al-Murra tribes were at war with the Manasir, Hale was told, and the situation was complicated by the fact that the king's tax collectors were in the area collecting the *zakat* tribute. But the 'Al-Murra tribesmen Hale had enlisted for the trip had not heard of any fighting with the Manasir, and Hale knew that the *zakat* was always collected in June and July, when the summer's lack of grazing forced the Bedu to camp on their home wells.

"He doesn't want a *Nazrani* out in the sands," said bin Jalawi philosophically, sipping coffee at a sidewalk café in the Al-Hufuf town square. "Not when the spirits have got everybody stirred up in this way. Even the *yakhakh* are animated. Perhaps, Tommo Burks, it is the end of the world."

Yakhakh were locusts, and in fact a net had been draped over the café's awning poles to keep the flying grasshoppers off the tables; every three or four years the insects migrated up from Abyssinia, and today the sky was actually darkened by clouds of them passing overhead toward Kuwait, as if the sun were eclipsed.

Hale drummed his fingers on the wooden table. "National Geographic he treats this way!" he said angrily. "I wish I *were* a journalist, *I'd* write a story about him." He frowned at bin Jalawi. "Can you . . . sell off the supplies we've bought, and the camels, and dismiss the men we've hired? I think I'll be buying a plane ticket back to Kuwait."

"Certainly." Bin Jalawi cupped his hand and rubbed his thumb across the inside of his index finger in a universal gesture. "The men will want pay for the time they've waited—I can distribute it."

I'll bet you can, Hale thought. "But could you secretly *hold back* some of the supplies, after making a big scene with trying to get the best prices in returning the rest of them?—and quietly keep a couple of the best guides on our payroll, after noisily firing the rest?"

"Alahumma!" said bin Jalawi; the phrase meant *to be sure* or *unless possibly.* "This would be in order to disobey the king—to be subject to arrest, in the company of an infidel *Nazrani* in the sands. A greater pay-scale would be required from the Creepo."

" 'You limpin' lump o' brick-dust,' " sighed Hale, quoting Kipling's *Gunga Din* at him, as he often did. "Yes, double the pay—it'll still be cheaper than hiring all ten of them at the old rate. And keep back six or eight of the best camels. Eight. I'll get somebody to board the Kuwait plane as Tommo Burks. And then I'll meet you and the camels and the two guides at the Jabrin oasis in . . . what, a week?"

"If we ride hard. And how are you going to get to Jabrin?"

"I'll drive a jeep there. The camel route from Hassa to Jabrin would be navigable in a jeep."

"The journey will destroy the jeep."

"Well, I haven't got to drive it back, have I? I'll ride one of the unburdened supply camels on the return trip, and just abandon the vehicle at Jabrin. And when you sell back the supplies, *don't sell the sled,* understand? Nor the ropes and shovels."

Hale had bought a sand sled that could be pulled by camels, and he was hoping the meteorite could be dragged to a gravel plain where an RAF aircraft could land.

"If the tribes get word of a *Nazrani* in the sands, it will be all they will talk about. Ibn Saud's men will hear of it."

"We'll be fast," said Hale confidently, "and if we meet any Bedu I'll speak only in order to return greetings, in Arabic with some northern accent like Ruwala—"

"And not get off your camel," added bin Jalawi. He had often told Hale that his huge English feet left monstrous footprints in the sand.

The 150-mile camel route from Hasa to Jabrin was mostly polished tracks slanting across gravel plains, but a number of times Hale did have to drive the commandeered RAF jeep over dunes, with the big 900-x-15 tires spinning heavily and sand thumping like deep water in the wheel wells. He had left Hufuf in the frosty dawn, but by the time he drove the jeep around the last sand ridge and finally saw below him the palm plantations of Jabrin, the sky was red with twilight, and a bandage from the jeep's first-aid kit was wrapped tightly around a splitting radiator hose, and the radiator itself had been patched by a helpful Bedu family at the last well, with a paste of flour and camel dung. The generator had been screeching for the last hour.

Through the jolting, dust-powdered windscreen he squinted around at the Jabrin basin. Though some of the tracts of palm trees were still flourishing in orderly rows, most were decimated and choked with wild acacia bushes, and several stretches showed only toppled, dry trunks. Until the jeep clattered down to the level of the oasis he could see the broken walls and foundation-lines of ruined buildings.

Salim bin Jalawi's party was camped on a flinty steppe by three well mounds, and out of sheer mercy for their eardrums Hale tromped on the brake pedal when he was still a couple of hundred feet away; and at long last he switched off the jeep's laboring engine.

The shrill whine of the generator blessedly squeaked to a halt, but in the sudden desert silence he felt even more conspicuous. He climbed stiffly out of the driver's seat and plodded around to the back, and as he unstrapped his two cases he squinted over his shoulder at the campfire and the tents and the humps of camels grazing beyond, and his nostrils flared at the warm aroma of boiled rice and butter on the alkali breeze.

The three men by the fire had stood up when the engine died, and

Hale straightened the dusty *kaffiyeh* on his head and then hefted his cases and stepped away from the jeep. In spite of the head-cloth's protection and the cloudy sky throughout the long day, he could feel the sting of sunburn on his nose and forehead.

He trudged slowly across the gravel to the fires, noting that the camels had already been watered—the nearest well mound had been cleared of sand and its cover of lumber and skins had been pulled away, to be conscientiously replaced before leaving tomorrow morning, and the mound, a cement of sand and a hundred years of accumulated camel dung, glinted with muddy moisture in the firelight.

"Al guwa," he called. *God give you strength.* These men knew he was English—a Frank, a nominal Christian, a *Nazrani*—but he wanted to say nothing to emphasize it.

"Allah-I-gauik," the three of them replied, civilly enough. *God strengthen you.*

"You camp right at the well?" Hale went on in Arabic when he had laid down his cases and embraced bin Jalawi. From one of the other men he accepted a small cup of hot coffee made from the well water, and drank it—it tasted fresh, but he knew that a laboratory analysis would show high concentrations of albuminoid ammonia, indicating contamination of camel urine in the well water.

"We are on the border of the desolation of A'ad," said the man who had handed Hale the cup. He was a lean, black-haired 'Al-Murra tribesman with a leather cartridge belt over his shoulder and what looked like an old single-shot .450 rifle propped against a camel saddle beside him. "Even the Saar tribes will have the sense to stay out of the Rub' al-Khali in these nights." He laughed quietly.

"Or even in the days," said bin Jalawi helpfully, crouching to sit by the fire again. "Men's hopes are confounded when angels bend their courses down to earth." Squinting up at Hale, he said, "I'll wager the *dibba* came to Hufuf, after we left?"

"Yes," Hale admitted. *Dibba* was the Arab term for locusts in the wingless, crawling stage, and armies of them often followed the airborne migrations. "Nothing extraordinary." In fact the *dibba* had advanced on Hufuf from out of the southern desert in a front four miles wide and two miles deep, and black masses of them had stripped the date trees so bare that they appeared to have been burned. When Hale had driven out of town at dawn, he had seemed to be driving over crunching black snow, and on the road he had seen half a dozen dog-sized monitor lizards springing up in the chilly air to catch strays from the low-flying last wave of winged locusts.

" 'Nothing extraordinary,' " echoed bin Jalawi in a thoughtful tone, and the other two Bedu muttered to each other as they spread their robes and sat down. "Perhaps to the Franks the end of the world is nothing extraordinary."

Hale found a place to sit on the windward side of the fire, and he accepted a plate of rice ladled from the pan that would recently have served as the camels' drinking trough. He dug in hungrily with his right hand, licking his fingers, for he had brought only bread and cheese to sustain him during the day's jolting drive.

"A few million bugs don't make the end of the world," he said to bin Jalawi around a mouthful of rice.

"It is *metaphorical,*" said bin Jalawi, using the English word.

In the twilight Hale could see several of the ruined forts of ancient Jabrin silhouetted against the purple sky. He knew that Jabrin had been a prosperous city long ago and that at some point the citizens had been driven out into the desert by a killing fever; the illness had abided at the place like a curse, and struck all the Arabs who had periodically made the attempt to live here since then. Oddly, travelers who stopped at the oasis never contracted the malady, and now the Bedu visited Jabrin only to use the wells and gather dates from the hundreds of date palms, which no one ever tended anymore.

Butterflies fluttered around Hale's face as he ate—little orange and black painted ladies—and bin Jalawi nodded somberly when he saw Hale brushing them away.

"You know better than to inhale one of them, bin Sikkah," he said, using Hale's Bedu name now that they were in the sands, rather than the city name Tommo Burks. "But don't crush them, or needlessly knock them into the fire."

"Poor ghosts," agreed one of the 'Al-Murra tribesmen. His gaunt face was sculpted into chiaroscuro gullies and prominences by the firelight as he too glanced around at the horizon notches that were the old forts. He wrung his hands for a moment as if washing them, then spread them to the sides, palm down. "At least they're the ghosts of men. South of here will be ghosts of other things."

Hale had read in the *Hezar Efsan* about ghosts of the A'adites. "The walking stones," he said.

"Uskut!" the man exclaimed; the Arabic word meant *shut up!* "Name them not!"

One of the butterflies had landed on bin Jalawi's palm, and he breathed softly on it, ruffling its wings but not dislodging it. "If you can hear," he said to it, "and think, remember us in your morning prayers; even the *Nazrani.*"

Hale smiled sourly, but he was sure that if the butterflies were indeed ghosts, they were fragments of identity too minimal to be capable of thought. He sniffed the stone-scented wind and thought that there was no sentience at all in the miles of dark desert surrounding them; far away to the north and south might be hidden isolated clusters of warm Bedu tents, with perhaps overhead in the dark sky the astronomical distortions that indicated the passage of djinn through the Heaviside Layer, but the Jabrin region felt empty.

He knew that the desert south of them would not be empty; and he tried to pray, but in spite of his best efforts he found that his mental *Pater Nosters* quickly degenerated into a sterile recitation of the London Underground stations. Once again he envied Elena her faith.

"Bug," he said in useless English to the fluttering nullity on bin Jalawi's palm, "in your orisons, be all my sins remembered."

When he had finished the rice and scoured the plate with a couple of handfuls of sand, he wiped his hands on his *dishdasha* robe and then unzipped the longer of the two leather cases he had carried from the jeep; he lifted out of it a slim Mannlicher 9.5-millimeter carbine and a canvas bag of loaded stripper-clips, and another canvas bag that contained four custom-machined iron ankhs, wrapped in linen cloths to prevent clinking. Doubtless his Bedu companions imagined that the second bag contained spare cartridges on clips like the first—they would be scandalized by the sight of the devilish ankhs—and Hale decided not to trouble them with an explanation of the Egyptian looped crosses until the party had reached the regions where their protection would be necessary.

Hale didn't have to goad his Bedu companions to ride hard during the cool January days; his only worry was that one or even all three of them might be missing at prayer time one dawn.

The wind was steadily at their backs from the north. When the sun was bright and there were high dunes to be crested—with the wind casting long dazzling streamers of sand from the topmost ridges, and the camels plunging single-file down the lee slopes to expose streaks of lighter-colored sand under the dark tan top layer—Hale dizzily felt that somehow they had climbed up into the sky and were plodding across the top surfaces of clouds. And when they crossed the desert's gypsum stone floor between dunes in thrashing rain, with the camels' hooves clattering among primordial seashells, he imagined he was in the vanguard of the Pharaoh's army, pursuing Moses across the floor of the Red Sea in the moments before the unnaturally sustained walls of water would break and crash back in.

And he came to appreciate the expertise of his guides; most of the covered wells were mounds identifiable by the camel tracks that led to them and the camel dung and date-stones that paved their surroundings, but several times he saw one of his guides ride directly to an anonymous sand hummock in a trackless landscape and confidently dismount and kick away drifted sand to expose the hides and timbers that covered a hidden well. Some of the wells they found had deliberately been left uncovered, either by raiding parties or by home tribes wanting to keep invaders from getting the water, and these wells had been filled in and covered by the drifting dunes. He was told that clearing the sand out of the shafts was not an impossible task for a tribe, and that in fact all the well shafts in the desert had simply been found, and cleared by the Bedu, rather than actually bored; the wells, cut straight down through red sandstone and white limestone, were reputedly the work of a very old civilization that had flourished in the days when great rivers had flowed across the Rub' al-Khali.

On the sixth day out from Jabrin they watered the camels and refilled the water-skins at the wells of Tuwairifah—and then they had left the last known wells behind, and they took extra care to strap the water-skins high up on the camels, secured against accidental bursting or puncture.

Under emptied blue skies the party of eight camels zigzagged onward southeast through the parallel dunes of the vast Bani Mukassar, keeping to the gravelly desert floor and crossing the dunes at shallow gaps that notched the mountains of sand like passes. All four of the travelers preferred to ride during the day, when the sun blotted out the malign stars, but twice when they had had to march for a long distance along a dune to find a crossing place, they made up for the lost time by riding at night—and though on one of these long, plodding nights there was no moon, the planet Jupiter glowed brightly enough in the sky to cast shadows on the dimly glowing sand, and Hale could see a faint luminosity around his companions and the camels. His party was now very far away from any outposts of men, and when he looked up at the stars of the Southern Cross in the infinite vault overhead, or gauged his course by the position of Antares in Scorpio on the southern horizon, it seemed that the postwar world of London and Paris and Berlin was astronomically distant and that he and his companions were the only human beings seeing these stars.

Riding or camping, they always spoke quietly at night; and even in the noon sun the oppression of the region kept his guides from indulging in the falsetto singing with which Bedu generally filled the time on long marches. They took turns standing guard while they were camped, and Hale saw that in the mornings one of his guides always paced out across the sands looking for the tracks of any stones that might have crept up out of the darkness to investigate the heat of their fire.

Hale saw a couple of larks and noted that the birds did not fly, but hopped along over the sand; bin Jalawi told him that this was to evade birds of prey, which would notice the moving shadow of a bird in flight. "They know better than to draw attention," bin Jalawi said ponderously.

Several times his companions shot hares, and though the Bedu only squeezed out the contents of the intestines before adding the carcasses to the rice pot, leaving the stomachs filled with whatever desert grasses the hares had grazed on, Hale found that his hunger outweighed his fastidiousness. Several times they saw foxes bounding across the gravel plains, and Hale dreaded the thought of eating one; but though desert foxes were considered lawful to eat, bin Jalawi told him that it would be madness to kill one in the region around Wabar. "Here they might be the old citizens," bin Jalawi said. " 'Honor him who has been great and is fallen, and him who has been rich and is now poor.' "

Hale's party reached the three wells of Um al-Hadid at sunset on January 27. The wells were in the bottom of a sand basin, and though they were recognizable by their characteristic mounds of stratified camel dung, the desert sands had filled them in long ago, and Hale saw no litter of date seeds around the mounds.

"The wells are long dead," said the elder of the 'Al-Murra guides, "but we camp here. Wabar is only half a day's ride farther."

They were not able to find any bushes or roots at all for a fire, and so their dinner consisted of dates and brackish Tuwairifah water. In the fruitless digging for roots Hale did find a broken ostrich egg; he pointed it out to his companions, for ostriches had been extinct in Arabia for fifty or sixty years.

"I'll bet it was laid and hatched right here," Hale said, turning over a piece of shell as he squatted over the find.

"Probably it was broken by fire-worshippers," said one of the guides grimly. "Bird eggs are anathema to djinn, and the fire-worshippers curry favor."

Hale was reminded of the story "Aleiddin and the Enchanted Lamp," a late and enigmatic addition to the text of the *Thousand Nights and One Night*. In the story, Aleiddin was at one point tricked into asking an obligated djinn for a roc's egg to serve as a dome for his palace; and in reply the djinn angrily refused to kill the Queen of the Djinn. Hale had never understood why the fetching of the roc egg should involve the death of a powerful djinn, and he sensed that he had found a clue to the explanation here, in this Bedu's remark—but the Bedu refused to say more, and Hale was too exhausted to press him. He thought of distributing the ankhs, but decided that it might now seem too much like the fire-worshippers currying favor, and he decided to hand them out tomorrow, before approaching Wabar.

The wind that had buffeted their backs for twelve days died to stillness during the night. Hale awoke when it stopped, and he lay there in his blankets on the sand for several seconds, staring up at the crescent of the new moon, wondering what sound had awakened him, before he concluded that the change had been the total cessation of the wind.

Only when he next awoke, shortly before dawn, did he notice that the 'Al-Murra guides had stolen away with four of the camels during the night.

Choking back a curse, he threw off his warm blankets and got to his feet to assess the supplies they had left; and they seemed to have divided the food and water evenly.

At least they had not taken the sand sled.

Salim bin Jalawi was at his dawn prayers, kneeling at a half-circle he had scored in the sand, bowing toward the west and Mecca. Hale looked around and did not see another line in the sand; the 'Al-Murrah must have left before prayer time, and were probably kneeling at a traced half-circle in the Tara'iz sands right now. Certainly they would not neglect it.

At last bin Jalawi stood up from the line in the sand and stared impassively at Hale. The sky in the east was pale blue and pink, though the sun had not yet appeared over the rim of the basin, and the still air was cold enough to make steam of both men's breath.

"If we ride hard," said bin Jalawi, "we could catch up with them."

"No," said Hale in a hoarse, tired voice. He scratched his bristly beard and yawned. "No, we will go on and get the egg—I mean, the big piece of iron. I hope four camels will be enough to haul it on the sled."

"The devil take your sled," said bin Jalawi mildly. He looked around at the sand basin they had camped in, clearly replaying in his mind the previous evening's search for fuel; and he must have concluded that it had been thorough, for he shrugged and said, "Allah gives and Allah is pleased to take away. Coffee must wait until we find wood at Wabar." He cocked his head then, listening, and he said, "They . . . return . . . ?"

Soon Hale could hear it too, the almost liquid sound of camel hooves in sand. He crouched by his saddle and pulled the Mannlicher carbine out of the oiled-wool scabbard, then scrambled on all fours up the northwest sand slope; he slid the rifle barrel up to the crest of the slope, and then with his hand on the stock near the trigger guard he slowly raised his head to peer over the basin edge.

The four returning camels in head-on view were the only figures out in the lunar dawn landscape—and though saddlebags flopped at their sides as they plodded this way, there was no rider on any of the saddles.

"*Fida' at al Allah!*" whispered bin Jalawi, who was now prone beside him. The phrase was one of farewell, meaning *In the custody of God.*

Clutching the carbine, Hale got to his feet and stepped slowly out across the still, icy sand to meet the camels. The beasts were walking normally, bobbing their big heads, and the saddlebags and water-skins didn't appear to have been touched.

The guides might have been shot by bandits or a hostile tribe—but he and bin Jalawi would have heard shots in this stilled air, and the assailants would have taken the camels; and Hale couldn't think of any other explanation . . . besides djinn. He was bleakly sure that he should have distributed the ankhs to the men last night.

The cold sky was a weight on his shoulders as he clucked his tongue at the camels and caught the reins of the leader. The beast lowered its head, and Hale slung the leather rifle strap over his shoulder and put his wool-booted foot on the camel's neck and let it lift him up off the sand toward the saddle. The sun was a red point on the eastern horizon, and Hale imagined that it was peeking at him as he had peeked over the basin rim.

There was no blood on the flat board of the saddle; only, caught in the folds of the blanket and on the saddlebag flap buckles, a scatter of jewelry. Hale stepped across from the camel's neck onto the small Oman saddle, and he knelt swayingly up there as he scraped and picked up a handful of the jewelry.

It was tiny sticks, some curved and some straight, made of glass and bone and bright gold; and not until he found a knobby round piece of gold as big as a marble and held it up to the light, and saw that it was a tiny scale model of a human skull, did he realize that the sticks were probably miniature sculptures of human bones.

He had heard Salim bin Jalawi's footsteps approaching, and now bin Jalawi was up on the saddle of another of the returned camels, and Hale glanced over to see that he too was gathering up scattered jewelry.

"La-ila-il-l'Allah!" bin Jalawi exclaimed abruptly, flinging the handful of gold and glass and bone slivers away from him in the dawn sunlight. "Drop them, bin Sikkah!"

The man's response had startled Hale so badly that he not only scattered the miniature bones but jumped right off of the saddle too. He landed unbalanced on his feet and sat down hard in the cold sand, the slung carbine barrel cracking him painfully over the ear. "What the hell?" he said irritably in English, getting quickly to his feet to dispell any impression of panic.

Bin Jalawi had climbed down with more dignity, but he was breathing fast as he led the camel forward toward the camp in the basin. "Djinn," he panted, "*duplicate* things. If they ponder a thing, sometimes a copy of that thing appears, made of whatever is at hand. In the desert the copies are generally made of glass, which is melted sand, or gold, which is in the sand. Somewhere up near the Um al-Hadid wells I know there is right now a stretch of sand that is *not* cold. And hot bare bones too, though they will have shaved some to make their models of others."

Hale was leading the camel he had jumped off of, and the two others were following placidly. "In miniature," he said.

"In *all* sizes, bin Sikkah! Djinn cannot comprehend differences in size, only shapes. These small copies stayed on the saddles, caught in folds—but by the Um al-Hadid wells there are now certainly bones as big as cannon barrels, made of glass—aye, and skulls a big as chairs, made of gold. We are lucky these camels weren't crushed."

Hale's forehead was damp with the sweat of nausea, and in order to appear unruffled he quoted an often-repeated speech from the *Thousand Nights and One Night:* " 'Thy story is a marvelous one! If it were graven with needles on the corners of the eye, it would serve as a warning to those that can profit by example.' "

Bin Jalawi snorted. "Your skull in gold will be more valuable than others, being solid all through. *Tawaqal-na al Allah!* We put our trust now in Allah. Let us quickly be finished with this business of dying, to save the trouble of making dinner."

Hale had slung the canvas bag containing the iron ankhs around his neck, and now he reached into it and pulled out one of the linen-wrapped crosses. "Carry this," he said, tossing it to bin Jalawi, "and perhaps you won't die. Don't unwrap it yet—it will hold the attention, distract the attention, of any djinn that might focus on you."

Bin Jalawi caught it and hefted it, then after a hesitation nodded and tucked it into a pocket in his robe.

Back at the camp they redistributed the bales and saddlebags among the eight camels and then they mounted and rode southwest.

After a few miles they found themselves riding over glittering black sticks that protruded from the sand and threw thin blue shadows, and for one chest-hollowing moment when he first noticed them Hale thought they were skeleton fingers; but the things shattered under the camels' hooves, and he realized that they were fragile fulgurites, rough glass tubes formed by lightning strikes, exposed now by the scouring wind of the previous days.

Ahead of them now stood a range of what the Bedu called *quaid*, solitary dunes two or three hundred feet high, which the winds had somehow not arranged into the usual long, regular lines; the northern faces were as steep as the sand grains would permit, and even in the stillness Hale could see patches of paler rose-colored sand appear as here and there the darker surface layer slid silently away.

A spot of still darker red bounded rapidly across the high crest of the nearest dune, right under the empty blue sky—it was a fox, running with apparent purpose—and the dark sand was falling behind the animal like a curtain sequentially dropped, exposing the rose underlayer—

—and suddenly the air throbbed with a loud roar like the harmonizing engines of a low-flying bomber. Hale flinched on his saddle at the sheer physical assault of the noise, and it was several seconds before he recognized the old rhythms—and then several seconds more before he realized that the drumming cycles were forming vast, slow words in a very archaic form of Arabic.

It was all Hale could do not to throw himself off of the high saddle and lie face-down in the sand—for the cyst of his own frail identity felt nearly negated by this "mountain, or one of the survivors of the tribe of A'ad" that was shaking the foundations of the world with its speech.

His stunned consciousness recognized the words for *Why come the sons of Solomon son-of-David to the Kingdom of A'ad?*—and he knew that no creatures who might in some sense survive here would know the term *Nazrani*. Their city had been destroyed by the wrath of Yahweh, the God of Solomon, long before Jesus of Nazareth was born.

Neither Hale nor bin Jalawi ventured an answer; and the eight imperturbable camels simply kept plodding forward toward a low gap in the sand between the dunes.

From the corner of his eye Hale saw another fox scampering across the ridge of the towering *quaid* dune that blocked the blue sky a hundred yards to their right. And as the ringing tones of the first dune shuddered away to silence this one took up the throbbing, rhythmic roar, repeating the same question.

Don't answer, Hale told himself, mostly to maintain his own distinct identity, as he rocked numbly on the saddle. *Don't reason with them.*

With a jarring thump that was almost drowned out by the syllables of the dunes, a geyser of sand shot hundreds of feet into the air from a point two hundred yards to the left; and as the upflung sand column began to dissolve into falling veils, another exploded up from the right. Abrupt collapses and avalanches in the slopes of two of the *quaid* dunes ahead made Hale think that similar detonations were happening under their weighty mass, and when he stared through the foggy rain of sand at the spot where the second geyser had erupted, he saw an age-weathered ring of stone exposed in the sand. It was a well. The wells of

Wabar were violently expelling the sand that must have choked them for more than two thousand years.

A quarter of a mile away to the left, another dune began pronouncing the resonant question, and more tan jets burst up from the desert floor on all sides, out across the plain to a distance of half a mile or more. Hale's nostrils twitched at a smell like cinnamon and old dry blood.

He was gritting his teeth, and tears were running from his slitted eyes into his beard. *They might not know the term* Nazrani, he thought, *but I am baptized. Is that what this dead kingdom is responding to, that spiritual polarization? Old St. John Philby came here—but only after he had renounced his own baptism and converted to Islam.*

He pushed the jangled thought away, unwilling to consider the notion that his baptism—"on the Palestine shore, at Allenby Bridge near Jericho"—might have made an important and recognizable change in him; and in any case he had more immediate urgencies.

Bumpy black objects as big as wrecked cars were rising out of the wells now, hovering in ripples of mirage over the masonry rings and glinting in the sun; Hale saw that they were made of stone, and when one of them, and then another, ponderously leaned to the side, the rim of its well was instantly crushed to an explosion of dust, and the black stones moved slowly forward, leaving behind them paths of deeply indented sand. A harsh, two-tone ringing had started up, as if in harmony with the repeated slow *basso profundo* syllables of the dunes.

Half a dozen of the black basalt rocks still floated heavily over their wells, but eight of the massive things—no, ten—more—were surging across the plain toward Hale and bin Jalawi from both sides and from behind. Their size made them seem to move slowly, but when Hale watched the steady extensions of their impacted-sand tracks, he saw that they were moving at least as fast as his train of camels. Two of the knobby boulders were closing in from the left and right like black spinnaker sails and were at the moment only a few hundred feet away; and at last he noticed in their bumpy contours the shelves of eroded shoulders, the outcrop of hip and breast. They were giant, broken, headless stone torsos, facing him and advancing, and the dizzying ringing noise was vibrating out of their black glass cores, as if in reiterated inquiry, or warning, or rage. The earth's harsh music seemed to be tolling the crystal vault of the air and shaking the remote clouds into dissipating mist.

Hale was panting in hoarse whimpers through his open mouth, and his memory and identity were indistinct vibrating blurs. He had forgotten how to turn a camel around, and his legs tingled with the unreasoned spinal intention of jumping down from the saddle and simply running away north, perhaps on all fours. Even in ruins this power was too much for a frail, short-lived mammal to bear.

But that indistinct admission stirred a spark of defiant anger in his mind. *Angels,* he thought, and holding a thought was like clinging to a filled glass while in free fall, *so be it; but I am a man.* He took a deep breath and raised his head; and from his all-but-abandoned memory he summoned a phrase from his Jesuit school boyhood: *Sin by sensuality, and you sin as a beast; sin by dishonesty, and you sin as a man; sin by pride, and you sin as the angels.*

"I," he declared out loud, though his voice was lost in the inorganic cantata of the dunes and the moving boulders, "can sin as well as any of you fallen angels." And even though he was forlornly sure that it wasn't true, that he was in fact simply sinning as a man, the deliberate intention served as an anchor for his otherwise-fragmenting identity.

Hale's hand darted into the canvas bag that hung on his chest, and as he fumbled out one of the linen-wrapped iron ankhs, he numbly saw that the advancing stones did not actually touch the sand, but impossibly floated over it, supported by some force that crushed the sand flat underneath.

He was able to glance to his right at bin Jalawi, who knelt resolutely on the saddle of the next camel; the scowling Bedu seemed defensive but secure, and Hale marveled at his Moslem endurance.

"Look!" he shouted at the stoic Bedu; and when bin Jalawi's slitted eyes turned toward him, Hale flipped the cloth off of the looped cross and pushed it up over his head, as he had done two and a half years ago in Berlin. In English he whispered, "S-submit, you b-b-loody d-devils."

The ringing sound became painfully shriller as the tall black stones rocked to a halt in the morning sunlight.

As in Berlin, he had had to *push* the cross up through the air to raise it, as if he were trying to move a spinning gyroscope, and now he had to brace himself on the saddle and flex the muscles in his left arm to drag the ankh through the resisting air to the left—but when he had done it, the torso stone on that side rocked back, cracking.

"Wave yours back," Hale yelled to bin Jalawi.

The Arab had retrieved the ankh Hale had given him and freed it from the linen cloth, and now he held it up and then slowly forced it over to his right; and with a hard clang the stone on his side broke into two pieces that toppled apart and thudded heavily into the sand, flinging up a cloud of dust.

Salim bin Jalawi looked back at Hale, his eyes bright. "In whose name do we . . . *kill* the ghosts of *angels?*"

"In the name of . . . George the Sixth of England!" Hale stood up on his knees to turn around and face the stones that had been advancing from behind them. The limbless, headless stone torsos had all halted out there on the northern sand plain, but Hale effortfully swung the ankh across his view of them and they fell back, several of them breaking apart and tumbling in pieces to the sand.

The camels had now reached the crest of the low gap between the dunes, and Hale shifted around and looked forward, down into a broad basin that stretched for a good third of a mile from side to side. Out in the center of it stood the black rings of two craters, each of them at least a hundred yards across and filled with rippled expanses of sand.

And as his camel began to step down the inner slope, the sky-filling noise from behind rang to a halt, and Hale's thoughts fell back into order.

He was panting as he dug his compass out of a saddlebag, and he tried to hold it steady as he bent his head to watch the rocking needle under the glass. It was swinging from side to side pointing behind him, toward the true north, but he was confident that it would point toward any big piece of meteoric iron if he could get close to it.

The basin appeared to slope away to flatness a couple of miles to the south, and he thought it would be easiest to drag the meteorite that way, and hope for gravel plains level and long enough to serve as a landing field for an RAF Dakota DC-3.

He stared at the jagged black crater walls as his camel train descended the slope toward them. In his book, old St. John Philby recounted having told his Bedu guides, *This is the work of God, not man.* The skeptical old Arabist had assumed that since this was clearly a meteor strike, it could not also be the site of the fabled city. Hale, though, had had the advantage of seeing the ghost guardians of the city and knew that he would put it differently: *This is the work of angels, not man.*

"You wait with the camels," he told bin Jalawi when they had reached level sand. "I'll trot around with the compass and try to get a reading on the iron stone."

The Bedu was still clutching the ankh in one hand. "Are we through with devils?" he demanded angrily.

"Apparently. For now. Keep that looped cross where you can get at it again in a hurry, though."

Salim bin Jalawi nodded and tapped his camel's neck to get it to kneel. Hale took one last fearful look back up at the gap through which they had entered the basin, then turned away and goaded his camel out across the drifted sand toward the craters.

The ragged black walls stood up from the desert floor like eroded masonry, and Hale morbidly wondered what sentries might patrol the topmost rims on moonless nights, and he was glad that he and bin Jalawi had arrived while the sun was still in the morning half of the sky.

Widely separated boulders of igneous rock studded the sand, hinting at broader craters; perhaps the whole basin was a cluster of meteor strikes. Wabar might have been a city of respectable size.

When he had ridden south of the western crater, Hale's compass became erratic—and two hundred yards farther on, when both the craters were behind him, the compass needle began pointing consistently in a direction that was ahead of him: south.

He goaded his camel into a faster walk; and when he saw a rounded stone that was brown, rather than igneous black, with the ridges of its surface islanded by the yellow sand that filled its grooves and holes and nearly covered it, he was sure that he had found the meteorite—the death of djinn.

It was roughly the size and shape of a big truck tire. It must weigh a ton, at least, he thought as he reined in his camel.

He glanced around from the height of the saddle, but the basin was still empty except for the distant figures of bin Jalawi and the kneeling camels to the north; and so Hale tapped his own beast's neck and then swung his legs off the saddle as the camel folded its forelegs and lowered its hindquarters to the sand. He hopped to the sand, gripping the stock of his rifle.

He trudged over to the half-exposed stone and then crouched beside it, brushing away the hot sand to see the texture of its uneven surface. It was pitted with spherical depressions, some as small as buckshot and some as big as tennis balls; he rubbed his palm over it, and it was clearly a metallic rock rather than a glassy one.

The sand around him was scattered with shiny dark pellets, and he picked one up. It was a smooth black glass oval, apparently formed from sand at very high heat; and he remembered that St. John Philby's Bedu guides had found things like these and had imagined that they were the scorched pearls of the ladies of Wabar. Hale scooped up a handful of the glass beads, shook the sand off them, and tucked them into the canvas bag at his chest.

He had just straightened up, intending to fire a shot into the air and summon bin Jalawi, when he heard the unmistakable cry of a parrot, not two hundred yards away—and it was followed by the crowing of a rooster.

The sounds had seemed to come from the larger of the two craters, northeast of him; he looked in that direction—and froze, his fingertips tingling.

The southwest face of the crater wall an eighth of a mile away had apparently been cut to vertical and then carved into gleaming black pillars and arches—how had he not noticed it until now?—and Hale was reminded of the city of Petra above Aqaba in Jordan, though the pillars and halls of Petra had been carved into solid red limestone.

Against the shadowy blackness of the central obsidian arch, he saw a figure that might have been a sitting man; then an arm was raised, and Hale knew that he and bin Jalawi were not alone in the waste of Wabar.

He unslung the slim Mannlicher and rocked the bolt back to be sure there was a cartridge in the chamber; and after he had closed the bolt he patted the canvas bag at his waist, and was reassured to feel the weight of the loaded clips. He began striding across the sand toward the strange black palace.

From this distance he could vaguely make out ornately carved lattices and minarets, but as he got closer, the details became blurred and irregular; and by the time he had approached closely enough to see the black beard and embroidered red robe of the man who was sitting cross-legged in the arch, the arch was nothing but a natural cavern mouth, and the meteor crater wall was just irregular bumpy black stone, ragged at the top edge.

What from farther back had appeared to be steps leading up to the arch were just tumbled black boulders, and Hale gripped his rifle carefully as he climbed up to the broad ledge on which the man sat.

The air was cool in the shadow of the tall cave mouth, and a breeze sighed out of the black depths as if a tunnel beyond led to underground caverns. A cluster of doves and chickens hopped around on the cave floor behind the sitting man, and a big green parrot stood by the man's robe-covered knee.

Hale was standing a dozen feet to the man's right, holding the rifle pointed in his direction—but he let the barrel swing down when he saw that both the man's hands were open and empty on his knees and that there was no sign of anyone else in the cave behind him.

The parrot cocked one glistening eye at Hale and squawked in Arabic, "What brings you to me, seeing you are not of my kind and cannot be assured of safety from violence or ill usage?"

Hale stared at it in alarm, and in his disorientation had even taken a breath to answer it, when the sitting man opened his mouth and spoke.

His voice was rich and deep as he spoke in archaic Arabic: "You are hungry. You have come a long way. Wash your hands so that we may eat."

The man leaned forward and began dipping his hands in the air and then rubbing one hand over the other, as if at an invisible bowl of water.

After a moment he looked up at Hale, his black eyebrows raised. "You stand while I sit? You do not join me at my table?"

Helplessly, Hale slung his rifle Bedu-style and elbowed the stock behind himself to sit down cross-legged on the rough stone a yard away from his host, facing him; and after a moment of plain embarrassment, Hale too began doing a pantomime of hand washing. What is this, he wondered dizzily, some ritual? Is this man insane? Could he simply be making fun of me?

Then the man flicked his hands and began moving his extended fingers from a point above his left knee to his mouth and back, his jaws working as if he were chewing.

"Do not be abashed," the man said. "Try some of this bread—note how white it is!"

Hale nodded awkwardly and pretended to eat a piece of bread, darting a nervous glance at the parrot.

"Have you ever tasted anything like this?" the man asked.

"Never," said Hale. He was sweating.

The man nodded with satisfaction. "You are a god?" he asked then.

"No," said Hale cautiously. "A man."

The smooth brown forehead above the topaz eyes creased in a mild frown. "But the ghosts of my people rose for you—and you drove them back." He waved a hand dismissively. "You are not of our covenant. Perhaps you are an agent of the one god. Why do you examine the killing stone?"

Hale understood that the man was referring to the stone he had found out on the sand, and he was guardedly pleased to hear his estimation of it confirmed. "I am going to take it away with me."

"That will not revive my people. My people are dead, irretrievably killed by it." He looked at Hale's hands. "I wonder to see you eating so sparingly. Do not stint yourself."

Hale again mimed eating a piece of bread. "It is not my purpose," he said as he pretended to chew, "to revive your people."

The bearded man smiled. "My people and I are secure from judgment. We have made a covenant with the Destroyer of Delights, the Sunderer of Companies, he who lays waste the palaces and peoples the tombs. We *stay here*. We do not go on, we do not face—"

The man had paused, so Hale ventured to complete the thought. "Consequences," Hale suggested softly. "Retribution."

"*Leveling*. We remain distinct."

At the sound of hooves in sand behind him, Hale spun up into a crouch, the rifle's stock fitting quickly to his shoulder and his eye looking over the gold bead-sight at the end of the barrel; but Hale recognized the camel that was still a hundred yards off on the sunlit sand to the northwest, and a moment later he recognized bin Jalawi riding it.

Instantly he scuffled back around to bring the muzzle to bear on the man sitting across from him on the cave floor, but the man had not moved; and Hale shakily crossed his legs again, lowering the barrel and tucking the stock behind him. He was profoundly glad that the Bedu was coming up.

"I think you are only a man," the sitting man said. "I am A'ad bin Kin'ad, king of Wabar."

Hale automatically lifted another piece of the imaginary bread. "Are *you* a man?" he asked, then opened his mouth and pretended to chew.

"I am half a man. I am the son of an angel by a human woman."

Hale recalled the giant *Nephelim* in the Book of Genesis, who were supposed to have had children by the daughters of men. He had read speculations that the *Nephelim* might have been fallen angels.

"Human enough to have survived the doom of your kingdom," Hale observed. He didn't change his expression, but he had to run his tongue around the inside of his mouth to be sure he had not actually eaten something, and he wished he had brought his water bottle with him when he had walked away from his camel—for his mouth was fouled with the woody taste of dry, long-stale bread.

The red lips smiled in the black beard, exposing white teeth, though there was no change of expression in the watchful eyes. "Human enough for half of me to have survived."

Hale breathed in and out through his open mouth, trying to lose the taste. "How did the . . . the killing stone . . . kill your people?"

A'ad stared at Hale as if at an idiot. "Know, O man, that it *fell* upon them. It, and others like it." He shook his head, then dipped his fingers over his right knee, by the blinking parrot's head. "Do try this meat. You have never tasted anything as exquisite as the seasoning of this dish."

"*Akh al-Jahala!*" cawed the parrot. The phrase meant *brother of ignorance.*

Oddly, this scene felt familiar in an agent-running context; and Hale realized that it was like debriefing an Arab agent who has lost respect for the handler and is about to stop cooperating. Get what you can, fast, he thought.

"Do you know about another kingdom of your father's tribe," Hale asked as he obediently pretended to pick a bit of meat out of an imaginary dish over the parrot's head, "on Mount Ararat—in what you would know as the land of Urartu, a peak called Agri Dag, the Painful Mountain? I believe the tribe survived the great flood because their kingdom was at the top of the mountain."

A'ad bin Kin'ad scowled, and Hale actually rocked back away from the rage that burned in the golden eyes.

"*Great flood?*" the king roared. "I am crippled, and my lands are dry desert, because of my denial of your one god. *I* evaded his wrath, half of me at least evaded the full killing and damning extent of his wrath, but the rivers of my kingdom are parched valleys now, my vineyards and pastures are dust under the sand! You are a man, but the ghosts of my people could see that you have not the black drop in the human heart. You talk to me about floods! In what flood did you wash out the black drop, as I, being half-human, never could?"

Hale just stared expressionlessly at the king of Wabar, ready to swing the rifle butt up very hard indeed under the man's chin if he should spring at him. He was to doubt it later, but in that moment Hale was bleakly sure that the man was referring to Original Sin, from the consequences of which Hale had supposedly been saved by baptism.

Abruptly the king relaxed and smiled. "But you need food. Taste that meat—the animals were fattened on pistachios."

Hale remembered the taste of bad old bread in his mouth, and irrationally he dreaded putting into his mouth the handful of air he held.

He hesitated. "What animals?" he asked.

"Eat. Would you dishonor my table?"

Hale looked over his shoulder when he heard boots chuffing in sand, and relaxed to see bin Jalawi just stepping up to the tumbled stones below the ledge, holding his rifle casually since Hale appeared to be at ease.

When he had clambered up onto the wide ledge, bin Jalawi swiveled his impassive gaze from the black-bearded king of Wabar to the parrot to the miscellaneous fowls in the cave. *"Salam 'alaikum,"* the Bedu said, formally, cutting a quick, questioning glance toward Hale.

"Indeed peace is on me," said the king of Wabar, "because of who my father was. I am A'ad bin Kin'ad."

Bin Jalawi's eyes widened; clearly he believed it. "There is no might nor majesty except in God the most high and wonderful!" he exclaimed, using a common Arab phrase to express awed surprise.

"Yahweh, Allah, Elohim," spat the king. To Hale he said, strongly, "Eat the flesh, damn you. Be a man, and nothing more."

Hale shuddered and flicked his right hand as though throwing something away, resolving to wash that hand soon, in water, or whisky, or gasoline.

"This place is a ruin, my lord," said bin Jalawi to the king. "Will you come away with us, on one of our camels?"

"O calamity!" shrilled the parrot, spreading its orange-spotted green wings and fluttering up into the air.

"To where?" asked the king in a voice as deep as rumbling in a desert well. " 'To the house no one leaves, where the mute crownless kings sit forever in deepest shadow and have dust for bread and clay for meat, and are clothed like birds in robes of feathers; and over the bolted gate lie dust and silence'?"

Hale recognized the man's words as the text of a Babylonian description of the afterworld, preserved in the Assyrian Gilgamesh clay tablets. He straightened his legs and slowly stood up, without taking his eyes off of the king of Wabar.

"Shall I walk?" demanded the king, opening the front of his embroidered red robe and flinging it back over his shoulders, scattering the clamoring chickens behind him. "Shall I ride a camel?"

Hale had flinched back with a smothered cry. The king's naked body from the waist down was made of rough black stone, with no seam or crack visible where white skin bordered black petrification—and millennia of sandstorms had grotesquely eroded the contours of the stone. The genitals were gone, and the projecting stone knees and thighs had been weathered flat, so that they looked more like frail flippers than a man's legs.

The robe must have been heavily padded, for the king's chest was just white skin sagging over ribs and collar-bones and prominent shoulder sockets; and the king's beard was patchy and white now. Hale could not see the robe on the cave floor, and he was suddenly sure that it had never been real.

"Stay," whispered the king through a toothless mouth. "Die. Learn to relish our food." One grimy, stringy white hand reached behind himself, and then he was holding a steel dagger by the point and nimbly cocking it back over his shoulder to throw.

Hale's brown hand snapped to the trigger guard of his rifle beside his hip, and in one motion he levered the short barrel up horizontal and pulled the trigger.

The ringing crack of the rifle shot was stunning in the cave mouth, and Hale couldn't hear anything as he instantly worked the bolt, ejecting the old shell and chambering a fresh cartridge.

By sheer luck the unaimed shot had punched a hole through the king's upraised forearm; and in an instant the wrist and hand had turned black, and the knuckles *clanked* when the suddenly heavy arm hit the stone floor.

"Jesus," said Hale blankly.

Tendons stood out in the king's shoulder and elbow as he tried to lift his stone hand; and the knuckles dragged on the ledge surface a little way, but did not rise. Behind him the dagger clattered to a halt on the cave floor.

"I am still secure from judgment," whispered the king, probably to himself. "I am still secure."

"We," said Hale, "are not." *Thank God*, he added mentally. He took a deep breath and let it out, and he found that he had to step back and flex his hand away from the gunstock to keep himself from firing an aimed slug through the king's heart, or through his head, out of sheer horror at the fact of him. "And we must leave you."

Then Hale and bin Jalawi were hopping down over the tumbled stones and sprinting across the sand toward bin Jalawi's camel, and beyond that Hale's camel beside the meteorite; and all Hale could think of was the coming effort of digging a trench up to the mass of iron, and winching it down onto the sled, and then hitching all eight camels to the sled for the laborious march south out of the accursed basin of Wabar. The radio case was in his saddlebag, and he had to tell himself forcefully that he must wait until they had found a gravel plain wide enough for an RAF Dakota to land on, before he dared use the agreed-on frequency to talk to a human being in the rational outside world.

13

▼

Turkey, 1948/Beirut, 1963

And the serpent said unto the woman, Ye shall not surely die;
For God doth know that in the day ye eat thereof, then your eyes shall be
opened, and ye shall be as gods . . .
    —Genesis 3:4–5

Hale and bin Jalawi had ankhs and rifles ready to hand as they flailed their shovels and secured the winches, but the ghosts of Wabar had been effectively knocked down, and the king was an inert figure in the portico of the black mirage-castle.

Between the two of them they managed to get the camels to drag the meteorite four miles south, out of the Wabar basin to a broad gravel plain at the edge of the Al-Hibakah region; and after they had freed the ropes from the heavily encumbered sled and tied a conspicuous long red flag to it, Hale used the radio at last, briefly, to give the RAF bases in Bahrain and Abu Dhabi a triangulation on the meteorite's new location.

He and bin Jalawi led the camels away to the northeast then, to arrive after five blessedly uneventful days at Abu Dhabi on the gulf coast. Here they sold the camels and got themselves on the ship's manifest of a lateen-rigged Iraqi *boom;* the old ship changed its name at every port, and stayed well clear of the steamer lanes, and safely landed its cargo of mangrove poles in Kuwait after only three days at sea.

A telegram waiting for Hale at his office let him know that the pickup had been successful—the pitted chunk of iron was now in the hands of the bewildered SIS, and Hale did not see it again until the middle of May, a little more than three months later.

By this time the old wartime Special Operations Executive had been officially dissolved for three years. The agency had been separated from Foreign Office control back in 1940, and placed under the supervision of the Minister of Wartime Propaganda, and after 1945 Hale's temporary seconding to SIS had been allowed to default into a permanent position. The CRPO was SIS cover, and Hale was on the SIS payroll, and he did field investigations for the SIS Head of Station in Al-Kuwait—but the SOE still functioned within SIS from a sort of administrative limbo, through Theodora with the secret sanction of one Cabinet minister, and Hale was still primarily an SOE agent.

The SOE had been covertly preserved solely in order to complete one operation—Declare.

In the early May of 1948 a decipher-yourself telegram arrived at Hale's Al-Kuwait CRPO office from Broadway Buildings in London. It was SIS orders to report immediately to Erzurum in eastern Turkey, but Hale noted the keywords that indicated that the message had been sent by Theodora, and so he knew the orders had to do with Declare; another clue was the fact that the telegram used the pre-1945 code term for Turkey, 45.000, rather than the new SIS term, BFX. The old code was obsolete, and had been compromised even during the war—Germany had been designated by the number 12.000, and Hale recalled hearing of Germans in a Brussels bar in 1941 drunkenly singing *"Zwofland, Zwofland uber alles."*

Kim Philby was the Head of Station in Turkey in 1948, working as First Secretary to the British Embassy in Istanbul; but Erzurum was more than six hundred miles east of Istanbul, and it was only a puzzled RAF commander who met Hale's plane and handed him orders to take a car from the RAF base motor pool and drive directly to an address in Kars, an old city of tsarist origin still farther east, near the Soviet Armenia border.

Hale drove east all day in a big borrowed Oldsmobile, over roads whose paving blocks were so unevenly sunken that he drove many miles through the stubbled fields alongside the pavement, and as the sun sank behind him and the road climbed up into the Allaheukber highlands he had to turn on the car's heater; the hill-slopes were green, but he didn't see any trees until the road began descending toward Sarikamis, a cluster of wooden houses and a couple of petrol pumps tucked into the shade of pine-wooded hills. Hale bought petrol for the car with American dollars and pressed on, and by twilight he had reached the cobblestone streets and the old wooden buildings of Kars.

The address Hale had been given was a hotel, very nineteenth-century Russian-looking with its steep roof and narrow lamplit windows. Hale parked the Oldsmobile at the stone curb alongside a row of newly planted hawthorn trees, and when he stepped across the dirt strip and the flagstone sidewalk to push open the front door, he found Theodora in the hotel lobby, sitting placidly on a long wooden bench that ran along one wall.

An iron stove in a corner was filling the lobby with hot air and the scent of burning ox dung, and Hale closed the door behind him and began to unbutton his coat; but, "Let's walk," said Theodora, getting up from the bench and lifting an overcoat from beside him, and Hale sighed and turned up his collar.

He followed Theodora back out through the creaking lobby door and across the sidewalk, and even as the northwest wind from Russian Georgia found the gaps between his buttons, Hale knew better than to suggest they talk in the RAF car. The sun had set behind them, and Hale trudged down the center of the darkening cobblestone street beside the tall figure of Theodora, waiting for the older man to begin talking.

At last Theodora spoke. "The story for the SIS is that tomorrow morning you're going to infiltrate some Armenians into the U.S.S.R. aboard the train that crosses the border by Kizilçakçak, thirty miles east of here. One of Biffy Dunderdale's operations, supposedly, run out of Artillery Mansions rather than Broadway, so that Philby won't expect to know the provenance. It's not too implausible that SIS would try it; Philby has had no luck running Armenians over the border—his have all been caught and killed within sight of the barbed wire."

"I daresay," said Hale dryly.

"I don't like him either, my dear, but hold your fire until you've got a clear shot. In any case, you *won't* be stuffing Armenians into the train's undercarriage tonight, so it's academic. Tomorrow you'll be at the border to watch the train go as if you had, and Philby will be along to *observe—*"

Hale almost tripped over a cobblestone. "Philby's out *here?*"

"He will be by tomorrow morning. He's Head of Station in Turkey, so of course he saw your orders; and of course he noted the inquiries you made to the Ankara desk last year, about Soviet activity around the Aras River. This present plan will go some way toward putting his mind at ease about those inquiries. Your story is that you and Dunderdale have been planning for months to put these Armenians across, so of course you wanted to know the lay of the land, right? In any case, directly after your tour of the border tomorrow, you'll be moving south—secretly."

"To Ararat," said Hale. As soon as he had got his orders to fly to Erzurum, he had guessed that this was to be the execution of his plan for the Shihab meteorite, and he had to clench his jaws now to keep his teeth from chattering at the imminent prospect; but it wasn't entirely fear that plucked at his tight nerves.

"Yes, indirectly," said Theodora. "You're to go by way of a Kurd village in the Armenian corner of Iran, so as to approach from the south, from the Agri district; these Kurds are like your precious Bedouins, they travel across borders virtually unregarded, and they've lived around the mountain for thousands of years." Theodora laughed softly. "The Khan of the village is an ally of the Crown. During the war, his men gutted the local RAF depot, ready with their rifles and knives to go to war with the whole English tribe; of course the RAF simply sent bombers in to level their villages, and the Kurds took their sheep and goats and fled up into the mountains, waiting for English soldiers to march in and fight properly, with rifles. But we simply sent in more planes, and the Kurds had no palpable enemy to fight, and their women hated living in caves, and finally they sent an ultimatum to our headquarters—'If you do not come down and fight like men, we will be forced to surrender.' Well, the RAF permitted them to, and the Kurds have been staunch allies of ours ever since."

Hale laughed. "They do sound like Bedu," he said, correcting Theodora's pronunciation.

" 'Half-devil and half-child,' " said Theodora, quoting Kipling. "Today is Tuesday—you'll have a day or so to go hiking with the Khan, and he'll explain the mountains to you, and Ararat in particular. The *big picture*. Do listen to him. By Thursday your meteor stone should be in place—you certainly did choose a *heavy* one, didn't you?—with its explosives attached and an Anderson bomb shelter set up nearby, and then you'll be helicoptered to the plain below Ararat, where you'll brief the commandos who'll be going up with you—demolition experts from the war—good men, hard to surprise."

"When is the Russian team going to arrive?"

"No sooner than Friday night, it seems. Ankara Station has been keeping track of a train that's been moving south from Moscow, with clearances south all the way to Erivan on the Turkish border—it's in Stalingrad now, bound south through Rostov and Tbilisi. Two known Rabkrin directors are aboard, as well as two renegade Catholic priests, ex-Jesuits—and there's a prominent Marconi radio mast over one of the boxcars that happens to be in the shape of an ankh."

Hale shivered in the chilly wind. "That does sound like the right lot."

"You and your commandos will be waiting for them. And when this Russian team arrives on the mountain, and has 'opened the gates,' as you put it, of your djinn colony, you will detonate your, your *exorcism.*" He peered at Hale. "In your proposal, you said you plan to *summon* them, down to where your meteor is. How do you plan to do that?"

"Blood," said Hale, trying to speak lightly. "Medical supply blood, a couple of bags of it. The Magians in the Hejaz mountains use fresh blood to call the creatures down for their worship, from out of the sky, and in Berlin the Arab ship was full of freshly dismembered bodies."

"Lovely," said Theodora quietly. "Well!—And once that little chore is over, back you'll go to your Kuwait haunts."

"Nothing to it," said Hale.

"I think it's a good plan," said Theodora. "If it works, we'll be able to put paid to Declare, and you can subside wholly into SIS. Face the challenging new postwar world, instead of grubbing about in—" He spread one hand, reluctant as always to refer to the supernatural.

"Devoutly to be wished," said Hale, nodding—but he was remembering the effort of dragging an ankh through the attention field of a djinn, as if the ankh were a scepter; and he remembered the shudder of awe at the sight of the angels bowing before him, or breaking—*Sin by pride, and you sin as the angels!*—and he wondered what secrets the king of Wabar might have been able to tell him. *What castles in the clouds . . . !*

"But in the meantime!" said Theodora, "there is a SDECE team in a hotel in Dogubayezit, roughly fourteen miles southwest of Ararat. You remember that the French secret service was in Berlin too, three years ago. God knows what *their* sources are—perhaps some other fugitive like our poor Volkov walked into a French embassy somewhere, and got a better reception—but I assume they too are aware of the imminent Russian expedition on the mountain. One of their team is a woman—"

Hale just nodded, keeping his eyes on the dirt road.

"—probably the Ceniza-Bendiga woman"—Theodora went on, and Hale could peripherally see that the old man was looking at him—"of fond memory. If you should meet her . . . try to stop the SDECE from interfering on Ararat, delay them at least, and try to find out what they know, what their source is. And tell her—she won't believe you, I suppose, but just for style—you can tell her the cover story about the fictitious Armenians you're supposed to be running, tell her just as much as Philby knows. The orders and the names and biographical details of the Armenians are in your room. Learn them, even though you won't be revealing them. Live your cover, right?"

"I'll fill out the orders," Hale said dutifully, "and learn their names and backgrounds . . ."

Hale was jolted out of his memories by a name that he had just recalled. He blinked around his room in the Normandy Hotel in Beirut—the sea beyond the fluttering white window curtains was indistinguishable from the night sky now, and the spools of the wire recorder were still slowly revolving. Hale gulped some of the soapy arak, and he wondered how many times Mammalian might have refilled the glass while Hale was lost in reminiscences—and how many times he might have changed the wire spools. The night breeze was chilly, and this strange new 1963 seemed like a year from a science fiction story.

Hale frowned across the polished table at Mammalian's impassive, bearded face in the lamplight. "One of the Armenians," he faltered, "one of the fictitious Armenians—"

"Was named *Jacob* Mammalian."

"Yes." Hale thought the other man too was shaken by this development. "Hakob, Jacob—did *you* cross the Turkish–Soviet border, then, in a train?" Hale asked.

Mammalian stood up to look out the window toward the muted roar of the invisible surf, and for a few moments Hale thought he wouldn't answer. "Yes," Mammalian said finally, "precisely then, in May of 1948. I had been an illegal Soviet spy working against Turkey, running agents in the military bases around Erzurum, until I was arrested in

1947. I had thought, until now, that it was the Soviet State Security who broke me out of the prison in Diyarbakir, and smuggled me onto the Kars train." He turned to face Hale, frowning. "And by God it was! When I got across to the other side, I was met in Leninakan by Soviet soldiers! Does your Theodora work for the KGB as well as the British Crown?"

"He certainly could have had planted doubles among the Soviets, secretly working for England. But why would he want to free you and repatriate you?"

"He must have *wanted* the Russians to try their Ararat approach, while you and your *meteorite* were handily in the area—and the Russians needed me in order to do it. I was their guide on the mountain then, as I am to be again now." He returned to the table and sat back down in his chair. "When I was twelve, Andrew Hale, the Ottoman Turkish Army invaded the Kars and Van districts of eastern Turkey and drove out all the Armenians they could catch, herded them like cattle south to what's now the Saudi Arabian desert. More than a million of my people died on that forced march. My family eluded the Turks and fled across the Aras river to Yerevan, on the Russian side; but Armenian fathers had been taking their sons up the mountain for centuries, each generation showing the next the location of Noah's Ark. I had seen it on several occasions by the time we fled, and as a young man I twice stole across the river, past the border guards, to climb up that gorge again."

Hale stared at the tanned, black-bearded man sitting across from him; and for a moment in his exhaustion he forgot about things like the whirlwind in Berlin, and the half-stone king of Wabar, and the djinn in the pool at Ain al' Abd. Instead he was remembering the day he had stumbled upon the church of Sainte-Chapelle in Paris in 1941, and how, in spite of his atheism, he had been awed to comprehend that some drops of Christ's blood had once supposedly been kept behind those stained-glass windows. And he remembered illustrations of Noah's Ark from his religious textbooks at the St. John's boarding school in Windsor, when his mother had still been alive.

"You," he said hoarsely, "have seen the Ark?" In 1948, Hale's expedition had not ascended high enough, before disaster had struck, to have any hope of glimpsing some trace of the fabled vessel; and they had gone up the gorge at night. "It's still *up* there, visible?"

Mammalian frowned impatiently. "Yes, Mr. Hale. Why would Theodora—"

"What—Jesus, man! What did it—*look* like?"

Mammalian reached toward the recorder, then visibly thought better of leaving an interruption on the wire. Instead he snatched up his glass of arak and drained it. "It looked—like a God-sized black coffin," he said, "with one end, about ninety feet of it, sticking out of the ice, over a cliff with a lake at the base. I suppose the Ark was about six stories tall. My father shot a musket at it."

Hale sat back. "Your father, Hakob, was a vandal."

"The wood was petrified," Mammalian said. "The shot bounced off. Now—"

"Why would he *shoot* at it?"

"It is inhabited, Andrew! Like a shell taken over by a hermit crab, a clan of hermit crabs. There were—voices, very loud voices, not human; and a face looked at us over the top. A—*very big* face."

"Oh." Hale nodded impassively, all thought of Sainte-Chapelle and his days at St. John's school dispelled. Somehow it had not ever occurred to him that Noah's Ark might still be whole and accessible; and the news that the holy vessel was the dwelling place of things like the monsters he had seen in those past years was inordinately depressing. "You were," he said, "asking about Theodora."

"Yes." The Armenian nodded and rubbed his forehead. "I wonder why Theodora led you to believe your Armenian infiltrators were imaginary."

Hale sighed, remembering one item from the list of his cover-story crimes as Theodora had summarized them in the conference room at Number 10 Downing Street five days ago: *Oh yes, and you took money from a now-deceased Russian illegal to break a couple of their agents out of a Turk prison and smuggle them safely back across the Soviet border; the illegal kept no records, so it can't be disproved. There's a good deal more, you'll be briefed in Kuwait.*

He did it so that my name would be on the SIS orders, Hale thought; I would certainly have been more circumspect if I had known that this "infiltration" was not only real but in effect a cooperative deal with the Russian secret service! Even back then, in 1948, the old man was laying the groundwork for my eventual disgraceful cover story, in case it might one day be needed!

And he remembered again his suspicion that Theodora intended to "establish the truth about him," have him assassinated, after this operation was completed.

"Why would he lead you to believe that?" Mammalian repeated. The man's hands were clenched into fists on the table. "And why would he nevertheless give you my correct name?"

"Well, since it turns out you were a real person, I suppose I needed your correct name to put through the SIS paper-work consistently," said Hale. "As to why he let me believe you were a fiction, invented to fool the SIS—I don't know. I suppose so that I'd know as little as possible, if the SIS or the KGB were to question me."

It chilled him now, in this disorienting 1963, to realize that he had been hiding from *both* services, in 1948. And he was even more of a fugitive from both now.

"But he deluded you," Mammalian said, "and freed me, so that the Russian Ararat operation could take place. You weren't to know that he *wanted* the operation to happen, *wanted* your men to run into opposition! Perhaps he *was* working for the KGB! Perhaps he is still!"

"No, that wasn't it." Hale rubbed his hands over his face. "He did want the Russians to awaken the djinn, but I'm sure he didn't know about your . . . about the ambush you set up for us." Set up with Philby's help, he thought. "Theodora believed that our Shihab meteorite couldn't kill the djinn until they had . . . opened their gates to your party, and in that way become vulnerable to our attack. The possibility of effective opposition from—you—was a regrettable necessity."

Mammalian was nodding, but skeptically. "That was and is true, that about the opened gates. Even buckshot bounces off, when the gates are closed. But I wonder if he is still deluding you—I wonder if he stage-managed it so that you would kill those two men last week in England and predictably flee to Kuwait, where we would predictably approach you."

Hale's chest was cold, for Mammalian was getting far too close to the truth—and he forced himself to frown as if at a difficult chess problem. "You think he's running me *now*?"

Mammalian laughed softly. "And perhaps for the KGB! I don't accuse you of dishonesty, my friend. I'm confident that if he is running you now, it is without your knowledge. I will certainly make sure that your Shihab stone is ground to powder and sifted into the sea! And even so, I may advise that we abort the operation. What did you learn from the Kurds?"

Hale's mouth was dry at the thought that the operation might be canceled, that he might not get a chance to avenge the men he had led to their deaths on that wild night fourteen years ago—in spite of what he had told Mammalian earlier this evening, he did want *vrej,* vengeance—but he forced a laugh. "How could he have had me followed—"

"That is my worry, Andrew. What did you learn from the Kurds?"

Hale wished for hot coffee, but didn't dare ask for it directly after a hard question; he had learned about Cassagnac's precious *amomon* thistle from the Kurds, and he was sure that Theodora did not want him telling this Rabkrin agent anything at all about the *amomon.*

"First I went to the train crossing at the border. Let me tell it in order. Guy Burgess was there, with Philby."

"Ah! I was there too, but hidden in the undercarriage of the baggage car." Mammalian topped up their glasses with the clear liquor and clouded it with splashes of water.

The railway line that crossed the border by Kizilçakçak had been the only train crossing along the entire eastern Soviet border; the rails had been laid for the old Russian five-foot gauge, and the nineteenth-century locomotive that traversed it twice a week ran from Kars to a station only three miles into the Soviet territory, after which it retraced the route in reverse, with the locomotive pushing from behind.

The train had come chuffing up from the west on that chilly spring Wednesday morning, white smoke billowing up out of its Victorian smokestack and trailing away over the three cars it pulled, and it screeched to a steaming halt on the Turkish side of the iron bridge that marked the frontier—the tall barbed-wire fence stretched away to north and south on either side, strung down the center of a broad strip of dirt that was kept plowed to show the footprints of anyone who might cross.

Khaki-clad Turk *askers* stood with rifles beside the weathered sign that announced KARS–SOVIYET SINIRI, the border between the Soviet Union and the Kars district of Turkey, and four Russian soldiers in green uniforms marched across the bridge from a black Czech Tatra sedan parked on the eastern side; two of the Russians were clearly officers, with blue bands around the visors of their caps and gold epaulettes on their shoulders, while the other two were plain *pogranichniki,* border guards carrying rifles with bayonets. The Russians and the Turks saluted one another, and the Turk soldiers handed over a sheaf that presumably was the train crew's passports and any bills of lading.

Hale was standing beside Philby and the stocky, red-faced Burgess in the shadow of a guard shack a hundred feet away from the tracks on the western side, and all three watched the two *pogranichniki* walk around the train cars, poking their bayonet blades into the spaces under the carriages.

"I h-hope your Armenians are s-s-*stoical* about a blade or two up their arses," said Philby softly to Hale. They were dressed in anonymous khaki for this dawn outing, and they were being careful not to be heard speaking English. "Though some m-might like it, I sup-s-suppose. Do you f-fancy any of those *pogranichniki,* G-Guy?"

Hale was making a modest show of glancing covertly at the train, and he wished the other two Englishmen had not come along to observe. Philby had insisted on driving them all out here in an embassy-pool jeep, and he *was* the Head of Station.

"Pooh!" said Burgess, pouting his full lips toward the Russian soldiers. "Slavs have shovel faces. *Slav* probably means *shovel* in some Balkan language."

"Be quiet," whispered Hale.

Burgess turned from Philby to give Hale a pop-eyed stare. Perceiving that Hale was annoyed, he went on in a mock-reasonable tone. "It's true. Look—you or I, if we were starving and saw a potato growing in the dirt, we'd dig it out and cook it." His breath was sharp with vodka, though the sun was hardly above the eastern hills. "But Slavic facial features are clearly evolved for diving right into the dirt to eat the potato, dirt and all, not bothering with the hands: the teeth slant out, there's no chin to get in the way, the cheekbones make fenders, and the eyes slant back and up, and the ears are set back to keep the dirt out."

Philby was laughing softly.

The Russian soldiers a hundred feet away had stepped back from the train cars, and on the locomotive's black flank the long connecting rods rose and shifted forward as the steel driving wheels began to roll and the train surged ahead, onto the bridge.

"Intermission," said Philby as the train picked up speed and the first of the cars rattled up the metal bridge. "Half an hour from now it will return, backward. We can check then for blood on the brake riggings and the axle-boxes."

Which there will of course not be, Hale thought, unless by coincidence someone really did sneak across this morning—and who would want to sneak *into* the Soviet Union?

"No," he said, nodding toward a watchtower that stood only a hundred yards away on the Soviet side of the border. "If they see a party hanging about to look at the undercarriage, they'll know we sent someone across. We leave now." He began trudging back toward Philby's jeep, and was relieved to hear the other two following him.

"What were the names of your Armenians?" called Burgess from behind him.

Hale stepped up on the jeep's running board and looked back at Philby and Burgess. "Laurel-ian and Hardy-ian," he said.

"Oh, see, he's a c-c-close-mouthed b-b-*boy*, Guy," said Philby, puffing up to the left side, where the Ford jeep's steering wheel was. "Don't even t-try to *draw him out* with your sut-suttee-*subtleties.*"

Hale sat down cross-legged on a coil of rope in the bed of the vehicle, and as Burgess grunted and hoisted his portly frame up into the passenger seat, Hale noticed for the first time a steel ring welded onto the dashboard on that side, right next to the brass plate that showed the gear-shifting positions. And when Philby had started the jeep and clanked it abruptly into reverse, Hale grabbed at the rope coil and found himself gripping an oblong steel ring knotted to one end of the line; glancing down, he saw that the oblong ring could be opened at a spring-loaded gate—it was a carabiner, a snap-link. He was sure that the rope was meant to be secured to the ring on the dashboard, to drag something; but why not simply moor the line to the hitch on the back bumper?

As Philby rocked the jeep around in the yard behind the guard shack and shifted into first gear, Hale groped among the rope coils under him to find the other end. And when he found it he recognized the release-pin housing of a weather balloon launcher.

The rope wasn't for dragging something—it was for towing an airborne balloon.

SIS business, he thought—but when he glanced up he caught Philby's gaze in the rear-view mirror, and Philby's eyes were narrowed with obvious displeasure.

Hale shrugged and dropped the end of the rope. "Weather balloon?" he said, loudly over the roar of the four-cylinder engine.

"Fuck me wept!" exclaimed Burgess, thrashing around in the passenger seat to goggle back at him.

"I'm doing," said Philby clearly, as if to prevent any further outburst from the drunken Burgess, "a top-pop-pographical s-s-*survey,* of the border r-regions out here. Operation Spyglass, we sussur-surveillance wallahs are c-calling it. And in order to m-measure atmospheric presh-pressure, and t-temperature, and relative you-you-humidity, we attach a *radiosonde* t-transmitter to in-sin-*instruments* on a wet-wet-*weather b-balloon,* moored to a mobile receiving station: namely th-this jeep." He cuffed sweat from his forehead as he steered the jeep along the dirt road back toward Kars. "Ultra-sensitive operation—k-keep it under your h-hat."

"Fine," said Hale easily, squinting out at the green hills. "Better you lot than me."

But as he kept a distracted expression on his face, he was remembering the balloon he had glimpsed over the incongruous Arab boat on the eastern side of the Brandenburg Gate in Berlin three years ago, in the oily warm rain—the balloon that had been engulfed, a moment later, by the sentient tornado. Like bait swallowed by a fish?—a lightning rod struck by lightning?

Philby had been in Berlin, then. Had he been monitoring that briefly glimpsed balloon, from a safe position on the western side of the gate?

Two alien thoughts had intruded themselves into Hale's mind on that turbulent night: *She walks in Beauty, like the night of cloudless climes and starry skies,* and *Zat al-Dawahi, Mistress of Misfortunes, look favorably upon our sacrifice!* He had been sure then that he had picked up the thoughts like a badly tuned radio receiving two signals at once, and now in the back of this rocking jeep he wondered for the first time if the intruding thoughts could have been Kim Philby's.

He recalled another night, nearly four years before that night in Berlin, when he had heard thoughts in an older man's voice, and had even tasted the Scotch the other man had been drinking. It had happened when he and Elena had used the old *clochard* rhythms to flee the Rue le Regrattier house in Paris and had ended up walking blindly all the way to the end of the Île de la Cité.

It seemed to him now that that voice too had been Philby's. And on the last night of 1941 he had seen Philby in a dream, in which Philby had split into two men; and that had been about seventy-two hours *before* Hale and Philby first actually met, in the interrogation room at Latchmere House in Richmond.

Hale swirled the milky liquor in his glass, and then gave Mammalian a look that he knew must appear frightened. "Why do I—seem to have some kind of psychic . . . *link* with Kim Philby?"

Across the polished table, Mammalian shifted in his chair and looked away. "I am not a theologian, Andrew," he said. "He is ten years older than you, nearly to the day, if your stated birthdays are to be believed. I will tell you this—the Rabkrin is now convinced that *both* of you must be present on the mountain, working together, for this attempt to succeed." Seeing Hale shiver, he stood up and walked around him, and as Hale stared into his glass he heard Mammalian pulling the window closed and latching it. From behind him the Armenian's voice asked again, "What did you learn from the Kurds?"

Tell him something he already knows, thought Hale. "I learned that, in 1942, British Army engineers in the Iraq mountains above Mosul had extinguished the 'burning, fiery furnace' that's mentioned in the Old Testament Book of Daniel—the perpetual natural-gas flare into which King Nebuchadnezzzar of Babylon threw Shadrach, Meshach, and Abednego. We had to, the Luftwaffe was using it for night navigation."

The Zagros mountain range was a vast snow-capped wilderness that extended from western Iran by the Persian Gulf up along the boundaries of Iran, Iraq, Turkey, and the Soviet Union. During the war the United States Army had run supply trains through the mountain passses to Russian bases on the Caspian Sea, and the Red Army had established transient outposts in the highlands above Teheran, but the Zagros Mountains had always belonged to the Kurds—who had been the Kardouchoi, described by Xenophon in the fourth century B.C. as "warlike people who dwelt up in the mountains," and who had been the Medes who stormed Babylon and killed King Belshazar at his feast.

Hale was to find that time passed unevenly in the mountains, free of all calendars; things seemed to happen either at once, or never.

On the evening of the same day that had started at the train tracks by the border crossing, Hale was pushing his way through a mixed herd of donkeys and goats up a narrow street toward the house of Siamand Barakat Khan, the chief of this small village in the mountains above Sadarak and the Aras River. The southwest half of the sky was blocked by snowy peaks rimmed with pink in the last rays of the sun, but the winter had retreated from these lower slopes, and Hale was sweating as he shuffled forward between the furry beasts. In order to be inconspicuous he was dressed in baggy blue wool trousers and a Kurdish quilted felt vest like a life-preserver, with the horsehair fringes of a turban waving in front of his eyes—but the valise that he held above his head with both hands contained a short-wave radio, much more powerful and compact than the old models he and Elena had had to use in Paris seven years earlier.

An RAF Chevrolet truck had taken him up the steep mountain roads to within a mile of the village, and after dropping Hale off the driver had turned back, hoping to get to the British outpost at Aralik before full dark.

The only herder that Hale could see for all this livestock appeared to be a boy who was walking behind the beasts and scraping dung into a sack—but even as Hale braced himself for the last push through the donkeys that blocked his way and the goats that bit at his vest, the crowd of animals was separating into twos and threes, trotting purposefully away down this alley or that toward their familiar stables. Hale was at last able to lower the valise and stride freely across the packed dirt to the gate of the Khan's house. Cold air down from the mountain peaks blew away the livestock smell.

Theodora had said that Hale would be expected and welcomed, and in fact the white-bearded Kurd who stood beside the gate stepped forward without unslinging the rifle from his shoulder and took Hale's free hand and lifted it to his forehead.

"A joyful welcome, Hale Beg," said the man in English as he released Hale's hand. He too wore a turban with the fringe that was meant to keep off flies, but it didn't appear to bother him. "How are you? Where have you come from? How are your children? I am Howkar Zeid." He spread his arms in a gesture that took in the boy with the bag of donkey dung, and two women in blue robes who were hurrying past on the opposite side of the twilit street, as well as Hale; "Siamand Khan invites you all to sup with him!"

Hale had had enough experience of Bedu greetings to recognize these as formalities rather than challenges. "I am well, thank you, Howkar Zeid," he told the man. He looked over his shoulder and saw the boy and the two women bowing and murmuring as they continued on their ways, and he guessed that the broadcast invitation had been a formality too, routinely declined. He was wondering whether he was expected to decline the invitation as well, when the old man took his elbow and led him in through the gate. Already Hale could smell roasted mutton and coffee, and again he was reminded of the Arab tribes.

The Khan's house was a two-story structure, a wooden framework filled in with alternating sections of mud brick and rough stone; the windows were dimly lamplit squares of cloth set back in rectangles of stone coping.

Hale took off his shoes, and then was led in his stocking feet through a shadowy hallway to a broad stone-walled room that was brightly lit by a paraffin lamp hung on a chain from a ceiling beam. The dirt floor was almost entirely covered with expensive-looking red-and-purple rugs, and Hale's host stood up from a European upholstered chair and strode forward across the floor.

Howkar Zeid was pouring coffee into tiny cups at an ornate black table in the corner, but Hale was looking warily at his host.

The Khan was dressed in a dark Western business suit and a knitted cap, with an orange silk scarf around his neck instead of a necktie; and Hale thought that even dressed this way he would have alarmed pedestrians in London or Paris, for the haggard brown face behind the white moustache was ferocious even in cheerful greeting, and the man moved on the balls of his feet with his big hands out to the sides, as if ready at any moment to spring into violent action.

Siamand Khan shook Hale's hand like an American, strongly and vigorously.

"My friend!" exclaimed the Khan in English as he released Hale's hand. His voice was a gravelly tenor. "Thank you for what you bring us!" He took a cup of coffee from Howkar Zeid and handed it to Hale with a bow.

Theodora had mentioned having sent a gift of rifles on ahead. "You're welcome," Hale said, bowing himself as he took the tiny cup.

"This is a radio!" the man observed, pointing at Hale's valise. Two moustached men in vests like Hale's and caps like the Khan's had stepped into the room from an interior doorway.

"Yes." Hale wondered if the man wanted it; and he supposed he could have it, once a helicopter had safely arrived in the level field Theodora had described on the village's north slope.

"You will need it, not. From the roof we can see Agri Dag and the Russian border—the Turks have set up torches along the border, poles as tall as three men, wrapped in dry grass, each with a bottle of fuel in a box at the base. My men are out below the mountain and along the border now, on horseback, and when the Russians arrive at the mountain my men will light all the Turks' torches, the whole length of the border." He laughed merrily.

Hale recalled that Agri Dag was the Turkish name of Mount Ararat. "The radio will summon me—or the arrival of a helicopter, here, will!—to go to the mountain," said Hale, "*before* the Russians arrive." He took a sip of the coffee—it was very good, hot and strong and thick with grounds, and the smells of cardamom and onions from some farther room were reminding him that he hadn't eaten more than a sandwich today. "They won't be starting for a day or so yet."

"Russians don't know what they think themselves, so how can you know? I have spoons and forks. You will dine with me?"

"I—yes, I would be honored."

"The honey is not such as to make you ill, of course," said the Khan, stepping back. The two men behind him now carried out into the center of the room a round copper tray barely big enough for the dozen earthenware platters on it. They crouched to set it down on the carpeted dirt floor, and then Hale followed the Khan's example and sat down cross-legged on the floor on the opposite side of the tray, on which he saw mutton kebabs and roasted quail and spinach and bowls of yoghurt. And he did see a jar of honey.

"I'm sure the honey's wonderful," he said. A flat piece of peasant bread and a silver fork and tablespoon lay on the tray in front of him, and when he saw the Khan using his own spoon to ladle food onto a similar piece of bread, Hale began doing the same.

The Khan was squinting at Hale across the crowded, steaming tray. "In England people do not suffer from the honey fits," he observed. "Bad headaches, then fall down like a dead man, and wake again healthy as a horse when the night comes. Even up here in the mountains it is uncommon—once when I was a child the children all got ill of it, and some of the men went down to the hills to search out the plant the bees had made the honey from. Those men are still alive today, black-haired and fathering sons! Even we children who only ate the honey are all still alive. This is what year?"

Hale swallowed a mouthful of roasted lamb. "This is 1948," he said.

"I was already a young man of fighting age when your Light Brigade charged against the Russian guns at Balaklava. I was there, at Sevastopol."

Hale realized that his mouth was open, and he shut it. The Battle of Balaklava had happened . . . ninety-four years ago. He remembered Claude Cassagnac's question to Elena, in the Paris cellar in 1941: *This-tles, flowers—plants; did Maly ever talk about such things with you, my dear?* And he realized dizzily that he believed what this Kurd chieftan was telling him. "What—plant," he asked hoarsely, "did the bees make the honey from?"

"Ah!" said the Khan, raising his white eybrows. "You thought I was thanking you for the rifles!" He laughed. "And I do! But six years ago your Theodora caused the English in Iraq to put out King Nebuchad-nezzar's fire in the mountains. The Magians, the fire-worshippers, they were dispersed from their monastery there, and so the angels on Agri Dag were left without their beacon and their human allies. And now the Russians have a man with them who they believe can get the angels to open the gates of their city." He set down a quail breast to clap his hands. "You will meet my wife."

Hale controlled his surprise. The Kurds, like the Bedu, were Sunni Moslems, and they nearly never introduced their wives or daughters to newly met Westerners.

A black-haired woman in baggy blue trousers stepped into the room from the inner doorway, and Hale didn't look squarely at her until his host had caught his eye and nodded toward her.

She was dark-eyed and stocky—her hairline was hidden by a row of gold coins that hung on fine chains from a braided cap, and the buttons on her short woolen jacket were mother-of-pearl. She returned Hale's gaze impassively.

"Sabry also was one of the children who ate the honey," said Sia-mand Khan. "Show Hale Beg the back of your jacket," he said to her.

The woman turned around, and Hale saw gold embroidery that

traced a complicated figure, with loops at the sides and curled, drooping S-shapes at the top; and after a moment he recognized it as the stylized image of a flowering plant.

"It is an old, old design among my people," said the Khan softly. "It is the *amomon*." He waved at his wife, and she bowed and withdrew into the farther room.

"Is it a . . . thistle," said Hale carefully.

"You have heard of it."

"I think so, just a little—a Hungarian Communist is supposed to have known about it. Uh, and the Russian secret service killed him."

"Some of the Russians want it, but are afraid of it; the secret police, the Cheka, are just afraid of it. When the angels die," the Khan said quietly, glancing toward the cloth-covered windows, "they go down to the house of darkness, whence none return, where their food is clay, and they are clothed like birds in garments of feathers."

Hale shivered, for he had heard of this ancient Hell only three months ago, from the half-petrified king of Wabar.

"But," the Khan went on, "their strength they cannot take with them to a place of such weakness, and so the strength disperses—but only their own kind can use it. Some of the angels, when they were thrown down from Heaven at the beginning of the world, became this plant, the *amomon*. These are very much asleep, ordinarily, bulbs that lie under the ground no livelier than rocks—but when the strength of killed angels washes over them, they sprout, and bloom." He bared his white teeth in a smile. "And the bees make the poisoned honey from their blooms, and we follow the bees, and we harvest them."

"*That,*" said Hale, nodding with comprehension, "is our gift to you. If we succeed, we will be causing the *amomon* to bloom."

"If you succeed in killing the angels on Agri Dag, dispersing their strength," said Siamand Khan, "come back to my village in the spring. Our Yezidi priests will prepare a salad for you that will let you teach horsemanship to the grandchildren of your grandchildren, as I have done."

Hale remembered Theodora telling him last night about the SDECE team at Dogubayezit. If I succeed, he thought, I will come back—and I will bring Elena with me.

"And I have a gift for you, Hale Beg," said the Khan. "A fragment of a ghost—"

Someone shouted outside the window, and the Khan stood up all at once, simply by straightening his legs. He looked down at Hale. "The torches are lit. The Russians are moving."

"Not yet," said Hale, struggling to his feet. "And certainly not at night."

"Come to the roof. I think you and I will not, after all, be able to go hiking in the mountains tomorrow."

Hale followed the very old man out of the room, past hung garlands of onions and peppers and a smoky wood-burning iron stove in the narrow kitchen, to a brick alcove and an ascending flight of steps made of split cedar logs. The steps ended in a little hut on the mud-plastered beams of the roof, and by the time Hale stepped out onto the crackling surface, Siamand Khan was already dimly visible standing at the parapet, looking north, his coat flapping behind him in the wind.

Hale joined him. The cold wind was from the east now, blowing the horsehair turban fringe and the blond hair back from his forehead; and he was glad the wind was cold, and that there was no oily smell on it. The moon was full behind the top edges of clouds mounting in the east.

Miles away in the night a string of bright yellow dots stretched across the black northern horizon, and when he had oriented himself he decided that they did indeed trace the Turkish–Soviet border.

The torches were lit; and he was bleakly sure the Khan was right too about the Russians having begun to move on Ararat. The train moving south from Moscow must have been a decoy. *I should have remembered,* he told himself—*they always leave before their official departure time.*

He hoped the French SDECE team in Dogubayezit was not aware of this, and that Elena would stay down on the plain tonight.

"I've got to get the radio up here on the roof," he told Siamand Khan, wondering if a helicopter could land in this wind. "I need to know if the meteor stone is at the mountain yet, and find out if they can land a—"

But he could already hear the distant, throbbing drone of a helicopter in the mountain gorges.

The Khan waved to men who had gathered in the narrow dirt street below. "Light the torches around the clearing!" he shouted. And when they had shouted acknowledgment and sprinted away, the Khan turned to Hale, his face invisible in the black silhouette of his head. "And I need to give you a talisman for your effort tonight. It is piece of black stone no bigger than your fist, but it was broken from one of the mindless stone ghosts of the djinn, which walk in the deep southernmost desert. Living djinn will be repelled by it, I think." He gripped Hale's hand. "Succeed—kill them—and then come back here in the spring."

▼

14

Mount Ararat, 1948

*Gilgamesh said, "I dreamed that we were standing in a deep mountain gorge,
and in it we two seemed to be like tiny insects; and an avalanche fell from the
mountain's peak upon us."*
  —Gilgamesh, II

The helicopter had been one of the new Bristol 171 Sycamores,
painted in brown-and-black mountain camouflage, and after its down-
draft had blown out half the torches that outlined the clearing, and the
craft had come to a rocking, momentary rest on its three wheels, Hale
had run crouching in under the whirling wooden rotors and climbed in,
and then the Alvis Leonides piston engine had roared like a machine
gun as the helicopter lifted off again. The engine was too loud for Hale
to have tried to talk to the pilot, even if the man had not been wearing
radio earphones, and so he just sat in the rocking passenger seat, clutching the black stone the Khan had given him, and watched the black
point on the gray horizon that was Mount Ararat swing ever closer as
the helicopter covered the twenty-six intervening miles at the speed of a
hundred miles per hour. Below his left elbow he could see the bright-
dotted line of the torches flickering past like slow tracer bullets.

The pilot was wearing khakis, and a beret that seemed in the darkness to be the same color. The wartime Special Air Service commandos
had worn a beige beret, but the SAS had been disbanded right after the
war; the War Office had subsequently created an SAS regiment within
the old Territorial Army regiment known as the Artists' Rifles, but Hale
understood that they wore a maroon beret. Had the old SAS survived,

covertly? Was this Ararat operation to be a joint effort between the fugitive SOE and the fugitive SAS?

The black shoulder of the mountain had eclipsed the purple western sky when the helicopter began descending, and though the pilot was showing no lights and Hale couldn't distinguish any features on the ground, the aircraft settled smoothly to a flexing halt on a level field of grass beside a dirt track. In the waxing moonlight Hale could see that this plain below the mountain was studded with angular boulders, and though he knew that they were just the rubble that had tumbled down the mountain out of the Ahora Gorge in one of the nineteenth-century earthquakes, he remembered the stone ghosts that had risen out of the dead wells of Wabar, and he gripped the Khan's black rock firmly.

The pilot had immediately killed the engine, and now he pulled off the headphones as the unpowered rotor blades began to clatter around more slowly.

"We're still three miles short of the gorge," the pilot said in a thick Yorkshire accent, "but I can't promise you the Russians didn't hear the motor."

"The Russians *are* up there? Is the *stone* even up in the gorge yet?" asked Hale as he levered open the door and stepped down to the solid, grassy dirt. The wind from the east was colder now, and he wished his felt Kurd vest had sleeves.

"Talk to *him*," the pilot said, nodding over Hale's shoulder.

Hale turned around quickly—and jumped, for a man in a gray windbreaker was standing only two yards away from him. And now Hale could see by the cloud-filtered moonlight that there were four men standing behind this one, and that what had appeared to be a low hillock was now revealed to be two camouflage-painted Willys jeeps and a stack of bicycles, with a tarpaulin settling to the ground behind them. All five of the men carried slung Sten guns, the characteristic horizontal magazines standing out from behind them like longsword hilts.

"I'm Lieutenant Colonel Shannon, Captain Hale," said the nearest man, without irony. "The Russian party came across the border about half an hour ago, dressed as Kurdish shepherds; we almost missed them—the *pogranichniki* staged a big crisis four miles south, with spotlights and gunfire, while this lot just walked across in the dark, through a hole in the wire, right under a watchtower that had its lights out; clear Soviet complicity. And the Turk soldiers at that point had conveniently been ordered to drive south to where the commotion was, as reinforcements. The Russians were met on this side by a party with a lorry; they all drove away up the gorge with their headlamps out."

Hale made a mental note to find out later who had ordered the Turk guards to leave their post. "And the Shihab stone, the iron meteorite?"

"We placed your stone high up in the Ahora Gorge late this afternoon, sir—it's been scored, incised, so as to fragment widely, and it's got two Lewes bombs tucked under it, delayed-action charges ready to be set. We were going to bring up the war-surplus Anderson bomb shelter, but there's clearly no time for that now—we'll leave it here." He nodded beyond the jeeps, and Hale noticed out in the dark field the curved corrugated-steel roof, like an American-frontier covered wagon, that had been such a familiar sight in the bombed lots of London four years ago.

The moonlight was bright enough for Hale to see the paler spot on the front of the man's beret, in the shield shape of the SAS cap-badge. Hale recalled that the SAS insignia had been a winged dagger over the motto WHO DARES WINS—and he recalled hearing that the shape of the wings had been modeled on ancient Egyptian drawings of scarab beetles. Maybe, Hale thought forlornly, these men won't be too skeptical about the ankhs.

The SAS had done deadly effective covert demolition work in North Africa during the war, as well as in Germany and Italy. Their only failures had reportedly been operations that had been planned by other agencies—and Hale hoped that this Ararat expedition, planned by the SOE, would not be another.

"Have you got the blood?" asked Hale—gruffly, for he was embarrassed to be speaking of the filthy uses of magic with these hard-bitten professional soldiers. "Medical supply bags?"

Shannon's voice was stoic as he said, "We have, sir—it's in the water bottle pouch of a set of '37 webbing, which you'll wear." He coughed and spat. "We can drive," he went on more easily, "and be up there pretty quick and noisy, or ride bicycles. A bit of hiking involved either way, where it eventually gets too steep for wheels. Nothing taxing."

Drive, Hale thought fretfully, or ride bicycles? "I hope you didn't score through all the bubble holes on the stone," he said, almost absently, as he pondered the choice. He wished he had time to brief these men properly, as Theodora had said he would have.

"The incised lines are zigzag, sir. We were told not to saw into any of the bubbles."

Hale was aware of the weight of the cut-down .45 revolver in the shoulder holster under his vest, but its two-inch barrel would be of little use for accurate shooting over any distance. "I believe you were instructed to bring a spare gun, for me," he said.

One of the men by the nearest jeep reached into the bed of it and hiked up another Sten gun, its skeletal stock making it look to Hale for a moment like some kind of modern orthopedic crutch.

"Right." Hale took a deep breath and let it out. "I think the sound of a jeep's motor would—"

He paused, for over the wind he could now hear the buzz of a distant motor, and from the sound and the cadence of gear-shifts he believed that in fact it was a jeep, somewhere out on the marshy plain to the south.

Exactly, he thought; you can hear the bloody thing for miles.

And then he heard a rumbling from the mountain—and even in the moonlight he could see the valley floor to the west *rippling,* in waves of shadow that were rushing across the grasslands toward him.

"Earthquake!" he said, crouching, even as the ground under his feet began to heave up and down like the bed of a speeding truck; and in spite of his stance, Hale sat down heavily on the jumping ground. The helicopter creaked on its wheels and the springs on the jeeps were squeaking as the vehicles rocked. The helicopter's six-foot rotors had stopped spinning, but were bobbing up and down now.

When the ground had steadied and the rumble had rolled away to the cloudy east, Hale rocked forward onto his hands and knees and looked back up at the mountain. The sharp outlines of the gorge were blurred by clouds like smoke, and he knew they were dust or snow, shaken up from the crags.

And he remembered the earthquake that had jolted the rubbled lot in Berlin, in the instant when the weather balloon over the Arabian boat had been engulfed by the living whirlwind.

"They've started," he said breathlessly, getting to his feet and stepping toward the nearest jeep, which had a spare set of suspension springs roped across the grille like an incongruously smiling mouth. "The djinn are awake now, they've opened their gates." He took a deep breath. "They're—goddammit, they're genies, right?—up there. Monsters, like earth elementals—no joke. Use the anchors, the iron crosses, as a shield, to force them back—the way they do with crucifixes to Dracula in the movies. Your lives depend on this." He was panting and sweating; the faces he could see were skeptical and noncommital. "We've got to drive—and fast. To hell with the noise, there's already a jeep banging around out here tonight."

"McNally," snapped Shannon, "you drive Captain Hale, behind the rest of us."

Shannon and three of his men sprinted to the other jeep as Hale vaulted over the rear fender of the nearer one and crouched in the gritty ridged-steel bed, snatching up the Sten gun. "Did you understand me," Hale nearly wailed, "about the anchors?"

Over the brief screeches of the jeep engines starting up, he could hear the men in the other jeep reply in the affirmative.

"Understood, sir," loudly echoed the man in the driver's seat of Hale's jeep, whose name apparently was McNally.

The headlamps were not switched on, but abrupt acceleration threw Hale back against the tailgate. "And you do understand," he added in a yell, "that this operation will involve the—the supernatural?"

"We have been told that, sir," shouted McNally over the roar of the engine. "And we'll believe it when we see it."

The other jeep was in the lead as they sped up the steep dirt track in the moonlight, and Hale hung on and tried to watch the looming mountain through the dust. He could not yet see any whirlwinds, or patches of refracted starlight in the sky, but he was bleakly sure that the driver would be seeing some sort of "it" very soon.

Hale reached under his shirt to pull free the canvas bag that contained his own ankh; the bag hung on a twine loop around his neck, and he let it bounce on the front of his vest like a heavy scapular, easy to reach. Then he remembered to pull back the cocking handle on the machine gun in his lap and let it snap forward, and to check the change lever to be sure the gun was set for full-automatic fire. He held the weapon ready, but kept his finger away from the oversized trigger.

Within a minute the two Willys jeeps had begun the ascent up into the gorge, both audibly shifting down into low gear. The road was muddy now, and the windscreen of Hale's jeep was soon spattered and

smeared; the two drivers still hadn't switched on the headlamps, and
Hale couldn't imagine how McNally could see to steer. Hale noticed that
even the brake lights of the vehicle ahead didn't flash, when it occasionally slowed.

A cluster of mud huts sat squarely on the delta slope of the gorge,
one of them half-collapsed now under its spilled thatched roof, and
beyond them the dirt road divided, one track slanting away south to
trace the foot of the southern cliffs and the other proceeding more
directly to the north wall of the valley. The surface of the northern path
was freshly imprinted with the tire tracks of a heavy lorry, but the driver
of the lead jeep steered his vehicle up onto the south road, at no less
than fifty kilometers per hour, and the one Hale rode in rocked and
bounced along right behind it.

They know where they put the Shihab stone, Hale told himself as he
clung to the jerrycan rack on the side panel, hoping the vehicle wasn't
about to capsize. And they know how to blow it up. My job is to . . . use
the blood to summon all the djinn down from the heights on the other
side of the gorge to the area around the stone; and duck for some sort of
cover when the explosion is due, with no bomb shelter, thank you, Jimmie; and then get myself and these men back down to the plain alive.

The Ahora Gorge was a long notch that slanted southwest up into
the heart of the mountain, between walls sheared nearly vertical by old
earthquakes, and all Hale could see in the deep moon-shadow darkness
was dimly glowing patches of snow beside the black path. Soon the
jeeps were grinding up a steeper track that was clearly not meant for
motor vehicles, still moving straight uphill along the south flank of the
gorge, and the wheels were spinning and hitching in slushy, pebbly
mud; looking across the narrowed valley toward the northern wall, Hale
could not see any sign of the Russian expedition on the faintly lighter
patches that were probably snowy clearings and slopes, but he was
cowed by the towering black cliffs that overhung the gorge on both
sides, and by the parapets and crenellations of snow visible in the
moonlight at the tops, right under the starry sky. The plain where the
helicopter had landed was more than five thousand feet above sea
level—the jeeps couldn't be far short now of the eight-thousand-foot
level, above which the Armenian shepherds had found that their sheep
died for no reason; and he wished he dared to shout to the commandos
in the jeep ahead of him, and tell them that the oppressive fear needling

this chilly air was a projection from the djinn, and not a naturally arising human response.

At least the Russians are over there on the northern side of the valley, he thought.

He was braced in the bed of the jeep, trying to lean out to see around the left side of the windscreen, when something began tugging at his vest. He repressed a shout, but he did scramble back against the tailgate, beating at his clothing; something in his pocket was moving, and his first thought was that it was a rat.

But his knuckles felt rocky hardness through the quilted cloth, and he relaxed a little when he realized that it was the stone the Khan had given him. Gingerly he reached into his pocket, took hold of it, and tugged it out into the air; and he was dizzily startled at how heavy it had become—and it was heavy *sideways*—it was tugging horizontally northeast, away from the mountain peak.

I should certainly hang on to it, he thought—if it's so magnetically repelled by the proximity of djinn, probably they will be repelled by it, as the Khan said.

But I don't want to repel the djinn, he told himself, trying to concentrate in the gusty, rocking jeep bed. And even if I *should* want to, soon, that will be—would be—a *mistake*. I need to make contact with the creatures that live on this mountain—to destroy them, but first to *see* them! Even if I could keep this stone hidden and somehow damped, the fact of having it in my pocket might be an overpowering temptation to use it, if this operation becomes too robust.

The stone was tugging away more strongly now—he had to use both hands to hold on to it, bracing himself with his feet—and he told himself that it would soon be repelled with such force that even if he wedged it against the floor it would drag the jeep to a wheel-spinning halt.

I have to let it go, he thought with cautious satisfaction—nobody can blame me. I do thank you for the kind intention, Siamand Barakat Khan! but—

He moved his head well to the side and then let go of the stone, and it went silently cannonballing away into the night behind them.

Hale brushed his palms on his vest and hiked himself forward again. He was committed to this now, like Ulysses tied to the mast, like Cortés after burning the ships on the Mexican shore.

And he realized that these five men were committed too. He glanced back, but of course the stone was lost in the darkness—perhaps it would tumble all the long way back to Wabar.

Suddenly McNally yelled something that sounded like, "Bloody horses?"

The jeep in front had slewed to a stop in front of a jagged white mound of snow that blocked the way, and when Hale heard McNally stamp on the brake pedal he grabbed the back of the passenger seat to keep from falling forward as his jeep halted.

And Hale's chest went cold in sudden fright when a man's voice rang out of the darkness ahead, speaking loudly in Turkish over the rumble of the idling engines—Hale didn't understand the words, but he thought he recognized the skewed vowels of a French accent; and at the same moment he saw the horses McNally had referred to: two four-legged silhouettes standing off to the right, dimly visible against the gray of the snow.

McNally had leaned sideways below the dashboard to unsling his rifle, and Hale knew that the four other SAS men must have done the same, and must be aiming their weapons toward the voice.

"Qui etes vous?" shouted Hale desperately. *Who are you?*

He could just make out the muzzle of his Sten gun in front of him, wobbling as the jeep engine chugged on in neutral.

The voice from the darkness was strained as it spoke again, in fluent French now: "Drop your weapons. Do you have shovels? Our companions are buried under this avalanche."

"Don't shoot," called Hale in English to the SAS men; then he took a deep breath and yelled, in French, "Is Elena with you?"—for clearly this must be the SDECE team from Dogubayezit, and he needed to know right away that Elena was not one of the people who were under the snow and certainly dead.

And sweat of relief sprang out on his forehead when he heard Elena's well-remembered voice cry, "Don't shoot them! Andrew Hale, is it you?"

"They're SDECE," Hale shouted in English, "French—allies. Elena! Yes!"

"Bloody hell," growled one of the men in the other jeep.

McNally had straightened up, and now he switched off the engine and began climbing out of the vehicle with his rifle still in his hands.

"We hike now," he told Hale quietly, "a bit farther than we planned. Even those horses would be no use from here on up. Now you've got a webbing to put on, with your—*medical supplies* in it."

The other engine had been turned off too now, and in the sudden echoing silence Hale could hear the rippling clatter of a waterfall somewhere in the darkness far ahead. The air was cold and thin in his nostrils, but seemed resonant as if with some subsonic tone, and he was humiliated to find that he had to force himself to let go of the familiar seat-back and climb down out of the jeep to the slushy alien ground, slinging his rifle. He could feel his knees shaking, and his hands were numb with cold.

"Andrew!" shouted Elena's voice. "Have you got entrenching tools? Help us dig!"

McNally was a blur in the darkness. "The stone is about a hundred yards up the slope, sir," he said, "up by the waterfall you hear."

Hale nodded tightly, though the gesture couldn't be seen. *I can't, Elena*, he thought. *I can't even order any of these men to. Why in hell did you have to come up here tonight?* "Where is the blood?" he asked McNally—

—and in Hale's head the question seemed to go on ringing, as—

—suddenly a blinding flare of white light ahead of him burned the silhouettes of McNally and the jeep's windscreen frame into Hale's retinas, and an instant later the night was shattered by the stuttering crash of gunfire.

Hale's hands were on the jeep's fender, and even through his numb fingers he felt hammering impacts against the vehicle's steel body in the instant before he dropped to his knees in the icy mud on the side away from the gorge's south wall. The sustained, deafening noise made it hard for him to unsling his rifle, and before he had got it into his hands he saw, by the razory-clear black-and-white illumination of the magnesium flare on the road ahead, the body of McNally tumble to the snowy mud by the right-front wheel of the jeep, his eyes wide and his throat punched open.

Black blood jetted from the wound—and Hale's mind keened in pure fear to see the glistening black drops move *slowly* in mid-air, like obsidian beads falling through clear glycerine.

He was still hearing his own voice ask, *Where is the blood?*

A gust of wind from the north knocked Hale against the muddy rear wheel, and his nostrils flared at the smell of metallic, rancid oil.

His balance was gone, and thinking that another earthquake was shaking the mountain, he raised the gun to shade his eyes from the flare light and squinted up at the overhanging masses of snow on the gorge crests—but it was the sky that made him bare his teeth in dismay. Even through the glare-haze he could see that the world-spanning black vault of stars was spinning ponderously, and the whole gorge seemed to be reciprocally turning the opposite way, with slow but increasing force.

And a voice like a volcano tolled down from the stony heights of Ararat then, exploding his thoughts away in all directions like frightened birds—its slow, throbbing syllables were in Arabic, and among them he caught the word for *brothers*—and his left hand closed on the canvas bag strung around his neck, with no more conscious volition than a frightened bug scuttling for cover. With his right hand he clumsily fumbled out the iron ankh.

The ankh seemed hot in his cold fist, and it served as an anchor for his thoughts: *Wave it, push them back*—

But when he pushed the iron cross up through the icy resisting air, it was abruptly snatched away upward, tearing the skin of his palm.

At the same time McNally's body had sat up in the white light, and now its arms flopped and then stood straight up over the lolling head; in the next moment the body had been yanked up onto its toes, and then right off its feet, so that it dangled unsupported in the air.

I should have held on to the Khan's stone, Hale thought despairingly.

And then his chest was suddenly constricted as if between a giant thumb and finger, and he was forcibly lifted up by an invisible strength, and just for a moment he was suspended in a half-kneeling posture, facing the jeep, with his knees off the ground and his toes in the mud. McNally's body fell away above him into the revolving sky, and Hale knew that he himself was about to follow the body up—

And in the Sten gun's trigger guard his right forefinger, neurally remembering the telegraph key, began twitching out the old hitch-and-skip *clochard* rhythm in firing the gun.

The muzzle was pointed at the jeep's right-rear tire, and snow and mud sprayed up into his face as the tire ruptured and the jeep's back end clanked down on the springs—but Hale's knees smacked into the mud as the invisible hand released him, and he made himself hang onto the jumping gun and keep blasting out the alien drumbeat.

In the few seconds it took for the magazine to be emptied, his pulse and breathing had taken on the pounding rhythm, and he let go of the gun and stood up to hammer out the beat on the lowered fender with his numb fists.

Then all the crashing sound ceased at once—not as though he had gone deaf, but as though a silent black surf had engulfed the gorge. The flare was glowing a golden orange now to his right, and the shooting certainly appeared to have stopped, though he could see spots of smoldering red in the darkness below the close south wall of the gorge, on the other side of the jeep. The Sten gun's ejected shells glittered in the amber light, and though the brass shells turned slowly they did not fall out of the air.

As if the rhythm that now defined him constituted a matched bandwidth frequency, he found himself taking part in a vertiginously bigger frame of reference, a bigger perspective.

He didn't seem to be in his own body anymore, nor thinking with Andrew Hale's mind. He was looking *down* on Mount Ararat now—and from a wider viewpoint than just two close-set human eyes.

Bending down over the gorge, he held McNally's body in a hand made of wind, and the upward-tumbling human body, with its random motions and unchanging appearance, was no less expressive than living men were. On another side of the McNally form he could see other men, and their constricted bendings held no meaning, and the clothes and hair that were their substances were as imbecilically constant as the shapes of the cliffs. Thought and identity consisted of moving agitation—the verb in the leap of stones, the whirling of mirth in infinite grains of sand in a storm, questions in falling rain and answers in the bubbling liberation of water into exploding steam—expressed across miles of desert or turbulent sea; and to this vibrant dialogue men could contribute only accidental statements, like the airplanes and bullets they moved through the air, or the narrow wave-sequences they projected from their mouths to kink the air and from their radios to flatten the fields of the sky.

Brothers. Only when men were split, mind as well as body, so that one half could therefore move in deliberate counterpoint to the other half, were they capable of expressing comprehensible thought. But this one that existed on both sides of the gorge had catastrophically been split *again*, and had therefore fallen back into opaque idiocy. It carried a *rafiq* diamond, an emblem of kinship with the rushing sky-powers, but

the message or request it had brought to the mountain was lost in conflicted motion.

Hale felt his subsumed identity flex with deliberate effort, and then
McNally's leg was a crushed ruin tumbling separate from the body—and
in the instant before he recoiled away from this incorporeal participation Hale *tasted* the hot blood and shattered bone and torn khaki.

The djinn were eating the men in the sky, and Hale, sharing their
identity because he had aligned himself with their peculiar frequency,
was doing it with them, in them.

Jesus, why didn't I hang on to the stone?

He forced his hands and his lungs to stop moving in step with the
rhythm, and horror had already made a staccato chaos of his heartbeat.

And then he sagged with sudden weight and was standing again
beside the jeep in the muddy gorge, in the icy wind; interrupted
screams crashed in on his ears, and some of the screams were echoing
down from the sky, and dark drops that must have been blood were pattering onto the jeep fender and onto his hands. Choppy bursts of full-
automatic gunfire still plowed the air, but the muzzle flashes were
pointed into the sky now—and then the steaming breath was crushed
from his chest as he was again tugged upward with frightening physical
force.

Automatically his fists again pounded the telegraph-key rhythms
onto the wet fender, and the breath in his throat choked out the
resumed beat in a series of grudged coughs.

With a dizzying flutter his heartbeat fell into the same cadence, and
the bigger perspective was at once his again, and this time he was aware
of another man participating in the alien indulgence—but the music
that defined this one was in a different key or octave, and he knew it was
the kind of man called a woman.

A thought of Hale's flickered across his subsumed awareness—it
was Elena. She too was evading the doom of the men by aligning her
frequency with the djinn, as they had both done in Paris.

And now she too was sharing in the consumption of the resisting
bodies that spun through the air over the snowfields of Ararat's peak.
Helplessly surrendering to the transcendent wills of the fallen angels,
the sparks that were Hale and Elena moved in concert with the angels as
the bodies were torn apart—and the two frail sparks had no choice but

to concede that it was only in wide-flying dismemberment that the men, in death, achieved something like coherent meaning.

Not all of the men in the gorge had been taken up into the sky—some had been killed and left to lie in the mud, and Hale was aware of three-squared that bent and unbent their autistic shapes to move down toward the plain, out of the mountain; but even the geometric patterns they formed as they moved were without conscious meaning, and along with the will of the skies he ignored them.

He found himself looking upward instead.

The highest of the moon-silvered clouds formed sweeping stairways to lattices and balconies among the stars, and the music was complete and comprehensible now with the base line of infrared radiation in the earth and the skirling arpeggios of the solar wind and ionized particles scattering in the vast halls of the upper atmosphere—the dance was eternal, defiant and endlessly fascinating, fast as a horizon-spanning arc of lightning and as slow as the shifting of the basalt-footed continents.

The knot of identity that was consciously Hale had to be careful not to flex away with the angels into the sky or into the stony heart of the mountain—he was diminishing as he held back from these seven-league steps—and after some period of time he realized that he was alone and small and discrete, and that he was Andrew Hale, Captain Andrew Hale of the fugitive SOE, twenty-six years old and . . . profoundly unhappy.

He was kneeling in the mud beside the shredded rear tire of the jeep, and the magnesium flare had gone out, leaving the gorge in darkness. Only the whistle of frigid wind against high stone cliffs intruded now on the mountain silence, and as Hale got shakily to his feet he knew that there would be no use in calling out to his SAS companions—they had either been killed in the ambush, or taken up alive into the sky, or had fled down the path.

Then he heard a scuffle only a few yards away, and a moment later a shrill neigh and the wet clop of hooves in the mud—apparently at least one of the horses had survived, and someone had succeeded in mounting it.

Hale had lurched quickly backward at the unexpected noise, and now Elena's voice called harshly, in French, "Who is there?"

Hale was ashamed to speak, after the horror of their shared experience, but he made himself croak, "Elena—it's me, Andrew."

"Ach! Stay away from me—*cannibale.*"

He glimpsed a rushing shape in the darkness and then the horse had galloped past him, its hooves thudding away down the invisible slope.

He wanted to shout the plural down after her—*cannibales!*—but he could only despairingly agree with her assessment of him. His earlier question rang in his head again—*Where is the blood?*—and he knew that the blood was on his hands . . . on his very lips, morally if not literally.

Elena had apparently taken the only remaining horse, but the other jeep was still here; and when Hale limped stiffly across the mud to it, he could make it out clearly enough to know from its stance that its tires were still inflated. Feeling immensely old and bad and sad, Hale climbed wearily into the driver's seat and forced his frozen fingers to press the starter—and when the engine roared into hot life, he clanked the gear-shift sideways into reverse and, hunching around in the seat to peer downhill through the steaming plume of his breath, began inching the vehicle back down.

After a few yards he realized that his panting had become sobbing.

Surely some of the SAS men had survived—they would know the jeep by its sound, and then they would recognize him in the dimness, if they looked closely. McNally is dead, Hale told himself, but the other four might still be alive—they'd have had a moment to dive for cover between the blaze of the flare and the start of the gunfire—they wouldn't know that I—participated in the deaths, some of the deaths, helplessly—

But he remembered the sustained full-automatic fire that had raked the jeeps, and he quailed. It had to have been Russians who had ambushed them—but how had Russians known to be waiting there, beside the south wall? Had the SAS men been observed planting the stone, or had they been betrayed by someone in the West?

After no less than an hour of rocking down the slope in reverse, frequently braking and shifting to low gear to climb back up when the right side of the jeep seemed to be tilting into the gorge, Hale found a wider clearing in which he was able to turn the jeep around and drive forward; and he switched on the one remaining headlamp as he drove, peering through the shattered windscreen at the surface of the mud track ahead.

And soon he saw the upright shapes of three men in the headlamp glare, plodding and limping down the rutted path. Two wore the dark windbreakers the SAS men had been wearing, and one had on the turban and baggy trousers of a Kurd. None of them turned around at the sound of the engine or the illumination of the headlamp.

His heart thumping, Hale slowed the jeep a few yards behind them. The Sten gun was long gone, but he fumbled the chunky .45 revolver out of his shoulder holster—and then he called hoarsely through the broken windscreen, "Get in the vehicle! I'll drive us down."

They had ignored the light and the engine noise, but Hale's voice seemed to galvanize them. The man in Kurdish clothing dove forward in a flailing cartwheel that carried him right off the path, and though the two SAS men stayed on the road, they were clearly insane—one began semaphoring wildly, hopping to use alternate legs as well as his arms and head, and the other turned toward the headlamps and dug his fingers into his face and tugged outward, as if trying to pull his head apart.

When Hale shifted the gearbox into neutral and ratcheted up the brake, intending to step out and try to grab them, they both went bounding away into the darkness, leaping high into the air at every step; to Hale they appeared to be trying to fly. In seconds they were lost to his sight.

Hale was sobbing again as he shoved the .45 back into its holster and released the brake and clanked the gear-shift back into first gear. He saw no more men on the slow drive back down to the plain, and he did not see the horse.

A cold rain began to fall as he drove the jeep across the dark miles of marshy road toward the spot where the Bristol Sycamore helicopter had landed. In the cloud-filtered moonlight he could see nothing on either side of the road except the grim boulders, and he had come to the conclusion that the pilot had flown the helicopter away and that he would have to drive twenty-five miles around the mountain to the town of Dogubayezit in the southwest, over God-knew-what sort of roads— when out of the corner of his left eye he caught a vertical thread of yellow glow in the night.

He stamped on the brake and peered in that direction, but he didn't see the glow again; he backed the jeep in a wide arc onto the south shoulder of the path, to sweep the area on the opposite side with the headlamp beam—and he caught a gleam of reflected light on metal.

He rocked the gear-shift into first gear and drove slowly forward across the road, and soon recognized the stack of unused bicycles. The helicopter was indeed gone. But though he had not seen the vertical glow again, he knew that it must have shone from the Anderson bomb shelter in the field beyond.

Instantly he switched off the light and the engine; and he hefted the .45 revolver and swung his legs stiffly down out of the jeep and stood up on the muddy grass. As he stole silently toward what he believed was the black hump of the bomb shelter, he saw again the gleam of yellow light, and he realized that it was lamplight inside the shelter, escaping through the gap at the hinge side of the door.

A British voice from the darkness startled him so badly that he nearly pulled the trigger of the revolver: "Drop the g-gun, I've got you in my sights. I've h-heard you c-coming for the last t-t-ten m-miles."

Hale didn't move. "Philby," he said, trying to speak levelly.

"Is it Andrew hay-hay-Hale?"

"Yes."

"Are you alone?"

"Yes."

"Ah, g-good. I've only got enough l-l-liquor for *two* m-men to get properly d-drunk tonight, while w-we w-wait for dawn. The road to dog-dog-*Dogubayezit* would be impossible at n-night, t-trust me."

Hale heard footsteps swishing laterally across the grass then, and a moment later the bomb shelter door was pulled open, spilling lamplight out across the wet grass.

"D-d-do step in, my b-boy—you m-must be f-fruh-freezing."

Hale saw a figure in Kurd jacket and trousers crouch to step into the shelter, but he caught a glimpse of the face, and it was Philby's pouchy, humorous eyes that glanced back at him.

Hale shoved the gun back into its holster and hurried out of the cold night into the glowing shelter.

The bomb shelter wasn't tall enough to stand up in, and Philby was already sitting cross-legged against the corrugated steel wall at the back, with the paraffin lantern by his right elbow on a low shelf. A tan woolen Army blanket had been spread over the five-foot width of the floor, and Hale sat down on it after he had pulled the door closed behind him and pushed the bolt through the hasp.

Several more blankets were folded and stacked on a shelf under the curved-over metal ceiling; Hale reached up and pulled one down, and then tugged off the soaked Kurdish vest and wrapped himself snugly in the dry wool. The rain was coming down harder now outside, drumming on the steel roof over his head.

He leaned back against the bolted door, but even at this opposite end of the shelter he was only six feet away from Philby's knees.

Philby was smiling as he twisted a cork into a nearly full bottle of Macallan Scotch and then rolled it across the floor toward Hale. Hale's numb fingers managed to grab it, but he used his teeth to pull out the cork and spit it onto the blanket by his boots. He tilted the bottle up, and the cold golden liquor seemed to boom like an organ chord in his chest, spreading heat and blessed looseness through his cramped muscles. Dried blood, he noticed now, spotted his knuckles and the backs of his hands. He lowered the bottle to take a breath, then lifted it again for another solid swallow, impatient for the sense of forgiveness he knew was alcohol's to bestow.

"Are all y-your SAS men d-dead?" Philby asked.

Hale wondered how Philby knew that an SAS patrol had been involved. "I thought the SAS was disbanded after the war," he whispered, exhaling richly volatile Scotch fumes.

"Like the SOE." Philby sighed, and recited, almost to himself, " 'When as a lion's whelp shall to himself unknown, without seeking find, and be embraced by a piece of tender air; and when from a stately cedar shall be lopped branches, which being dead many years, shall after revive, be jointed to the old stock, and freshly grow; then shall the posthumous end their miseries, Britain be fortunate, and flourish in peace and plenty.' " For a moment he was glaring furiously at Hale. " 'Read, and declare the meaning.' "

Hale blinked at him in genuine bewilderment, careful to show no response to the word *declare*.

Philby hooded his eyes in a smile. "Sorry—Shakespeare, the prominent B-British playwright—*Cymbeline,* Act Five. Do you th-think that didn't . . . b-b-*bother* me, as a child? 'A lion's whelp,' 'without seeking find'? What were you all d-d-*doing* up there? I *am* the Head of Station in T-T-Turkey. First a commotion on the So-So-Soviet border down by Sadarak, and th-then a thousand rounds of ammunition f-fired off in the ha-ha-Ahora G-Gorge!" He was still smiling, but Hale had blinked the exhausted blurriness out of his eyes, and he thought Philby looked desolated, as if by some enormous disappointment.

"I—heard it," said Hale. "I drove around up there, but I wasn't able to find out what was going on. Shooting, evidently, as you say." He wondered what Philby would say when he got a look at the bullet-riddled jeep.

For the first time it occurred to him that his career, SIS or SOE, was probably over, after the disaster this operation had been. He took another sip of the Scotch, and then his hands had loosened up enough for him to shove the cork into the bottle and roll it back to Philby.

Philby opened his mouth to speak, then appeared to think better of it. " 'A lion's whelp,' " he said again, catching the bottle and uncorking it for a liberal swallow. "My f-father is Harry St. John f-f-Philby—have you h-heard of him?"

Author of *The Empty Quarter,* thought Hale. "Noted Arabist, I believe."

"Who was *your* ff-f-father?"

"A Catholic priest, according to the village gossip."

Philby nodded owlishly at him. "Have you ever h-heard of Rudyard Kipling?"

Hale sighed. "He wrote a book called *Kim.* I have read it."

"Ah! Well, my f-father gave me that n-nickname, because I reminded him of the b-b-boy in that very book. I was b-born in Ambala—that's in-in—in *India,* Andrew!—in 1912. I spoke H-Hindi before I learned hig-ig-English. When and where were you born?"

"1922, in Chipping Campden, in the Cotswolds."

"Or possibly in polly-p-p-Palestine, as your SIS records c-claim. Were you khh—chriss—*baptized* in the J-Jordan River? My f-father t-took me along with him on a t-t-trip to collect s-samples of Jordan w-water, the year after your b-birth."

"I certainly don't recall."

"Y-you were in Berlin thruh-three years ago, and n-now here you are at rahrah—Arararah—Agri Dag, damn it." He raised his eyebrows. "Do you have queer d-dreams on New Year's Eve?"

Hale forced down his alarm and made himself smile quizzically. "I suppose so. And then wake up with a hangover."

Philby nodded. "Let's pass the t-time with a game of c-cards," he

said. He tipped the bottle up for another mouthful and set it down carefully, and then dug a pack of playing cards out from under his blue
Kurdish robe. Hale noticed for the first time that the man's robe was
nearly as soaked as Hale's vest. "Poker," Philby said as he opened the box
and spilled the red-backed cards into his hand.

Hale laughed mechanically. "With promissory notes?" he said. "I'm
afraid I left my notecase at the hotel in Kars."

"And I b-brought a j-jewel, but I'm afraid I s-s-*swallowed* it. D-Did
you know that poker d-derives from an old purr-Persian card game,
known as As-Nas? It was an ancestor of the F-F-French Ambigu as well.
We can play for *her*."

Hale could feel the Scotch beginning to do its good work. He
blinked at Philby in the lamplight. "Her? Who, this Ambigu?"

Philby pouted his lips and shook his head. "You know who I
m-mean. She appears to f-fancy b-both of us, so the l-loser of this hand
will agree to stay-stay out of the other m-man's *way*, fair enough? Elena
Ceniza-Bendiga."

Hale's face burned with suddenly renewed humiliation—
Cannibale!—and he wished the bottle was up at his end. "I won't play,"
he muttered. He recalled Elena's headlong gallop down the lightless
mountain path. "She may be dead, in any case."

"Then it's p-probably academic, isn't it?" Philby's face was heavy and
expressionless, his lower lip hanging away from his teeth; Hale was
reminded of the gargoyles on Notre-Dame. "We can play for her," Philby
repeated, in a voice that made Hale think of heavy clay.

Dimly Hale realized that this was a moral choice, possibly an important one. But there was no God, and Elena loathed him; and through his
mind flickered a bit of Swinburne's verse: *We thank, with brief thanksgiv-
ing, whatever gods may be, that no life lives for ever; that dead men rise up
never; that even the weariest river winds somewhere safe to sea.* No resurrection, no judgment. The bottle rolled across the blanket and rapped
his knuckles, and he picked it up. "Very well," he said hoarsely. "Five-
card draw?"

Philby's charm had returned in the crinkling of his eyes and the
quirk of his lips. "She's not dead, by the way—she rode past here twenty
minutes ago, on a horse. No, not five-draw. A different derivation of As-
Nas, I think," he said as he began shuffling the cards in a lazy, overhand
style. "Seven-card stud—high-low—declare, not cards-speak."

Again Hale made himself show no reaction to the word *declare*. "High-low?" he asked. "Low hand splits the pot? How can that work? We can't split *her,* the way . . . the way King Solomon offered to split the baby those women brought to him."

The thunder of rain on the roof was redoubled, and the ground under the steel floor shook with an aftershock of the earthquake, or perhaps at the impact of a close lightning strike. Fleetingly Hale thought of the rough glass fulgurites he had found in the Rub'-al-Khali desert three months ago.

Philby had paused in his shuffling to stare speculatively at the curved, ribbed ceiling. "You're insane," he remarked in a conversational tone, "to invoke that name here, tonight. But you have, at least, summoned witnesses! No, we won't split her. High hand wins her, and the low hand wins this."

Holding the deck of cards in one hand, he reached with the other inside his robe, and then tossed out onto the blanket a thick roll of buff-colored paper.

Hale stared curiously at it—it appeared to be a manila envelope, tightly rolled up and tied with a ribbon. Red wax had been smeared across the ribbon and over an ink signature on the outside of the envelope, and the paper was speckled with half-dried red drops, blotted in spots with a dampness that must be recent rain.

From where he sat, Hale could read the signature's last name—*Maly.*

Hale widened his eyes at Philby.

"I was supposed to get that in '37, from an old friend, a Soviet agent I had . . . doubled, and was running in England. An inheritance, last-wishes type of thing. I only got it tonight, and even so I had to take it off of a dead man."

"And it is what?"

"It's the true Eucharist, the guide to it, anyway; it's the reason Stalin purged the GRU in '37—what you'd have called the Razvedupr, during your Paris days. Did you know that even the GRU cooks and lavatory attendants were killed, in that purge? The illegals in Europe had stumbled on a discovery, learned it from the Communist Polish Jews who had fled to Palestine, in the 1920s, and run the undercover Unity network there. At first it was just a—well, you must have stumbled across it—a sort of beat, or cadence, used in telegraphy, to project signals better. But the illegals eventually discovered that this sort of cadence could evoke peculiar aid in all sorts of situations. Eventually this man"—he reached forward to tap the rolled envelope—"discovered how it could be used to—if used in a certain symbiosis—prevent death."

At the word *death* the shelter shook with a hard gust of shotgunning rain.

"Yes!" Philby shouted at the roof. To Hale, he went on, "You know the *amomon* plant—your Kurds must have told you about it."

Hale turned up one palm. "Remind me."

"It's what my father searched for in the Rub' al-Khali desert, what Lawrence found and chose to die rather than use; it's—well, it's the way to avoid the 'truth to be found on the unknown shore,' be sure that you won't 'without seeking find.' Stop anyone from establishing the *truth* about you, hmm? Evade the"—the corners of his lips turned down ironically—" 'the *wrath of God.*' "

"*Not die,* you mean," said Hale. "Directions are in that envelope."

"Your position is gone, you do know that, don't you? You're out of a job, old son; so why bother acting skeptical now? Yes, in this envelope! It's . . . it's partly a crude musical score, I'm told, and partly a recipe, for the preparation and *awakening* of the angel that slumbers in the thistle." He smiled. "You were brought up a Catholic—evade the Last Judgment, husband your precious sins—live forever, without the necessity of a resurrection!"

"And you're willing to gamble *that* against"—Hale paused to gulp some more of the Scotch—"just for an unobstructed way with Elena."

Philby opened his mouth as if in a laugh, but if there was any sound it was too soft for Hale to hear over the drumming of the rain. "I'm confident I'll get *this* again," Philby said, "if not entry to immortality on a higher level of access. *You'll* never see it again, that's certain."

And no djinn died on the mountain tonight, Hale thought dully. There will be no poisoned honey for the Kurds next spring, and I won't be bringing Elena to the village of Siamand Barakat Khan. But I *might* be able, back in the Nafud or Summan regions of the desert outside Kuwait, to find and kill a djinn; and then the following spring take a party of the Mutair out to look for blooming thistles . . .

Live forever, evade the wrath of God.

The taste of khaki, and blood . . .

He shuddered. "Deal," he said.

Thunder broke in vast syllables across the sky outside, and Hale remembered that Philby had said his reference to King Solomon had summoned witnesses. And it occurred to him that Philby was not so much playing here to gain something as to make Hale "cast lots" for Elena, betray his love of her. Philby was supposed to be a master at getting Soviet agents to defect—was he playing here simply to get Hale to damn his own soul?

But the cards were already spinning out across the blanket, two down and one up. Hale was showing a three, and his hole cards proved to be a pair of nines. Not a bad start toward the high hand.

Philby's showing card was an Ace—good either way.

"We're both already all-in," said Philby in a voice like rocks rubbing together. "No further betting." He dealt two more cards face-up—Hale got a seven; Philby got a four, and was looking good so far for making the low hand.

Philby's eyes were as empty as glass. "She's staying in Dogubayezit," he groaned as he flipped out two more cards. Hale got a ten, no help, and Philby got a six, looking very good for the low hand. "And she's got her own room, at the quaintly styled Ararat Hotel! I've got my jeep here, I can drive us to town at dawn, and the holder of the high hand can sneak right up to her room then, hmm?" His stiff demeanor made the jocularity of his words grotesque.

Hale's face chilled as he realized that Philby's two hole cards might be Aces, giving him three of them. Philby might have a lock on the *high* hand.

What have I done, here? thought Hale, trying to will away the fog of alcohol. Will this game have real *consequences*? Am I *giving* her to Philby? *Her*, to *Philby*? With a sickness in the pit of his stomach he realized that he couldn't back out of the hand now—he would simply be forfeiting the entire pot. And Philby had said there were *witnesses*. Hale remembered wondering if Philby was trying more to damn Hale's soul here than to win; and he realized that Philby had lost his stutter in the last minute or so, as if another entity, a devil, was speaking through his lips.

"She doesn't—Elena doesn't—*fancy* you," said Hale thickly.

Two more cards flipped out: Hale got a nine, giving him three of them now, and Philby got an eight. The rocking lamp flared and dimmed.

Philby's voice was an echoing growl: "Do you think that will matter, after this?"

The bomb shelter shook with a gust of wind, or thunder, or an after-shock—the earth and sky seemed to be agreeing with Philby.

"Last card," said Philby in a tone like the hollow crack of artillery; "down and dirty." He dealt each of them a card face-down, and Hale picked his up from the shaking floor with trembling fingers. The welded seams of the shelter were creaking now as the little structure rocked in the wind like a boat on a turbulent sea.

Down and dirty. The whole bomb shelter was vibrating now.

Hale's last card was another seven, giving him a full boat, nines over sevens. That was a good high hand—but Philby might conceivably have a better high hand, Aces-full, or even four Aces. If Hale declared high and then lost, he would lose the entire pot: Elena's safety from Philby and the immortality, both. And even if he should choose to abandon Elena to Philby, and try for the immortality—declare low—Philby could easily have a better low hand than Hale's terrible pair of sevens and could declare that way, and again win the whole pot.

Philby looked at his last card and then placed it back on the shivering blanket, still face-down. "We need tokens, for the declaration," he said peevishly, "to hold in our fists until the count of three—one token to declare for the low hand, two for the high, three for both ways. Do you have six . . . pennies, pebbles, matches?"

Slowly and thoughtfully, Hale dug his fingers into the canvas pouch that had contained his iron ankh.

And after a few seconds he tossed out onto the blanket six of the scorched black glass beads he had picked up from the sand by the mete-orite, in Wabar.

And as the beads bounced on the blanket, the whole bomb shelter was abruptly kicked over sideways, and the western wall of it punched Hale in the head as the lantern flew against the opposite wall and shat-tered—and then the creaking structure had ponderously rolled all the way over, and Hale tumbled to the ceiling on his right shoulder, his knees following in the constricted somersault to thump against some part of Philby; spatters of burning lamp oil had splashed across the blankets and the clothing of the two men, and Hale scrambled up, his feet slipping on the flaming curved ceiling, and wrenched back the bolt of the inverted door. He butted it open with his head.

Cold rain thrashed against his face and cleared his nose of the smell of burning wool and hair, and he threw himself over the top of the doorway and then jackknifed out onto the puddled grass, rolling over and over in the darkness to extinguish all of the flaming paraffin that had splashed on him.

He supposed Philby had climbed out too, but Hale could only clutch the wet grass and sob into the mud, for the whole earth was booming and resounding and shaking under him, and he was irrationally sure that God was striding furiously across eastern Turkey, looking for him, to throw him into Hell, as he deserved.

Hale closed his eyes lest their glitter should give his position away, and he tried to burrow his body into the mud.

I was afraid, because I was naked, and I hid myself.

After some hundreds of heartbeats, the ground stopped jolting under him, but Hale could still feel an intermittent subsonic vibration swell and fade deep in the earth, and he was drunkenly sure that it was God's wrathful attention sweeping the landscape. *I let go of the Khan's stone, because I wanted to command the djinn*, he thought despairingly; *I participated in the deaths of my men, in order not to be killed myself; and I tried to trade Elena for eternal life.* He kept his face pressed into the wet grass.

The rain dwindled away and stopped before dawn, and the earth was quiet, waiting for the sun. The moment came when Hale dared to move—he got up stiffly on his hands and knees in the windy darkness, cowering, but no shout from the sky knocked him back down; and he crawled to the inverted bomb shelter and pulled himself up to peer in through the open door. The fires had burned out, and when he climbed cautiously inside he discovered that Philby was gone. Hale wrapped himself in charred, rain-damp blankets and closed his eyes.

He awoke with a jolt at the screech of a starter motor in the dawn air outside; gray sunlight was slanting into the steel box through the open door, and he disentangled himself from the smoke-reeking blankets and climbed stiffly out onto the grass, shivering and squinting around at the plain and the mountain.

A gray Willys jeep sat on the north side of the upended bomb shelter, and the scarecrow figure of Philby was hunched in the driver's seat, fluttering the accelerator now to keep the cold engine from stalling. God only knew where the man had waited out the night.

Hale limped wide around the crumpled corrugated-steel walls, plodded across the wet grass to the vehicle, and wordlessly climbed into the passenger seat. Philby swiveled on him a look that was devoid of greeting, or of anger, or even of recognition; and eventually he clanked the engine into gear and began motoring across the bumpy field to the road that would take them to Dogubayezit.

Hale saw that the two-foot length of the rope he had seen yesterday in the jeep's bed was knotted now to the ring on the dashboard, and he saw that its end was hacked, as if by frantic blows of a knife edge; the fibers of it were curled up and blackened, and the tan dashboard paint around the steel ring was charred. Hale thought that the ring was even bent upward.

The other end of the rope, now gone, had been attached to a weather balloon mooring.

He tried to comprehend the huge thought: this jeep was used to awaken the djinn last night. This is the jeep I heard driving on the plain, just before the earthquake. The man who was driving this vehicle last night was almost certainly working for the Soviet team.

Hale looked away, out at the boulder-studded grass plain in the watery sunlight, and he kept his breathing steady.

Hold your fire until you've got a clear shot, he told himself as his heart thudded in his chest and he thought of the five lost SAS men. Plain revenge is seldom the shrewdest move in espionage. It might have been Burgess—but could Burgess be an active Soviet agent in this without Philby's complicity?

Hold your fire.

Neither man spoke, or even glanced again at the other, as the jeep bounced over the muddy road and the red sun slowly rose at their left, over Soviet Armenia.

Philby did not slow down as he drove through the silent main street of Dogubayezit, past the Ararat Hotel, and straight on toward the road that would take them back to Kars.

At Erzurum Hale was able to use an RAF radio to send a long decipher-yourself signal to Theodora in Broadway Buildings. In it he reported his failure, and he reported too his suspicion that Philby had participated in the operation, working on the Soviet side. Nearly immediately he received a telegram, but it was from the SIS personnel office rather than from Theodora. It was orders—he was to get aboard the next RAF flight to London and then report immediately to C, who in 1948 was Stuart Menzies.

And Hale had not seen Jimmie Theodora again until January second of this year, 1963, in Green Park.

When he had got out of the cab at Broadway Buildings by St. James's Park in London he had thought again, for the first time in many years, of the old Broadway Tower in the Cotswolds and of how he used to hike out across the stubbled fields to stare at its medieval-looking turrets and limestone walls when he had been a boy. The SIS headquarters at Broadway Buildings had long since lost for him its storybook associations with that old isolated castle, but now it seemed almost as remote.

The guard at the reception desk had recognized him from the wartime service, and after showing the man his orders-telegram Hale had been directed straight to the "arcana," the fourth-floor office from which white-haired old Stuart Menzies guided the worldwide concerns of the postwar SIS. The courtly old man had stood up from his desk to shake Hale's hand, but had not seemed to know exactly what Hale's work in Kuwait had been; and clearly he had not heard from the Turkish station about the recent disaster on Mount Ararat.

Perhaps imagining that Hale was simply a wartime agent demobbed very late, C had advised him to make a new life for himself in the private sector.

"I understand you were reading English at an Oxford college before we recruited you," Menzies had told him kindly. "Go back to that, pick up your life from that point, and forget the backstage world, the way you would forget any other illogical nightmare. You'll receive another year's pay through Drummond's in Admiralty Arch, and with attested wartime work in the Foreign Office you should have no difficulties getting an education grant. In the end, for all of us, '*Dulce et decorum est pro patria vanescere.*' "

▼

15

Beirut, 1963

"All women are thus." Kim spoke as might have Solomon.
  —Rudyard Kipling, *Kim*

Elena Teresa Ceniza-Bendiga awoke in an unfamiliar bed before dawn, from a dream of Madrid; she was alone in the dark, and it took her several seconds to remember that she was nearly thirty-nine years old, and that she was in Beirut. After leaving Kim Philby last night in the bar of the Carlton Hotel on the southern shore, she had taken a series of cabs to the St. Georges Hotel and paid cash for a room on the northwest corner of the second floor, overlooking the beach and the terrace.

She could hardly remember Madrid before her parents had been killed—she could call to mind the sunlit palaces along the tree-lined Gran Avenida de la Libertad, and the metal barrel of the strolling *barquillero,* with a wheel on the top of the barrel that she would spin to see how many *barquillos* her *centavo* would buy; the *barquillos* were light sugared wafers, and when she won more than three of them her father made her carry the rest home in her handkerchief. And she remembered taking her first Holy Communion at San Francisco el Grande, on the city's western bluff . . . solemn in a white dress, receiving on her tongue the wafer that was the body and blood of Jesus . . .

Then in April of 1931 King Alfonso had fled Spain, and riots had erupted in the streets—and on a stark Sunday afternoon in May, seven-year-old Elena had stood over the sprawled bodies and spilled blood of her father and mother, on the pavement of the Gran Via in front of a burning church.

Young Elena had apparently gone quietly mad and stopped eating for a while after that, and she recovered from the brain fever in the boardinghouse owned by her aunt Dolores. Her parents had been devout Catholics, members of the Accion Popular—but her aunt told her that the fascists of the Accion Popular had covertly set fire to the church themselves, in order to lay the blame on the Socialist Provisional Government; Elena's deluded parents had threatened to go to the *guardia civil* with the story, and had been killed by the fascists.

Only after her stay in the Lubyanka prison in Moscow did it occur to Elena to doubt her aunt Dolores's version of the story.

Tia Dolores was a Communist, and she enrolled Elena in the Pioneros youth organization, where the children had made big cardboard hammer-and-sickles and five-pointed Red Stars and learned to revere Lenin and Stalin and the Workers' Paradise. When the army rebelled against the government and the Loyalist guns had fired on the barracks and driven the soldiers out of Madrid, Elena's aunt had joined one of the citizens' militias and got a couple of rifles from the Loyalist Ministry of Defense, and the old lady and the little girl had practiced marksmanship by shooting at the statue of Christopher Columbus in El Retiro park. At night Elena sat through Party meetings in the unheated Palacio del Congreso, under a framed photograph of La Pasionara, the nun-like old woman who was one of the Communist deputies in the Loyalist parliament and whose radio and street speeches could rouse the sick from their beds to take their places at the barricades—and on the walk home through the Madrid streets afterward, Elena and her aunt had looked as pale as drowned corpses, for all the streetlamps and automobile headlights had been painted blue to be less visible from the air.

The right-wing Nationalists had taken Spain's army with them when they had rebelled, and the Loyalist army was just men in rope-soled shoes and coveralls and token red sashes, and women in smocks and forage caps, all equipped with unfamiliar rifles. Elena could still recall the sporadic banging of amateur target practice echoing in the streets—and she could recall too driving out the north road in a requisitioned Ford truck one morning in the summer of 1936, shouting *Viva la Republica* with everyone else, to stop the rebel army at the pass in the Sierra de Guadalarrama.

And the ragged militia had stopped the army, for a while. Twelve-year-old Elena had fired her rifle at a soldier that day, and had seen him fall; and that night she had not slept, and by the next morning she had come to the endurable conclusion that her parents had been fools, and that all priests were liars, and that there was, as Tia Dolores insisted, no God at all besides Man himself.

Her aunt was killed while crossing the Puerta del Sol one afternoon in August, struck in the spine by a stray Loyalist bullet.

Children were recruited for spy work because of their anonymity; Elena joined one of the International Brigades and learned the uses of wireless telegraphy and code groups and one-time pads, and she met the Communist Andre Marty in Albacete. She watched Marty shoot a British spy, and from Marty she learned more about the Communist Party which had replaced God in her chilled heart.

She had become an agent of the Soviet Red Army at the age of twelve—and in November of 1936, when the Nationalists had advanced all the way up to the Carabanchel suburb of Madrid, she had been ordered by Moscow Centre to take up new duties in Paris.

Escorted by a gruff old Soviet military advisor whose name she never learned, she traveled with hundreds of other fugitives north to Jaca in the foothills of the snowy Pyrenées, where they got on a bus full of Soviet officers and foreign journalists. Elena had sat by a window and watched the fir trees along the steep road disappear in the thickening mists as the bus labored up the Portalet Pass to halt at the French border, and while the Customs officers searched the bus, she had got out to sniff the cold mountain air and stare at the surrounding mountains—but when the bus had got under way again, and had driven down the Route des Pyrenées on the French side of the mountain range and stopped for petrol at Lourdes, she did not get out. The Blessed Virgin, Mary the Mother of God, was said to have appeared to a French peasant girl in a grotto at Lourdes eighty years earlier, and miraculous cures were now common here—and Elena was superstitiously afraid that her atheism might be cured by some supernatural intervention of the Virgin, and that her little red forage cap with its red star might be left among the stacks of discarded crutches and wheelchairs that were supposed to line the path to the grotto where Mary had appeared.

Elena stood up out of the hotel bed and crossed the carpeted floor to pull back the curtains—the Mediterranean Sea was purple, and the sky was red in the east over the Normandy Hotel. From the balcony outside her door she would be able to look down on the terrace where Philby would be meeting his Soviet controllers later this morning.

She thought of the CIA men who had braced her and Philby last night at the Carlton Hotel, and she considered the idea of using her radio to muster the SDECE team and exfiltrate Philby today, right after his meeting here, as he had suggested last night. She had dismissed the idea then, but now it seemed to be the prudent course. If she left him in play here, it was too likely that the CIA would kidnap him, or that the Soviets would pull up stakes and shift their base of operations out of Beirut, or even that Philby would crack, and have to be killed by one side or the other.

She did have to admit, against huge reluctance, that Philby's offer to defect seemed genuine after all. When she had tried to kill him a week ago, she had planned to report that his offer had been a trap, a Soviet plot calculated to embarrass the French Pompidou Cabinet. And even after her ill-considered assassination attempt had failed, she had still hoped to find actual evidence that he was Soviet bait. She had wanted— she *still* wanted—an excuse to kill him, and thus erase the most shameful episode of her life; if she brought him home alive, that episode would surely be part of his recorded biography, and she would almost certainly have to resign.

She sat down on the bed and picked up her purse. Down behind the long-barrel .38 revolver was a pack of Gauloises with a book of matches tucked into the cellophane, and she lit a cigarette and drew the smoke deep into her lungs.

But if she brought Philby back alive, and if his deposition proved to be as valuable as it seemed likely to be, she would have delivered a damaging blow to Moscow, even as she ended her own career. And truly she hated Moscow as much—and as personally—as she hated Philby.

She didn't want to let herself think, yet, about Andrew Hale; late last night she had composed a crash-priority inquiry about his current status to SDECE headquarters at the Quai d'Orsay in Paris, and tonight she would tune in the Paris bandwidth for an answer.

On New Year's Day of 1942 she had left Andrew sleeping in the room on the Île de la Cité and begun the first leg of her trip to Moscow. Her introduction to the Workers' Paradise had been the Tupelov ANT-35 two-engine airplane that had flown her out of Tbilisi—the pilot told the passengers in halting German that the plane had been built without a lot of *eitelkeit*, vanity, and this had proven to mean that there were no upholstered seats or safety belts or, apparently, wing-flaps; in order to take off, he ordered all the passengers to crowd up to the front of the plane so that he would be able to get the tail up, and even so the airplane cleared the fence at the end of the airfield with so little room to spare that Elena, pressed against a window, was able to see the individual barbs on the wire as it whipped past under them. Instruments too were apparently an *eitelkeit*, for the pilot never took the plane higher than five hundred feet and was clearly following the highways visible below.

When the plane landed at a small snow-plowed airfield on the outskirts of Moscow, she was met by Leonid Moroz, the Moscow council member and Red Army intelligence liaison who was to be her boss. Elena quickly learned that she had not, in fact, been called to Moscow to be killed—Moroz was working with Section II of the Operations Division of the GRU, and he had been ordered to construct a new identity for Elena as an expatriate Spanish heiress, and to infiltrate her into Berlin. Moroz was pitifully anxious that the plan should succeed.

Elena was given a couple of furnished rooms on the Izvoznia Ulitza, a street of gray five-story buildings outside the Sadovaya ring road on the banks of the western loop of the Moskva River. She soon gathered that her flatblock was a prestigious address—the forty or fifty other flats in her building were occupied by wives of Soviet officers who were stationed at the front—but she also noticed that the walls of the concrete structure were four feet thick and that its narrow windows faced the Mojaisk Chaussee thoroughfare and the Kiev railway station; clearly the place had been built as a defensive fortress. And she hoped that if the Germans were to approach Moscow she would be given a rifle and allowed to participate in the defense.

Leonid Moroz was a Party member and took pains to look like one. The dark pouches under his eyes were a sign not only of virtue—indicating that he worked at his desk until the small hours—but of status as well. Party members were beyond having to bother with dressing as the common people did, and Moroz was vain about the double-breasted jacket he always wore with all three buttons fastened—it was too tight, but it had a velvet collar. His only concession to the proletariat was his cloth cap, and Lenin was always portrayed wearing one.

Moroz frequently called Elena to his office to describe in vague terms the studying she would have to do to perfect her cover, and to discuss with her the current state of the war, and to ask her to type letters. His office was always so cold that Elena had to wear an overcoat and scarf; Moroz had three telephones on his bare desk, though he never made any calls and they never rang, and the only furnishings aside from an implausible dozen straight-backed chairs were framed photographs of Stalin, Marx, and Molotov.

The GRU, or Razvedupr—the Chief Intelligence Directorate of the Army General Staff—had been purged to the ground in 1937; and then after the Army had assembled a completely new staff for its intelligence directorate, all of its residencies abroad had been purged again in 1940—and Elena knew at first hand that the Razvedupr illegal networks in Paris were being rolled up last year, in 1941. The man behind the purges was Lavrenti Beria of the NKVD, and Moroz lived in fear of him. Moroz often made lunch of the pickled herring and vodka he kept in his desk, and once after drinking several inches of the vodka he told Elena that Beria was personally charming, an urbane little bald-headed flatterer in spectacles—but that he used the NKVD to kidnap attractive young women off the Moscow streets so that he could rape them; husbands or fathers who protested were never seen again. Moroz had been given the GRU-liaison post when he had become a member of the Moscow council, and he was desperate not to be connected with any error that might draw the placid, murderous gaze of Beria.

"Why does he want to uproot any plant, any feeblest seedling, that grows out of the Army's intelligence efforts?" mourned Moroz more than once. "Is there truly something inherently perilous in an Army intelligence agency, so that it needs to be exterminated to the last man every few years? Beria is Stalin's man, as the monster Yezhov was before him. The Army was founded by Trotsky—do you suppose that's why Stalin must at every season sow salt in that scorched earth?" Moroz had already confessed to Elena that he wrote poetry.

Elena knew that Trotsky had been killed more than a year ago in Mexico; but she knew too that Stalin feared the man's posthumous influences. Trotsky had been the founder of the Red Army, directly after the Revolution, as well as Lenin's commissar of foreign affairs; and he had been a close confidant of Lenin's, and was rumored to have helped Lenin organize a number of Soviet agencies so independent and secret that now Stalin himself could only guess at them. Perhaps there was some subterranean agency that Stalin especially feared, one that consistently tended to surface in the GRU, which was the agency founded to deal with threats against Mother Russia from abroad. Had some defensive posture proven more horrifying to Stalin than the foreign threat it was meant to counter?

Elena remembered Andre Marty executing alleged Trotskyites in Spain, and she remembered her suspicion that Marty was actually eliminating agents who had drifted into some transcendent order.

Sometimes Moroz thrust his hand into his pocket as he voiced his worries about Beria and the NKVD, and Elena guessed he was making the gesture known as *fig v karmane,* the fig in the pocket—the *fig* was the thumb thrust between the first two fingers in a clenched fist, expressing the universal "fuck you" defiance; but *v karmane* meant *in the pocket*—furtive, fearful. For all his frail charm, Moroz lived by the Soviet bureaucrat's maxim: *ugadat, ugodit, utselet,* pay attention, ingratiate, survive.

"*Nichevo,*" Moroz would say, dismissing the subject—she gathered that the word expressed something like a despairing *What's the use,* and a fatalistic *So be it.*

But Elena made a determined effort to love Moscow. She was allowed to supplement the basic diet of black bread and cabbage by buying food at a restricted General Staff shop, and she tried to buy only Russian items such as garlic sausage and eggs and Caucasian tea, and ignore the powdered milk and peanut butter, which were likely to be United States Army rations donated through the Lend-Lease program. But nearly half of the cars on the boulevards were American Lend-Lease Studebakers and Dodges. She never saw refrigerators in the shops and never saw a refrigerator car in the trains at the Kiev station.

She got used to the street loudspeakers that played the "Internationale" every morning at dawn and broadcast incomprehensible speeches all over the city all day long; and she made allowances for railings that came loose under her hand and new brick walls that had no mortar at all in some spots and were lumpy with excess in others; but she couldn't bear the smell and the crowds at the public baths, and made do with towels and cold water in her room—but a dated chit from a bathhouse was necessary to buy a train ticket, and when heavy snow forced her to take the train to Moroz's office she would buy a bath-chit on the black market. When the trains broke down, a porter would walk through the cars and take the electric lightbulbs out of the lamps so that they wouldn't be stolen.

Elena learned to scan the newspapers that were posted in display cases on the street, looking for the Cyrillic symbols for Moroz's name in the lists of Party officials; she had noticed that the lists weren't arranged alphabetically, and gathered that the order of the names indicated their current standing with the Politburo.

And she noticed that Moroz's name had fallen to the bottom of the list on the day after she met the Middle Eastern woman on the Sadovaya ring road by Arbat Street.

Elena had stopped at a sidewalk kiosk to spend a ruble on a scant shot of vodka, when she noticed the metallic glint of jewelry on a woman standing beside her; the popular costume jewelry was stamped out of colored plastic, so Elena assumed the gleam had come from one of the state medals that Muscovites always wore. But when she turned to look, the exotic face of the woman distracted her—it was a dark face, veiled across the nose and mouth so that only the glittering brown eyes could be seen under the black braided hair, and in spite of the intense cold the woman was dressed in a length of dark blue cloth draped over the shoulders and wound around the waist to hang in folds like a skirt. Her feet were bare on the pavement.

And even as Elena told herself that she must help this lost for-eigner, must get her indoors somewhere out of the snow and find shoes and a coat for her, she noticed that the woman's bare feet were in the center of a patch of cleared wet pavement; the woman's feet had melted the snow on the sidewalk to a distance of nearly a yard; and now Elena could feel the heat that radiated from her, as palpable as radiant energy from a furnace.

The jewelry, Elena noticed finally, was a string of gold rings around the woman's neck; and interspersed among the rings were holed lumps of steel and gold. Elena had seen many Muscovites with stainless-steel teeth—dental porcelain was scarce.

The woman rocked her head to the south, staring intently into Elena's eyes—and Elena's face was suddenly hot, for the gesture and the look had somehow conveyed an urgent sexual invitation, if not an order. One of Elena's molars was gold, and she could imagine it strung among the lumps and the rings on the woman's breast.

But Elena turned away and ran down the Arbat Street sidewalk, skidding on the ice and fearful of pursuit but somehow taking comfort in the grid of electrified streetcar wires that made a net overhead. When she stopped under the harsh neo-Gothic pillars of the Foreign Ministry and looked back, the woman had not moved—or only a little, perhaps: surely she seemed a little closer, a little bigger against the background of gray buildings, than she would have if she had not moved.

And the next day, when Elena checked the display copies of *Pravda*, the Cyrillic symbols for "Moroz" were at the bottom of the list of Moscow council members.

She walked on past the newspaper display and then turned up a side street to the left, away from Moroz's office.

She felt like a swimmer out far past any thing to cling to, with the bottom leagues away below her flailing legs. If Moroz had been arrested, how could she safely find out? If he had been, she herself would surely share in his ruin. Her faith in the Party was subsumed in her terror of Beria—*Each morning the NKVD executioners were given their rifles and their vodka*, Cassagnac had said only three months ago, *and after they had shot their dozens and bulldozed them into pits dug by convict labor, they went back to the guardrooms and drank themselves insensible.* And even more recently Marcel Gruey, Lot, had told her, *Cassagnac said that this generation of the Soviet secret services will be killed in their own turn before long, and that the next lot is likely to be more reasonable.* But how could she take any evasion measures here? She had no contacts, she didn't know the city, the nearest border was more than three hundred miles away at Latvia, and she didn't even speak the language yet beyond a few utilitarian or slangy phrases.

She simply walked, east down the Gertsena street toward the medieval bastions that studded the gray Kremlin wall. She saw several police officers—mostly women in blue skirts and berets, directing traffic—but it wasn't uniformed figures that would threaten her. And she saw old women bundled up in coats and scarves, shuffling along the sidewalks in heavy felt boots, sweeping the snow into the gutters with crude brooms. Elena envied them their secure identities.

She had walked past the northernmost towers of the Kremlin. The buildings she passed were pillared palaces now, and she knew one of them was the Bolshoi Theatre—but she hurried past without looking up at the Corinthian columns, and tried to step along in a businesslike way as she made straight for the shadows of a cobbled pedestrian underpass.

When she came up into the gray daylight again on the far side, she heard music—a song that Marcel Gruey had sometimes sung, an American song called "The Atchison, Topeka and the Santa Fe"—echoing out across the snowy sidewalk from a hotel whose name she was able to figure out phonetically: Metropol. The clarity and imprecision let her know that the music was being produced by a live band rather than a radio speaker, and she hurried across the street and up the hotel steps. If she could meet some man, and get him to take her home, she could at least establish a temporary shelter from which to reconnoiter.

A moustached old man at the door mumbled something to her, and when she cocked her head enquiringly, he said, in English, "Thirty cents." Uneasy that he had so instantly identified her as a foreigner, Elena gave him a ruble coin and hurried past him—into a corridor that opened on an ornate nineteenth-century ballroom, with a fountain and a marble pool out in the middle of the polished wood floor.

At the checkroom she handed her overcoat across the counter. Three girls in lumpy ski pants arrived right behind her, chattering in Russian, and they began hopping on one foot and the other to pull the pants off, afterward smoothing the dresses that they had worn crumpled up under the pants. Elena's face went cold and expressionless to see two men in Red Army uniforms stepping up the hall now—but they were laughing as they took off their overcoats. Clearly they too had come simply to dance.

Elena shuffled nervously into the ballroom, eyeing the young men who seemed to be without partners. Everybody in Russia seemed to have come to the Metropol—men in coveralls were dancing with young women in wrinkled gowns, helmets rocked on the belts of gyrating soldiers, and even the aproned waiters were tap-dancing as they carried drinks on trays; Elena even heard English sentences, and after peering around spied a table of obvious Britishers drinking watery Zhigulovsky beer. Her first thought, instantly scorned, was to try to give them a message to take to Marcel Gruey, to poor gallant Lot—but she didn't even know his real name, and in any case he was a sadly deficient Communist.

Elena had just steeled herself to approach a studious-looking young man whose dance partner had been deflected away by one of the Red Army soldiers, when she found herself in the arms of a lean-faced man who smiled at her with steel teeth. "Bless me," the man said.

She nodded, recognizing the old Paris Razvedupr code: *Things are not what they seem—trust me.*

"You'll have to tell us," the man remarked quietly in her ear in French, "how you knew to avoid his office this morning. You were right—he's gone, and so would you have been. We might or might not have been able to get you away from them. But why didn't you simply follow her, when she approached you in her ring yesterday?"

Elena knew who it was that he must be referring to. *"Her* ring? The Sadovaya?"

"With her . . . earring stones? anchor stones? . . . installed around the periphery, at Patriarch's Pond and Gorky Park and the Kursk Station, to keep her from becoming . . . disoriented?" The French word was *désoriente,* and he laughed as though he had made a joke.

He had whirled her to an arch on the other side of the high-ceilinged room, and he stepped back and let her last dance step link her arm through his, so that now they were walking down the corridor beyond without having paused.

Another man was holding open an outside door, and Elena found that she had been escorted down a set of cement steps and into the back seat of a black Ford sedan before she could catch her breath. She wondered if she would ever see her overcoat again.

The man who had met her on the dance floor glanced at his wristwatch as the car accelerated away from the curb, driving in a counterclockwise loop around the block and then speeding north up the Neglinaya boulevard. "Moroz is probably dead, by now," he said, still speaking in French. "The NKVD has learned about your Palestinian lover in Paris." He laughed and shook his head. "A Palestinian radio operator! You would be food for Zat al-Dawahi yourself if we hadn't been tracking you closely. Moroz planned to send you to Berlin?"

"Who are you?" Elena demanded. "Hiding me from the NKVD—you're not Russians!"

The driver turned his head around to look at her, and she quailed. Under a wool cap his hairless face was pure Cossack, with high cheekbones and slanted eyes. "We are the oldest Russians," he said harshly in barbarous French, before turning back to the street ahead. "Our organization was old before Lenin returned to Petrograd from his Swiss exile in 1917," he went on, "and Lenin blessed us and committed into our hands the protection of Russia."

"The secret protection," agreed her escort. "Stalin and his NKVD hate the measures we take, and so we protect the motherland while hiding in foxes' earths that are secret even to the secret service, true to the old covenant. Andre Marty noted you, in Spain, and would have killed you as soon as he didn't need your wireless telegraphy skills any longer, if we hadn't used the GRU to summon you out of Madrid. Marty wrote a report to the NKVD, in which he said you were particularly dangerous—you were baptized but nevertheless sensitive to the most-secret world, and you were nearly virgin, still, in '36." The word he used was *vierge,* a term often used in speaking of unexposed photographic film.

"I *was* a virgin then!" protested Elena; and a moment later she could feel herself blushing.

"A virgin in the sense of not having killed anyone," her escort explained. "Marty said you had shot a Nationalist soldier, but it was before you had reached puberty, and we think you have probably killed no one else since, and never anyone up close. A soul's first few bloody murders have a sacramental power that must not be spent promiscuously."

"We were at war," said Elena now. "It was not a murder!"

The man shrugged impatiently. "Killing, execution, riposte, establishment of truth. We don't want you wasting any more of your baptized sanctity until you can spend it effectively." He looked away from her, out the window at the old women sweeping snow from the sidewalks. "And not in Berlin."

These *are* Russians, she told herself; and they apparently want me to perform an assassination. She remembered her sleepless night after shooting the Nationalist soldier at the Sierra de Guadalarrama pass, but she took a deep breath and said, "I am at the command of the Party."

"The Politburo consigns you to us with her left hand," dryly said the man she had danced with. "Our headquarters is in the Commissariat for Foreign Affairs on the Kuznetsky Bridge, where we still operate out of the Spets Otdel, the Special Department, of the NKVD. They don't quite know who we are, and our very presence in so secret an institution forbids them to inquire."

Elena never saw her flat on the Izvoznia Ulitza again—she was quartered now in a single-story log cabin in one of the "Alsatias" down at the southwestern bend of the Moskva River, by the Lenin Stadium. The

Alsatias were rookeries dating from before the Revolution, tangles of old streets and open sewers that had been slated for leveling and reconstruction before the war had intervened. The Alsatias were a perfect sanctuary for "hooligans"—criminals and deserters—and in fact a fugitive division of Azerbaijan troops had lately taken up residence in Elena's neighborhood, and frequently could be heard firing their Army-issue rifles at the cavalry patrols who enforced the midnight-to-five curfew. Elena's roommates were Betsy, an American-Armenian woman who, lured by the promise of a farm of her own in a new Armenia, had moved from New Jersey to Moscow in 1935 and irretrievably surrendered her American passport, and Pavel, a Roman Catholic priest who was generally too drunk to speak. Elena gathered that they were all working for the same unnamed agency, but it was never discussed.

The man who had danced with her at the Metropol told her his name was Utechin, and he led her with cheery confidence through the mazes of the Soviet secret world. As his secretary, she went with him to the offices of various commissars and ministers, always having to pass through two sets of padded-leather doors with brass plates over the key-holes, to discuss everything from weapon shipments to the selection of operas to be performed at the Bolshoi. Once she watched him preside over the disposition of a shipment of American Lend-Lease leather—the Army wanted it all for boots, and the Minister of Health wanted some of it for the construction of artificial limbs, while the Minister of Trade wanted enough to make a lot of industrial belting; Utechin later prepared conflicting reports to make each of them imagine that he had got what he had wanted, while in fact a full third of the leather was diverted to partisan groups in Astrakhan and Baku on the Caspian Sea coast, for the construction of assault-coracles—boats powered by outboard motors, each with a .50-caliber machine gun mounted at the stern. "The hulls have to be animal-stuff," Utechin told her merrily, "for our *allies* there to be able to distinguish our boats from the Germans'."

And he took her on tours of graveyards. In the Vagankov and Danilovskoye cemeteries they shoveled away the drifted snow to note the patterns of little holes punched upward out of fresh graves, and Utechin pointed out that the graves of the affluent dead had more such punctures than those of the poor. "The rich can afford gold teeth and jewelry," he told Elena once as they made a picnic of vodka and hard-boiled eggs and bloodwurst on a snow-covered grave mound. "It's only right that they should be called to give them up at the end. There is too much gold anyway, in our country—teeth from the dead, plating from the old church domes. If our angel wants our gold, so be it."

"*Nichevo*," Elena had agreed bewilderedly, reaching for the vodka bottle.

He nodded. "Drink more," he told her. "A fledgling agent should live more in drunkenness than in sobriety, in order to achieve distance from the deformity which is bourgeois conscience."

The preserved body of Lenin had been moved to Kuibyshev when the Nazis had begun their advance toward Moscow, but Utechin took her to the empty mausoleum, right across the broad expanse of Red Square from the palatial GUM department store. Utechin showed a pass to the guards at the tall portal, and he and Elena walked into the mausoleum and followed a counterclockwise route to a set of descending stairs, then turned right several times to get to the crypt room. Net zero, Elena thought.

Though it was empty, the glass coffin in the middle of the floor was brightly lit by electric lights. "If the Politburo has any sense," whispered Utechin as he ran his hand over the glass, apparently feeling for pits or scratches, "they will leave him in Kuibyshev. Why tease *her* with this?"

Elena was afraid she knew who Utechin referred to—and her suspicion was confirmed only a day or two later, when she received her ideological confirmation at the Spets-Otdel office on the Kuznetsky Bridge.

Utechin fed her six glasses of vodka before sitting her down in a chair across the desk from him. "You are elevated? Out of the twitching, gag-reflexing body? Good. Listen to me, girl—Mother Russia has a guardian angel, a very literal one. She can take a number of physical forms—you met her in one form, on the Sadovaya ring. In her remote youth she was known as Zat al-Dawahi, which is Arabic for Mistress of Misfortunes, but we call her Machikha Nash, Our Stepmother . . ."

And so, in the uncritical credulity of drunkenness, Elena had learned about the supernatural creature who had been captured on Mount Ararat after the earthquake of 1883 had knocked down the old confining drogue stones; and she learned that the guardian angel demanded deaths in return for her protection of the Soviet empire—such a constant cascade of deaths that Utechin's agency had been forced to assist and even encourage the NKVD in its insane wholesale purges. Elena was told that the great famine in the Ukraine during the winter of

1932 and 1933 had not been an accidental consequence of collectiviz-
ing agriculture and relocation of the land-owning farmers, the despised
kulaks; the famine had been deliberately set into motion, and the
Ukraine had been cut off from the rest of the world by heavily armed
OGPU detachments at the Kiev and Ukrainian–Russian borders.
"Machikha Nash demanded sacramental cannibalism," Utechin said
blandly, "and the starving Ukrainians provided it for her, in the interval
before they became her food in turn."

And, finally, in order to "divest her of the Judeo–Christian spiritual
gag reflex," she had been driven to the Lubyanka, only three blocks east
of the Metropol Hotel, and taken down many flights of stairs to the basements. After fasting and being kept awake by electric shocks for forty-
eight hours, she was shown the ring of huge rectangular stones in one of
the remotest chambers, each stone with a loop carved at its top, and
inside the ring she saw the crushed, skinned, and eviscerated bodies that
had lately been offered to Machikha Nash; and she was taken to a cell full
of Polish and Romanian women, and was allowed to talk to them in pid-
gin German for a few minutes before being forcibly restrained while they
were brutally and deafeningly killed by guards with machetes; and after
she was finally allowed to eat, she was told something abominable about
the stew she'd eaten. Throughout the three-day ordeal she was prevented
from sleeping and was constantly forced to choke down glass after glass
of harsh vodka.

At last she was marched into a wide, tiled room that shone a sulfurous yellow in the light of an electric bulb that hung on a cord from
the ceiling; two wooden chairs stood facing each other across fifteen
feet, with a drain in the floor between them. Elena was tied into one of
the chairs and given a hypodermic injection, and then an old man in a
white coat came in and talked droningly to her as he swung in front of
her eyes a tiny, anatomically perfect gold skull. After some time a young
woman was brought into the chamber by a couple of aproned guards;
the girl was dressed in a blood-spattered smock that was a precise copy
of the one Elena wore, and she had clearly been chosen because of her
strong physical resemblance to Elena—auburn hair, thin face, sunken,
haunted eyes. She too appeared to have been drugged, and she didn't
struggle when the guards tied her into the other chair, facing Elena.

"This woman is you," the old doctor told Elena in guttural English
as he stood behind the girl, with his hands on her shoulders, "and you

are sitting right here, you can feel the ropes that confine you; the chair out there toward which I am looking is empty." He was staring down at the top of the girl's head as he spoke, though Elena was finding it difficult to focus her eyes. "You feel my hands on your shoulders, don't you?"

Elena did—and when the doctor lit a cigarette and leaned down to blow smoke in the girl's face, Elena smelled the burning tobacco. After some unguessable period of time, punctuated by more injections and electric shocks and many administrations of vodka through a rubber hose, Elena found that she was able to see from the girl's eyes, and she could see that the doctor was right—the chair across the room was empty.

At last the old doctor stood away from her, with his back to the empty chair, and Elena saw him draw a revolver from the pocket of his lab coat. "Now you will be killed," he informed her. He pointed the gun at her face, and she saw his finger whiten inside the trigger guard.

A wall seemed to break in Elena's mind—and in the instant before the gun's muzzle exploded in stunning and obliterating white light, she thought, *Santa Maria, Madre de Dios*—

And when consciousness, but not light, returned to her, along with the sensation of lying on a cold stone floor, the voice in her head resumed where it had left off, simply because she had no thoughts of her own: *—ruega por nosotros, pecadores, ahora en esta hora de nuestra muerte.*

Pray for us, sinners, now in this hour of our death. Because there were no thoughts in her head, her concussed memory simply repeated the prayer over and over again.

Another voice was saying similar words in the dark, in insistent Spanish and Russian, and she tried to attend to the other voice's sentences too.

Then she was alone, lying in darkness for some period she could not estimate, without food or drink. She was able to move, and feel with her palms the texture of the stone floor and walls, and she could remember being hypnotized and told to identify herself with the girl who had been shot, but she was not at all certain that she was not in fact herself dead. And after the lights were turned on at last, and Utechin unlocked a barred door to run to where she lay and tip a glass of cold clear water to her cracked lips, she explained that the string she had tugged from her smock and tied into a series of knots had been her attempt to number the days of her confinement.

Her identity came back to her slowly. She pretended to have become the cold, truncated Party operative that they had worked so hard to make of her; and she kept deep within herself the memory that the string had been a makeshift rosary, and that in the long darkness she had made a binding vow to the Virgin Mary, the Mother of God. In the years to come, she was to tell only two people of that vow—Andrew Hale, and Kim Philby.

For two weeks she was allowed to rest in a yellow-brick dacha in the village of Zhukovka, on the Moskva River outside of the city. When she wasn't sleeping she went for long walks in the green pine woods, never forgetting that she was being observed, careful not to move her lips or make the sign of the cross as she prayed.

And the day came when she saw the trim figure of Utechin striding up the path from the direction of the Moscow road, stepping around the laborers who were digging trenches to stop the Germans if they should get this far east.

In the kitchen of the dacha, over glasses of Caucusus tea—she was no longer required to drink vodka, which was fortunate since she could no longer bear the medicinal smell of it—Utechin told her, "You will now be called on to commit your second killing, the first real murder of your life. Is Elena Ceniza-Bendiga willing to spend her soul for the Party in this way?"

She smiled at him. "Elena Ceniza-Bendiga is dead—she was shot in the face in the Lubyanka basement. I will be happy to give the Party anything I have that was hers."

She thought she caught a fleeting wince of sadness in Utechin's face; but then he went on in a businesslike tone, "You and I will travel to Cairo. The German General Erwin Rommel has driven the British Eighth Army to a point west of Tobruk, in Libya, and we believe that Rommel is being assisted by the efforts of a very elderly scholar operating from a residence in the City of the Dead below Cairo, the ancient cemetery. You will kill that old scholar."

Elena spread her hands. "Show me the way."

That evening at dusk they boarded an Aeroflot Tupelov ANT-35, and took off on the first leg of the journey that would take them to Baghdad, Tel Aviv, and ultimately to Cairo.

▼ ▼ ▼

Elena had seen photographs of the Pyramids of Giza and the Sphinx, and so when the two-engine Tupelov had at last flown west over the straight silver blade of the Suez Canal and banked south over the Nile Delta in its descent toward the Heliopolis airfield, she gasped at her first sight of the Sphinx through the airplane window.

"He has moved!" she exclaimed to Utechin, who was sitting in the seat beside her. "The Sphinx is on top of one of the pyramids!"

This seemed to alarm Utechin, who leaned over her to look down.

"Ah!" he said in evident relief as he slumped back into his seat. "No, child. That 'pyramid' under her chin is a support made of sandbags, thousands of them stacked up—to keep her head from falling off, if German bombs strike nearby. The three pyramids are still where they belong, west of her."

Elena leaned forward to peer back, and now she could see that the triangular slope under the scarred stone face was of a different tan color and texture than the three ancient stone monuments that dented the blue sky farther away. Elena knew that the Sphinx was a portrait of the Pharaoh Chephren, a man; evidently Utechin had confused it with the murderous female Sphinx of Greek mythology.

"Keep faith," muttered Utechin, apparently to himself, "and so will we." When Elena raised her eyebrows, he said, "The scholar in the City of the Dead knows of me; but, since he does not know I am coming to him, there can be no—*truth* to be established—for me in Cairo, on this trip."

But when they had landed and carried their valises out to the sidewalk to flag down a taxicab, Utechin was sweating through his sport coat, in spite of the cool breeze that rattled in the palm fronds overhead; and as he climbed into the back seat of the battered cab, he handed Elena a book-sized zippered leather case.

It was so heavy that she guessed it contained a handgun.

"American .45 automatic," he whispered to her in French as she hitched up her skirt and climbed in beside him with the case in her lap like a purse. "1911 Army Colt. You must be familiar with it from Spain. If we are cut off, cornered by anyone—use it on them."

Elena laughed easily, for she had long since decided to walk away from the Rabkrin in Cairo. "And promiscuously use up one of my sacramental bloody murders?"

Utechin's sweating face clenched in a frown that made him look ill. "Do as I say," he said softly. He tapped his lapel. "I am prepared too— and if you should fail to come to my assistance, you will not have any more heartbeats than I."

She stared at him curiously as the cab accelerated away from the curb. "But if we have killed our consciences," Elena said, speaking more loudly to be heard over the roaring automobile engine, "surely it was because there is no God?—and if there is no God, what is to be feared in dying?"

"No God," said Utechin, nodding rapidly as he stared out through the taxicab window at the narrow-windowed white houses. "Marx said that, but Marx was no Russian. The NKVD says that, but the NKVD is an army of witless thugs. We have never said that. We work to circumvent Him."

"Like a bull in the arena," said Elena, forcing herself not to smile. "Ah, you will divert Him with your capework, and leave Him blinking stupidly at empty sand while you steal around behind Him."

"This . . . merriment of yours may be an appropriate posture," Utechin said irritably; then he gave her a weak smile. "But it is certainly a trying one. Could you please put on a becoming solemnity, at least until after I've been able to catch up on my drinking schedule?"

Elena nodded obediently, and didn't speak until the taxicab had squeaked to a halt at the curb in front of Shepherd's Hotel on Port Said Street.

"Let us walk around a few blocks and view the layout of the streets before we go in," Utechin said as he climbed out. Elena had seen the United States star emblem on B-25 bombers at the Heliopolis airfield, and now she was staring at an American jeep swerving through the traffic of trolley cars and donkey carts on the broad boulevard; and Utechin added, "It will not be American soldiers, repellent though I grant you they are, who might assail us. Watch for . . . Egyptians, Arabs."

And in the crowded street Elena saw flashes of many Arabic faces— from the toothy grins of ragged brown boys crying for "Baksheesh!" to the white beards of Moslem elders, and she was nervous—even though she knew that Machikha Nash was confined within the borders of the Soviet Union—each time she met the eyes of an Arab woman staring at her from the slit above a black veil. It occurred to her that Utechin's target might be forewarned, and that Utechin's head and her own too might be centered in the sights of rifles in high windows even now. She hoped she might soon find a Coptic Catholic church—with luck, the priest wouldn't even understand the language in which she would make her lengthy Confession.

  . . . that I have sinned exceedingly, in what I have done, and in what I have failed to do . . .

The architecture of the city had been plaster-fronted white houses and domed mosques at the northern end, but on this street nineteenth-century European buildings had intruded among the older houses, making the traditional overhanging latticed balconies look frail.

"That is the French Embassy," said Utechin, nodding toward the Romanesque doorway of an ornate stone building front, "covert head-quarters of the French secret service. They are hand-in-glove with the British Special Operations Executive. So is the American OSS, in the American Embassy, another block down this street."

Elena had gathered that the British SOE contained a secret core that was the Western equivalent of the Rabkrin. Among Andre Marty's Communists there had been rumors of a vast old British operation known as Declare, and from the way Marty had especially devoted his energies to killing any British agents who seemed aware of a supernatural element in the war, Elena was confident that Declare, if it existed, was opposed to the secret Soviet cult of Machikha Nash.

They had stepped off the curb and were crossing Port Said Street, among a mixed crowd of Europeans, Egyptians, American soldiers, and half a dozen goats that were being herded by children in loincloths and baseball caps. Elena unzipped the leather case Utechin had handed her.

On the sidewalk she slipped her hand into the case, and her palm fit familiarly around the .45's grip. The safety catch was up, engaged, cocked-and-locked—and she thumbed it down. Finally she took a deep breath and pointed the concealed gun at Utechin's back. "Look," she said.

Utechin's face went blank when he turned around and saw her hand inside the case. He stopped walking, and leaned against a lamppost. "Explain this, please," he said. The concealed muzzle was now pointed at his abdomen.

"We will walk into the French Embassy," Elena said. There was a quaver in her voice, but her hand was steady. "We will surrender to their secret service. Defect."

Utechin licked his lips. "And . . . why?" he asked hoarsely.

"Because we are in front of it. If we were another block down the street, we would surrender to the Americans."

He shook his head slowly, an expression of both sadness and surprise on his damp face. "Ach, Elena, so soon! It is my fault, for not taking more time with you." And then he said, in Russian, *"Take the death now."*

A spot on her forehead stung with a sudden chill, and the breath stopped in her throat and her knees began to fold—and she realized that she must have been given a precautionary post-hypnotic order to *die,* as if of the gunshot that had killed her double in the Lubyanka cellar, upon hearing this Russian phrase a second time.

But though she fell hard to her knees on the pavement, she was able to raise the hidden .45 and keep it pointed at him; and the spot of chill on her forehead was now hot, as if a priest had marked the Ash Wednesday sign of the cross there with still-smoldering palm-frond ashes; and she realized that the words of the post-hypnotic order had got tangled with the words of the *Ave Maria* that had been droning in her head both before and after the shot had been fired—*ruega por nosotros, pecadores, ahora en esta hora nuestra muerte—*

Pray for us, sinners, now in the hour of our death.

Apparently the inadvertent parallel had disrupted the lethal grammar of the order, broken its imprinted lines like a double exposure.

Utechin hesitated, and then he abruptly crouched, falling backward as his right hand sprang up and under his lapel.

Elena hammered her gun hand downward to follow his sudden drop, and she twitched the trigger three times rapidly.

Only the first shot fired, for the recoiling slide snagged on the inside of the case—but when she brought her right hand back down into line after the recoil, she saw that Utechin was lying flat on his back, with a spreading spot of bright red blood on his white shirt over the solar plexus. His eyes blinked once, and then simply stared up at the cloudy sky.

Elena was dimly glad that she was kneeling as she stared at the body, for she was suddenly dizzy, and she was reminded of having seemed to die when the girl in the Lubyanka basement was killed. *We don't want you wasting any more of your baptized sanctity,* Utechin had told her in Moscow, *until you can spend it effectively.* At last, after no more than three stretched-taut seconds, she forced herself to look away.

The noise had been loud enough, but, muffled by the leather case, had not obviously been a gunshot; and the fact that Elena had fallen to her knees in the same moment that Utechin did had made the pedestrians duck away, fearful of whatever had apparently knocked these two down.

Glancing up at the rooftops now to suggest the idea of a sniper, Elena scuttled on her hands and knees up the gritty stone steps and through the swinging glass doors of the Cairo French Embassy.

Once inside, she got to her feet and walked directly to the reception desk. The man behind it had got to his feet to peer past her at the street, and she waved at him to catch his attention.

"I am a Soviet agent," she told him in French, speaking clearly though her vision was blurred with tears of a vast, almost impersonal grief, "and I have just killed my handler. I wish to defect—and to report a Nazi collaborator who has been working out of the City of the Dead here in Cairo, assisting the German General Rommel."

And after long interrogation in Algiers, she had been recruited into Colonel Passy's wartime Central Bureau for Information and Military Action; she met other ex-Communist agents in the BCRAM, and in 1944, by which time the French secret service had been incorporated into the Direction Generale des Services Spéciaux, she was surprised and delighted to be assigned to work with Claude Cassagnac.

The DGSS counter-Machikha team in Algiers was deliberately assembled along the same lines as the American President Wilson's Inquiry group of 1917, which had included experts on ancient Persian languages and the Crusades, and the British Admiralty's Room 40, which during the First World War had included a scholar of the early Church fathers and the code-breaker Ronald Knox, who had become a Catholic priest after the war. The DGSS team also included a number of physicists and geologists and an astronomer.

The result of their researches had been the bullet, lathed from a nickel-iron Shihab meteorite, which Cassagnac had fired at Machikha Nash in Berlin in June of 1945.

▼ ▼ ▼

Now, nearly eighteen years later, Elena crushed out a cigarette in an ashtray piled with cigarette butts, and she crossed again to the window of her room at the St. Georges Hotel. The sun from over the Jebel Liban mountains east of Beirut made the sails and the seagulls glow white against the dark blue Mediterranean, and she knew that the tables on the terrace below her door would be crowded with hotel guests having breakfast. She glanced at her radium-dial wristwatch— but Philby would not be arriving there with his Soviet handlers for hours yet.

She walked barefoot across the carpet to the bathroom, and she began brushing her long white hair without turning on the light or glancing into the mirror.

Do you want to see a monkey?

Andrew Hale had been in Berlin in 1945, doing Declare work for the looking-glass SOE; her hair had been as white then as it was now, having grown in that way right after her . . . three days? her week? . . . in the Lubyanka cellars.

She didn't want to think of Andrew Hale, nor of what she would have to do if she met him—*wasting what's left of your baptized sanctity, and this one would surely spend any last whiff of it that might still remain—* and so she thought instead of her other one, the third man in her life after Hale and Cassagnac, whom she would apparently not be permitted to kill: Kim Philby.

But her time with Philby had been in Turkey, in May of 1948, and of course Andrew Hale had been there too.

Cannibale, she had called Hale. *Nous cannibales* would have been fairer. We cannibals.

In the Ahora Gorge on that terrible night she too had quickly figured out that using the old Parisian *clochard* rhythms was the only gambit that would save her from the supernatural death that leaned hugely down out of the turning sky. The other members of her French SDECE team were either killed in the Soviet ambush or, worse, were pulled away into the sky by the ravenous djinn that had somehow been summoned down from their mountain-peak fastnesses—and because she had aligned her mental rhythms, the rhythms of her very identity, to those of the inhuman djinn, she had found herself intolerably *participating* in the aerial dismemberment and devouring of her fellows.

—And she had not, she admitted, been helpless in that participation. Like Andrew Hale, she *could* have stopped drumming and breathing and pulsing the rhythm, could have stepped out of the dance—but then she would have been just another human figure on the ground, prey for the djinn.

She had told herself that she was not responsible for the deaths of the SDECE men—that they were being killed in any case, and that she herself would have been killed if she had not . . . psychically *flown along* with the creatures that were tearing the men apart in the sky and eating them—but on that dawn, when she had at last ridden the horse all the way back across the muddy Aras plain to the clapboard Ararat Hotel in Dogubayezit, she had been convinced that she was a murderess.

She curtly told the base team at the hotel that the other operatives had all been killed and that this operation too had been a failure, and she made them pack up their radios and drive back to the pickup site in Erzurum—but she had stayed on at the hotel, alone, lying in her muddy clothes on the bed in her room, drinking cognac and watching the slow ceiling fan and desperately hoping that Andrew Hale would come to her there. She had not locked the door. She wanted to beg his forgiveness for what she had called to him last night on the mountain; and she thought that if they were together, talking, the enormity of what they had done might diminish. In Paris he had told her that he had been raised as a Catholic—perhaps he might find some way for her to assimilate what she had done: some way to take hold of the sin, voluntarily bear the weight of it, and then lay it before an outraged God in gross presumption on His mercy.

Later in the morning she had heard the motor of a jeep grind past on the dirt street under her window, but it had not stopped, and by the time she had blundered to the window and clawed the curtains away from the frame, the vehicle had driven on out of sight.

She threw herself back down across the bed, sobbing. Hale would not be coming. There was no way to diminish the magnitude of what she'd done. Man had been created in the image of God, and probably cannibalism was the "sin against the Holy Ghost," for which there was no forgiveness in this world or the next.

She slept heavily, and when she awoke with a start in darkness she thought for several seconds that she was lying in the Lubyanka basement, shot through the head.

That nameless Moscow girl had been killed on Elena's account.

Utechin had killed the wrong girl. If Elena had died there, she might have died in sanctifying grace, not in certain mortal sin, as she was now.

All she could do to put an end to her restless self-loathing was to finish the job Utechin had mismanaged six years ago. She had neglected to cork the cognac bottle, and it had soaked the mattress, but she was able to get several more swallows out of it.

At last she sat up and fumbled around among the litter on the bedside table until she had found a box of matches. When she had lit the lamp on the table, she shook out the match and drew her gun from the holster under her mud-stiffened jacket.

It was a semi-automatic Swiss SIG, standard issue for the SDECE, chambered for the French 7.65-millimeter cartridge. She popped out the magazine that she had emptied on the mountain and dug a heavy magazine from her jacket pocket and slid it up into the grip until it clicked.

Belatedly she realized that it had been the sound of a jeep motor that had awakened her—but it didn't matter. It would not be Andrew Hale, for he would certainly be on his way back to London by now, or to wherever it might be that he was stationed—and if it were members of her SDECE base team that had missed the pickup and come back here in the jeep, they could not stop her.

She pulled the slide back against the resistance of the recoil-spring, paused, and then let it snap forward. A cartridge was in the chamber now, and of course the safety was off. Her nostrils twitched at the smell of gun oil over the cognac fumes.

She could hear footsteps in the corridor outside her room door.

She hefted the pistol and held it up to her forehead, butt out, with her right thumb inside the trigger guard. Straight through the center of the forehead was how the Moscow girl had been shot. This gun had been tucked under Elena's arm while she slept, and the muzzle ring was warm. Aunt Dolores, she thought, give me strength.

She heard the squeak of the doorknob and let her eyes focus past her thumb to the door. The knob was turning—and she waited, curious in spite of herself, as the door creaked open.

But the man who stepped into the room's dim lamplight was not Andrew Hale. It was the unpleasant stuttering Britisher from Berlin, the onetime chief of Section Nine, now SIS Head of Station in Turkey—Kim Philby.

He stared past the gun butt at her left eye. "Am I interrupting?" he said.

He had spoken in English, and she forced herself to frame an answer in that language. "I'll only be a moment," she told him.

He smiled and slowly closed the door at his back. "I say, could this wait—half an hour? I won you in a card game last night—well, it was interrupted, but the other fellow is long gone, and I believe I did have the high hand—and—well, damn it—it does just seem too *bad* of you to *kill* yourself the moment I arrive! What do you say? Twenty minutes!—for a spot of fornication? You and I halfway did it on New Year's Eve in 1941, proxy or vicarious or something. Hey? There's a good girl!"

She reversed the gun in her right hand and lowered it, pointing it at him. For a moment neither of them spoke, and she was trying to figure out if this was a humanitarian gambit on his part—distract her with insult so as to have a chance to talk her out of it—or if he really had meant what he had said.

"That would be a mortal sin," she said carefully. "Adultery, even—I happen to know you're married, Mr. Philby." She had also read that he suffered from a terrible stammer; but he seemed to be talking smoothly enough right now.

"Ceniza-Bendiga," he said. He waved at the wooden chair against the plaster wall. "Do you mind if I sit? Thank you. Spanish, that is. Mortal sin! Are you a Catholic?"

"Devout," she said with a nod.

"Ah! I'm an atheist myself, sorry. I thought you lot were down on suicide."

"Will you do me a favor, Mr. Philby?"

"If you'll do me one." He smiled and held up his hands, palms out.

"*Will* you? This is a—" She shifted on the mattress. "A deathbed request."

I will," he said levelly. "If you will." Clearly he had meant what he had said a few moments ago.

She was sick at the idea, and at the abrupt immediacy of it. The fumy brandy surged up into the back of her throat.

But what if it's all you can do? she thought. It is all you can do. And who are you now to treasure scruples, souvenirs? You have abdicated yourself.

She waited several seconds, but there was no providential interruption. "Very well," she whispered. She took a deep breath and went on, "So listen. I will be missing an appointment I made six years ago—breaking a promise I made. It can't be helped, but—when I was in the Lubyanka, and it seemed that they were going to kill me, I made a promise to the Virgin Mary—she doesn't like communism, you know. I made a vow. Will you swear to keep it for me?"

Philby shifted uneasily in his chair. "Why were you in the Lubyanka?"

"I was being trained as an agent. I was an atheist then—my mother and father were shot down in a Madrid street by the right-wing Catholic monarchists in 1931, right in front of me; and when I was twelve years old I was a wireless telegrapher with Andre Marty. But in Moscow I saw the true face of communism. Will you swear on your own mother and father to keep my vow for me?"

Philby puffed out his cheeks. "Well, that's not really *my* line of *territory*. What was the vow?"

"I told the Virgin: 'If you will intercede with your Son to get me out of Russia alive, I vow that on my—' " Elena frowned. "I wanted to give it time, selfishly wait until my youth was safely gone, I think—I said, 'I vow that on my fortieth birthday at high noon I will light a candle for you right here in Moscow, at St. Basil's Cathedral in Red Square, in the heart of your enemy's kingdom, the way you put your heel on the serpent's head.' And I promised her that I would—"

After several seconds Philby shook his head and raised his eyebrows. "What's the harm of being honest now, here? On your deathbed?"

"Oh God," Elena sighed. "I promised her that I would be a chaste wife from then on. I didn't want to embark on it too soon, there was a young man—gone now—"

"Chaste," said Philby impatiently, "do go on. I don't need to hear about your tiresome *young men*. Whom were you going to be married to, in your old age?" Philby himself was then forty-six.

"I vowed that I would not marry *until* then, and that—that I would consider marrying—I was delirious—that I would take whomsoever she might elect to show me, after I had lit the candle. You see? I was humbly placing the selection in her hands. I think I imagined Prince Myshkin." The gun was wobbling in her grip, and she told herself that she must soon return it to its position against her forehead. "If there is a man

there, in the cathedral when you light the candle . . . give him my
regrets."

Philby nodded. "I can do that much—no prayers. When would be
your fortieth birthday?"

"April the twenty-second—in 1964."

"My calendar is free on that day, as it happens." Philby stared at her
in evident perplexity. "You're about to—*kill* yourself, but you still
believe all this business?"

"I wouldn't kill myself if I *didn't* believe this business." She shivered.
"Sin has real weight."

"What, your men dying on Mount Ararat last night?" When she
didn't answer he shook his head and laughed, clearly not yet satisfied
with her situation. "You know, I've never understood . . . *faith.* 'Do the
stars answer? in the night have ye found comfort? or by day have ye seen
gods? What hope, what light, falls from the farthest starriest way on you
that pray?' " She had realized that he was quoting something, and now
he waved deprecatingly and said, "Swinburne."

"Yes," she said. When he raised his eyebrows, she went on, miserably, "Yes, the stars answer. God answers."

Philby opened his mouth, then frowned and closed it; he appeared
to shiver, and when he finally spoke, it was more quietly. "What d-does
H-H-He say, ch-child?"

Elena blinked tears out of her eyes. "He says, 'Whom wilt thou find
to love ignoble thee, save Me, save only Me?' " She sniffed. "Francis
Thompson."

"I n-know it," he said. " 'Yet I was sore adread lest, having Him, I
must have naught beside.' " Philby seemed agitated. "Tell mmmm—tell
me!—when you g-go to your s-sacrament, of C-C-Confession!—do you
really have a f-firm purpose of am-amendment?"

"Yes. It might not seem possible later, but—yes. 'To sin no more.' "

"And in b-baptism you were freed of the—w-weight of s-s-sin? The
b-black drop in the h-human heart?"

"Yes, I was."

"I—" He sighed and shook his head. "But for m-me that would be
g-going b-back to point zz-zero! At forff-forfeit-forty—at m-my age! It's
not for m-me, my dear. Too much tie-time invested." He slapped his
open palms on the thighs of his trousers and stood up. "But sss—suicide
is n-not for you—'the Everlasting hath fix'd his canon 'gainst self-

slaughter,' you n-know. Is this *doubt,* do you d-doubt that your *ggg*—your *God*, will f-forgive you, as p-promised? Or is it p-plain shame? 'I was afraid because I was naked, and I hid myself.' *O santisima Elena!*—are you s-simply *ashamed* to approach H-H-Him as . . . just one m-more sinner, as b-bad as the rest of us? You w-w-won't *play,* if you c-can't wear the *halo?*" He laughed gently. "You're n-not the-that egotistical, surely?" He took a step toward her across the threadbare carpet. "Test your m-monstrous villainy, my dear. Either sh-shoot *me,* or give me the g-gun." He walked toward her with his palm out.

Elena's hand twitched, as if to fire the gun at him or turn it on herself while she still could, but when his palm was below hers she opened her trembling fingers and let the gun fall.

Quickly he popped out the magazine, and he tugged the slide back and forth several times, ejecting the round that had been in the chamber. Finally he dry-fired the gun at the ceiling, and when it had clicked harmlessly he tossed it clattering onto the floor.

In her suddenly renewed drunkenness it seemed echoingly loud.

Elena covered her face with her hands, and all at once she was sobbing at the appalling prospect of living until tomorrow, and the day after that—and she only realized that he had sat down beside her when the mattress tilted under her.

In the morning he had been gone, but he had left a note on the bedside table under her retrieved gun, signed with a hasty pen-drawing of three interlocked, leaping fish. The note had been brief: *On second thought, I don't think He'll forgive you. I've reloaded your SIG. (Through the roof of the mouth is better, by the bye.)*

She could tell by the weight of the gun that the full magazine had been replaced, but she had truly not believed that he would actually have chambered a live round, until she roused all the chickens and dogs of Dogubayezit by blowing out the hotel window with a tentative pull of the trigger.

Yesterday evening, in the Normandy Hotel bar, Philby had said to her, *I have a fucking bullet hole in my head; do take note of the fact that you have not got one in yours.*

That had been before he had learned that Elena had been the one who had shot him.

She remembered lying prone in the darkness on the office building roof, seeing that familiar pouchy face in the yellow square of the bath-room window across the street, divided into fleshy quadrants by the cross-hairs of the telescopic sight. He had turned away, toward the mir-ror, and she had centered the cross-hairs on the back of his head, and squeezed the trigger.

Even with the silencer the shot had sounded like a hammer-blow on a door, and she had hurried away to the fire escape, mentally preparing the report she would encode and radio to the SDECE headquarters in Paris—OFFER WAS A TRAP, DISCRETIONARY VERIFICATION OF THE DECOY BECAME NECESSARY—but later when she listened to the police band to confirm the kill, she learned instead that Philby had been taken, alive, to the American University Hospital.

She should have known that his birthday-of-record would not be his real one. And she could not deny now that his offer to defect was clearly genuine; the SDECE team would exfiltrate him, and soon the service would learn that she had slept with a Soviet agent directly after the infamous 1948 catastrophe in the Ahora Gorge.

Trying to kill Philby had not been part of her orders, had not been for the defense of France—it had been sheer attempted murder, a mor-tal sin. The next morning, with as much "firm purpose of amendment" she could muster, she had confessed it at the St. Francis Roman Catholic Church on Hamra Street.

She tied a towel around her white hair, put on a pair of oversized sunglasses, then opened her hotel room door and inhaled the chilly sea air.

She stepped to the rail and looked down at the crowded tables under the bright red umbrellas on the terrace—and fell back against the stucco wall, her heart racing and her face suddenly cold.

Andrew Hale was sitting at one of the tables, blinking up at a waiter.

▼

16

Beirut, 1963

"Will they kill thee?"
*"Oah, thatt is nothing. I am a good enough Herbert Spencerian, I trust, to
meet little thing like death, which is all in my fate, you know. But—but they
may beat me."*
 —Rudyard Kipling, *Kim*

The waiter said, "Here's a list. Gin . . . Scotch . . . brandy . . . vodka . . ."

Hale's attention had been caught by the man's first sentence, and
vodka made four. "Right," said Hale hastily, "vodka." God! he thought;
after a night of arak! Why couldn't the fourth word have been *beer?* But
his thudding heartbeat had instantly become more rapid, for this was
the old SOE recognition code; though of course the waiter might not be
a player at all, might simply have sized Hale up as a man who needed
strong drink this morning. Hale squinted up against the sunlight at the
clean-shaven young waiter. He appeared to be Lebanese.

"On the rocks," Hale added.

The table was on a railed cement deck on the Mediterranean-facing
side of the St. Georges Hotel; a red umbrella shaded half of the table
from the pre-noon sun, but Hale had chosen one of the white-painted
wrought-iron chairs in the direct sunlight. Sweating seemed to lessen
his headache, and his white shirt was already clinging to him.

Hakob Mammalian had knocked at Hale's hotel room door at about
ten o'clock, an hour ago, and said that Philby wanted to meet them up
the street at the St. Georges Hotel, rather than at the Normandy; and
Mammalian was now standing only six yards away, at the rail overlook-

ing the beach and the white sails on the blue sea. Hale had got perhaps four hours of sleep after the long, recorded interview. At least he couldn't remember any dreams.

"Shall I tally the bill now, sir?" the waiter asked.

Hale frowned in thought. I've got to think of a contrary and then a parallel or an example, he told himself. "Rather than me pay cash now," he said haphazardly. "Why don't you simply bill it to the Queen." He caught the waiter's eye and raised an eyebrow toward Mammalian. *For God's sake,* Hale thought, *don't say anything here to compromise my cover!*

The waiter smiled and nodded. "Do be careful not to overindulge, sir," he said. "If you were inebriated on the street, you would be *arrested*—and taken to *jail.* Very routine, happens with frequency."

He stepped away from the table to take Mammalian's order, and Hale peered after him uncertainly. *Had* that been the deliberate recognition signal? Had Hale just been ordered to fake drunkenness so as to be arrested, and presumably receive his long-delayed Declare briefing in the local jail—or had that simply been a friendly warning from a plain hotel employee? He would have to assume the man was an SOE operative, and that it had been deliberate.

Hale heard Mammalian order coffee and arak, and then the big Armenian was shuffling back to the table, his blue-striped gown flapping in the wind.

"He's right," said Mammalian as he pulled out another chair and sat down. "You shouldn't get drunk."

The sea breeze was pleasantly cool on Hale's forehead, but he would have to be moving soon. He had to bolt this drink and then get out onto the Avenue des Français, where, if he had understood the waiter correctly, *sûreté* officers were waiting to arrest him. "A sober traitor will cost you a lot more," Hale said, putting irritation in his voice.

"Does it sting you, valuably, to use ugly words like that?" Mammalian was staring at him curiously.

" 'Sober'?"

" 'Traitor.' You were born in Palestine, and the service you worked for planned to kill you even before you fled, a week ago. Do you suppose that in 1948 they went looking for the SAS men in your party who had gone mad on the mountain? Well, perhaps they did—to kill them, 'give them the truth.' No, my friend, you are simply devoting all of your energies and recollections now to a new cause—one that will allow you to sire children in the next century, and the century after that."

" 'Take the cash in hand, and waive the rest,' " quoted Hale, shaking his head. "Children in another century! How is all this live-forever stuff supposed to happen, precisely?"

"You are skeptical, after all that you have seen!" Mammalian bared his white teeth in a grin. "Perhaps you will become the consort of a goddess, Andrew Hale, and share in her immortality. Perhaps you will have a djinn for a body slave, who will protect you from every ill, even from age. If all else fails, you will eat a salad of enchanted thistles, and never die. Believe me, the 'cash in hand' will be the most trivial of your rewards. You do a service for angels here."

"And for Russians."

"The angels do not distinguish among our nations."

Seem reckless and belligerent, Hale thought. "The Russians . . . *kidnapped* one of your angels," he said, "in 1883, didn't they? Took it back to Moscow, moored it with drogue stones, anchors, in the Lubyanka basement and at the Soviet borders. I would think his fellows—" He remembered the thing he had seen in Berlin, and corrected himself: "*Her* fellows, would look unkindly on that."

Mammalian's face was expressionless. "If we—when we succeed, on the mountain, this time—" He raised a hand hesitantly. "You needn't fear that there will be injustice."

Hale quickly looked over his shoulder, as if impatient for his vodka—for Mammalian, hungover himself, had given away more than he had meant to, and there was no advantage for Hale in seeming to have noticed.

But Hale was certain now that Mammalian's loyalty here was to the djinn themselves, and not to the Rabkrin. And Hale wondered if Mammalian had even been a devout Communist during the Rabkrin attempt in 1948.

In fact the waiter was now striding back toward their table, carrying a tray; and neither of the seated men spoke as the two glasses and the coffee cup were set down on the glass tabletop. But as the young man was stepping away Hale called, "Another vodka here, please! And a cold Almaza beer with it to put out the fire." He bolted the glass of vodka in two hard swallows.

The waiter nodded without looking back.

"You will be useless before noon, at this rate!" exclaimed Mammalian in dismay. "And Charles Garner drinks arak!"

Hale's nose stung with the vodka fumes, and his eyes were watering. "I'm worse'n useless now," he said, carefully pretending to be more drunk than he was. "And I don't wanna be Charles Garner. I wanna be Tommo Burks."

Mammalian frowned and stirred his coffee, and Hale recognized, from the other side now, the agitation of a handler dealing with a skittish agent. Mammalian appeared to decide something, and stared straight at Hale. "Have you ever," he asked, "met a woman, an Arabic woman, with a string of gold rings around her neck? She would not have spoken."

Not bad, Hale thought. Last night I didn't bother to mention the woman I saw by Hitler's Chancellery in Berlin in '45, but I do remember her, and it's interesting to learn that she *figures* somehow. Apparently I was *likely* to meet her!

But he had to get onto the street, get his briefing, before he met Philby.

He stood up, so unsteadily that the table rocked and nearly spilled Mammalian's coffee and arak. "I won't—incidentally—work with Kim Philby. See. He told the Russians—he told *you*—where my SAS team was going to be, in the Ararat Gorge. The Ahora Gorge. Know, O Armenian, that I quit. Sod you all."

He walked quickly away between the other tables, artfully bumping one with his hip; he heard a glass roll and then break on the cement deck as he reached the top of the stairs that led down to the hotel driveway; a chair's legs scraped as it was pushed back, and hurried footsteps were coming up from behind him, but two uniformed *sûreté* officers were even now tapping briskly up the steps from below.

Hale deliberately snagged his shoe behind his calf and tumbled forward, driving his shoulder into the midsection of the officer on the right; somehow all three of them wound up sitting and bumping and flailing down the steps to the parking lot pavement, and before Hale could even pull his legs down off the bottom two steps, he felt the ring of a handcuff close on his wrist and ratchet shut.

While the policemen were barking questions at him in French—through the ringing in his ears he caught the word *ivresse*, drunkenness—Hale squinted back up the stairs; but Mammalian had apparently decided not to interfere in a civil arrest. The only person peering down was a tanned woman in big sunglasses and a towel wrapped around her head.

The Beirut Municipal Jail was in one of the modern buildings at the Place des Martyrs, only seven blocks south off of Weygand Street, and when the police car rocked to a halt in an alley beside the Direction of Police, Hale was pulled out of the back seat and marched in through a side door.

Briefly he glimpsed a crowded yellow waiting room, with civilians and uniformed officers standing in lines before a row of windows under fluorescent lights, and then he was pushed along a narrow beige-painted corridor and around a corner.

This stretch of the corridor was momentarily empty except for a brown-haired Caucasian man in a damp white shirt, who stood with his hands open at his sides and stared straight at Hale with something like apprehension; and in the same instant the two *sûreté* officers let go of Hale's arms and took hold of the stranger's, and a door was pulled open at Hale's right.

In the dimly lit office beyond the door, a bald man in a jacket and tie beckoned to Hale impatiently. "Here's a bloody list," he whispered, "one-two-three-four."

Hale heard a scuffle ahead of him and looked up in time to see one of the *sûreté* officers drive a fist into the face of the brown-haired stranger who was now being led away. Hale took a long step sideways into the office.

The bald man winced at the sound of the blow as he pulled the door closed behind Hale.

"They hit him?" the man asked. "Sit down," he said, waving toward a wooden chair beside a gray metal desk. The smell of hot coffee drew Hale's attention to a chugging urn on a nearby table even before the man said, "Or help yourself to coffee."

Hale nodded and stepped to the table, and he looked around as he held a ceramic cup under the tap—the room, lit by an electric lamp on the desk, had no windows—and he sat down in the chair while the bald man turned a key in the door lock and walked around to the other side of the desk.

"Yes," said Hale, setting the steaming cup on the bare desktop. "They hit him."

"I am sorry." The man shrugged and smiled. "Verisimilitude!"

Hale nodded sourly and touched his own left cheek, wondering when and how he would be given an identical blow. Soon, probably, since bruises change appearance quickly.

"Somebody will shortly be bringing in a photo of his face," Hale guessed.

"I expect so—well, a drawing, probably. To make it match. You gave the Rabkrin all the '48 math?"

Hale only became aware that his shoulders were stiff with tension now that his muscles began to relax. "That *was* the orders," he said, watching the man carefully. "Yes, I gave them everything."

The man nodded. "I'm heartsick," he seemed to say, and Hale's face was abruptly cold; but the man quickly added, "I'm sorry, that's my name, H-*A*-R-T-S-I-K. Polish. You're Hale, I know. Pleased to meet you. No, you did the right thing, all that math was bad. And if you gave them some extra stuff too, we can afford it; it'll just enhance the look of the old math, and with luck Declare is within a week or so of shutting down for good."

"They're going to destroy the Shihab stone," Hale said. "They may be on the mountain now, to get it. Mammalian said it's still up in the gorge, on Ararat."

"They're welcome to it, now," said Hartsik. "Two months ago we sent a team of undercover agents up there to make rubber castings from it. They had to go up with a truck, and winches, to make it seem that their purpose was to retrieve the stone itself. They did get the rubber molds safely down, though several of the men were killed by the Turk oscars." He raised his eyebrows. "More verisimilitude—the Rabkrin was strongly led to believe that we went up to fetch the stone. It's been guarded, since."

More deaths on my account, thought Hale. "What," he asked wearily, "did I do wrong? In '48," he added, seeing Hartsik's incomprehension.

"Oh! Convex versus concave. You mistook the mold for the bullets." He pulled open a drawer of the desk and picked out a couple of irregular gray metal balls, which proved to be lead when he spilled them from his palm onto the desktop and they thudded and didn't bounce. "These were cast from the mold they took on Ararat in November."

One of the balls wobbled across and clinked against Hale's coffee cup. He slowly reached out and picked it up between his thumb and forefinger. It was egg-shaped, and though it was heavy it forcibly reminded him of the black glass pellets he had found at Wabar and had later thrown down in the bomb shelter below Ararat.

Peering more closely at the thing, he noticed that it was incised with two fine equator lines at right angles, one around the middle and one around the ends.

"Three-dimensional crosses," said Hartsik, "or wheels buggered out of usefulness by being folded into three dimensions, if you like, *completed*—on an oval, which is a sphere with two internal hub-points, two *foci*. Mathematical severance of the geometric core. It's the experience and expression of *end-of-message*, for djinn, and it will impose shutdown if it's delivered spinning clockwise fast enough to match their own rotation, so that it becomes an integrated part of them. They can't help but take it in—they're hypnotized by right angles and ovals, like the shape of an ankh. Morbid of them, really."

"If—my team—had been able to blow up the stone—"

"It would have been useless. For one thing, the open bubbles on the stone wouldn't have created reciprocal *balls*, just . . . *bumps*, even if they struck impressionable mud. These leaden balls have been finished, trimmed. Djinn cast this shape when they die, they *become* hundreds of these balls, of all sizes, made out of whatever's at hand; it's as if they crystallize terminally into this configuration. The concave impressions in the Shihab stone are just the molten stone's plastic response to the death-shape. You know what the djinn tend to be made of, from moment to moment—wind, dust, snow, sand, agitated water, swarms of bugs, hysterical mobs. All that stuff is already thoughts in fluid motion. You need to intrude a new memory—a seed-crystal, the physical experience of death." He opened another drawer and hiked out a half-full bottle of Laphroaig Scotch. "Your exploded stone would have done no good—but a plain chicken's egg, with the crossed-parallel lines scratched into the shell, might have worked, if you'd thrown it up in the air so that it was spinning." He waved the bottle. "Purify your coffee?"

Hale was dizzy with the vodka he had bolted half an hour ago, and he shook his head.

"I'm to bring—*those*," he said, waving at the lead balls, "up the gorge, this time? Will we be going all the way up to the Ark itself?" He was still depressed at the thought that the djinn were occupying Noah's vessel.

"Well, it's *not* the *Ark*, it seems," Hartsik said, clunking the bottle down on the desk; "not Noah's ship."

"It's not?" Hale was surprised at the extent to which this news cheered him. "You're sure?"

"We've been busy on all this since you've been in storage. The situation has been clarified by study of overflight photos and a couple of furtive expeditions. In '43 the Americans were flying provisions from the U.S. air base in Tunisia to the Soviet base in Brivan, and Ararat was right in the flight path, and we've got hold of films the pilots took; and then the Geodetic Institute of Turkey did an aerial survey in '59, and our Turkish station was able to get prints of the relevant area. The American National Security Agency even consented to what appeared to be a most-secret request from the Foreign Office, and sent along some recent photos taken by their prototype Ryan 136 drone. Of course, even with the Foreign Office the NSA is circumspect—a photo of Ararat isn't intrinsically secret, but the mere fact of an overflight photo-survey of that area, the Russian–Turkish–Iranian border, is; and they often employ less-than-their-best photographic equipment on such flights because anybody can deduce the specifications of the camera that was used, by examining the photographs—resolution and instantaneous-field-of-view and so on. Still, altogether we've been able to establish that a formation in the Anatolian Akyayla range, some twenty miles southeast of Ararat, is probably the real, Biblical Ark. It wasn't visible in the wartime photos—we believe it was exposed by the earthquake in '48." Hartsik gave an uncertain wave. "Which you doubtless recall."

Hale ignored the mention of the earthquake. "Twenty miles south?" He shook his head slowly. "But . . . what's the thing Mammalian saw on Ararat?"

"Well—according to the old Arabic *Kitab al-Unwan*, at least—the Devil, or Iblis as the Arabs call him, survived the Flood because of clinging to the tail of the ass, who was in the Ark; and some rabbinical writers claimed that the giant Og, king of Bashan, saved himself by hanging onto the ship's roof eaves. We think that when the Flood started"—Hartsik shrugged deprecatingly—"something malignant had a boat of its own, and hooked a tow-rope onto the Ark."

"And ran aground on Ararat and cut the tow-line, while the real Ark went down with the floodwaters and landed farther south."

"Exactly."

Hale was glad that Noah, at least, was safely out of this. "But what am *I* in all this?" he asked. He remembered the djinn at Ain al' Abd saying, *This is the Nazrani son.* "Who is my father?"

Hartsik sighed. "More relevant is who is your—" he began, but he was interrupted by a knock at the hallway door. "Excuse me." He stood up and crossed to the door, his hand darting inside his tweed jacket. In Arabic he said, "Who is it?"

From the hallway a man's voice replied, "Farid, Hartsik."

Hartsik turned the key in the lock and stepped back, then relaxed and let his hand fall to the desktop when a short man in a blue Lebanese *sûreté* uniform stepped in and closed the door behind him. Hale saw that the Arab was holding a childish pencil drawing of a man's face with a ring drawn below the left eye. The Arab's eyes narrowed to slits as he gave Hale a grin that exposed many gold teeth. "Smite you now," he said in English.

"Don't put the whisky away," Hale told Hartsik. Then he turned around in his chair to face the Arab, and he closed his eyes. "Right," he said through clenched teeth. "Go."

For a full two seconds nothing happened, and Hale was about to open his eyes in a squint when the man's bony fist abruptly crashed against his left cheekbone. Hale's head snapped back, and for a moment his headache, and nausea induced by the metallic taste of the impact, made thought impossible; finally he took a deep breath, swallowed, and opened his eyes. His left eye was blinking rapidly and was too full of tears for him to see out of it.

The fist had been turning as it hit, and Hale could feel the sharp burn of a cut below his eye and a hot trickle of blood running down his cheek.

"Too hard," said the Arab. "Other man not bleed."

"Well then, go hit him again," said Hartsik impatiently in Arabic. "Now get out of here."

The Arab bowed and left the office, and Hartsik closed the door and turned the key. "Your double is being questioned," he said as he crossed to the desk and resumed his seat opposite Hale. "You'll get a transcript of the interrogation, but he's been coached to say he's Charles Garner, an expatriate British journalist, and to deny being in Beirut for any purposes other than business and dissipation. We happen to know that one of the clerks here is in the pay of the Soviets, and that clerk has been called in to work on his day off, so that Mammalian will be told by an eyewitness that you revealed nothing and were told nothing."

Hartsik was holding the bottle over Hale's coffee cup, but Hale twitched his fingers at it, and when the other man handed it to him he tipped the bottle up for a liberal mouthful. After he had swallowed it, he opened his mouth to inhale the warm fumes.

"Who is my father?" Hale said thickly.

"Harry St. John Philby," said Hartsik. "Kim Philby is your half-brother."

Hale's breath had stopped—but a moment later he nodded slowly, remembering the times he had dreamed of Kim Philby, and had seemed to hear Philby's voice in his head. Had Philby suspected this? *Our Hajji which art in Amman . . .*

"He," Hale said unsteadily, "the old man, he—raped my mother—" Tears were running down his cheek from his left eye.

"Apparently," said Hartsik, "not. Old Philby was the British political agent in the court of King Abdullah of Trans-Jordan, in Amman, just on the other side of the Jordan River from Jerusalem, where your mother's religious order was working in a British Army hospital; and by all reports he was, er, handsome and charming. Thirty-seven years old at the time, probably quite a—well. St. John seems to have been troubled by the fear that Christianity might be . . . real, the true story. Specifically he was afraid of Roman Catholicism, with all its . . . nasty old relics and sacraments and devotions, the whole distasteful Irish and Mediterranean air of it. He apparently thought that if he could persuade a so-called bride of Christ to forsake her vows—seduce her, I mean—"

Hale nodded impatiently. "I didn't suppose he tried to force wealth on her."

"Right. Well, he thought this would disprove the nun's whole faith, you see, expose it as a morbid but harmless hypocrisy—like citing Popes who have had illegitimate children. I do wonder how Catholics justify—"

"Infallible, not impeccable," snapped Hale; and he wondered why he was bothering to defend his forsaken old faith at all. "The Russians want both of St. John's sons up on the mountain—working together this time. Why?"

"Because St. John's dalliance with your mother was a very costly mistake for him—and for the Russians. Young Kim was supposed to be a human emissary to the djinn, taking the long-dormant job over from the Arab royalty—the son of King Saud relinquished an ancestral *rafiq* diamond to Kim, in 1919, when Kim was seven."

"*Rafiq?*" said Hale, puzzled. "Do you mean in the Bedu sense? An introducer or guarantor?"

"Right, a member of the other tribe, who'll vouch for you. Kim was supposed to be this person; and even now the diamond serves its *rafiq* purpose. Kim was given the djinn sacrament when he was an infant, deliberately, by his father. St. John received it by accident—he was born in Ceylon, and on that day a streak of light like a comet shot south over the Bay of Bengal and lit up several Ceylonese villages—but after that St. John was baptized, which blunted the non-human grace of it. St. John made sure that Kim was never baptized."

"Uh," said Hale, "djinn sacrament?"

"The splitting?" Hartsik raised his eyebrows, then shook his head in disappointment. "Huh. You remember the story in First Kings, about the two women who came before King Solomon? They had a live baby and a dead baby, and each woman claimed the live one was hers. According to the Bible, Solomon called for a sword and offered to cut the baby in half."

"Yes. It always seemed implausible to me—that the lying woman would agree to that, would say, 'Yes, cut him in half.'"

"Well, sure—because actually Solomon *didn't* call for a 'sword' to settle the argument. The old copyists put in the word *sword* because it seemed to make more sense than the word that was in the oldest manuscripts—it began with the Hebrew letters *cheth* and *resh,* as *sword* does, but it was a neologism—paleologism, I suppose—a combination of *blasphemy* and *destruction* and *potter's wheel,* which are all spelled similarly."

A potter's wheel, thought Hale—a changing form, rotating. "A djinn," he said. "Solomon called for a djinn."

"Right. Apparently Solomon really was able to confine the djinn, abbreviate and summarize their tumultuous thoughts down to something he could pop into a jug and then seal with"—he pointed at the lead balls on the desk—"a threaded cluster of those. Threaded, see? So that they'd have to be rotated, assimilated, for the djinn to get out; and assimilating those would kill the thing. In any case, if you expose a *tab-*

ula rasa infant to the attention of a djinn, there's a bond formed—neither side can help it, the child has no defensive mental walls yet, and the djinn is no more able to *not* look into the child's eyes than water can *not* run downhill. The djinn almost *adopts* the child, recognizes it as family. Djinn apparently perceive humans as autistic—"

Hale suppressed a wince, remembering having shared that perception in the Ahora Gorge.

"—but they can tell that a baby is *new*—it's not the child's fault that it can't express anything. Now this procedure, this sacrament, is fine for inter-species relations, but it's hard on the child—the shock of it polarizes the child's mind, as if you were to freeze a glass of gin and tonic—you'd wind up with liquid gin and solid tonic, right? The child becomes two children; that is, the child is able to be in two places at once, literally." He shrugged. "It's not so implausible that the lying woman in the Biblical story was willing to settle for half of such a split."

"Jesus. This was done to Kim Philby?"

"Very shortly after his birth in India, yes. And until he was ten years old he was verifiably able to be in two places at once, and he seemed destined to be the *rafiq* to the djinn. But then St. John had to go and father an illegitimate baby—you—who was born on Kim Philby's tenth birthday. December thirty-first, both of you, though your birthday has always been given as January sixth, so as not to rouse Philby's suspicions, and he has always claimed January first as his own. But you were both born on the same day in the solar year, you see? The night sky was the same again on your birthday as it had been on Philby's, and the djinn in their literal way confused you with Philby. The *two* of you became the polarized pair, and Philby wasn't able to be in two places at the same time anymore."

Again there was a knock at the office door; and when Hartsik got up and unlocked it to let Farid in, the Arab said, "I now smite the other man too hard. He bleeds more than this one."

Hartsik stamped his foot on the floor. "For God's sake, Farid! Very well, hit this fellow again, carefully, and then get out of here." He glanced at Hale and shrugged. "I do apologize, old man."

Hale stared at the Arab in disbelief. "No," he told Hartsik. "I'll just smear blood around."

Hartsik shook his head. "This has to be perfect, I'm sorry. Mammalian will be very suspicious in any case—you must be a precise match for the man who's being interrogated."

Hale sighed deeply and turned toward Farid, bracing himself again. "If this becomes necessary one more time," he told the Arab tightly, "I'll smite *you,* I promise."

"Has to be perfect!" protested Farid. "Hold still, please."

Hale closed his eyes and gritted his teeth, and the fresh, hard blow on his already bruised cheekbone rocked his head and brought bile to the back of his throat; and he had to lower his head and breathe spittily through his mouth to keep the rainbow glitter of unconsciousness from filling his vision.

He didn't see Farid leave, but over the ringing in his ears he heard the door click shut.

Hale took a deep breath and rocked his head back to blink at Hartsik out of his right eye. The man was relocking the door. "Does Philby know?" Hale asked thickly. "That he and I are half-brothers?"

"Not that we know of. He might well suspect that St. John had an illegitimate child, and that the birth ruined Kim's prepared destiny; broke it in half."

"Broke it. So Philby and I are two halves of one person."

"Well, in a sense." Hartsik walked back to his chair behind the desk and sat down. "We suspect that you've been able to hear each other's thoughts, in the season when the sky has assumed the definition of you; and probably you dream each other's dreams then. And you do appear to—" Hartsik paused, awkwardly.

"Don't hesitate," Hale said, "to add insult to injury."

"Well, Philby appears to have got—this is imprecise, you understand, armchair speculation—he appears to have got all the family feeling, the—practically *obsession,* in his case—with hearth-and-home, parents and wife and children. He's been married three times, and he's got five children. He has, though, no comprehension of loyalty, duty. Those qualities all seem to have flowed your way."

"And the Russians want—because the djinn require—the entire *rafiq* to be present."

"That's it. You were both there in the gorge in '48, but not working together. They couldn't see you properly. This time they will open their gates to the two of you—and *you* will kill them."

"How?" Hale waved at the lead balls on the table. "Shoot them with these?"

"Yes—a lot of them, cast in a much smaller scale. Birdshot caliber. Several shops in Beirut are now manned with clerks who will sell you prepared shot shells and an American derringer, chambered for the American .410 shell and rifled to the right so that the pellets will emerge in a pattern that's turning clockwise as it expands, to match the spinning of the djinn if you fire upward. The djinn will assimilate the shot pellets—which is to say, assimilate the experience of death. Dying, they will no doubt throw spontaneous egg-shapes of their own, made of mountain stone or whatever is at hand, and ideally a chain-reaction will ensue. You will buy several boxes of shells—but you must save one shell for Philby."

Theodora had mentioned this, but Hale had not known then that Philby was his half-brother. "What about his protections?" Hale asked, mainly just to slow this discussion. "His Achilles-heel date isn't due to come round again for nearly another year."

"The protections aren't against self-injury. You are virtually him, in this context; that will be especially true on Mount Ararat."

The other half of me, Hale thought. *The hearth-and-home half of me.* "Very well," he said unsteadily, "I'll shoot him." He may be my brother, he told himself, but Philby is still the man who betrayed my men in the gorge. I can shoot him for that.

"You are not to kill him. Do please pay attention. You are not on any account to kill Philby, even to save yourself. You are to shoot him in the back, from a sufficient distance so that the shot will penetrate widely around his spine but not be focused in any kind of tight pattern. We certainly don't want the 'rat-hole' effect! The goal is to leave him able to walk away, to Moscow, with at least one pellet in his flesh that cannot be removed surgically."

Hale's arms were suddenly cold. "She's a *ghul*," he whispered, using the Arabic word for djinn who haunt graveyards and eat the dead in their graves, extracting up through the soil as souvenirs any bits of metal—rings, gold teeth—that the cadavers might have contained. "A *ghulah*," he corrected himself, using the feminine form.

"Very good, Mr. Hale! Yes, she is. And when—"

Hale remembered Mammalian's question this morning. "And she sometimes appears as an Arabic woman with a string of gold rings and gold teeth around her neck, right? I've met her. And since 1883 she has been the guardian angel of Russia."

"Machikha Nash, the Rabkrin call her. Yes. And—"

"And!" interrupted Hale, "if Philby goes to Moscow, after this—and I presume he'll be given no choice—he'll eventually die there. He'll be buried in a Moscow cemetery."

Hartsik's eyes narrowed in a smile. "Ex-act-ly. And the guardian angel will not neglect to devour him, and to draw up, in her spiral way, the metal that is in him, including at least one of these shot pellets. And she will thus assimilate into herself the shape of djinn death." He sat back. "And she will die, and the Soviet Union will lose its guardian angel. I can't imagine the U.S.S.R. surviving Philby by more than three or four years."

Hale recalled what Prime Minister Macmillan had said six days ago: *I suppose we can't simply shoot spies, as we did in the war—but they should be discovered and then played back in the old double-cross way, with or without their knowledge—never arrested.* And Hale thought that Macmillan would be pleased with the way Theodora had orchestrated this use of Kim Philby.

It seemed to call for a drink. Hale picked up the Laphroaig bottle and took another aromatic mouthful from the neck of it. "In London," he said hoarsely, "I was told that Philby does not want to participate in this expedition to Ararat; that I'll have to threaten him to get him to go along. What's the basis for his reluctance?"

"That's right. His father—your father—died, here in Beirut, a little more than two years ago. I'm, uh, sorry."

"Stop it." Hale could hardly remember the text of *The Empty Quarter,* which his father had written; and that book was his only link to the old man. Any feeling of . . . *loss,* here, he reminded himself, would be sheer affectation. But he did remember standing on the steep escarpment at the windy Edge-of-the-Wold when he had been a boy, looking down at the roofs of Evesham and the River Isbourne on the plain below the Cotswolds highlands, and speculating that his father was a missionary priest "somewhere east o' Suez," and imagining how the two of them might one day meet. And then he remembered walking across the grassy quad at the University College of Weybridge on many late afternoons in the 1950s, picturing an eventual reunion with Elena. How shabbily these fond dreams work out, he thought—and he was glad that Farid had hit him again, for he was afraid that some of the tears leaking from his swollen left eye were tears of purest self-pity.

"What did Philby's father have to do with it?" he asked harshly.

Hartsik took Hale's cue. "Philby's father was always very protective of Kim; clearly he blamed himself—altogether justly—for having crippled the boy's standing in the supernatural world by indulging his own—his—"

"Lust for my mother."

"Well, not to put too fine a point on it. Now old St. John saved the life of a fox in '32, in the Empty Quarter desert, the Rub' al-Khali—his Bedouins were going to kill it, but St. John intervened and set it free. He may have been able to tell somehow that this particular fox contained a djinn, who had been abridged down into this form—in any case, it did, and in gratitude the djinn gave St. John certain powers over foxes— even over fox furs. Several times St. John used this power to protect Kim. When Kim was a war correspondent in Spain in 1936, St. John gave him a mad-looking Arab coat with a fox-fur collar, and he told Kim to wear it whenever he was in peril, especially on his birthday. Kim still has certain magical protections, as you may too, but they become transparent on his birthday—*vos anniversaire*. And sure enough, on December thirty-first of 1937, Kim was in a car that was hit with an artillery shell; Kim was wearing the fox-fur coat, and he came through with a scratch, though the men with him were all killed—and St. John, who was in Alexandria at the time, was knocked down, bleeding from the ears. Neither of them was seriously hurt, you see—the fox-fur magic dissipated the blow."

"I assume that protection has been gone since 1960, when the old man died."

"Well, it's gone *now*. But Philby didn't really lose it until three months ago, in late September of last year. On *Easter* of '62, he got hold of a fox cub—he named it Jackie, and kept it in his apartment in the Rue Kantari here. The animal reportedly liked whisky, and would sometimes suck on the stem of a pipe. And Philby was still gung-ho to go along on the Rabkrin expedition to Ararat, to become at last the full-fledged *rafiq* to the djinn. And then, on September twenty-eighth, precisely on the second anniversary of his father's original death, someone pushed the fox off the balcony of Philby's apartment while he wasn't home. The animal died, and Philby spent two days weeping drunk, and then he began surreptitiously trying to get out of the expedition; he wrote to *The Observer,* the paper he writes articles for, asking for London leave—and he's been trying to defect to France—and if the SIS offers him any kind of immunity deal, he will want to leap at it."

Defect to France, thought Hale; that must be why Elena is in Beirut. But why did she try to *kill* Philby?

Don't even think about her, he told himself. "Easter of last year, Philby got the fox?" he said, forcing himself to concentrate on what Hartsik had said. "A good day for rising from the dead, I suppose. Where had the old man's ghost been, in the intervening year and a half?"

"Haunting the Bashura cemetery, where he was buried—only about three blocks south of here on the Rue de Basta. St. John was a convert to Islam, you know—what the Turks call a 'Burma,' which is to say a turncoat, not someone to be trusted. According to Arab folklore, two angels, Munkir and Nakir, visit a man in his grave right after his burial and quiz him on his faith—if he acknowledges Allah, they let him rest in peace; but if he believes another faith to be true, they thrash him with iron maces until his cries are heard 'from east to west, except by men and djinn.' "

Hale smiled. "Did a lot of dogs howl, locally, after St. John was buried?"

"We didn't notice. But the SIS Beirut station picked up a heavy traffic on the service bandwidth; it was *en clair,* but they thought it must be code because it was all nursery rhymes—'the man in the moon came down too soon,' 'but when she got there the cupboard was bare,' 'how many miles to Babylon'—that kind of thing. The SIS triangulated the signal and found that it seemed to originate in the Bashura cemetery, but they could never find a transmitter, and the signal faded after a month, and they blamed the vagaries of the Heaviside Layer; but we in Declare knew that it was St. John's ghost, catching hell from the Moslem angels."

"I wonder what faith he believed was the true one."

"Maybe your mother is laughing in *her* grave," Hartsik agreed magnanimously.

"So what would the fox have provided, in this Rabkrin expedition, that Philby cannot do without?"

"The same thing as always—dissipation of a blow, sharing an injury, taking the brunt of it, even; and old St. John's guilt was so strong that he never refused. Kim loved his father, which is to say that he needed him;

needed him to take Kim's punishments, mainly. You see, becoming the *rafiq* to the djinn will be an ordeal. Kim is not properly split, because of your divisive birth, and in the ceremony on the mountain he will be called on to face one of the djinn, eye to eye, be recognized by it. The old sacrament. He didn't fear this in '48, because he was wearing his fox-fur and his father was in Riyadh. Even four months ago he was eager to try Ararat again, because he could bring along the live fox that contained his father's identity—if anyone's mind was to be broken, it would be good old long-suffering St. John's. But now Philby is alone—and he's afraid that the sacrament, undiluted, will leave him half-witted, or insane."

"Did Declare kill the fox?"

"No. Guy Burgess did, acting for the Rabkrin. The Rabkrin would *prefer* that their *rafiq* to the djinn be a little simpleminded; and Philby is too sneaky and ambitious by half. Burgess has always been Philby's handler for the Rabkrin—he understands him, having known Philby since they were schoolmates at Cambridge; Philby used to call him 'your Demoncy,' because his full name is Guy Francis de Moncy Burgess. And Burgess has undergone the djinn sacrament too."

"He has? I had the idea he grew up in England."

"That's right, in Hampshire. But his father was born in Aden and was on the staff of the rear admiral in Egypt during the First World War. And apparently his father was 'embraced by a piece of tender air' at some point in those eastern lands—he requested early retirement in '22 and returned to his family in Hampshire, but two years later young Guy was awakened in the middle of the night by his mother's screams, and he got up and burst into his parents' bedroom." Hartsik pursed his lips. "The house was dark. He was thirteen years old. His father had expired in the midst of sexual intercourse with his mother—Guy's mother was pinned beneath the corpse, and it may have been simply that that had set her screaming—but young Guy could see over her head, out the window his father must have been facing, and the boy found himself eye to eye, exchanging recognition, with the far-traveling 'piece of empty air' that had followed Guy's father all the way from Egypt to Hampshire: a djinn, perhaps not bothering to assume a completely human aspect." Hartsik shrugged. "Burgess is now a hopeless alcoholic, and a flagrant homosexual."

Hale's eyebrows were raised, and he was remembering, with some sympathy now, the rude drunk he had met at the Turkish–Soviet border in 1948. "Hard to blame him."

"Well, really. Burgess apparently derived no pleasure from being able to be in two places at once—he seems not to have had much control of his double, which probably embodied his Eton-and-England loyalties. The double nearly took over after the Molotov–Ribbentrop non-aggression pact in '39. Finally Burgess simply *ran over* his double, in Dublin, during the war—drove a car over the thing. After that, there was nothing left of Burgess but alcoholism, homosexuality, and petulance." Hartsik shrugged. "Many have prospered in the espionage trade with no more."

Hale opened his mouth to say something, but was stopped by a knock on the office door; and even with his aching, swollen eye, he managed to give Hartsik a ferocious scowl as the man got up from the desk again.

It was Farid, this time carefully carrying a steaming cup. "Now they have thrown coffee onto the fellow's shirt," Farid explained.

Hale thought of his hours-long confession last night to Mammalian. For your penance, he told himself bleakly, take two blows to the face and a cup of coffee down your shirt. And I'll be lucky if that's the extent of it, here or on Ararat.

"Tell them I said to take it easy, for God's sake," said Hartsik shrilly. "Mr. Hale, I feel terrible about this—"

Hale just hiked his chair around to face Farid. "Get it right," he said through clenched teeth.

The Arab bent over and carefully splashed gouts of the hot coffee onto several areas of Hale's white shirt. Hale breathed deeply through flared nostrils and made no sound as the hot coffee scalded his stomach. At last Farid stood up, frowning and swirling the coffee that was left in the cup. Hale restrained himself from stretching out his leg and kicking the cup up into the man's face.

"An artist should know when to walk away," said Hartsik tightly. "Go."

After Farid had bobbed back out into the hall and pulled the door closed, Hartsik did not sit down again. "I'll tell you the rest briefly, before those *sûreté* decide to break that poor man's legs. If your threat to Philby is effective, and he agrees to continue with the Rabkrin operation to Ararat, you will keep your wristwatch set to the correct local time; if Philby refuses, or if three days go by without a clear decision from him, you will set your watch six hours off—and then Kim Philby will find that his next glass of gin has been flavored with a poison that will get past any magical protections, birthday or no birthday. Holy water and—well, you're Catholic, aren't you?—you don't want to know. At any rate, the old Rabkrin recognition phrase is: 'O Fish, are you constant to the old covenant?" and the answer is—"

" 'Return, and we return,' " said Hale. " 'Keep faith, and so will we.' " He stared bleakly up at Hartsik. "Philby must have known that since he was a child—because I have."

Hale was hurriedly shown photographs of the room in which his double was being interrogated, and then photographs of the officers who were asking the questions—a cup had been drawn in over the hand of the one who had thrown coffee on the prisoner. After that Hale was given a scrawled transcript of the questioning session and was made to read it several times. He had to admire the way "Andrew Hale" had stuck to his cover story—and the script was good, with the sûreté gradually becoming convinced that this really was just some British journalist named Charles Garner. To judge from the transcript, the sûreté officers had even been gruffly apologetic at the end.

At last Farid led into Hartsik's office the man who had pretended to be Hale. Hale stood up, wondering who this unlucky Declare operative was. Looking at the man's face was like looking into the forty-five-degree intersection of a pair of mirrors—Hale winced to see a duplicate of the jagged cut in his own left cheek, and the extent of the silvery bruise under his eye. He was even disoriented for a moment when he licked his lips and the other face didn't do it too.

"I owe you a drink, when all this is over," Hale said to the man.

"Not arak," said his double.

"Right." Hale was aware of being drunk, though the hour could not yet be noon, and he bit his tongue against the urge to ask the man if he had heard from Elena.

"This mistreated gentleman," said Hartsik, waving at Hale's double, "will stay here in my office until nightfall, and then leave in Arab dress, with his face concealed. In the meantime, one of the Rabkrin team has come to the station here to take you back to your hotel." He stared at Hale. "It's the one called Kim Philby."

Hale nodded. "I know what to say to him."

Hartsik unlocked the door and swung it open. "We won't speak again," he said quietly as Hale stepped out into the hall; "if you get into unmapped territory, improvise."

Hale nodded, as much to the two *sûreté* officers who stood in the hall as in acknowledgment of Hartsik's remark; and then he was escorted back down the hall to the yellow-painted waiting room. The police did not hold his arms now—Charles Garner had officially proven to be a harmless drunk.

Kim Philby was leaning against the wall by the alley door. He was wearing a sport coat and a tie, but his pouchy face was spotted and pale, and he was frowning.

My half-brother, thought Hale as he walked away from the police, toward the door.

"I was t-told it was you," Philby said. He peered at Hale's face. "They d-did m-mess you up, rather, didn't they? There's no bail to be p-paid—apparently they feel that your mistreatment here has been pa-pa-payment enough. I'd have said you rated another biff or two, but the *sûreté* and I d-don't always see eye to eye." He waved toward the wire-mesh glass door. "We'll walk. I was also t-told you're likely to be d-drunk. You can walk, can't you?"

"I can walk."

When they had stepped down to the alley pavement and crossed to the far sidewalk, Philby began talking in a low voice that barely reached Hale's ringing ears. "Your indulgence of t-temper and intemperance th-this morning may have caused this operation to be can-can-*canceled*," he said, and Hale thought there was a note of suppressed satisfaction in his voice. "You had better h-hope otherwise, because I don't m-mind telling you that Mammalian will simply v-v-verify you if he does abort it, casually as swatting a fly. You were always a blundering f-f-fool, Hale, but this—"

Hale was suddenly very tired, and the prospect of walking a mile or so with Philby in this hectoring mode was beyond bearing. Brace him now, Hale thought, if only to change his tone.

"O Fish," Hale interrupted, "are you constant to the old covenant?"

Philby stopped walking, and Hale had to halt and turn around to face him. "I want to buy a couple of guns," Hale added. "Where's the nearest shop for guns?"

"Return, and we return," said Philby hollowly, staring at Hale in evident puzzlement. "Keep faith, and so will we. What do you m-mean?" he added in a cautious tone.

"It's the Rabkrin exchange, Kim. You answered it correctly. We proceed."

Philby stirred and began walking again. "B-But that's—that's old. How l-l-long have you been—? *You?* And it's very high; not many p-people know that challenge. I don't think Mammalian knows the exchange." Hoarsely he said, "Who—*are* you?"

"It's higher than you suppose, Kim. I'm not Rabkrin. Have you forgotten the bargain you made with Theodora in '52, at the Turkish–Soviet border? I've been sent to remind you of it. An SIS representative will shortly be contacting you here, offering you immunity in exchange for your total memoirs. You will pretend to cooperate, but you will not tell him anything about Rabkrin or the Ararat operation, and you will not return to England."

Philby had stopped again. "You can get g-guns at one of the import shops on Allenby," he said absently. "Jimmie's anachronistic SOE . . . that was t-t-*ten years* ago. And now you—has there truly b-been a British secret s-service that I was not *aware* of, all along? Was L-Lawrence one of *you?* How far in—" Philby's pale face had lost all expression, but Hale could recognize baffled rage. "Are you with the fabled D-D-*Declare? You?*" He held out his hands and slowly closed them into fists. "Cassagnac's murder!—your old c-crimes—your flight from England last week—this has all been c-*cover?*"

They were on the Weygand Street sidewalk now, and the wind from the north carried the salt smell of the Mediterranean, and Hale stared at Kim Philby in the late-morning sunlight and didn't bother to keep scorn out of his voice. "I was recruited by Captain Sir Mansfield Cummings in 1929, when the SIS headquarters was in Whitehall Court. I've been a Declare agent since the age of seven." He held up one hand. "And *you* have been one, since the SOE doubled you in 1952. You agreed to participate in any operation the Soviets might want you for, as a covert British operative; the alternative offered then was that you would be killed, and that is still the only alternative. *Are* we clear on that? You won't fly back to England—you won't defect to France—Mammalian won't cancel the Ararat operation—and you and I will go up the mountain with him. And immediately that's done, you will defect to the U.S.S.R.—cross at the Aras River—and live out the rest of your life behind the Iron Curtain." Hale's lip quivered as he resisted an impulse to spit. "There won't be any pay; you won't need it in Utopia."

Philby had recovered himself and begun chuckling while Hale spoke, and now he laughed out loud. " 'O Bre'r Fox!' " he said, " 'just don' throw me into yonder briar patch!' Defect to France! My dear f-fellow, as I understand this, you're *ordering* me—on pain of d-death, no less!—to go to Ararat and become something akin to a g-g-*god,* and then retire to the c-country that has been my motherland since I was a b-boy!"

But Hale had noticed the beads of sweat on Philby's hairline. "A half-wit god," Hale said, not without sympathy, "Pa Fox being dead."

Philby's smile was gone, though his mouth was still open. "True," he snapped finally. "And frankly Moscow d-does sound like 'the house whence no one issues, whose inhabitants live in darkness, dust their bread and clay their meat, where over the bolted gate lie dust and silence.' " He gave Hale a squinting smile as he resumed walking, and in a particularly Oxbridge accent he said, "You seem awfully confident that I will not elect to be killed, rather. Do you remember Thomas Browne's remark in *Religio Medici?*—'I am not so much afraid of death, as ashamed thereof.' "

But Hale remembered the words of the half-stone king of Wabar: *I am still secure from judgment. We do not go on, we do not face . . . leveling.* And he guessed that Philby had always arrogantly lived on the assumption that although he might airily betray his country, he would never be so ill-bred as to . . . use the wrong fork, not be able to hold his liquor, not be able to quote Euripides in a proper Attic accent, *be afraid to die.* For all his treason, Philby was a product of the old British Raj, a graduate of Westminster and Cambridge accustomed to upper-class privilege, at home in the Athenaeum and Reform clubs of Pall Mall. But Hale suspected that, having renounced loyalty and honesty and faith, Philby would find that courage had correspondingly become an undercut platform, not able to take his weight. Philby might hate the idea of being a living prole in Moscow, but not as much as he hated the idea of being a dead aristocrat in Beirut.

"Yes," remarked Hale, trudging along beside his half-brother, "I am awfully confident of that."

Philby was silent for several steps, and then his only reply was a cry of *"Serveece!"* to one of the white taxicabs cruising past on Weygand Street; and there were already three Arab passengers in the cab as Hale and Philby climbed into the back seat, so it was only natural that the two spies did not speak until they had alighted on the curb at the Normandy Hotel.

"B-brace yourself for f-forty lashes," said Philby to Hale as they climbed out of the cab.

Hakob Mammalian was waiting for them on the steps to the lobby, but he hurried across the sidewalk to where Hale and Philby stood, and without speaking he took hold of each of them by an elbow and turned them back toward the lanes of the Avenue des Français, and the blue sea beyond.

The three of them strode out across the breezy street, Philby and then Hale waving their free hands in apology as cars honked at them and donkey drivers shouted.

When they had reached the far sidewalk and stepped down from the pavement onto the hot pale sand, Mammalian turned to Hale and stared angrily into his face. Mammalian's right hand was inside his blue-striped robe. After several seconds he reached up with his free hand and prodded Hale's bruised cheek with one finger, and then scratched with his nail at the fresh cut.

Hale flinched back. Even though he was only wearing a shirt, he was already sweating in the direct sunlight. "What the hell, Hakob!" he protested.

"My hand is on a gun," said Mammalian curtly. "Open your shirt."

Hale sighed. "I assume you'll tell me why," he said as he began unbuttoning his coffee-stained shirt.

Mammalian prodded Hale's bare stomach, looking into his eyes as Hale winced.

"When the *sûreté* was questioning you," Mammalian snapped, "you said the arrest was like a dog. What kind of dog?"

"I, I told them it was a dog that wouldn't hunt," said Hale, remembering the remark from the hastily scrawled transcription he had read before leaving Hartsik's office. It had in fact not struck him as the sort of thing he would say.

"What did you mean by that?"

"It's an—ow," Hale said, for Mammalian was still palpating his stomach. "Would you stop? It's a saying. It means a plan that won't work out; I meant that their arrest would not stand up—I wasn't guilty of anything."

Mammalian squinted at Philby. "Is that a common saying?"

Philby blew out air through his pursed lips. "Sure, one h-hears it."

At last Mammalian stepped back from Hale, his right hand still inside his robe. "You were out of our sight for an hour. In a *police station*. Tell me one reason why I should not abort this mission."

"Yes, yes," said Hale, nodding, "I do see your point of view. I would worry too, in your place." He shrugged and looked up and down the beach. "Let's see—you know some of what was said. Do you know it all? Did it sound as if the police and I were talking in a code? Any of the three of us here could recognize code exchanges, I think."

"No," said Mammalian. "It did not sound like a code. But if you are an SIS plant, a Declare plant!—then there might have been only one thing you needed to learn or convey; and any one phrase could have accomplished that. *A dog that won't hunt!*"

Hale mentally cursed his double for not speaking more simply. "If we were exchanging a code phrase, why would we choose something so awkward?" He touched his cheek. "I don't care if you do abort it—as long as that doesn't involve giving me the truth."

"It would involve that. And right now I am inclined to abort it."

"He w-wanted to buy a g-gun, after he was released," put in Philby helpfully. "S-several guns."

Hale didn't bother to comment on that; and Mammalian flicked his fingers in the air impatiently. "Of course he would want to be armed, in any case." After scowling at Hale for ten more seconds, Mammalian turned to Philby. "You have experience with the British secret service, and with this man—and it is in your interests that this Ararat plan not fail. Is it your feeling that we should abort it, or go ahead?"

Hale did not look at Philby—live prole or dead aristocrat? he thought—and finally, after a pause, he heard Philby sigh and then mutter, "I—" Peripherally Hale saw him wave a hand as if uncertain how to proceed. "Declare?—low on the l-list of likelihoods, I think. If H-Hale was really b-being run by Theodora, there wouldn't be any n-need for a last-minute c-conference at a police station. Let's—ah, God!—let's proceed with it as p-p-planned."

In Philby's hesitant speech Hale had caught the phrase, *I declare low.*

And he knew that the three words had been a reference, for him, to the interrupted high-low poker game the two of them had played in the bomb shelter below Mount Ararat nearly fifteen years earlier; Philby was conveying his decision, his cowardly decision, to choose life.

"Well, I do concur," Hale said, trying not to breathe any more deeply than he had been doing a moment earlier; and he glanced at his wristwatch to be sure the hands were set for the correct local time.

▼

Book Three

Mount Ararat

▼

17

Mount Ararat, 1963

He pointed throught the window—opening into space that was filled with moonlight reflected from the snow—and threw out an empty whisky bottle.
"No need to listen for the fall. This is the world's end," he said, and swung off. The lama looked forth, a hand on either sill, with eyes that shone like yellow opals. From the enormous pit before him white peaks lifted themselves yearning to the moonlight. The rest was as the darkness of interstellar space.
—Rudyard Kipling, *Kim*

The morning breeze down from the high glaciers was positively Arctic.

Kim Philby had photographed Mount Ararat extensively during his posting as SIS Head of Station for Turkey, a job that had lasted from February of 1947 through September of 1949. Using as cover the SIS surveying operation code-named Spyglass, he had taken pictures of the Ahora Gorge from every angle, climbing as high as the 8,000-foot level to get clear pictures of the bottom slopes of the valley over the gorge, the glacier-choked Cehennem Dere. He had studied the accounts of previous explorers—Archbishop Nouri of the Nestorian Church in India, who at the Chicago World's Fair in 1893 had made a plausible claim to have found the Ark on Ararat five years earlier; Hardwicke Knight, who in 1936 had climbed the western face of the Ahora Gorge in search of a legendary ruined Armenian monastery and found instead, at about the 14,000-foot level, a huge structure of ancient black timbers protruding from the glacial moraine; and the American Carveth Wells, who was reportedly led to the Ark by Armenian shepherds in 1943. Philby had not been able to fly a helicopter so near to the Iranian border, but Guy Burgess had relayed to him a sheaf of photographs taken in the mid-'40s from Mikoyan-Gurevich fighter planes out of the Soviet air base at Erivan—prints that clearly showed a boxy black shape overhanging a glacier lake near the Cehennem Dere, at the foot of the higher glacier known as Abich I. Each of these photographs included in the frame another MiG, flying at a lower altitude, as if to establish a Soviet claim.

The MiG photographs had been taken during the summer—the lake would be frozen now, in late January.

Mount Ararat was of primordial volcanic origin, and its slopes were littered with "pillow lava," smooth igneous stones formed when the magma had flowed out under sea water. And although the mountain had sunk, so that it was now surrounded by a moat-like caldera of snake-infested marshes, its nearly 17,000-foot height was imposing because it stood virtually alone on the Kars-Van plain, the northernmost sentinel of the Zagros mountain range.

Until the death of the fox in September of last year, Kim Philby had lived for the day when he should finally climb up to the structure that folklore had mis-identified as Noah's Ark, and take at last his destined role as human emissary to the djinn—*rafiq* to the spirits of the air.

Now that his father was irretrievably lost, though, his only hope was that Hale's Declare operation would ignobly succeed and that the djinn would all be killed before he could be subjected to the devastating *recognition* of the inhuman powers that inhabited the high glaciers.

Standing now on the broad face of the Cehennem Dere glacier above the Ahora Gorge, Philby looked back at the two white nylon tents, and at the two motionless Spetsnaz commandos in their white parkas, holding their white-painted automatic rifles; and he leaned his weight against the bitter wind and tried to comprehend the fact that the rest of his life lay north of this point—and east.

He shuffled around in the snow to peer through his goggles in that direction, the heels of his boots squeaking on the compacted dry powder; mists in the middle distance blurred the cliffs of the Ahora Gorge below him, and against the white blur of the winter sun he could not see the Aras River, twenty miles away to the northeast. But if today's climb were successful, he would be crossing that river, that Rubicon, tomorrow, never again to recross it. He would be greeted as a hero in Moscow, no doubt—he had been honorarily awarded the Soviet Order of the Red Banner after his assistance in placing the drogue-stone in Berlin in 1945, and had even been shown a photograph of the medal, with its red-and-white striped ribbon, gold-wreathed medallion, and enameled banner. He would be able to take physical possession of it, soon, and wear it to . . . state dinners at the Kremlin. Evenings at the Bolshoi.

He had never even bothered to try to learn Russian.

Truly he had always imagined that he would live undercover—*know, not think it*—for the rest of his life; that he would one day return to England with Eleanor, and there attend cricket matches, write for the *Times,* send his sons to Winchester and Cambridge. He had won his Commander of the British Empire in '46, and that was only two ranks below being knighted! And he would always have been warmed, as he watched the Derby from the Members' Stand at Epsom or drank malt whisky with the lawyers and journalists in the Garrick Club, by the secret knowledge that he had done more to undermine this capitalist decadence than any other Soviet spy in history.

He had to tilt his head now, to see down the gorge past the fluttering fur fringe of his parka. The action reminded him of trying to see with the bandage on his head, back in Beirut.

Nicholas Elliott, who had been Head of the SIS Beirut Station until Peter Lunn had taken over in October of last year, had returned to Lebanon thirteen days ago. He had telephoned Philby the next day, a Friday, and proposed a meeting at the flat of Lunn's secretary. Philby's head had still been taped up with gauze then, and when he arrived at the flat the first thing he had said to Elliott had been, "You owe me a drink. I haven't had one since I did this to my skull on my birthday, ten days ago." Not strictly true, any of it—his skull had been cracked by Miss Ceniza-Bendiga's .30-caliber bullet, and he had been drinking like a champion ever since—but Philby had been smiling confidently as he spoke, holding out his right hand. Only three days had passed since Andrew Hale had frightened and insulted him on Weygand Street, and he'd been eager to numb the smart of that humiliation in reminiscences of braver, grander days.

Philby and Elliott had become friends at War Station XB in St. Albans during the war, and later in Broadway the two SIS men had worked together at trying to design a non-Communist postwar Germany—though, unknown to Elliott, Philby had seen to it that all the proposed agents were safely killed before the war ended. In 1948 it had been Elliott who had found a Swiss nerve specialist for Philby's second wife, after her incautious curiosity about Philby's work with Burgess had begun to cause her to lose her mind; and later, in the dark winter of '51, after Burgess and Maclean defected and Philby was suspected of complicity, Elliott had been Philby's staunchest defender in Broadway. Eventually Elliott had helped Philby get journalism work with *The Observer* and *The Economist,* and had steered a lot of under-the-table SIS work his way, mainly so that Philby wouldn't starve.

But on that Friday afternoon in Beirut nearly two weeks ago, Elliott's eyes had been cold behind his horn-rimmed glasses, and he'd said, "Stop it, Kim. We know what you've done. You took me in for years—and now I'll get the truth out of you, even if I have to drag you to Ham Common myself. I once looked up to you—my God, how I despise you now. I hope you've enough decency left to understand why."

Well, it had been the SIS confronting him at last, hadn't it—and, as Hale had said, they were offering immunity in exchange for Philby's full confession. *You will pretend to cooperate,* Hale had told Philby, *but you will not tell him about the Ararat operation, and you will not return to England.* And so Philby had flippantly conceded his guilt and typed out a rubbishy confession, admitting only to having spied for the Comintern and claiming to have quit in '49, when the Attlee government's reforms had "disproved Marxism." God!

But it had all gone down well enough with Elliott.

Elena Teresa Ceniza-Bendiga had sidled up to Philby at the Khayats Bookshop in Avenue Bliss the next day, and over the stacks of *Life* and *Paris Match* she had told him that the SDECE was prepared to exfiltrate him to France right then, from the bookstore; a news delivery lorry was in the alley behind the shop, its engine idling. He had put her off, said he needed to clock in with Mammalian first, and had got her to agree to meet him again by the Pigeon Grotto on the cliffs at Chouron Street, that evening—and then he had gone back to the Normandy Hotel and told Mammalian that the French SDECE agent Ceniza-Bendiga was in Beirut, and that she had approached him with a defection proposal; he told Mammalian when and where he had agreed to meet her, and he had then gone upstairs and got drunk alone in his room.

Philby had not seen Elena since then. Perhaps Mammalian had killed her—Philby hadn't asked.

Nicholas Elliott had taken Philby and Eleanor to dinner that night at Le Temporel, and both men had tried to talk and laugh as if their old friendship had not been a betrayal from the start. Poor Eleanor had sipped her wine nervously, glancing from her husband to Elliott and back, clearly aware of the forced tone. In the men's room Philby had passed Elliott two more typewritten pages of chicken-feed confession.

Two days later Elliott had flown back to London, telling Philby that Peter Lunn would take over the interrogation and make arrangements for Philby's return to England. Lunn had clearly been embarrassed by the spectacle of a Cambridge-and-Athenaeum-Club man confessing to having been a Soviet spy, and Philby had no difficulty in postponing their first meeting for a week—and then on the night of the twenty-third, the Rabkrin expedition had left Beirut.

January twenty-third, Philby thought forlornly.

Now, shuddering in mountaineering boots and a parka on a windy glacier 13,000 feet above sea-level, Philby allowed himself the useless fantasy of reconsidering his decision. He could have stayed with Eleanor, his wife of very nearly four years. Perhaps the SIS and the MI5 together could have protected him from facing "the truth" at the hands of Jimmie's ultra-covert old SOE, in England, at least—but he didn't believe that. According to legend, Declare had dealt with the code-breaker Alan Turing, and T. E. Lawrence, and even Lord Kitchener, drowned off the Scapa Flow in 1916. Philby clenched his mittened fists in frail bravado. Very well, so what if they *would* have killed him, eventually? Or even as soon as he was released from interrogation at Ham Common? He could have died as a loyal husband and father. *If I should die, think only this of me: that there's some corner of England that is forever a foreign land!* The thought made a hash of Rupert Brooke's scansion, but Philby smiled at it. And in the eighteenth century Edward Young had written, *Death loves a shining mark, a signal blow.* But more recently Eugene Fitch Ware had countered it: *We fixed him up an epitaph, "Death loves a mining shark."* And it was something more like a mining shark that Philby had become, in his furtive career—burrowing, hiding, voracious, without conscience.

And, he was honest enough to admit to himself, profoundly afraid of dying. *Meet your Maker . . . !* At least if vile Hale was successful here, there would be a very large-scale dying of djinn. The idiotically ghoulish *amomon* thistle would be blooming in the wastelands, probably even in Soviet Armenia. And he still had Theo Maly's sealed instructions.

What had Maly called it? *A more profane sort of eternal life.*

To his credit, he felt, Philby had actually tried to give his children the better sort of eternal life—though admittedly he had been maudlin drunk each time. Did it still count, he wondered now on this cold flank of Mount Ararat, if it was administered by a drunk? A resolutely *atheist* drunk? With the older four of his children he had found opportunities to spill water onto their heads, and then, while seeming to try to wipe it off, covertly make the feared Papist *sign of the cross* on their foreheads— he had cringed to do it, and his teeth had actually hurt each time as he had mumbled, *I baptize thee in the name of the Father, and of the Son, and of the Holy Ghost, amen*—but in the case of poor young Harry, his youngest son by his previous wife, Philby had eventually resorted to pushing the boy out of a rowboat on the Dog River, near Ajaltoun in the Lebanon mountains, mumbling the hated litany as he'd pulled the boy back aboard and pushed the wet hair out of his eyes, up and then sideways.

And he was always aware of the power of birthdays and anniversaries. The zodiac wheel was in precisely the same position again on such days, and the events they commemorated were in a sense repeated in all their vulnerabilities, renewed in their purposes.

And so *of course* the Rabkrin expedition had left Beirut on the twenty-third of January! At five o'clock on that rainy evening, with no warning, Mammalian had given him a passport in the name of Villi Maris and ordered him to get into a Turkish truck bound for the Syrian border. "We go now," Mammalian had told him. But Philby and Eleanor had been expected at a dinner at the house of the First Secretary of the British Embassy on that night, and Philby had simply demanded to be allowed to call Eleanor and tell her to go on without him, that he would meet her there later. Mammalian had eventually given in and driven him through the downpour to a telephone kiosk from which he could make the call. When Philby had dialed the number, thirteen-year-old Harry had answered the telephone, and in every hour since then Philby had wished that Eleanor had picked up the extension, so that he could have heard her voice one more time; but in the rain-drumming telephone kiosk, with Mammalian scowling at him over his dripping beard in the open doorway, Philby had only dared to say, "Tell your m-mother I'm— g-going to be late, H-Harry—my b-boy. I'll m-meet her at the B-Balfour-Pauls' at eight." While he had fumbled for words to say more, Mammalian had reached across him and pressed down the plunger.

The next day, the twenty-fourth, would have been Philby's and Eleanor's fourth wedding anniversary.

Till Death do us part, Philby thought now as he blinked rapidly to keep tears from spilling down his cheeks, where they might freeze the snow-goggles to his skin. Thin veils of dry snow were blowing past him down the snowpack slope, like white dust.

Off to his left he could see a couple of the others lumbering out of the nearest tent, looking like polar bears in their hooded parkas and boots. One was Mammalian, the tallest; the other would be one of the Turk Rabkrin agents. There had been no snow last night, and they were standing in the darker, tromped-flat area around the tents. The commandos who had been standing watch slung their white Kalashnikov machine guns and began trudging to the farther tent—hourly rotation of watch, Philby recalled.

"*Sutle ekmek!*" called one of the Turks to Philby, his voice thin in the chilly air. *Bread and milk*, and it would be sour milk.

"*Ben onsuz yapabilirum,*" Philby shouted to him across the snow. *I can do without it.*

"And briefing," called Mammalian over the wind. "Synchronizing our watches, girding up our loins for battle, revelations of secrets not to be divulged down in the lowlands. Come in here."

Philby sighed a gust of steam and plodded back across the wavy snow, planting his boots in the same holes they had made when he had walked away from the tents; and the sky was too overcast for him to throw much of a shadow. Perhaps he was not really walking back to the tent at all.

Oddly, and he smiled wryly at it, he was feeling an extra bit of guilt here—Hale and I didn't finish that poker game in 1948, he thought, but I took the whole pot anyway: I had Señorita Ceniza-Bendiga the next day in Dogubayezit, and I kept Maly's *amomon* instructions too.

Andrew Hale looked up from his cup of tepid tea when Philby came stamping back into the tent.

Hakob Mammalian was right behind him, followed by the surlier of the two Turks, Fuad.

"Sit," said Mammalian as he ponderously lowered himself into a cross-legged position on the rubberized canvas floor, scattering floury

snow from his boots. Philby and Fuad sat down, and the Turk by the little paraffin stove began handing disks of flat bread to Hale, who passed
them to Mammalian. Hale was just wearing his tan wool liner gloves,
and he could feel that the bread was hot.

"When we were here in '48," Mammalian said, his breath steaming
in the razory cold air, "we did not come this high. We did not presume
to *knock at their door*, but called them down to the gorge. We were cautious because of some old stories—St. Hippolytus wrote in the third
century that climbers who tried to ascend Ararat were thrown down to
the valley floor by demons; and in the fourth century, Faustus of Byzan-
tium recorded the story of an Armenian bishop, Jacob—"

Fuad snorted around a mouthful of the bread. "An Armenian named
Jacob!" he said in English. "Was *he* a saint?"

"He was," said Mammalian imperturbably. "And he climbed partway
up the mountain, hoping to see the Ark. Where he slept, a spring burst
out of the rocks; we passed that spring in the gorge yesterday, by the
cairn of rocks that marks his grave, though the shrine that used to stand
there was destroyed in the 1840 earthquake. He too found himself
abruptly at the foot of the mountain—but he had been carried there by
an angel, who gave him a piece of wood from the Ark and told him that
it was God's will that he not attempt to climb the mountain. That piece
of wood is today in the Armenian Orthodox monastery in Echmiadzen,
in Soviet Armenia. The angel was a Christian one, and knew that Jacob
might be killed if he climbed higher. With my own eyes as a boy I saw a
demon face staring angrily from the Ark. Perhaps we Armenians are in a
privileged position; my father and I were not molested."

"The mountain does not belong to Armenia," said Fuad. "It is in
Turkey. Why do you Armenians have it on your coat-of-arms?"

"Does the moon belong to Turkey?" asked Mammalian. "It is on your
flag." He gave Fuad a dismissive wave. "But"—he shrugged—"in fact
men of many nationalities have ascended to the Ark and survived; and in
this century the djinn have been more quiescent, possibly because one of
their number is abroad now, in Russia. In 1948 our group on the north
side of the gorge was not attacked, but our covering party below the
southern cliffs, as well as a British and a French group that tried to sabotage our operation from that side, were nearly all killed—many men
were lifted away into the sky, doubtless to be thrown down onto the
plain, as Hippolytus described."

Hale passed the last piece of bread, not taking any for himself—the thought of eating nauseated him, and he almost gagged at the thought that the bread smelled like khaki—and he touched the lump in his pocket that was the special derringer he had bought a week ago in Allenby Street in Beirut. He made himself stare back at Mammalian with no expression.

"But," Mammalian went on, steepling his fingers in front of his beard and glancing from Hale to Philby and back, "the djinn did speak, that night. They said, in Arabic, 'Answer whom? The brothers are divided.'"

A moaning gust of wind from the peak bellied the tent wall behind Mammalian and snapped the outer flap like a flag; Hale's nostrils constricted at a cold whiff of metallic oil over the bread-and-rubber smell of the tent.

Mammalian shucked the leather mitten off of his right hand and began unsnapping his parka. "Wear your drogues outside your clothing!" he barked.

Hale hooked a finger into the leather thong at his neck and drew out the flat rectangular stone Mammalian had given him yesterday, at the camp by the trucks on the plain. The stone was the size of a thick playing card, with a protruding ring at the top, and a cross had been grooved across its matte face.

Each of the five men in the tent was clutching one of the stones now; and over the long course of ten seconds the keening wind outside diminished away to silence. Hale was braced for the ground-tremors of an earthquake, but none came.

His pounding heartbeat didn't slow down. He didn't think it had slowed to less than a hundred beats per minute in the last forty-eight hours, and in his sleeping bag on this rubber floor last night he had not got more than two hours' restless sleep.

Mammalian tapped his drogue stone. "These are better than your Egyptian ankhs," he said to Hale. "When Gilgamesh tried to take a boat to where the immortal Upanishtim could give him eternal life, do you recall that he nearly made the voyage impossible when he broke the 'things of stone' with which the boat was equipped? They were stone anchors in this shape, but more than just the kind of anchor that keeps a boat from being swept away. These fix the attention of the djinn, and thus impede new intentions."

"What brothers?" rasped Philby. Hale looked at him—the man's face in the parka hood was pasty and he was staring at the ridged rubber floor. "What brothers were divided?"

"The two sons," said Mammalian, "of Harry St. John Philby. They are yourself and Andrew Hale. This is the truth."

Philby stared at Hale then, and Hale almost looked away—Philby's wet eyes were wide with hurt, and something like loss, and even sorrow. "I d-did know it, *suspect* it," Philby said thickly. "I—d-damn me!—I s-s-some-t-times thought I s-saw—*him*—in y-you."

Hale had to take a breath to speak. "And treated me accordingly?" The words came out with more bitterness than he had intended to show, and he glanced down at his boots to hide any tears that might well up in his own eyes. The lost father I used to daydream about, he thought. Have I seen him in you, Kim? I wouldn't have known.

"You h-had n-no—*right*," Philby choked.

"Nor say," said Hale shortly.

"Together," said Mammalian in a loud voice, "you will approach their castle, today. Together you will be the one person who was consecrated to them in 1912, in Amballa."

Ten years before I was even born, thought Hale tensely. Mother, why in the name of *Heaven* did you—

He glanced again at Philby, and thought he caught a flicker of wild, fearful hope there. *No*, Kim, Hale thought in sudden specific alarm—I will not serve as your fox; your father was *willing*, but I will *not* consent to sharing the ordeal of the djinn sacrament with you. Aloud, he said to him, trying not to speak quickly, "Did you ever go through the espionage-paramilitary course at Fort Monkton?"

Philby blinked. "Y-Yes, in '49."

"I did it in '46. You remember the litany? 'Would you kill your brother?' " It hurt Hale's jaw to speak so much. "We both answered yes to that. *Don't* expect a lot of brotherly love, right?"

He hoped that was innocuous enough not to rouse suspicion in Mammalian, and at the same time a clear enough message to Philby—*If you tell them about me, about this Declare infiltration and sabotage, you will go through with the djinn sacrament, as the Rabkrin has planned—alone; and you will live ever after as a pampered imbecile in Moscow, never again able to read, or think.*

He saw the hope die in Philby's eyes as the import sank in, and Hale took a sip of his cooled tea to cover his frail relief: clearly the psychic sharing did have to be voluntary. *Our father,* Hale thought, *loved you very much, Kim.*

"Brotherly love," echoed Philby emptily.

"—is not called for here, fortunately," said Mammalian. "Plain professionalism will suffice. We are going to be ascending to the Abich I glacier today, and then traversing it to the top slope of the Parrot glacier. We may get snow, and the winds are constant, but no storm is expected. It will be dangerous nevertheless—the traverse will be across a convex snow surface at about a thirty-degree angle, so avalanches are a real possibility—and of course there are deep crevasses in the ice— but," he said, rocking his head toward the other tent, "our Spetsnaz commandos were chosen because they have mountain-climbing experience, and we'll all be roped in a line. It is what they call a static rope. Not much *climbing* should be required—simply follow the directions of the leader. If a man near you should fall into a crevasse, try to plunge your ice-axe into the surface near you, to moor yourself; and if *you* fall in, just hang there—don't thrash or struggle, lest you pull the rest of us in after you."

"Jesus," said Philby.

"Prayer, I think," said Mammalian judiciously, "would be contraindicated. We will all carry our automatic rifles, but it's unlikely that we'll encounter opposition at this point; nevertheless you will have a full magazine loaded and a live round in the chamber. Radios are not likely to work this close to the Ark and its inhabitants, but we have flare-guns, and since we are so close to the Soviet border a Mil helicopter will be here in less than ten minutes if we fire them."

Mammalian paused and reached up to one of the hang-loops for his bottle; the liquid in it was cloudy, arak already mixed with water, and certainly it would be as cold as he could ask for. After he had uncorked it and taken a swig, he went on, exhaling licorice fumes, "In addition to the natural hazards of mountaineering, many climbing parties upon this mountain have been troubled by . . . irrational irritability and fear among the climbers, even abrupt insanity. Equipment has failed, inexplicably. These are evidences of resistance by the inhabitants of the peaks. We appear to have experienced nothing of the sort so far on this climb, which perhaps means that we are not unwelcome, but that condition may change when we get onto the higher glacier. So if you find yourself suddenly angry, or afraid, or disoriented, remind yourself that it is not a genuine, justified emotion! The Spetsnaz have been told this too, as clearly as seemed advisable. Simply stop, breathe deeply, recite the multiplication tables. And we have drugs that might help counter these effects."

He looked beside him at Philby, then at Hale. "The Ark is on a ledge, over a lake," Mammalian said. "It should be accessible, and we have enough men to dig it out if it is not. The two of you are to approach it, together. Don't bother to try to walk in step or anything of that sort—it will be enough that you are side by side." To Philby he said, "You have the *rafiq* jewel."

"I contain it," said Philby.

"As in 1948." Mammalian took another sip of the arak and then corked the bottle and smiled. "As if that would stop us from taking it from you, if such was our purpose! The two of you may shout to the vessel, if there is no immediate response, but I think the Ark will open for you, at the mere approach of . . . the completed son."

"And what," asked Hale, not having to feign anxiety, "do we do then?"

Mammalian spread his hands and smiled. "Improvise."

Hale nodded. That was what Hartsik had told him too. He remembered the djinn confined in the pool at Ain al' Abd saying, *This is the Nazrani son*—and he remembered the king of Wabar telling him, *The ghosts of my people could see that you have not the black drop in the human heart.*

Prayer, I think, Mammalian had said here, *would be contraindicated.*

"Could I, er, have a bit of your arak?" Hale asked.

"I've got Scotch," said Philby suddenly, "and gin. Both." He was looking at the floor again.

Hale gave him an uncertain glance. He had seen Philby drinking from a steel water bottle that he had topped up last night from a bottle of Gordon's gin, so Hale said, "Well, gin, actually." He clenched his teeth, then made himself say, "Thanks."

He was peripherally aware of Mammalian smiling ironically at him.

Improvise.

Hale had been improvising without cease ever since Mammalian had ordered him into the Bombard inflated motorboat in the storm surf below the Normandy Hotel on the rainy night of the twenty-third. And his calculations had become more complicated when he and his escorts had joined the rest of the team at the camp below Ararat last night.

Philby unsnapped a water bottle from a webbing harness on the floor, and Hale reached across to take it from him, willing his fingers not to tremble.

When the time came, Hale would shoot his derringer upward, into whatever form the djinn assumed; perhaps he could do it with the little gun held down by his belt, so that it would not be obvious that he had fired it, or even that the noise had been a gunshot. There might well be other, covering noises. But how wide would the shot spread, out of the gun's short barrel?—widely enough to blow Hale's face off? And then—the djinn would *die*? What ferocities might that involve? If he had to shoot more than twice, he would have to reload, and then aim. What would the Spetsnaz commandos make of that? Short work was what they'd make of *him*. And he had to save one round to fire into Philby's back.

He took a big mouthful of Philby's gin, and let it sting his mouth for a few seconds before swallowing it.

"Thanks," he whispered more sincerely, handing the water bottle back to Philby.

"Up," said Mammalian, slapping his hands onto his thighs. "Fuad and Umit will stay here—we take up our rifles and . . . ascend!"

The big Armenian was cheerful as he stood up again and began refastening the snaps of his parka; and Hale remembered coming to the conclusion, on the St. Georges Hotel terrace eighteen days ago, that Mammalian's loyalties in this operation were to the djinn themselves, and not to the Rabkrin.

Hale got to his feet, glad that the climbing pants were so thick as to hide the shaking of his knees, and he pulled the snow-goggles down over his eye sockets and the bridge of his nose. His crampons were slung at his belt beside the head of his ice-axe, and he shuffled to the corner of the tent and picked up one of the white-painted Kalashnikovs. It weighed about ten pounds with the full thirty-round magazine attached in front of the trigger guard, but its weight was comfortable when he had slung it over his shoulder Bedu-style. Five spare magazines clicked in his pockets as he shifted to tug the leather mittens on over his liner gloves.

The tent had been cold, but he shivered when he had stepped out onto the snow and the icy wind found the gaps at his throat and wrists. Ice dust was sweeping down over the snowpack from the peak like the ghost of a fast, shallow stream, and he was glad that their route would not be taking them higher than the 14,000-foot level. Even under clouds the white glare of the snow field was dazzling, and the cornices of the Abich I glacier to the west glittered like diamonds.

He sat down on the trampled area of ice outside the tent to strap the steel-spiked crampons tightly onto the soles of his boots. Under the trampled snow the surface of the Cehennem Dere glacier was black, impregnated with lava dust—and he remembered the black glass beads he had found at Wabar, and then he thought of the oval shot pellets in his derringer.

The thought that he would be firing at least two shells of those pellets today made his belly flutter so loosely that he was afraid he might wet his pants; but he felt an aching tightness in his chest, as if his lungs were struggling against his closed throat for fresh air while he was submerged far under water. I'm forty-one years old, he thought as he took deep breaths of the frigid air to try to dispel the feeling. I didn't die at Ain al' Abd three weeks ago—will I really finally do it today?

Pot's right, no more bets, showdown.

He remembered his dismay at finding himself committed to a hand of cards without having honestly looked at the stakes, fourteen years ago. Had he been doing it again? But if the stakes were too frightening to consider, and the game was already lost, what value could there be in clear comprehension?

"All I can do is play out the hand," he whispered. "I can't change anything at forff-forfeit-forty—at my age."

He stood up, still breathing deeply of the thin, icy air, and used his teeth to tug tight the wrist strap of the left mitten. The ten Spetsnaz commandos had filed out of their larger tent, and for the moment Hale avoided looking at them. Even seen peripherally they did look bulky, and he had to assure himself that a 7.62-millimeter round would easily penetrate even the thickest layers of leather and nylon weave and kapok fiber. He tugged his bulky parka hood over his head and trudged forward behind the rocking white rifle-barrels slung on the backs of Philby and Mammalian.

One of the Spetsnaz commandos pointed at Hale and barked some syllables in Russian. Hale forced himself simply to pause, and not to shuck his right hand free of its mitten to grab the Kalashnikov stock.

Mammalian turned around to face Hale—his black beard below the gleaming snow-goggles was already powdered with ice dust, but was still a conspicuous spot in this white sky world—and he called, "He says you will kill someone accidentally, holding your gun that way. Sling it the way they do."

"*Da!*" yelled Hale obediently. But when he pulled the sling off over his head and then put it on again, the rifle barrel was pointed down, so that one yank on the barrel would bring it back to the Bedu position. The Spetsnaz seemed to be satisfied.

West of the tents the white slope climbed toward the tumbled chunks of ice at the foot of the Abich I glacier wall, and down here at the level of the tents one of the Russian commandos had begun axing out a square, yard-wide step in the snowpack. Another was lashing three snap-link carabiners at fifteen-foot intervals on a long white rope, and when he had finished he beckoned to Philby, Hale, and Mammalian.

He clicked the carabiners one by one onto similar links at the fronts of their climbing harnesses, so that the three men were attached to the rope.

The Russian muttered something, and Mammalian laughed and translated: "Our borscht-blooded friend says we are three babies that must be leashed."

Neither Philby nor Hale had any funny rejoinders.

The Russian who had chopped out the step in the slope was now crouched in front of it, digging at the vertical wall of snow he had exposed. When he stood up and began speaking to one of his fellows, Hale could tell by the man's tone that he was not happy. Hale peered at the exposed surface of snow, and saw that the Spetsnaz had scooped loose snow and ice out of several horizontal layers—apparently the snowpack was not uniformly dense.

Hale was the last man on the rope, and he walked up to where Philby stood, dragging the slack behind him. "Is that bad, do you suppose?" he whispered to Philby.

"This is all bad," Philby muttered. "Our father has doomed us both."

The Russian was speaking, and Mammalian waved backward at the two Englishmen; then he turned and said, "The ice is subject to shearing, sliding. Avalanche is a—real possibility."

"Well, we knew *that*, for heaven's sake," snapped Philby.

"Uh," Mammalian went on, translating, "it will be more dangerous when we are moving *across* the slope, above—rather than straight up it, as here. Make no noise—tread lightly, not stomping—and—don't speak."

One of the Spetsnaz, whose white machine gun was equipped with a folding stock and a collapsible bipod at the muzzle, walked downhill past Hale and knotted a lighter line onto the trailing end of the rope and clicked his own harness carabiner onto the bight of the knot. The three amateurs were now bracketed at either end. The rest of the Spetsnaz had attached their harnesses along the far half of the long rope with similar knots, and now the procession had begun to move up the white slope, in single file.

After Mammalian and then Philby had begun plodding forward, Hale took up the pace, hearing the crunch of the Spetsnaz's boots start up behind him.

Hale could feel the grade of the hill in his calves, for with the crampon-spiked boots it was not possible to walk on his toes; but the mild ache was pleasant for now.

Soon the men at the front of the rope had stopped at the foot of the thirty-foot glacier wall, and after Mammalian and Philby and Hale had walked close enough for the rope to lie slack on the ground between them they halted too. The Abich I glacier was gray-white in cross-section, and Hale was staring up at the overhanging cornices of snow and ice when he noticed that the leader had begun to climb the bumpy, gullied wall.

The man moved upward in a contorting but graceful series of moves, like slow-motion bullfighting; at one point he would stretch out a leg to hook an outcrop with his instep, at another he would wedge his forearm or elbow into a gap in order to reach higher with the other hand, and once he simply pulled his whole weight up a yard like a man doing chin-ups. He paused near the top to hang a loop of slung rope on the face, and then after climbing up another yard he stopped below a gap in the overhanging cornice, unslinging his ice-axe to reach up and prod the surface with the pointed butt end of it.

At last he climbed up to the gap and jackknifed through it and out of sight; and a moment later another man was moving up the face, in rapid scrambles, and the line had begun moving again.

Hale was dizzy at the thought of making that ascent himself. There wasn't enough slack between himself and Philby for him to hope that the men at the crest could simply lift them up like sacks of coal—clearly some *climbing*, some supporting of his own weight, would be required. Under all his clothing he could feel sweat on his chest, and suddenly his mittens seemed as clumsy as the fins of a fish. Was one supposed to take them off?—they were thonged together through a loop at his collar.

But when Mammalian went flexing and reaching away up the face, Hale saw that although the man was climbing, he was at the same time giving some of his weight to the rope, which was being tugged up from the top—and his mittens were off, swinging loosely behind his belt. I can do that much, Hale thought, shucking off his own and flexing his hands in the liner gloves; and when Mammalian had disappeared over the cornice and even Philby was halfway up the face, puffing and grunting and scrabbling with his crampon spikes at the ice, Hale stepped gamely up to the face and found that it was not difficult. With the rope taking his weight at his waist and tugging upward, he even found several times that he had to pause before stepping up to the next hand-hold to allow the rope to come taut again.

Then he had rocked over the lip in the cornice gap and was crawling across snow, the drogue stone swinging below his chin. Only one of the Russian commandos was hauling the rope up now, and the others were squatting on this new slope.

They were on the Abich I glacier now. It was more steeply inclined from south down to north than the Cehennem Dere had been, and it was mostly bare ice, with pockets of snow clinging to the face only where cracked, compacted sections of ice had been pushed up to make steps.

The air stung the inside of Hale's nose, too cold at this height to carry any smells except a faint tingle like sulfur. Hale pulled his mittens back onto his aching, numbed hands, and the exposed patches of his face stung as if with a burn. He shifted around to look southward up the mounting slope to the peak, still three thousand feet above, and he quailed at the lunar remoteness of it, and of the white streamers of snow that trailed away from the peak across the gray sky.

Mammalian was standing by the slack rope beside him, looking down toward his boots. Hale followed the direction of his gaze and saw a smoothly oval two-inch hole cut into the ice.

"A borehole," said Mammalian, speaking loudly to be heard over the static-like roar of the wind, "from one of the scientific expeditions. Round, originally—the glacier flow has made it elliptical."

Hale just nodded. Hartsik had said that the djinn had no problem with elliptical *holes*. Well, Hale had brought some elliptical *solids*, a few thousand of them, packed tight for now in .410 shot shells.

Too soon the Spetsnaz were all on their feet again, and then one by one, as if through an invisible bottleneck, they were moving out in single-file across the glacier face. In less than a minute it was Mammalian's turn to start forward, and then Philby's, and then Hale was plodding out onto the glacier, his crampon spikes clashing on the ice.

They were walking up a convex slope. The surface was bumpy and cracked, but it seemed solid enough, and the few yards-wide gaping crevasses they skirted were conspicuous. *If I could kill the man behind me with one round*, Hale thought with a sort of dazed abstractness, *I could probably catch the other nine with a couple of careful bursts—they're all within a ten or twelve degree wedge in front of me. Twenty-nine bullets for nine men; well, ten men, I suppose, counting Mammalian.*

But he didn't know how much mountaineering skill would still be required before they reached the Ark; and if even one of the Spetsnaz was not killed outright, Hale would find himself the target of very professional return fire; and anyway he knew he could not shoot men in the back. Especially not Hakob Mammalian.

The rubbing-alcohol wind was stinging his cheeks and forming ice crystals around his nostrils. I can at least put the load of birdshot into Philby's back, he thought despairingly—and as long as I don't kill him, as long as he can still flee to Moscow, that will have turned over the hourglass on the Moscow *ghula*, Russia's guardian angel, Machikha Nash. She'll die shortly after Philby does, and he's already fifty-one; and the Soviet Union should collapse within only a couple of years after that; assuming Declare's math is right, now. And I should be able to fire at least one shell into the djinn too, before the Spetsnaz cut me down.

Play out the hand.

He was light-headed, almost drunk, and he watched his alternating boots scrape the ice as if they were images on a movie screen. He had not seen Elena again after that late afternoon three weeks ago when he had stood in the doorway of the Normandy Hotel bar and watched her kiss Philby. He had had no clear chance to ask Philby about her, and truthfully he hadn't tried to make a chance—she had presumably been part of the SDECE team with plans to exfiltrate Philby, back when Philby had still believed he had the luxury of considering a defection offer, and in any case Philby would assuredly not have told Hale anything that could have been helpful to her; and Hale was bleakly sure that her only response to the sight of Andrew Hale now would be to try to kill him.

At least she didn't look up and *see* me, that afternoon at the Normandy bar, he thought now, bitterly. At least she didn't see me. That's warming consolation to take with me to . . . to "the house whence no one issues."

At least the Babylonian myths hadn't said anything about it being *cold* there! The tightness in his chest, a feeling like the useless urge to breathe underwater against a resolutely closed throat, was stronger.

He had been daydreaming, and he only realized that he had passed the crest of the glacier and was now plodding through calf-deep snow on the lee side when a hard yank at the waist of his harness webbing snapped his head back and pulled him forward off his feet; he jerked his head back down and saw that he was falling toward snow, but the snow surface was breaking up in chunks and tumbling away below him into deep shadow, and the rope was a tight line slanting steeply down.

Hale landed with his knees on snow-padded ice but his chest out across the rope, over a black abyss; and an instant later his hands had clamped like vises onto the rope's taut length. He was hanging over the pit of a bottomless-looking crevasse, and he was stable as long as he didn't move: he was a downward-pointing triangle, with his solidly braced knees being the two secure points of it. He had hit the rope with his face, and his snow-goggles had been knocked down over his chin—his eyes were stinging in the sudden cold.

From behind him he could hear a rapid metallic hammering, and from far away ahead, on the other side of the abyss, he could hear Mammalian shouting English words at him; but most of Hale's weight was on the rope, and he was squinting straight down into the darkness, watching the diminishing fragments of white snowpack fade into the black.

Hale didn't breathe, or think. Coils of intenser blackness were moving, far away down there, like gleams of reflected absence-of-light on vast shoulders and ribs and thighs. The mountain wasn't tall enough to encompass the downward distance Hale's gaze seemed to be plumbing—he must be looking down into the heart of the earth. He became aware of two spots of a blackness so absolute that he had to look away, dazzled, fearing that he would blind himself by staring straight into them; and then he was glad that he had looked away, and he clung even more tightly to the quivering rope, for he realized that the two astronomically distant orbs of blackness were eyes.

Wisps of radiant vapor flicked up past his face, but he knew they indicated no heat below—he guessed they were simply the chunks of ice and snow that had fallen in, twisted by tidal forces until their very molecules had been wrung apart and the atoms dispelled in all directions.

Hale's own eyes were blinded by frozen tears. Even though he was not looking down into the pit, he could feel the attention of the thing down there stretching his identity.

What was down there would unmake him, though afterward the stuff that had been him would fly away into the sky here, into the upper air, perhaps to trouble radio broadcasts with idiot recitations of nursery rhymes.

Pot's right, no more bets, showdown.

The Destroyer of Delights, the Sunderer of Companies, "he who layeth waste the palaces and peopleth the tombs"—call it Death, call it the Devil who had brought Death to Adam and Eve. *I was afraid because I was naked, and I hid myself.* He would never be found, if he hid here. He needn't fire the derringer at all.

Lay down your losing hand, he told himself, and forfeit everything.

A line from Rupert Brooke echoed in his head: *And I should sleep, and I should sleep.* How much longer could he have been expected to keep on being Andrew Hale, alone?

It would be easy to free himself from the rope and plummet down to what waited; and in this vertiginous instant it seemed to be inevitable. *I've lost my father, I've lost Elena—I can save Theodora the trouble of verifying me, and lose myself, at last.* Already one of his hands, without his volition, had shucked its mitten and crawled to his waist, and was clutching the carabiner snap-ring. One squeeze of the spring-loaded gate, and then all he would have to do would be shift his weight to one side or the other.

He had been aware of Mammalian's voice shouting at him, as if from the other side of the sky, but now he heard a phrase—*for God's sake, man!*

And it seemed as if he could hear him because Hale had surfaced from deep, cold water. His throat could now open at last in surrender to the insistence of his lungs, and he was breathing in great gasps while his lips formed unvoiced syllables; and when he made himself listen to what he was saying, he heard, *hallowed be Thy name, Thy kingdom come, Thy will be done . . .*

Hale strained to raise his head, blinking and squinting to see around the frozen tears. He was just able to lift his head high enough to make out Mammalian, sitting twenty feet away in the snow on the far side of the fissure. "What?" shouted Hale to him, in a rusty voice.

"Do you want to live, or die? Please be honest."

One more bet, after all. Double or nothing.

Hale bared his teeth at him before letting his head drop back down. "To live, Hakob." He could feel that his innermost shirt was slick with sweat.

"Then go ahead and unsnap your harness," Mammalian called to him patiently, "but then grab the line again, and *crawl backward.*"

Hale's hand was already on the carabiner, and now he squeezed the gate and freed himself from the link lashed to the rope; instantly his hand was back on the rope, and with infinite care he pushed himself backward, feeling his knees slide back up the slope behind him, inch by inch, until the edge of the ice crevasse was under the heels of his hands and he was able to crawl back across the glacier surface on all fours.

Then strong hands had grabbed him under the arms and pulled him back up the slope. He saw the shaft of an ice-axe standing up from the snow, and the taut uphill length of the rope was looped around it and then moored to a piton that had been hammered into the ice a yard away—clearly the Spetsnaz behind him had managed to use the axe as an anchor, and had then protected the mooring with the piton. Several of the commandos were on this side of the crevasse now, and Hale could see by their tracks in the snow that they had freed themselves from the lead section of the rope and walked around the uphill side of the hole.

Their faces were snow-dusted white masks below the crusted lenses of the snow-goggles, no more human-looking than their steel and nylon equipment, and Hale quickly pulled his own goggles up into place to hide behind a similar mask.

The rope was still bent sharply into the hole—Philby was hanging at the low point in the middle, and he was upside-down. All Hale could see of him was the baggy knees of his white climbing pants.

A new rope had been spliced onto the old one on this side, and now four of the Spetsnaz held it taut while another of them pried up the piton. Then they were slowly feeding the newly extended rope out, hand over hand, while their companions on the far side of the hole pulled the other end in; Philby's knees began to wobble away, toward where Mammalian sat.

The Spetsnaz who had levered the piton out of the ice now scuffed across the snow to Hale and stared at him through white-powdered snow-goggles. Then he pointed from Hale to himself and waved back along the tracks that led around the crevasse to the other men on the far side. "Hah?"

Hale nodded.

The two of them trudged uphill and along the crest of the glacier for several yards, and then back down to the snowy lee side. The Spetsnaz was leading, and by pointing he conveyed to Hale that they were to follow the already trodden track, presumably to avoid another collapse—which would be fatal, since the two of them were unroped at the moment. Hale nodded to show that he understood, but reflected that the bit of ice that had given way under Philby had already been walked over by ten pairs of boots. Like the Russian ahead of him, Hale walked in a tense crouch, with his ice-axe half-raised in his right hand.

By the time they got to where Mammalian was now standing, Philby had been drawn to the crevasse lip and pulled up onto the snow.

Mammalian glanced at Hale, and just from the set of his mouth Hale could tell that he was frowning. "Do you need a pill, a stabilizing drug?" Mammalian called to him. "It looked from here as though you were suffering from 'abrupt insanity'—trying to free yourself in order to drop down into the hole."

"Optical illusion," Hale assured him, speaking loudly enough to be heard over the wind. But in fact he suspected that it *had* been a supernaturally induced temptation that had seized him as he had hung over the gulf. And when the choice had finally been between breath and death, Hale had found himself saying the *Our Father*. Certainly he didn't want to talk about it now, and he looked away from Mammalian.

The commandos on the far side of the crevasse had walked back around and were laying the rope out across the snow on this side—to let the fibers relax, Hale guessed. Philby was lying on his back and panting steam like a locomotive, his drogue stone upright in the snow beside his head.

In Berlin in 1945, after Hale had crashed that truck back onto the western pavement of the Brandenburg Square and he and Elena had run back to the restaurant where they had met Philby earlier, Elena had asked Hale, *But do you imagine that you are an atheist, still?* He had said he didn't know, and she had said that he was not honest. Had she been right, had he simply not wanted to admit that he was at core still a believing Catholic? It *was* a terrible thing to admit, freighting an already difficult world with supernatural responsibilities and consequences. Was he actually admitting it now? The idea of facing some kind of judgment for the actions of his life set his heart thudding with an extra dimension of terror.

The Spetsnaz commandos had lifted sections of the rope and were lashing themselves onto it, and one of them marched over and clicked the first moored carabiner onto Mammalian's belt; then he glanced at the men near Philby and barked something in Russian.

Philby was hoisted to his feet, and he managed to limp over to Mammalian and Hale. His face was beet red under the glittering snow-goggles, and Hale was suddenly afraid that the man might have a stroke or a heart attack right here.

"Are you all right?" Hale asked him quietly, having to speak directly into his face to be heard. "You could call for a rest. It can't be near noon yet."

Philby just shook his head, swinging the drogue stone that hung at his chest.

A moment later Philby and Hale had been snapped into their places in the line, and one of the Spetsnaz said something to Mammalian.

"Now we descend the Parrot glacier," the Armenian told Hale, "to the ledge on which rests the Ark itself. The way is treacherous, and our Russians will cut steps in the ice for us."

The men in the front of the line began walking over the snow, stepping carefully up onto the shelves where the glacier had buckled, and eventually it was Philby's turn to move. He seemed to stride forward easily enough, and Hale fell into step behind him.

Hale touched the lump under his parka that was the derringer. Soon now, he thought. Should I be praying?

Though the helicopter that swept through the Seyhli valley east of Dogubayezit was painted mottled gray-and-white to match the sky, and bore no markings, by its sleek lines it was recognizable as a French Aerospatiale Alouette III—but the same model had been purchased by the military operators of many nations, including nearby Syria; and in any case it was racing over the grasslands at a height of only a hundred feet, and was not likely to show up on Turkish radar, nor to have been noted by anyone but the taciturn Kurdish mountain tribes when it had crossed the Turkish border in the remotest wastes of the Zagros Mountains to the south. It had taken off an hour ago from the bed of a truck outside Khvoy, in the desolate northwest corner of Iran, and two seven-tube 70-millimeter rocket launchers were mounted low on either side of the fuselage.

Acquisition and equipping of this particular helicopter, and transporting it to Khvoy, had taken the SDECE more days than it should have, but Elena Teresa Ceniza-Bendiga had insisted on the Alouette III—three years ago one of these aircraft had made successful landings and takeoffs at a height of nearly 20,000 feet in the Himalayas, in midwinter. She had, after all, no idea how high up the slopes of Ararat the Rabkrin team intended to climb.

She sat on the corrugated-steel deck beside the armament control panel in the stripped cargo bay, rocking with the sharp lifts and descents of the racing helicopter, puffing a Gauloise.

The departure of the Rabkrin team from Beirut three nights ago had taken the SDECE by surprise; Elena had been monitoring the surveillance by radio from a motor yacht off the north Beirut shore, for since the night of January 12 she had not dared set foot in the city.

On the evening of the seventh she had encoded and tapped out a message to SDECE headquarters in the Quai d'Orsay in Paris, saying that Philby's defection offer appeared to be genuine, accompanied as it was by all the authentic signs of confusion and dislocated pride that one looked for in a ripely breaking defector; but then she had not been able to speak to Philby again until five days later, when he went into the

Khayats Bookshop on Avenue Bliss, momentarily alone. He had been evasive then, too hearty in his greeting, and all the caution-warnings in her head had sounded when he proposed meeting her that night at the Pigeon Grotto cliffs.

She had kept the assignation, but she brought along a full covering team of SDECE street-play experts—known as *gamins des rues*—and she stood on the inland side of the street, on the entry steps of Yazbeck's all-night pharmacy. And even against the backdrop of a public building, she had been shot at.

She had made sure to maintain a six-foot distance from every pedestrian, and, on the frail theory that a sniper required two full seconds to bring the crosshairs of a telescopic sight to bear on a target, she had been moving constantly, with many abrupt about-faces. In such a crowded, public place, with the whole Rabkrin team still *in town,* any kind of full-automatic fire seemed ruled out. Her legs were twitching with the urge to tap out one of the old *clochard* nothing-right-here rhythms, but she was afraid that such a move would hide her from Philby's notice, if he did show up.

She had been wearing body-armor under her coat, and her hat weighed ten pounds with the steel-and-resin-and-ceramic laminate of its low-hanging crown—but this was as perilous a game as tightrope-walking, and she made herself do it mainly in atonement for having prematurely tried to shoot Philby eleven nights earlier, on the evening of New Year's Day. Surely this ordeal, putting herself in the way of a bullet, was adequate penance!

A rifle bullet would have penetrated any of her protections—but by standing on the inland side of the street she had apparently disrupted any plans for placement of a rifle, and so it was just three fast 9-millimeter handgun rounds that hammered her hat and punched her twice in the spine. The impacts threw her forward onto her hands and knees on the sidewalk, but the *gamins des rues* were on her in an instant, and dragged her limp body into the pharmacy. The body armor had kept the bullets from reaching her, but the shot to the head had stunned her.

She had been bundled into the backup vehicle, a flower-decked hearse, which accelerated away to a boat dock by the Place Côte d'Azur south of the city. Philby's status was switched from exfiltration-target to a proposed assassination-target; but orders for an assassination would have to come from the Quai d'Orsay, and anyway Elena had been the only assassination-qualified SDECE agent in Beirut, and she was ordered to control the stalled operation from a boat in the north-shore marina.

Philby had moved furtively after that, and the Rabkrin team had set up a protection cordon around his apartment building on the Rue Kantari, and the apartment's curtains were always drawn.

Andrew Hale had been kept even more secluded by the Rabkrin, after his arrest for public drunkenness on the morning of the eighth.

It appeared that Hale really had defected to the Rabkrin side; Claude Cassagnac had been killed at Hale's house in England three and a half weeks ago, and the SIS stations really did have Hale on their urgently-detain lists all over the Middle East. The cover identity the Rabkrin had given him must have been very solid, to get him through a sûreté interrogation. Oddly, the SDECE had not been able to get a transcript of the interrogation from the police.

According to protocol, she would also need authorization from the Quai d'Orsay to kill Hale—if she proposed doing it in Beirut. But the counter-Ararat operation had already been approved, and it included a provision that *all* members of the Rabkrin team might be killed, if they made it onto the slopes of Mount Ararat.

Elena had requested the Alouette III, with specific modifications, and she told the SDECE to get the French diplomatic corps to work on calling in favors from the Iranian Pahlavi government—the helicopter needed to be trucked to some remote spot in the northwest corner of Iran, near the eastern Turkish border.

The Iranian government had been hard to convince—a national election was scheduled for the twenty-sixth, and the progressive White Revolution party didn't want to provide any excuses for anti-Western sentiments—and so the helicopter, and the peculiar warheads in its four-nozzle 70-millimeter rockets, had not been ready and in place until the twenty-second; and on the very next night the Rabkrin team had surreptitiously left Beirut.

From the rain-swept deck of the yacht, Elena had actually seen one member evacuated.

Beirut had been a neon blur through the sweeping veils of rain on that night, and from the crackling speaker of her radio in the main cabin she listened to her surveillance agents out there in the city complaining about stalled cars and flooded intersections. They had lost Philby, but hoped to regain contact at a dinner he was going to that night at the house of the First Secretary of the British Embassy. Immediately after that transmission she had heard a motorboat laboring through the storm surf outside, and she had snatched up her binoculars, unlocked the cabin door and gone swaying out onto the deck.

She had barely been able to see the boat through the rain. It had been a flat-bottom inflatable Bombard rescue-craft with an outboard motor at the stern, and it was showing no lights. As she watched, the ponderous rubber boat rocked over the low waves and slid up the beach below the Normandy Hotel.

The Normandy was where the Rabkrin team had been staying.

Dimly in the reflected glow from the hotel windows she had seen two figures waiting on the beach; one of them got into the boat, and then it was pushed away, back into the whirling surf.

She had gone back inside and picked up the radio microphone. "I think your target won't show up at the dinner," she told the surveillance team. "I think he's bolted. I think they all have."

She had poured herself a glass of brandy then, for the Rabkrin team appeared to be on its way, after all, to Mount Ararat. The SDECE force had failed to stop the Soviet operation in Beirut, and she had not turned Philby—but the Alouette III was at last in place in Khvoy, and within a couple of days Philby and Hale would both be on the mountain.

She wondered if she had meant things to work out this way all along.

The Rabkrin party would climb to Noah's Ark—and then all of the witnesses of her shames would be together in one place: the djinn with whom she had participated in the deaths of her men in the Ahora Gorge in 1948, Kim Philby who had heard her secrets and been permitted into her bed, and Andrew Hale, whom she had loved.

The 70-millimeter rockets in the seven-tube rocket launchers were cyclotol explosive packed in shells lathed from Shihab meteoric steel. A barrage of them should take care of everyone.

In her earphones now she heard the helicopter pilot say, *"Une dizaine minutes."* Ten minutes or so to target. Out the port windows she could see through the ground mists the white south shoulder of Ararat, still twenty miles away. She threw her cigarette onto the helicopter deck and ground it out under the toe of her boot; then she turned to the armament control panel and clicked up the switch that armed the rocket launchers. The green STANDBY light went out, and the red ARMED light was now glowing, right next to the red light that had all along been indicating that the gun-firing solenoids of the .50-caliber machine guns were activated.

"Montrez-moi," she said into the microphone by her chin. *Show me.*

▼

18

Mount Ararat, 1963

This is a tale of those old fears, even of those emptied hells,
And none but you shall understand the true thing that it tells—
Of what colossal gods of shame could cow men and yet crash,
Of what huge devils hid the stars, yet fell at a pistol flash.
   —G. K. Chesterton, *To Edmund Clerihew Bentley*

One of the Spetsnaz commandos had taken an end of static rope down the lee face of the Parrot glacier slope in a controlled *glissade*, using the butt end of his ice-axe as a rudder while he slid down the convex snow surface. When he reached the house-sized chunks of tumbled ice at the glacier's next broad step, fifty yards below, he plowed to a halt and began climbing over the broken serac toward the east, away from the supposed Ark site, while the men up at the top of the slope slowly fed out more rope and the slope between them grew steeper. Hale estimated that the Spetsnaz paid out thirty feet more of the rope. At last the man below waved, indicating that he had found a good place from which to proceed, and the Spetsnaz at the crest walked to a point over him and hammered pitons into the ice for mooring two descending static lines.

Two of the Spetsnaz immediately crouched and lashed themselves to the ropes somehow, and then hopped backward and began descending the ice slope in long, descending bounds.

Mammalian and Philby and Hale were to descend separately. Hale was to go first, and one of the Russian commandos knelt down in the snow with Hale and tied a yard-long looped cord to Hale's harness carabiner and then tied the free end to the descending rope in a fist-like Prusik knot; and he made Hale practice yanking on the knot and then flicking it upward, to show Hale that the knot would slide down the rope if it was loose but would grip the rope tightly if weight were put on it.

The man gestured down the slope. The wind from the peak was flinging spirals of dry snow against them with increasing force, and it was easy for Hale to lift the cord and slide back and down. His legs slid out from under him in the snow and the cord tightened as he fell to his knees, but a moment later he had got his spiked boots under himself and had done it again, descending a good three yards and landing upright and balanced.

The glacier grew steeper as he progressed downward, and when he was halfway to the bottom, he felt a thrumming in the rope. He looked up and saw that one of the Spetsnaz was leaping and sliding down above him, and Hale began to spring farther out from the ice slope with each jump and to let more of the rope buzz through the Prusik knot before reaching out with his toes to slow down and put weight on it.

At last he was hanging with his boot-spikes dangling a yard above a patch of snow between two truck-sized ice-boulders. One of the Russian commandos standing below him took hold of his boots and pushed him upward, and Hale used the slack to slip the loop of cord right out of his carabiner; then he waved, and when the man let go of his boots Hale dropped and sat down, jamming the barrel of his slung machine gun into the snow.

He got up and stepped away from the rope, trying to peer through his ice-clotted snow-goggles. From the shadows on the west side, another of the Spetsnaz reached out and caught Hale's hand and drew him along the narrow, back-slanting ledge to a sheltered hollow under an ice cornice. Hale swiped a mitten across his goggle lenses.

The close landscape was all enormous surfaces of black stone and white ice tumbled together at slanting angles, with the wind whistling through it all as if the whole mountain were rushing up into space; there was no ground, and Hale was belatedly nauseated at the thought of having unsnapped himself from the rope to drop the last yard. The empty vault of gray northern sky in front of him was somehow obviously a high-altitude view, and he held on to the carabiner at the front of his harness, automatically blinking around for something to snap it onto.

The Spetsnaz who had led him into the shelter now tugged him farther along the ledge; and mercifully it widened out as it slanted to the left, and after a few scuffing steps for which he had to brace himself with his hands against the stone walls, Hale stepped forward past the Russian and hopped down onto the flat ice of a long frozen lake, its surface littered with gravel and chunks of ice like bomb-shattered concrete. The steep mountain shoulder stood up from the ice-lake fifty yards in front of him, with the Parrot glacier blocking the sky ahead of him and to his left; twenty or thirty feet behind him was the margin of the lake and then the infinite void.

He let his gaze rise from the ice-flat to the cliffs that were the body of the mountain, fifty yards away—and then through the veils of snow he saw the black wooden structure that loomed out from the glacier and shadowed that side of the frozen lake, and the only thing that kept him from falling to his knees was the recollection that this was not in fact Noah's Ark.

The thing was huge, probably six stories tall, and rectangular—more like a long building imbedded in the ice than like any kind of ship. It hung above him out there, viewed almost end-on, and he could see that the underside was flat; the roof, which extended out past the high walls, was nearly flat, with a low peak at the center. The blacker squares of windows fretted the top edge, and a rickety wooden staircase, clearly of newer origin, had been erected across the flat front face and down to the ice.

Snow whirled in dust-devil arabesques across the lifeless ice of the lake below the thing, and in the atonal whistle of the dry wind Hale was sure he heard familiar chords, as if the mountain were a vast Aeolian harp, wringing music from currents that came down raw from the stars. Under it all throbbed an alliance of subsonic tones that resonated unpleasantly in the tiny pulsing focus of Hale's ribs and made connected thought difficult.

Derringer, he told himself as he stumbled out across the ice; then, in terrified derision and self-contempt, *Derringer? I'd do them more harm throwing it at them.*

His balance was going—he had to keep glancing at the surface under his boots to assure himself that he was still vertical—and he sat down hard on the ice, resolved at least not to kneel. He clutched the drogue stone that hung in front of him, glad of the cross cut in its face.

From over the shoulder of the mountain, on the side by the Abich I glacier, he heard booming and cracking; and then the earthbound thunder sounded to his right, and he saw that it was the noise of avalanches, galleries and valleys of snow moving down from the heights and separating into fragments, then tumbling and exploding into jagged bursts of white against the remote gray sky before they disappeared below his view.

The cracks and thunders made syllables in the depleted air, but they didn't seem to be in Arabic. Hale guessed that they were of a language much older, the uncompromised speech of mountain conversing with mountain and lightning and cloud, seeming random only to creatures like himself whose withered verbs and nouns had grown apart from the things they described.

The music was nearly inaudible to Hale's physical eardrums, but in his spine he could feel that it was mounting toward some sustained note for which *tragedy* or *grandeur* would be nearly appropriate words.

Silently in the vault far overhead the clouds broke, and tall columns of glowing, whirling snow-dust stood now around the black vessel, motionless; Hale reflected that it must be noon, for the shining columns were vertical. The mountain and the lake and the very air were suddenly darker in comparison.

The columns of light were alive, the fields of their attentions palpably sweeping across the ice and the glacier face and the mountain, momentarily clarifying into sharp focus anything they touched; for just a moment Hale could see with hallucinatory clarity the woven cuffs of his sleeves.

Angels, Hale thought, looking away in shuddering awe. These beings on this mountain are older than the world, and once looked God in the face.

Which they will never do again, he told himself, and which I may, God willing. Against this spectacle he mentally held up his remembered view of Sainte-Chapelle in Paris, especially as he had seen it in a dream, in which the cathedral had been the prow of a ship laboring through a black ocean.

He rocked forward on the gravel-strewn surface, and by pushing downward with his hands he was able to stand up, shakily.

He looked back toward the gap he had climbed out through, and saw two unsteady figures step down onto the ice—one had a snow-whitened beard, and he knew they were Mammalian and Philby.

A new, louder note grew out of the mountain's resonance, and resolved itself, incongruously, into the whine of a turbine engine. The sound was droning from the void behind him, and Hale rocked around to look northwest—and he was disoriented to see the nose and glittering edge-on rotor disk of a helicopter hanging out there in the sky. It was growing in apparent size, clearly speeding toward the Rabkrin position.

Even as he watched, two spots of fluttering white glare appeared below the onrushing cabin; but only a moment later the craft was climbing and banking to the east, and the machine-gun slugs blew a vertical series of bursts of white spray from the glacier face and then expended themselves away among the higher ravines as the helicopter, its guns still chattering in the thin air, disappeared with a roar over the mountain shoulder.

It had been one of the new French Aerospatiale Alouettes, and before it disappeared Hale had seen the *fasces* tubes of rocket launchers slung under the fuselage.

Why hadn't they fired the rockets?

Probably they would on their next pass.

In her earphones the pilot was angrily demanding an explanation for Elena's abrupt order to veer east.

She ignored him and clung to a stanchion on the port bulkhead, staring through eyes blinded with tears at the two accusing red lights on the armament control panel.

She had switched on the machine guns as the aircraft had climbed up for a sweep, and her finger had been poised over the button that would have sent a volley of rockets into the grotto where the obscene black structure protruded from the glacier and the tiny figures of the men were so conveniently clustered; but one lone figure had been out on the frozen lake, struggling to its feet—and she had somehow recognized the posture.

It had been Andrew Hale, and in another moment the shattering tracks of the machine-gun patterns would have stitched right over him.

Into her head had flashed an image of his bloody hand outside the garret window in Paris, when the Gestapo had been within seconds of breaking down the door, and she had heard again his voice in Berlin saying, *I will not say good-bye ever.*

And reflexively she had ordered the pilot to veer hard east. The move had required that they climb steeply, and in a moment the aircraft had flown right up over the glacier. But she believed the tracks of the bullets had missed Andrew Hale.

Out the starboard window she watched the clouds keep wheeling past—clearly the pilot was coming around for another pass.

And she remembered that the pilot too had an armament control panel on his instrument board.

Mammalian was shouting, but his voice barely reached Hale. "The angels must think the helicopter was ours! Approach them, quickly!"

Philby, propelled by a push from Mammalian, was lurching blindly out across the ice toward Hale. And Hale could feel the man's approach in his mind, could feel the agitation of Philby's fears and jangled memories aligning themselves with his own to form some bigger, other mind.

Father, where are you? I'm your son—we're your sons, we're your son—

The inhuman music of the sky seemed to respond, and the dust-devils of snow were dancing over the ice. The smell of metallic oil on the icy air was exotic, exciting.

I will not have this, Hale made himself think. I will not be the restored half of Kim Philby. God help me. Hale bit the mitten off of his right hand and thrust his hand into the deep pocket of his parka.

Behind him sounded the abrupt ripping roar of full-automatic gunfire. Hale spun on the ice, crouching and blinking through the frosted lenses of his goggles—but the gunfire was not aimed out toward himself and Philby. Mammalian was shooting at the Spetsnaz commandos.

Hale choked out an involuntary whimper as he turned back to face the Black Ark on the far side of the ice.

And it wasn't a black wooden structure overhanging the ice now. The stone flank of the mountains was soaring obsidian arches and columns, and the ice cornices against the sky were gone, replaced by minarets shining in the sun, and the clouds were higher terraces and balconies of milky crystal, mounting away to the zenith. The towers of light stood in parallel out on the broad ice-paved square, each one wide as a house and taller than the mountain's peak, and the crescendo of their inorganic singing was shaking clouds of snow from the high glacier crest and calling up answering verses in the mind that was Hale and Philby.

A cold white light was shining out of the high windows of the black structure, *flowing* out of it, to join the columns of living sunlight.

Hale felt his mouth drop open, and he could feel Philby's mouth opening in the same moment, though Philby was twenty feet behind him; and now the welcoming towers of light had overlapped and entwined to become a figure whose brightness was nearly intolerable to human retinas—in the corona of glare, Hale could make out molten golden shoulders, a chest as deep as the Ahora Gorge, a vast face shining with challenge—

Hale felt Philby's knees buckle, and so Hale was kneeling too, helplessly, his kneecaps thudding against the pebbled ice. The golden angel was tall, leaning down over them because it would crack the sky if it stood up to its full height—

If he had not withstood the stressful attention of djinn many times before, Hale's identity would simply have imploded under the psychic weight, dimly grateful for the escape into oblivion; as it was, he was able to hold on to his diminished self, but the urge to surrender to this nearly divine being, this higher order, was overwhelming. To oppose his will to this force would simply be to shatter his will, shatter his very reason. *I will give in to it* was his concussed thought; *live in the kingdoms in the clouds, learn their secrets, share their power over men—*

But his mouth was suddenly sour with the taste of the imaginary bread he had eaten with the king of Wabar in 1948, and with the taste of the dish he had refused then but had helplessly shared with the djinn in the Ahora Gorge three months later—

—blood and khaki, the SAS men he had led up to their deaths—

Hale's identity recoiled from the memory, and for one teetering moment his self was his own. He hastily made the sign of the cross, clanking the derringer barrel against his snow-goggles as he shouted, "In the name of the Father!" out into air that was incapable now of carrying any merely human voice—and then he pointed the blunt little steel barrel up at the angel—

And he pulled the trigger.

Even as he did it, his mind screamed in protesting grief and loss. *What you might have had—!*

In slow motion his fist moved up with the recoil, and a churning smear of fire hung in the air. He thought he heard a groaning wail from far behind him—it might have been Mammalian's voice, Dopplered down to a bass register.

Slow as a flight of arrows the shot pattern was spreading out as it rushed up into the sky, its pattern rotating to the right as it expanded. The light of the towering figure became the enormous flare of an explosion, but Hale levered back the hammer of the little gun and fired the second shell. Again the shot sped visibly through the billowing air, like an expanding wheel turning.

Then with a shearing scream the hot shock-wave punched him over backward, and he was sliding north, skating on the barrel of his slung Kalashnikov, toward the edge of the abyss. He was lying on his back, and he spasmodically arched his body to press his weight down onto the crampons laced to his boots. The grating of the points in the ice vibrated in his shinbones, and in seconds he had bumped to a halt against someone's legs.

The air was agonizingly shrill with the prolonged whistling scream. Hale's ribs and legs were being hammered with stony missiles, and his exposed face stung with abrading sand; the lenses of his goggles had been cracked into star-patterns by the blast, and he clawed them off before these ferocious gusts could punch the glass wedges into his eyes.

He rolled over to protect his face from the flying debris—perhaps an avalanche had crashed down into the grotto, though he couldn't see why it should *keep on* bursting this way—and his hand closed on the upright head of an ice-axe imbedded in the ice. Philby had arrested his own slide, and possibly Hale's too, by unslinging the axe and driving its point into the surface of the frozen lake.

Balls were rolling and clicking around on the ice by Hale's hand, and he picked up a golf-ball-sized one and squinted at it in the dimmed daylight—the thing was made of ice and egg-shaped. It was the shape of djinn death.

Hale hunched around under the battering rain of ice, and saw that Philby's face was bloody—one of the flying hailstones had apparently struck him. Hale grabbed the carabiner at Philby's belt and began tugging him back toward the tumbled stones at the east edge of the lake. But Philby was clinging to the shaft of the ice-axe, and Hale had to get up onto his knees in the shotgun wind and throw his weight onto the shaft to rock it loose from the ice; and when Philby's anchor had tumbled flat to the ice, unmoored now, Philby turned his goggles toward Hale and then appeared to comprehend Hale's gestures.

The two of them began crawling back across the ice. Hale was grateful for the flat surface, because his balance was gone—from moment to moment he felt that the frozen lake was tilting out over the void, or folding in the middle to spill him down into the black abyss where Death still waited for him, but he forced himself to judge his position only by what he could see between his hands below his face, and he could see that he was not sliding across the ice surface. The razory whistling seemed to be the shrieks of predatory birds.

Tears were freezing on his face, and he had to keep rocking around to look over his shoulder, to be sure Philby was still crawling along behind him through the rain of ice and gravel.

In heavy gusts Hale did have to pause and brush aside the tumbling eggs to see the surface of the ice under him; after one burst that nearly knocked him over onto his side, Hale saw that some of the skittering balls were marbled red-and-yellow, and broke in red smears across the ice when he brushed them aside, and he knew that the body of at least one of the Rabkrin party had shared in the expression of djinn death.

At last Hale climbed up over the tumbled ice chunks at the eastern end of the lake, and when he had pulled Philby through the narrow gap onto the slanted ledge, they were protected from most of the grapeshot barrage of ice. Hale banged the barrel of his Kalashnikov against the rock and shook snow and ice out of the muzzle.

The air was still shaking with a shrill infinity of whistling and crashing, and Hale had to lean down and shout into Philby's face: *"Back to the ropes!"*

Philby's eyes were invisible behind the snow-goggles and his face was a mask of frozen blood, but he nodded.

A flash of white glare threw Hale's shadow across the slanted ice ahead of them, and an instant later the mountain shook under his knees and a whiplash of stone fragments abraded the exposed surfaces. Hale's eyes were stung, and he fell back against the bulk of Philby, and in his mind he was again curled up in a London gutter in 1944 when a V-2 rocket had struck nearby.

The helicopter must have come back for a second sweep, and fired the rockets this time.

Calling on the last reserves of his strength now, Hale straightened up and tugged Philby up onto his hands and knees and then dragged the man along the ledge toward where the static ropes hung. Hale's eyes were watering and burning, and he peered forward with his eyelids nearly shut.

The ledge narrowed and the wind from behind was a fluttering air-flow pressure between Hale and the rock wall he was trying to hug, and he had to let go of Philby's collar and hope the man would crawl along behind him. At last Hale scuffed around the last outcrop on his right and saw one of the swaying ropes ahead.

Two of the Spetsnaz commandos were crouched against the wind on the ledge by the rope, holding their Kalashnikovs across their knees, and at the sight of Hale one of them straightened up and began firing from the hip.

The shock-wave of the shots thudded in Hale's ears and he saw stone fragments bursting from the rock wall to his right—and in the old Bedu reflex he yanked up the barrel of his own gun and squeezed the trigger.

His burst blew the front of the man's parka into a haze of flying kapok shreds, and Hale immediately edged the vibrating barrel over to cover the second man, who spun away in another cloud of white lint. Both bodies tumbled out away from the rock wall and disappeared below, toward God-knew-what glacier or moraine. The gun had stopped jumping in his hands, the magazine emptied, and he uncramped his finger from the trigger. Ejected brass shell-casings rolled on the ledge.

Apparently some recognition signal had been required, and Hale had not given it.

Hale looked back. Philby had managed to unsling his own white Kalashnikov, and he had it pointed at Hale's back; but as Hale watched, he lowered it and then pulled the sling over his head, with the white rifle barrel poking up over his left shoulder. He spread his hands.

Hale nodded and then sidled over to the ledge below the rope. Both ropes were still there, but one of them had been blown up by the wind and was now looped over a stone spur twenty feet overhead and to the left; the end of the other one swayed at the level of Hale's eyes. He gripped the end with both hands and tugged, but he knew he didn't have the strength to pull himself up hand over hand.

He squinted at the bumpy stone wall, trying to look for hand and footholds and to ignore the lines of red drops, which had already frozen over; and at last, not roped to anything, he fitted his left foot into a crack in the rock face and then kicked himself up to grip an outcrop with his left hand. He scuffed his right foot against the stone, trying to find a purchase for the front point of his crampons, and then he felt Philby take hold of his calf and lift his foot to a solid projection. Hale straightened his right leg, and now he was high enough to reach out with his right hand and catch the rope.

His Prusik knot—or somebody's—still hung on the rope, down at the level of his thigh; he hiked his hand down the length of the rope until he was able to grab the knotted cord, and he was careful to slide it back up the rope gently, so that it would not tighten. The icy wind battered against his face and his unprotected eyes. When he had worked the knotted cord up to a point level with the carabiner at the front of his harness, he pulled the rope in and with numbed fingers held it against the snap-link while he thumbed open the spring-loaded gate.

After a full minute of fumbling and cursing into the wind and trying to blink past the ice that was frozen onto his eyelashes, while the fingers of his numbed left hand cramped and stung as they gripped the rock outcrop behind him, he got the loop of the Prusik knot into the carabiner link, and then he let his weight sag against the rope, bracing himself on the rock wall with his crampons and letting his aching arms hang.

"D-damn you!" shouted Philby from below him. "What about m-m-me?"

"I'll free the other rope," called Hale. "Don't shoot me." Hale flapped his arms and flexed his constricted fingers, then began climbing up toward the point from which he would be able to reach the snagged rope; he quickly caught the trick of leaning forward to give the Prusik knot slack when he wanted to pull himself up and then leaning away from the rock when he wanted it to belay him.

When he had grabbed the other rope, he pulled the whole length of it across to him, coiling it loosely over his lap, and he saw that several of the Prusik-knotted cords were hung along the last yard of it; but before he let it all drop down to where Philby waited, he unsnapped the front of his parka to reach into an inner pocket. Very carefully he pulled out a box of .410 shot shells, and he gripped the brass of two of them between his teeth and pulled them out as he closed the box and tucked it away; then he reached into the outer pocket and drew the derringer.

He pushed the button behind the exposed trigger and swiveled the locking lever around in a half-circle and swung the hinged barrels up away from the frame. He pushed up the extractor and lifted the spent shells out of the barrels, then took the fresh shells from between his teeth and fitted them into the barrels. At last he closed the gun and locked it and replaced it in his pocket, along with the two spent shells.

"Here!" he yelled, letting the rope spill off his legs to hang slack down the rock face a yard to his left. He peered down past his legs at Philby's upturned face.

"Is it long enough?" shouted Hale.

"Yes!" came Philby's call from below.

Thank God. Hale had not wanted to try cutting and splicing it. "Fit the bight of a knot into your snap-link!"

"Aye aye," shouted Philby.

Within ten minutes they were both sitting cross-legged, panting, on the wind-swept crest of the Parrot glacier. They had pulled up one of the ropes and freed it from its piton, and now it lay coiled beside Hale. It was an unwieldy pile. He had unslung his Kalashnikov and fitted a fresh magazine into the receiver in case the helicopter might reappear, but the racing wind had not abated since he had shot the djinn by the Black Ark, and he didn't think the aircraft would dare approach the mountain now.

Philby swung his frosted, blood-blackened face toward Hale, and his eyes were invisible behind the sky glare on the goggle lenses. "Shoot the other rope," he said, loudly to be heard over the wind.

Hale thought of Hakob Mammalian, conceivably still alive down there on the northern face, making his wounded way to the ledge and finding both the static lines gone. "No," he called back to Philby, wearily standing up and slinging his gun. He bent down to pick up the coil of rope, then straightened with it and began plodding up the crest, toward the windward side of the glacier. "Come on, the sun's past noon."

From behind him he heard Philby say, "D-damn you! Then I'll d-do it."

Hale spun clumsily around, his crampons grating on the ice as he dropped the coiled rope, and Philby was standing, and had already unslung his own Kalashnikov and was lifting it to his shoulder.

The derringer felt extraordinarily heavy in Hale's right hand as he drew it and raised it to point it at Philby's back, and cocking the hammer against its tight spring seemed to take all of his remaining strength.

Am I my brother's keeper?

Philby was aiming, and had not fired yet.

Hale touched the derringer's trigger with his forefinger, and the little gun flared and hammered back hard into his palm.

Then his knees hit the snow, and Hale was simply too exhausted to try to re-cock the derringer or raise the barrel of his machine gun.

Through watering eyes he peered past the retinal glare at the silhouette of Philby.

The man had fallen to one knee, and his head was down, and he was making a noise, a flat monotone wail. *The voice of thy brother's blood crieth unto me from the ground,* thought Hale, fearful that he might have been standing too close to him. How wide would the shot pattern have spread in twelve feet?

"Are you dying?" Hale croaked. He blinked around at the infinity of snow. He could melt some between his palms. "I can baptize you."

Then with a shout of pain Philby had straightened up and turned, and Hale saw that the muzzle of Philby's Kalashnikov, though wobbling, was pointed straight at him.

"*If,*" grated Philby, "I t-try again to shoot the r-rope, will you—" He inhaled with a near shriek. "Will you sh-shoot me, again?"

Hale stared through a red haze of exhaustion into the ring of the wavering muzzle. He took a deep breath, wondering if Elena might have been aboard the French helicopter. "Yes," he said.

Philby's answering howl was lost in the battering roar of the machine gun, but Hale could see that the muzzle flare was slanted away to the left side of him; and after three deafening seconds the gun stuttered to a ringing halt, its thirty-round magazine emptied.

Then Philby was on his knees in front of Hale, shaking him weakly by the shoulders, and the mouth opened in the frosted black face and Philby was screaming, "I would n-not shoot my own f-family!" The wind was strengthening, flinging clouds of obscuring snow over them and down the slope behind them. Philby fell back, his hands clasped across his chest in evident pain. "C-can we!" he said loudly. "Get down off th-this, to the Cehennem Dere?"

Hale nodded. He recalled that the Spetsnaz had left the piton in the edge of this glacier, between the cornices over the level where the tents had been. He would find the little iron ring, if he had to crawl the whole length of the glacier edge.

The south sides of the tents were nearly buried in fresh snowdrifts, and Hale and Philby had blundered a dozen yards past them in the flying white haze before Hale happened to look back and see the rectangular shapes. He waved to catch Philby's attention, and pointed back.

Philby had to walk stiffly around in a circle to look back; and then he didn't nod, but waved his left hand weakly, and began trudging heavily in that direction, leaning into the snowy wind.

Hale tugged his machine gun forward, into the Bedu position—God knew what the response of the two Turks would be to the return of only two of the thirteen men who had gone up the mountain. Ahead of him, Philby laboriously unslung his own machine gun and limped forward carrying it.

Hale peered through nearly blinded eyes at Philby's back; he thought he could see a couple of the tiny pin-holes where the birdshot had penetrated, but of course there was no blood visible on this outermost layer of clothing.

"Fuad!" roared Philby as he stepped up to the tent entrance. "Umit! Open up in the n-name of the KGB!"

The wall of the tent fluttered, and then snow was being punched away from the tent entrance from the inside; at last Hale saw yellow lamplight through a vertical slit between rubberized canvas flaps, and a gun muzzle pointed out.

"You m-mad sod," shouted Philby, "p-put that down. Who d-do you sup-suppose it is out h-here that knows your n-names?"

Enough snow had been shoved away so that the flap could be pulled open, and Philby was a shaggy silhouette against the lamplight as he blundered inside. Hale pulled his numb feet quickly through the snowdrifts to enter right behind him.

The still air of the tent burned on Hale's face as he let himself collapse into a sitting position. One of the Turks was at the tent opening, but the other seemed to be closer. Philby fell heavily to his knees and demanded the bottle of arak, and Hale rocked his head in an emphatic nod. Philby had brought his flasks with him onto the mountain, but of course there was the risk that the liquor in them might by now be far below the freezing temperature of water, though still liquid, so that one mouthful would freeze teeth and tongue and throat.

Through his watering, ice-crusted eyes Hale could see only blurry silhouettes and a yellow glow that was the paraffin lamp, but he could make out the shape of one of the Turks standing over him.

"Where are the others?" the Turk asked, his voice ringing in Hale's ears.

"C-close the tent," rasped Philby. "Where's the arak? The others are all d-dead."

"Dead!" said the Turk, and his suspicious tone made Hale sure that it was Fuad. "Did you kill them?"

"Of course, F-F-Fuad, t-two middle-aged Englishmen k-killed ten spit-spit—fucking—Spetsnaz. The elite so-so-Soviet *commandos*. You fool."

Hale could blurrily see the bottle in Philby's hand—it appeared to have been uncorked, but Philby was simply holding it.

Hale bit off the mitten and liner glove from his right hand, and then reached out clumsily. "Infirm of purpose," he said hoarsely, "give me the liquor."

Philby tipped the bottle up to his lips first, and Hale heard gurgling; then the bottle was in Hale's hand, and he lifted it and swallowed several mouthfuls of the warm, stinging, licorice liquor.

"A F-French helicopter," said Philby, exhaling, "strafed us, f-fired explosive rah-rah-rockets." Hale could feel his gaze, and then Philby added, "I c-caught some shrapnel, in my b-back. I'll w-want medical attention."

"I'm sure they'll be ready to treat injuries," said Hale, "at the air base in Erivan." You're crossing the border, remember, Hale thought— you're defecting now, not going back to Beirut. "You've got a flare pistol?"

"In the back!" sneered Fuad. "You did not run as fast as the shrapnel, quite, eh?"

Philby was silent for several seconds, and when he spoke it was to answer Hale. "There's a f-flare piss-piss-*pistol* in the tent, y-yes." Hale heard him shift, and then the bottle was taken out of Hale's hand. "You w-wouldn't care to—c-come along? Hero's w-welcome."

"In the Workers' Paradise," said Hale. The ice was melting off of his eyelids, and he was blinking around to assure himself that he could still see. "No, thank you. I was hired help for this enterprise. This failed enterprise."

"We c-can't fire the fluh-flare yet," said Philby. "Snowstorm. W-wait until they can s-s-see it."

"I need a pair of snow-goggles," Hale said.

"The helicopter w-will l-land right here," said Philby. "Twenty p-paces from the t-tent."

"And I'll be gone by then," said Hale. "If I was to go to Erivan with you, I might not ever get back across. And if I wait here, the Soviet agents might not care to let me just walk away. Which," he added, "I am going to do as soon as I've rested here. Oh, and I'll want the key to one of the trucks."

"No spare goggles," said Fuad with satisfaction.

Philby had pulled back his furred hood and tugged his goggles down below his chin; the top half of his face seemed bone-white in contrast to his blackened mouth and jaw. Now he reached up with both hands and pulled the snow-goggles off over the top of his head; and there was wry humor in his pouchy exhausted eyes as he held the goggles out toward Hale.

"I won't need them," he said. "Umit—give him the keys to the Dodge."

Hale saw Fuad open his mouth to object, then shrug.

Umit crouched by a tin box on the rubber floor and opened it, and when Fuad nodded he tossed a ring to Hale.

"A waste," said Fuad. "You will surely die before you reach the truck, if you leave now." His glittering eyes fixed on Hale. "A waste of the truck key, I meant."

Hale groped for the key, and when he had closed his stinging fingers on it, he carefully dropped it into the pocket with the derringer.

"Let's put it to the test," he said.

Philby was smiling sourly at him. "They'll k-kill you, you know," he said softly. "Don't l-look for g-gratitude."

Fuad and Umit would suppose he referred to the KGB, or the GRU; but Hale knew he meant the SIS, the secret SOE—he meant Jimmie Theodora.

"That had occurred to me," Hale said. He fitted the snow-goggles over his eyes and the bridge of his nose and began pulling his gloves back on. "I suppose we won't meet again," he said to Philby.

"In this world or the next," Philby agreed. "I can't say I'm sorry."

"Certainly not."

Hale struggled to his feet and pulled the parka hood forward over his head. He reached for the white Kalashnikov, but Fuad was suddenly pointing a revolver at him.

"The machine gun stays here," said Fuad. "Do you think I would hesitate killing you?"

"I th-think he would n-*not* hesitate," said Philby thoughtfully. "Do p-put it to the t-test, if you like."

After a moment Hale straightened, his hand still empty. "Fair enough," he said.

He shambled to the tent opening and climbed through, over the mounded snow that still half-blocked it. The wind outside instantly leached out of him all the scanty warmth he had absorbed in the tent, and it was all he could do not to shout with the shock of it.

His course was easy—downhill. The climb back down to the Ahora Gorge would be over broken serac, and should be easy enough if he took it slowly. After that would be just the long walk back down the gorge path, on the other side of the gorge from the path down which he had driven a jeep in reverse in 1948; but this time he would be leaving behind him avenged ghosts.

The snowstorm had faltered to a silent halt before he was out of the gorge, and the wind had shifted around to the north by the time he stumbled up through knee-high green grass to the three trucks on the plain; and when he had climbed into the cab of the Dodge truck and started the engine, he simply sat in the cab with the motor running and the heater blowing hot air at him. After a while he unsnapped his parka and contorted on the seat to pull the heavy garment off, but he did not rouse himself to clank the gear-shift into reverse until he saw, faintly over the high white shoulder of the mountain, the luminous chalk-line of the flare against the gray sky.

The Soviet helicopter would be rushing overhead within minutes. Hale backed the truck around, then shifted into first gear and began steering the truck along a shepherds' track that stretched away to the east, away from the mountain and Dogubayezit and all of civilization. The Soviet border lay twenty miles ahead, but he did not intend to drive quite that far.

▼ ▼ ▼

The red sun was hovering over the distant peak of Ararat in his rear-view mirrors when Hale regretfully abandoned the truck in a snowdrift halfway up one of the narrow horse-cart tracks; he got back into his damp parka, climbed down from the heated cab, and proceeded up the steep track on foot, hoping to find the shelter he sought before dark. And though the sun had set by the time he reached the village in the Zagros Mountains, the gray sky was still bright enough for him to recognize the two-story stone house on the narrow main street, and his nostrils flared at the remembered smells of mutton and hot coffee on the icy wind.

Exhaustion robbed his vision of depth, and he stumbled on the cobblestones; but he didn't fall until he had at last reached the very gate.

He might actually have lost consciousness for a few moments; when he opened his eyes he was lying on his back on the stones, and a white-bearded man in baggy blue woolen trousers and a quilted felt vest was staring down at him. The old man hadn't unslung the rifle that rode on his back, but one brown hand was on the stock.

"Howkar Zeid," said Hale hoarsely. In English he added, "How are you?"

"It is Hale Beg!" said the old man wonderingly in the same language. He took his hand from the rifle and crouched to slide one arm under Hale's shoulders, and then he had effortlessly straightened up, hauling Hale back up onto his feet. "How are you? Where have you come from? How are your children?"

Hale knew that the questions were unthinking formalities, but he said, "I am—tired to death. I've come from—Hell, I think. My family is all lost. All lost." He sighed, though the effort of it nearly cost him his consciousness again. "Siamand Khan said I might come back." It had been nearly fifteen years ago, but Hale had at last fulfilled the Khan's request. "I'm early," Hale added. "He said to come back in the spring."

Howkar Zeid led Hale through the remembered shadowy hallway to the same broad whitewashed stone room in which Hale had dined with the Khan so long ago. Red and purple rugs shone in the yellow paraffin lamplight, and Hale sat down heavily to unsnap his soggy boots and tug them off before he stood up again and stepped across the dirt-floor threshold.

Siamand Khan was dressed in the same sort of trousers and vest as Howkar Zeid this evening. Hale remembered him as he had looked fifteen years ago, in a Western business suit and an orange scarf around his neck instead of a tie; but Siamand Khan still wore the knitted cap, and his stride was still graceful as he stood up from the long bench that spanned the far wall, and his brown face behind the white moustache was as ferociously cheerful as ever.

"My friend, sit!" he said, taking Hale by the hand and leading him to the middle section of the bench, on which lay so many cushions that Hale was able to rest his arms on them when he had sat down. To Howkar Zeid, the Khan called, "Coffee and cigarettes for our guest! A dish of pears from the cellar!"

Hale's vision was flickering. "I have just come down from Agri Dag," he said, his voice just a rasping whisper now. "The angels are killed. The *amomon* will bloom this spring. If I could—eat, and sleep here tonight—"

"You are nearly used up, my friend," said the Khan gently. "You will stay with us until your strength returns—indeed you will stay until spring. You and I will be able to go hiking in the mountains after all."

Hale had to keep focusing his eyes to remember where he had come to. When his vision blurred, he seemed again to be dozing over his one-time pads in the janitor's room on the roof of the house in the Rue le Regrattier, dimly aware that there was an emergency and that he should hurry down the stairs to Elena's room and awaken her; and he imagined that Jimmie Theodora, black-haired and somehow younger than Hale now, was giving him instructions he should be paying attention to, in the office in Whitehall Court with the candlestick telephones on the wall and the models of airplanes and submarines serving as bookends in the cluttered shelves on the wall; and finally the murmur of the Khan's words blurred away into the remembered voices of his grandfather and his mother, quarreling about some troubling passage in Scripture, and—in the moments before consciousness left him—he was weakly resolved to climb the narrow old stairs of the house in Chipping Campden and crawl into the old eighteenth-century box bed, and abandon himself at long last to dreamless sleep.

▼

Declare

▼

Moscow, 1964

Kim stole out and away, as unremarkable a figure as ever carried his own and a few score thousand other folks' fate slung round his neck.
—Rudyard Kipling, *Kim*

Ah, Love! could thou and I with Fate conspire
To grasp this sorry Scheme of Things entire,
Would not we shatter it to bits—and then
Re-mould it nearer to the Heart's Desire!
—Omar Khayyám, *The Rubáiyát*, Edward J. FitzGerald translation

Batsford House in Tunbridge Wells had been one of the English country homes that had been turned over to the SOE during the war, and the sweeping green lawn visible from the south kitchen window still showed the humps of bunkers and trenches that had been dug for infiltration practice and to keep German aircraft from landing. A dozen cows were visible in the middle distance now, cropping the grass around the old mounds. The morning sun was shining in brightly enough to show too the heating and water pipes that the SOE had installed along the high stone wall and ceiling, above even the unreachable topmost row of copper skillets, but the old man was grateful for those alterations. Somehow the mess officers had hung too a vast government-issue print of a cow in profile, with dotted lines outlining the various cuts of beef, right up under the ceiling, and no one had ever managed to take it down in the more than twenty years since.

The vaulted eighteenth-century ceiling arched thirty feet above the flagstone floor, and as he struck a match on the windowsill and puffed his pipe alight, Jimmie Theodora recalled several conferences that had been held right in this kitchen, at the battered old table that stretched across more than twenty feet of the space between the window and the huge fireplace. In January of 1944, when the south lawn had been a small village of snow-covered tents, Winston Churchill had met here with Theodora and Bertram Ramsey and Arthur Tedder to privately assess Eisenhower's proposed SHAEF, the Supreme Headquarters Allied Expeditionary Force that was to be run by the Americans, and to discuss the most-secret details of Operation Overlord, which in June of the next year had been decisively put into effect as the Normandy invasion. And before that, twenty-year-old Andrew Hale had interviewed Turkish and Russian fugitives at this table, gradually assembling the history of the Russian involvement with eastern Turkey and Mount Ararat. Twenty years later, Operation Declare had finally been consummated and closed, and Theodora had at last been able to retire—at the age of seventy-three!—to tend the gardens here at his old ancestral home.

And now his retirement had been compromised. A cable from the SIS's new headquarters in Century House on the south side of the Thames—Broadway Buildings no longer!—had arrived yesterday, and it appeared that MI5 was involved as well. It all promised no end of bother and embarrassment, and even some faint risk of legal trouble; and personal, face-to-face humiliation, if some hasty sort of establishment-of-truth couldn't be arranged quickly in Helsinki.

In the forty-eight hours since receiving the cable Theodora had not tried to mobilize the old leave-behind networks to arrange it—not, he realized now, because of any admittedly valid doubts about the viability these days of the networks, but because he felt he *deserved* some degree of humiliation, even of punishment.

Andrew Hale had apparently walked into the British Embassy in Helsinki two days ago. He had dictated a cable to Century House, proposing terms according to which he would take a flight to Heathrow Airport outside London. More than a year after the successful termination of Operation Declare, Hale wanted to return to the United Kingdom.

On reflection, Theodora was not surprised to learn that Hale was still alive. In July of last year the Soviet paper *Izvestia* had announced that Kim Philby had been made a citizen of the Soviet Union, but

Theodora knew too that Philby had been rushed to the Semenskoya clinic outside Moscow on the twenty-eighth of January, for treatment of a gunshot wound. That would have been Hale's work, as ordered. And Hale's had not been one of the burned, frozen bodies that had been recovered from below the Parrot glacier by the Turks last summer. That Hale could have disappeared for a year in the Middle East was hardly a surprising idea. Nor was Theodora surprised to learn that Hale wanted to come home, now, at the age of forty-two; he remembered that in the briefing at Number 10 Downing Street, fifteen months ago now, Hale had proposed retiring after Declare to the Cotswold village where he had grown up.

Hale was approaching the British secret services cautiously. Clearly he knew that he had been slated for verification as soon as the djinn had been slain on Mount Ararat.

It had certainly been obvious to Theodora that Hale could not go on being in the picture afterward. Theodora recalled his late-1962 conversation with the leveraged minister who gingerly sponsored the fugitive SOE, after the minister had objected to the idea of killing Hale: *Think about it, man!* Theodora had said. *By agreeing to have Hale send Philby to Moscow with a skin-full of Shihab-shot, the Prime Minister is authorizing a pre-emptive strike against the Soviet Union! That's what it is, if our math is correct. Nobody's indoctrinated for this. We may have to kill you. I may have to kill myself. Even if Hale doesn't succeed, he would be in a position to stir up enough old evidence to make it plausibly clear that we did attempt exactly that—and by demonstrably sorcerous means! The Prime Minister! McCone at the CIA wouldn't give us Manhattan street maps, after that. Hale will be a hero if he can pull off this Ararat operation—but we've killed bigger heroes, famous ones, to keep this a secret.*

It had been true then, a year and a half ago, and it was still true now. The SIS interrogation center wasn't at Ham Common in Richmond anymore—with a pang Theodora recalled recruiting Hale into the SOE there, in the corridor outside the kitchen at Latchmere House, in February of 1942—but Hale would have to be lured back, and debriefed, and then given a Cold War hero's retirement: a quiet, painless death, and the undisturbed, enduring disgrace of his last cover.

And Theodora would probably have to face Hale, before it was all over. He remembered the young ex-nun he had found in Cairo in 1924, living in a Misr al-Qadimah flat with her priceless illegitimate child, the issue of St. John Philby's folly; and he remembered meeting that child again when the boy was seven years old, on the day his mother brought him to the SIS headquarters in Whitehall Court. Theodora recalled now that the boy Andrew had nearly passed out from hunger in that interview, having fasted since the previous midnight in order to take his first Catholic Communion. And Theodora could still recall the long conversation he had had with Hale in the ruins around St. Paul's Cathedral in the late summer of 1941, among the antique wildflowers whose entombed seeds had been liberated by the German bombs.

And Hale had ultimately proven to be worth the long, costly investment. Theodora's battles with eight Prime Ministers and five Chiefs of the SIS, even his brief imprisonment on suspicion of treasonous acts in the first weeks of 1942, had been vindicated: the power on Mount Ararat was killed. And if Kim Philby would eventually die in the Soviet Union, preferably right in Moscow, the Soviet Union would lose the guardian angel that had protected Russia since 1883.

I do owe it to Hale to face him one more time.

At the other end of the enormous stone room, the door creaked open.

"Bring the car around to the front drive, would you, Nigel?" said Theodora thoughtfully, rapping the dottle out of his pipe on the ancient table. To London, to London, he thought—to arrange a spot of humiliation for myself.

"Nigel is still in Southborough," said the well-remembered voice of Andrew Hale. "I'm taking over for him for the rest of the day."

Theodora opened his mouth in a laugh that was too quiet to be picked up by any microphones that MI5 might have installed. "Well, I don't want the car anyway," he said lightly, "now that I think of it. I believe I'll go for a walk in the gardens instead."

Of course he came over early, the old man thought. He learned that from the GRU during the war. I should have expected it.

Theodora noted wryly that his heartbeat was suddenly rapid.

At last he tucked his pipe away in the pocket of his corduroy jacket and looked toward the door.

Hale had apparently been in sunny climes—his face and hands were tanned a dark brown—and his sandy hair was newly gray at the temples. He hadn't shaved recently, and the bristles on his chin were white. No doubt it had been a stressful year. The man was dressed in Nigel's clothes—white shirt, black jacket and tie—though his shoulders were broader than Nigel's, and Theodora doubted that he would be able to button the jacket.

Hale's right hand was in the pocket of the black trousers.

Theodora unbolted the door that led right out to one of the smaller gardens, having to rock the bolt to get it to slide back—probably it had not been opened since 1945—and when he had pulled the door open he walked carefully down the old stone steps, the grass-and-stone-scented morning breeze ruffling his fine white hair.

He heard Hale scuff down the steps after him.

Theodora's boots crunched along the gravel path that led to the sundial. The kitchen sundial at Batsford House was on a mound, and the triangular sections below the iron gnomon were each planted in a different variety of thyme—silver thyme and bright yellow-and-green variegated thyme on the morning slope, darker creeping thyme on the afternoon decline. Theodora stepped up to the crest of the mound, crushing the noon *thymus vulgaris,* and turned around to face Hale.

"You're late in reporting, sir!" Theodora said. "It was in January of last year that I sent you out. I remember saying that I believed you'd be back within the month."

Hale nodded, but he was glancing back at the high south wall of the house, a cliff of uneven tan stones and widely separated windows. "I was here, during the war," he said. "Had no idea it was yours." He glanced at Theodora with neutral, pale eyes. "Batsford, Theodora."

"A widowed Lady Batsford married a cloth merchant Theodora around the time of Waterloo. It used to be grander—one of the bedrooms still has a railing across the middle of the floor, so that any king who might be visiting could greet his subjects without getting out of bed. Two Earls once got into a serious fight in that room, the issue being which of them was to have the privilege of dressing George the Third. Bloody noses, broken furniture—I believe George wound up having to put on his own shirt. And I remember standing right here at night, as a boy—this would have been late '90s, 1900—and looking up to watch the servants carrying torches across the rooftops, as they made their way to the bedrooms in the turrets."

"Of course I've got a gun, Jimmie," said Hale.

"Of course you have," Theodora agreed. "And some sort of proposal, I imagine."

"I trust I'm still . . . on the rolls. I want to be sent out one more time, and then I want to retire here. Scotland, Wales, I don't care. Ireland, even. I came in through the London Docks yesterday, on a Canadian passport—it was a friend who sent the cable from Helsinki. I wanted to have a chance to discuss terms privately, before a lot of definitions were made, photographs taken."

"Terms," said Theodora.

"Well, I've got it all down in a little book, haven't I? Declare. With enough names and dates to make it convincing; and it's compelling reading too—T. E. Lawrence, the Dead Sea Scrolls, Kim Philby, Noah's Ark. A Belgian solicitor has it, and if a New Year's Day goes by without me having sent him a Christmas card, the whole works will be sent to every newspaper in the United States, and in Europe—oh, and *Pravda*. When I turn sixty-two, twenty years from now, I give you my word I'll destroy it. By then I doubt anyone will still care."

"Scopolamine," sighed Theodora, "sodium Pentothal. Plain old torture."

"A photograph of myself in with the Christmas card, every year. With a newspaper visible, to establish the date. The solicitor has a large staff, many offices, and he does a lot of international crime work—bodyguards, security—he's tremendously cautious."

Theodora shrugged, conceding the point. " 'Sent out one more time,' " he said.

"To Moscow, under journalist cover. SIS can arrange that easily enough. I want to cash out the Machikha Nash account. Khrushchev can be the last Premier of the Soviet Union."

Hale was proposing to kill Kim Philby, his half-brother, and thus set into motion the chain of events that would culminate with the *ghulah*-guardian angel ingesting the Shihab-shot from Philby's buried corpse.

"Well, Khrushchev wouldn't be the last anyway," Theodora said, stalling. "I doubt the Soviet empire would come crashing down *immediately* after the guardian angel was killed, and it doesn't look as though Khrushchev will last out the year. Russia had a bad harvest last year, and he had to use hard currency to buy wheat from the West. The KGB had to become grain brokers, and the KGB head, Shelepin, wants Khrushchev out. Leonid Brezhnev seems to be the likeliest replacement."

"Is my brother covering himself with glory, over there?"

"Well, no. It turns out he's what they call a 'secret collaborator,' not a Soviet intelligence *officer,* as I'm sure they had told him he would be. He's got a nice apartment, and access to a chauffeur-driven car, but he's apparently drinking a good deal, and his main value to the KGB is that he's still being debriefed, these fourteen months later. The only actual work he's doing is for the Novosti news agency—and his work needs to be translated. He's never learned Russian."

"Cremation is very common in Russia," Hale said. "If he dies years from now, as just an embarrassing old drunk left over from a previous regime, he's likely to be cremated."

And the precious shot pellets will be melted, thought Theodora. I won't live that long, but it *would* fret me to die thinking that the main operation of my career had not come to full fruition.

"Right now," Hale went on, "the people who vouched for him are still in charge, unwilling to concede that he's nothing but a drunk old Englishman. If he dies a hero's death now, a properly vindicating death, he'll be buried with honors at one of the Moscow cemeteries. Buried."

"What would be a hero's death?" asked Theodora. "A vindicating death?"

"He must be shot, killed, publicly and conspicuously, by an Englishman who can be proved to have been working for the SIS. Simple logic—if we considered him worth killing, obviously he must have been a Soviet hero."

Theodora laughed incredulously. "My dear boy, do you have any conception of the havoc that would cause? Consider the abuse the United States endured when one of their mere U-2 spy planes was shot down over Russia four years ago! It would not start World War III, I suppose, but we would lose all credibility worldwide—the present Conservative government would collapse, we'd have Harold Wilson and the Labour Party in charge!"

"Haven't you got—I seem to recall—*ears,* in Number 10 Downing Street? How likely is it that this Conservative government will survive the year in any case? The Profumo scandal drove Macmillan out last year—how long do you think Douglas-Home can hold the Conservative reins?"

"Until a general election, in October," Theodora said glumly. "And then, yes, I do happen to know that we'll have Harold Wilson for Prime Minister. And I have similarly good reason to believe that Wilson will not . . . expand the scope of the secret services."

"Then it's now or never," said Hale. "The Conservatives may as well have some decisive *reason* for going out, don't you think?—not just the declining pound and rising interest rates."

Theodora was nodding, squinting out across the newly green spring lawns. "It's impossible, my boy. You'd need a real SIS purpose in going to Moscow, a plausible cover story for Whitehall, and you could never sell the Foreign Office on any particle of what you've told me."

"What would be a plausible cover story to sell to the Foreign Office?"

"Well! Just for the sake of argument—something fairly low-key, routine administration type of thing." Theodora swiveled on his heels, crushing the thyme. "The KGB resident in London, Nikolai Grigoryevich Begrichev, has been increasing the size of the residency outrageously; and all these Tass representatives and cultural counselors are servicing the Soviet trade delegations and the Soviet students at our universities, all of them active agents—MI5's mobile surveillance operations are already completely compromised. And it's likely to go on escalating. And the Foreign Secretary knows that a Labour government will only be interested in appeasement, not any saber-rattling. And our embassy in Moscow is simply a KGB snuggery—we are required to hire all the maids, janitors, chauffeurs, even *translators,* from the Moscow Burobin employment agency, which is simply a branch of the KGB Second Chief Directorate, the counter-intelligence directorate. If the SIS could get some evidence of Burobin treachery, it would serve as an excuse for Douglas-Home to expel a good number of the Soviet Embassy staff in London. It would arguably be the last chance to do that."

"Most natural thing in the world, then, for the SIS to send an agent to Moscow under journalistic cover. An old wartime leftover agent; experienced but ulitmately unreliable, as it will turn out."

Theodora revolved on the sundial, staring blankly at the lawns and high walls of Batsford House, as he estimated the flurry of decipher-yourself telegrams that would erupt from the Moscow embassy after Philby's assassination—and then the international headlines, the outraged statements by Khrushchev, and then by Douglas-Home. Lyndon Johnson would weigh in with denunciations, McCone would scramble to distance the CIA from the lunatic British secret services.

But two or three years from now, he thought, the Soviet Union would stop being a Union. The gross, artificially maintained flower of communism would lose its hothouse protection, and it would wither in the unhindered winds of the world, and brash young weeds would spring up from the fallow Russian ground and choke it.

"You'd have to find your own gun," he said at last. "Whitehall could not possibly provide you with the gun."

Hale kept his face expressionless and simply nodded, but he felt the tension of the last thirty hours relax out of his shoulders. "I can find my own gun."

"I gather you don't intend to be caught, but you *do* intend to be identified, as a British SIS agent. Do you seriously think a retirement identity for you in the United Kingdom is a question that need occupy me?"

"I'll make my way back across the Channel," said Hale.

Theodora frowned, possibly with genuine concern. "You've got plenty of field experience, my boy, but you've never been on the wrong side of the Curtain. It's a whole other world. Moscow was Looking-Glass Land even when I was there with Lockhart and Reilly, back in the innocent days of 1918, when our great plan was to capture Lenin and Trotsky, and then pull off their trousers and parade them through the streets in their undershorts, to make laughingstocks of them." The old man smiled, showing the shape of his skull under the wrinkled, parchment skin. "We were MI1C in those days, and the Petrograd station chief vetoed our idea; but I still think that would have nipped the whole Communist enterprise in the bud."

"I'll nip it in the . . . sere and yellow leaf." Hale released the grip of the Seecamp .32 in Nigel's trouser pocket and stretched in the chilly spring morning breeze. From somewhere high up on the stone wall he could hear pigeons cooing, and the sound made him sleepy—he hadn't slept or eaten or changed his shirt for thirty hours, and above the spicy scent of crushed thyme he could smell his own old sweat. "Do keep in mind too that I'm the only one who can *do* this. If you establish the truth about *me*, then you won't ever be able to do the same for Philby, much as you might one day wish to. He's vulnerable to injury on his birthday, of course—but you know the Kremlin will keep him in a bomb-proof subterranean vault on *that* day, every year; and on any other day of the three-hundred-and-sixty-five, the only person who can get past his magical defenses to injure him is the one other person who also *is* him, at least according to the angels' silhouette-recognition cards."

"But they're all dead. The angels."

Hale stared at Theodora. "Jimmie. The ones on *Ararat* are all dead. With luck. But in Arabia, Egypt, India—no. *China*, even, probably."

"Oh. No, of course not, I do see. China. Hmm."

Watching the old man's sagging gray face now in the morning sunlight, Hale thought that in fact Theodora had *not* known that Declare had killed only one major colony, albeit probably the biggest colony in the world, of djinn. And for several seconds Hale didn't speak, but let Theodora arrive on his own at the conclusion that the destruction of the Soviet Union must stand as the major accomplishment of the old man's career. And don't forget the risk of cremation if you wait, Jimmie, Hale thought.

"I came across the Channel on a French cattle boat," Hale added finally, with some tension, "because I can't fly in an airplane over about ten thousand feet anymore. I learned that bit of data on an Air Libyan flight out of Kuwait a month ago—the plane had to land in the gulf, off Bahrain, with half the fuselage ripped off. The spirits of the upper air are still up there in the Heaviside Layer, and they're aware of me when I get up that close to them; and they're—angry at me, still."

"Really." The old man was staring off across the lawns, nodding slowly. "That must have been exciting. You'll have to travel by boat, then, and overland by rail—but that will look good, actually, not at all the behavior of a modern *spy.*"

He sighed heavily. "Yes, very well, I'll get you reactivated and assigned to Moscow, under journalistic cover, with orders to investigate the Burobin employment agency. Human interest angle, ostensibly, focus on the little people who keep the show rolling, as it were; hobbies, filthy ethnic foods, framed pictures of the old Bolshevik parents on the shabby apartment walls. There are still newspapers that will let us force a foreign correspondent on them. And then—I'll be as shocked as anyone else, if you do something crazy while you're in Moscow."

"And of course in the meantime," said Hale gently, "you'll make sure that any old *verification* orders concerning me are switched off."

"Oh, my dear, I'm sure there never was anything like that!" Was there an ironic glint in the old man's eye? "You insult me. But of course I will get on the telephone and explain your status. It might be best for you to stay here tonight, not try to go into the city. Right? We should certainly have you in Moscow by the middle of April, even at your slow rate of travel."

That will do, thought Hale. He allowed himself to sit down on the damp green grass.

He recalled a story in the *Thousand Nights and One Night,* in which a poor traveler had been hired by a jewel merchant to allow himself to be sewn into the skin of a freshly killed mule. When it had been done, an enormous eagle snatched up the dead mule with the traveler hidden inside and flew to an otherwise inaccessible mountain peak, and the bird flew away in surprise when the man climbed out of the carcass. He found that the mountain-top was littered with human and mule bones, but also that the stones lying about were all jewels; and, from the valley below, the jewel merchant was calling up to him to throw down as many of the gems as he could lift. The traveler obediently flung down more than two hundred fabulously valuable stones, but eventually he paused to rest and called down a question about the route he would have to take to get back down—and at that point the jewel merchant gathered the jewels scattered in the valley, packed up his own mule and departed without a backward look. The abandoned traveler had pressed onward up the mountain and eventually after many hardships found a green valley, where he met and fell in love with a daughter of the djinn. She had loved him too, and had taken him down the mountain and dwelt with him as a human woman for a year. At the end of the year she had flown away—and the grief-stricken traveler had found his way back to the city where he had started; the jewel merchant did not recognize him, and hired him again to be sewn into a fresh mule skin. And this time, after the eagle had carried the carcass to the mountain-top and taken flight after a living man crawled out of it, the traveler ignored the jewel merchant's cries from the valley and threw down no jewels, but set off at once for the remembered valley where he might once again find the daughter of the djinn.

"I'll impose on your hospitality for a bath," he said, "and some food and drink—and sleep."

And then, he thought, you can sew me up, Jimmie.

Theodora drove Hale to London two days later in his old Continental Bentley, but instead of crossing the river to Century House he proceeded to Artillery Mansions near Westminster Hall. London Station ran a department from Artillery Mansions known as DP4, which was in the business of inserting SIS agents into eastern Europe and Russia—students, businessmen, journalists; as a lowly DP4 operative, Hale would be beneath the notice of Dick White, who was still C.

Theodora's proposal was approved without objection by Dickie Franks, the DP4 chief, with routine authorization from the Foreign Office, and at the end of the week Andrew Hale boarded the Polish liner *Topolewski*. After three days at sea, with stops at Rotterdam and Copenhagen, Hale arrived at the Baltic Sea port of Danzig in northern Poland. His British passport identified him as Varnum Leonard, a non-staff foreign correspondent for the *Evening Standard,* and its pages were stamped with many visas from Eastern Bloc countries such as Czechoslovakia and the German Democratic Republic; and in the Brest railway station on April 8, the passport's last empty page was stamped with the red star of the U.S.S.R. visa.

Across the Soviet border now, he boarded a crowded train that took him over the course of several days through Minsk and Smolensk, and finally on the evening of Sunday the twelfth he watched through his sleeping compartment window as the outlying villages of Moscow, quaint snow-covered log cabins and narrow lanes animated with horse-drawn sleds, gave way to paved streets and new apartment buildings with television antennaes on the roofs. It was full dark by the time his train squealed to a steaming halt in the Belorussia Station on the Leningrad Prospect, only a short Metro ride from the apartment which Intourist had assigned to him on the Sadovaya Samotechnaya ring road.

His apartment building proved to be an elegant Stalinist-baroque ghetto for Western journalists, insulated from surrounding buildings by high cement walls and a sentry box manned by KGB agents in police uniforms. During his first days there, he picked up from the other foreign correspondents the habit of referring to the broad avenue on which they lived as "Sad Sam." The term was just a two-syllable abbreviation to the Burobin Russian interpreters who generally accompanied the journalists out into the city, but for other Westerners it carried a flavor of good-humored desperation. The other correspondents always spoke of coming "into" or going "out of" the Soviet Union, never saying simply "to" or "from," and even the ones who were most at-home in Moscow, speaking the language and knowing where the bars were, were careful to schedule frequent trips back out to London, or New York, or Rome, or any other place where the standard drink was not "a hundred grams" of vodka, and where people didn't select a wine by its alcohol content, as in "give me something at 19 percent."

Hale quickly learned enough phrases in the Russian language to apologize and ask directions, and he began exploring the city without an interpreter—the Intourist and Novosti Press Agency authorities permitted this, since all press releases were censored and no photographers could be obtained except from Novosti.

Moscow within the Sadovaya ring was physically daunting—the streets and squares were vast, though automobile traffic was sparse, and it seemed to Hale in his first days that the industrial-Gothic architecture of the Stalinist skyscrapers, crowned with giant red stars that lit the night sky like the Devil's own landing-lights, were contrasted only by the medieval bastions and towers of the Kremlin wall and the new blocks of modernist pre-fabricated apartment buildings, which appeared to have been assembled with rust streaks and pock-marks already applied. Later he found the Bolshoi Theatre with its ornate Corinthian pillars, and the wrought-iron balconies and bridges and hanging lanterns of the vast GUM department store on Red Square, but these were forlorn remnants of the tsarist nineteenth century—like the palatial Gastronom 1 on Gorky Street, where grim-faced shoppers now waited in long lines to buy turnips and bottles of cheap red and blue syrups under the old gilt cherubs and chandeliers.

On the Moskva River embankment he stared at the twelve-foot-by-thirty-foot movie posters, trying to puzzle out the names of the stars, whose faces he didn't recognize; farther up the embankment, outside the Kremlin wall by the Taynitskaya Tower, he could sometimes hear the scuffle-and-thump of a volleyball game, presumably among the guards, on the other side of the high wall; and for half an hour one day he watched a flock of crows busily dropping chestnuts down the top of a drainpipe on the tower and flying down to the pavement to retrieve the nuts when they rolled out at the bottom, and then flying up to do it again.

He felt like one of the birds. He had two things to do—and now that he was so close to defining the course of the rest of his life, he was postponing considering either of them.

When he had gone to the GUM department store he had seen the colorful spires and onion domes of St. Basil's Cathedral, standing like some fantastic Walt Disney island hundreds of yards away at the south end of Red Square, and he had stared at its crimson walls and gold-and-blue spiraled domes. And when he realized that he was so anxious about his imminent intrusion there—on the twenty-second of April, forty years after 1924, only a week away now—that he was afraid to approach it, he made himself walk all the way across the plain of the cobblestoned square, past the ranked snow-plow trucks and the raised cement ring of the Lobinoye Mesto where criminals had been publicly beheaded in the tsarist days, to the the cathedral's rococco north arch. He walked up the stone stairs beyond and found that the tall doors stood open, with the cavernous aisles of the sixteenth-century church dimly visible inside.

With one finger he made a tiny, furtive sign of the cross on the front of his overcoat, and he stepped over the threshold onto the polished stone floor; and then—defensively, afraid to hope—he occupied himself with noting the placement of the doors in the far walls and the width and separation of the towering pillars, only peripherally aware of the chandeliers and the ranks of saints painted in luminous fresco on the high walls.

His heart was thudding alarmingly in his chest as he left the church and strode away across Red Square, and in his head he was telling himself, *She may not be able to come, she may have forgotten, she may be dead, she certainly hates you.*

But he had brought along a package from the remote Zagros mountain village of Siamand Barakat Khan, and he did need to find Kim Philby—though not in order to kill him: Hale also had two Scandinavian Airlines tickets that he had purchased with a *casse geule* passport in Finland late in March. The names and passport numbers for the tickets had not yet been filled in.

Philby's was of course a famous name in Moscow, especially among the Western journalists, some of whom had known him during his six years as a correspondent for *The Economist* and *The Observer* in Beirut. It had only been in July of last year that British Secretary of State Edward Heath confirmed that Philby had been the legendary "third man" in the Burgess and Maclean spy scandal of 1951, and Philby had arrived in Moscow in a season when spies were trendy—everyone was reading Vadim Kozhevnikov's *Shield and Sword*, a novel about a brave Soviet spy in World War II, and the youth newspaper *Komsomolskaya Pravda* was running a serial about the adventures of a beautiful KGB girl named Natasha—but Philby seemed to have become a recluse.

None of the journalists could tell Hale how to find Philby, and he didn't dare to show more than casual, morbid interest. A *New York Times* man told Hale that he had seen Philby dining at the Aragvy Restaurant by the Bolshoi Theatre with two KGB men, who were distinguishable as such because they had been wearing the new pale-green fedoras available only in the privileged hard-currency stores; and a woman from *The Saturday Evening Post* told Hale that she had seen a man who looked like Kim Philby trying, speaking English, to order a new Pagoda brand washing machine in a parking-lot black market on the southern loop of the Sad Sam.

The most recent Moscow telephone directory had been published in 1958, and the four-volume set had gone out of print immediately and had never been reprinted. Journalists and Muscovites amassed private telephone directories by writing down and sharing the names of all the parties they had got by wrong number connections—which were frequent—but none of these informal telephone books that Hale could get a look at had a listing for Philby.

Hale made no effort to live his journalistic cover story. He walked by the Aragvy Restaurant every day at noon and dusk, hoping to glimpse Philby, and in the evenings he nibbled cucumber-and-tomato *zakusi* in the bar of the Metropol, drank vodka at the Sovietskaya and purple vermouth *koktels* at the Moskva—but he did not succeed in catching a glimpse of his half-brother.

When there were only three days left until the twenty-second of April, Hale reluctantly decided to look for Philby among the Gray People. This was the name given by the Sad Sam journalists to the Western expatriates who had defected and become Soviet citizens, and who all seemed to work for the Foreign Languages Publishing House, paid by the line for translating the speeches of Party members into English. They were said to be a furtive colony, inordinately proud of their various shabby treasons, and sure that the CIA or the SIS or the SDECE would pay dearly for the chance of arresting them. And all of them would reportedly turn pale with envy at the sight of a valid Western passport.

It was bad form to try to socialize with them, and Hale understood too that any such efforts were likely to draw the attention of the KGB, with the probable consequence of revocation of one's visa, and speedy expulsion from the U.S.S.R.

Hale had considered simply going to St. Basil's Cathedral on Wednesday the twenty-second of April, without visiting Philby first. But he did want to be able to fly out of the Soviet Union, afterward.

And Hale finally found the Gray People on the afternoon of Tuesday the twenty-first, in Khokhlovskaya Square on the eastern loop of the Sadovaya Samotechnaya ring road, at the black market for books. Here, unmolested even by the city police, the Moscow intellectuals in their shapeless clothes sorted through stacks of books in the watery sunlight, looking for Arthur Miller's *The Crucible* and Benjamin Spock's *Baby and Child Care* and illegal mimeographed copies of Pasternak's *Doctor Zhivago*. The many mimeograph texts, stapled or sewn with yarn, were known as *samizdat* and were illegal, lacking the Glavlit stamp of approval; aside from the Pasternak, these blurry texts seemed to be mostly modern poetry, anti-government satire, crude witchcraft, and pornography.

The native Muscovites were easily distinguishable from the Gray People. The latter tended either to cluster together in threes and fours or to visibly avoid their fellows, and their voices were quieter, petulant, and nervous.

Hale picked out one middle-aged man who had snapped, "Leave me alone, will you?" to another man in English, and Hale followed him when he began shambling away alone with—good sign!—a *samizdat* copy of Mikhail Bulgakov's satire of the Stalinist regime, *The Master and Margarita,* wrapped tightly in brown paper.

Hale managed to hurry around through the linden trees in front of his quarry, so as to approach him from ahead; and he made sure to have a British ten-pound note in his hand when he spoke.

"Excuse me," Hale said, smiling, "I appear to be lost. Do you know the city well?"

The man had flinched at the English sentences, but his eyes were caught by the banknote—Hale had been in Moscow long enough to know that this hard currency, unlike the flimsy rubles, would be honored in the elite Berioska stores in the downtown hotels, where it would buy fabulous items like American cigarettes and Scotch whisky.

"Where did you want to go?" the man asked finally, in a south-of-the-Thames British accent. His face was pale, and he didn't look around. On the broad lanes of the Sadovaya ring road to Hale's right, a few drab Moskvich and Zhiguli-Fiat sedans roared past, but no pedestrians were nearby.

"I need to find an old pal of mine—his name is Kim Philby. I can't seem to get his phone number from Information."

"I—don't know him."

"Well, you don't need to *know* him to have heard where he lives, right? This tenner is yours if you can tell me."

The man sighed, blowing stale vodka fumes at Hale. "I know who he is, of course. I suppose you're a journalist—or an SIS assassin. It's as much as my life is worth to tell you where he lives."

"No doubt. But it's also worth a British ten-pound note. Which would you rather be sure of having?"

The man licked his lips nervously, his fingers flexing on the paper-wrapped book he carried.

Hale was watching his eyes, and from long practice saw the flicker that meant he would lie. " 'O fish,' " said Hale then, impulsively, " 'are you constant to the old covenant?' "

The man blushed deeply. "I was never—out there I was never—*damn* you! No, I don't mean that, it's only—" His hairline was suddenly beaded with sweat, and he appeared to be blinking away tears. "I was a clerk in the Admiralty Military Branch, and I only photographed documents having to do with NATO naval policy. I thought I was doing it for the WPO, the World Peace Organization, in Austria! NATO is just a tool of American imperialism . . ." He had been looking at the pavement, but now he met Hale's gaze, sickly. He sighed, and then in a hoarse voice said, " 'Return, and we return. Keep faith, and so will we.' "

Hale spoke gently. "Where does Philby live?"

"Is this a test? You must know." He shrugged. "I don't know the address. At Patriarch's Pond, they say." He yawned, and Hale recognized it as a reflex of tension, not boredom.

Hale knew he should leave now, but he was shaken at how well his gambit had worked. "You weren't working for the WPO," he said. "When did you learn who you were really working for?"

"Even when I defected," the man said in an injured tone, "I thought I was working for the KGB. All of us did, or for the GRU, or the Comintern, or something. Something *rational*. It's only when we've surrendered our passports and we're *here*, for *life*, that we learn we work for . . ."

"For . . . ?" pressed Hale, impatient now to get away from this doomed specimen.

The man looked up at Hale with a bent smile. "You know who she is."

Hale nodded reluctantly. "Machikha Nash," he said.

The pale man gave a whinnying cry, and he glanced anxiously past Hale at the lanes of the ring road; and almost immediately his face blanched as white as bone, and the eyes rolled up in his head a moment before his knees, his book, and then his forehead smacked the sidewalk pavement.

The chilly spring breeze was suddenly rancid in Hale's nostrils with the smell of metallic oil.

As the man's still-shivering body toppled over onto one hip, Hale stepped away from him and glanced over his shoulder at the street.

Sunlight glittered on the teeth of the robed, dark-eyed woman on the far pavement—but Hale could see the individual gold rings and teeth strung around her neck, so she must actually have been much closer than that; and then it seemed that the ring road was rotating on the axis of the Kremlin, in fact on the axis of the tomb in which Lenin's preserved body defied decomposition—the image had sprung into his head—and although the woman's black, hungry eyes held his gaze, he was aware that the white sun was moving around the horizon.

He opened his mouth to speak the first words of the *Our Father*, but realized that he had forgotten them; and so he quoted the words he remembered Elena saying, on the deck of the Arab boat on the east side of the Brandenburg Gate, in Berlin in 1945: "*Santa Maria, Madre de Dios, ruega por nosotros pecadores—*"

The dark woman was more clearly on the far side of the lanes now; and her teeth were bared in a snarl. The street had stopped seeming to spin. Hale was able to break his gaze free from hers, and he walked away heavily, as clumsy as if his legs had gone to sleep.

The first time he looked back she seemed to be closer, seemed to be standing between him and the body of the unfortunate Admiralty clerk; and Hale tried to make his numb legs work faster. But when he peered over his shoulder again, a few seconds later, she was nowhere to be seen— the sidewalk was empty except for the tumbled body a hundred feet back, and no figures at all stood between him and the bleak windows of the office buildings on the far side of the street.

He walked until he saw a northbound bus unloading passengers, and he hastily climbed aboard, paid his five kopeks, and then during the course of an hour rode the bus for one and a half circuits of the Sadovaya ring, counterclockwise.

He climbed down from the bus by the Tchaikovsky Concert Hall at the Gorky Street intersection. He recognized the nineteenth-century stone steeples and office buildings, for he was only eight blocks northwest of the Aragvy Restaurant; and the old residential neighborhood known as Patriarch's Pond was two blocks further south on the Sad Sam ring, in a warren of narrow lanes around the pond that was filled every winter to provide a rink for skating.

The sun was already sinking behind the tall pines of the zoo park, and the sky had begun to take on the soft silvery glow of far-northern sunsets, with only the faintest tinges of pink.

As he began walking south along the sidewalk, Hale reached inside his overcoat to pat the pocket of his jacket, and he was reassured to feel his passport and press credentials; if he was stopped by the police or the KGB, his journalism cover would stand up here—*Pushkin Square, the lovely old narrow lanes, the graybeards playing dominoes under the linden trees . . .*

He turned right, into a cobbled street overhung by Muscovy plane trees, and he felt as though he were fencing. He knew that if Philby lived in this area every pedestrian would be watched, and he walked down the center of the cobblestone street for now, not making any feints toward the shingle-roofed stone houses on either side. Prewar apartment buildings were looming through the budding branches ahead, and it was likely that Philby would be put up in one of those places, where tighter security could be maintained.

The lane zigzagged past tiny parks with cement tables set out on the grass, though any dominoes players had by now retired for the evening. Hale could smell wood smoke from the old chimneys, and boiling cabbage, but he didn't see any pedestrians until he stepped into the littered entryway of one of the apartment buidings; as soon as he was in out of the wind, a man in a black overcoat strode down the sidewalk on the other side of the street, and Hale suppressed a smile at the sight of the green fedora on the man's head.

A twitch of the blade, Hale thought, but not a full parry. This isn't the building. He dug a pack of Trud cigarettes out of a pocket and shook one out and struck a match to it. Half the length of the black cigarette was an empty cardboard tube.

He stepped back out onto the sidewalk and resumed walking in the direction of the pond. Soon the street curved away to the west, and an alley was the only route by which to move farther south, but he didn't hesitate before stepping into the shadows between the high brick walls.

The windows he passed were painted over, though he heard voices behind a couple of them, and the vertical iron pipes radiated heat. Just as he came out the far end of the alley, he heard a soft scuff echo behind him.

Hale was in a cul-de-sac now, with flower gardens in the gaps between the old yellow-brick houses on his left. The view to his right was blocked by one of the prewar apartment buildings, an eight-story gray-faced stone edifice with butcher-paper packages and milk bottles visible in the windows, between the insulating double panes of glass.

Hale took a deep draw on his Russian cigarette, and a throat-full of hot air let him know that he had used up all the tobacco in it. He ground it out under his heel and began walking out across the pavement toward the apartment building.

Immediately two men in green fedoras had stepped up from a set of basement stairs, and they made straight for Hale. One of them asked a question in Russian.

"*Dobriy vyechyir,*" said Hale amiably. It meant *Good evening.* "*Vi gavrarityeh pa angliski?*" he went on. "*Nyimyetski? Frantsuski?*" *Do you speak English? German? French?*

In German the KGB officer said, "Let me see your passport. What are you doing here?" His companion had stepped to the side, probably to have a clear shot at Hale.

"I am an English journalist for the London *Evening Standard,*" replied Hale in German. With his right hand he pulled open his overcoat, and with two fingers of his left hand he slowly drew out his passport. "I wish to write an article about Pushkin Square and the picturesque old neighborhoods around it."

"This is a restricted area," the KGB agent said, handing the passport to his companion. "You are staying at the hotel on the Sadovaya Samotechnaya?"

"Var-noom Leeyonard," said the agent with Hale's passport, and it took Hale a moment to realize that the man was pronouncing the name on the passport, Varnum Leonard.

Hale nodded. "That's right."

"*Joor*-nalist," the man added.

"Right again."

"Do not come here again," said the first man, waving Hale back the way he had come.

Hale retrieved his passport, nodded apologetically, and walked back toward the alley. The cul-de-sac was in deepening shadow, and he noticed that there were no streetlamps.

A committed parry, he thought with satisfaction. That's the place. And probably there'll be a new shift of guards tomorrow morning.

At the alley-mouth he glanced back, and he saw a pair of lighted windows on the eighth floor of the apartment building. Are you at home, Kim? he thought. I hope you're an early riser—I need to be at St. Basil's Cathedral at noon.

The prospect of his visit to the cathedral was much more troubling than the thought of cornering Kim Philby tomorrow morning.

That night Hale sat up drinking Glenlivet Scotch whisky with the *New York Times* man, watching Russian television on the fourteen-inch black-and-white television set in the lobby of their Sad Sam hotel. One of the two available channels was airing a special on collective farms in the Ukraine, with lots of footage of modern harvest combines moving through fields of wheat; the other channel featured a show about steel-workers, and Hale and his companion stared befuddled at a view of white-hot steel ingots bumping down a ramp.

"I've got to get out again soon," the *New York Times* man mumbled as he switched off the set and got up to stagger toward his room. "I'm starting to root for their Five-Year Plans."

Hale nodded sympathetically, but sat for a while with his whisky and stared at the dark television screen. From another room he could hear a radio playing some rock-and-roll—a song called "*Sie Liebe Du*," by a Hamburg group called, apparently, The Beetles.

She loves you, the lyrics meant. *Ja, ja, ja.*

Nein, nein, nein, he thought bleakly, refilling his glass. *She loved me, she loves me not.*

Abbitte tun, the lyrics advised. *Apologize.* But I didn't do what she believes I did, he thought; and if I had done it, no apology would be possible.

Hale wondered if Theodora could have set it up that way deliberately: killing Claude Cassagnac and then blaming Hale for the death, just to preclude any renewal of intimacy between Hale and Elena in Beirut. Theodora would have wanted to minimize any involvement by the French SDECE—though in fact the SDECE did manage at least to blow the Black Ark site to smithereens, moments after Hale had delivered the death-blow to the djinn. Once again he wondered if Elena had been aboard that unmarked French Alouette III helicopter, and if she had been the pilot who had veered off or the machine-gunner who had nearly given Hale the last truth; and he wondered if she believed he died there. She must know Philby survived—anybody in the world who read newspapers knew that.

For the first time in many years, he let his mind dwell freely on his last night in Paris in '41 and on his last night in Berlin in '45.

I can't not try, he thought, putting down his glass and struggling to his feet to climb the stairs to his room.

He wound his alarm clock, set the alarm hand at six o'clock and fell asleep in his clothes. In his dreams he took Elena's hand and ran across the bumpy pavement of Red Square, fleeing from KGB agents in green hats, but when he paused by the river embankment and looked back at her, the creature he had by the hand was the dark-eyed Arabic woman with the wedding-ring necklace, and she lifted his hand to her lips and began to bite off his fingers.

At eight the next morning Hale stood in chilly sunlight over two old men playing dominoes on one of the cement tables near Philby's apartment building. Hale had managed to nick his chin while shaving, and now a blob of white cotton was stuck below his lip; he consoled himself with the thought that it was a disguise of sorts—or at least a distraction. And his graying sandy hair had not cooperated with the comb, and now stood up in spikes in the back.

Hale had brought along a Russian-language edition of Tolstoi and a bottle of vodka in a paper bag; and he had borrowed a shapeless wool coat, a leather hat with ear-flaps, and an ill-fitting old pair of bell-bottom trousers. Altogether he felt that he looked like a native, not worth special scrutiny by the KGB.

The spring thaw had definitely arrived upon Moscow. Green buds and even tiny pink flowers dotted the black boughs of the apple trees; Patriarch's Pond itself, which he could see through a gap between two houses, had thawed out in the middle, with broken ice clinging around the grassy shore.

At nine Hale saw two alert men emerge from the basement stairs at the foot of Philby's building, and though they were wearing snap-brim felt hats, with the eccentricity of having no dents in the crowns, he guessed they were KGB; and it was confirmed when Philby himself came blinking up into the sunlight right behind them.

Hale realized that in spite of his pouchy face Philby had always been slim; he wasn't any longer. It was a stocky, gray-haired figure that came lumbering across the pavement, and his features were coarser, blunter, now. Hale had been sitting on a bench, trying to puzzle out the Cyrillic syllables in the Tolstoi and taking an occasional mouthful of the chilly vodka, and now he stood up. He opened his book and folded it around with the pages on the outside, and then closed it again, to make a furtive white flash. It was a standard SIS sign.

And Philby saw it from thirty feet away. The man's eyes lifted from the book to Hale's face, and Hale caught a gleam of surprised recognition, quickly concealed. Kim Philby stopped walking and frowned up at the sky for a moment, then shrugged out of his heavy overcoat—and while he was getting his arm out of the sleeve, he gave Hale the old SIS hand-signal that meant *Follow, at a distance.*

Fair enough, thought Hale cautiously as he ambled across the cul-de-sac at an angle behind Philby. I've got three hours before high noon. As soon as he saw that Philby intended to walk down Spiridonovka Street, Hale hurried around a block to get in front of Philby and his KGB escorts. Now Philby could see him and cooperate in maintaining visual contact, and the KGB men, for all their deadpan vigilance, had apparently not considered that someone might be following Philby from in front.

This neighborhood, inside the Sadovaya ring and south of Patriarch's Pond, was all foreign embassies—the American Embassy was only a block or two ahead—and Hale wondered if Philby intended to dart into one and ask for asylum. Hale could have told him that all the embassy chauffeurs and maids would be Burobin agents, KGB.

But Hale kept walking ahead, glancing into windows or up at the street-spanning rooftop banners in order to glance back peripherally and make sure that Philby was still behind him. He knew enough Russian to translate the text of only one of the huge red banners—GLORY TO WORK. It seemed a depressing thought.

When Hale had walked past the crenellated bell tower of a Russian Orthodox church, he glanced up at the clock and then let his gaze fall behind him—and he saw that Philby had stopped on the sidewalk by an arch that led into the church grounds.

Hale paused to lift his bagged bottle and take a sip, feeling safe in facing back along his track to do it, and two full seconds later Philby stepped through the arch. The two KGB men followed, though Hale thought he saw them exchange a glance before they too disappeared.

Hale quickly shuffled sidways into the recessed doorway of a restaurant on the other side of the street, and after putting down his bottle and tossing his leather hat and the blob of cotton, he shrugged out of his coat and pulled its sleeves inside-out before putting it back on; then, hatless, and with the coat's pink-satin lining on the outside now so that he seemed to be wearing a decrepit Oriental smoking jacket, he retrieved his bottle and emerged from the doorway and strode purposefully across the street to the stone arch. He took a deep breath and stepped through.

The arch led into an old walled cemetery, and Hale walked forward out of the shadow of the wall into a patch of still sunlight. For a moment he smelled the grass and the tulips, but then he caught the familiar whiff of rancid oil. His eyes were watering in the sun glare.

He was suddenly dizzy, and after only a few more steps along the gravel walk he gripped a bronze double-barred cross on the nearest gravestone to keep from falling. A thought that was not his own echoed in his head: *What brings thee in to me?*

Hale glanced around for Philby—and he saw only the two KGB men, who were striding between the upright stones in evident alarm.

Philby had evaded them—but where was he? Hale took a deep breath and stepped away from the gravestone.

And he noticed with a sort of ringing tunnel vision that he was casting two shadows across the gravel—or, rather, that he stood *between* two shadows, with no evidence that his own body was stopping the sunlight at all. He raised his arm, and so did the shadow a foot away to his right. He looked up to his left, where the person casting the other shadow should be standing, and for a moment he saw the back of his own head, with the hair still standing up in spikes, and saw below it the shoulders of the crazy-looking quilted pink-satin coat.

A moment later the vision was gone, and aside from his two shadows he seemed to be alone on the gravel path.

His left leg flexed forward into an involuntary step, and in his left ear he heard a whisper: "Walk back out. Drink your vodka as you go."

In his disorientation Hale would have gone along with almost any proposal, and he obediently lurched back toward the arch, tipping the bottle up for a slug of vodka.

He saw bubbles wobble up through the clear liquor, and heard them gurgling, but no liquid reached his mouth. Then his arm was pulled back down, and the whispering voice in his ear said, "Ahh," and Hale could smell vodka fumes over the metallic oil reek. "Straight ahead, across the street," the voice went on, "there's a park where drunks sun themselves, two blocks away, just alleys to get there."

Hale stumbled out through the arch and swayed and shuffled across the street like a man with a concussion. When he had stumbled up onto the far sidewalk his left leg flexed again, and he wobbled away in that direction. If the KGB men had observed him at all, they must have dismissed him as an unsignifying drunk.

Within a few steps Hale had turned right, off the Spiridonovka; and when he had walked one block down an alley that led away to the north, past windowsill flower boxes and the back doors of old wooden houses, he regained his balance. Out of the corner of his left eye he could see Philby walking along beside him now, and he could hear Philby's boots crunching on the pavement; but Hale didn't look directly at him for fear of overlapping him again. Hale did notice with relief that his own shadow stretched ahead properly from his own feet now, and that Philby's was moving normally beside it, not alarmingly close to it.

As if this ordinary sight were a signal, Hale's heartbeat was suddenly very fast in his chest, and he was panting. "What—" he said hoarsely, "—happened?"

"I often duck in there, or into any cemetery," said Philby quietly, his own voice sounding a little strained, "when I want to lose my escorts. The guardian angel is present in such places, and when *she* is focusing on me, *other* people seem to have difficulty doing it." He took a deep breath and sighed gustily. "I guess you're my other half, right enough, my ten-years-delayed twin—today she obviously mistook you and I, authoritatively, for one person." Hale saw the shadow of Philby's head lift and turn in profile toward him. "Not very flattering to me, I must say," Philby added. "What *is* that garment?"

"Overcoat," said Hale shortly. "Inside-out."

Neither of them said anything more until they had reached the park Philby had mentioned, a narrow grassy square with wooden benches around the periphery. And several of the old men on the benches were holding bottles.

Hale and Philby found an unoccupied bench in the far corner, and sat down heavily enough to creak the boards.

Philby was staring at Hale. " 'What brings thee in to me,' " he said, " 'seeing that thou art not of my kind and canst not therefore be assured of safety from violence or ill-usage?' "

"The way in which I *am* of your kind outweighs all the rest," Hale told him, his voice still shaky. "I've come to propose a trade." His heartbeat was slowing down, and at least he was able to speak without gasping. "Do you still have Theo Maly's instructions for preparation of the *amomon* root? Specifically a *copy* of those instructions?"

Philby stared at him blankly. "Yes."

"Well, I want a copy. In exchange for that, and for one other thing, I will give you directions to a dead-letter box, a *dubok,* that I've found here in the city. In the *dubok* is an inhabited *amomon* root, wrapped up in waxed paper and rubber bands. It's my suspicion that the Soviet authorities will not have seen fit to provide you with one."

Philby shifted on the bench, then held out his hand for the bottle, which Hale passed to him. "Where," Philby whispered after he had taken a swallow, "did you get a live *amomon* root?"

"In the Zagros mountains, last spring. The djinn-kill on Ararat was massive—there were whole hillsides of blooming *amomon* thistles."

"Ah," Philby said. "Yes, there would have been."

Hale took the bottle back and lifted it for another sip. He had to keep reminding himself that Philby had cold-bloodedly betrayed Hale's men in the Ahora Gorge in 1948, for what Hale was proposing here was a cruel fraud: even if Philby should correctly ingest an inhabited *amomon* root, his bloodstream would spin the primitive djinn past the Shihab shot pellets that were probably still imbedded in his back, and the *amomon* djinn would be killed instantly, uselessly. There could be no *amomon* immortality for Philby, though Hale needed him to believe that it was possible.

"What is the 'one other thing' you want, in exchange?" asked Philby.

"The diamond that Prince Feisal gave you in 1919," said Hale, making himself speak without emphasis. "The *rafiq* stone."

Philby was laughing softly, his puffy face gray in the cold sunlight. "Oh, Andrew! And here you are, devoted boy, in Moscow, on her fortieth birthday! Like Gershwin's Porgy, looking for Bess! I daresay you've got airline tickets, and so you need the *rafiq* diamond in order to fly out of the Soviet Union with her, unmolested by the angry angels at cruising altitudes! To where, boy? Back to your Bedouins?"

Hale's whole body had gone cold. "She—t-told *you?*" he said—and remotely it occurred to him that Philby had lost his own stammer. "*You?*"

"I've always been good about remembering birthdays," Philby said placidly. "Yes, in Dogubayezit she told me about her vow, on the day after nobody succeeded in the Ahora Gorge. Nineteen forty-eight, you must remember it. She made a prayer to the Blessed Virgin, right?—when she was imprisoned in the Lubyanka here, during the war: 'I vow that on my fortieth birthday at high noon I will light a candle for you right here in Moscow'—O Mother of God!—'at St. Basil's Cathedral in Red Square.' Very devout young lady, I gathered, though she and I—" He chuckled and shook his head, then said, clearly reciting, " 'Blue the sky from east to west arches, and the world is wide, though the girl he loves the best rouses from another's side.' " He glanced at Hale. "That's—"

"Housman, I know." Hale ignored the implication. He hadn't allowed for Philby knowing that Elena was supposed to be at the cathedral on this day, and he reconsidered the lines-of-compulsion in his proposed deal with him. "I will give you directions to the *dubok* that contains the inhabited thistle root—it should be testably genuine, able to animate cigarette ashes placed near it, or to wiggle the legs of freshly killed flies, for example, small agitations—and as soon as I have Maly's directions and the *rafiq* diamond—"

"My wife Eleanor is living with me here in Moscow," Philby interrupted. "I don't think you met her, back in Beirut, did you? Lovely woman, but her passport expires in July, three months from now, and she's determined to be back in the United States by then. She's got a daughter there, by a previous marriage. She loves me, you understand, but she doesn't want to become just one more of the ring-road birds."

Hale decided to let Philby ramble—it was dangerous to let him control the conversation this way, but Hale might learn something that could be useful as leverage. "Ring-road birds?" he said.

" 'Dust is their food and clay is their meat, and they are clothed like birds in garments of feathers,' " Philby said. "Have you met them, the expatriates who've defected, given up their old citizenships—in the service, as they come unhappily to learn, of *her*? I swear their breath doesn't *steam*, on winter days!—as if they have no more body heat than trees, or *lichens*. When it was clear that Eleanor couldn't be dissuaded from catching an Aeroflot flight here to join me, my old pal Nicholas bloody Elliott took her to a London cinema and made her watch *The Birds*, that new Alfred Hitchcock movie. Have you seen it? Attractive, independent-minded young lady undertakes troublesome travel to be with the fascinating man, but brings down on herself the injurious wrath of the ordinarily timid fowls, and ends up in shock, mute and infirm. I could be a, a *king*, among that sad population . . . if I was willing to let go of what shreds of humanity I still possess."

"I met one of them yesterday," Hale said. "He—pitched over dead of fright, while I was talking to him."

Philby laughed and shook his head. "They're frail," he agreed, "individually. In a group, though, they have a certain spiteful power. And their eyes just glitter with sick envy when they learn that Eleanor still has a valid passport! Even Donald Maclean simply shivers when she speaks of flying back to—New York, London. And she *is* resolved to fly out, in June. And so"—he shrugged and smiled—"I will be without a wife, my boy! I think it was Hemingway who said that the state of being married is unimaginable until you've entered it, and then once you've been married you can't ever imagine *not* being. I've had three wives, and I'm vigorous enough for at least one more."

"What if," said Hale unsteadily, "Elena doesn't . . . *want* you?"

"Do you think that will matter? Here? *Droit de komissar,* my boy!" Philby reached out one blunt-fingered hand to tousle Hale's hair affectionately, but Hale flinched back when he felt a blade cut his scalp.

Philby was unfolding a handkerchief now and scraping onto the mono-grammed silk the shred of bloody hair he had cut off with a tiny folding knife.

"There," Philby said with satisfaction as he refolded the handker-chief and tucked it away. "Cheat me now, and I'll have the Mother of Catastrophes on you like a bloodhound, long before you can walk to the nearest border crossing. I don't relish the idea of summoning her and *conversing,* but I would make a point of it, in this case."

Hale's left hand was pressing his scalp above his ear, and he could feel hot blood matting his hair. He was nervously aware that he had lost control of this meeting. "I'm not going to cheat you. The terms I propose—"

"Are irrelevant, Andrew!" Philby slapped his palms on his knees and stood up. "Excuse me for a moment, would you? while I talk to these good comrades."

Then Philby had strolled away across the grass toward the old men on the benches, and he had pulled a wad of banknotes from his pocket.

Hale set the vodka bottle down on the bench beside him to grope for a handkerchief in the breast pocket of his inside-out overcoat—his scalp was still bleeding, and his left palm was red with blood. This was not going well at all. But surely Philby wanted the *amomon* root!

And Hale needed the *rafiq* diamond. He did not want to have to try to take trains and boats out of the Soviet Union—and he certainly didn't want to *walk* out.

Philby was striding back to the bench now, with a cigarette-pack-sized cardboard box in his hand instead of the bills.

"How could there *not* be a gambler," said Philby cheerfully as he sat down on the other side of the bottle, "among a crowd of Russian alco-holics? You recall Dostoyevsky!" The box he was holding was, Hale saw, a red pack of playing cards. "No, Andrew, the terms of our deal were defined fifteen years ago! The *rafiq* diamond resided in my *guts* then, and it stays with me now, though not so intimately; I was on Ararat too, a year ago, I too incurred the wrath of the stratospheric angels just as much as you did, and I might want to travel by air myself one day." When Hale just stared at him, Philby explained patiently, "The thing is, we never finished our *card game.* Seven-card-stud, high-low declare—the high hand wins Elena Teresa Ceniza-Bendiga, the low hand wins the *amomon* procedure." He held up his hand. *"And—all three* of the roots you brought are part of the *amomon* unit, and go in the pot. I know you brought one for yourself too, and one for Elena."

Philby was right, of course, beyond plausible contradiction—Hale had hidden two other inhabited roots in the journalists' hotel in the Sad Sam.

"Yes," he admitted.

Hale kept the angry frown on his face as he pressed the handkerchief to his scalp. But this was a rout. He had hoped to exchange one of the magical thistle roots for the diamond, and then go away on his own to meet Elena; now, though, the jewel seemed to be a lost cause, and it looked as though he'd be lucky just to be able to be the one to meet Elena! And Philby had cut a piece out of his scalp! For the first time, Hale had some professional respect for Philby as an agent-runner.

Hale must at least seem passionately to want the *amomon,* for the sake of letting Philby seem to have won something by taking all three of the roots; but of course in the end Hale would declare high. He had brought along the two other *amomon* roots simply because he'd *had* them, and they had value; and because it had seemed too high-handed for Hale to decide, for Elena, that she did not want to avail herself of the magical longevity the *amomon* offered.

But he was sure she would reject the option. She was, after all, a practicing Catholic, as Hale had been himself now for more than a year, and taking immortality from a fallen angel was hardly in accord with Catholic doctrine.

In fact, Elena would almost certainly reject *Hale,* if he approached her in the cathedral. And the djinn-thistle, supplemented with Maly's instructions, would *probably* give him genuine immortality, if he won it.

Suddenly, sickeningly, Hale was very far from sure that he did not want to be the one to win the *amomon.*

"You want," he said carefully, "to deal a hand of—"

"No, my boy, that would call for fresh rules, fresh definitions! Wild cards, cut-for-the-deal, dealer's choice, no end of arguments! No, I simply want to finish the hand that was interrupted by the earthquake in 1948. Here are cards, here are the players—here's the church and here's the steeple, open the doors and see Elena! If you won't play, if you forfeit the game, you *lose*—and I'll at least be the one to go meet Elena in an hour, and I'll have a good try too at getting the KGB to wring the *dubok* location out of you."

Hale's forehead was chilly with a dew of sweat. "But those cards were scattered."

"I remember mine. And I remember what you were showing on the board—a three, seven, ten, and nine, of different suits. Do you remember?"

Actually, Hale did remember the hand, with hallucinatory clarity; he remembered too the rain drumming on the corrugated steel roof of the little war-surplus Anderson bomb shelter, and the tan woolen Army blankets, and the bottle of Macallan Scotch that they had rolled back and forth between them. "Yes. And you were showing an Ace, four, six, and eight; the six and the eight were diamonds. But are we to—*trust* each other, to choose the same hole cards we held then?"

"That's an insulting remark from an Oxford man to a Cambridge man. And in any case it's high-low—unless one of us declares both ways, each of us gets half the pot. The girl—or life everlasting." Philby stretched, yawning. "I wonder if she's kept her looks, our Elena? The white hair fetched me, I must say." He smacked his lips and blinked at Hale. "You could probably kill me, right now—the old Fort Monkton skills—but of course then you'd never see Maly's instructions. And I took the Fort Monkton course too, remember, and I do have my little knife."

It was riskier than Philby had said. The ranks of the hands would be almost superfluous, since Philby would certainly choose new hole cards to maximally improve his own hand in one direction or the other, high or low, and he would assume that Hale would do the same—it would be more important here to guess which way the other man would declare.

Philby leaned back and spoke into the sky: " 'We have set the seal of *Solomon* on all things under sun,' " he said, reciting from Chesterton's *Lepanto* now, " 'of knowledge and of sorrow and endurance of things done.' " He smiled at Hale. "That will have called witnesses, don't you think? You spoke the name of Solomon in that bomb shelter, if you recall, and it did summon attention then."

Hale could feel a pressure against his mind now—not the full, thought-scattering scrutiny of a corporeal djinn, but a quiver of alien attention, and he thought the grasses were moving more than the wind could explain. He exhaled to clear his nose of a new whiff of the metallic oil smell.

Philby had moved the vodka bottle and was sorting through the cards, now laying one face-up on the bench, now tucking one under his thigh. After a minute there were three cards under his thigh and the predetermined Ace, four, six, and eight lying face-up.

He held the remainder of the deck out toward Hale. "Now find yours."

Hale's scalp seemed to have stopped bleeding, and he shoved the handkerchief into his overcoat. He took the cards and stared at Philby's exposed cards as he slowly shuffled through the deck. Philby could have selected a two, three, and five for his hole cards, giving him the perfect low hand, if he wanted to go that way. Hale couldn't even construct a hand that would beat it. Or Philby could have chosen three Aces for his hole cards, which would give him four of them—a *high* hand Hale couldn't possibly beat.

But Philby could not have assembled a hand that would assuredly win *both ways*. The best he could do for that would be the Ace-to-five straight, and Hale could have three more nines hidden, and the four-of-a-kind would beat the straight.

Hale began laying out the cards he had had showing in 1948: the three, the seven, the ten, the nine.

The declaration alone would be the verdict—if they both chose in the same direction, Philby would win.

Hale coughed to conceal an involuntary sigh. All delusions aside, he knew which way he had to declare.

Hale chose three cards at random for his hole cards and wedged them under his knee. Beyond Philby he saw that several of the old drunks had got up and were shambling away, doubtless troubled by the itchy resonance of the supernatural attention that Philby had summoned by speaking the name of Solomon.

Philby was digging in a pocket of his trousers. "I'll fetch us six kopeks, for the declare," he said breathlessly. When he had pulled out a handful of coins and begun fingering them, he squinted up at Hale. "Don't you wish it were *our* birthday, today, instead of Elena's, and we could read each other's minds?"

"I think we can anyway," said Hale.

Philby frowned, and suddenly Hale guessed that Philby had assembled the Ace-to-five straight, and arrogantly meant to declare both ways—confident that Hale would declare for low, that Hale would choose the good chance of immortality over the uncertainty of Elena's dubious reception.

"She hates you, you know," Philby said quickly. "In Beirut she learned that you had supposedly killed that Frenchman, that Cassagnac fellow. She told me—word of honor!—that she meant to kill you."

"I don't doubt it," Hale said, reaching across to select three coins from Philby's palm. He shook them inside his cupped hands like dice. "I'm willing to put it to the test."

Philby forced a hearty laugh. "There spoke bluff! She's forty—she hates you—and there is an infinity of other women in the world." His gaze focused past Hale then, and he drew in a sharp breath. "Ach, and now the groundlings have arrived."

Hale made himself look around slowly, and he was afraid he would see the peculiar hats of the KGB—but the figures that had shambled into the park were thin, pale-faced men and women in shabby over-coats. Hale saw tweeds, and tartans, and even an unmistakable Old Etonian tie. These were the Gray People, the ring-road birds. *I could be a king among that sad population,* Philby had said. They made no sounds, and almost seemed to ripple with the breeze.

For Philby to declare low here would be the equivalent, in the context of this crowd, of Arthur pulling the sword from the stone. It would be declaring, *To hell with love, and eventual payment of the death I owe to God. I willingly choose this existence of bitterness, envy, and cherished lies, on the condition that I can be assured of it for eternity.*

Hale was certain that it was what Philby would choose, would *have* to choose, now that Hale's own decision had been made to seem problematical. If Philby were forced to choose between love and grubby security, the course of his life would have left him no alternative but to choose grubby security.

"I'm willing to put it to the test," Hale said again. He slid two coins into his right fist and held it out.

Philby rubbed his hands together for nearly a full minute, baring his teeth in a grimace of indecision—and then at last he made a fist and struck it hard against his chest. "Mea culpa!" he whispered.

"Declare," said Hale, opening his hand to show the two coins.

Philby lowered his hand probated, and he opened his fingers and let the single kopek drop into the grass.

The air seemed to twang, a released tension felt in the abdomen rather than heard.

All Hale had won, after all this, had been the right to go meet Elena, as he had planned to do all along.

"The *r-roots*," Philby was gabbling, "wh-wh-where are the *roots?*"

Hale stood up and looked at his watch—he had twenty minutes to get to St. Basil's Cathedral on Red Square, a bit more than a mile away to the east. "Two are in a high cupboard in the kitchen at the journalists' hotel on the Sadovaya Samotechnaya, behind an old wooden tray; the other is in the bookstore next door to the Ararat Restaurant, behind the red-leather collected works of Marx. You can unleash Machikha Nash on me if you don't find them. Oh, and—" he held out his hand. "Here are your two kopeks back."

"Keep them," snarled Philby, "to be p-put on your *eyes*, after you're d-d-*dead!* What can you h-have left, thirty summers, at the m-most? And the last duh-duh-*dozen* of them impotent, s-senile! How many is th-thirty? Three prints of your h-hands in mud!"

Hale had turned and was striding away across the grass, and behind him Philby raised his voice nearly in a scream: "While I'll be y-you-*youthful* still, d-drinking claret, reading Shakespeare, f-f-fathering children! You l-*lost* here today, Hale! Don't doubt it! You l-lost!"

Hale paused at the alley and looked back. Kim Philby was sitting on the bench, still shouting, but he was surrounded now by the Gray People, and seemed as insubstantial as any of them.

Enjoy the illusion of immortality, thought Hale sadly, O my brother. The *amomon* djinn will die as soon as you digest it. If I've got thirty years left, you've got twenty. Two prints of your hands.

"You l-l-lost!" came Philby's voice, sounding thin and birdlike at this distance.

Hale smiled tightly as he turned away.

No, he thought as he hurried down the sun-dappled cobblestone alley toward the lanes of Spiridonovka. Whatever the outcome, I declared high.

Hale made himself walk, rather than run or even jog, down the wide quarter mile of paving stones toward the fantastic spires of St. Basil's

Cathedral on the hazy middle-distance horizon. His watch showed only eight minutes to noon, but he was wary of the Soviet Army honor guards in their gray fur hats and gray uniforms with bright red collar tabs and epaulettes. Clusters of Army guards marched across various empty quadrants of the square, and individual guards stood like buoys at the widely separated corners of the line of Moscow citizens that stretched like a boundary fence across the square, enclosing the concrete bleachers and terminating at the temple-like mausoleum in which Lenin's preserved corpse could be viewed. In the eleven days he had been in Moscow, Hale had twice seen these guards knock a person out of the line and pummel him to the stones for some apparently minor violation of security, and he didn't want to attract their attention today at all.

It was far too late now to pull the long, quilted sleeves back through his overcoat and put it on correctly; it would take some minutes to walk all the way past the longest, bleacher-spanning segment of the mausoleum line, and he would have to march the whole distance with the pink-satin lining-side of the garment out, looking like a performer in some crude satire on Chinamen, or Tibetans. And it was the fashion among the *stilyagi,* the stylish young Moscow hooligans, to go about anarchistically hatless; but at least Hale's graying hair and ludicrous coat would save him from being mistaken for one of them.

Hale had not eaten for more than twelve hours, and the vodka he had drunk with Philby was making him dizzy. A hundred yards away to his left rose the gray stone arches and towers of the GUM department store, as sternly grand as the Houses of Parliament; far off ahead of him to his right the Saviour's Tower stood up from the brick-red Kremlin wall, incongruously crowned with a giant red star; and straight ahead, its bulbous blue-and-gold striped domes looking like bellied sails on a sultan's ship of state, St. Basil's Cathedral loomed on the broad, gently rippled sea of paving stones.

Hale was trying desperately to convince himself that Philby would not send KGB agents down here to arrest him and Elena. Hale knew that Philby had been a turned agent, working for the SOE against the Soviets, since 1951; and at a KGB trial he could testify that Philby had cooperated in the Declare sabotage of the Rabkrin expedition on Mount Ararat a year ago. Surely the mere accusations would be likely to get Philby into trouble!—and Theodora had said that Philby was not highly regarded by the Soviet authorities these days.

Like any competent agent, Hale had his passport and money in his pockets—along with the Scandinavian Air tickets, two seats booked on a flight leaving tomorrow morning from Vnukovo Airport, bound for Stockholm. He couldn't use his—perhaps he could give one to Elena, if she needed it.

Then a thought occurred to him that almost brought him to a halt—what if Elena had also incurred the wrath of the Heaviside Layer angels by participating in the destruction of the Black Ark last January, and what if she had tried since to fly above 10,000 feet? Hale had only survived the djinn-attack on his Air Libyan Caravelle turbojet in February because the crippled plane had been able to land in the Persian Gulf.

If she's dead, he told himself steadily, then she won't be here. She may not be here anyway. See to it that *you're* in the church, at noon.

He pushed back the bunched pink sleeve of his coat to look at his watch—it was twelve right now. The cathedral was still a hundred yards away, and he broke into a jog; but after only a few paces he slowed back to a walk, his heart thudding and his face suddenly chilly.

A dozen men in dark brown uniforms stood in the shade around the cathedral's north arch. Even from this distance Hale could see campaign ribbons on their chests, but their visored caps made them look more like policemen than soldiers. Hale had no idea what agency they might represent; and he wondered if they were on the watch for *him*.

Hale knew he cut a peculiar figure here; and after a moment he felt a hot tickle of blood run down behind his left ear, and he realized that his brief jog had opened the cut in his scalp.

I can't go in to see if she's there, he thought helplessly. Even if they're not after me, I'd be drawing needless attention to her.

But what if they're after *her*? If Elena is in the church, lighting the candle she promised to the Virgin Mary, unaware of this dragnet outside, I could at least provide a distraction.

His ribs tingled almost with vertigo at the thought, as if he had been standing on the narrowest, highest coping of the Saviour's Tower, looking up.

He could probably walk past on the right, safely—and then just trudge all the way down to the foot of the Moskva River Bridge. And leave Elena to whatever action was going on at the cathedral. She wasn't expecting Hale, after all, and probably wouldn't welcome the sight of him.

In the end he simply couldn't do it. You didn't go to all the trouble to get yourself sewn up in a mule skin, he thought, and let yourself be carried by the eagle all the way up to the inaccessible peak, just to try to find a way to climb back down.

He walked straight ahead into the shadow of the bulging domes, and when the uniformed men saw that he was going to pass among them, he nodded politely to the ones who were staring coldly at him. Trying to look like a Russian, he stepped between two of them and tapped up the stone stairs as if he had every sort of legitimate reason to be visiting the cathedral. He didn't look back, but only glanced at his watch as he gripped the vertical brass handles of the ten-foot-tall gold-paneled doors. He was only a minute and twenty seconds late.

The doors weren't locked. He pulled them both open, and peered into the chandelier-lit dimness of the vast church.

There was no crucifix visible anywhere on the high walls he could see from the entry, and no pews to interrupt the expanse of polished-stone floor, but the walls and the broad pillars were dense with the frescoed silhouettes of saints and angels and apostles.

There were policemen in here too, a number of them—it was hard to know how many, for each of the tall pillars that stood up from the floor was as wide as a car viewed head-on; but there were at least six of the uniformed figures standing at various points across the dim nave. Hale didn't glance squarely at any of them, but he imagined that the intrusion of his ragged self must have drawn the unfriendly attention of every one of them.

He couldn't just stand in the doorway.

A tiny constellation of candle flames lit the low reaches of the gold walls in a far corner, and when he began slowly walking across the floor toward the glow, he saw three or four black-hooded women kneeling in front of an iron table with the candles arranged on it in ranks. The candles were tall thin tapers, not the short votive candles in jars he remembered from his youth. The place should have smelled of incense and frail missal-pages, but the only scents he was aware of were damp stone and a diesel taint on the cold air that he had let in from outside. At least he could detect none of the rancid oil reek.

Two of the policemen were standing immediately to the left of the kneeling women, almost leaning against the frescoed wall; Hale pretended to be indifferent to them.

He hesitated and stopped when he was still a dozen feet away from the candles, and he stared at the backs of the women; and his heart began thudding even before he was sure that he recognized the figure and posture of the woman closest to the wall.

She was here, she had arrived safely this far, at least, after all the perilous years and betrayed loyalties. Was she about to be arrested now, and taken back to the Lubyanka?

For more than twenty years she had occupied Hale's thoughts and brightened or tormented his dreams, but the only period in which the two of them had known each other, lived and worked and eaten and joked together, had been the three months in Nazi-occupied Paris, at the end of 1941, more than twenty-two years ago.

During his years as a lecturer at the University College of Weybridge, he had imagined one day meeting her again, and courting her, and marrying her; but under the gaze of the police in this cold Moscow church, those daydreams seemed all-of-a-piece with the bright, naïve ambitions of his Cotswolds boyhood, and he didn't dare to hope for anything at all now, not even continued liberty.

He stirred himself and walked forward, digging into the pocket of his corduroy trousers for Philby's two kopeks. The women were kneeling on a black leather kneeler in front of the candles, and Hale lowered himself down onto the yard of it to Elena's right, so that she was between him and the nearest policeman; and Hale reached out to drop the two coins into the slot in the iron money box.

They fell to the floor of the box with a noise that seemed as loud as a couple of .22 shots.

From the corner of his left eye he could see that she was looking at him, and he was resentful that he dared not meet her gaze.

He saw her right hand move—she had made the sign of the cross. He crossed himself in turn, and he was genuinely praying to God too when he said softly, "*Segne mich.*"

The words were German for *Bless me.*

It was the old GRU Rote Kapelle code phrase: *Things are not what they seem—trust me.* Though he had spoken in a near-whisper, the words echoed back down at him from the remote arched ceiling.

He forced his hand not to tremble as he reached out and picked up one of the matchboxes on the iron table, and he managed to light one of the matches on the first strike. He held it to the curled black wick of one of the candles that had been extinguished, and shook it out when the wick flared in a tall yellow flame.

He made the sign of the cross again and stood up, staring at the candle flame and trying to see Elena as clearly as he could in his peripheral vision. Her white hair was conspicuous under the black hood, and he could make out her big Castilian eyes and the smooth, graceful sweep of her jaw.

God knew what she made of him, with his graying hair and strange, blood-spotted clothing.

He turned away and began walking toward the south entrance, where the tall doors stood open and he could see a segment of distant gray overcast indented by the Moscow skyline south of the river.

No one stopped him as he scuffed across the stone floor past the massive pillars. He stepped out between the open doors into the cold breeze, and walked down the first couple of steps, and then he heard someone's footsteps behind him.

Two or three of the uniformed men stood at the foot of the stairs, but Hale slowed and let the person behind him gradually catch up. It was Elena, heartbreakingly slim and straight in a long black dress. He let himself look into her face finally, and though there were new lines under her eyes and down her cheeks, her blue eyes were still youthful, and vulnerable.

He let his left eyelid flutter in a faint wink, and then he had stepped ahead and was leading the way left, toward the sidewalk on the eastern side of the cathedral island. He could hear the tap of her shoe-soles on the cement behind him, and he didn't look around to see if the policemen were watching them.

When they had reached the sidewalk, where the wind was swirled into eddies by the curtained black ZIL limousines that swept past, one of them possibly transporting Brezhnev himself from some meeting of the Communist Party Presidium at the Kremlin Palace, Hale whispered back over his shoulder, "I'm Varnum Leonard, journalist for the London *Evening Standard*. Solid cover until this morning, but now Philby's talked to me, I'm compromised." He was dizzy, and he took a deep breath. "I did not kill Cassagnac."

From behind him she said softly, "Gitana Sandoval, Spanish movie producer, location-scouting via Intourist."

And both of us, Hale thought, are in the old GRU records, and certainly in the more recent KGB records too—not to mention Rabkrin—if anybody should be interested in checking.

He could hear clocking footsteps approaching from some distance behind, and he shuffled for two paces and nearly tripped, for he had instinctively begun to tap out the old *clochard* nothing-right-here rhythm—but in nearly the same instant he had remembered the uses those rhythms had been put to in the Ahora Gorge fifteen years ago, and he had awkwardly tried to resume his former pace.

Elena's shoes had scuffled on the pavement too, for a moment; and now she was again walking normally. Ultimately, Hale thought with a sort of solemn pleasure, we both know which way to declare.

The footsteps behind were closer, and sounded like boots. Elena was walking beside Hale on his right now, and she took hold of his hand, and squeezed. "I knew, after a while, that you had not," she said quietly. "I knew when I ordered the helicopter to veer east."

She was holding his hand so tightly that he could feel the fast beat of her pulse; and a moment later he realized that it was precisely matching his own, as if they were one person on the sidewalk.

With her free hand she fetched up from her coat pocket a little mirror—apparently the same old tortoise-backed one she had had in Paris—and when she held it out in front of them, Hale could see her face and his, half-overlapped in the cracked glass.

The footsteps from behind faltered, and then broke from a concerted group into unmatched individuals—and then the policemen had passed them and were craning their necks to peer up and down the lanes of this south end of Red Square, as if, Hale thought giddily, they were watching for a taxi.

"Grace," said Elena. "Not magic."

"I have airline tickets," said Hale, "but I can't fly and I can't go back to England. I'm more or less going to have to *walk* out, and God knows across which border."

"You remembered my birthday," she said, still holding his hand tightly, though she was staring past him at the cathedral. "Did—did Philby?"

"Yes. We played a game of cards, to decide which of us would come to meet you in the cathedral. The loser to win three of the inhabited *amomon* roots."

"Immortality!" she said. "He was happy to lose."

"Not *happy*—resigned. I was happy to win. I would have come even if I had not won."

She laughed, and it was the first time he had heard her laugh since Berlin in 1945, nearly twenty years ago. "Walking out," she said, "would be easier for a couple than for one person alone."

They were a peculiar-looking couple—the man in the clownish overcoat, who had fired the shot that would one day topple the Union of Soviet Socialist Republics, and the woman dressed in black like a Spanish *duena*, who would at long last become his wife—but they attracted no attention at all as they strolled away hand-in-hand past the southernmost corner of the Kremlin Wall and on to the embankments of the Moskva River.

▼

Afterword

Kim Philby died in the early morning of May 11, 1988, of arrhythmia of the heart, at the KGB clinic in Moscow. His last words were in reply to a telephoned congratulations on the anniversary of the Soviet victory of 1945: "What victory?" Philby said.

He was buried in the Novodiverchy cemetery near Red Square.

The Union of Soviet Socialist Republics collapsed three and a half years later, in December of 1991; Mikhail Gorbachev resigned as Soviet President on Christmas Day.

▼

Author's Note

In my experience stories never write themselves—but they do often *suggest* or even strongly *indicate* themselves. Being a John le Carré fan, I happened one day to read his introduction to *The Philby Conspiracy,* by Page, Leitch, and Knightley, and I was so struck by the mysteries surrounding Kim Philby and his father that I read that book, and then Boyle's *The Fourth Man*—and it soon became evident to me that a novel could be woven around these characters and events. Eventually I discovered that, in fact, novels such as Ted Allbeury's fine *The Other Side of Silence* had already been.

But as I went on to read Eleanor Philby's *Kim Philby: The Spy I Married,* and Borovik's and Modin's books providing the KGB perspective, and Philby's own *My Silent War,* I found that the incidents that intrigued me were the apparently peripheral ones. I kept being nagged by a feeling that the central element of the story had been almost completely omitted, to be derived now only by finding and tracing its fugitive outlines.

In a way, I arrived at the plot for this book by the same method that astronomers use in looking for a new planet—they look for "perturbations," wobbles, in the orbits of the planets they're aware of, and they calculate the mass and position of an unseen planet whose gravitational field could have caused the observed perturbations—and then they turn their telescopes on that part of the sky and search for a gleam. I looked at all the seemingly irrelevant "wobbles" in the lives of these people—Kim Philby, his father, T. E. Lawrence, Guy Burgess—and I made it an ironclad rule that I could not change or disregard any of the recorded facts, nor rearrange any days of the calendar—and then I tried to figure out what momentous but unrecorded fact could explain them all.

After all, why *did* Philby spend two days in drunken grief when his pet fox fell to her death in Beirut, in September of 1962? In Nicholas Elliott's autobiography we're told that Philby and Eleanor brought the fox back "from a visit to Saudi Arabia,"[1] and Philby himself, in an article published in *Country Life* in 1962, describes the fox as chewing pipe stems and licking up whisky; Eleanor notes that they "were all desolate"[2] at the fox's death, but the only other time Philby gave in so to grief was at the death of his father, precisely two years earlier.

The garment Philby was seen wearing in Spain on the evening of December 31, 1937, after the car he was in was struck by a Russian artillery round, has been described by both Anthony Cave Brown in *Treason in the Blood* and Phillip Knightley in *The Master Spy* as a woman's moth-eaten coat; the implication being that some Good Samaritan had draped him in it. But Philby himself, quoted in Genrikh Borovik's later and more authoritative *The Philby Files*, says, "I looked so picturesque that I later read somewhere that someone had put a woman's fur coat on me after the explosion. In fact I was wearing the coat my father had given me, which he had received from one of his Arab princes. It was a very amusing piece of tailoring: bright green fabric on the outside and bright red fox fur on the inside."[3]

And at the end of the "Bitter Waters" chapter in St. John Philby's *The Empty Quarter,* he describes being led by a fox to a meteorite in the Arabian desert. The elder Philby, in fact, devotes an appendix to "Meteorites and Fulgurites," and in *Declare* I respectfully adhere to his description of the Wabar meteor–strike site (at least until the supernatural intervenes). In another appendix he notes that "The Arabs believe that some stones in the desert walk about, leaving a track in the sand. They attribute this

---

[1] Nigel West, ed. *The Faber Book of Espionage* (London: Faber and Faber, 1993), p. 336.

[2] Eleanor Philby, *Kim Philby: The Spy I Married* (New York: Ballantine Books, 1968), p. 6.

[3] Genrikh Borovik, *The Philby Files* (New York: Little, Brown, 1994), p. 100.

remarkable power to the work of spirits,"[4] though earlier in the book he says, "I reserved judgment on the 'walking stones' until they could be produced to perform in my presence."[5] Also in *The Empty Quarter* is St. John's description of his dreams in the Rub' al-Khali desert: "My dreams these nights were nightmare vistas of long low barrack buildings whirling round on perpetually radiating gravel rays of a sandy desert, while I took rounds of angles on ever moving objects with a theodolite set on a revolving floor. It was the strangest experience of my life."[6]

In his autobiography, *Arabian Days*, St. John mentions the comet that blazed across the sky on the Good Friday of his birth; and Knightley, in *The Master Spy*, recounts the story that the infant St. John was left behind in Ceylon and discovered later as one of a pair of identically dressed babies being nursed by a "gypsy" woman. This reminded me of the account, in 1 Kings 3, of Solomon offering to split the baby claimed by two women—a story that had always seemed to me insufficiently explained.

In *The Master Spy* we're told that St. John "took up the collection and study of early Semitic inscriptions in Arabia and increased from some two thousand to over thirteen thousand the number of known Thamudic inscriptions."[7] And in Brown's *Treason in the Blood* we learn that St. John Philby took possession of T. E. Lawrence's personal files covering the years 1914 through 1921.

What would have been in those files, which were subsequently "lost"? *Something* had happened to Lawrence in the Syrian town of Dera on the night of November 21, 1917, after the failure of a covert operation of his own near the north end of the Dead Sea; in his book, *The Seven Pillars of Wisdom,* on which he spent six years plagued by self-doubt and the theft of an early draft, Lawrence claimed to have been captured by Turkish soldiers and raped by the Turkish governor of Dera. But his grisly account does not fit with the facts and timetables, and according to George Bernard Shaw, Lawrence "told me that his account

---

[4] H. St. J. B. Philby, *The Empty Quarter* (New York: Henry Holt, 1933), p. 378.
[5] Ibid., p. 81
[6] Ibid., p. 164
[7] Phillip Knightley, *The Master Spy* (New York: Knopf, 1989), p. 20.

of the affair is not true."[8] In 1922 Lawrence joined the RAF under an
assumed name, and when this disguise was exposed he joined the Royal
Tank Corps under another. What ordeal could have been so stressful
and *outre* and secret that homosexual rape was a more mundane cover
story?—and left him with an apparent tendency to manifest multiple
identities? Preparatory to the inquest on Lawrence's death in 1935, a
witness was officially told not to mention the "black car or van"[9] he
claimed to have seen passing Lawrence's motorcycle moments before the
fatal crash.

A year earlier, working for a Russian secret service, Kim Philby had
photographed his father's secret papers, and those papers would have
included the lost Lawrence files.

Philby was recruited into the British secret service by Guy Burgess,
and many have speculated that Burgess had pre-emptively recruited him
into a Soviet one before that. The *in media res* death of Burgess's father is
mentioned in Andrew Boyle's *The Fourth Man;* and in *My Five Cambridge
Friends* the retired Soviet agent-runner Yuri Modin notes the "persistent
rumor that Guy had once actually run down and killed a man in Dublin
during the war."[10]

I found many clues, many "perturbations," especially when St.
John's obsession with Arabia led me to the various versions of the *Thousand Nights and One Night.* From the stories in that primordial text I was
able to deduce the nature of the forces called djinn—their peculiar
attachment to objects and physical arrangements—and to speculate on
the insistently recurrent image of a "Castle of the Mountain of Clouds,
which, built by one of the djinn who revolted from the covenant of
Solomon, was cut off from the rest of the world."[11] In his translation,
Richard F. Burton mentions stories of the Devil trying to get aboard the

---

[8] Lawrence James, *The Golden Warrior: The Life and Legend of Lawrence of Arabia*
York: Paragon House, 1993), p. 213.

[9] Ibid., p. 361.

[10] Yuri Modin, *My Five Cambridge Friends* (New York: Farrar, Straus, Giroux,
1994), p. 10.

[11] Joseph Campbell, ed., *The Portable Arabian Nights* (New York: Viking, 1952),
p. 569.

Ark, and says that "people had seen and touched the ship on Ararat."[12] And when at last I had calculated the nature of a big-but-unrecorded fact that could have caused the perturbations, I went looking for evidence of it.

And it was all right there in Kim Philby's life. Anthony Cave Brown notes that in 1919 Prince Feisal had formally given young Kim a twenty-carat diamond, and I did not invent the designation or function of a *rafiq*. Philby was SIS Head of Station in Turkey in 1947 and '48, and in his coy autobiography, *My Silent War,* he explains, or does not quite explain, his proposed "photographic reconnaissance of the Soviet frontier area . . . I called it Operation Spyglass . . . it would give me a cast-iron pretext for a long, hard look at the Turkish frontier region . . . I had learnt long before, while working for the *Times,* some of the tricks of dressing implausible thoughts in language that appealed to the more sober elements in the Athenaeum."[13] And a page or two earlier: "After a first summer of reconnaissance, I would be better equipped for a more ambitious programme in 1948."[14] In *The Philby Conspiracy* I learned that he "kept an odd souvenir of the period which in later years he displayed in his apartment in Beirut: a large photograph of Mount Ararat which stands on the Turkish–Soviet border."[15] The rope attached to the dashboard of Philby's jeep is described in *Something Ventured,* the autobiography of Monty Woodhouse, who was SIS Head of Station in Iran in 1951.

The explanation I arrived at was, admittedly, a fantastic one; not one that le Carré would have come up with, I daresay. But when I had fitted the djinn postulate in among all the published facts, they all fell satisfactorily into place at last, and suddenly made "sense." Even my protagonist, Andrew Hale, was suggested by the fact that St. John Philby and young Kim did collect samples of water from the Jordan River in the summer of 1923; according to Anthony Cave Brown, "The collection

[12] Richard F. Burton, trans., *The Book of the Thousand Nights and One Night* (New York: Heritage, 1962), p. 479.
[13] Kim Philby, *My Silent War* (New York: Grove Press, 1968), pp. 175–76.
[14] Ibid., p. 173.
[15] Bruce Page, David Leitch, and Phillip Knightley, *The Philby Conspiracy* (New York: Doubleday, 1968), p. 195.

had a purpose. It was claimed that the water contained special proper-
ties, and for centuries it had been drawn at that point and sent to England for christenings; they [St. John and Kim] would send the water to
the British Museum to establish whether it really contained holy proper-
ties."[16] The implied previous baptism there, and St. John's evident concern about it, gave me the shape of Andrew Hale.

In his Moscow retirement Philby insisted that he had fled Beirut in
1963 aboard the Soviet freighter *Dolmatova*—though he was "short-
tempered" when interviewer Phillip Knightley pressed him for details—
but according to Eleanor, "I believe he walked a good deal of the way,"[17]
and in *The Philby Conspiracy* we hear that "Philby told one of his children that he arrived in Moscow with his feet heavily bruised from a long
and difficult walk."[18] Early accounts of his escape have him crossing the
border near Ararat, and in conversation with Knightley published in the
last chapter of *The Master Spy,* Philby is quick to cut off a discussion of
his old photograph of Mount Ararat. Knightley, and Chapman Pincher
in *Too Secret Too Long,* agree that immediately upon his arrival in
Moscow Philby was put into a KGB clinic.

And Philby, though an unbaptized atheist, did always seem to be
uneasy with Christianity, particularly with Roman Catholicism. Brown
recounts Philby's claim of having suffered a nervous breakdown at Westminster School because of the "unending Christian instruction"[19] and
also describes a visit Philby paid to a Roman Catholic ARAMCO political agent in Riyadh, shortly after St. John's death—they discussed
Catholicism, and Philby was so knowledgeable and at the same time so
nervous about the faith that the agent wondered if he were not a lapsed
Catholic considering reconciliation. Nicholas Elliott's wife was a practicing Catholic, and in his autobiography Elliott mentions a cocktail party
at which Philby mockingly asked her if she really did have "a firm purpose of amendment" each time she went to Confession; and I don't

---

[16] Anthony Cave Brown, *Treason in the Blood* (New York: Houghton Mifflin, 1994), p. 75.
[17] Eleanor Philby, op. cit., p. 72.
[18] Page, Leitch, Knightley, op. cit., p. 290.
[19] Anthony Cave Brown, op. cit., p. 133.

think it's too presumptuous to see in Philby's banter a trace of wistful envy.

In her book, Eleanor Philby recounts how in 1963 Nicholas Elliott, having failed to persuade her not to fly to Moscow to visit Philby, took her to a cinema that was showing the Hitchcock movie *The Birds*. Elliott bought her ticket but then left her to watch it alone, presumably hoping that the movie might effectively make a point that he could not convey. Into his silence I've presumed to fit the admittedly extravagant—but, I think, consistent—premise of this story.